Frag Box

Books by Richard A. Thompson

Fiddle Game
Frag Box

Frag Box

Richard A. Thompson

Poisoned Pen Press

Poisoned Pen Press
6962 E. First Ave., Ste. 103
Scottsdale, AZ 85251
www.poisonedpenpress.com
info@poisonedpenpress.com

Printed in the United States of America

This one is for Helen.

Acknowledgments

The creative process never occurs in a vacuum. I am enormously indebted to the following people for their unstinting help with this project:

Jim Woodward, who fleshed out the landscape of 1960s Detroit for me;

Tate Halverson, who kept my descriptions of Vietnam-era Army organization accurate;

My long-suffering writing buddies, Peter Farley and Ingrid Trausch, who gave me priceless ongoing critical analysis and moral support;

And of course, Margaret Yang, my indispensable beta reader and soul mate.

As usual, my humble thanks are quite inadequate.

frag. [1] A fragmentation grenade. [2] To explode a fragmentation grenade. [3] To kill or wound one's superior officer, from the fact that a fragmentation grenade was often the weapon of choice.

Paul Dickson,
War Slang: American Fighting Words and Phrases from the Civil War to the War in Iraq, Second Edition
Potomac Books, Inc. (formerly Brassey's, Inc., XXXX)

frag pot. A place for collecting money to induce somebody to kill an officer; from the fact that the preferred container was often a helmet, or "pot."

Common G.I. slang, Vietnam War

frag box. The same as above, only in civilian life.

Charles Victor, veteran

Prologue

Eveleth, Minnesota
Early March, 1968

It was twelve degrees below zero when he got off the bus. He still had fifteen miles to go, but Eveleth was the end of the line, as far north as the Greyhound would take him. He would have to hitch hike the rest of the way to the town of Mountain Iron, where his parents had a tiny house. Neither the town nor the house nor the parents were much to come home to, but they were what he had.

After four years in the service, three of them in Vietnam, he had finally had enough. The Army had dangled a big wad of money and some stripes in front of him, but this time, he didn't bite. He mustered out and went back to the World.

His class A uniform and greatcoat were no match for the cold, and he had nothing to cover his hands or ears. He decided to get a few shots of antifreeze before starting the rest of his trip, and he walked the two blocks to Main Street, weaving between mountains of shoveled snow that towered above his head.

Downtown, upstairs over an appliance store, there was a VFW bar. He assumed he would be welcomed there. With his uniform and his ribbons, he might get a freebie or two, or even a ride home. Who knew?

At the side of the appliance store, he opened a frosted-over glass door, kicked the snow off his polished jump boots, and climbed the stairs.

Upstairs was a workingman's bar, with a small hardwood dance floor that hadn't been varnished in thirty years and cheap paneling on the walls, adorned with stuffed moose and deer heads and phony looking lacquered fish. Beams of feeble late afternoon light from a few narrow windows pierced the smoke and dust and illuminated a big American flag on a floor standard and some dingy patriotic bunting over the bar. Under the moose head, a movie poster of Jane Fonda in her sex-kitten role from *Barbarella* had obviously been used as a dartboard, with the moose also getting his share of random punctures. The tables and chairs were all stacked and pushed against the outside wall, but that didn't matter, because the seven or eight regular patrons all sat at the bar.

They looked interchangeable: dumpy-looking retired or out-of-work men in dirty baseball caps, plaid shirts, and Osh Kosh work pants held up by wide suspenders. Their Chippewa or Red Wing boots rested on the brass rail, showing rubber soles worn to banana-shaped profiles. They also wore expressions of well-practiced boredom, and they hunched low over the bar, nursing flat beers, trying to keep an all-day buzz going on a scanty mining pension or an unemployment check. They did not chat. The bartender was younger, though definitely not young, and he wore black slacks and a white shirt with a crumpled clip-on bow tie.

Near the door was a jukebox with selections by such worthies as Whoopee John, Frankie Yankovik, and The Six Fat Dutchmen, but it wasn't playing. This was not a place for music. Everything here was yesterday, elsewhere, and too bad.

All eyes turned when the young sergeant came in with a cloud of frigid air. He took off his greatcoat and hung it on a peg, dumping his duffle on the floor nearby. Most of the regulars turned back to stare into their beers, but some of them smirked and exchanged knowing looks.

"Anybody looking to buy some cookies?" said one of the smirkers. "I think the Girl Scouts just came in."

The soldier ignored him and took a stool near the center of the bar.

"Beer and a bump," he said.

The bartender made no move to get him anything.

"You a member?"

He couldn't believe what he was hearing. He spread his arms wide, to display his chest full of ribbons, including a purple heart with a bronze V in the proper position of honor, top row, inside.

"Well," he said, "I am damn sure a veteran, and of the foreign-ist goddamn war the politicians ever made. What else you gotta have?"

"This place is for members only," said the bartender, now folding his arms and tilting his chin up aggressively.

"Aah, give the kid a drink," said a voice from the end of the bar.

"Who the hell asked you?"

"He wears the uniform, he's entitled."

"Not if he ain't a member. He ain't entitled to diddly shit." That brought a chorus of muttered agreements from up and down the bar.

"That's bullshit, and you know it," said the lone dissenter on the end, a stumpy, bowlegged troll with a barrel chest and a full white beard. He detached himself from his stool and came over, his hand extended.

"Luther Johnson," he said. "I was with the Seabees in Burma."

"He was with the Salvation Army in Bumfuck, is where he was," said another regular. "He has a half a beer, he gets all confused."

"No, he don't. The two are the same thing."

"Throw the both of them out, Mack."

"Fucking-ay. We don't need their kind here."

"Charlie Victor," said the soldier, taking the hand. That brought a whoop from the others.

"He not only couldn't beat the enemy, he took their name!"

Johnson stood his ground. "Can that shit," he said. "I'm a paid up member, and Charlie here is my guest. Pour him a drink."

"You ain't paid your tab in two weeks, Luther," said the bartender, though now he moved to get a glass from the counter behind the bar.

"Well, it ain't the end of the month, is it? I ever stiff you on it?"

"Just don't be calling yourself paid up, is all I'm saying."

"Listen, mister civilian barhop, you can—"

"How much is his tab?" said Victor.

"What do you care?"

"How much?"

"I dunno without looking it up. Twenty, maybe twenty-two or three bucks. Mind your own business, soldier boy."

The soldier reached into his wallet and dug out a twenty and a five and slapped them on the bar top.

"My friend Luther is all paid up, okay? Now give us both a drink."

"I can pay my own way, kid."

"No shit. And I can fight my own battles."

"Really?" The voice belonged to somebody slightly younger and a lot bigger than Johnson, though still cut from the same common mold. He slid off his stool and came up behind them, doing his best to look imposing despite a sagging beer belly and unfocused eyes.

"Seems to me all you candy-ass, druggie Viet Conga boys know how to do is whine, get high, and lose."

Somewhere in a primitive part of Victor's brain, old wheels began to turn, mixing dark impulses into explosive slurry, begging him to add a detonating spark. But he ignored it with a force of pure will, also ignored the fat, belligerent drunk.

"Are we square now, or what?" he said to the bartender.

The bartender didn't answer, but he poured a shot of rye and slammed it down on the bar, deliberately slopping some over the side. Then he drew two beers and put them on the bar top as well. After he had scooped up the money and stuffed it in the till, he walked back to where the soldier was throwing back the shot and pointedly spat into his beer. The cogs turned a notch farther and the juices started to approach critical mass.

"Just exactly what is your problem?" said Victor as calmly as he could.

"His problem's same as our problem," said Beer Belly, now coming close enough to poke him in the arm. "His problem is that we won our war. We didn't protest and we didn't run off to Canada and we didn't get high on dope and badmouth our country. We didn't fuck up."

"What makes you think I did?"

"Well you damn sure ain't won, have you?" The bartender again, and Victor turned back to stare into his eyes.

"And just exactly which war did you win, Mr. Bowtie?"

"Well, I, um—"

"He don't have to have been in any war to respect the guys who was. He knows how to act. But you phony jungle heroes with your pussy berets don't even know how to do that. You screw around and you keep this damn war going, and pretty soon some real Americans are going to have to go over there and die."

"Like his precious kid," said Johnson.

"What about it? My kid is college material, is what he is. His hockey coach pret' near said so. This asshole here's nothing but mine slag. That's probably why he got drafted; they always take the trash first. And if he couldn't finish the job, he shoun't a come back."

The final bit of machinery clicked. To Victor's surprise, though, the wave of rage that flooded through him was cold, quiet, and supremely controlled. And he knew exactly what he was going to do with it.

"You know what's wrong with war?" said Victor. "I mean, three tours in-country and two purple hearts, and I didn't figure it out until just now. Do you know?"

"Easy, man," said Johnson. "Maybe you should—"

"Oh, now we're gonna get the peace and love speech." Beer Belly turned sideways to play to the rest of the regulars, but before he could say another word, Victor took the glass with beer and spit and smashed it against the side of the man's head. Foam and blood ran down his pasty face, obscuring one smashed eye. The other eye bulged, matching the astonished "o" of the mouth below it. The man howled but didn't go down, so Victor gave him a solid jab to the solar plexus, dropping him in a blubbering heap.

Behind him, Victor heard Johnson say, "Whatever you're reaching for under that bar, Mack, it better be made out of chocolate, 'cause I think you're about to eat it."

Victor whirled around to see the bartender pull a sawed-off baseball bat from under the bar. But before he could do anything with it, Johnson pounded the man's forearm with the side of his fist, pinning the arm to the bar top. The hand went limp. Victor snatched the bat and shoved the end of it into the man's mouth, grabbing a fistful of greasy hair with his other hand, preventing him from backing away.

"What's wrong with war," he said, staring intently into the bartender's eyes, "is that the wrong people always die."

Johnson said something he didn't hear, and the bartender tried to say something but couldn't. Victor shoved the bat down his throat, as hard and as far as he could. He felt things tear and break and squish, and he gave himself over utterly to the delicious black rage that flooded his brain.

Up and down the bar, nobody else moved. No beers were drunk and nobody spoke as they waited in frozen terror to see what the crazy Vietnam vet would do next.

The lunatic went around behind the bar, where the bartender now lay on the floor, convulsing and making choking, gurgling sounds. Victor ignored him. He slammed two handfuls of shot glasses up on the bar and poured them full from two bottles of liquor he picked up at random, one in each hand. He sent the glasses sliding up and down the bar, distributing them, then continued to pour. He doused liquor on the bodies on the floor and flooded the bar top.

"Drinks all around," he said. "On the house." In the background, he saw Johnson go over to the pay phone on the wall and rip out the receiver cord.

"Drink, you sonsabitches," he screamed, "or I swear I'll kill every fucking one of you!"

They drank.

Over by the phone, Johnson made a gesture toward the door.

"Time we got out of here, kid."

He nodded, held up a finger in a gesture that said "just one minute." Then he took out his Zippo lighter and calmly lit the puddles of booze.

What the rest of the regulars said or did after that, he would never know. Nor did he know what else, if anything, he did to them. The next conscious memory he had was of himself and Johnson running over brittle-crusted snow to jump on an ore train that was laboring up a grade on the edge of town. Twenty miles later, just outside the Erie Mining plant, they swapped it for a ride on a trainload of processed taconite pellets, headed for the dockyards at Duluth. It was blackest night by then, and the temperature seemed to drop almost as fast as the train speeded up. They huddled on the machinery platform at one end of a big hopper car, holding onto the framework with arms looped around steel bars. Neither of them had gloves, and they didn't dare grab the frigid metal with their bare hands. Somewhere between Hoyt Lakes and Duluth, Luther Johnson froze to death.

"So it's true in the World, too," said Victor. "Always the wrong ones who get killed."

He jumped off the train in West Duluth, dumped his uniform, except for the boots and fatigue jacket, in a dumpster at a truck stop, and started hitchhiking. South. In a Catholic church across the street from a gas station in Cloquet, he stopped long enough to light two candles, one for Luther Johnson and one for himself. He was not a Catholic, but it seemed like the right thing to do. Then he continued heading south.

He never made it back to Mountain Iron, to the father who had once told him to go off to war. He settled in St. Paul, finally, sometimes living on the street, sometimes with a former hooker in Lowertown, in the wino district.

"It's always the wrong ones get killed," he told her, when one of their fellow winos died from drinking antifreeze.

"Well, why don't you quit your whining and do something about it?"

So he did.

Blood Game

It was a day for pocket billiards, snow, and death. The snow came in the late afternoon, in fat, globular flakes that swirled in the eddies of the urban canyons, stuck to the rough brick of old buildings, and covered the streets in a layer of slush for cars to splash onto pedestrians. On the windows of Lefty's Pool Hall and Saloon in downtown St. Paul, they dribbled down the dirty glass and made mushy heaps on the sills, leaving crooked, wet trails behind them.

I was inside Lefty's at the time, shooting eight ball with Wide Track Wilkie. And while the hapless man on the street below was lost in a world of pain and despair, we were lost in the click of the balls and the smell of smoke and stale beer and the electric tension of money being put in harm's way.

Lefty's is an old-fashioned pool hall, a walkup flight above a not-quite-downtown street, with high ceilings and lazy Bombay fans and green-shaded hanging lamps. It has pool tables with real leather pockets and no coin slots, and snooker and billiards tables, too. And it has high, multi-paned windows. You have to stand on tiptoe to see anything out of them except the sky. It's an easy world to get lost in.

Wilkie likes eight ball, because it's slow and it gives him a lot of time to hustle side bets. I like it because it lets me get more mileage out of finesse than power, which means I can beat him sometimes. At snooker, I almost always can. At nine ball, never.

He can sink the money ball on the break one time out of every six, and those are odds that I can't ignore. And I am nothing if not a believer in odds. So for our separate reasons, we agreed to play straight eight.

Back about a hundred years ago, in the shiny chrome city of Detroit, I worked for my Uncle Fred, a bookie and numbers man and the smartest handicapper I've ever known. He taught me that the secret to all of life is nothing more than being able to figure the correct odds. That, and knowing who the house is and always betting with it.

After he went upstate for the second time, I used his money to start a bail bond business, which I figured was as house as you can get. And I was doing okay, with more cash flow than any of Fred's games produced and none of the risk. But I forgot his second secret to life, which is never to be your own customer. I foolishly used my office to recruit some talent for a caper that went not at all well, and I wound up having to flee The Motor City for good. I kept my old name, Herman Jackson, since it's a common enough one, but I changed everything else. I started a new bail bond business and a new life in St. Paul. It's the capital of Minnesota, of course, and I suppose that makes it important, but I always think of it as an uneventful old shoe of a city, which was exactly what I wanted.

Now I spend my days quietly, playing low stakes pool in Lefty's and writing get-out-of-jail cards for small-time losers too stupid to stay there. I bet only the smart odds, and I spend a lot of time looking over my shoulder.

Sooner or later, I suppose, that had to change.

That afternoon, the odds didn't seem to matter. I was on a roll, and I had just dropped the seven ball with a long-green shot as soft and subtle as destiny's whisper, leaving the old timers in the place thumping the butts of their cues on the floor in muffled applause.

"Nice," said Wilkie.

"I thought so," I said.

"Yeah," he said, rocking on his heels and making the floor groan in the process. "Slicker than snot on a doorknob. It ought to make you feel so good, Herman my man, you forgive yourself in advance for missing the next one, which you are definitely going to do."

"You wish."

"I know. Look it over, man."

I looked. I had only the solid-colored black eight ball, the money ball, left to shoot, while Wilkie still had three striped balls on the table. But the eight was backed up in a corner, frozen against the end rail and totally hidden by the thirteen. In the other direction, down the table, there wasn't enough English in a whole bottle of Beefeater's to let me miss the nine and fifteen and do a two-cushion double around the far corner. I could do a deliberate scratch, without touching the eight, and stay in the game, but that would give Wilkie another turn at shooting, which was never a very good idea. For reasons I will never fathom, I decided to go down with style.

"Massé," I said.

"You can't be serious."

"Have you ever known me otherwise?"

"A hundred bucks says you can't make it."

I looked over the setup again. He was right; I couldn't make it.

"A hundred to my twenty," I said.

"Five to one? Are you nuts? I wouldn't give my sweet old grandma five to one."

"If I had your grandma shooting for me, I'd give you three to five. But you're so damn sure I can't do it, you ought to be willing to be a little sporting."

"Hey, I am a little sporting. I promise not to bounce on the floor while you're setting up to miss. Five to three, then; my hundred to your sixty."

"You bounce on the floor, and all bets are off." Wilkie is over four hundred pounds on the hoof. When his stomach rumbles, so does the earth around him.

"I said I wouldn't, didn't I?"

I looked at the shot again and made a few practice strokes. It really was a terrible setup. A massé is a bizarre shot where you actually stroke the cue ball vertically, as if you were trying to drive it straight down into the table. But you hit it off center, and it goes drunkenly spinning off, waltzing around the ball you have to avoid and back to the one you want to hit. Sometimes. It's never all that easy to do, let alone with exact control. And with the eight ball frozen against the cushion, this one had to be perfect. But for any event in the entire universe, there are odds. And if the odds are right, you have to play. That's another secret of life, which my uncle Fred did not teach me. "Four to one," I said, "nonnegotiable."

"Remind me never to buy a used car from you. All right, against my better judgment, your lousy twenty-five bucks to my hundred."

"I've only got twenty on me, Wide. I told you that up front." And truth to tell, I shouldn't even be risking that. My cash flow situation just then was a disaster.

Wilkie groaned. "I'll carry you, Mr. High Roller."

"Nope." I shook my head while he looked as if he were about to blow a gasket somewhere in his vital machinery. "I never play for what I haven't got. You know that."

"Listen, Superchicken, if you—"

"Call the cops!"

All heads turned to a shapeless character in a dirty parka and watch cap, charging in the main door and screaming at Lefty, who was at his usual spot behind the bar.

"They killed a man out there!"

"Who did?" said Lefty.

"The hell difference does it make, who? Call the cops, will you? And gimmie a beer. And a shot, while you're at it."

Part of the crowd went to the windows and gave out a bunch of noises like, "awgeez," and "willya lookathat?" The rest of them headed for the door. I leaned toward a window.

"Screw that," said Wilkie. "Take the damn shot."

"Who's dead?" I said, looking over the setup with the eight again. It didn't get any better with further study.

"Looks like old Charlie Vee," said one of the voices at the window.

"Oh, shit," I said, and my shoulders sagged. "You sure?" I suddenly had a sinking sensation in my stomach and no interest in the game at all.

"Hard to tell for sure from here," said the voice. "He's messed up awful bad."

I put down the cue stick and headed for the door, leaving Wilkie to fume about the bet. The first shouts of anger and denial inside my own head were already drowning him out.

I didn't know if Lefty had made the phone call yet or not. When I passed him, he was pouring the drinks for the bearer of ill tidings.

"Friend of yours?" said Lefty. "The dead guy, I mean?"

"Customer," I said. At least, that was the short version.

"Always a bitch, losing a good customer."

I didn't bother to stop and explain it to him.

I don't generally look out the windows of Lefty's once in five years, but if I had done so ten minutes earlier on that day, I'd have seen it. I'd have seen them back him up against the wall and punch him in the chest and stomach until he gushed blood from his mouth and the strength went out of his legs and he sagged down against the bricks. I'd have seen when they pushed him all the way down, until he was flat on his back, and one of them stood on his chest while another one finished the job with a heavy boot. And when they spilled whatever was left of his soul onto the cold concrete, along with the addictions and nightmares he carried from the jungles of a distant, dirty war, I might have screamed. I might have. The sky was dim and gray at the time, but it was still daylight. I could have seen it all, and I could have screamed for him.

And I should have.

It makes absolutely no sense and does no good to say so, but I know I should have.

◇◇◇

The wet, wind-driven flakes hit me in the face and insinuated themselves inside my open collar and up my shirt cuffs, reminding me that I had run out without a coat.

Across the street, there were a dozen or more spectators ahead of me, clustered in a semicircle about ten feet back from the body on the sidewalk. Gawkers, drawn irresistibly to the sight of violent death but still wanting to keep a certain sterile distance between it and themselves. From somewhere far away, I could hear the first sirens. I pushed through the crowd and had a look, instantly regretting it. The guy at the window had not been exaggerating about how messed up the dead man was.

The face was a deflated soccer ball, smeared with blood and draped in overlong gray hair. And the body shape was masked by the countless layers of old clothes that street people collect. At first glance, it could have been anybody. But there, unmistakably, was the threadbare khaki fatigue jacket with the faded sergeant stripes and the frayed Air Cav shoulder patch. There, also, were the thick-soled work boots, their brown leather daubed endlessly with black shoe polish, to try to make them look like combat boots, because Charlie couldn't get any real combat boots at the free store on West Seventh Street. And there were the big, once powerful hands, now cruelly deformed by arthritis, with a blue tattoo of a coiled cobra on the back of the right one. I knew all that well enough, and a good bit more. It was Charlie, all right. In some ways, he was still a complete mystery to me, but I knew him when I saw him, even in this sorry state.

Charles Victor was his real name, and yes, he did once have to go to Vietnam with that most unfortunate of handles. What they called him over there, I didn't know, but I imagined that he must have had to be one hell of a soldier, just to keep from being shot by his own people. He had a lot of stories, but who knew how many of them were true?

Whatever he had really done, he never got over it. I didn't know if he fit the orthodox definition of post-traumatic stress syndrome, but for my money, he could have been a poster child for it. In Southeast Asia, the war was over decades ago. People go there as tourists now. The war in Charlie's soul went on every day, and no sane person would go there, ever. He left the jungle, but it never left him. It was always sitting on his shoulder like a dark, leathery gargoyle, waiting to trip him into quiet madness and horror. If he was violent, I never saw it, but I did see times when he just wasn't present in the real world at all. Whether for that reason or others, he never held a regular job or had a home or a woman or wanted anything from life but anonymity and oblivion. And he finally got both of them, but as usual with him, he paid way too much.

But then, there's a lot of that going around. By rights, I shouldn't have cared. What was he to me, after all? A customer, and not a very big one at that. But there was another link there, not so easy to put a name on. Sometimes I had the feeling that his story, if I knew it well enough, would also turn out to be my own. And as with my own, I knew I hadn't heard it all yet. For the moment, though, I felt sick. And at least part of that sickness was called guilt.

Footprints

"What about you? You see anything?" It was a challenge, not a question. The cop throwing it at me was fortyish, red-faced, big, and belligerent. His expression made it clear that I had damn well better have seen something, if I knew what was good for me. Otherwise, my presence on the street was an insult to the universe in general and him in particular.

"I just got here," I said, shaking my head.

"Yeah? Well, just get someplace else. The thing I do not need around here right now, is I do not need any more goddamn rubbernecks."

He had a point. So far, he was the only police presence at a scene that was drawing a crowd faster than the free bar at an Irish wake. If there had been any useful evidence in the fresh snow, the mob had already obliterated it or stuffed it in their pockets for souvenirs. Not good.

Down near the end of the block, there were still a few sets of distinct footprints, but even as we watched, a big, square-shouldered kid in a black nylon wind breaker and a stocking cap came around the corner and began pushing them into the gutter with a shiny new aluminum snow shovel.

"Now that's really sweet," said the cop. "Priceless." He looked over at me, as if he was waiting for some kind of reaction. When I gave him none, he hustled off to intercept the shoveler.

There was some conversation I couldn't hear, some pointing and shrugging and less-than-polite gesturing, and a baton poked in the kid's chest a few times. Finally the kid took his shovel and went back the way he had come. As he flipped the bird to the cop behind his back, I noticed he wasn't wearing any gloves. I also noticed that he hadn't been shoveling the whole sidewalk, merely the strip where the footprints had been. Or was that my imagination? The cop didn't seem to notice or care. He came stomping back to me, looking like Moses coming down off the mountain, with fire in his eye and heavy indictments on his mind.

"You know," he said, "after fifteen years on the job, I've developed a terrific memory for faces. You look exactly like the guy I just told to get his ass out of here." He must have had a circulation problem in his left hand, because he was rhythmically beating on his gloved palm with his nightstick now.

"I can identify the victim," I said.

"You said you didn't see anything." The baton came out of his left hand, and both it and he were suddenly at full cock.

"I didn't, but I know the dead man."

"Is that all? Well, it so happens that I also know him. That's why they call this my turf, you know? He's a bum named Cee Vee, a nobody, lives in a box down in some boofug Dogpatch ditch. And some cokeheads or meth freaks decided to punch his lights out and then liked it so much that they just couldn't stop themselves. Case closed."

"His name was Charles Victor," I said.

"The hell, you say. Now you can give me yours." He took out his notebook and flipped it to a page that looked like as if it was already full of doodles and phone numbers.

"Herman Jackson."

He started to write, and I peered over the edge of the pad enough to see if he had written Charlie's name, too.

"You're starting to piss me off, Herman Jackson. You want to know the remedy for that?"

"No."

"That's good, because—"

"Did you get the name of the kid with the shovel?"

"Jesus, you just don't take a hint, do you? He's a kid with a shovel, okay? Another nobody, also saw nothing. The guy that owns the hardware store around the corner gave him five bucks to shovel the walk, he says. Big mystery. You happy now? Get the hell out of here."

"Did you notice he wasn't wearing any gloves?"

"Your point?" He stopped writing, sighed, and gave me a pained look.

"Would you be out shoveling with no gloves?"

"No." He stuck the notebook back in his pocket and pointed the baton menacingly at my chest. "What I'd be doing, is I'd be over here trying to get rid of some smartass wants to tell me my job. Some guy who's about to get smacked for his trouble, he pushes it just a little bit farther."

"But he—"

"The detectives will be here in a little bit, also trying to tell me my job, and when they do, I do not want you around helping them. Got it?"

I could see I was arguing with a parking meter, so I stuck my hands in my pockets and started to go. "There is one thing the detectives are going to want you to have found out," I said over my shoulder.

I took three steps back across the street and was stopped by the handle end of the black baton, hooked over my shoulder.

"You got one shot," said the cop. "One. What are they going to want me to know?"

"There is no hardware store around the corner. There's nothing but the back doors of a lot of offices and a hole-in-the-wall shoe repair shop."

"Look, the kid said—"

"Wow, you don't suppose he lied to a cop, do you? Why would he do that?"

"Shit," said the cop. "Sam bitch! Listen, mister smartass Herman Jackson, you do not talk to the detectives, you got that? You do *not*." Then he spun on his heel and ran off in the direction of the now-shoveled street corner, shouting into his radio on the way.

It seemed to me he had a lot of funny attitudes for a cop. It also seemed that he didn't know his own turf very well. Or else he belonged there even less than I did. I tagged along behind, just to see what the detectives were not supposed to.

But when I rounded the corner, the street was empty. I walked a bit farther, to put the street light behind me, and squinted into the darkening urban landscape. Two blocks away, cop, kid, and shovel were running away as fast as they could. They were already far enough off to be hard to see clearly, but it sure looked as if they were together, rather than one chasing the other. Another quick block, a turn into a side street or alley, and they were gone.

I went back the way I had come, turned the corner again, and looked over at the crime scene. The first squad car was just arriving. The first one. And I knew, absolutely, that the cop I had talked to wasn't coming back.

I wanted to kick myself for being so slow on the uptake. It had puzzled me when I said I knew the victim, and instead of getting interested, the cop got pissed. That's not how cops are supposed to act. It should have set off my radar. And I should have also wondered how this guy just happened to get to the scene so fast.

Should have.

I didn't go back toward the body, to tell a new set of cops who the victim was. For all I knew, the uniform I had talked to was really a cop, and if so, I wasn't sure how I should play the scene. Whatever the guy was, I was sure he had at least witnessed the murder, if not had a hand in it. Sticky. You don't hand off that kind of information unless you're sure of the people you're handing it to.

Instead, I headed back to Lefty's to find Wilkie and see if he was carrying. Because if I was going to try to follow Officer Pissed Off and his shovel-toting friend, I definitely wanted a gun in my pocket.

◇◇◇

Wilkie was gone when I got back to the pool hall, so I borrowed a piece from Lefty, despite his being not all that happy about the idea.

"I get held up while you're off with that, I expect you to make good on my losses," he said.

"You get held up a lot, do you?"

"What's that got to do with anything?"

"That's what I thought." I retrieved my leather coat from the rack by the door and stuffed the gun in the pocket. It was a short-barrel .38 revolver, and if Lefty could hit a robber with it from anything more than three feet away, he was a damn sight better shot than I was. But it was what he had. A street preacher I know called The Prophet would say the karma of the moment was structured that way, which was not so different from my Uncle Fred telling me to play the hand I was dealt. Either way, I went with it.

We don't really have a part of town called Nighttown, but that's how I always think of it. East of downtown and north of what's left of the old Soo Line freight yards and the warehouses they used to service, the land falls away sharply to a low, weedy area that never quite knew what to do with itself except be a place for the Mississippi to flood into every spring. A bit north of there, the general slough forks into two distinct branches, Swede Hollow to the east and Connemara Gulch to the west. The high ground between those two is called Railroad Island. The buildings suddenly get a lot seedier and farther apart there than in downtown, mixed with scattered vacant lots and impromptu junkyards that are overgrown with weeds and favored by strange animals and stranger people. There are still a few shacky houses and apartments and some small industrial buildings, like plating factories and chop shops, but a lot of the area is just wilderness. The urban removal programs of the sixties wiped out most of the old slum housing and marginal businesses and replaced them with nothing. I guess somebody thought that was progress.

Neither of the gulches is a good place to go alone and after dark. The high ground may or may not be any better, depending on which alley you go down. A deputy sheriff friend of mine first got me calling it Nighttown because, she says, there are a lot of ways for your lights to go out there, ways that have nothing to do with the sun going down. Somewhere down there, "under the wye-duct," Charlie may have had his cardboard box, the one that wasn't warm enough. And that general direction was where the cop and the kid with the shovel seemed to be headed. And though I knew he was still lying on the sidewalk across from Lefty's, I had the strong feeling that somewhere down there, Charlie was waiting for me. Waiting for me to set things right.

Nighttown

The cop and the kid had a big head start on me by the time I got back from Lefty's, but rush hour had been over for a long time and the snow continued to fall, so there weren't a lot of competing footprints to confuse things. I followed them east for four or five blocks, then north and east, across a bridge over the Interstate ditch and into an area of old factories and warehouses, somewhere near Railroad Island. The streetlights got very far apart there, and about a block past the bridge, they disappeared completely. I was beginning to wish I had hit Lefty up for a flashlight as well as a piece.

Over behind an old industrial building that had been partly made into artists' lofts and partly abandoned to squatters, some street people were huddled around a trash fire in an old barrel. They were a younger and tougher-looking bunch than the usual pack of lost souls and dehorns that hang around in that area, and if I'd been smart, I'd have probably just kept walking. But there was no more pristine snow, and no more distinct tracks. They were my last hope for picking up the trail again.

I headed over to see what I could learn from the great unwashed.

"Here comes another one."

"Another what?" A second shapeless bundle of rags looked up from the fire.

"Sit-ee-zen, man, what you think?"

"Nah, this one ain't no citizen. This one ain't got no ramrod up his ass, like that last dude."

"Bet he ain't got no badge, neither."

"Does he gots money, is what the thing is."

"I can think of some ways to find out."

"Think of one that don't get us all busted."

"Shit, man."

"Shit is right. You think I'm playin' y'all here?"

"Shit."

That seemed to be the consensus, all right.

There were five of them altogether, and I found their talk about *another* sit-ee-zen more than a bit interesting. But before I was likely to hear any more of it, there was some physical protocol to take care of. A little respect, a little threat, a little reward. Not the way the cops do it. Let them know you're not afraid of them, but let them wonder if they should be afraid of you. Easy, easy. First, though, find a place where they can't get behind you.

I caught the eye of the big black guy who was doing most of the talking, held up my last twenty from the pool game, and let him get a good look at it. Then I went over to a niche in the back of the closest industrial building, an inside corner by a loading dock. He looked at his buddies as if wanting their approval. They didn't react, which was good news. It meant they probably weren't a regular gang. The big guy shuffled over to me, and the others followed about five yards back.

"Rough night to be out," I said.

"'Pends on if you with you friends, man."

"Yeah, well it's always good to have friends," I said. I took the .38 out of my pocket and let my arm hang by my side, partially lost in the folds of my coat. Then I rotated the piece outward, toward him, giving him just a bit of a look.

"I'm real scared, man. So what you lookin' for, with your big-assed strap and your little bitty double sawbuck?"

"Two guys, a cop and a big kid, came by here maybe fifteen minutes ago, tops."

"You shittin' me? That's it? You ain't lookin' for ol' Cee Vee's squat?"

That got my attention, but I tried not to show it too much. I tore the twenty in half and gave him one piece of it.

"First, the cop and the kid," I said.

"For that crappy piece of paper? Go fuck yourself."

"Listen, man, what's your name?"

He glared at me for a while, just to show me he didn't have to tell me if he didn't want to. Then he did it anyway.

"Linc."

"Okay Linc, tell me. You know about the stick and the carrot?"

"What's that, some rock group?"

"That's the two things you can get, to make you feel like talking to me. Twenty is all the carrot I've got. After that's gone, we go to the stick. Trust me, you don't want that."

"You a cop?" said one of the other worthies, who was sidling his way up to me along the dock face.

Didn't I wish? If I were a cop, I could call for backup. I took a deep breath and tried again.

"No. I'm also not a fed or a social worker or a preacher or a politician. And that means I don't have anybody I report to or any damn procedure I have to follow. Think about that for a minute."

Number three continued to crowd in on me, and the momentum started going the way I had hoped to avoid. Oh, well.

I made a sudden jerky movement, as if I were trying to get away from the guy. He took that as an invitation, which it was, to stick out an arm and lunge for me. I grabbed the arm and pulled him in the direction he was already moving, only a lot faster than he wanted to go. As he lurched by, I kicked his legs out from under him, letting him sprawl on the ground in front of me. Then I put one foot on his neck, hard, swung Lefty's .38 up into full view, and pointed it at the guy who had been moving in from the other way.

"Five guys, six bullets," I said. "I can make that work. Or you can all split an easy twenty bucks and get the hell out of here." With my left hand, I waved the torn bill in front of me. "Your choice. You don't look stupid to me. How do you want to play it?" And I gave them about two seconds of a totally phony smile.

"Cool," said the big one with the other half of my twenty.

"Cool what?"

"What I says is we all play it cool, man." And he held up his hands, palms toward me, and backed away half a step.

"I think you're smarter than your buddy under my foot here," I said. "So how about cop and the kid?"

"Yeah, okay. They come by here, jus' like you say. Then they take a cab."

"What the hell does that mean?"

"Somebody in a big black set of wheels come by and picked them up, is what."

"What kind of wheels?"

"Big, is all I know. Not a stretch, but a 98 of some kind. One of them high mothers."

"Like a SUV? Escalade, maybe?"

"Yeah, maybe. I dunno."

"Was the kid in cuffs?"

"Nah, they was tight, man. Wasn't no bust or shit goin' down. Them rims come for them, is all."

"And which way did the rims go?"

"That way." He pointed toward the gulch, deeper into Railroad Island.

"You're sure? They didn't head back into town?"

"What I said, man. Back that way. That enough?"

"We're getting there. Now tell me why you asked me about Cee Vee's pitch."

"She-it, man, that's the flavor of the day. First a couple of suits come by askin', back this afternoon, a dude and a broad. Broad was bad, too, but she didn't bust a move or nothin' and they didn't pay us. They just flash around these fancy ID cards an' all, wasn't even real badges."

"Feds?"

"Maybe, some kind."

"And who else?"

"Short, fat dude with a big overcoat and a funny hat, maybe two, three hours ago. He didn't have no fancy ID, but he gave us fifty presidents."

"And what did you tell him?"

"You got fifty, man?"

"I already told you I don't. We're almost home free, man. Let's make it work, here."

"Yeah, well, we didn't really have no cipher to give him, no how, so we made up some shit. Kinda like the shit we tole the suits. Tole them Cee Vee's box was down under the viaduct, whatever the fuck that is, 'cause that's what he allus use to say. An' we tole them the viaduct was down in Sheeny Gulch, which who the hell knows?" He hooked a thumb in the general direction behind his back.

"So, what did they all do?"

"Do? What you think, man? They all go down there, is what they all do."

"What about the guy with the ramrod up his ass?"

"Who?"

"Aw, hell, and we were doing so well there." I stuffed the half of the twenty back in my pocket.

"Oh, you mean *that* dude, the one we was talkin' 'bout when you come up? Looks like a jarhead with a cheap suit? He got out of the wheels."

"The wheels that picked up the—"

"Yeah, yeah, that one."

"And you weren't going to tell me about him?"

"I thought I'd keep the story short, you know? He didn't talk much, no how. I s'pose he coulda been making sure nobody followed the wheels. Thought he was hot shit, gives us a hard stare for a while like he's lookin' to rumble some. Finally he just splits."

"Let me guess…"

"Down to the gulch. It was like a regular fucking parade, man."

"This is good," I said, and I handed the other half of the bill over to him. "Thanks, Linc."

"You gonna let Mingus, there, up?"

"He fuckin' well better," said the head that was down by my foot, "or when he does, I'm unna—" I stepped down a bit harder, and he grunted a bit and then shut up.

"Back off thirty paces, and he's all yours."

They walked backward, back to their trash barrel, and I slowly lifted my foot. Mingus, if that was really his name, pushed himself up fast to a hands-and-knees position, looking pissed. But before he could jump up to his full height, I stuck the barrel of the .38 up against his nose and let him have a good look at it.

"Don't do anything stupid, Mingus."

He stared cross-eyed at the piece for a moment, then shook his head vehemently. I let him get the rest of the way up, and he hustled off to join the others. When they started their own muttered, low conversation again, I turned and walked away, toward the reportedly popular gulch.

I let out the breath I'd been holding for longer than I could remember.

Fifty yards later, I was in a totally unlit area of weeds, rocks, and trash. A short way ahead, it got even darker, as the snow gave way to the utter black of Connemara Gulch, gaping below and beyond me. Or maybe it was just some railroad ditch. I wasn't that sure of where I was anymore. I couldn't tell how far it was to the bottom, but the way down looked steep and treacherous. There had to be a better route. Right or left? I picked left and walked along the edge of the gully for a while, and sure enough, I came to a crude roadway with a gate across it where it dropped down into the hollow. And standing with one hand on the gate was a guy who must have been the ramrod-ass that the village people had liked so much. Stiff posture, military-style brush cut on his light hair, and a dark topcoat that hung on him like a tent that was one size too big. And even in the dark, I could tell he wore a look that said, "I'm in charge here, and you are lower than whale shit." One of my favorite types. I wondered if I could find an excuse to shoot him.

"This road is closed," he said.

No "mister," no "sir," not even a "please." Wow, he really did want to impress me with what a badass he was. And for all I knew, he really was. He was big, anyway. He had his hands shoved deep in his coat pockets, and I had the impression I did not want him to take them out.

"Because you say it is? Who are you, exactly?"

"You have no business here," he said, in non-reply. "Move along."

"I asked who you are," I said.

"I'm Mister Colt." He opened his coat and let me see that he had two semiautomatics in holsters, in addition to a compact submachine gun that he had just pulled out of a pocket. "And your name is Mud. Some people are about to get hurt here, and unless you haul ass now, you could be one of them. This has nothing to do with you."

That was way too much firepower for me. "Thanks for the warning," I said. I kept my hands at my side, turned around and walked back into the shadows.

In the black gulch below, somebody was switching on powerful flashlight beams. They looked as if they were on the bottom of the ocean. Then there was a bunch of shouting that progressively got louder. Some of it sounded hysterical, all of it angry. Soon there were crashing noises to go with it and then sporadic automatic weapons fire.

And there was the smell.

What the hell was it? A gasoline smell of some kind, but not like what you whiff when you fuel up your car. Kerosene, maybe, or the kind of gas they use in camp lanterns.

As I thought about it, the gulch below lit up with the orange glow of tents and sleeping boxes and piles of rags being torched. Somebody, or rather several somebodies, were moving through the gulch, setting fire to everything in sight and driving a frantic clot of ragged derelicts in front of them.

I stared, dumbfounded, transfixed. I felt the hair on the back of my neck stand up, and my ears roared with my own pulse. Why the hell did they have to use fire? I hate fire. Let me die any way but that.

For a while, I watched the pyrotechnics display and the shadowy crowd of refugees move farther down the gulch, away from me. And seeing nothing to be gained down there but trouble, I turned away. I didn't know where Square Head was by then, but I decided he was right: I had no business down there.

As I walked back the way I had come, fresh out of ideas and purpose, I found the snow shovel.

Business as Unusual

The next morning, I blew the dust off the remote for my TV and listened to the early morning news as I worked on my first caffeine fix of the day and my nourishing, balanced breakfast of White Castle hamburgers and bread-and-butter pickles. The incident at the trash barrel bothered me. I had pulled a gun on a man I did not really want to kill, and that can't happen, ever. Once a gun is out, it takes on a life of its own, and all your careful plans for anonymous existence can suddenly be nothing but yesterday's daydreams.

As troubling as all that was, the fires down in the gulch were worse, if only because I had no idea what to make of them. The media, of course, wouldn't know how to tell me the complete or accurate truth if their ratings actually depended on it. But they might at least tell me something about the superficial events. That would be a start.

But the early news said nothing about a commando raid on homeless people or any mysterious fire in Connemara Gulch. On three different channels, male-female anchor teams flirted ever so mildly, giggled at their own inane jokes, chatted about the latest squabbles between the City Council and the Mayor, and offered advice on how to prepare your lawn for winter. They also promised to give me the morning traffic reports and some high-powered weather information after only sixteen or twenty more commercials. I quickly remembered why my remote control is all covered with dust. How can people listen to that shit every day?

Before I left for my office, I called the non-emergency number for the police and got a female desk sergeant with a phone voice that radiated don't-mess-with-me with thorns on it.

"A man named Charles Victor was killed outside Lefty's Pool Hall last night," I said. "I'm wondering if I could talk to the detective who has that case."

"And your name is?"

I told her.

"Are you calling from your own phone?"

"Yes, I am."

"And you have information on what case, again?"

"The murder of Charles Victor." I almost said I didn't have any information, but I could see how far that would get me. As it happened, it didn't make any difference.

"We have no such case on record, sir." If her voice had been any colder, my phone would have been icing up.

"Maybe you just don't have the name. He was a homeless person."

"We have more than one John Doe homicide currently open, sir. Could you give me some more information?"

"This man was beaten to death last night, in front of Lefty's Pool Hall."

"And you were a witness?"

"No. I just have some information about the victim. I'm a bail bondsman, and he used to be a client of mine." I also had the shovel, of course, but somehow I didn't feel like sharing that information with her.

"That would be Detective Erickson's case, sir. He's very busy right now."

"How about if we let him decide that? Could you transfer me, please?"

"I'll tell him you called, sir. If he needs your information, he will get back to you. I have other calls to take here."

"Can I talk to some other detective, then?"

"To which detective did you wish to speak?"

"I have no idea. Any detective."

The line went dead, and I could swear the receiver was flipping me the bird. I wondered what time the shift changed at the cop shop, so I could try again with a different professional asshole. Meanwhile, I wrote down the name of the detective, put on my coat and headed for my car.

Outside, I was able to figure out, even without Super Duper Doppler Radar, that last night's snow was melting, though the sky was the color of dirty dishwater and could spit some more of the stuff at any time. The sun was nowhere in sight and there was just enough wind to get your attention. It was all very October.

I took my usual route downtown and parked the BMW 328i in the Victory Ramp. I mostly park there because I love the name. I like to think Winston Smith would have parked there, if the Thought Police had let him have a car. Then he could have made it with his darling Julia in the back seat, and he wouldn't have had to worry about all those nasty rats. It may not be great literature that way, but it's a favorite fantasy.

Walking from the ramp to my office, I bought copies of both the *St. Paul Pioneer Press* and the *Minneapolis Star and Tribune* from some paperboys disguised as tin boxes. If they contained anything about the fires in the gulch, it wasn't on the front page of either. A quick flip of pages showed me that it also wasn't on the first page of the Local News sections. What on earth was going on here? The *Strib* was often a day late in reporting local events on this side of the river, though they sometimes made up for it with better detail. But the *Pioneer* should have caught it. Hell, it was practically in their back parking lot. On a slow news day, which it was, it should have made big headlines. Or Charlie's murder should have.

As usual, Agnes, my indispensable Lady Friday, general manager, and confidante was at the office ahead of me. I think she does that just to make me feel guilty. She isn't aware of this, of course. Someday I'll explain it to her.

She had already opened the mail and was having a nice dialogue with her computer, while off in another corner, Mr. Coffee was talking to himself in some belchy-gurgly appliance creole.

I threw the newspapers on my desk, hung up my coat, and picked up a letter from the top of the stack. It was hand written on three sheets of lined yellow legal paper, the kind that cops give perps to write their confessions. The assault upon the language spoke for itself, but at least it wasn't in crayon. And it was fairly polite, in its own way. It also came in a neat white envelope and was actually legible.

Agnes smirked when I picked it up. Not a good sign. I smoothed out the smudged paper and read:

Dear Mr. Jackson Bail Bonds

I am writing about a bond you sold me that din't work. I mean, they let me out of jail and all, even though I had to come back later, but I din't enjoy it. I found out my woman run off with the bus driver lives down stairs from us if you can believe that shit and I din't have no money to go get some ass or some booze on account of the bond and the lawyer. So my brother he come home from the U S Army where he was on absence of leave and I told him how I wasn't getting none and even if I was to get unconvicted, I'd have to give the lawyer a bunch more money, too, which I ain't got. So him and me we got all sad together and then we got some Colt 45 and got all lickered up a little and decided to go rob the Army Navy Surpluss Store on Payne Avenue. Just to even things up, like. But there was a alarm in the store, wun't you know, and we got caught and now I'm back in the slam, and my brother too. And because of the first bond I can't get no new one cause there dam sure pissed at me this time.

So I just thought. I no you ecsplained to me that I don't never get my bond money back, not in anny real money or nothing. But I thought maybe since the first bond din't work and I ain't got no more money since we got caught before we finished robbing the Army Navy Surpluss store, maybe you could see your way clear to make a free bail bond for my brother so he can get out of this awful place and go back to the U S Army and go get his self killed in some forn country like Irack, like a real solder. He is a good man and it seems like the least you could do for your country any how.

I hope I don't have to add that I still have lots of friends on the out side who can find out where you live, if you no what I mean.

My brother's name is Vitrol, like the hair tonic, and last name same as mine. Help him out, can you, and we will be all square again.

Your frend in boundage,
Remo Wilson but my friends call me Trick

God, I love this business. It's not the money; it's the class of people you get to meet. I snatched a cup of coffee from the gurgling machine, pouring it quickly so not too much would drip onto the hot bottom plate. The plate hissed at me from under the pot, telling me I hadn't been quick enough.

I looked over the letter again. I could only count it as another triumph for the adult literacy program at the County Workhouse.

"Why do you always have to do that?"

"That? What that?"

"Pour yourself a cup of coffee before it's done brewing."

"Oh that that. Because it's better then. And a lovely good morning to you, too, Agnes. Know anything about lifting fingerprints?"

"Of course it's better then. That's because all the gunky, bitter stuff is in the last cup that drips through. Good morning."

"Then maybe we should shut it off before it gets to that part." I took a sip and found the morning's brew, as expected, really rather good. Later, it would be progressively more like battery acid.

"Sometimes it's abundantly clear to me why you're not married, Herman. Fingerprints off what, the coffee pot?"

"No, off a snow shovel." *It had better not be abundantly clear, or I'm in a lot of trouble.*

"You can't be serious."

She went back to pecking at her keyboard, which is a sure sign that she sees she's talking to a crazy person and would really rather not deal with it just now, thank you. Or maybe she was disappointed that I wasn't going to talk about the deeply moving letter from my friend in boundage, Trick.

I noticed, not for the first time, that she actually looked her best with a mild mock scowl, concentrating on her computer through a pair of thick glasses. Agnes is a hard person to describe, even harder to remember, somehow. It's as if she had no prominent features to focus on. I had known her for eight years, and I still looked at her and tried to remember who it was she reminded me of. She had one of those oddly familiar faces that are neither young nor old, always pleasant but a bit self-deprecating, almost perky, almost pretty, almost sexy. Almost. Sometimes I wonder if I ought to be closer to her, but I'm not. And sometimes I wonder if she would like to change all that. But then I forget to wonder more. She definitely looked nice, though, scowling through her glasses.

"Of course I'm serious," I said. "In the movies, they're always talking about dusting something for prints, right?"

"Yes they are. So?"

"So, what's the dust?"

"How should I know? Fluorescent bath talc, probably."

"That sounds reasonable. Got any?"

If looks could kill, my day would have ended, right then and there. I decided to change the subject.

"I got my Visa statement yesterday."

"Does that have something to do with fingerprints?"

"No, that has to do with you not cashing your last two paychecks."

"Well, what did you expect? You can't be writing payroll on credit, Herman. That's worse than going to a loan shark."

"No, it's not. Visa won't break my legs if I don't pay them."

"Herman, it's economic suicide."

"More like slightly postponed disaster. Trust me, Ag, I can afford to go into debt better than you can afford to go without being paid." I really couldn't, but my only other options at the moment were to sell the BMW or go into one of my secret escape caches.

"Look, Herman, we can…"

Her voice trailed off as she was distracted by something out in the street, and her expression changed from plain vanilla anxiety to real, double Dutch resentment.

"Here comes trouble," she said.

I turned to follow her gaze and saw a shapeless middle-aged guy in a sharp brown pinstripe. He crossed the street against the light without looking to either side, as if he either didn't care about getting run down or simply expected everybody to get out of his way. Once across, he looked up, turned, and headed toward my door. I had never seen him before.

"Friend of yours, Aggie?"

"Not on the best day he ever had. He's been here a few times, looking for you."

He was not a big man, but he had a certain presence, and his round face seemed on the verge of a sneer, as if he knew he intimidated people and was glad of it. He wore what was left of his brown hair slicked straight back under a classic dark fedora, a hat so out, it was back in again, and he walked with his lump of a chin out, as if it were a badge of authority. He dressed expensively but with just a touch too much flash, I thought, like somebody who spends all his time running away from an impoverished past. Or maybe some street muscle who has just graduated to middle management and doesn't yet know how to shop. He didn't look as if he was carrying, but his suit coat was cut large at the chest, possibly to hide the occasional holster.

He let himself in, and when he spoke, his voice was gravel and oil, with a certain smugness to it and an accent I couldn't quite identify. Some sub-species of New Yorker, possibly.

"Mr. Jackson?"

"The very one." Following Agnes' lead, I did not offer him my hand, but I did give him the courtesy of not glaring.

"My name is Eddie Bardot, Mr. Jackson, I represent—"

"The mob," said Agnes.

"Oh, please." He gave me a stage smile and held up his hands in a palms-forward gesture of innocence. "Let's not get melodramatic here, shall we?" He jerked a thumb at Agnes and said, "Missy Four Eyes here doesn't like me coming around your office. I think she's afraid I might make a pass at her."

And I swear to God, he gave me a wink. I didn't think anybody ever did that anymore. I was not charmed by it, nor by the fact that he liked to stand less than two feet away when he talked to me.

"You can take your 'missy' and your 'four eyes' and go wander off a cliff somewhere," said Agnes. For her, that was pretty nasty, and I wondered what this guy had said to her in my absence.

"Maybe we should talk privately," he said to me.

"Maybe we shouldn't. How about if you just quit talking about Agnes as if she weren't here, and we'll see how that works? And back off, while you're at it. We're not conspirators or lovers, so get out of my space."

He backed off a step, but not as far as I would have liked.

"All right, look, maybe we all got off on the wrong foot here. Let's try again, okay? I represent…"

He looked pointedly at Agnes, to see if she was going to interrupt him again, but she merely stared at him with one eyebrow raised.

"I represent," he went on, "a, um *group* of businessmen who are investing heavily in the bail bond business. You have a very nice little operation here, Mr. Jackson, but the word is, you have a cash flow problem."

"Oh really? And whose word would that be?"

"With a bigger block of capital, see, and some better connections, some better layoff options, you could be—"

"Squeezed out," said Agnes.

"I thought she wasn't going to interrupt me."

"I didn't hear her say that. I thought you weren't going to talk about her as if she weren't here."

"Could I please just finish what I came here to tell you?" The color was starting to rise in his face now, the veneer of civility beginning to wear thin. *Silk over slime,* I thought. *Soon it will begin to seep through.* But he went on in almost the same tone, with just a bit more open hostility now.

"You're a successful businessman, Jackson. You know what that means in this day and age?"

"You bet. It means I can be fussy about who I talk to."

"It means," and he paused slightly and drew himself up to his full height, "that you are a prime candidate for being bought out. In case you don't know it, that's a very big deal."

"Oh, I can see that, all right."

"You think I'm joking? That's the American dream now. Nobody tries to make it on their own anymore. The real jackpot is when you get successful enough that the big boys want your operation. And they do."

"And why do I care what they want?"

"Oh, you care, believe me. You're about to find out how much you care. Anyway, you never think about retiring young? No more sweating the recovery rate of your bounty hunters? No more wondering if anybody knows you only run an eighty percent layoff rate? Think of all the trips you'd like to take, maybe with—"

"Don't even think about using that phrase again," said Agnes.

"What she said," I said. "Just who are these so-called big boys, by the way?"

Bardot reached into an inside pocket and produced a business card, which he handed to me with what I'm sure he thought was a significant look. It was an expensive-looking, low-key bit of embossed printing, and under his name, it said "Amalgamated Bonding Enterprises." Without an "Inc.," I noted.

"This tells me diddly squat," I said. "I'd like to know just exactly who all these wonderful, amalgamated, unincorporated folks are." I stuck the card in my shirt pocket without being properly awed by it.

"Oh, big people. Very big, very important. Venture capitalists, entrepreneurs. Totally above reproach."

"Who?"

"Well, they like to keep a low profile. You know how it is."

"No. How is it?"

"Mind your own damn business, is how it is." Finally, the smile was completely gone, the gloves off. "This is a real opportunity here, Jackson."

"You're absolutely right."

"Excuse me?"

"About minding my own business. That's what it is. My business. And that's what it stays. It's not for sale and it's not open to extortion."

"Everything is for sale, Jackson. And everybody has their pressure points."

"In your world, maybe. So what happens now? Do you send Guido and Dutch over here to tip over my vegetable stand and break my windows, just to show me you're serious?"

"Do you really take me for a thug, Jackson?"

"'I would you were so honest a man.'"

"What's that supposed to mean?"

"It means get the hell out of here."

He sighed and turned around. "It always starts this way," he said. And without waiting for my brilliant retort, he left, once again crossing the street against the light and without looking either way.

"Nice fellow," I said, "but very confused."

"How did he know about your layoff rate, do you suppose?"

"You picked up on that, too, did you, Aggie?"

"He made it hard to miss."

"It could be a guess on his part," I said, not really believing it, "but if so, it hit awfully close to the truth. I'm sure that's one of the things he wants us to contemplate while he's gone."

"I take it you're expecting him back."

"Oh, I think we can count on that. And the next time, he'll have something to up the ante with."

"What do you think his 'big, important people' really want, Herman? Is this whole act really just simple extortion?"

"It's some kind of extortion for sure, but I don't think it's so simple. I'm guessing they really do want to buy my business, but not before they've screwed it up somehow, so it's not worth much of anything."

"I don't like this, Herman."

"You're right, Aggie, you don't like this at all."

The phone rang, and since Agnes was still looking a little stressed out, I picked it up.

"Jackson Bail Bonds."

"Herman?"

"Speaking."

"Yeah, say, Frankie Russo here, Herman. I just wanted to let you know it was nothing personal."

"Of course it wasn't. What are you talking about?"

"Jumping bail."

"Your trial isn't for four days yet."

"Yeah, well I can't be there, is the thing."

"Are you crazy? Failure to appear is a worse offense than the one you're charged with, which is completely bogus anyway. If you hadn't mouthed off to the judge, you'd be ROR. You said it yourself: the cops just want to harass you because they can't legally close down your strip joint like the Mayor so dearly wants them to. If you skip, you'll be doing just what they want."

"Yeah, well, I gotta skip."

"Why on earth?"

"'Cause this guy named Eddie stuck a gun in my face and told me to, is why. He threatened my family, too."

"Son of a bitch."

"Yeah, that would be him, all right. Look, I gotta go, okay? You take care."

"Hey, wait—" The line went dead.

Frank Russo's bond was for twenty-five thousand. And because he was no flight risk at all, I had carried it on my own.

"Call Wilkie and tell him we've got a jumper for him."

Layoffs and Other Labor Problems

It's a funny business, writing bail bonds. People like to say it's like the insurance business, but it's not. Except when it is. In any absolute sense, I'm usually not a bondsman, but a bonding agent, in exactly the same way that the guy you buy your car insurance from is an insurance agent. He doesn't personally insure your car; he just represents a big company that does. And that is what the pinstripe goon, Bardot, was talking about when he referred to laying off the bonds.

The thing is, he wouldn't have used that term for it unless he had some kind of background in a different business altogether. Like bookmaking. "Laying off" a bet is what a bookie calls it when he has somebody make a legitimate bet at a legitimate track, to insure himself against a nasty loss on some suddenly popular long shot or other. And the fact that Bardot used that term meant that he also knew I would be familiar with it. And he wanted me to know that he knew.

He also knew how much of it I did. Laying off, that is. Nobody lays off everything, because there are some clients that are just no risk at all, and you may as well carry them on your own and pocket the full bond fee. Like Frank Russo. There are others that just don't fit any legitimate, regular profile, though they are still perfectly good customers. Those you also carry on your own, if only because you can't sell them to your backup company.

And then there are the bail junkies.

You can't daisy-chain insurance policies. That is, you can't buy a policy against having your roof blow off, say, and when the roof *does* blow off, buy another one against getting water damage, and when that happens too, because now you have no roof, get still another one against getting sick off the mildew and mold, and so on. What sane person would write such a string of policies?

A bail bondsman, that's who. He can make a lot of money at that game, because strange as it sounds, there are people who are bail junkies, and they really, really want that daisy chain. It's almost as if they don't know they're free unless they have to keep paying for it.

So Bud Everett, for example, a good customer of mine, gets busted for getting falling-down drunk and painting some rather uncomplimentary things on the Mayor's car, after he accidentally breaks the rear window and mistakes the back seat for a urinal. That's not what the citation says, of course, but that's the important part. And because it's the Mayor's car and not yours or mine, everybody knows good old Bud is going to do some time.

To that end, the arraigning judge sets bail at five thousand dollars, which he knows damn well Bud can't raise. In any sort of just world, that would be a direct violation of the Eighth Amendment to the US Constitution, but we passed some quibbling laws a long time ago to make the issue of unreasonable bail go away. Nowadays bail is supposed to be unreasonable. That's what it's for.

But even though Bud couldn't raise five thou to buy his soul back from the Devil, he somehow manages to come up with five hundred, which he uses to buy a five-K bond from me. Which obliges me to insure his appearance in court, right?

Wrong.

Also wrong is the idea that I'm going to get some kind of security deposit from him so as not to be out anything when the guy craps out on both me and the court. It's a nice thought, but not only would he not know five thousand if it rang his doorbell looking like Ed McMann, he also very much does not own a thing in the world that's worth that much. His beat-up car probably has more than that against it in outstanding parking fines.

But I write the bond anyway, because Bud Everett is one of my regular nonviolent, nontoxic, recidivist bail junkies.

When his trial date comes up, he fails to appear, as I had no doubt he would. Or rather, wouldn't. That should mean that I or my layoff bonding company, if I had used one, has to cough up the full five thousand dollars.

But the thing is, the court doesn't really want the money, they want *him*. So they give me ten days to produce the little nimrod, figuring I know where to find him, which I do because he's an old regular. He's out in his ex-brother-in-law's old junker of a camping trailer, in the woods up by Forest Lake. He's drinking boilermakers and watching soap operas and bitching to anybody who will listen, which mostly means his dog, Thumper, about how he doesn't want to go to court because he knows he will get a raw deal and he didn't really mess up the Mayor's car all *that* bad, and the asshole had it coming anyway.

So I send Wide Track Wilkie out to talk to him. He works as a bounty hunter when he's not shooting pool, and he persuades Bud that he really ought to do the standup thing, if he wants to retain the ability to stand up, period. And they both go off to the courthouse together.

But not to trial.

He's already missed his slot in the court schedule. That's how this whole scenario got started in the first place. And since there are always more candidates than slots, it has been given to some other worthy. His original trial will now have to be rescheduled and he will be informed of the new date by postcard, no less. That's if he's still walking around free. But what he's in court for *this time* is to get arraigned for jumping bail, or FTA, failure to appear.

That's not as bad an offense as the first one, since it didn't involve the mayor's car and also since he didn't try to run away when Wilkie went to pick him up. So this time bail is set at a mere one thousand, for which Bud can buy a bond from me for another hundred. I have no idea where he gets the extra c-note and probably don't want to know, but he does, and the game begins.

That's right, it merely begins.

The next time his court date comes up, Bud will again be in a drunken pout, since that's the only way he has of dealing with authority, and he will again fail to appear. And once again, Wilkie will go have a little heart-to-heart chat with the lad and bring him downtown for yet another arraignment. And with the backlog in the courts showing no sign of ever getting caught up, this scene can now replay itself roughly every one or two months, for just about forever. That means that for as long as good old Bud does not decide to face up to all his past charges or, even less likely, get a sudden flash of ambition and flee the jurisdiction, he will pay me an average of about fifty dollars a month to be permanently bonded.

And the absolutely hilarious thing is that he will find this a perfectly acceptable arrangement.

I have anywhere from one to a dozen clients like Bud at any given time, and while you can't get rich off them, they can definitely help pay the rent between the big customers. And at the moment, I dearly wished I had a bunch more.

But somebody named Amalgamated Greedy Guys, or whatever the hell it was, wanted them all, enough to scare off one of my clients. Or maybe they just wanted a big slug of money to make them go away and lose interest in me.

"When hell freezes over."

"Excuse me?" said Agnes.

"Talking to myself again," I said. "Sorry. Probably means I forgot to take my meds."

"There are worse problems to have, Herman." She gave me a sort of indulgent big-sister kind of smile.

"Yes there are. And we probably have them, too. Here come some more suits. More gangsters, you suppose?"

She looked out the window, to where I was gesturing with my coffee cup.

"They look more like government," she said. "Feds, I'd guess."

"I believe that's what I said." I opened the door for our new guests, a tallish, athletic-looking man and woman, maybe late thirties, in matching black business suits. The guy wore a dark red tie, the woman a black velvet choker with a tiny cameo pin. Other than that, they looked pretty much the same, except that her legs were better, and I was glad she let them show. Both of them—the people, not the legs—wore tight-lipped expressions that showed they took themselves very seriously.

"Mr. Jackson?" Her voice was deep and throaty, as if she routinely took just a bit too much Dewar's in the evenings, and she had a heart-shaped face with puffy lips that seemed made for whispering. But her manner was all business. Oh, well. Another perfectly good fantasy, shot right to hell. I wondered if this could be the pair of feds my trash-barrel informant had been talking about.

"I'm Herman Jackson. How can I help you?" I held out my hand, but instead of shaking it, the Persons in Black held up some kind of plastic ID cards. Feds, definitely.

Not FBI, though, but Secret Service. I was surprised. Did the President need a bail bond?

"I'm Agent Krause," she said, "and this is my partner, Agent Sladky. We are informed that you, Mr. Jackson, are the bonding agent for one Charles Victor."

"Was," I said.

"Excuse me?"

"I was his bonding agent. He was murdered last night."

Agnes dropped her hands in her lap and gave me a look of wide-eyed astonishment. The two agents were unreadable.

"Then you owe him no further service." She said it without pause or hesitation, as if she had rehearsed the speech. I had no idea what she was driving at.

"I didn't owe him any prior service, either," I said. "He hasn't been bonded by me since the last time he got sent to the Ramsey County Workhouse, last winter. How is it you know about me being his agent, by the way?"

She ignored the question completely. "Whether he had a bond or not, you were holding something for him, I believe?"

"You mean some kind of standing security object?" I shook my head. "When he needed a bond, Charlie always gave me cash for security. And when he got out of the Workhouse, he took it back."

"If he had that kind of money, why would he come to you for a bond at all? Why would he come to anybody for one? That's not even a good lie." Agent Sladky should have continued to let his partner do the talking. He had a slightly nasal, high-pitched voice that made him seem too young for the job. His comment about the lie didn't help any in that department, either. Was there any experienced G-man or cop who didn't expect to be routinely lied to by everybody?

"He didn't trust the court to give him his money back again. He didn't trust any government of any kind, period." I shrugged, to show them that it was Charlie's choice entirely and also a matter of great indifference to me if they believed it or not.

And in any case, I really didn't have any of his money at the moment.

The woman took over again, and I had to admit that I liked hearing her speak. "Well, then, Mr. Jackson, if you will just turn over your files on the man to us, we won't bother you any further. The originals. All of them. You may keep your own copies, of course, but we require the originals. Oh, and any other little item you may have been holding for him, your denial notwithstanding."

"No."

"I beg your pardon?"

"I said 'no.' That means no."

"People do not find it wise to say no to the Secret Service, Mr. Jackson." She eyed me in exactly the way a hawk looks at a very small mouse.

"Well, I'm seldom accused of being wise."

"We have subpoena and warrant power, you know. For any records we might decide we want to see for any reason, not just his. Think about that for a moment. We can turn your past inside out, if we want to."

"Then I suggest you do so, Agent Krause. Do your warrants usually include permission to burn homeless people out of their camps, by the way?"

"I don't believe I know what you're talking about." But her eyes said otherwise. Both agents' façades of cool, self-assured control had wilted. I thought the guy, Sladky, even looked a bit afraid. The woman mainly looked pissed, but quite possibly that was her regular, default posture.

"How could he possibly know—?"

"He doesn't. Shut up, Agent."

"I told you we shouldn't have gone down there. We could have just as well—"

"Sladky, will you please shut up? We're in front of a subject, you know." To me, she said, "We're done here."

She turned on her heel and headed for the door, and her partner followed. Her shoes had some of those compromise high heels that looked as if they had started out as spikes but had melted and squished. They still clicked importantly when she got to the tiled threshold, though. This was a woman who definitely knew all about creating presence. Mostly a threatening one. I found it interesting, though, that she seemed even more hostile toward her partner than she was toward me.

"You'll be seeing us again," she said without turning around.

"Imagine my anticipation."

They both left without another word, leaving the door open, which I took as a classy substitute for slamming it. I shut it in my most restrained manner, and Agnes and I watched them go.

"Well, you certainly handled that well," she said.

"Thank you." I always like it when she lies for me.

"Can you really stand to have them turn your past inside out, by the way?"

"Not really, but one person trying to strong-arm me was enough in one day, Ag. My willing victim quota was all used up. Mostly, though, I can or can't stand it, depending on how far back they go."

"Uh huh. These are federal agents, Herman. They will go back to when God first created dirt and J. Edgar Hoover used it to blackmail somebody."

"That would definitely be too bad. I was sort of hoping they would get tired of the game before then." After about fifteen years of history, to be exact. I had a squeaky clean record back to 1987, when I first came to St. Paul. One could even say it's so virtuous, it's boring. I worked long and hard to make it that way. But try to look farther back, and you will run into a lot of gaps.

Officially, nominally, Herman Jackson, St. Paul bail bondsman, never convicted, arrested, or even suspected of a major crime, was born in 1953 in Manley, Iowa, a tiny farm town that has now almost entirely vanished into the fields of corn and soybeans around it. Its empty Main Street has only a few boarded up buildings left, and even fewer residents, none of whom remembers me. There were church and school records once, but nobody knows what happened to them. Even the tombstone from which I got my birth date is gone, its little plot of ground now busy pushing up barley or oat stalks. It's a wonderful place to be from, since nobody can ever say for sure that you're not.

A really persistent researcher might conclude that between Manley and St. Paul are just too many blank pages to be believed. Awkward, but hardly damning. And even with the research capacity of the federal government, it would be awfully hard for somebody to find a link back to Detroit and a bonding agency abandoned when its principal was implicated in a murder (innocent, I swear) and an insurance fraud (that's another matter altogether.)

Hard, but not impossible. And somebody who knew exactly what to look for might even find a cold case file in Detroit that points to an even colder case file in Toronto that actually contains my fingerprints, the only place on earth that does, other than St. Paul.

The links are all very convoluted, their discovery highly unlikely. And that's good, because bringing them to light could very well spell the end of life as I know it. Against that eventuality, I keep an escape kit in a locker at the Amtrak depot, plus extra cash in two locations out state. If I ever have to use them, I can never, ever come back.

And if I am too slow in making that decision, I will lose the chance forever. I'm not ashamed to say that scares the hell out of me.

Agnes is the only person who knows anything about any of this, apart from my Uncle Fred, the career bookie who is currently doing hard time in the Michigan's Upper Peninsula and can be trusted to be at least as discreet as any other con. Even Agnes doesn't know all the particulars, though she does know that she may someday have to do a rearguard stalling action while I make myself nonexistent. She gets all teary when we talk about it, so I seldom do.

"What about that other thing, Herman? Are we holding anything for Charlie Victor?"

"Nothing that they would really care about."

"Then what's the big deal? Let's give them his files and wave goodbye as they leave."

"It's a matter of principle, Ag. Never give bullies what they want."

"Even when they have the authority to demand it?"

"Especially then."

Massé and Fugue

Athletes like to talk about muscle memory. You make the perfect free throw or the ace tennis serve or the flawless triple axel, the theory goes, and you should immediately do twenty or a hundred more. Then when crunch time comes, even if your mind has degenerated into a useless collage of past disasters, your body remembers how to make the moves.

That's what they say.

I had no idea what I was going to do about my cash flow problems or the pinstriped mobster or the feds whom I had deliberately pissed off or the flames I had seen from Railroad Island or even about Charlie Victor's cigar box, which I had told nobody about, not even Agnes. So I decided to work on the problem that I at least knew how to approach. If the athletes are right, that is.

I left the office and headed back to Lefty's, to practice the pool shot that sooner or later I would have to perform for Wilkie, or else give him his twenty bucks as a forfeit. I can do things like take unscheduled time off, because I own the business. Hard working, sweet-hearted Agnes can't, because she doesn't. Life is not fair.

I gave Lefty back his .38 and got an arched eyebrow and a pointed look at his watch in return. Then I got a large mug of beer, a bowl of salted-in-the-shell peanuts, and a rack of balls, and I rented a table that was as far from Lefty's perch at the bar as I could get. I told him I wanted to be left alone to practice. What I really meant was that I didn't want him noticing me practicing a shot that is famous for turning a cue ball into a deadly airborne missile and also for ripping up the felt on the table. In fact, a lot of pool halls have signs on the wall prohibiting massé shots.

"What are you practicing?"

"Three-cushion banks."

"Wow. Tough stuff."

He didn't know the half of it.

I left the rack with eleven balls in it on a windowsill, putting only the cue ball, the eight, and three striped balls on the table. I picked the shortest cue stick I could find and chalked the tip until there was a little cloud of blue dust floating around it. Then I swallowed a slug of beer, put an unshelled peanut in my mouth so I could suck on the salt, and began.

I started out with a simple draw shot, hitting the cue ball below center and giving it enough backspin to go straight away from me, then change its mind and come straight back. It didn't work very well. The amount of backspin I was able to give the ball was different every time. I pulled an emery board out of my pocket, turned my back to Lefty to hide what I was doing, and proceeded to rough up the cue tip. After that and some more chalk, it worked a lot better. I got in the habit of chalking after every shot, which everybody knows you should always do anyway and nobody ever does.

I did a dozen more draw shots, progressively increasing the angle of the cue stick with the horizontal. As it approached dead vertical, I could get the ball to come back beyond the place where it had started. Sometimes it skipped and bounced a little along the way and sometimes it wobbled a bit, but mostly it worked.

This was pretty exciting stuff. I wondered if they knew about it at MIT or Cal Tech.

It was also pretty trivial, compared to what I had come here to try. I took another slug of beer, shelled and ate a bunch of nuts just to stall a little longer, and finally got down to hitting the ball off-center in two directions at once.

That's kind of a slippery concept, and it doesn't do to think about it too much. But not thinking about it wasn't working worth sour owl shit, either. I could get the ball to go away to the right and come back to the left or vice-versa, but there was no way I could get it to go away *a little* to the left and come back even more to the left.

I decided it was all a matter of point of view, and I tried the shot with the cue in the same place but with me facing a different way. That was a little better.

Finally, I set up all five balls in their original locations, closed my eyes for a moment, and meditated on the mystical state of being Minnesota Fats and a Zen archery master, all at once. Then I tried the massé shot exactly fifty times. I almost made it twice. The odds were getting better, though I seriously doubted if my muscles had learned a thing yet. I decided it was time for another beer.

As I was heading back to the bar with my empty mug, I was met by a short, pasty-faced blimp in a rumpled three-piece sharkskin suit and a striped dress shirt with a pin collar. He also had a hat that I don't know how to describe. A real independent thinker. I hadn't seen pin collars since the mid-nineties, or sharkskin since never mind when. And I had never seen a hat like that, though I thought it might have been what was once described as a pork pie.

"I was told I might find Herman Jackson here. Would that be you?"

"That would be me, yes." *And I was told a fat guy in a suit and a hat went down in the gulch last night. Would that be you?* "And you are?"

"G. Harold Mildorf, Attorney at Law. My card." He pulled a business card out of his vest pocket, showed it to me, and then put it back, just as the Persons in Black had done with their plastic ID cards.

"You have a client who needs a bond, Mr. Mildorf?"

"You mean a bail bond? Certainly not. I don't practice criminal law. In fact, I try not to even practice civil law with people who might possibly be criminals. Is there someplace private where we could talk?" He looked at the cane-backed spectator chairs around the perimeter of the hall as if they might be about to attack him, his bushy eyebrows nearly meeting as he formed them into a frown.

"Lefty's in the morning is about as private as anything you're liable to find. Pick up a stick and pretend you're shooting pool, and I guarantee you nobody will pay the slightest attention to us." Not that there was anybody else around anyway.

He obviously didn't like the idea, but he took a cue stick off a rack on the wall and walked back to the table. I suddenly became aware of the empty beer mug in my hand.

"I was just going to get myself another beer. Would you like anything?"

"Do they have food?"

"They have the usual bar food. Fried stuff, microwave pizza, that sort of thing. The burgers are pretty good."

"I'll have two burgers and fries and a large beer."

"The beer, I'll get you. The other stuff, I'll order, and Lefty will bring it over when it's ready."

"Lefty. So there really is such a person. How fearsomely droll."

"You're holding the cue stick by the wrong end, by the way." I left him to ponder the subtle geometry of tapered wood and went back to the bar, where I ordered his little snack.

"On your tab?" said Lefty.

"No way. I don't even know this guy."

"Oh yeah? Well, he knows you. He was watching you shoot pool last night."

"Really?"

"Almost the whole time. Came in after you'd already started, asked me to point you out. Another beer?"

"I suddenly lost my taste for the light buzz. Give me a new mug of beer for my spectator friend and a cup of coffee for me."

"Is that on your tab or not?"

"The drinks, yes. For everything else, G. Harry there is on his own."

"Got it. I'll collect cash when I bring the stuff."

"Can't say I blame you."

We were talking about a lawyer, after all.

I went back over in the corner and found G. Harold Mildorf pushing the eight ball around the table with his stick, scowling at it in intense concentration.

"I don't believe you've stumbled onto your secret vocation, Mr. Mildorf. There's nobody here to impress, so why don't we just sit down and wait for your food?"

"Really? I thought I was doing rather well."

"Trust me, you don't want to enter any high stakes tournaments." I gestured to a couple of chairs over by the windows, and we ambled over that way and sat down. I found a small round table that was only slightly wobbly and pulled it over in front of us.

"I don't really have any papers to lay out," he said.

"How very un-lawyerlike. But you do have about four and a half pounds of food on the way."

"Oh, yes. Well then, a table by all means."

"While we're waiting for it, why don't you tell me what's on your mind?"

He looked around the entire place, working his mouth in odd ways and squinting, as if some silent spy might have snuck in while we were looking at chairs. Then he leaned over close to me and said in a low, conspiratorial tone, "Charles Victor."

"He's dead." I think I upset him by speaking in a normal voice. He deepened his already monumental scowl.

"The body on the sidewalk?"

I nodded.

"I feared as much. The whole point of my being here, in fact. You see, I am the executor of his estate."

Good thing I wasn't sipping my coffee at the moment, because I would have definitely choked on it.

"Estate? Charlie had an estate?"

"But of course."

"Get the hell out of here."

"Excuse me? My food hasn't arrived yet."

"It's an expression, Mr. Mildorf. It means 'I can't believe what you're saying.'"

"Oh, I see. Get out of the hell, yes, um… Let me assure you, I am entirely in earnest. He had an estate, and you, Mr. Jackson, are his sole heir. I am empowered to give you this." From an inside jacket pocket, he produced two or three pieces of paper that had been folded into business-envelope size. As he handed them over, he again scanned the room in all directions.

"A copy of his will," he said. "Only two pages, and not terribly eloquent. But it definitely names you as his one and only beneficiary. He even mentions his father, someplace up in the northern part of the state, so there can be no question of him merely forgetting that he had one. He mentions him, curses him, and excludes him. All very legal. You get everything, as you can see."

I stuffed the papers in the inside pocket of my suit coat without looking at them.

"Besides his cardboard box and some occasional walking-around money, what does 'everything' consist of, exactly?"

"Ah yes, well, therein lies the problem. I don't honestly know, you see. Not exactly how much, and not where it is, either. I know he had something, because he paid my fee in cash and didn't quibble about the amount. And he claimed to have something he called a frag box, which he said contained thirty thousand dollars, but I never saw it. Aren't you going to read the will?"

"What's the point? Aren't we exactly where we would have been if you had never talked to me?"

"We most certainly are not. I have now delivered the will, as I am legally charged to do. That is not a trivial thing, you know. Don't you at least want look at it?" He pointed with an index finger, looking as if he really wanted to pull the papers back out of my pocket.

"Later, maybe. Tell me about this frag box thing."

"You realize, of course, that if you weren't his sole heir, I wouldn't be able to discuss it with you at all."

"But you just said that I am."

"And so you are, sir. Do you know what a frag *pot* is, by the way?"

"I know what it was in Vietnam. Charlie told me."

"Enlighten me, if you would."

"Basically, it was a pile of money to pay for an assassination. Usually it was kept in an extra helmet, which is where the name 'pot' came in, but it could have been kept anywhere. When some troop had an officer who was really despised, they would start the collection. And every time the guy pissed somebody off again, a little more cash would get thrown in. When the pile was finally big enough to be worth risking a prison sentence, somebody would waste the officer in question and collect the reward. The preferred method of killing was with a grenade or a mine, which would leave no fingerprints or ballistic evidence."

"Aha. A fragmentary weapon, and hence the word 'frag,'" said Mildorf, nodding.

"I believe the word you want is 'fragmentation.'"

"Just so. Mr. Victor assumed I already knew all that, which made him a little hard to follow at times. Tell me, do you think this practice actually did happen?"

"Some people say it was really quite common, especially toward the end of the war, when the morale was all in the toilet."

"Well, then, maybe the box is believable, too, who knows? Mr. Victor claimed to have a box in which he was accumulating money to buy a political assassination."

"Really? Did he say who the target was?"

"He did not. And since it involved a criminal activity, I didn't ask."

"But whomever it was for, now the money is all mine."

"Exactly so."

"But only if I can find it."

"Correct again. I think there were supposed to be some instructions to you in the box, as well. As his executor, it would be up to me to enforce them. But since I cannot ethically enforce an illegal behest, and since I don't have the box anyway, I think it's safe to say all that is moot. Unless, of course, you already have the box?"

He took a large drink of his beer, which immediately reappeared as sweat on his forehead and cheeks. He took a tissue out of a back pocket and mopped at his brow. But through it all, he kept his eyes on me. If he was looking for a "tell," I disappointed him utterly. Then his hamburgers arrived, he paid Lefty, and nothing else could compete for his attention for a while.

"I don't suppose you have any idea why Charlie didn't tell me all this himself?"

With his mouth full of hamburger and onions, he nodded absently, then looked around and held both hands up with greasy fingers spread. I handed him a napkin, and he wiped first his hands and then his mouth before he spoke.

"Thank you. He might have wanted to, but he was trying to stay out of sight, as it were. When he came to see me, he snuck in the back way, through the fire escape stairs."

"That's not like him."

"If you say so, I believe you. But when I met him he was definitely running scared."

"Do you know of what?"

"I think he knew he was about to be murdered."

"Did he say that?"

"In a roundabout way. He found it ironic. He said, as I recall, 'After all these years, somebody is keeping a frag pot on me.' And then he used one of those colorful expressions I can never seem to remember. Something about a card."

"A death card, maybe?"

"Yes, that's it. Thank you. He said somebody had a death card for him. Or he himself had one; I don't remember which. Does that mean anything to you?"

"The ace of spades," I said. "Usually from a deck of cards with a military unit insignia on the back. Have you told the police any of this?"

"I have told you, Mr. Jackson. My legal duty is now discharged."

He gulped down the rest of his food and beer, stood, belched in a most undignified way, and started to leave.

"Stay a second," I said. "What about Charlie's body?"

"I'll play your ridiculous game. What about it?"

"What happens to it? Do I need to make some kind of arrangements?"

"You are the heir, not the next of kin. If you made some kind of arrangements, I'm sure nobody would argue with you. But you don't have to do anything. I assume they will keep the body for evidence for a while and then do whatever they do with homeless dead people."

"Which is what?"

"I have absolutely no idea."

He turned to go again, and this time, I let him. He did not look back at me, but he continued to cast hunted looks everywhere else.

I watched him leave, and wondered what, if anything, I should do about him. Even more, I wondered what I should do about Charlie's body. I hoped they wouldn't burn it. Then I remembered the will.

I pulled the papers out of my pocket and unfolded them. The first page seemed to be all preamble, with Mildorf's business address and Charlie's military service number, which was all he had in the way of ID. There were a lot of wheretofores and inasmuchas-es and *ipso factotums* that finally got us to the second page, where the real meat was. Once you got to it, it took only about half a page more for Charlie to call himself sane and me his heir. His scrawling signature, in real lawyers' blue ink, took up half of the remaining space, leaving a couple inches at the bottom that had something else written on it.

Printed in block letters, all caps, in pencil, it said simply, "YOU ARE BEING WATCHED." If it was true, it was definitely too bad, because somewhere out there was a box that might just contain thirty thousand dollars. And I rather badly needed twenty-five.

I decided I had hit enough pool balls for one day.

Fox and Geese

As I stepped out of the door from Lefty's, I scanned the sidewalk and the parked cars for a tail, but I couldn't spot one. But then, if it was any good, I wouldn't, would I? In a standard cougars-and-rabbits operation, there would be at least four shadows, two on each side of the street. Of course there was also the distinct possibility that G. Harold Mildorf was a babbling lunatic, which would also mean that I wouldn't spot a tail, because there wouldn't be one. But my gut instinct was that G. Harold was correct. And at some other level, I think I wanted him to be. Maybe I had acquired a will in more ways than one. It was time to engage the enemy.

I paused in front of Lefty's a bit longer, to let a couple of young black women pass in front of me. One was tiny and fragile-looking and incredibly pretty. From her size alone, I would have said she wasn't yet a teenager, but she had an air of quiet sorrow and dignity about her that made her look much older. She was pushing a baby stroller. Her friend was bigger, and there was nothing either pretty or quiet about her. She was also pushing a stroller, walking with something between a waddle and a swagger, gesturing wildly, and running her mouth non-stop. Since they were going in my direction, I fell in about ten paces behind them. But I could have heard the big one from a block away.

"So I says to her, 'What you trippin' on me about, bitch? Cramped chickenhead like you ain't got no call to be dissin' me.

Shit, you ain't even got no call to live.' An' she couldn't think of nothin' to say to *that*. Humph!"

She looked over at the small woman with a flash of triumph in her eyes. But the other one made no reply of any kind. She simply continued to look down and push her stroller at a slow, deliberate pace.

Getting no reaction, the big one decided to try again, with a slightly amped-up script.

"So I says to her, 'You better back off, bitch. You think you so phat, but I munna take you…'"

I decided that ten paces hadn't been nearly far enough. I stopped and took out a cigarette that I didn't really want and took my time lighting it, as if I couldn't concentrate on such a complicated task and walk at the same time. The stroller pushers were going awfully slowly, but I was determined to stall around long enough to let them get at least a half a block ahead of me.

That was when I spotted the first one.

Across the street and a little behind me, a tallish, nondescript guy in a dark nylon windbreaker and a mad bomber hat was suddenly taking a great interest in a storefront window. Innocuous enough, except the particular glass he was looking into belonged to a store that had been out of business for some three or four years. Now the place was used to store furniture that had never been taken out of its shipping cartons.

If they were running a classic box, Mr. Windbreaker's partner would be on my side of the street, maybe a half a block back. I looked back that way and saw a medium-height man in a crumpled raincoat walking away from me. He hadn't come out of Lefty's, or I would have noticed him there. And there weren't any other businesses in that block. Cougar number two. Three and four would be another half a block back.

I stayed where I was and smoked for a while, making no attempt to hide the fact that I was looking at the guy across the street. He kept his back to me, facing the glass, hands in pockets, pretending to be interested in the unremarkable display of boxes and dust. When I turned and headed east, back toward Lefty's, he seemed to hesitate for a moment. Then he, too, headed east. Ten seconds later, I looked at my watch, put on a phony expression of dismay, and did an abrupt one-eighty, once again heading west.

My man on the other side of the street suddenly had an overwhelming need to make a call on his cell phone. I thought I could pretty well imagine the content.

I think I might have been made.

Then you have been, idiot. Get out of there.

Of course, it was also possible that I was supposed to make him. They might let me have a glimpse of the scrubs, just so I wouldn't look too hard for the A-squad. That's assuming that I was worth a multiple-person surveillance team in the first place. If so, then my stock had gone up dramatically since I became the heir to a phantom estate and a cardboard box in some unknown location, a box that might have also been a frag pot.

I suppose I should have been flattered. I hadn't been the subject of that kind of interest since my Uncle Fred was being investigated by the feds for some trumped-up RICO charge. I was one of his collectors back then, so I got watched a lot by shadows that were ludicrously easy to spot. Back then, the FBI agents, even when they were working undercover, were strictly required to be clean shaven and wear a coat and tie at all times. But none of them made enough money to buy anything but off-the-rack suits and imitation silk ties. J. C. Penney's spies. I thought they were adorable.

I dressed better than any of them. In my early twenties, I thought of myself as a young professional, even though the job sometimes required more muscle than polish. I wore tailored wool-blend suits and button-down shirts made of the new permanent-press cotton blends. I preferred the wide ties that were popular then, but I wore narrow pineapple-knits, just to needle the feebes. I knew they weren't allowed to have them, because Mort Sahl, the comedian, always wore one. J. Edgar Hoover thought Sahl was a communist, and he hated him.

Fred's numbers and bets always came to him by phone, but the money came to about two dozen collection points around the city, mostly in bars, corner groceries, and laundries. I made the rounds several times a week. Any time I accumulated more than about three hundred dollars, I would feed it into a hidden box that I had welded behind the dash of my '72 Barracuda. It started its life as the housing for a defroster blower, so even if you stood on your head to get a look back there, it looked as if it belonged. If anybody ever demanded to know why I had $300 cash in my pocket, I would say I was going to buy a car from a friend. If they had been smart, they would have put some pressure on me by threatening to arrest me for failure to register for the draft, which was a federal misdemeanor. They had me there. The draft officially ended in 1973, but you were still legally required to register. But the feebes were never anything resembling smart. When Uncle Fred eventually went away for bookmaking, it was an undercover unit of the Detroit PD that nailed him. They weren't hampered by cheap suits.

Things were easier back then. Back then, it was a game. Now, my anonymity and maybe even my freedom were starting to feel a bit fragile, and it was not a good feeling at all.

Ahead of me, the so-I-tole-that-bitch monologue was still in full boom, though the extra distance helped a little.

"She so full of shit, I don't even mess with her. I just slap her right in the face."

Again, no reaction from the small, sad woman.

"That's what I do, all right. I slap her right in the face, knock her down, one time. She couldn't believe *that* shit. And then I says, 'Listen, bitch…'"

They stopped for a red light at Cedar Street, and I turned and walked south, leaving them behind me. I had no doubt that the loud one would keep retelling her story until Ms. Sad Eyes either became suitably impressed or told her she was full of shit. I was betting on her doing neither, and I wondered how many more times the routine would be replayed and how much more it would escalate. In half a block, it had gone from a story of mere bad-mouthing to one of physical violence. In another few blocks, it could well be up to murder.

Somewhere once I read the number of times we can tell the same lie before we start to believe it ourselves. It was rather shockingly small. Something less than thirty. That probably meant that by this time tomorrow, the motor mouth would seriously believe she had assaulted somebody. That's if the offending other person even existed.

And maybe that didn't even matter.

That got me thinking about Charlie. He had decades to tell his stories. By the time I heard them, did they have anything at all to do with reality? Would he even know?

I thought about the day I first met Charlie Victor a little more than four years earlier. He had come into my office to ask about a bail bond, even though he was obviously not under arrest at the time.

Jackson Bail Bonds is the totally unglamorous name on my storefront, picked because "Herman Jackson, Bail Bonds" would have been just as unglamorous, as well as longer. But that's who I am and what I do. The sign is unilluminated, some would say just like its owner, and painted in a lettering style that the sign company called "Railroad Gothic." I think I liked the name more than the appearance. It called up images of wizened, colorful hobos with bizarre stories to tell. Under the main sign is a smaller one, in red neon, that says "24 Hour Service," with a phone number to call when the office is closed. Agnes says that's my lighthouse beacon, competing with the blue-lit crucifix of the Souls Harbor Mission over in the wino district north of Lowertown, for the traffic of souls lost in the night. That's what she says, that is, when she isn't complaining about the fact that the 24/7 service means she has no social life whatsoever. I never did have one, so I don't worry about it.

Charlie walked in during regular business hours and said, simply, "What's it cost for a bond?"

"For a friend?"

"No, man, for me."

"What did you do?" I said.

"When?" He looked behind him, as if there might be a train wreck in the street that he hadn't noticed, one that he might be blamed for.

"When you did whatever you did that you need a bond for."

"If I'd already done it, I couldn't be here now, could I? I mean, I'd be under arrest, wouldn't I?" He looked at me as if he were talking to a total idiot.

"That would be a problem," I said, "yes."

"Well, there you are, then," he said. "I ain't done nothing yet. I want to know what it costs first."

And they say there's nothing new under the ancient sun.

"Let me get this straight," I said. "You're contemplating doing some kind of crime, but first you want to know what the bail will be if you get caught?"

"Oh, I'll get caught, all right. I don't know how to do much, but I know how to get caught, all to hell. I wouldn't waste your time, otherwise."

"Of course not." And there I was, indeed.

I motioned him to my classic Motel Six lobby chair, even though Agnes shot me a look that clearly said, "Don't you dare!" She gets a little nervous when we have clients who look as colorful as they really are.

Bonding is a funny business, and in some ways, she has never gotten used to it. Bonding is safe, is the thing to remember. In a system that is full of attitude and even rage, people almost never get mad at the bondsman. It's a little like being a ringside doctor in a prizefight where lethal weapons are allowed. The fight stops momentarily, you assess the damages and do what you can about them, and then the bell rings and the chaos starts all over again. A lot of the customers don't even remember you.

I once had a guy in my office, in cuffs and leg irons, who tried to attack the cop who was escorting him. He used his feet and teeth and head, but he mostly just managed to get the living crap beat out of him. But he never made a move of any kind toward me. When it was all over, the cop was kneeling on the guy's back with a nightstick jammed down on his neck.

"You gonna bond this guy?" he asked.

"That's a trick question, right? A sobriety test?"

"I got to hear it officially," said the cop.

"No, I'm not going to bond him. Is that official enough?"

"Perfect." He jerked the man, who was still officially only a suspect, to his feet and bopped him once more on the ear, just for punctuation. Then he hustled him out, ignoring a sputtering tirade about police brutality.

"You don't know who you're fucking with, pig." The man was screaming, despite split lips and missing teeth. "Someday I'm gonna get out, and I'll find you and spill your blood and wipe your woman's face in it. And then I'll start on her." Then he turned to me, and in a completely calm voice said, "Sorry about the mess on the carpet, man."

"Hey, no problem," I said. He was a suspect, all right. At least, I sure as hell suspected him.

Anyway, Agnes watched the whole scene in appalled silence, and since then, she keeps a .38 revolver in her desk. As far as I know, she has never fired it, and I have never made it an issue.

I managed to look somewhere else as Agnes eased open the drawer where she kept her heat. Then I offered our possible new client a cup of coffee.

He took a look at the carafe on the table in the corner and said, "You got to be kidding."

"Some people are happy to get it," I said. I mean, gee, it wasn't all *that* old.

"Some people are happy to get a shot of radiator juice," he said, "but that don't make it bottled in bond. What do I look like, a goddamn bum?"

I looked him over before I replied. He had a wedge-shaped face that was too large for the rest of his body, and he made a lot of sudden, jerky motions with it, like a cat who's been out on the streets too long and can't ever relax. It was hard to tell with all the rags he wore, but I thought he must have had a powerful frame and broad shoulders once. Now he had a permanent stoop and one hand that was curled with arthritis, though he still carried himself with a certain stubborn dignity. Ex-military, I decided. Maybe that unit patch on his old fatigue jacket was real, at that. There was something else, too, some quality that made me think that he was down but definitely not out.

"Actually," I said, "you look more like a hobo."

"A connoisseur," he snorted. "I come in to ask about the cost of a bond, and I get a goddamn connoisseur of untouchables. A gourmet of street people."

"I used to be," I said, "but it's harder to tell them apart nowadays."

"Yeah? Well, I'll help you out. I used to be a stockbroker, okay? Had friends in high places, money in low ones, and prospects up the wazoo. But I got sick of all that crap, and I dropped out of the system to give all my time to helping the oppressed, legalizing pot, and freeing Tibet."

I had no idea what kind of response that was meant to evoke, so I gave him none. After I had looked blank for half a minute, he spoke again, this time with a lot less energy.

"That was a joke," he said. His shoulders suddenly sagged even farther, and his face fell. His mind had switched to a different channel.

"Oh," I said.

"About lost causes, see."

"I see. And you're into lost causes? Or is that the joke?"

"You shitting me? I *am* a lost cause, son. I been down so long, it looks like up to me."

This time I laughed, and so did he. And for reasons I couldn't begin to explain, I knew I was going to like the guy.

"So tell me about this crime you're planning on getting caught for," I said.

"Well, I haven't picked one yet. I mean, you got to see what opportunities come your way. And you gotta be careful, too. Purse snatching is good, but if you pick some hyper old broad with gardening of the hearteries, say, she can get a stroke or a heart attack, and all of a sudden, it's murder. And breaking and entering is okay, but if you pick a place that's got too much money inside, that can turn into big-time hard time, too. What you want is some nice little felony misdemeanor that will get you ninety or a hundred in the County workhouse, and no hard feelings. Smashing a window on a cop car is all right, as long as you make sure there's no damn dog behind it, but sometimes—"

"Are you telling me…"

"Winter's coming on, Harold."

"It's Herman."

"No, it's fall. And pretty soon, my cardboard box down under the wye-duct just ain't gonna cut it anymore."

"I think it's time to brush up on your O. Henry," said Agnes from her keyboard.

Good grief, was that really what this was all about? Were we about to play out "The Cop and the Anthem," about the bum trying to get thrown in jail for the winter? If so, I was sure it would be without the surprise epiphany at the end.

"What's a wye-duct?" I said.

"It's like a bridge," he said, "only not over a river. It goes over some train tracks or a road or something. You know, like in the old song: 'Oh, I live under the wye-duct; Down by the winny-gar woiks.'"

"Oh, that old song." Huh? Where the hell was he from, anyway, an old black-and-white movie? "So you're looking to get locked up someplace warm for the winter?"

"The County Workhouse," said Charlie, nodding vigorously and looking suddenly gleeful. Another channel switch. "Not just someplace. And for sure not the damn jail."

"Then why do you need a bond?"

"So I don't gotta sit in *jail* while I wait for my hearing to come up so I can get my sentence and go to the *workhouse*."

"So instead, you sit in your box and freeze?" I said.

"Life's a bitch, Howard."

"Herman."

"Him, too. See, the timing is everything. Just like in war. You ever been in combat?"

"No." At least, that's not what it was called. In the part of Detroit where I grew up, the streets were never exactly peaceful, except when the night people were asleep and the working stiffs were off at their jobs. Or maybe when there was a free barbeque at the UAW hall. So I knew a bit about timing, but I still didn't get why he wanted the bond. "What's so bad about sitting in jail for a week or so?"

He gave me a pained look, then spoke slowly and carefully, as if it were explaining a difficult topic to a retarded child. He tapped his finger on my coffee table to empathize each syllable.

"Jail," he said, tapping and then pointing to the brick building a little over a block away, "is not like the workhouse." Tappity-*tap*. "Jail is full of *crazy* people!" Big bunch of taps. "You can get *hurt* in there."

I had absolutely no argument for that.

Since he might actually be about to become a paying customer, and also just because he seemed to need it, I walked him over to the Gopher Bar and Grill on Wacouta and bought him lunch. We had Coney Islands, the house specialty, and mugs of draft beer, and after a few follow-up beers plus a shot or two to cut the bubbles, he got that faraway, changing-channels look again, and we both traveled back to the jungle on the other side of the world.

In Country

South Vietnam
1965

On Charlie's first night in country, he was put with a company on perimeter night-guard duty at an artillery firebase. They manned a string of two- and three-man foxholes fifty yards outside their own concertina wire, well into the fringe of the bush. Their orders were simple. "If you see any VC trying to sneak up with sapper charges, kill them."

The catch was that they couldn't see anything at all.

Nobody had any night vision goggles or even any flares, except for one of the sergeants, who had a sniper rifle with a starlight scope. A few grunts had brought flashlights, but they didn't dare turn them on, for fear of drawing fire. And the jungle in front of them was as black as only true wilderness can be.

Their only other order was that no matter what happened, they were not to leave their foxholes.

Charlie was in a sandbagged foxhole with a goofy kid from some wide spot in the road in Georgia and a big black guy from some ghetto in Washington, D.C. The kid was named Junior Sauer, and the black guy called himself Bong. Charlie thought they were either screw-ups or nut cases. But even so, they knew the territory and the drill, and he didn't.

"This is a bullshit detail, man," said Sauer.

"Uh huh," said Bong. "What you think they put us on it for? We get overrun, it don't matter, because the firebase is all safe back behind us yet. But we get attacked and kill some gooks instead, then the lieut back in the hooch gets a nice little pat on his West Point ass for upping his body count. So he puts nothing out here but fuckups and FNGs, dig? Which one are you?" He gave Charlie a gentle poke.

"What's an FNG?" said Charlie.

"Fucking new guy. What I tell you, Junior? Nothing out here but us disposables."

"Well, it's still bullshit. Hey new guy, you carrying anything?"

"Am I carrying anything? Are you serious? I think I'm carrying every damn piece of gear the Army ever bought."

"Jesus, Bong, was we ever that new?"

The big man laughed. To Charlie he said, "He's talking about dew, Man. Something to get high on. Some Mary Joanna or some uppers or something."

"You can't get high on guard, for chrissake."

"Sure you can. Sarge don't care. You watch; he'll be one of the first ones firing up a joint. Acid's no good, though. Guys on that stuff do crazy shit, like try to fly or go playing around with grenades. You try dropping any acid, I'll kick your ass."

Charlie decided he had just been thrown into the snake pit, with the unfortunate handicap of being sane.

Then the last sliver of red-orange sun slipped over the horizon, and faster than he could have believed, blackness slammed down on them like the lid of God's coffin.

The entire world disappeared.

Charlie literally couldn't see his hand in front of his face. He couldn't even tell which way was up, which gave him a sense of falling. His face felt hot and prickly and he suddenly found that he had trouble catching his breath. He was glad he didn't have to run anywhere, because he was sure his legs wouldn't work any more.

"Hey new guy, where you from?"

"The Iron R...., um, Minnesota."

"The Iron Rum-in-a-soda. Never heard of that place, did you, Junior?"

"No way, Bong. They got dark like this in Rum-in-a-soda?"

"Sure. Um, ah, no. I don't know. Down in the mines, maybe. Is it always like this?"

"No, man, sometimes it gets real dark, you know?"

He could hear Junior giggling, and it should have pissed him off, he knew, but he just didn't care. So much for all the bullshit about brothers-in-arms that they fed him in Basic.

Basic.

In Basic, the targets were all exactly fifty or a hundred yards away. In Basic, you could always see the targets, and they didn't shoot back. And in Basic, the people around you were dependable, and if they didn't know what they were doing, the sergeant did.

Basic was Fantasyland.

He didn't know what this place was.

Then the big 155-millimeter long toms ripped open the night with their thunder. The ground trembled, and multiple shock waves and flashes of yellow-white strobe light came from behind the foxholes. Somewhere, miles away, some forward patrol had called for artillery support, and the firebase was pouring it out.

Charlie looked at the jungle in front of him in flashbulb blinks. Had it looked like that in the daylight? Were there new shapes there now, advancing between glimpses, hiding, coming to kill him? He hugged his M16, pressed the barrel against his cheek and smelled the oil. Had he used enough? Metal corroded in the jungle, he had heard, while you were still putting away the cleaning rag. And corroded M-16s jammed, were already famous for jamming. Hell, they would jam if you gave them a dirty look.

He wanted to cry.

He wanted to be very, very small.

He wanted to die.

No, that was wrong, check that thought. He wanted to live, but he wanted to quit being so very afraid. Hell, he didn't know what he wanted, except that he wanted to be anywhere at all except where he was. And he hated the goddamned Army.

Then, as suddenly as they had opened up, the big guns fell silent, and all he could hear was the rock music. Jesus H. fucking Christ, some idiot had turned on a boom box!

"Is everybody here completely nuts?" said Charlie.

"Shit, man," said Junior Sauer, "that's what this war's all about. Make the world safe for rock and roll, y'all. Ain't no other reason to be here."

"Yeah, but—"

"What's it matter, anyhow?" said Bong, somewhere in the darkness. "You think Charlie don't know where we are, after that salvo? He damn sure got us all zeroed in now."

They heard a rifle shot from off to their left, and the radio died. Charlie figured the sergeant with the night scope had shot it. Whether that was true or not, it touched off a hailstorm of fire up and down the line. Red tracers from the company's three heavy machine guns went streaming off into the jungle, and the chorus of rifle and pistol fire around them became deafening. Now and then, somebody tossed a grenade into the bush, just to up the ante. People were screaming as they fired, some of them standing up in their foxholes.

Charlie didn't know what to do.

"Fire your weapon, man!"

"At what? I can't see a damn thing."

"It don't matter. We put enough lead out there, won't nothin' get past it. Hell, we'll kill the fuckin' bugs."

"But we don't have—"

"Will you goddamnit fire your fucking weapon?"

So Charlie fired his M-16. He fired until his magazine was empty and then he locked in another one and kept firing, caught up in the blind frenzy that was sweeping through the company.

And he found that as stupid as it was, frenzy was better than fear.

After a few minutes, a sergeant came by and tapped them each on the forearm and shouted at them to cease firing. And they did so, for just about as long as it took for the sergeant to move on to the next hole. Then the shooting started again, as furiously as ever.

Eventually they ran out of ammunition.

Up and down the line, the foxholes fell silent. And as the frenzy died out, soldiers checked their luminous-faced watches and realized they still had almost six hours of watch left to stand, with no ammunition. They fixed their bayonets, stared intently into the dark, and didn't speak.

It was the longest night of Charlie's life.

The next day, the tension dissipated with the first morning light, replaced by a mind-numbing fatigue and a vague sense of shame. They straggled back through the wire, to where the lieutenant who commanded the company was waiting for them, hands on hips, jungle cammos flawlessly cleaned and pressed, jump boots gleaming like patent leather. His mouth was a single, stern slash, his eyes inscrutable behind dark aviator glasses. As they shuffled past him, he returned their salutes with exaggerated crispness.

Charlie couldn't remember how close he was supposed to get before he saluted, and he probably waited too long. Thus, he committed the Army's most unforgivable mistake: he let himself be noticed by an officer.

"Stand fast, Private!"

"Yes, sir."

"You don't say 'yes sir' to that order, shithead, you just do it. Why aren't you holding your salute?"

"Well, you said——"

"I said stand fast. I did not say fuck off."

Charlie added a frozen salute to his braced posture and thought about how much he hated the Army. The lieutenant did not return his salute.

"Did you learn anything last night, Private?"

What could he say to that without getting into trouble?

"Sir, yes sir."

"All you men stand fast! Private Shithead here is going to tell us what he learned from your pathetic little mad-moment fireworks binge last night."

Jesus, he just wasn't going to let it go, was he?

"Let's hear it, Private. Loud and clear."

And before he had time to think about what he was doing, the words came tumbling out of his mouth like heretical lemmings, gleefully bound for self-destruction.

"Sir, I learned that there is a great lack of leadership and direction in the field. Sir."

And that was how Charlie came to be designated as the company's replacement tunnel-rat.

He survived as a tunnel rat for over nine months, which was long enough to get a betting pool started on the date of his eventual death. Short-timers always bet on tomorrow or the day after, but more and more, the smart money was saying that he might actually survive his tour of duty.

In a country full of ways to die, clearing the VC tunnels was notable for being one of the worst. If you ran into an AK-47 round or a poisoned punjii stick or one of those hard-to-see, blink-quick, deadly little green snakes that were everywhere, it was an open question whether or not anybody else in your unit would even go down after you and pull out your body.

But as he survived more and more descents, Charlie started to get deadly, too.

He learned to hear and even sense bodies in the pitch dark and he learned when to pursue and waste and when to retreat or hide. He found that if he plugged his ears up with huge wads of chewing gum, he could drop grenades into lower, intersecting tunnels without giving himself a concussion. He learned to shoot by feel, in places so dark that he couldn't see the sights on his guns.

He acquired a pair of .45 pistols, called John Wayne rifles, a seven-shot .38 revolver, and a long machete that he filed down to make into a sort of double-edged sword. He also got a three-foot-long bamboo stick that he taped an extra flashlight to, so he could light the tunnel ahead without giving away his true location.

The gear gave him confidence, and the confidence gave him time. Time to learn how to be invisible and time to learn to kill. He learned to kill in very confined quarters, at very close range. He learned to kill without hesitation or remorse or even thought. He began to be famous. He was known as Chazbo the Tunnel King.

He was a great disappointment to Lt. Rappolt.

Then one day his company abandoned him.

◇◇◇

It was a high profile, supposedly high-percentage operation, with reporters and TV cameras. Three full companies were choppered into the bush around a ville that I-Corps was sure was a VC sanctuary, if not an actual stronghold. The plan was to surround the ville on three sides, kill off the VC who stood and fought, and drive the rest of them off into a low mountain pass, where another two airborne companies waited in ambush.

It was textbook air-mobile tactics. It was guaranteed to work. Officers like Rappolt actually accompanied their own troops, though not in the first wave of choppers. It was a photo op for an officer on the way up.

And it was "fugazi" from the get-go, the Nam-era name for SNAFU.

For openers, the place was abandoned. There was nobody there but a few chickens and pigs, who seemed to mock the American troops as smugly as did the empty huts.

There were a few baskets of rice and other foodstuffs, and when the grunts kicked them over, they blew up. There were also a few weapons, which they didn't touch. And there were a few tunnel entrances. Rappolt let himself be photographed dropping a grenade into one of them. Then he sent the photographers away and sent for Charlie.

Charlie waited a few minutes for the smoke to clear, dumped all but his essential killing gear, and dropped into the biggest and most complicated underground maze he had yet been in. After he passed three branching points, he backtracked to the beginning and started all over again, this time spreading a trail of baking soda behind him. He had learned that baking soda worked better than a string, which the enemy could move.

He found a lot of shafts leading back up to more entrances into the village. He found two large galleries where troops had probably slept and an electrically lit medical dressing station. From there, a string of bare light bulbs lit a long tunnel in a direction he thought was back into the mountains. He jerked on a wire from one of the bulbs, and far down the tunnel, something exploded and took all the lights out with it.

He turned his flashlight back on and followed the trail of white powder back the way he had come. To press farther ahead was practically asking to trip another booby trap or walk into an ambush.

Twice on the way back, he thought he heard a sound coming from a cross-gallery, and he emptied his .45s into the opening as he passed it.

When he finally came back out into the daylight, he looked at his watch and was surprised to see that he had been underground for almost two hours.

And his entire company was gone.

He ran through the ville, first in disbelief and then with a rising feeling of pure panic. It couldn't be. Not even the dead were totally abandoned, unless the company was under such intense attack that it was impossible to take them out. But there was no sign of any battle here at all. No shell casings, no burning huts, no smell of cordite or HE in the air. His people had simply flown away and left him down in the tunnels.

But they had left a radio.

He found it not far from the first tunnel hatch, and a little red light and some static seemed to say that it was operational. He keyed the SEND button and spoke, surprised to find that his panic was now almost totally replaced by anger.

"This is Private Charles Victor, Golf Company. You guys left me, over."

When the handset had nothing to say in reply, he tried again, this time forcing himself to remember to release the sending button after he talked. He got an immediate response.

"What's your radio code, soldier?"

"How the hell should I know? I'm not a radioman; I'm the guy you left behind, okay? Over!"

"That's a negative on swearing over the air, private. Try again, with the code for the day, and this time, tell us where you are. Over."

"I'm wherever Golf got choppered today, where do you think I am?"

"That would be a classified location, over." The voice continued to be infuriatingly calm.

"Well of course it is, you dumb fuck! I didn't ask you to broadcast it, I just want you to come back and get me. The sun goes down here, this place is going to be nothing but void vicious."

"You were told not to use profanity on the airwaves, private. And if you have no radio code and no location, there's no way we can..."

"What kind of dumbfuck tripwire vet am I talking to? GET ME THE HELL OUT OF HERE!"

"You are talking to Lieutenant Rappolt, soldier, and you're either an imposter or somebody way out of line. Either way, without a code, you're SOL. Over. And. Out."

Charlie shouted every obscenity and swear word he knew into the radio. Then he threw it on the ground and kicked it several times. Then he shot it. Finally he hunkered down on the ground and wept.

And when he had wept long enough, he picked up his gear and walked into the jungle.

Faux Box

My shadows had managed to become invisible now, but I was sure they would still be with me. *Maybe I should write Charlie an obit*, I thought, and I smiled at the reaction that would have gotten from him. And then I did a mental double take and thought maybe that was exactly what I should do. In a way, anyway. First, though, I wanted to set up a little street theatre.

I headed up the Fourth Street hill and back toward my office, but I went on past it and then across the street and down the block to Nickel Pete Carchetti's pawnshop. Its name is Pawn USA, but I always call it the Emporium of Broken Dreams.

An old-fashioned jingle bell clanked as I went in the door and saw Pete brooding at his usual perch behind the teller's cage. With a jeweler's loupe stuck on his troll-like forehead, he looked like one of the seven dwarfs, just back from the mines. Grumpy, to be exact. His bottle of Pepto-Bismol was on the counter in front of him, half full, and I guessed his Panzer-class heartburn was staging another major offensive.

"Herman, old friend." He raised his chin by way of greeting and gave me his idea of a smile. Then he took a swig of his pink elixir. "All by yourself, for a change, instead of bringing me one of your sleazy clients with some piece of junk to hock. I feel honored. No doubt you came to take me out to lunch."

"After you called my customers sleazy?"

"Well what do you call them, pillars of society?"

"Pillagers, more often. But you're not exactly in the carriage trade, either, you know."

"Hmm. No, I guess not. I had a great-grandfather who was, sort of, but they called it something different back then." He sighed, spread his hands on the counter, and stared up at some invisible object to his left.

"Like robbing trains?"

"Stagecoaches."

"Much more elegant. I need a cigar box."

"Excuse me?" His eyes snapped back down and refocused, and he looked a little pissed that I had interrupted his reverie.

"You know, one of those little wood things with phony brass hinges and circus graphics on the lid? I think cigars used to come in them once, though I can't honestly say I've ever seen any."

"I know what a cigar box is, Herman. I'm an educated man. What I don't know is why you would come to me for one. Try maybe an antique store. Hell, try a cigar store. I'm not in the box business."

"I will make no comment on what kind of business you're in, Pete. Do you have one or not?"

"I might could find one. Mind telling me what you want it for?"

"It's kind of a long story."

"So give me the made-for-TV version."

"Okay, the short take is this: it's possible that I'm being followed right now. If that's true, I want my shadow to see me come out of a pawn shop carrying a ratty-looking old box that you just might have been holding for me."

"That all sounds very B-movie-ish. Which by the way, I got a good assortment of. I even got Beta."

"Beta is deader than Elvis, Pete."

"No it's not. It's good stuff, always was. I got the players, too, is the thing. Give you just a hell of a deal on a whole package."

"We were talking about boxes, I believe."

"Yeah, yeah, all right then." This time he gave me his Oscar-quality sigh. "You care if anything is in this box?"

"It might actually be better if there is."

"How about a pasteboard item that's held together by a couple of big rubber bands and is full of some costume jewelry that's so crappy, even I can't peddle it?"

"Sounds perfect. Stick a phony claim ticket on it and it will be better yet."

"The things I do for you."

The box turned out to be white, with a picture of a two-corona owl on the front, and it looked suitably junky and also light-colored enough to be seen from a good distance away. I borrowed a Magic Marker from Pete, peeled back the rubber band temporarily, and wrote:

CHARLIE VICTOR—-HIS BOX
OPEN WITH CAUTION

I smiled at my handiwork and gave him back the marker. He didn't charge me for the box.

"But you realize, of course, that now you really do owe me a lunch?"

"Fair enough, Pete."

"Damn straight it is. Just don't make good on it until you lose your tail, whoever it is, okay? What I do not need in what's left of my wretched old life is a bunch of cloak and dagger shit, is what."

"Got it." I put the box conspicuously under my arm and headed back out into the crisp air. Time to visit the fourth estate.

Three blocks later, I was back on Cedar, at the main office of the *Pioneer Press*. The place had a grand lobby at street level that actually contained nothing but a desk for receiving mail, a lot of photomurals, and a big spiral staircase that led up to the skyway level. There, a pretty receptionist at a tiny desk managed to look cheerful and sweet while she mostly told people to go away.

"I'd like to talk to a reporter, please."

"Do you have a news story for us, or are you concerned about one that we've already printed?"

"I'm concerned about one that you should have printed but didn't. I'd like to find out why."

"And what is your point of view, sir, if I may ask?"

"I was a witness." What a nice way of asking me if I'm a nut case with an axe to grind. I gave her what I hoped was a bland smile, just to show her I wasn't dangerous.

"A witness to…?"

"A fire." *That's good, Jackson. Keep it simple. Stay away from the conspiracy-theory stuff.*

"You mean like a house fire?"

"More like an area fire, down in Connemara Gulch."

"Like a brush fire, you mean? I don't think we—"

"Not brush. Something directed at homeless people. Somebody was deliberately torching their campsites."

"I think you should be talking to the police, sir."

I just never seem to listen to my own advice.

She began punching buttons on her console, but not 911, I noticed. Their own security, more likely. I was obviously making the poor young woman feel threatened. Now she was sending for the people with the white coats and truncheons.

"In fact, sir, I can…" She ran her free hand through her hair, frowned once, hung up her receiver, picked it up again and punched some different buttons.

"I'll talk to this gentleman, Pam." The unexpected voice of calm came from a petite, dark-haired woman with a perfectly tailored suit and a bemused look. She had come out of the passing skyway pedestrian traffic, coat folded over one arm and thin leather gloves in her other hand. The receptionist named Pam looked surprised and relieved, and she gave the newcomer a palms-up gesture that said, "your funeral."

"I'm Anne Packard," she said, shifting her coat to her left arm so she could offer me her hand.

"Herman Jackson. Pleased to meet you."

"Herman Jackson the bail bondsman?" Her grip was surprisingly strong for a woman's, and she held it longer than I expected. I looked at her face again and saw alert and probing eyes that had little laugh creases at the corners, a sharp nose, and thin, not-quite-smiling lips. She reminded me of a psychotherapist I once knew: very pleasant to chat with, but you wanted to be damn careful what you said to her. And she already knew who I was, which was more than a bit jarring.

"I'm impressed," I said. "I didn't realize I was known to the press."

"You should be impressed. It's part of being a reporter, and I work at it. I know the names of all the businesses that I pass regularly. Sooner or later, I will know all the faces and stories that go with them, too. You, however, have just missed your big chance to impress me. You're supposed to say, 'Oh, wow, Anne Packard! I read your column every day! Great stuff.'"

"Didn't I say that? I was sure I said that. I certainly thought it. I probably thought 'witty and incisive,' too."

"Nice try. Tell you what, though: buy me a cup of coffee at the little deli over there, and I'll listen to your story anyway."

"I was hoping for a real reporter. No offense."

"A *real* reporter? You mean instead of a *mere* columnist? Well, I was hoping for a *real* scoop from an unimpeachable source, and a *real* Pulitzer Prize for writing it. No offense. How about if we both take a chance here?"

"When you put it so charmingly, how could I refuse?"

"God, I hope your story is better than your pickup line."

Was that a pickup line? I hadn't thought so, but in any case, we walked over to a little hole-in-the-skyway C-store and mini-deli that had wrought iron chairs and tiny tables, right out in the pedestrian traffic across from Pam's desk. I got us two regular coffees in Styrofoam cups and we settled down to talk newspaper talk.

I told her all the parts of the previous night's events that didn't sound like lunatic raving. The very short version, in other words. I did not say anything about the kid with the snow shovel or my being followed.

"Between a murder right downtown and the fire in the Gulch, I thought at least one of the two stories would have found its way into your paper," I said.

"Don't be so disingenuous. You also think the two stories are related."

"Okay, you got me. I wouldn't have thought so, except that some street people over in Railroad Island told me a couple of federal agents were there last night, looking for the dead guy's squat."

"His what?"

"His nest, his patch, whatever you want to call it. The cardboard box he lived in."

She nodded her understanding, and I went on. "This morning, the same feds were in my office, looking for something they thought I was holding for him. Turns out, they're Secret Service."

"Are you sure they're the same agents?" She had started taking some notes on a miniature steno pad, which I took to be a positive sign.

"No. To be perfectly honest, I have no proof of that at all."

She looked up from her writing and gave me a very penetrating look and the tiniest hint of a smile, and I figured I had just passed some kind of credibility test.

"Drink some coffee," she said.

So I did.

While I tasted dark, too-hot coffee and plastic, she produced a cell phone and made three calls, taking a lot of notes and frequently furrowing her brows. I sat back in my chair and stared at the ceiling, making a show of not trying to hear her conversation.

Finally she put the phone back in its clip-on belt holster and once again stared thoughtfully into my eyes while she tapped the eraser end of her pencil on her note pad.

"Very curious," she said.

"What is?" If *she* was very curious, that could be very good for the home team.

"I have some good sources in Fire, Police, and the County Morgue," she said. "Nice folks, people who don't bullshit me or try to freeze me out."

"How handy for you."

"It usually is. Today, they're all sounding a bit on the phony side. And they're not even being very clever about it. The official story is that the fire was a brush fire, probably accidentally set by homeless people trying to keep warm."

"Brush doesn't usually burn very well in a snowstorm, does it?"

"I'm not sure. And the official story on your homeless guy is that he died of exposure."

"I agree. Exposure to brass knuckles, exposure to boots, exposure to some very nasty people. The question is, why are the cops trying to whitewash it?"

"Drink some more coffee." She dug her phone back out and made two more calls, taking still more notes. Then she scowled at her notes, tried some of her own coffee, and looked back up at me.

"Neither of your stories would have made the morning edition. Our usual deadline is four p.m. But my editor says we aren't running anything on them this afternoon, either. We're sitting on the death story as a courtesy to somebody who wants to see who comes poking their noses into it."

"Meaning me."

"I would say so. Interesting, though, how he doesn't say who the favor was for, and he also does not use the word 'murder' at all."

"But that would explain my visit from the Secret Service, wouldn't it?"

"It could explain why they picked you to visit," she said, "but not why they were interested in this dead person in the first place." She drank some more coffee and did some more scowling at her notes. "It's also interesting that my editor told me to forget about the whole business."

"Does it work, telling a reporter to do that?"

"You bet. It just about guarantees that I will investigate further. And it also allows him to deny he ever told me to."

"Neat. So now what happens?"

"That depends on how serious you are, Mr. Jackson."

"Me? Serious?"

"Serious enough to take a little walk with me?"

"To Connemara Gulch?"

She nodded. "Show me where you saw what you saw."

"Absolutely."

As she was getting her coat back on, I happened to look down at Pete's cigar box and get a sudden inspiration.

"Listen, this box is sort of heavy to lug around. Could I leave it with your receptionist, Pam, until we get back?"

"What's in it?"

"Just some low-grade client collateral." I hoped I said that loud enough for Pam to hear and remember.

"Sure, why not? Pam?"

"No problem, sir." She was, I'm sure, delighted to be rid of me so easily.

As Anne Packard and I set off down the skyway at a brisk pace, I noted the location of the security cameras in the reception area. I liked the setup.

"Ms. Packard—"

"Call me Anne."

"Anne, then. Do you by chance know anybody who can lift a fingerprint off a snow shovel?"

"Is that a trick question?"

Sheeny Gulch

My informants from the night before were nowhere to be seen as I led the way through the industrial debris at the rim of the Gulch. The snow was all melted now, leaving scores of little rivulets dribbling down toward the hollow and hundreds of puddles that weren't draining anywhere at all. I was glad I wasn't wearing any shoes that had cost more than sixteen-fifty at the outlet mall. Anne Packard's, I noticed, were much more sensible than mine, rugged-looking things that were almost like low hiking boots. I wondered if she kept a pair of classy-looking heels at her desk. Then I wondered what she looked like in them. I wondered a lot of things that I had no business thinking about at all.

"Are your street people, the ones you said saw the federal agents, still around?" she asked.

"I don't see them," I said. "And we're just as glad for that, since neither of us has a sidearm."

"A cell phone is better," she said. "Nobody attacks you if they can see you can call for help. You don't carry one, I take it?"

"I'd rather die."

"Well, it's good that you understand your options so clearly."

The road down into the gulch didn't look nearly as steep as I remembered it.

"This is where I watched it from," I said. "This gate was closed and had some burly type guarding it, but he left when the commotion started down below."

"And you didn't follow?"

"Nope, I chickened out, pure and simple."

"You obviously have no reporter's instincts."

"Also no unnatural desire to go in harm's way. I expect to die someday, but I'm really not ready for it just yet."

"Well, there are no flames now. Let's go see if they left any traces."

As we descended on the rutted gravel roadway, I began to feel more than a bit foolish. Things looked so ordinary in the daylight. What did I really expect to find, a ten-ton pile of ashes? Anne Packard led the way, and I saw her looking over her shoulder at me from time to time. I was sure she could read my mind.

Down in the trough of the gulch, there were several sets of train tracks, some rusted and some shiny from recent use, piles of old railroad ties, a lot of scrub brush, and all kinds of assorted rubbish. There was still some snow in the shaded areas under bushes or trees, but most of it was gone, leaving just wet stones and mud. A lot of the underbrush and the rubbish looked blackened, but the effects of mildew, random trash fires, and spilled creosote and oil were impossible to distinguish from what we were looking for. Now and then, Anne would poke at a black branch on a scrubby tree, to see if the soot on it was fresh. Then she would throw me a look that I was sure said, "You brought me here for *this*?"

I was rehearsing an apology when she pushed aside a burned head-high poplar, stopped, and said, "Oh my God."

"Something?" I said, rushing to catch up to her.

"Dog."

"Dog?"

"Dead dog," she said. "Burned. And look at the tracks in what's left of the snow."

I looked. It had been a big dog of some kind. Now it was a grotesque, blackened corpse, and it had left deep marks in the snow and dirt, as if it had tried to burrow into the earth to stop the fire, or at least the pain. And most telling of all, what was left of its fur still smoked faintly. I wanted to cry for it.

"What do you think?" she said.

"I'll tell you what I don't think. I don't think this dog died from a trash fire set by homeless people."

"No. Not from careless cigarette smoking, either." She pulled a tiny silver camera out of her purse and began weaving around, looking for a good angle. "Pity," she said. "I don't think we can print anything this heart-rending. Why would anybody do such a thing?"

"They was tryna make an example, is what."

We both turned around to see that the voice came from a shapeless, pasty-faced woman with about three scarves on her head, oversized rubber boots on her feet, and uncounted layers of clothes everywhere else.

"First they beat up on some of the guys, and when that didn't do no good, they started burnin'. They had cans of gas or somethin', an they burnt our stuff and then they burnt the dog, said they'd do the same to us. Poor thing screamed something awful. Finally they shot it."

"Who?" I said. "Who were they?"

"Who wants to know?"

"Press," said Anne, producing a business card and a winning smile faster than I would have believed possible.

"Strib?" said the bag lady, squinting at the card. "The good one?"

"*Pioneer Press*," I said. "The local one." Anne gave me a dirty look.

"Oh, that one."

"Tell us what these people wanted," said Anne, starting to shoot pictures of the woman.

"What's in it for me? You got some money for me?"

I started to reach for my wallet, but Anne pushed my hand down and said, "You'll get your picture in the paper. Maybe you'll even get quoted. Would you like that?"

"Really? Front page?"

"That's up to my editor. I'll do what I can."

"Will you bring me a copy?"

"Sure. Lots of copies."

"Will you tell everybody how I lost my job at the bank when I wouldn't fuck the manager?"

"Tell us about the people who killed the dog."

"I'd really like to see that asshole reported on. Bet his fat-assed wife and ugly kids don't even know—"

"The fire? Please try to stay on track, miss, um...?"

"Glenda." She furrowed her already wrinkled brows and nodded. "I think so. Yeah. I started hitting the juice just a little harder than I should a few weeks back, maybe, and sometimes I forget some stuff. But I'm pretty sure it's Glenda. Like the witch, you know? I don't s'pose you got any red? I remember real good with a shot of the red."

Swell, I thought. *My only corroborating witness, and she turns out to be a wino with Alzheimer's.* But Anne didn't seem dismayed in the slightest.

"Think hard, Glenda. Concentrate. Tell us exactly what happened and we'll get you fixed up with something to drink afterward, okay? What did these people who burned the poor dog want?"

"Well, shit, the first time, they wanted Charlie."

"The first time?"

"They was here twice," she said, nodding. "The first time was in the daylight, and they was looking for Charlie, only he wasn't around. Then they came back after dark and wanted Charlie's box, is what they said. Lots of people was looking for that thing, all freaking day and night. They said they found his squat, but his box wasn't there. That didn't make no sense to me. I mean, his squat *was* his box, wasn't it? Anyway, first there was Elmer Fudd with his weird hat and then and then these guys with the guns and the gas cans and finally these two Bobsey Twins in black suits. The twins told them they better go. They was mad."

"And did you know where this box was?"

"I didn't, but I think some of the guys mighta. I don't think Charlie even lived here. He hung around here a lot, but when night'd come, he'd go someplace else. We didn't tell nobody nothin', though. We wouldn't. People don't understand that.

After you lived on the streets for long enough, you can't be threatened anymore, is the thing. What do people got, to scare you with? Pain? Cold? Hell, they's old friends. Death? Who gives a shit? A broken arm or leg? That's a trip to a nice warm hospital with good food. I got to admit, the fire was pretty scary, and they had some really big guns, but killing the dog mostly just pissed us off. I mean, he wasn't a *great* dog or anything, but he didn't hurt nobody."

"So who were the guys with the guns?" I asked again. "More agents? Cops?"

"Don't put words in her mouth," said Anne, half under her breath.

"No, man, they was soldiers."

"You mean like uniform security guards?"

"You gonna tell me what I mean now? When I say soldiers, I mean soldiers. They didn't have their regular uniforms on or nothin, but you could tell. The way they talked, the way they moved. Even the way they had their hair cut. And they all had those funny looking boots they wear nowadays, the kind they don't have to polish?"

"Herman, why don't you go and get us some coffee and something to eat."

"Sausage biscuits," said Glenda the Witch. "I like them."

"Sausage biscuits," said Anne.

"And some red."

"And a bottle of wine," said Anne. "Glenda here has a lot of things to tell me, don't you dear?"

"I'll curl your fucking hair, is what."

"There's a sweetheart. Run along, Herman."

Forty-five minutes later I was back, with the finest gourmet sandwiches that the SuperAmerica in Lowertown had plus a bottle of red wine so cheap, I wondered if it was safe to drink. I picked it mainly because it had a screw top. I figured if I had gotten one that needed a corkscrew, Glenda the Witch might just have opened it with a brick and wound up drinking the broken glass. Somebody once told me that was the homeless person's equivalent of having it on the rocks. The guy who told me that thought it was a joke.

When I got back, Anne Packard was sitting on a large rock, letting Glenda talk into a hand-held tape recorder, nodding encouragement now and then. They stopped when they saw me.

"Did you get the good stuff?" said Glenda.

"Did you earn it?"

"She did, Herman. Go ahead and give it to her."

Glenda opened the bottle first and had a big slug. She paused and looked off into space for a moment, as if she was pondering some great truth, and then she had another, bigger than the first. Then she screwed the top back on and made the bottle disappear somewhere inside her layers of clothes. Finally, she dug greedily into the paper bag with the sandwiches.

"How many ketchup you get? Looks like two."

"That would be because two is what it is."

"Didn't your mama teach you nothin? Something's free, you take all of it you can get." Her face darkened and she rummaged harder. "Ketchup, mustard, salt, napkins. Them are staples, man!" Her voice was rapidly escalating to hysteria-pitch.

"I'll remember, Glenda." To Anne, in a much lower tone, I said, "Time to leave."

"We're not quite done."

"I'm afraid we are." I gently took an elbow and tried to steer her away. Meanwhile, Glenda was working herself up to full frenzy.

"Next time? What the hell good's that do me, that 'next time' shit? You go back and get the rest of that stuff now, or I'll kick your ass, is what I'll do." She was screaming now. "Who the hell you think you are anyway? You come down here with your fancy clothes and your camera and shit, and you think you can cheat me. You think I'm nobody but…"

We walked away and left her ranting. When we got back up on high ground, Anne said, "What on earth was that all about?"

"Apparently Glenda is a mean drunk. Also a bipolar one, with maybe a touch of schizophrenia or alcoholic dementia here and there."

"But she only had the two drinks."

"You don't have a lot of experience with winos, do you? After enough years of pickling their brains in the sauce, the well-known trend of 'increased tolerance' starts to go the other way. They might go through a quart a day for years, and then one day they find they can get higher than a kite just by licking the cork."

"That's terrible."

"Well, yes. Life on the street is terrible. Maybe that's what you ought to be writing about. Not that it's exactly a new topic."

"So are you telling me that all the stuff I just got from her is just drunken delusions?"

"No, I'm not. She's probably never really sober, but she was at least dry when you were taping her. Did she say she was dry when the soldiers came to the gulch?"

"I think so. She had a lot of stuff to say, most of it totally beside the point, but I think she said that, yes."

"Then you should be all right. The cops would write her off because they couldn't count on her in court, but you don't have that problem."

"No, I only have the problem of getting two corroborating sources. Sometimes I think it might be easier to be a cop."

"Do reporters actually do that, that two-source business?"

"I do."

Back downtown, we went up into the skyway system at its eastern end, through the lobby of the former Buckby-Meers Building, where I'm told there used to be a real Foucault pendulum. I've never figured out what purpose it served, taking the pendulum out. A block or two farther on, I pointed to another deli and gave Anne an enquiring look. She pointed to her watch and shook her head, no, and we headed back toward her office.

"So what do you think?" I said. "Do you have a story?"

"Oh, it's a story, all right. But I can't see what it's about yet. It's at the stage we call holding a monster by the tail. I still need the hook, something to hang it all on. Until I get that, I really can't write it."

"That makes sense. I don't know what it's all about, either, but I intend to find out."

"Well, when you do, give me a call. Here's my card, with my direct line. I'll write my cell phone number on it, too." She proceeded to scribble as we walked, looking up from time to time.

"And here's my office," she said. "So I'll say goodbye now. Pam, would you please give this gentleman back his box?"

"Some people from his office came and picked it up, Miss Packard. They said he needed it right away." She smiled sweetly, as if she were expecting a pat on the head.

"What did they look like?" I said.

"Well, like you two, sort of. Business people. Not crooks or anything."

"A man and a woman?" I said. "Dark, severe clothes, very formal, superior manner?"

"Yes, that sounds right. So they were your people, then?"

"No, they were not. I think they were spooks, actually, but I would definitely like to see the tapes from your surveillance cameras for that time slot."

"I don't know if we can do that."

"Herman," said Anne, suddenly very serious, "that wasn't it, was it?"

"What wasn't what?"

"Don't be cute. Was that Charles Victor's box, the one everybody is supposed to be looking for?"

"No, it was a decoy. And somebody just bit on it."

"But you know where the real one is?"

"Possibly."

"Now you're being cute again."

"Let's say I can lay my hands on *a box* that used to belong to Charlie. He thought it was important for somebody to keep it for him. I have never looked inside it."

"Is that my hook?"

"I won't know until I look inside it, will I?"

"Fair enough."

"You can go with me to get it, if you want. First, though, I think we should go visit your friend at the County Morgue."

"Why on earth?"

"I'm Charlie's sole heir. I can claim his personal effects, whatever they might be. And I should do so before they all get shipped off to some lab that won't tell us what they find."

"Pam? Sign me out for the rest of the day."

Fire in the City

Anne's contact person down at the Morgue turned out to be a young lab technician named Brian Faraday. It was obvious that it made him very nervous, having us back in the restricted spaces. It was also obvious that he was totally infatuated with Anne and would do almost anything to keep from displeasing her.

Looking at Charlie's body didn't tell us much, apart from the fact that both life and death had been very cruel to him. His meager collection of personal possessions wasn't just a fountainhead of information, either. Brian wouldn't let me have any, but he let us have a look at them, in a zippered plastic bag that was on its way to the evidence room in the main cop shop. So apparently they were calling it a homicide, after all.

There wasn't much there. There were his original army dog tags, of course. Why he had kept them all this time, I couldn't imagine, but I knew the police had used them to ID him more than once before, since he had held neither a driver's license nor a Social Security card. There was a small comb with a few teeth missing, a pocketknife, a combination can opener and corkscrew, a few coins, a dirty bandanna. Half a candy bar. And an ace of spades from a deck with the horse-head insignia on the back. The death card he had told his lawyer about.

"Air Cav," I said, pointing to it.

"Are you an expert on military insignias?"

"Not even slightly. But that was Charlie's old outfit. He had a shoulder patch on his fatigue jacket, just like it."

The bag also contained some kind of key, a stubby little brass thing, very thick and solid.

"I don't suppose we could get something to drink," I said to our host. "Coffee or a soda, maybe?" Anne gave me a perplexed look and I nodded my head ever so slightly, trying to cue her to go along with me.

"Um, you're not going to hang around here or anything, are you?" said young Brian, even more nervous than before.

"No, no. I, ah, just got a little queasy, looking at poor old Charlie back there. I could really use a little drink of something to settle my stomach."

"Maybe a can of pop?" said Anne. "Thanks so very much, Brian."

And the moonstruck lad was off in a flash. As soon as he was out of sight, I dug a stick of gum out of my pocket, peeled the wrapper off it, and made two quick imprints, one each of the end and side of the key. Gum was hardly the preferred medium for a pattern, but it was what I had. Then I held the key out to Anne with the face that had a serial number on it toward her.

"Shoot," I said. "Close-up, if you can."

"I can."

She shot three quick pictures of the key and we immediately stuck it back in the plastic bag. Then I put the stick of gum back in its wrapper and slipped it into my shirt pocket, where it wouldn't be too likely to get bent out of shape. As I was tucking it away, the lab techie came back, bearing a hopeful smile and a can of iced tea.

"Jesus," I said under my breath. "Why did he pick tea? I really hate tea."

"Not today, you don't," said Anne, out of the corner of her mouth. Out loud, she said, "Oh, that's so thoughtful, Brian. Thank you again."

While he beamed at her, I put a tiny bit of the nasty brew in my mouth and a bunch of it down the drain of a service sink. My memory was dead-on correct, for a change; I really do hate tea. I pretended to drink a bit more and then asked Brian the thing that had been eating at me.

"What happens to the body?"

"We keep it for a while, until we know for sure if the detectives want any other tests done. After that, if nobody comes to claim it, we cremate it."

"You burn it." I didn't like that idea at all.

"Well, that would be how you cremate somebody, yeah."

"Yeah but I mean…" I drew in a deep breath.

"It's not like he's going to feel it, or anything."

"Don't we have something like Potters' Field in Minnesota? I mean—"

"Cremation," he said, folding his arms and shaking his head. "We do it right over there."

He pointed at something that looked like an antique furnace, bulky, rusty, and machine ugly. In fact, it looked a lot like the furnace from my old pad in Detroit.

And suddenly, there it was. With a gasp and a chill, I had tripped back to a time and place I was sure I had left forever, never wanted to think about again. I was back in Detroit in the blistering summer of 1967. I was fourteen years old, and in a broken-bottle landscape backlit by burning buildings, I was running for my life.

◇◇◇

You hear the term "Rust Belt" a lot these days, but I don't believe in it. A lot of the old factories along the Detroit River have moved out or just shut down, but Henry Ford's River Rouge plant and GM's Cadillac factory farther to the north are still cranking out shiny chrome-trimmed monsters, the railroads are still busy feeding the iron giant and hauling away its products, and the diners and bars and dance halls are full every night. Everybody works and plays. Everybody is singing Motown, and everybody is buying tickets to tomorrow. Life is good.

Pretty good, anyway. The folks who have good jobs work hard and get by. Those who can't break into the unions or the decent housing, which mostly means blacks, don't. They tend to be some of Uncle Fred's best customers, since their chances in the normal world are rotten to none. Sometimes that translates into despair but just as often it morphs seamlessly into rage. And sometimes the two are hard to tell apart. When the heat goes up in the center city, there seems to be plenty of both.

There are neighborhoods where a white boy like me has no business wandering around on his own. And there are others where no kid of any color wants to let the sun go down and find him still on the street. That's too bad, since a lot of my Uncle Fred's customers are in those neighborhoods, and sometimes it's my turn to help with the collections.

Besides the normal bookie business of taking bets on horse races and sports contests of all kinds, my uncle also sells tickets to the New York lottery, since Michigan doesn't have one of its own. He lets me take the orders on the phone. I copy down the requested number and read it back to the caller, along with their name and address. When I've sold twenty or so, I call one of half a dozen numbers for our layoff men in New York itself, and he calls me back a little later to confirm that he's bought the actual tickets. We charge our customers five dollars for a fifty-cent ticket, don't mess with the quarter or dollar tickets at all. In the unlikely event that the customer's number actually hits, we split the winnings right down the middle. I've only seen that happen once, and I was dumbfounded to hear an out-of-work upholsterer's helper bitching about only getting thirty-five thousand dollars.

On a good day, when nobody wastes my time with a lot of chitchat, I can sell a hundred and twenty tickets, make a record of who I sold them to, and get the actual tickets bought, some thousand or so miles away. My pay for all that is ten percent of the markup, or forty-five cents a ticket, which translates to fifty-four dollars a day.

That is just purely one hell of a lot of money for a teenage kid, more than enough for me to have my own place, upstairs over a rundown hardware store on the near West Side. Fred calls it "a two-room flop, upstairs over a used paint store," but it's a big deal for me. I don't intend ever to go back to high school or to my mother's house up on Seven Mile, with its floating array of boyfriends whom I refuse to call stepfathers. I intend to be a mojo numbers man, just like my uncle.

We have several freelance contractors working at collecting the five bucks a pop from all those customers, and I don't know what their cut is, except that it's more than mine. But that's okay, because their job is tougher.

Once or twice a week, Uncle Fred tells me to tag along with one or another of them, just to see all the facets of the business close up, practice for the day when I'm big enough to pinch-hit at any position. For those trips, I don't get paid anything. It's just on-the-job training. I carry a sturdy leather gym bag to put the money in and a baseball bat to protect it with. Uncle Fred doesn't let me carry a gun.

I usually go with a big Irishman about twice my age, named Gerry Phearson, or Jerp for short. He's ten feet tall and has baseball mitts for hands and bulldozers for feet, and everybody says he looks like John Wayne with stringy red hair. They also say that if you get him mad enough, he can kick a hole in a cinder-block wall or bite the numbers off a billiard ball.

He likes me. When people say, "Hey Jerp, who's riding shotgun for you today?" he will tell them, "Me little brother, boyo, and don't you be giving him no grief, or I'll let him break your kneecaps for you." We drive around in a beat-up '59 Mercury and park any damn where we like.

The heat wave this July is brutal, and we have all the windows down and wet rags on our heads. Swamp Arabs, Jerp calls us. I think we look so totally stupid, we're cool. We're overdue to collect on about a hundred bucks worth of tickets up in Highland Park, where the first big Ford plant was once, and over on the near West Side. There were some riots over there a couple nights ago, and we stayed away from the area to let it cool down. On Twelfth Street, right in the heart of the neighborhood, the cops made an early morning raid on a blind pig, and a hundred or so drunk customers decided they would rather attack the cops than stand around waiting for a fleet of paddy wagons to show up and take them off in chains. To hear the news reports, it turned into a major war.

But we've had blowups before, between angry blacks and angrier white cops. The situation ought to be cool enough to touch by now.

Rounding the corner off Grand Boulevard onto Dexter, I can see that cool is exactly what it is not. A huge crowd of blacks, mostly young men, is swarming over the street, while behind them, buildings are going up in flames, one after another. We might have another ten minutes before the whole sky is covered with dirty brown-black clouds and the cinders come raining down everywhere. Off to the east, I can see the flashing lights of some fire trucks, but it's obvious they're never going to get through the mob.

There's gunfire now, too. I can't tell if any of it is aimed at us, but there's a lot of it.

"Jerp, I hate to be the one to say it, but maybe we should get the hell out of here."

"We've still got collections to make, lad. It sets a bad precedent, letting a fish off the hook over a little thing like a riot."

"What about the guns?"

"Which ones?"

Which ones? Is he crazy? "The ones that seem to be going off all around us just now."

"Ah, those. Sort of like Sunday in Belfast, isn't it? Makes a body homesick, it does. Now, if one of our customers had a gun, that might be different. I'd have to make him eat it, wouldn't I? But these guns have nothing to do with us at all, at all. The jungle people are shooting up their own, most likely. Or they're shooting the cops, which of course would be a terrible shame."

I can see there's no point talking to him. He's got himself set on showing me how unflappable he is, I guess, and once he makes up his mind, you might as well argue with a statue. Typical Irish, my Uncle Fred would say. Rock solid from the ground up, right through the brain.

I wish I felt as cool as he acts. I've got a prickly little animal running around in my gut that says the day is going to get very ugly before it's finally over.

The crowd gets closer and larger, and Jerp steers the big Merc' over the curb and through a trash-strewn parking lot as some rocks and bricks start to hit the car and a lot of guys are swinging big sticks and surging toward us. Behind us, a Molotov cocktail goes up with a dull "whoof," maybe meant for us, maybe not.

Jerp is picking up speed now, despite people swarming in on all sides. Wire grocery carts and trash cans go flying off the front bumper and into the crowd, as he tries to get enough momentum up to crash through the cyclone fence at the back of the lot.

A metallic screech, a lot of jolts and tearing noises, and we're through, heading down a wide industrial alley. All around us, black men are grabbing sticks or metal bars, pounding on the car as we plow through them. Occasionally we bounce a sweaty black body off the grille.

"Lock your door, lad."

He doesn't have to tell me twice.

More gunfire. Loud, hoarse barks that I recognize as shotgun blasts, and other higher-pitched popping that must be pistol fire. A few bodies down on the pavement now, some of them in spreading pools of blood. We sure as hell didn't shoot them. I wonder who did.

If all that weren't enough, now we have machine gun fire. Tracer rounds are stitching a line across the second story fire escapes of a clapboard tenement down the street. The neon line of bullets comes first, the brrt-brrt noise a second or two later, sounding muffled. The shooter is a long way away, maybe as much as a mile. He's shooting at something else altogether, something we will never see, or at nothing at all. But what goes up must come down, and unfortunately, it's still lethal.

"Herman, lad, do you know how to drive?"

"Yeah, sure." The car has an automatic transmission. How hard could it be? I look over at him and I see blood coming out of his mouth and the big, meaty hands white on the steering wheel.

"Jesus, Jerp—"

"Just grab the wheel, will you? You don't have to worry about the brake, because we're not stopping. Head for downtown. The old Michigan Central train depot. The place has been next thing to abandoned for years. We ought to be able to find a place inside there to lay low for a while and maybe stash the money. Or if we can't, we'll take a train out. If we try to get back to the office with the dough and run into the cops or the National Guard, they'll relieve us of it, and that's a certainty."

He lets go of the wheel and floors the gas pedal, and I suddenly find out that steering really isn't very tough at all, if you don't care what you hit.

We're back on Grand, heading east and south, the big engine pushing us up toward seventy. I blow the horn at anything that gets in our way, bounce off a few busses and cars, and mostly aim right down the center of the street, ignoring all the traffic lights. Jerp is breathing in gasps now and clutching a red handkerchief to his side, but he's still conscious and his eyes look clear.

Two blocks ahead, I see a wall of khaki. The National Guard or the Army, hundreds of them or maybe thousands, with trucks and jeeps, are blocking off the street, advancing en masse.

"Ease off, Jerp. I think we're okay now."

"With that lot? Bollocks. First we have to stash the money."

"It's only money, Jerp. There will always be money. We have to get you—"

"It's the responsibility, is the thing. We lose somebody else's money, we're no better than that riffraff we just left. Find a place to stash it, I say!" He's screaming through clenched teeth now, and again I see there's no point in arguing.

"We're not too far from my place," I say. "I've got a secret stash in the basement of the hardware store that we—"

"Go for it, lad!"

I make the corner onto Hobson on two wheels, and Jerp eases off on the gas a bit and lets me maneuver into the side streets.

"Almost there," I say. "How are you holding up?"

"Alls I need is a short beer and a shot of Bushnell's, and I'd be singing 'Molly Malone.' Shut up and drive."

Three more turns and we're there. Jerp can't seem to find the brake pedal, so I throw the shifting lever into Park. The transmission makes a noise like a mechanical pig being slaughtered, but finally the rear wheels lock up and we skid to a stop in the alley behind the hardware store.

"Quick now, lad."

As if he had to tell me. The streets are deserted here, but I can hear shouting mobs not that far off. I grab the gym bag, pile out of the car, and use my key to let myself into the service entry of the store. Lights off, everything deserted. I wonder where Mr. Holst, the owner, would go, if he decided to evacuate his own neighborhood. Where would anybody go?

Down in the basement, I open up the fire door on the old monster coal furnace that has long ago been replaced by the new gas-fired Lennox. I stick my body half inside the fire chamber, pick up the edge of the sheet of asbestos board that covers my own personal money stash, and throw the gym bag under it. As I shut the door and sprint for the stairs, I hear gunfire out in the alley.

Oh, shit. We cut it too fine.

Maybe I should have brought Jerp inside with me. Maybe I still should. Go ask. But my feet aren't moving. It feels safe in the basement. And I am so very afraid. I dither and hesitate and wait, for what, I don't know. And then I see the smoke at the top of the stairs. The bastards have torched my building.

Stairs three at a time, kick the back door open again, don't bother with turning out the lights. The deadbolt will relock itself, if there's anything left to protect. Just be sure you've still got your key.

Back outside, the sunlight is blinding. I put my hand up to shield my eyes, just in time to catch a blow from a club. Jesus, it feels like my forearm is shattered. With my other hand, I swing the baseball bat, lashing out blindly in all directions. I catch at least one set of shins and maybe a head or two, and I'm able to clear a little free space around myself.

Everything looks black and white but slowed down now, like an old movie being run in slow motion. I must have a lot of sweat in my eyes, because it's getting hard to focus.

Down the street, somebody yells, "Hey man, they broke open Ullman's!" That would be the neighborhood liquor store. The mob surges that way and loses interest in me. I make a final clearing swing or two with the bat and head back to where I left Jerp and the car.

Neither of which is there anymore.

What the hell?

He was hurt too bad to drive off himself, but if somebody was just boosting the car, wouldn't they have dumped him out first? I climb the steel fire escape from my own pad, to get a better look over the crowd, but even so, car and Irishman are absolutely, totally gone. And as I perch there, they are joined by my pad, my building, my stash. And all my dreams. The building is going up so fast, the flames are already scorching my back.

I bound back to ground level and fight my way through the fringes of the crowd to some fairly clear street to the south. Then I start to make my way back toward downtown, running from one hiding place to another. The old Michigan Central train depot, Jerp had said. If he was capable of moving under his own power at all, that's where he would go, and that's where I should go, too.

Get there before dark, though, boyo. If you don't, you're just as likely to be killed by somebody inside the building as out.

How long is it until dark, anyway? The day is already about thirty hours old and looking like a place with no end.

Is that as fast as you can run, Herman? Cry, if you have to, maybe also scream. Piss your pants, if you think that helps anything. But whatever you do, do not stop running. Because once that goddamn sun goes down, the only white folks left on these streets are going to be the very quick and the very dead.

Jerp, where the hell are you?

"Herman?"

I blinked.

"Are you all right, Herman?"

"Sure." Not even slightly.

"Do you want to claim this body?" said Brian.

"I'm not sure what I want yet." I gave him one of my cards. "Don't burn him without calling me first, okay?"

Dead Man's Key

We thanked Brian for all his help and went back out on the street.

"Well, that certainly didn't gain us much," said Anne.

"Maybe, maybe not. How quick can you get me a print of that key photo?"

"If we go back to my office, I can run one in two minutes, flat. What are you going to do with it?"

"Take it to a pawnbroker friend of mine who also happens to be a locksmith, see what he makes of it."

"And also have him make you an illegal copy?"

"Are you so sure it would be illegal? I mean, I really am Charlie's heir, you know."

"I think I don't want to hear about it."

"You're probably right, you don't want to."

We walked back to the skyway reception area again, and I did a poor job of making small talk with Pam while Anne took her camera to some inner sanctum to do her thing with it. As good as her word, she was back in less than five minutes with an eight-and-a-half by eleven color print.

"It's a little grainy at this enlargement size," she said, "but the serial number comes up all right."

"That should do very nicely. If it's a real key, from a real lock company, my guy should be able to look it up."

"The bad news is, we shouldn't have come back here."

"Oh?"

"I ran into my editor, who was tactless enough to remind me that I have a deadline for a column I haven't started yet. I'm going to have to pass on going to see your locksmith."

"Tell you what: you go do your column and I'll go do the things you don't want to know about. And later this evening, I'll take a look inside Charlie's box and call you on your cell if I find anything that looks important."

"Call me no matter what you find. I won't shut the phone off until I've heard from you."

"Deal."

"Later."

"Happy column." I thought about inviting her to a romantic candlelit dinner of takeout Chinese with a cigar box instead of a fortune cookie. I thought about it rather a lot, in fact. But if she was sending me any of the right signals for such a venture, I couldn't read them. I sighed slightly and headed back down the skyway.

Nickel Pete's was only a couple of blocks away, but instead of going straight there, I took the skyway system all the way to the City Hall Annex. Whether my friendly shadows had found my phony cigar box amusing or not, I figured they would still be following me.

At the Annex, I took the elevator to the basement, then picked a lock to let myself into a stairwell to the sub-basement. Some remnants of my old life skills are handy at times. I re-locked the door behind me and went down to the original boiler room, now covered in dust and cobwebs, where I waited. Five minutes later, somebody rattled the knob from the other side. Then he kicked the door twice. Then nothing.

I waited another ten minutes, then headed back north through a maze of forgotten storage spaces and mechanical rooms. All of the sub-basements on that block are connected, and I finally came back out into the daylight through a freight elevator at the far end of the block, where I turned up my collar, put my head down, and sprinted the block and a half to Nickel Pete's pawn shop.

He was about as happy to see me as he had been the last time.

"It's too late for lunch now, Herman, so what kind of weird favor are you going to hit me up for this time?"

"Good to see you, too, Pete. Always a pleasure. I have a picture to show you."

"Is it pornographic? Will it awaken long-forgotten urges and incite unwise adventures?"

"Afraid not." I unfolded the print and laid it out on his counter, along with the impressed stick of gum, which really hadn't fared all that well in my pocket.

"Then what's the point?"

"Just look at it, will you?"

He looked.

"Do you have a book of some kind where you can look up the serial number of that key?" I asked.

"What for?"

"Is this what they call a senior moment? To tell what it is, of course."

"I don't have to look it up, I know what it is. It's a Master."

"That's probably why it says 'Master' on it. I picked up on that already. Can you look up the serial number and tell me what it fits?"

"Obviously Herman, you were having a little nap when I said the word 'Master.' Master only makes padlocks."

"So?"

"Millions and gazillions of padlocks. The most you might find out is the name of some hardware wholesaler, who is most likely out of business for ages now."

"Why do you say that?"

"Because the number is only four digits. That baby is *old*, Herman."

"Well, bat shit, Pete."

"Now I expect you're going to ask me if I can make you a copy, using nothing but the photo and that mangled piece of chewing gum for a pattern."

"Pete, you really should have made a career on the stage. You can read minds perfectly."

"How nice for me. But instead, I'm stuck here, breaking the law and putting my locksmith's license in jeopardy." He let out a profound sigh and headed for the back room. "The things I do for you."

It was favorite line of his.

While Pete made the key, I watched the storefront and main door, looking for shadows on the other side of the glass that I might want to hide from. Then I grabbed the phone from Pete's side of the counter and called Wilkie's cell phone.

"Harra." He always answers that way, and I have never figured out what it means.

"Hey, Wide, Herman here. How's your work load?"

"Your man Russo hasn't left town yet. Unless he tries to leave the country, I can't grab him before his trial date, so I got one of my second-stringers keeping an eye on him."

"That'll work. So are you available for something else?"

"Well, seeing as how I failed to pick up any loose change last night when my eight-ball shooter split on me, I could use a little something, you know? Not for tonight, though. I got a date."

"Would that be with the ugly broad from the Minneapolis cop shop?"

"Hey, watch your mouth. She's a nice person."

"Me? You're the one who always calls her that. I've never even met her. Anyway, is that the lucky lady?"

"So?"

"I'm wondering if you can hit her up for a favor."

"The number of dates she gets? I can hit her up."

"Now who's saying mean things about her?"

"Well it's not like she's listening, is it? What are you after?"

"Go by my office and pick up a snow shovel that's wrapped in a black plastic trash bag. Don't open it unless you've got gloves on. I need somebody who knows what they're doing to see if they can pull some fingerprints off it."

"And then see if those prints are on record."

"Well it would be a pretty pointless exercise otherwise, wouldn't it?"

"What do I use for an excuse?"

"You'll think of something."

"But this is a bounty hunting job, right?"

"We'll call it that, anyway." Wilkie doesn't have a PI license, and sometimes we have to do a little creative labeling of the work he does for me. Bounty hunting doesn't require a license.

"Who am I hunting besides Russo?"

"Whoever's prints are on the shovel."

"Uh huh. And who am I hunting before I know who that is?"

"Joe Kapufnik. The Duke of Paducah. I don't care. Have Agnes pull a couple of names out of our 'long-gone' file. And tell her I said to give you a couple hundred retainer out of petty cash. Take your friend someplace nice."

"Hey, you're right. I'll think of something. Anything else?"

"One other thing. This one's a little more open-ended and not so quick. See what you can find out about a guy who calls himself Eddie Bardot, claims to work for something called Amalgamated Bonding Enterprises. He was in my office this morning, so my security tape will still have him on it. Aggie can print you a still photo off it, if you see a frame you like. Either his name or the company's could be phony, but he doesn't look as if he ever changed his face. Give it a shot, okay?"

"What are you liking him for?"

"I'm not sure. He comes off like old Mob, but he could be just a freelance shakedown artist trying to look that way. Before I decide how to deal with him, I need to know if he's connected."

"Time and expenses-plus-ten?"

"That's the drill, only I might not be able to pay you right away."

"I can wait. I'm on it."

"What's your girl's name?"

"None of your business."

"Odd name. Say hi for me."

Pete brought me the key, and I left.

Charlie Victor's Box

I left Pete's by the back way, through an L-shaped alley, and went straight to the Victory Ramp, where I retrieved my BMW, after carefully looking over the undercarriage and the wheel wells to see if it had acquired any bugs or bombs. If it had, they were extremely tiny, so I decided they couldn't hurt me.

If my tail included one or more vehicles, I couldn't spot them. But just to be on the safe side, I took a very indirect route home. I crossed the Mrs. Hippy on the Robert Street Bridge and wandered around the river flats for a while, then headed up the Wabasha hill to the top of the river bluffs, to an area known as Cherokee Heights. There I got on the high end of the long, straight, severely sloping High Bridge and went back down across the river again. But at the bottom of the bridge, I made a strictly illegal U-turn and headed back up. As I went back the way I had come, I did a mental inventory of the oncoming traffic.

White Taurus with Parks and Rec markings, blue Corolla with about a dozen little kids in the back seat, dark green Mini Cooper with a lone woman in it, kind of cute, red Chevy pickup with dopey-looking decals and a couple of young guys with backward baseball caps, dirty black Hummer, some kind of small Pontiac in metallic brown. All of them had Minnesota plates, except for the Hummer, which had no license on the front.

At the top of the bridge, I turned right onto a narrow parkway, went around a couple of blocks, and finally turned back south onto Smith Avenue, heading across the bridge yet again. And again, I looked at the oncoming traffic.

Dodge Intrepid, Honda Civic, big box Chevy, PT Cruiser, Hummer.

A dirty black Hummer with no front plate. Very careless, guys.

Unfortunately, the glass on the monster was too dirty or too heavily tinted for me to see who was in it.

The speed limit on the High Bridge is forty. But if I were going to pick up a cop, my goofy U-turn would have already done the job. So I took the rest of the bridge at seventy. At the bottom of it, I ran the gear box on the 328i down into second and made a hard left, accelerating through the turn in a nice, four-wheel power drift, just on the verge of out of control. Forty going in, sixty coming out, and gone in a blink. Any Hummer trying that would be found upside down, a quarter of a mile down Smith Avenue. I blew into the tangled web of narrow streets to the north and west, made a few more turns, and finally parked the car in the customer lot of a body shop. Then I locked it and walked back south through the alleys, to my condo. I didn't see the Hummer again.

My condo is a two-story stone-clad row house, in the middle of an attached cluster of six others just like it. They are a hundred and twenty years old, restored and gone to seed again more times than anybody can remember anymore. If the stone on the outside were dirtier and rough, instead of newly sandblasted and smooth, and if the whole building were located a couple thousand miles farther east, you would call it a brownstone. It has high ceilings, multi-paned windows, and walls that you couldn't punch through with a bazooka. And it's on a short side street that gets no through traffic at all. I like it.

I checked both front and back doors, to see if they had been worked on. They have electronic lock monitors that Pete rigged up for me. If either of them had been opened while I was gone, all the monitors would be flashing tiny red lights at me. Inside, a light on my phone would also be flashing, but no message would go out to the police or anybody else. Satisfied that everything was as I had left it, I went back outside to an old-fashioned sloped cellar door on the end of the entire building complex and worked the combination on the padlock.

The townhouses have the unusual feature of having a single, undivided common basement. Since that has been a violation of about sixteen kinds of building and fire codes for a century or so, the last set of renovators solved the problem by giving no unit any direct access to the space. Instead, the basement has an unbroken fireproof ceiling with no stairs going up into anybody's house, including mine. My furnace and water heater are in a closet off the kitchen.

Silly as it sounds, that makes the basement a good place to hide things, if only because most search warrants will not be written to cover a space that isn't exactly in the same building. At least, I thought so. The general clutter of cardboard boxes and broken appliances and antiques with no names would make searching a real undertaking, too. But the real goodie was the dirt floor. I had done nothing any more clever with Charlie's box than put it in a plastic bag and bury it. I buried it right in front of the basement's only door, where I figured the dirt would get packed back down quickly by whatever traffic there might be. Then I left a small shovel for myself inside an old laundry tub, as far from the door as it could possibly be.

I don't know if any of that was really clever or not, but it worked. The box was still there.

It seemed awfully large for a cigar box, but it clearly had a label that said Rigoletto Palma Cedars, so I didn't think it was a tackle box. It was well made, out of solid wood, with brass hardware, and it had a stamped-on trademark of some importer on it. I threw the plastic bag in the trashcan by the back alley and took the box inside. I put it on the kitchen counter while I reset my lock system. Then I checked for any obvious booby traps or notes warning of booby traps on the box. Finally, I flipped up the brass hasp and opened it.

It was full of junk. War medals, old coins, expired coupons, free passes to places that didn't exist anymore. Bus tokens for lines that had made their last stops ages ago. Also lists of names and phone numbers, and mailing addresses torn from yellowed envelopes. Little people's treasures, the kind of crap that the kids closing out their parents' estates never know what to do with.

And at the very bottom of the box, there was a ledger. An old-fashioned green-page ledger and a loose-leaf scrapbook, showing what people gave him and what they wanted in return, with inserted notes in dozens of different writing hands.

At first I thought they were all the stuff of pure fantasy, vouchers to be drawn on the First National Bank of Neverland. But the more of them I read, the less I thought so. Charlie had often said that for all his other faults, not the least of which was being a self-proclaimed murderer, he was always a man of his word. His markers were good, he said, and I believed him. But these were some damned strange markers.

A typical note in the scrapbook read, "Here's these two ten dollar bills I been saved since my graduation party at the rehab center, twelve year ago. I never touch them till now. Bet them along with what you want of your own on Bottom Jewel in the Exacta, and if he wins, put everything in the pot for B."

There was a date on the note, and when I looked up the same date in the ledger, I found the following entry:

Bottom Jewel 40:1 to win, 25:1 to place. $800 to pot, 6/29/97. Tally now $17,250. Hook says he wants an even 20k. Balance to big box.

It wasn't possible. I mean, Bottom Jewel was possible, but no way Charlie accumulated thirty grand, or even seventeen, by always betting on the right horse. Where the hell did he get the rest of his money? I took the papers to my dining room table, where I could spread them out a bit. Then I laid out a fresh pack of cigarettes and a clean ashtray from the living room and a bottle of Scotch and a tumbler from the hall closet, and sat down to go to work.

I looked for entries in the ledger that had dollar amounts but no references to any bets, and then I looked for notes with the same dates. The first one I found blew me away.

> Wells Fargo Downtown. Six guards, all armed. Two of them know how to handle themselves. Security cameras too high to spray or disable. Vault closed. $200 to big box.

There was a similar note for the Bremmer Bank, which was also downtown, and several for grocery or liquor stores, which were not.

I was stunned. Burnout case or not, Charlie was apparently coherent and focused enough to be a point man for a bunch of professional robbers. It would have been easy enough for him. Bumble into the lobby, practice a little aggressive panhandling, and get himself thrown out by the security staff. He could pick up a lot of information that way, and after they threw him out, people were unlikely to bother to have him arrested.

So it was possible that Charlie had a large stash, at that. Then the question became what he did with it.

Partway through the second Scotch, I found a list of names. No notes, just names. Some had check marks in front of them. They were not famous names like the President or some senator or T. Boone Pickens, but I knew a few of them. One was a judge, one a parole officer, and one a cop. They all had checks by their names and if memory served, all of them were dead.

It suddenly occurred to me that in his own strange and twisted way, Charlie had been in the business of selling hope. It was a very angry and bitter variety, the hope of some hated authority figure getting offed. But it was hope, all the same, the stuff that made somebody's life just a little more bearable. Real or phony, he was in the business of letting little people believe they had a way to fight back at the establishment.

Of course, he had also been in the business of making the Secret Service and some kind of nameless military types extremely nervous. Nervous enough to kill him? I didn't know, but I intended to find out. I took another sip of Scotch, a very small one this time, and started to add up the numbers in the ledger.

One other thing mystified me: if everything I was seeing was what it seemed, why had Charlie let me hold the box for him? He had given it to me two years earlier and never asked to see it again. Curiouser and curiouser.

An hour later, I called Anne Packard from the wall phone out in my central hallway and told her I had found her hook. The doorbell rang in the middle of our call.

"Are you expecting company?" she said.

"No, and it's too late at night for the Jehovah's Witnesses or the cute little girls selling cookies. Hang on a minute, will you?"

"I'll be here."

I put down the phone as quietly as I could and quickly went back to the kitchen and took my .380 Beretta out of its plastic bag in the vegetable crisper of the refrigerator. As I passed the phone again, the little red light was flashing frantically.

A Deal With the Devil

My house has a storm entry, with about four feet between the inner and outer doors. I peeked through the edge of the leaded glass in the inner door and saw that my intruder was a familiar figure. I flattened myself against the adjacent wall and let her finish picking the inner lock. As she was opening the door, I threw a phone book down the hallway, and when she leaned forward to see what the noise was, I hooked my left arm around her neck, pulled her the rest of the way into the room, and pressed the Beretta against the base of her skull. She tried to put an elbow into my chest, but she had a poor angle, and it was easy to deflect. She also tried to stomp on my instep, but her aim was bad and all she managed to do was flatten my big toe a bit. She had a lean and athletic body, but she had definitely been neglecting her martial arts training.

"Good evening, Agent Krause. I'll take your sidearm now, please."

"You'll take your hands off me, is what you'll do. I have a no-knock warrant."

"I don't care if you have the goddamn Magna Carta. I'll take your weapon. Now. Spare us both the embarrassment of me pulling it out of some kind of holster between your thighs."

"You're putting yourself in a lot of trouble here, Mr. Jackson. For assaulting an agent, you can get thrown in a hole so deep and black, the best lawyer on earth will never find you."

"Is that what you told Charlie you were going to do to him? Is he dead because he believed you and let down his guard?"

"You don't really think that, do you? That's insane."

"So are black holes where lawyers can't find you. For all I know, so's the whole damn Department of Homeland Conspiracy. Now give up the piece." I pressed the barrel of the Beretta harder into her neck.

"All right," she said. "Just stay calm, okay? I'm going to move really slowly."

She started to reach down toward the hem of her skirt with her right hand, and I told her to stop and switch to her left. She did. And slowly, as she had promised, she produced some kind of very narrow, compact semi-automatic. Not standard Secret Service issue, I thought.

"Put it in my left hand," I said.

"Take your left hand off my neck."

"Actually, that's my forearm on your neck. But give me the gun, and we'll be all done with that, too."

She put the weapon in my hand, barrel first, and I told her to turn it around the right way. When she did, I held it out in front of us, reached down with my little finger, and tripped the lug to drop the magazine out. If she was impressed with that fantastically dexterous maneuver, she withheld her applause.

"Do you have a round in the chamber?"

"The place I carry that thing? Do you think I'm crazy?"

"No. Disagreeable, but definitely not crazy." But I flipped the safety off and pulled the trigger, all the same, pointing the gun at the floor. It really was empty. Then I let her step away from me and gestured to the living room and its big, overstuffed couch. When she sat down on it, I gave her back her gun.

"I'm going to show you the warrant now, okay?" She made a move toward her handbag, but I grabbed it away from her.

"No. Not okay."

"You need to see what you're violating, here."

"No, I don't. You need to see that I don't give a damn. If I shoot you, I'm not violating anything, I'm defending my home.

Any jury in the nation would say so. But if I decide you can be trusted, then maybe you don't need the warrant anyway."

"Oh, really? That's not how you were talking last time we met."

"I've been thinking since then that I might be open to some trading."

"We don't trade. We insist, and we get."

"We? I don't see your partner, Agent."

"He's probably inside the back door by now, about to come in here and blow you away." But she wasn't looking toward the back of the house. Instead, her eyes were turned down and to her right.

"No, he isn't. And from the look on your face, I don't believe he's coming, either."

There was also the small matter of the silent alarm. If her partner really were at the back door, I would be seeing two flashing red lights on the hallway phone, instead of just one. But I saw no reason to tell her that.

"Do you seriously think I would come here without my partner?"

And suddenly I saw it. And it was hilarious.

"You dumped him, didn't you?" I said. "I could see back in my office that you don't like the little twerp. But you don't trust him either, do you? That's why you came here alone. You probably didn't even tell him what you were up to."

"Goddamned arrogant little prick." She folded her arms tightly and found something to study in the pattern of my carpet.

"Him, or me?"

"I mean, stupidity is one thing, but aggressive, gleeful, pompous stupidity is inexcusable."

I guessed she meant him. I was starting to like this conversation a lot.

"Does he hit on you, too?"

She unfolded her arms and slapped the couch on either side.

"God! What is it with you guys? I mean, is that a given? No, he doesn't hit on me. That has too much finesse for him. He tried to rape me, is what he did."

"Oh, shit." Suddenly it had stopped being funny. "I'm sorry for you."

"You think *you're* sorry? Talk to him. I gave him a case of smashed balls that left him walking funny for a month. But that was just a gesture. I'm going to ruin that asshole's career, and I don't mean sometime in the distant future. I really am an agent, you know. I can—"

"Relax, Agent. I respect your professionalism, even if your partner doesn't. And you might still make a success of tonight. First, though, I want to know why you're interested in Charlie Victor." And just to show her how trustworthy I was, I put the .380 in my back pocket.

"You talked about a trade. What do I get?"

"If your story makes sense to me, maybe you get Charlie's box."

"The one you said you didn't have?"

"That's not what I said. But in any case, how bad do you want it? Would it really hurt all that much to simply tell me what you're up to?"

"Why is it any of your business?"

"Jesus, you just don't give an inch, do you? He was my friend, okay? I want to find out why he was killed. And right now, you and your partner are the best suspects I've got."

She sucked in her lower lip and scowled at the ceiling for a moment. "All right," she said, finally. "I'll tell you what I can. We have reason to believe your pet homeless person was going to hire an assassin to kill the President."

"Jesus, Mary, and Joseph."

"That would be an understatement."

"Wouldn't that take an awful lot of money?"

"Not necessarily. There are plenty of people out there who will try it just for the thrill or the fame. And some will take any fee at all, just to show that they are professionals."

"Which they are not, in that case."

"Maybe not, but they're still potential killers. A lot of agents have died for assuming that nut cases can't also be deadly."

"You said you had reason to believe Charlie was lining up a hit man. What reason?"

"That's classified."

"Screw classified. I thought we were talking about a trade here."

"Somebody sent the President a threatening letter."

"Charlie?"

"No, somebody else. Somebody said they were fed up with the President's treatment of poor people, so they had decided to contribute to the frag pot that some homeless guy was keeping on him. The letter didn't give his name."

"Did the letter call it that? A frag pot?"

"Actually, it called it a frag *box*, as I recall. That's a new term, I believe."

"And the postmark led you here?"

"And the postmark led us here. And we talked to poor people and social workers and jailers and priests. And we talked to a lot of homeless people."

"And you killed a dog or two."

"We don't do that sort of thing, Mr. Jackson."

"Be cruel to animals?"

"Be cruel to anybody, out in plain sight."

"So who did?"

"That, I am not free to tell you."

"But you know, don't you?"

"I'm not free to tell you that, either."

"Thank you. What about the black Hummer, the one that's been following me?"

"Now you're being paranoid. We had a walking tail on you for a while. But a Hummer? Get real. Who would use a stupid, obvious vehicle like that for surveillance work?"

"That's the question, all right. Who would?"

"Not us, I can assure you. That's all you get. Now it's your turn."

"Okay, I buy at least some of it. Tell you what: I'll give you Charlie's box if you let me finish looking at the contents first."

"I want to be there when you do."

"Sure, why not?" I stood up and gestured to her to do the same.

"So where is it?"

"On the table in the next room."

"You son of a bitch!"

"That has been observed, yes. I have some single malt Scotch on the table, as well as the box, by the way. Can I offer you a drink?"

"You must realize I'm on duty."

"Of course you are. Yes or no?"

"Why not?"

What a remarkable evening this was turning out to be. I gestured Krause toward the dining room, and I went back to the kitchen to get another glass. But first, I went back to the hallway and picked up the phone.

"Still with me Anne?"

"Yes."

"Could you hear all that?"

"I might have missed a word or two while I was getting my tape recorder, but mostly, yes. I love it. I don't know how much of it I can publish, but I love it."

"You probably won't be able to hear us when we move to the dining room. I'll hang up now and call you again when I get done with my disgruntled agent."

"I'll be here."

Back in the dining room, I gave Agent Krause a cut glass tumbler.

"Ice?"

"Never."

"A woman after my own heart."

"I seriously doubt it."

"Do you have a first name other than Agent?"

"No."

Right. Agent Agent, then. She had let down her hair enough to tell me that she hated her partner, but if I thought that meant we were going to be friends, I could just forget it. In fact, it probably guaranteed that we wouldn't be.

I settled into reading the last of Charlie's ledger and finishing my notes. Sometimes she looked over my shoulder, but mostly she wandered around the room, looking at my things and putting a serious dent in the Scotch supply. At a glass case on top of my buffet, she paused overly long.

"Do you play, Mr. Jackson?"

"You're looking at the violin? No. The only thing I play is a pool cue. The violin is a gift from an old friend, a sort of memento."

"Really? I would have thought you would be musical."

"Why would you think that?" I didn't look up from the pile of papers.

"Well, music is mathematical, they say."

"They do say that, yes. What's your point?"

"Didn't your name used to be Numbers Jackson?"

I was glad my back was to her, because that was a real kick in the guts, and there's no way my face wouldn't have told her so.

"I can't imagine where you would have heard that," I said. And that was absolutely the truth. Numbers Jackson was actually the nickname of my Uncle Fred, not me. But that was still way too close to home. And how the hell had she found it?

"You know, this box really doesn't tell us anything about who the hired assassin was going to be," she said.

"If anybody," I said.

"Oh, there was somebody, all right. Or there will be. And I am going to find him. But of course, your friend Victor can no longer help me, so I need somebody else."

"Well, we all have needs." I started dumping all of Charlie's junk back into the box.

"Yes we do. And you and I are going to help each other with them. Because, you see, *somebody* is going to go down here."

"I assume you mean for the murder of Charlie Victor."

"No, Mr. Jackson, I mean for the conspiracy to assassinate a president, the case that I am going to get a commendation for solving. A commendation and a new partner. Do we understand each other quite well now?"

So there it was. Find the hit man or invent one, because Agent Agent said so. And Agent Agent also knew a name from my blighted past in Detroit and maybe a lot more. Worst of all, I had foolishly hung up the phone, so I had neither a witness nor a recording of the extortion. So as much as it galled me, I would have to play by her rules. I gave her a silent nod, just in case she had some kind of recording device of her own. Then I put Charlie's box in her hand.

"Don't forget to pick up the magazine for your gun on your way out," I said.

"Thanks for the drink." She smirked and left.

There was a time when her threats would have seemed laughable. Not so long ago, either, but another era. Now we have the insultingly titled Patriot Act, and anybody who has read even a snippet of it and not been scared witless wasn't reading very carefully. As a bondsman, I knew all too well that it's an extremely fine line that decides which side of the law you are on. And if you have no rights, that's very, very bad, because all too often, the law is enforced by the Agent Agents of the world. And besides not getting their facts right, they have no more professional integrity than a pack of hungry wolves. I had thought she was annoying. Now I knew she was downright scary.

I stood at the front door and watched her drive away in a featureless government sedan, then reset the door alarm and called Anne Packard back and gave her a short version of the encounter.

"Did you get enough notes from the ledger for me to do a write-up, I hope?"

"I tried, anyway. I also got an address that my lady spook might not have noticed."

"Oh?"

"The box itself had what I thought at first was an importer's stamp on it. But when I looked closer, I saw that it was really drawn onto the box by hand, with a felt-tip pen or some such."

"Why is that important?"

"The address was in Mountain Iron."

"As in Mountain Iron, Minnesota?"

"The very one."

"Herman, I'm not inclined to think there are a lot of cigar importers on the Iron Range."

"Neither am I. I'm thinking it's either a place where Charlie had a stash, or the address of his father, which could be the same thing. I'm going to go have a look."

"When?"

"Tomorrow, early."

"I'm coming along."

Northland

Before dawn the next day I picked up Anne Packard in front of her office and we headed north in my BMW. She was dressed in professional woman's casual: slim-fitting khaki pants tucked into suede boots, a soft emerald green turtleneck sweater under a wool car coat, her usual thin, tailored leather gloves, and some tiny gold loop earrings. The earrings seemed to set off the gold flecks in her eyes, which I hadn't noticed before. The lady had style. She also had coffee and pastry in a white paper bag and an appropriate look of cheerful determination.

For the first thirty miles of I-35, we met a steady stream of headlights from inbound commuters. After twenty miles or so, she said, "Good grief, is it always like this?"

"Scary, isn't it? Apparently, life on your own little half acre up by Forest Lake or Scandia, with unleashed neighborhood dogs and strange snowmobiles in your yard and raccoons in your attic, is so wonderful that it's worth getting up at five every damn morning to follow somebody else's bumper for an hour or more. Personally, I don't get it."

"Sometimes it's nice being a newspaper person," she said, nodding. "It means you have to be aware of current trends, but you aren't allowed to judge them."

"I don't think I'm wired that way."

"No, you don't seem to be. So what was your idea of the golden age?"

"The what?"

"You know, the time when everything was right with the world? The time we ought to go back to? Everybody has one."

"Oh no, you don't."

"Excuse me?"

"I know you reporter types. You're trying to trick me into rhapsodizing about the good old days when cholesterol was good for us, nobody rigged elections, and a gallon of gas cost less than a small loaf of bread. Then you can give me some clever label, like 'pre-postmodern reactionary obstructionist,' and you won't have to think about who I really am any more. Not on your life."

She chuckled. "I usually try for something shorter than that."

"Like 'renaissance man,' maybe?"

"I was thinking 'curmudgeon.'"

"I'm not old enough to be a curmudgeon. How about post-renaissance man?"

"Have a doughnut. They're the postmodern low-cholesterol kind."

"Thank you, I will."

We had the northbound lanes pretty much to ourselves, but I stayed at just barely above the speed limit, figuring that with that much traffic in the southbound lanes, the State Patrol would have a presence somewhere nearby. Fifty thousand people, all driving bumper-to-bumper and too fast were bound to need some guidance sooner or later.

Finally, around the town of North Branch, the traffic thinned out to nearly nothing and the dirty gray sky started to get back-lit with something that passed for dawn. I poured some more coffee from my own Thermos, switched off the cruise control, and let the machine have its head a little, running a constant throttle rather than constant speed. The sprawling 'burbs fell away behind us, and we cruised into the land of black-green pine and cedar forests, with occasional tiny farms so poor, all they could raise were blisters and junked cars. The road behind us was empty. I increased my speed a bit more and settled into the rhythm of machine noise and passing landscape.

"Have you been up on the Iron Range a lot, Herman?"

"First time," I said.

"You're originally from…?"

"Iowa."

"What did you do there?"

"Not much."

"Married?"

"No."

"What made you come to the Twin Cities?"

"That's a long and not very interesting story."

"This is a long trip. Did you have some trouble back there?"

"Nothing worth talking about."

She laughed. "Wow, you don't give much away, do you?"

"No, as a matter of fact, I don't."

"Then why are you traveling with a newspaper person?"

"Because of Charlie Victor. I had this strange notion that he shouldn't just die on a sidewalk in front of a pool hall and get ignored, as if he had never even existed. I thought his story ought to be told."

"I can understand that. So tell me his story, then."

So I did. I told her how he always bought a bond from me in the fall and I told her most of his in-country stories from the jungle. I did not, of course, tell her how his being abandoned in the tunnels reminded me of a dumb kid running scared in Detroit. But I told her quite a lot.

"What about the fragging business?"

"Ah, yes. How could I have left that out?" I told her.

It took Charlie seven weeks to walk out of the jungle, a lot of which was spent hiding and all of which was spent being lost. He didn't know where his firebase was in the first place, so he didn't try to go back there. But he remembered when they were being choppered into the ville that they had turned above a river and then gone fairly straight the rest of the way. He figured if he could find that river, he could follow it downstream until it joined with some others, maybe even the Mekong, and eventually led to civilization. There were a lot of patrol boats out around the Delta, he had heard. If nothing else, he ought to be able to get picked up by one of them. He knew which way his platoon had come into the LZ. He left in the opposite direction.

He took all the gear and ammunition that he could carry, but he only had food and water for about two days. Water was the biggest problem. He had canteens, but no safe place to fill them, and he wasn't sure if he trusted his standard-issue purification tablets. He had heard about some kind of big tree that sent all the water from its branches down to its roots every day at sundown. You could hear it gushing inside the soft wood, the story went, and if you slashed open the bark, you could drink it.

Just before sundown on his third day, he made camp in a deep thicket of alien-looking trees in triple-canopy forest, and he slashed the bark of every different kind of tree he could see. He stayed awake all night long, listening, but he never heard any gushing and he never got a drink. The next morning, he saw that he had made so many slashes, he might as well have set up signs pointing to his camp. After that, he resigned himself to filling his canteens with paddy water or from puddles where he saw animals drinking.

He changed his attitude toward enemy patrols, as well. At first, he hid from them. Then he got to wondering if some of them might be just as careless and unmilitary as his own squad. So he followed a patrol during most of one day. When they settled down into a crude camp for the night, he snuck up and killed the sentry with his knife and took his food and water. He also took an AK-47 and a lot of ammunition. He figured if he had to get into a firefight, he didn't want the VC to be able to distinguish the sound of his firing or his muzzle flashes from their own.

It was a good strategy. Two nights later, he tried the same thing again but accidentally awakened one of the sleeping grunts. He wound up killing the entire squad with a couple of grenades and the stolen assault rifle. Things were definitely looking up. He joked to himself that as long as the VC kept patrolling the jungle, he could live there indefinitely.

At some level, though, he knew that if he kept it up long enough, the VC would mount an operation to hunt him. He had no idea how long that might be, but he tried not to dally in the jungle, waiting for it.

He fell into a routine. He traveled at night, hunting enemy patrols whenever he was out of food and water. During the day, he hid and slept, usually as high as he could get in some very leafy tree. But he never slept more than a couple of hours at one time, constantly waking up and rebriefing himself on who he was and what he was doing. He told himself he was a panther in combat boots, silent, deadly, and remorseless. He told himself he was young, fast, strong, and invulnerable. He told himself he was a legend, that the VC were afraid of him. He told himself a lot of things to keep from facing how wretched and alone he felt.

Eventually, he found the river. By then, he had contracted malaria, dysentery, and every kind of bug bite and body parasite known to the rain forest, which was a lot. Weak from dehydration and hunger, he built a crude raft and simply let himself drift downstream. After three days on the water, he floated into a backwater of the Mekong, where a firefight was in progress between three US Navy "Pibber" patrol boats and a small fleet of armed sampans. The Navy won, and Charlie was picked up with the rest of the flotsam.

He spent three weeks in a hospital in Manila, mostly getting his intestines rehabilitated. When he had first walked into the jungle, he was six feet, two inches tall and weighed a hundred and ninety-five pounds. When he was picked up, he weighed a hundred and forty, and he never again seemed to be able to stand straight enough to be over six feet. The Army gave him new uniforms, corporal's stripes, and a bronze star. Then they sent him back to his old platoon. Nobody in authority would talk to him about bringing court marshal charges against Lieutenant Rappolt.

Rappolt was still there, and Charlie might have been willing to forget about the whole abandonment episode, as happy as he was to be alive and not an FNG anymore. But the idiot leut kept harping on it. He told Charlie that he, by leaving him at the ville, had made him into a better soldier, had forced him to overcome his own inadequacies. He finally went so far as to tell Charlie he had made him into a man.

"Well, I sure do thank you for that, sir," said Charlie, as he plunged his K-bar knife under Rappolt's rib cage and up into his heart. "I probably couldn't have done this, otherwise."

Later that day he was burning his bloodstained fatigues in a honey pot when Bong, who was now also wearing corporal's stripes, brought him a big wad of money.

"I figure this is yours now, man."

"What is it?"

"The frag pot, baby. All of it. I was the official keeper. We been collecting on that asshole ever since you been gone and a long time before you even got here. Thanks, man. Anybody ever needed to die, it was that mufucker."

And that was how Charlie learned how the system worked. After that, he became the regular keeper of the frag pot. And he signed up for two more tours of duty, always with the stipulation that he could stay with his old outfit. He didn't quite understand why or how, but he felt as though he had inherited a duty to protect his squad mates from more Lieutenant Rappolts. And as luck would have it, there were several of them.

Iron Country

A hundred and sixty miles north of where we started, the interstate freeway that had been steadily easing eastward made a more
abrupt turn that way, plunging down into the Lake Superior
basin to head for Duluth. I split away from it on Minnesota
33, through the town of Cloquet, following a sign that said
"Range Towns."

What I expected to find there was not so certain. Charlie had
said that he hated his father so many times that I had to believe
it. But maybe hating him was not the same as not trusting him.
The old man could still have been his banker. And in any case,
the address on the cigar box did not get there by accident. He
meant me to read it, of that I was sure. Time to find out if he
also meant me to follow it.

North of Cloquet, the landscape turned open, rocky, and
white. The lasting winter snow cover had already arrived, broken
here and there by windswept outcroppings of black rock. The
buildings got more run down and farther apart and the farm-
steads disappeared altogether. We crossed the Saint Louis River
and linked up with Trunk Highway 53, which headed straight
north, four lanes with a wide center median, though it had lots
of signs telling me it was not a freeway.

Anne had been napping under her coat, and now she poked
her head out and looked around.

"Where are we?"

"Forty miles south of the town of Virginia. We're all out of coffee, I'm afraid."

"This is quite a road. It must have cost more to build than the total value of all the towns that it connects."

"Maybe there was more to connect, back then. Now, neither the road nor the towns look like much."

"No. And it takes fewer and fewer buildings to even qualify as a town."

"Three," I said. "I've been counting. Anything more than three, and it's a town plus a suburb."

"But there aren't a lot of those."

"No, there surely aren't."

To me, it felt like a good place to get away from, the kind of country that makes you appreciate a new set of rubber and a well-tuned engine. Because if your car ever died and left you to walk back to civilization, you could be in for one damned long trek across the windy steppes.

I put the pedal down a bit more and blasted past places with unlikely names like Zim and Cotton and Cherry. As we approached Eveleth, I could see a featureless pillbox called the U.S. Hockey Hall of Fame perched on a hilltop, standing guard over an abandoned two-story motel with weeds and scrub trees growing out of its pavement. I took the exit off the non-freeway.

"Is this it?"

"No, this is Eveleth. Charlie claimed to have killed a man here once, in a VFW bar upstairs over an appliance store. I thought I would just go and see if there is such a place."

"See if there's such a place as a cafe, while you're at it. Those politically correct doughnuts aren't staying with me very well."

"I'll look for a sign that says 'Bob Dylan ate here.'"

"Just look for a sign that says 'Open.' That's as much as you're likely to get on the Range."

She was right. Eveleth wasn't quite a ghost town yet, but the closed stores outnumbered the working ones by a big margin and the streets were almost empty of traffic. The only second-story bar we found was a BPOE, rather than a VFW, and it was over a union hall, not an appliance store. Both it and the hall looked closed. There was no sign of a Greyhound bus depot. Was that an indication, I wondered, of how close to reality Charlie's stories came?

We found an open diner on Main Street, where we sat and looked at stuffed and mounted fish, old license plates, and display cases of antique carnival glass, while we ate "world-famous Taconite Burgers" and "authentic Cornish pasties." They were surprisingly good. The pasties could be had "with or without," and I had to be told that the commodity being referred to was rutabagas. I had mine without and did not regret the choice.

The waitress, a pretty, self-conscious girl who didn't look to be more than nineteen, didn't know where the bus used to stop, but she did know that the appliance store on Main Street used to have something else upstairs before they had a fire.

"That was back before I was born," she said.

Things were looking up.

The cook, an aging black man who must have overheard our conversation, stuck his head out of the kitchen.

"The bus used to stop at the big front porch on the hotel, a block over east," he said, pointing. "Not no more, though. The place ain't even a hotel no more, got turned into a 'partment building, years back. There wasn't nobody wanted to ride the bus no more, no how."

"Did you come here on that bus?" said Anne. She took his picture.

"You're a smart lady. Yeah, I come here on that bus. Got off at that hotel in nineteen and fifty-two. Lots of jobs down in the Cities then, but you had to come a long ways north before it wasn't still the South, if you know what I mean."

"We know, believe it or not," I said. Anne gave me a look of surprise.

"Yeah? Anyway, so I come here and I been flipping them burgers ever since. Now I suppose you'll be wanting to know where Bobby Zimmerman grew up before he got to be Mr. Hotshot

Bobby Dylan and picked up some kind of accent ain't nobody on the Range or anyplace else ever heard before."

"Actually," said Anne, "we couldn't care less."

"I was right; you're some kind of smart lady." He grinned broadly while she took one more picture of him.

I pulled back onto the highway and headed north again, checking my mirrors as I got back up to cruise speed. There was nobody behind us. Ten miles later, the road curved left to swing around the southwest corner of Virginia, which looked as if it might actually be a real city. I cruised up a big hill on its west side, ignoring the signs for skiing areas and mine tours, and took the exit for Highway 169, westbound. My next stop should have been Mountain Iron. If it was still there.

It was a diamond interchange, with a stop sign at the end of the ramp.

"Apparently we have to choose between new and old Highway 169," said Anne. "On your map, I don't see that distinction."

"The new one looks like some more of the same wide, four-lane, non-freeways they have here. I'd be willing to bet it wasn't even there when the address got written on the cigar box. I say we take the old road."

"Spoken like a true investigative reporter."

"Which I am not. That's why I have one with me." But I took the old road, all the same. We left the fringes of Virginia behind us very quickly and settled into a sedate fifty-five miles an hour on a narrow, two-lane highway that was built following the path of no resistance, making wide curves to avoid rock formations and gullies. Six miles out, it made a particularly sharp s-curve. A few dozen simple box-like buildings clustered around the road in crude rows, as if they had all fallen off the back ends of trucks that took the curve too fast. Since then, they had not been fixed up. I would have said they were all abandoned, except that some of them had smoke coming out of rusted tin chimneys.

"I think we have arrived at Mountain Iron," I said.

"How can you tell?"

"It has a little bitty water tower and a post that used to hold up a stop sign. If that's not civilization, I don't know the stuff. We're looking for Third Street."

"This place doesn't look as if it ever had three streets, and I mean back in its boom days."

"You think they had boom days here?"

"Well, maybe an eventful afternoon now and then." She had the tiny silver camera out again and was shooting as we drove.

The street signs were infrequent, to say the least, and were as badly rusted as the chimneys, but we found one that said Third and turned down a street that had exactly six tiny houses on it before it quit at a big pile of rocks and some stunted pine trees. I made a U-turn at the rock pile. Charlie's father's house, if that's what it was, was the last one in the row.

It was maybe twenty-four by twenty feet, tops, with asbestos shingle siding in an indescribable color and a covered porch with empty flower boxes on the rails. There was no smoke coming out of the chimney, but there were vehicle tracks in and out of the unshoveled driveway. Out in the back yard, half covered by snow, there were a couple of plastic lawn chairs and a barbeque made out of half a steel drum.

Next to the house was an ancient pickup, so rusted that its fenders wiggled in the light wind. It had tracks going to it, but not fresh ones. On the rear bumper were a couple of faded stickers that said "UNION WORKER AND PROUD OF IT" and "BAN IMPORTED STEEL." I thought that was hilarious, considering that the truck was a Toyota.

"Chez Victor," I said. "White tie optional." I pulled up at the place where a curb might be buried, if there were any.

"You're not going in the driveway?"

I shook my head. "That set of tracks is from some kind of vehicle with big tires and a lot of ground clearance. If I try to go in there, my undercarriage will bottom out on the snow and we could spend the rest of the day trying to shovel it out."

"Do you have a shovel?"

"No."

"Good call, Herman. Park in the street, every time."

The snow turned out to be mid-calf height, and by the time we got to the front porch, my sixteen-fifty shoes were candidates for the trash bin. There was a doorbell button next to the door, but it was hanging away from the wall by its wires, so I pounded on the door instead. Then I shaded my eyes and peeked in through the tiny glass.

"Anything?"

"There's a light on in there, but I can't see anybody moving around." I pounded again, waited twenty seconds, then tried a third time.

"Maybe he's in the study, working on his rare book collection," she said.

"Books are probably all rare in a town like this. I think more likely, he just doesn't want to talk to anybody. A lot of old people turn into hermits. Let's have a look at the back door."

We slogged through more of the deep snow, past the pickup and around to a porch that was smaller than the front one and had no roof over it. The combination screen-storm door was swinging in the wind, its spring broken or disconnected. The door and jamb behind it had both been badly gouged by some kind of heavy tool. Again, I shaded my eyes and peered into the gloom.

"Well, he's there," I said.

"So, aren't you going to knock?"

"Do you have your phone handy?"

"Of course. Why?"

"See if you can get us a local sheriff of some kind. I think Charlie's father is sitting in a kitchen chair, with his head half on the table in front of him."

"What do you mean, his head half on the table?"

"I mean somebody blew his brains out."

"Oh. Oh, dear Jesus." She fumbled in her purse, then began punching buttons. I squinted to see better through the dirty glass. The light was pretty poor, and the line of sight wasn't the greatest, but I could definitely see an ace of spades in the dead man's hand. It looked as if it had been stuck there after he had died, just for somebody like me to see.

The Law of the Range

The sheriff was a collection of middle-aged sags and bulges squeezed into a heavily starched, too-tight uniform. He also wore cowboy boots, a Smokey Bear hat, and about thirty pounds of weaponry and gear. His name was Oskar Lindstrom, and he seemed as much in denial as in charge.

"You know, for a long time I thought I was going to retire from this job without ever having a murder to handle."

"That's really too bad." *I'm sure the murderer did it just to spite you.*

"We got a coroner in Virginia, don'cha know, but if I want a crime scene crew, I'll have to either ask for help from Duluth PD or call the BCA, over to Bemidji."

"I think you ought to have a crime scene crew, Sheriff." *Do I have to make the call for you, too?*

"Well, yeah, I guess so. I'll maybe just have a preliminary look myself, though, anyhow. You said you and your wife were here to see the victim?"

"She's n…" Anne stomped on my instep, hard, and gave me a penetrating look with a tiny shaking of her head. I didn't know if her pantomimed "no" applied to telling the sheriff she wasn't my wife or telling him she was a reporter, so I did neither.

"She's what, you say?"

"Excuse me," I said. "I tripped on the step, there. I was going to say she's just along for the ride, Sheriff. I came here to tell Mr. Victor that his son is dead."

"You call him Mr. Victor? Hell, he wasn't anybody special."
He put on a pair of leather gloves before trying the doorknob.
The door swung away from him easily, without needing the
knob turned. He walked into the tiny kitchen, stomping snow
off his fancy boots, and I followed.

"I don't know his first name. The street address was all I had."

"Jim. Or James, I guess. His name was James Victor. I've
known him all my life. He was an asshole, I don't mind saying.
The kind of guy would pick an argument with a post, just to
stay in practice. And now he's messing my life up again, giving
me a murder case. So, you couldn't leave notifying him up to
the authorities, then?" By which he clearly meant himself.

"His son was a homeless man. I'm sure the police have no
idea who his next of kin was."

"So that's what became of him, huh? Turned into a bum?
Doesn't surprise me, I got to say. But you knew where to find
his next of kin. Why was that, I wonder? And who the hell said
you could follow me into the house, here?"

"Oh, wasn't that all right? I'll be careful not to touch anything." Sure, I would. Anything I wasn't going to take, that is.
"I just thought we could all get in out of the cold."

"It isn't in out of the cold, just out of the wind. Looks like the
furnace hasn't been lit for some time. That half a cup of coffee
on the counter is froze solid."

The card in the dead man's hand looked identical to the one
they had taken off Charlie's body, but I was obviously not going
to get a chance to look at it closer. Meanwhile, Anne had her
little camera out and was holding it waist-high, partially hidden
by her purse, shooting everything in sight. Not that there was
much to shoot, other than the body. I couldn't tell if the rest
of the place had been trashed or if Mr. James Victor was just a
terrible housekeeper. Either way, it was a mess.

And so was he. There wasn't much left of his face, but what I
could see looked as if he had been beaten before he was shot. He
was also tied to the chair, and there was blood on the floor that
didn't look as if it had anything to do with the gunshot wound.

"Why was that, again, that you came all the way from down Minneapolis?"

"St. Paul, actually."

"Same damn thing. Now you've had time to think up an answer, so what is it, then?"

"I wrote a bail bond for Mr. Victor's son once, and I sort of befriended him. I figured if I didn't come and tell the old man, nobody would."

"You couldn't call him, then?"

"That would be pretty cold, Sheriff," said Anne. I liked that better than what I had been going to say. Obviously this was a woman who could think on her feet. She had put the camera away now and was easing her way back toward the door and making gestures that said, "let's blow this pop stand."

"Yeah, okay, I guess it would a been, at that. Now get on out of here. This is a crime scene, ya know."

"Happy to help out."

"Wait on the porch a minute, though. I need your name and address before you go. I would say 'don't leave town,' like they do in the cop movies, but hell, you can't hardly go across the street here without leaving town. That's a little joke, see?"

I smiled politely and gave him one of my cards, both of which seemed to make him very happy. I wrote my license number on the back of it for him, and he wrote "Mr. and Mrs." ahead of my name on the front. Then he shook my hand and gave Anne what might have been a salute, and herded us off the porch.

"Charlie said his father worked in the mines," I said. "I don't suppose you know what he did, exactly?"

"He's been retired for a lot of years now," said Lindstrom, crowding us further off the porch. "I think he used to drive truck, though. One of those big off-road monsters, you know? A Euclid or a Cat, or something."

"Oh really? So, not underground work, then?"

"You kidding? There haven't been any working underground mines on the Range for forty, fifty years. Used to be, you could take a tour through the main shaft of the first one, at Tower-

Soudan. But open pit was the wave of the future, don'cha know, except there's not even much of that anymore. The ones who cashed in their pensions before it all went to hell, like Jim there, they were the lucky ones. So what makes you ask, then?"

"Just curious." I tried for a nice, sincere-looking shrug. "Nice meeting you, Sheriff."

Back in the car, Anne said, "Do you suppose he really will call the BCA and get a proper investigation going?"

"I wouldn't bet on it. He seemed awfully glad to finally be left alone at the scene. You're in the newspaper business. Do you know anybody on the Duluth paper?"

"As a matter of fact, I do."

"Maybe you should call them up and give them an anonymous scoop. If our sheriff has press coverage, I'm sure he'll do everything by the book."

"I like it." She dug her phone out and started scrolling through some kind of list. "What was all that business about the underground mines, by the way?"

"There was hardly anything in James Victor's house that didn't look as if he got it at a rummage sale fifty years ago."

"I would agree. So?"

"So why did Mr. Victor, who never was an underground miner in the first place, have a shiny new pickaxe leaning against the wall in a corner of his kitchen?"

"I give up, why?"

"How soon do you have to get back to St. Paul?"

"Where are we going instead?"

"Tower-Soudan."

"Is that all one place?"

"I have no idea."

Night Life on the Range

I took Minnesota 169 back to the interchange on the west edge of Virginia and headed north again. I thought about going into the town to buy some hiking boots and some flashlights, but the day was already getting late, and I didn't know how much more of Anne's time I could burn.

"Why did you want to let the sheriff think we were married, by the way?"

"Did that make you uncomfortable?" said Anne. "I'm sorry."

"Not uncomfortable, just perplexed."

"If I had told him I was a reporter, then I'd have had to cover the murder story."

"I suppose you would have, yes. What would be wrong with that? I'd have waited for you."

"I'm not actually supposed to be here, is the thing."

"You said your editor told you to back off the story, knowing that you wouldn't."

"That was before. What he told me later, when I was filing my column, was to pursue it if I thought I just had to, but strictly on my own time. So if I admit I'm here, I have to take a vacation day."

"Do you have one to take?"

"I never seem to have any to take. I use them up as fast as they accumulate, nursing hangovers and working on the Great American Novel."

I looked over to see if she was putting me on. She gave me an open face and a palms-up gesture.

"A hard-drinking novelist? That's actually respectable, in some quarters. Do you shoot elephants and write about bullfights and wars?"

"No, I shoot pictures and write about bail bondsmen with mysterious pasts."

I shot her another look and was met by twinkling eyes and a mouth on the verge of a huge smile.

"Made you look," she said.

"Twit."

"Now tell me about Iowa."

"Never happen."

"Why?"

"It's too boring."

"You're a bad liar, Herman."

Maybe so, but I can stonewall with the best of them.

Tower-Soudan turned out to be two places. You come to Tower first, and if you blow right on past it because it's so small, you come to Soudan less than a quarter of a mile later. And to your amazement, you find that Soudan is even smaller. Somebody once told me that you can estimate the population of a small town by counting the number of blocks on Main Street and multiplying by one hundred. If that's true, then Tower had about three hundred people and Soudan didn't have any. But it had a big monument telling us we were in the right area.

The mine that Sheriff Lindstrom had talked about was on the north side of Soudan, and it wasn't nearly as closed-looking as he had implied. In fact, it had been turned into a state park. The skeletal framework of the pit-shaft hoist tower, unsheltered from the weather, poked maybe sixty feet up in the air, looming over an assortment of buildings and platforms and trails that meandered down a steep embankment.

The whole park complex looked bigger than the town on the other side of the road. A sign said that the underground mine tours were closed for the season just then, but there were lights on in the buildings, and the complex was obviously still staffed and open. As far as I could tell, the underground mine and a couple of open-pit ones beyond it were still in operation, even. I pulled into the outer parking lot, which was neatly plowed, and stopped but did not get out.

"I'm afraid I've dragged you off on a wild goose chase," I said. "I'm sorry."

"What were you expecting, Herman?"

"Something abandoned and boarded up. Charlie was an old tunnel rat. If he was going to hide a box of money around here, I figured he would pick a place that was underground. And I was hoping the new pickaxe was what he had used to break in, and we could follow the scratch marks or some such."

"I see," she said. "And where did his father fit in with all that?"

"Well, there was a gap or two in my theory yet."

"Hmm."

"I really am sorry."

"Well, it's not as though you're the first person who ever wasted my time. And I got the story of the second murder, anyway, for a tie-in. Tell you what: find a place to buy me a dinner that doesn't include lutefisk, and we'll call it even."

As she spoke, the windshield began to get spotted with the first flakes of another snowfall. It wasn't exactly a blizzard yet, but it was enough to make the visibility rotten for the trip back to St. Paul. I sighed.

"Swell," I said.

"Looks nasty, doesn't it?"

"It looks like we're cursed, is what it looks like." I flipped on the wipers and switched the duct control to full defrost.

"Let's wait it out, then. We're far enough into the Range to get blizzards that can stop a sled dog. The world will not end if I don't get back until sometime tomorrow. I'll say I was covering the cranberry harvest in Brainerd, or something. You can use my phone to call your office in the morning, if you want."

"Does Brainerd have a cranberry harvest?"

"It does now. Look for a motel that doesn't predate the Second World War."

I sternly pushed aside the thoughts that were gleefully crowding into my consciousness.

"We're not going to find any four-star resort hotels, you know," I said.

"Then we'll have to find some other kind of attraction, won't we? Think like a reporter, Herman; learn to take advantage of what's around you."

Unbelievable, the straight lines people give me.

We went to a little strip mall on the outskirts of Virginia, to buy a few things. I went into a drugstore and bought a throwaway shaving kit and a toothbrush, and Anne went I don't know where and bought I don't know what. Then we drove back to Eveleth and took adjoining rooms at a motel whose only commendable feature was that it was an easy walk to the place where we had eaten lunch.

If we were about to become lovers, we weren't admitting that to ourselves yet. And the more I thought about it, the worse idea I thought it was, anyway. Sooner or later, people who are physically intimate become intimate in other ways, too. And of all the people I could not let that happen with, a newspaperwoman was close to the top of the list. But that was no reason we couldn't have a nice dinner.

But then, she said it first. Even to myself, I'm a bad liar.

The snow was getting thicker by time we hiked back to the main street. The temperature wasn't really bitter, but the wind made it feel worse than it was. We hunched into our coats and hurried. Fortunately, it was only three blocks.

The cafe was a lot livelier than when we had last been there. A folding partition had been rolled back to open up a much bigger dining room, with a bandstand, a bar, and a small dance floor. We took a booth in a corner, and a cheery fortyish waitress whose nametag said she was Madge brought us menus.

"Friday night," she said, "so I guess you know what that means, then."

"Um," I said.

"Let me guess," said Anne. "The special is all-you-can-eat fish fry."

"You got it, honey. Beer-battered walleye. And the Paul Bunyan drinks until eight o'clock, of course."

We ordered drinks and studied the menus. Over in the opposite corner of the room, a trio with matching black slacks and embroidered vests was pumping out schmaltz. A tallish blonde played a button accordion, accompanied by a bearded guy with an acoustic guitar. The third member of the combo looked like a refugee from a sixties jug band. He played a washboard with an assortment of bells and horns attached to it and sang into a microphone. Out on the dance floor, a few couples were doing something that might have passed for a waltz.

"The pretzels are zalty, the beer flows like vine," sang Mr. Washboard, in a faux accent that was probably supposed to be German. "After sixteen shmall bottles, the band she sounds fine. Ve laugh und ve dance und ve haff a good time…"

To my amazement, they really didn't sound too bad.

"Do you dance, Herman?"

"Only after the aforementioned sixteen small bottles or so. And by then, I would probably just fall down."

"I could teach you."

"You could get very frustrated trying, anyway. Where did you learn?"

"Political rallies."

"Get out of here."

"No, it's true," she said, shaking her head. "My father was a state senator from northern Wisconsin. He'd go to fundraisers in roadhouses and dance halls in little towns out-state, and the party faithful would listen to speeches and drink beer and dance the polka. I was too young to drink, so I had to learn to dance. Otherwise, I wouldn't have had anything to do at all."

"Where was your mother all this while?"

"Sitting home, mostly, disapproving. She refused to go out on the campaign trail. I'm not sure if she thought it was immoral or just undignified. Sometimes I think she was a closet Methodist. But she loved my father deeply, so she just sulked a little and kept quiet about it."

"That's a nice story," I said, meaning it. "Does that somehow lead to a career in journalism?"

"Partly, maybe. I surely saw plenty of reporters doing it badly. But even when they were sloppy with their stories, they seemed about as independent as a person can get and still be drawing a salary. It looked like fun."

"How come you never went into TV news? With your looks and poise, it seems like a natural evolution."

She shook her head again, though now she was smiling and blushing a bit. "That's not real journalism," she said. "I guess when it comes to my profession, I'm a curmudgeon, too. In my world, you're just not an honest-to-god reporter unless you write for a paper."

The waitress brought us our drinks then, a gin and tonic in a huge old-fashioned soda-fountain glass for Anne and a Scotch with a short beer for me. She asked if we were ready to order, and Anne told her to bring us some munchies for now, onion rings and spiced bull bites.

"Is that okay?" she said to me.

"Sure. Just what us health-food nuts always order."

"I figured as much. So. Pay me back for my nice story. Tell me about your father."

I sighed. "You just never give up, do you?"

"Not me. Bulldog Packard of the Mounties."

I took a sip of scotch and tried to think what I could tell her that would be consistent with rural Iowa.

"I don't remember my father," I said, which was the truth. "My mother claimed he died in the Korean War, but I don't recall her ever getting a government pension check. I think he just split."

"I'm sorry for you. Did you blame yourself for that?"

"Not really. I didn't come to that conclusion until I was fairly old. When I was a little kid, I thought it was cool to have a father who was a war hero."

"Even though he was dead?"

I shrugged. "I had plenty of friends who wished their fathers were dead. They probably envied me."

"And your mother?"

"My mother." I took another sip of scotch. "What can I tell you about my mother? She waited tables at a blue-collar bar, where she was probably also one of the best customers. She put..."

I had been about to say she put me in an orphanage when I was eleven, but then I realized that small towns probably don't have orphanages.

"She put?"

"She didn't want me around. I spent a lot of time with my uncle, out on a farm."

"Was that nice?"

I thought about running the phones for Uncle Fred and finding that I had a lot of money.

"It was okay," I said. "It was interesting." And I was amazed to realize how much of what I had just told her was true.

"And you never married?"

"Well, I hadn't ever seen a marriage up close that worked, you know? I couldn't figure out why people wanted it. What about you? Your ring finger doesn't look like it's ever worn anything."

"I guess I never saw one that worked, either." But her eyes wandered when she said it, and she toyed with a phantom ring on her left hand, telling me the real story. I touched her glass with mine and gave her what I hoped was an understanding smile.

Our food came, and we laid into it. We liked it so well, we ordered more of the same, plus some stuffed potato skins, rather than what she called "an honest meal." And we had more drinks, of course. And after fewer than sixteen but more than I could easily count, she really did get me out on the dance floor. I don't know if the dance I wound up doing had a real name or not. But just as the singer over in the corner had promised, we danced and we laughed and we had a good time. She was an easy person to be with.

It was past midnight when we walked back to the motel, leaning on each other. The wind had died down and the snow had changed to puffy, floating flakes that actually managed to make the dirty old town look postcard-pretty. We indulged in a very chaste goodnight kiss and let ourselves into our respective rooms.

Running in the Dark

Our rooms had a connecting door, in case we wanted to call them a suite. I had no idea if the doors, one on each side, were locked, but I assumed so. The walls were paper thin, and through them, I could hear water running in Anne's room, presumably the shower. A cold one? I should be so irresistible.

Still fully dressed, I lay on the bed for a while and listened to the rushing sound, wondering if there was something I might have said to make my sexy journalist fall into my arms in an erotic swoon. Probably not. This was a very in-charge kind of woman, even back when she was busy trying to drink me under the table. If she had an incurable fever for me, I figured she would have come right out and said so.

It had been a long day and a surprisingly energetic and alcoholic evening, and I should have been ready to crash into oblivion, but I didn't feel even slightly like it. I got up and looked at the connecting door. The sound of the shower stopped, but no matter how long I looked at the door, it didn't open.

I sighed just a little, shrugged, and paced over to the windows. I pulled back a drape and looked idly out at the parking lot with its strange-colored sodium lights illuminating the falling snow. And froze.

A black Hummer had just pulled into the parking lot next to my 328i, and some large and dangerous-looking types were piling out of it.

They were dressed in black topcoats and dark slacks, like the big gatekeeper at Railroad Island, two nights ago, except that they also wore ski masks and carried some very heavy-looking firearms.

I went quickly over to the connecting door again, clicked open the deadbolt, and opened it. Almost instantly, I heard the bolt on the matching door in Anne's room click as well, as if she had been waiting there. She pulled it open a bit and I immediately shoved it the rest of the way and pushed her back into the room.

"Oh, that's romantic," she said. "Really charming. I think I may have made a big mistake here."

She was wearing some lacy, low-cut panties and the soft green sweater and quite possibly nothing else, and she nearly made me forget why I had opened the door. Nearly.

"We've got to get out of here."

"Why on earth?"

"And I really do mean *now.*"

I shut the door and threw the deadbolt, then took her hand and pulled her into the bathroom, where I unlocked the small window above the toilet and began to push it up.

"Herman, have you gone completely insane?'

The window had been painted shut for a long time, and opening it was doable but slow.

"I mean, if this is your idea of how to—"

From next door, we heard the sound of breaking glass and a few seconds later, the eardrum-splitting bang of an explosion.

Anne immediately joined me in pushing on the window, and it slid the rest of the way up suddenly, with a crash and some clunking of jiggled sash weights. A few white flakes and a lot of frigid air blew in from the black rectangle. While I shut the bathroom door and wedged a soggy, folded-over bath mat under it, she climbed up and put her upper body through the window. And as much of a panic as I was in, I still had to admire the sight of her taut, shapely legs and round buttocks. I hoped I would live long enough to see them in better circumstances.

"I'm not sure I can do this, Herman."

"We don't have a choice. Hurry."

"But how do I land?"

"Any way you can." I gave her behind a very unkind push and she disappeared through the opening.

"Get clear!" I said. I grabbed a pair of thin foam slippers from the floor and threw them out the window, then dove after them. In the bedroom behind us, there was another explosion.

It wasn't much of a drop to the ground, but I remembered how fragile things like wrists and necks are, and I did a tuck-under on the way down and landed on my shoulder blades with only minor agony. Anne had used her hands to break her fall and was getting up slowly, nursing her left wrist. I put an arm around her waist and helped her up, then tossed the slippers in front of her.

"Step into those," I said, "and then let's move."

"Where?" She picked up the slippers, rather than putting them on, folded her arms in a protective gesture, and started to run where I pointed.

"Out to the alley first. It's been plowed clean, and we won't leave tracks."

We ran down the alley for fifty yards or so, past a jumble of garages and small outbuildings behind a block of houses. At a yard that had a cleared sidewalk in the back, we turned into a tiny fenced garden, ducked behind a corrugated potting shed, and chanced a look back.

Nothing. Nobody behind us. I was wishing I had taken a moment to grab my coat, and I could only imagine how cold Anne must be feeling. She put her slippers on, finally, but they can't have helped much.

Then we heard the snarl of an over-revved engine, and the Hummer came tearing around the end of the motel. It went to the far end of the alley and stopped, and two men with flashlights got out. Then the big vehicle sped down the alley, past where we were hiding, and let another man out at the opposite end of the block.

We were bracketed.

We ran through the back yard and around the house, just in time to see the big SUV cruise around the corner of the street, moving slowly now, checking out front yards with a spotlight. There was no way we had enough room to cross the street in front of it and not be seen.

"Back," I said, and Anne needed no further coaching. We ran back the way we had come and tried the side door on a garage.

Locked.

But the second garage we came to, larger than the first one, was unlocked, and I pushed it open, pulled her inside, and shut it as quietly as I could. The lock on the door had no turn button on the inside, so I looked around for something to block it shut with. By the light of my trusty Zippo, I found a big double-headed axe hanging on the wall. I rested the end of the handle on the floor and wedged the head into the crack between the jamb and the door. I stayed there and held it, just in case I hadn't wedged it tight enough, and gave Anne my lighter.

"Try to find another one," I whispered.

"Another axe?"

"Another thing that could be used as a weapon. Tire iron, pry bar, anything. But keep the lighter away from the windows."

She faded into the darkness and came back a short time later with a crowbar and a blade from a rotary lawn mower.

"Good job. You get first choice." She picked the crowbar.

"Herman, I'm scared."

"Relax, Anne. And keep your voice to a whisper. We're going to make it through this." I had absolutely no idea how.

The garage was not small, but most of it was filled with the massive hull of some kind of cruising sailboat.

"See if you can get up and inside that thing," I said, pointing. "If they break in, I'll try to draw them away."

"I can't ask you to do that."

"Now would be a good time," I said. "And quietly."

She gave me a soft kiss on the cheek, which I found totally surprising and rather touching, and disappeared into the dark interior.

We waited silently in the dark for maybe five minutes. I wondered how clear our footprints were in the new snow, then pushed it out of my mind as just one more thing I couldn't do anything about. Then something bumped against the outside of the garage, and I could dimly hear voices. The lock handle on the overhead door, by the bow of the boat, rattled. *Shit!* I had completely forgotten to check that one.

"This one's locked," said a voice.

Thank God for small favors.

"What about the man-door?"

"Checking it now."

Suddenly somebody on the other side of my wedged door was jiggling the knob.

I grabbed the mower blade in my right hand and held it over my head, ready to strike down on the first thing that came through the door. With my left hand, I held the axe in place. If somebody decided to shoot through the door, I was a dead man. Or through the wall, for that matter. The place really wasn't built all that solidly. Its only good feature was that it had only two very small windows, and they were set high off the floor, where an ordinary person couldn't look through them without standing on something.

The doorknob jiggled again and somebody pushed on the door at the same time. It moved maybe a quarter of an inch before the wedging action of the axe head took hold and stopped it. I resisted the enormous urge to push it back to where it had been.

"No joy," said the voice outside.

I heard another bump against the side of the garage, and I continued to hold the mower blade high, ready to strike with it. Then a couple of powerful flashlights turned the glass on one of the windows opaque yellow-white, while the beams swept around the interior, probing, accusing.

I abandoned my post by the door before the light got to it, diving under the boat. The hull seemed to be supported by some kind of a cradle, rather than sitting on a trailer, and there was barely room for me to squeeze under it. The discs of light continued to dance around, but they couldn't reach me. I forced myself to breathe normally, hoping to put myself into a state of calm control by some reverse body language. It didn't work. Some very old impulses were resurfacing. Very old. But I wasn't very old anymore. Suddenly I was fourteen again, and quite sure I was about to die.

The Chill Below

Michigan Central Station is the only building left standing in the center of Detroit's old downtown, other than the twin office towers behind it. The towers are vacant and abandoned now, the lower-level windows boarded up. The train station is still in use, but it looks like a derelict, too, surrounded on all sides by blocks and blocks of empty landscape, where all the buildings have been leveled and replaced with nothing.

I see it suddenly, as I break out from the alley between a bank and an insurance company building, still running. My lungs are on fire. I would tell myself to stop and take a few deep breaths, but that won't do it. I need a lot more oxygen than that. And I will need more yet. I put my hands on my knees and bend over for a moment, resisting the urge to puke. Then I straighten up and move on.

I can clearly see the station now, but there's no way I can get to it. The space between it and me is full of cops, guardsmen, and rioters, all beating the shit out of each other. It looks like a battle scene from the Trojan War, only with firearms and smoke canisters.

Over near the terminal building itself, there is a beat up car beginning to catch fire back by the gas tank. It looks just one hell of a lot like Jerp's Mercury.

Forget about the troops. Forget about catching your breath. You can get through, somehow. You have to. Jerp could still be there. But even as I start running, I see the flames spread.

Then the gas tank blows, lifting the ass end of the car six feet off the ground.

What the hell do I do now, besides try again to catch my breath? Get someplace else, anyplace else. Not back downtown. I just came from that way, and it's no good. Run. Move, damn it!

Away from the terminal building, toward the river, three or four sets of train tracks bend away from the main lines and disappear into a black tunnel, plunging down to go under the Detroit river. Nobody in his right mind would go there on foot.

So I do.

Maybe twenty yards into the tunnel, stumbling over rocks and railroad ties that I can't see, I find a string of freight cars, just sitting. The doors all look shut, so I climb under a car and scrunch up behind one of the big wheels. Clutching my baseball bat, the only protection I have besides my young, fast legs, I hug the track ballast and pray that I won't be seen.

Stay here, stay here, stay here. Wait this thing out.

I stay until the sun goes down and the urban battlefield behind me is empty of people, lit by the occasional burning car or trash fire. Even in a real war, people eventually get tired and go home, I guess. Walk back over and check the Mercury for Jerp's body. Nope, empty. Well, that's something.

Suddenly I remember that my pad has been torched. Where to go? Where to spend what's left of the night? Where to sleep? God, I need some sleep.

Six-by-six Army trucks with fifty caliber machine guns mounted on them are patrolling the streets now. There's probably a curfew, and the troops are spooked and strung out, shooting anything that moves. And here and there, people who aren't so easy to see are shooting, too.

Back to the tunnel, is all I can think of. My freight train is still there, but I no sooner get under it than it starts moving, filling the dark with clanking, screeching noises. There's no place else to go, so I flatten out and let the train pass over me. Nothing hits me, so I guess there's more room than I had thought. I don't care what Uncle Fred says; if I get out of this alive, I'll never go collecting without a sidearm again. After the train is gone, I go deeper into the tunnel, clear down to where I imagine I can hear the river rushing overhead. There are more trains, later, but they don't frighten me anymore. I'm busy listening for other things, waiting out the night. And feeling very frightened and very, very ashamed.

"Herman?"

And quite suddenly, it was over. Really over. Its power was gone, and not because Anne had called my name, but because somewhere deep in the back of my psyche, the right machinery had finally clicked and I knew I could redeem myself by my own hand. I had come a long way since Detroit, dragged myself up to adulthood and self-sufficiency with no help from anybody. And the terrible memory of that boiling summer had been easy to push away, never to be looked at again. But Charlie Victor's death had brought it back and it made me see, finally, the link between us that I hadn't been able to put a name on. Charlie had been abandoned by his comrades-in-arms. And to my shame, I had been an abandoner of another comrade. Sooner or later, I had to atone for that. I decided it would be sooner.

"Herman?"

The flashlight beams were gone, and Anne was leaning over the gunwale above me.

"Herman, where are you?"

"Keep your voice down. We don't know if our new friends are completely gone yet."

"Okay, my voice is down. Come and see what I found."

I dragged myself out and up and took the object she was holding out to me. It was a double-barreled shotgun.

"I don't believe this," I said. "Is it loaded?"

"I think so. There's some kind of shells in it, anyway, but I didn't pull them out to see if they were live. I was afraid I might drop them and loose them in the dark. I didn't find any extras."

I cracked the breech and carefully pulled out one shell. It was about the right weight and had a closed end, so I pronounced it live. I put it back in and snapped the weapon shut again. Suddenly I had a whole world of options.

"Can you see out the garage windows from up there?"

"They're awfully dirty, but I'm up high enough, yes."

"How did you get up there?"

"There's no ladder, but there's a sort of step thingy by the rudder that works pretty well."

I found the thing she was talking about and hoisted myself aboard as quietly as I could. The garage windows were dimly lit from outside by a single streetlamp in the middle of the block. I saw no silhouettes of anyone looking in. I leaned out a bit farther and saw parts of an empty alley.

"We need to find out if they've really gone."

"How about if we curl up together in the cabin of the boat and get warm for a few hours first? No, make that a few days."

"We have to know."

"And how do you suggest we find out?"

"I'm going back outside."

"I was afraid you'd say something like that."

We agreed on a secret knock, and Anne secured the door behind me. I immediately ducked into a shadow and began to work my way down the alley. I tried to move like a commando looking for a sniper, grabbing cover wherever I could, keeping my eyes moving, always pointing the shotgun where I looked. Nobody.

I hugged the shadows, forcing myself to take my time. Across the alley from the bathroom window that Anne and I had bailed out of, I hunkered down behind a garbage can and looked and listened.

The window was dark. It should have still been lit. I watched the snow drift silently down in front of it and it suddenly occurred to me that it was the most beautiful thing I had ever seen. Here I was facing almost certain death, and I was thinking that the snowfall in an alley behind a third-rate motel was the stuff of picture post cards. I almost laughed. And somehow I knew that now I could do whatever it took to survive. Or at the very least, I could save her. And that would be good enough.

I looked for movement or light in the window, the glow of a cigarette, the green spillover from a night-vision scope. I listened for a careless bit of chitchat or a scuffling footfall. I breathed deeply and counted my breaths. After thirty, I finally decided there was nobody there, and I moved on.

I wondered if the intruders had killed the night manager at the motel before they came for Anne and me. When I came to a spot across from the end of the motel, I broke cover and ran as fast as I could across the alley, flattening myself against the back wall. I risked a quick look around the corner, then a longer one. Again, I saw nobody. I turned the corner and moved along the end wall of the building, shotgun shouldered and up.

And quite suddenly, the jig was up. Four men in black came ambling around the corner, carrying their weapons loose and low, talking with each other, not looking at me. I cocked both hammers on the ancient shotgun, and they froze and looked up. And again, I knew I could face death and not blink.

"The first one of you who raises his weapon, gets his head blown off." I was surprised at how steady my voice was.

"You seem to be a little light in your math skills," said the one in the right center slot. But he kept his weapon where it was and with his free hand gestured to the others to do the same. He seemed to be the one in command, and I aimed the shotgun squarely at his head.

"Not really," I said. "I have two shots and there are four of you, and that's way too bad. It means I can only kill you and one other guy before the others drop me. But I can do that, and I will." God, I loved that voice. Hell, even I believed that voice.

But would he? He and the others were backlit by the spillover from the parking lot floods, and I couldn't read their expressions at all. They remained motionless for what seemed like hours, and so did I. Finally the same man spoke again.

"I don't think you'll shoot anybody in the back. You win, for now. We're leaving. Let's go, men. Slow and easy." And still keeping his gun at sling-arms, he turned slowly on his heel and walked away from me.

After a skipped heartbeat or two, the others followed suit. I walked quickly backward to the corner of the building, to use it for cover in case it was all a ruse. I kept the shotgun leveled at them. But they kept on going. A minute or two later, I heard car doors slam and an engine start. When I ran over to a dumpster at the edge of the parking lot and ducked behind it, I saw the Hummer cruise out the driveway and on down the road.

I permitted myself to tremble. I avoided walking anywhere for a while, because I was sure my legs didn't have a bone in them. And as I leaned on the dumpster and stared off at the dark streets, I saw flashing red and blue strobe lights, first a long way off, then closing rapidly. The law had arrived.

Ships in The Night

My new favorite sheriff, Oskar Lindstrom, led the parade in his Explorer, followed by a couple of deputies in unmarked cars and then a fire truck. When they got close enough to have me in their headlights, I put the shotgun on the ground and stepped forward, away from it. The sheriff got out of his vehicle and squinted at me, as if he couldn't believe his eyes. He had his revolver out and up, but when he recognized me, he relaxed a bit and pointed it at the sky.

"Some folks don't seem to know when to get out of town," he said.

"It's that small town hospitality," I said. "You just hate to leave it."

"Yeah, I'm so sure. So you stick around and blow up a motel room, just to be doing something?"

"We didn't do it, we had it done to us. I'll tell you the whole story, but first I think we ought to go check on the motel manager. He could need medical attention." I walked toward the motel office with the sheriff at my side. The others trailed behind us. As we walked, I gave Lindstrom a quick version of what had happened. He put his gun back in its holster and walked with his hands on his hips, shaking his head a lot and scowling. He looked as if I had personally brought him more trouble than the entire rest of his law enforcement career.

"Well, I can't imagine anybody making up something like that," said the sheriff. "So who do you think these people are, then?"

"I have no idea."

"I think you have a lot of ideas. You just don't like sharing them."

I was starting to think he might be right. Maybe I knew a lot more than I thought I did. Or I was about to.

The motel manager had been gagged and tied up but was otherwise undamaged. Apparently it had been one of the other motel guests who had called nine-one-one. We checked our rooms next, and to my amazement, there was very little damage beyond the broken window and a couple of kicked-open doors. If the sheriff hadn't gotten a call from somebody other than me, I'd have had trouble convincing him there had been any explosions at all. *Concussion grenade*, I thought. *Not meant to kill, just to stun and shock.*

"So, is that your shotgun back there?" said Lindstrom.

"No. I borrowed it from a garage with a big boat in it. We ran away and hid there when the goons came."

"That would be Elmer Carlson's garage. He's a retired carpenter, built that boat from scratch. Used to be, when his wife was alive, it was his place to go get away from her. He'd go out and pretend to work on the boat and then get drunk and pass out. She's been gone for a long time now, died of cancer, and he's confined to a wheelchair, has a nurse look in on him a couple times a day. So there's probably been nobody in the garage for years now. I'm surprised it wasn't locked. Where's your wife, then?"

I nodded my head in the general direction of the alley. "Still hiding in the boat. I have to take her some clothes."

"Well, I think maybe we're done with you here for now. Take your time. Have a shot of old man Carlson's booze, if you find it. He'll never be back out there. See me again before you leave town, though, hey?" He gave me a card.

"Sure, no problem."

I grabbed up everything from both our rooms and headed back out to the alley. Along the way, I picked up the shotgun again.

◇◇◇

It took Anne a while to respond to our secret knock, and for a brief moment I wondered if she had been attacked by a fifth member of the patrol, if that's what it was, while I had been drawn away.

But the third time I knocked, I heard the axe being pulled out, and then the door opened away from me. When Anne saw I was alone, she put down the crowbar and hugged herself again.

"Are you okay?" I said.

She nodded. "I was back in the boat again, and I wasn't sure I ought to come out. The question is, are *we* okay?"

"Yes. Anyway, we're clear for now," I said. "The bad guys are gone and the—"

"How can you be so sure?"

"Because I pointed my trusty shotgun at them and they got in their car and left."

She gave me her penetrating, skeptical stare again. I gave her what was probably a goofy-looking grin and nodded my head. "Yeah." I laughed at the sheer wonderfulness of it. "Just like that. I couldn't believe it, either. They ran off just before our friendly sheriff showed up. He's back at the motel now. I brought you your clothes. Maybe you'd like to—"

But instead of taking the bundle out of my hands, she wrapped her arms around my neck and kissed me long and hard. I pushed her back for a moment, just so I could put the shotgun out of the way, then kissed her back. Wonderful, euphoric stuff, escaping from mortal danger. Just about the best aphrodisiac there is.

"You're running on adrenalin afterglow," I said. "You should—"

"Come and see what I found," she said, still ignoring her clothes, though she should have been turning blue by now. She took my hand and led me back to the transom of the boat. We climbed aboard, then stepped down into the cabin.

"There's power," she said. She flipped a switch and a tiny light came on in the overhead. There was also a small electric space heater on one bulkhead, and she turned it on.

The cabin was small, but cleverly laid out. The entire bow of the boat was one big, triangle-shaped bed, upholstered in some kind of red plush fabric. Farther toward the stern, there was a bench seat and a fold-down table and a lot of shelves and mesh slings, with various kinds of gear in them. On one shelf, there was a case of beer in long-necked bottles and a quart bottle of Canadian Club.

"I don't think I want to go back to that motel room just yet, Herman."

"We probably shouldn't. If the nasties come back, that's where they'll look for us, not here. And we have more or less official permission to stay in the boat."

"Really? How did we get that?"

"The owner is a shut-in. The sheriff gave us his blessing to mess around in the garage."

"Mess around. I like that." She pulled the cap off the whiskey bottle and took a slug, then held it out to me. "Buy you a drink, sailor?"

"I don't think you want to be doing that," I said. "You're just a bit on the emotionally fragile side right now, you know."

"True, true," she said. She put down the bottle and wiped her mouth on her sleeve. Then she reached farther back on the shelf and picked up something small.

"Forget about the booze, then. Look at what else I found." She put it in my hand. It was a condom in an unopened wrapper.

Considering what the sheriff had told me about the owner of the boat, there was no way I believed Anne had found it there. She had to have bought some at the mall in Virginia and put one in the elastic band of her underpants. There was also no way I was going to tell her I knew that. Not for the first time, I marveled at my utter inability to read a woman, and I was grateful that Anne hadn't had the same problem with me.

Her mouth found mine again and this time, I did not push her away, even slightly. I put my hand under her sweater and pulled her against me, then laughed in spite of myself.

"What are you finding so funny, there, Iowa Jackson? I'll have you know I've been—"

"Your rear end is cold."

"Oh, that." She chuckled quietly. "Well, I wonder why? I'm cold all over, you know?"

"There's a cure for that." I pulled down the collar of her sweater and nuzzled her neck.

"Well for God's sake, let's get to it, then." She unbuttoned my shirt and, I swear, climbed inside it with me. Then she wrapped her legs around my torso and we traveled to that place that has heat and resonance and intensity but no name. Somebody once said that when you make love, the dogs don't bark. Time doesn't exist and neither does fear. I hadn't been to that place for a very long time, and it was nice to be reminded.

Much later, we treated ourselves to a drink of whiskey and a can of cashews that we found on another shelf. It was warm in the cabin by then, even hot, and after a nightcap and a snack, we made love again, much more slowly this time, savoring it all. Then we curled up together and slept the long, blissful sleep of people recently delivered from death.

I have to say Elmer Carlson had built himself a damn nice boat.

The Morning After the Night Before

Dawn came with real sunlight, for a change. It streamed into the high east window and bounced around the garage a little before finally finding its way into the boat cabin. That made it dissipated, but still friendly.

The little space heater had been running all night, and the cabin was now much too warm for comfort. I stepped out into the rear cockpit and enjoyed the feel of the frigid air on my body. I looked at my watch. Only a little after eight. All things considered, it wouldn't have surprised me if we had slept until noon. A heavy hangover wouldn't have surprised me, either, but as far as I could tell, I didn't have one and wasn't going to get it. Never underestimate the curative powers of adrenalin and sex. Either one or both.

Anne was still asleep, and I grabbed my clothes out of the cabin and dressed in the cockpit. Then I went back to the motel to retrieve my car and get us some coffee from the lobby. The motel clerk did not seem to be my friend anymore.

"I could charge you for the damage to those rooms, you know."

"I get attacked in your motel, and you want to charge me for the experience? You're lucky I'm not a lawyer."

"Um. You're not, are you?"

I shook my head and gave him a reassuring smile. I was feeling much too good to get sucked into an argument, and anyway, he was looking more confused than angry. Obviously, nothing in his two-year community college degree had prepared him for this kind of incident.

"Did you call your insurance people?" I said.

"Sure, right away."

"And you're not hurt and neither is anybody else and you will be getting a police report to substantiate what went on, right?"

"I guess."

"Sure, you will. So relax. You'll have a good story to tell down at the corner saloon."

"I don't go to those places."

"Right. Me either. Tell you what: give me four cups of coffee and a cardboard box to carry them in and we'll call everything square."

"And then you'll go, right?"

"And then I'll go." Nice young man, but he really needed to do something about all that negative thinking.

I put the coffee on the roof of my BMW, took a flashlight out of the trunk, and lay down in the new snow long enough to check the undercarriage for bombs or bugs or other assorted bits of unwanted baggage. Seeing nothing amiss, I brushed myself off, got in with my coffee, and fired it up. Going around the corner of the motel into the alley, I punched the gas and did a short power slide, just for the pure joy of it. Then I went more sedately the rest of the way and stopped by the garage in the middle of the block, to collect Anne.

She was dressed by the time I got there, but still in the boat. We popped the lids on two of the coffees and sat with our feet hanging over the gunwale, eating Elmer Carlson's cashews and getting ourselves recaffeinated.

"Well, Herman, now you know my worst secret."

"I do?" I shot her a quick sideways look. "And what might that be?"

"What I look like in the morning."

I looked again, a little more critically.

"If that's the darkest secret you've got, I would say you have nothing to worry about."

"Well, you would say that, wouldn't you? Whether it was true or not."

"Damn right I would."

She chuckled and took another handful of cashews. They went surprisingly well with the coffee.

"I don't suppose we can go back to the motel and use the bathroom and clean up a bit?"

"As a matter of fact, we can. The clerk was so happy to see me go that he forgot to get our keys back. And anyway, it's not as if he's going to rent the rooms out again right away, with two broken doors."

We shut off the lights and the heater, and Anne wrote a thank you note and stuck it in the empty cashew can. On the way out, I bent a piece of wire I found hanging on the wall into a crude lock pick, and I used it to lock the door behind us. After all, who knew what sort of riff raff might be wandering in?

We drove back to Anne's room, since that was the one that still had all its glass intact, and while she disappeared into the bathroom, I used the bedside phone to call Agnes and tell her I'd be back in the office sometime in the afternoon.

"Is she cute?"

"I can't imagine who you're referring to, Aggie."

"Oh, good. She is cute. I'm glad for you, Herman."

"I don't know why you always think—"

"Wendell called, by the way." She always refers to Wilkie by his real first name. "He says he's got something for you. And a Detective Erickson from the SPPD called later. You want that number?"

"No, thanks. He made me wait. Now it's his turn. Anything else?"

"I, um, guess not. Not really." The energy had suddenly gone out of her voice altogether.

"Tell me, already."

"It's really nothing, Herman."

"Has that asshole Eddie Bardot been bothering you again?"

"He scares me, Herman. And that gets me mad at myself for being so silly, since he doesn't really do anything very threatening."

"What does he do, exactly?"

"Yesterday morning, he tried to leave an envelope full of money on your desk."

"What did you do?"

"I threw it out on the sidewalk. I told him he could pick it up or not, as he liked, but I certainly wasn't going to do so."

"Good move. So did he leave then?"

"He did, but later he came back. He hangs around. I think he only does it because he knows you're not here. He makes what he thinks are cute little sexual innuendos and says I should be nice to him because you aren't going to be around much longer."

"Does he, now? Next time he comes back, in fact the next time you even see him coming down the street, call Wilkie right away, okay? Tell him I said we need the trash taken out. I'll be back as soon as I can."

"Thanks, maybe I will."

"Not maybe. Do it."

"Drive safely, Herman."

"See you, Ag."

I hung up and dialed Wilkie's cell phone, but all I got was his voice mail. "I'm not here now, see?" said the recording. "So I can't talk to you. When I'm back, I will. You can leave a message, if you want to, and I might listen to it."

I waited for the beep and then left a message asking him to look in on Agnes. Meanwhile, Anne had come out of the bath. We left our keys in the room and headed out.

Sheriff Lindstrom's office was a new building just off the new Highway 169, not really in any town. His deputy gave us some coffee in real cups, and we settled into some visitor chairs in front of Lindstrom's desk in his inner office.

"I did a little write up of the business last night," he said. "Maybe you could look it over and sign it for me?"

"Sure," I said, and I began to skim through my copy. It was written in first person, as if it had been taken as dictation from me, so I felt free to edit it. When I came to references to Anne as my wife, I crossed them out and wrote in "girlfriend." That made me smile, and I wondered what she was writing on her copy.

"By the way, Sheriff, has your coroner determined when James Victor was killed yet?"

"Um, well, it's not so easy, you know. The heat turned off in the house, and all. Ah, why, ah, would you be wanting to know that?" He was visibly uneasy with the topic.

"Well, I was just thinking." I paused and looked into his eyes, and he did not hold the contact.

"Okay, then," was all he said. "You're allowed to think."

"I was thinking that if James Victor was killed more than three days ago," I said, "then maybe the killer or killers came to the old man to find out where the kid was."

"Oh, like that. I see. That could be, I guess."

"I was also thinking that yesterday at the murder scene, and again last night, you were awfully nice to me. Not suspicious or authoritative at all."

"Hey, I'm a nice guy. Just ask Marty out there."

"He's a nice guy," said the deputy from the desk in the front office.

"Sure you are. But I think you also knew you didn't have to suspect me of any wrongdoing, because you knew you had already seen the real killers."

"Just what the hell are you saying?"

"They came here, didn't they? To ask how to find old man Victor. And of course, you told them."

"Well, why wouldn't I? Not that I'm saying I did, mind you. That doesn't mean I had anything to do with—"

I held up my hands and shook my head. "I wasn't implying anything of the sort." I signed his report and pushed it back across the desk to him. "People ask for directions, you give them some. Nothing wrong with that. What did they say, that they were old army buddies, trying to get a line on Jim's kid?"

"You're pretty damn smart, you know that? You want a job as a deputy?"

"Hey!" said Marty.

"Yeah, they were here. I guess it can't hurt anything if you know that. They had an address for old Jim, but they couldn't find the whole damn town of Mountain Iron, they said. You wouldn't believe how much of that I get."

"Yes, I think I would. And you say they also asked about Jim's son?"

"They asked, but I didn't have anything to tell them. I'm thinking Jim didn't, either. One time he bitched to me about how his kid only sent him one lousy postcard in the last twenty years. He knew it was sent from St. Paul, but that's about it."

"Really? Did you tell them that?"

"Hell, no. I didn't like them. Bunch of arrogant, pushy types, acted like they owned the world and everybody should kiss their asses. So I didn't feel like telling them diddly."

"So when did James Victor die?" said Anne, also pushing her report form across the desk.

"It's iffy, like I said. The coroner says he could have died as much as a week ago. The guys who came here were five days back. Happy? Now, have you two got anything else to tell me? Like maybe who these guys were?"

"I wish I knew. They seem to be tied to Charlie Victor's past in Vietnam somehow, but they're way too young to have been there when he was. And they seem to be military, but I don't think they're part of any kind of actual operation, even a rogue one. That's as much as I know, and I'm not even sure I know that." I got up and headed for the door. On my way, I said, "The police detective in St. Paul who's working on Charlie Victor's murder is named Erickson. You might want to give him a call."

"Another St. Paul smart guy? I can hardly wait."

"I really think he—"

"I'll call him, I'll call him. Are you gone yet?"

"Ciao," said Anne, and we were, indeed, gone. But we didn't head south just yet. We went back to James Victor's house.

Yellow CRIME SCENE tape was wrapped around the entire house several times, and the site was full of tire tracks and footprints. Anne took a picture of it.

"Did you tell the sheriff we were coming here?" said Anne.

"Of course not. He'd have just told me not to."

"So now we can pretend we didn't know any better?"

"I was thinking more of getting in and back out fast enough that we don't have to pretend anything."

"That's a good plan. What are we looking for?"

"A postcard, with a twenty-year old postmark on it, the one Charlie's father bitched about. You want to stay in the car and play innocent bystander?"

"Not on your life."

The back door was still unlatched, and when I looked at it more closely, I saw that the strike plate had been completely ripped out of the jamb. I swung the storm door out as little as possible, and we managed to slip inside without breaking the plastic tapes.

Inside, the place was pretty much as we had seen it the last time, except that now, of course, James Victor's body was gone. I had been wondering how the cops were going to make the famous chalk outline of the body, since it had been sitting in a chair. To my disappointment, they hadn't even tried. Maybe they only do that in the movies.

The rest of the house was an even bigger mess than the kitchen. Drawers dumped, upholstery cut open, everything thrown all over hell.

"It doesn't look as though our crime scene techies were very neat," said Anne, and she took some more pictures.

"I'm thinking this is the way they found it."

"Our bad guys' handiwork?"

"It would fit." I had also noticed some possible bloodstains in the living room, which I had not pointed out to her, and I wondered if the pickaxe in the kitchen had been used for some purpose quite different from digging ore. The crime scene people had taken it, in any case.

In the bedroom, the threadbare mattress on an old brass bed frame had been slashed, dresser drawers dumped, and even the dresser mirror had been smashed, then spun around backward and the paper backing torn open. Shards of slivered glass crunched under our feet.

"I think we're a day late and a postcard short, Herman."

"Maybe, maybe not. Sometimes people trying to be intimidating get in a frenzy and don't look carefully." I rotated the broken mirror back to facing the correct way. And stuck in the frame, in places that still had pieces of glass left, were some ticket stubs from a movie theater, a menu from a pizza joint, a church program from some long ago Easter, and an old postcard.

"Hello," I said.

"Something?" said Anne.

"Could be," I said, pulling it out. "It almost looks *too* old, though."

"Let's see it. No, it isn't. It's one of those nostalgia replicas, like they sell at the History Center gift shop. It's meant to look like something from before World War Two, but it's really not."

"It looks like a picture of a downtown park."

"Kellogg Park, the way it looked back in the streetcar days," she said. She flipped the card over. It had Charlie Victor's signature and James Victor's address on it, but nothing else. No greeting, no request for money, no message of any kind. I squinted at the tiny printing in the upper left hand corner, telling us what the picture on the other side was.

"That doesn't say 'Kellogg Park,'" I said.

"No, it has the older name for it: Viaduct Park."

And my mind flashed back to that first day in my office, when Charlie had told me about his cardboard box "under the wye-duct."

"What's under this park?" I said.

"Under it? Second Street, I guess, or most of it. The whole place is built sort of like a double-deck bridge, with a sloping street below and a park up on top."

"And under the sloping street?"

"Some hollow spots where street people hang out, I think."

"And I bet they sing, 'Oh, I live under the wye-duct; down by the winny-gar woiks.'"

"What on earth does that mean?"

"It means we just hit pay dirt. Lets get out of here."

The Road to the Wye-Duct

The road back to St. Paul seemed shorter than it had on the way out, but maybe that was just because it was familiar now. We skipped our new old favorite restaurant in Eveleth and instead had a late brunch in Hinckley, at a place with a tin tree on a telephone pole for a sign. It had a cloud of bluish smoke coming out of the kitchen exhaust, and it smelled like hot cooking oil and burning beef. In other words, it smelled wonderful. Inside, it also smelled like coffee and fresh bread, and I knew we'd come to the right place. I had the house special stew and Anne had some kind of large salad, with greens that were freshly flown in from Mars, I think.

"How's the stew?" she said.

"It's famous. The menu says so."

"Well, then, what else is there to say?"

"Actually, it's very good."

"I'm glad. How was the sex?"

If I'd been swallowing, I would have choked. Instead, I laughed and said, "You just don't beat around the bush about anything, do you?"

"First rule of reporting," she said, shaking her head and grinning wickedly. "You don't find out anything if you don't ask."

"All right, then, Lois Lane, the sex was wonderful. Does this mean we're going to do it again?"

"If we're lucky. Now comes the time when it gets really, really good for a while, before it all starts to go south."

I shot her a surprised look and found that she was holding her coffee cup with both hands and staring off into space with a sort of dazed look.

"Why should it all go south?" I said.

"Because it always does."

"That's really—"

"You worry too much, Herman. First we get the good time, and if it's really good, it makes it all worth it."

I couldn't help but wonder what had happened on all those political fundraisers besides dancing the polka. Whatever it was, it must have been terribly sad. And I was sure I shouldn't ask about it.

"What about my story?" she said, blinking her eyes back into focus. "Do we know any more than we did yesterday, apart from the fact that the homeless guy had a father who was also murdered and some goons who look like they *might be* military have been chasing us?"

"We can speculate, is all."

"I'm a reporter from the old school. I don't let myself do that. You do it for me."

"First of all, now that I've seen them up close, I would definitely agree with our witch, Glenda—"

"It was actually Glinda, in the Oz stories."

"Are you going to let me speculate or are you going to correct a bag lady's personal mythology?"

"Speculate, Herman."

"Okay. So I agree that our thugs are military types. And Charlie was murdered by some kind of gang, so that would also make these guys our best suspects. But they're way too young to have been in Vietnam when he was. So why do they care what he did when he was there?"

"I give up, why?"

"I don't know yet. But my gut feeling is that everything that's happened so far is somehow tied to his time in the jungle."

"But we have no proof of that."

"Not a shred. Put that aside for a moment and consider something else. Two somethings. One is that if these guys had really wanted you and me dead, I, at least, would be."

"You don't think they were afraid of your big, bad shotgun?"

"Not for a minute. If I had been a real target, they'd have paid the price and taken me out."

"So what did they really want with us?"

"Could be they thought we had a line on Charlie's stash of money, but I think it's more likely they were just trying to scare us off."

"That plays okay," she said, "but we still need a reason."

"They haven't found the money yet. And until they do, they don't want to fold up the tent and go off to wherever they came from. So while they're hanging around, they would rather you and I quit poking into their affairs."

"Absolutely maybe," she said. "What's the other something?"

"Timing. They killed Charlie's father before him, and they killed him quick. I mean, they beat on him some first, but when they were satisfied they had what he knew, they shot him in the head. 'We're done with you now, old man. Bam!' No screwing around."

"But when they killed Charlie..."

"When they killed Charlie, they took their time. I'm thinking they maybe even told him they had killed his father first, so he could think about it while he died."

"That sounds like a crime of passion, not a treasure hunt."

"It does, doesn't it? It sounds like a blood feud. They meant to kill Charlie and his father all along, and the money was just a little sideshow, an unexpected bonus."

"'Blood Feud' is a good headline," she said, making a little frame with her hands. "'Blood Feud Has Roots in Vietnam War' is even better. But whose blood, besides the Victors'?"

"That's the question, all right. Charlie said he killed, or collected money for killing, several officers. Could one of them have had a buddy, a classmate from West Point, whatever? I don't know. I think we need some personnel records from Charlie's old outfit. Last known addresses, so we can talk to whomever is left of them, see what they know."

"I don't know if the Army would give those out to a reporter. Maybe if I pretend I'm writing a book... Hmm. No. I just don't know." Her face said that she did know, and she wasn't happy about her prospects.

"I know a sort of renegade hacker who could possibly steal the information," I said.

"You know some strange people, Iowa."

"This is undoubtedly true."

"One other thing bothers me: how did the goons find us at the motel?"

"I thought about that, too," I said, thoughtfully stirring my coffee. "They were following me the day before yesterday, but we didn't have anybody behind us when we headed north, and I checked the BMW for a homing device before I left town. So that leaves your cell phone."

"When I called the sheriff from Mountain Iron? So they homed in on the signal? That seems a little far fetched."

"If they had the right equipment, they wouldn't have to. Modern cell phones broadcast their position every time they're in use. All they had to know was your number, and they could have gotten that from my phone records."

"That would only get them to Mountain Iron. How did they get to the motel in Eveleth?"

"They cruised around looking for a 328i. There aren't a lot of them on the Range, you know."

"Like one?"

"Just like that."

The last of my stew had turned cold, and I let the waitress take it away and bring me fresh coffee and a piece of apple pie that turned out to be about two inches high and sprinkled with enough cinnamon and sugar to open a small bakery. Anne looked at it longingly.

"I'm sure they have more," I said.

"You're a vile seducer."

"I certainly hope so."

She signaled the waitress, pointed at my plate, and held up two fingers. The waitress smiled knowingly and went off to get another piece.

The pie was something to die for, but our dessert was interrupted by Anne's cell phone.

"Now you know why I don't carry one of those damned things," I said. She waved a hand to shush me, turned away and spoke quietly into the infernal device. It was a short call.

"My editor," she said.

"How thoughtless of him."

"You don't know the half of it. How fast can you get me back to my office?"

"Well, I think the 328i will do something like Mach oh-point-twenty-five. If there are no cops out and you aren't afraid of flying, I can have you back in an hour."

"In one piece, would be nice."

"For some people, everything has to be perfect."

I didn't bother to tell her that I had another reason for wanting to fly down the highway at a speed that was probably insane. Far back, almost out of sight, I had again spotted a black rectangle that could definitely be a Hummer. Our military gang was not done with us yet.

Echoes

I dropped Anne at the *Pioneer Press* building, put the BMW back in the ramp, and walked to my own office. I turned the corner onto my block just in time to see my friendly shakedown artist, Eddie Bardot, picking himself up off the sidewalk. He glared at me as I walked by but said nothing. Pretty soon his hat came flying out my office door, and he scrambled to grab it before it got run over by a passing garbage truck.

I couldn't resist nodding to him and giving him a sardonic smile as I opened the door and went inside.

Agnes was at her usual place behind her desk, looking as if she just ate a canary, feathers and all, and Wide Track Wilkie was standing in the center of the storefront window, fists on his hips, watching Bardot go.

"Hey, Wide."

"Herm." He nodded absently.

"I see you've met our friendly wannabe bonding tycoon."

"Asshole had the nerve to tell me to fuck off and mind my own business. You believe that?"

"Shocking," I said. "Also very disrespectful."

"Yeah, that's what I said, too. Didn't I say that, Miss Agnes?"

"Well," said Agnes, "not exactly. I seem to recall your words were a bit shorter than that."

"Yeah, whatever. Anyways, I had to slam him into the wall a couple times, just to see how good he bounced."

"And did he?"

"Not worth a shit."

"So you told him to have a nice day and invited him to leave?"

"Just like that."

Agnes snorted. Now they were both grinning.

"How about your research?" I said. "Do we know anything more about him?"

He lost the grin, wrinkled his brow and shook his head. "Not much. The word on the street is he's some kind of outcast from the Chicago mob, but he's got no record under the name he's using right now. Maybe this will help." He reached in the pocket of his trench coat and pulled out a well-worn leather wallet.

"This is his?" I said.

"Not anymore."

Agnes chuckled and shook her head in mock disapproval.

"Does he know you've got it?"

"Not yet."

"Better and better. Let's just see what we can see here. Then we'll copy what we need and throw the wallet out on the sidewalk for him to come back and find later."

"I'm not leaving any money in it."

I pulled out maybe two or three hundred in small bills and gave it to him. Then I pulled out three different drivers' licenses in three names, some credit cards that matched each of them, and one of those little envelopes that you get at hotels, to hold your key and tell you what your room number is. I handled them all by the edges. I took them over to my copy machine, copied both sides of everything, and put it all back together.

"Does the wallet itself have your prints on it?" I said to Wilkie.

"It would have to, yeah."

"I meant on the inside."

"No. I didn't open it."

I took a tissue from a dispenser on Agnes' desk and wiped down the entire outside of the wallet. Then I threw it in a drawer of my own desk and locked it.

"What happened to leaving it on the sidewalk?"

"I just got a better idea."

"Which is?"

"You're better off not knowing. What about the other thing, the fingerprints from the snow shovel?"

"That's another big awshit. We lifted some okay prints, but they're not in the criminal info computer."

"You still have them?"

"Sort of. I've got a CD that describes them to a computer. Or I think that's what it does."

"That's even better. Do you happen to know if The Prophet is still in business at his old digs?"

"The crazy guy? As far as I know."

"He's not crazy, he just marches to the beat of a different kazoo."

"He talks to people who aren't there, Herm. And I mean without using a phone."

"Well, there is that, yes. But he also talks to just about any secure data base you can think of."

"And we need that?" His face told me he was hoping for a no.

"We need it, Wide. I'm thinking our fingerprint might be in a military or government file. But you don't have to come along, if you really can't stand the guy."

"Well, I'm already in the game, you know?" He sighed. "I'll see the next card."

I told Agnes that if Anne Packard called, she should give her Wilkie's cell phone number. Then he and I headed for the door.

"Have a nice day, Miss Agnes."

"Why, thank you, Wendell. You, too."

He insisted that his only name was The Prophet, so that's what we always called him to his face. To ourselves, we mostly called him the Proph. In the summers, he lived in a junker of a step van that was permanently parked in the alley behind a defunct furniture store. He spent his days misquoting scripture and dispensing pearls of incomprehensible wisdom to anybody who would listen. But when the weather turned cold, he moved back into an old two-story brick building on the far East Side, next to some railroad tracks. I think it used to be a switch house or some other kind of railroad maintenance building, back when there were lots more tracks and the BN&SF was the Soo Line or even earlier, when it was the Great Northern or the Union Pacific.

Whatever railroad it was, it lost interest in the building a long time ago but didn't bother to wreck it, and The Prophet had been squatting there for several years. He stole power from a nearby transformer that didn't get looked at much and phone service from who knows where, and he supported himself and his ersatz ministry by engaging in some of the most effective hacking known to nerd-dom. I had used his services before.

Like his van, the building was painted with a lot of strange proclamations, like crude, oversized bumper stickers. "Yah! Is my god!" done in six-foot-high shadow lettering and four colors was the most prominent. Off to the sides were slogans that hadn't been rendered quite so elaborately. "THE LIVING ARE NOT NEARLY SO ALIVE AS THE DEAD ARE DEAD," was one. Another said, "He that diggeth a pit shall fall in it," and a partially painted-over one said something about "A Land Flowing With Bilk and Money." The over-painting said, "The meek shall inherit the earth, complete with windfall profit, state, dog, and syn taxes."

There was a door on the side of the building facing the tracks. Wilkie pulled it open, and we found ourselves looking into a small black closet with a full-length mirror facing us. We stood there a while, looking at ourselves looking stupid, and then the ceiling spoke.

"Praise Yah!" it said, in a tinny voice.

"Yeah?" I said.

"You pronounce it wrong," said the ceiling. I smiled, because we had had this exact conversation before.

"There's a lot of that going around," I said.

"Pilgrim? Is that you?"

"In the willing flesh. Wilkie's with me."

"Praise Yah, already," said Wilkie, looking disgusted. He knows that I'm the only one who gets to go inside without saying that.

"Make it!" said the ceiling.

There was a loud buzzing noise, and one of the walls of the closet turned into a door that popped open. We went through it, bumbled around two more corners, and finally emerged into the main building. Most of the windowless room was taken up by a huge workbench covered with multiple-screen computers, printers, and a dozen other gizmos that I couldn't identify. Tangles of wire were everywhere, as were little plastic boxes that had colored lights blinking in no identifiable pattern. Behind it all, in a rattan peacock chair, sat a small, wizened black man with a full beard and a Nike headband. He smiled broadly at us.

"Welcome to my inner sanctum," he said. "You have been a long time wandering in the wilderness, Pilgrim."

"Well, there's a lot of it out there."

"Disheartening, is it not?"

"What's with the new door setup?" said Wilkie.

"You like that?"

"No."

"It repels bad joss." He continued to smile as if Wilkie hadn't spoken. "Good joss meanders and insinuates and can always get in, but bad joss travels in straight lines and gets reflected back by the mirror. Also, it can't get around all the corners."

"Told you," I said.

"You never."

"Yah told me you would come," said The Prophet.

"Well, he always does, doesn't he?" I said.

"I bet he doesn't say when, though, does he?" said Wilkie.

"He said you would be seeking enlightenment. Have I told you how the world tripped into the beginning of its present utter, irreversible madness in 1955, when people wanted coffee tables and picture windows?"

"Yes," I said.

"Really? How was it?"

"Long."

He frowned a bit and pursed his lips. "Hmm. Maybe I did tell you. What is it you seek today?"

"Is information the same as enlightenment?" said Wilkie.

"No," said The Prophet. "Enlightenment, if you can find it, is free. Information costs. If it's illegal, five hundred, minimum."

"Steep," said Wilkie.

"But worthy of it," said the Prophet.

"'A good name is rather to be chosen than great riches,'" I said.

"Very good, Pilgrim. Proverbs, Chapter 22. But Ecclesiastes says, 'Wine maketh merry, but money answerith all things.' Five cee won't ruin my good name or your profit-and-loss sheet."

If he only knew.

"'A word fitly spoken is like apples of gold in pictures of silver,'" I said. You have to do a lot of homework to dicker with The Prophet.

"Could be," he said. "Have you got one?"

"Sure. 'The race is not to the swift, nor the battle to the strong, but that's the way the smart money bets.'"

He looked at me for a while with some surprise on his face. Finally, he broke out into a smile.

"That's not bad," he said. "I can use that. All right, for the sake of your golden words, two-fifty, but it could go up if the stuff gets tricky."

"Fair enough."

I laid five fifties on his desk, and we got down to business. "Army personnel records," I said. "Vietnam era."

He began massaging two separate keyboards with great concentration, shutting out anything else we might say for a while. I noticed that although his chair was straight off the set of some Tennessee Williams play, it was nevertheless fitted with swivel castors, and he had a good time whizzing around on them, sometimes for no apparent reason. Finally he stopped and asked me for some more specific direction.

"I need the roster of a company that was in-country in about 1965. Echo Company, with the First Air Cavalry."

"Brigade and Battalion, Pilgrim."

"Excuse me?"

"The First Air Cav would be a division. It splits into brigades, then battalions, and then finally companies. That's a lot of damn heathens."

"You seem to know an awful lot about army organization, for a holy man."

"When the walls of Jericho came tumbling down, I said *Kaddish* for the people buried under the rubble. I was a chaplain in the Fifth Roman Legion at the time. When the—"

"You've also got an organization chart on the screen in front of you," said Wilkie.

"To download is to know, oh great one."

Wilkie snorted. The Prophet continued to work mouse and keyboard. Sometimes I wished he weren't so useful, so I could tell him how full of shit I thought he was.

"So a division is how many souls?" I said.

"Ten or fifteen thousand, with bodies attached."

"That could cost fifty bucks just for the paper to print it out," said Wilkie. I could stand for him to be a lot less helpful at times.

"Let's attack it from the other end," I said. "Find the record of Charles Victor, and see what unit he was in, back then." I gave him Charlie's service number, which I had pulled from one of his bond files.

"Which year, Pilgrim?"

"Work that backward, too, if you can. Go for a time when he was a newly minted corporal."

He fired up a second screen and did a lot of looking back and forth between the two of them.

"July, 1966. Looks like the company had three platoons, about twenty people per. You want all of them?"

"What I really want is the last known address of each of them."

"You're a hard taskmaster."

"Remember the golden apples."

"Hmm. I'll write a short program to pull them up. Perhaps you would like a cup of my famous tea while you wait?"

"Is it hallucinogenic?"

"Only a little. It will not affect your ability to drive, I think."

"Um. Got any coffee?"

"Timid souls. There's instant over by the sink, hot water in the carafe." Wilkie and I helped ourselves, and the Prophet got back to work. After a while, he punched a last key, and machines began to click and whirr on their own. Now and then, a list of names would come out of the printer.

"Anything else, while we're waiting for that to finish?"

Wilkie reached into an inside pocket a pulled out the CD in its plastic envelope.

"Fingerprint," he said. "Put into some kind of electronic code, I guess. It's not a picture anymore, anyway."

"And you want me to check it for a criminal record?"

"Nah, we already tried that and came up dry. We were thinking maybe it would be in the Army's records."

"Ah." He took the disc and fed it into yet another machine. Almost too fast to be believable, he said, "It's there, all right."

"And?"

"Classified."

"How the hell can a Fingerprint be classified?" said Wilkie. "I mean, aren't all these files we're looking at classified? Why can't we look at it anyway?"

"This is classified the way the true name of Buddha is classified, big man. I mean, *nobody* has the key to this."

"Black ops?" I said.

"Could be. That, or the man simply had a friend in records and put the lock on it himself. Some sojourners prefer to go about anonymously."

"Isn't that the truth, though?"

196 Richard A. Thompson

"Anything else?"

"One thing," I said. "While your machine is still back in 1966, see which brigade Charlie was in."

"Easy. Q.E.D."

"Why brigade?" said Wilkie.

"Because I think that's the highest level that still has a commanding officer who is actually in the field, with the troops." And therefore could have been assassinated in the field. Also because I had a hunch, but I wasn't sure enough of it to say so just yet.

"Got it," said the Prophet.

"Now see who commands that same outfit today."

That took a little longer, but he got that, too.

"The name of the soul is Rappolt."

"No way," I said. "I'm sorry to be the one to tell you, Prophet, but you screwed up. You're still back in the sixties, and Rappolt was a lieutenant."

"Not so. Look for yourself. Colonel John S. Rappolt, the Third. He took command less than a year ago."

"Well, I'll be go to hell."

"Not in my inner sanctum, you won't."

"What's the big deal?" said Wilkie.

"We're not looking for a service buddy, after all," I said, "we're looking for kin. John Rappolt was the name of the first officer Charlie ever fragged."

"Not that common a name," said Wilkie.

"It sure isn't. I'm thinking this is his son."

"Could be a grandson, by now."

"I don't think so. Not an immediate enough link. I'm thinking it's somebody who grew up fatherless on account of Charlie and has been pissed off about it ever since. Somebody who took a long time and went to a lot of trouble to find out who to kill. Can you get me a picture of him, Prophet?"

"Coming out of the printer now."

It was a face I had never seen before.

"Wide, you were in the Army, weren't you?"

"Don't remind me. Yeah, I was in Desert Storm."

"So tell me: if a colonel decided to go off duty and off the radar to kill somebody, who would he trust to go with him?"

"That's easy. He'd take his sergeant major."

"Isn't that two people?"

"It's a hybrid rank," he said, shaking his head. "It's the battalion commander's link to the grunts, and the two of them are usually tighter than cell mates."

"And what about the others?"

"A sergeant major would have a few enlisteds who are more loyal to him personally then they are to the army. It wouldn't be hard to find a few to go along. In the current crop of grunts, there would even be some who would make the trip just for the chance to break some rules and raise a little hell."

"Who pays for this supposed operation?"

"Rappolt, of course. He's a full colonel, Herm. He's got money coming out of his brass ears."

"That much?"

"Hey, it's an officers' corps. Always was, always will be."

I looked back at the Prophet and said, "Can we find Rappolt's sergeant major?"

Two minutes later, we had the name of a Sergeant Major Robert Dunne.

"You want a picture of him, too?"

"Yes."

His picture shouldn't have surprised me, but it did. A line at a time, the machine spat out the face of a fiftyish man in full dress uniform. He'd worn a uniform the last time I saw him, too, but not that one. It was the beefy-faced cop that I had followed into Nighttown.

"Do you have a fax?" I said.

"Is the Pope a child molester?" He spread his palms outward and grinned.

"I take that for a yes. I'll need a regular phone, too."

"Secure?"

"It doesn't matter."

"Then I don't have one."

"All right, then, secure."

"Twenty bucks, Pilgrim."

"You're something else, you know that?"

"I am the thing nobody knows how to cope with: a genuine holy man with business sense."

"Wide, loan me your phone, okay?"

"Some people just don't believe in free trade." The Proph went off somewhere to sulk.

I called Anne at work and got her fax number, so I could send her all the stuff we had just printed. But she had something else on her mind, as well.

"I'm glad you called," she said. "I think I know where your dead man's tunnel is."

The Road to the Jungle

Anne had found out about the tunnel quite by accident, chatting with an old-time staffer at her newspaper about the problems of interacting with the pressmen, who were across the river and a mile away. Email was all well and good, he said, but it was better when the presses were just down the street, at Fourth and Minnesota.

"They were? How did they get the big rolls of paper there?" she had idly asked. "Don't they always come in by rail? There are no train tracks on Fourth Street, never were."

The answer was that there was a long, sloping tunnel that ran down from the basement of the old press building, south, under Kellogg Boulevard, under Kellogg Park (né Viaduct Park,) and finally down to a small warehouse by the railroad tracks. The tunnel daylighted on the Mississippi river flats, at the base of the limestone bluffs that hold up Downtown. When the press building was wrecked and replaced with a parking ramp, the little warehouse down by the tracks was also leveled, and the tunnel was simply sealed up and abandoned.

I let Wilkie and The Prophet listen in on my phone call with Anne. It turned out that The Prophet also knew where Charlie's tunnel was. Silly soul that I am, I had neglected to ask him. He knew most of what went on in the homeless community, but he never volunteered anything that wasn't either for enlightenment or for sale.

"That place is full of bad joss, Pilgrim. Maybe demons, too. And it's all linear, so you can't dodge them. Nobody ever followed your man Cee Vee in there. Nobody even talks about what's in there."

"Where is the entrance, exactly?"

"Trust me, you do not want to go there."

"I have to."

"Then may Yah! protect you."

"Where?"

He told me.

I had promised Anne that I wouldn't go in the tunnel until she could get clear of her office and maybe bring a photographer with her. That would be about two hours, she said. Tight, but doable, if everything went right.

I drove back downtown from The Prophet's place and dropped Wilkie off at Lefty's. He didn't like the idea of being cut out of the action, but I told him I had to do some things that were better done without any witnesses. That, he could dig. I went to my office and took a few things out of my desk, including the copy of Charlie's Master key and Eddie Bardot's wallet. Then I took my copy of Charlie's will, penned a quick note to myself and headed out.

"Leaving again so soon?" said Agnes.

"Got to. Can't let the bad joss catch up with me."

"Well, I definitely know who you've been talking to. Where will you be, if anybody asks?"

"If anybody asks, you think I went to Lefty's."

"And if I ask?"

"I'm off to play tunnel rat. I also need you to make a couple of phone calls for me, but not just yet."

"Honestly, Herman, why don't you just give up and get a cell—"

"Don't even start, Agnes."

◇◇◇

The rail yard that used to cover the river flats below Downtown is almost all gone now, mostly ripped out and replaced with contract-only parking lots. That makes the base of the bluff not so easy to get to anymore. I parked a quarter of a mile to the west, near the sally port entrance to the County Jail, took a flashlight out of my trunk, and walked back east, under the Wabasha Bridge. I followed the limestone rubble at the bottom of the looming wall of stone, skirting the parking lots that were baking in the late afternoon sun.

There were a lot of openings in the bluff face that had been plugged up with concrete or bricks. Most of them were quite high up, including a lot of them right under the steeply sloping roadway of Second Street. But down at base level, almost blocked by fallen stones and sand, was one that had not been simply bricked in. It had a rusty steel door built into the brickwork, with a hasp and a padlock. I took the copy of Charlie's key out of my pocket and tried it.

Click.

I swung the door toward myself, and it drew with it a breath of musty, cold air. It smelled like wet limestone and dead rats and failed dreams. It smelled like fear. I pulled the door open as far as it would go, clicked on the flashlight and walked into Charlie Victor's nightmares.

The machinery for moving the big rolls of paper was still there, sort of a trough-shaped skeletal steel framework with rollers on the cross-frames and a heavy chain running down the center. The chain had big hooks on it at regular intervals, and it looked like something out of a mechanized slaughterhouse for elephants.

The rusted conveyor took up most of the tunnel width, but there was room enough to walk alongside it on the left. Service access, probably. I imagined that once in a while a roll of paper would fall off the frame or get stuck, and some poor bastards would have to go into the tunnel and fix it. I also imagined that they didn't like the job much. I wasn't quite ready to start using terms like "bad joss," but the place did not have a good feel to it. I found myself walking with my shoulders hunched. Whether you think you're claustrophobic or not, the thought of about a million tons of earth above your head is going to be oppressive. There also seemed to be a draft at my back, which didn't help my mood any.

I had left the door fully open, but a dozen steps into the tunnel, it provided no light at all. I turned around now and then to satisfy myself that it was still there, an increasingly small white rectangle in a universe of black. Not an auspicious thing, having the light at the end of the tunnel behind your back.

My flashlight was woefully inadequate, and I used the steel framework like a banister, to keep myself oriented and to pull myself up at times. The tunnel floor was a soft, yellowish sand, almost a powder, and it sloped upward fairly steeply. Walking up it was a lot of work. Now and then something would drip onto my face and arms, cold and startling. If it was something other than just water, I didn't want to think about it. And then there was the other thing.

I didn't call it a ghost, and I didn't think it was the Prophet's demons, either, but there was definitely some kind of *presence* in the tunnel. And somehow or other, it was both with me and waiting for me to arrive. Was the Prophet's instant coffee hallucinogenic, as well as his tea? Would he have told me if it was? I let my guts feel what they wanted to and forced my feet to move forward in spite of it. I had a job to do. I did not have to be comfortable doing it.

After maybe fifty or sixty yards, I came to a smaller tunnel, crossing the main one, with some kind of pipe in it. I tried shining my flashlight down it to see if it looked worth exploring, then shone it on the floor to see if there were any obvious footprints going into it. That's when I saw the first of the white powder.

It crossed the path of the pipe and made a sort of one-pronged arrow, pointing deeper into the main passage. What was it Charlie had told me about marking his path in the VC tunnels?

I never used string, Harold. Somebody can move string on you. Some kind of white powder is better, some flour or baking powder, or something. You got to put it off to one side, so you don't accidentally scuff it out, but it never moves on you. And the enemy don't have any of the stuff.

It wasn't a lot lighter in color than the sand of the floor, but now that I knew what to look for, I spotted lots more of it, always directing me farther up the main tunnel.

I passed another small pipe tunnel, then a bigger cross-passage that looked natural, rather than man-made. It looked irregular and deep, and the draft I had felt at my back seemed to be flowing into it. And there was a string on its floor, leading straight away from me and into the darkness. I smiled and continued the way I had been going. I imagined hearing Charlie chuckle and say *I knew you'd be too smart for that one, Herbert.*

I must have been under Kellogg Boulevard by then, deep underground, where the temperature should have been a constant fifty degrees or so. It felt colder. I remembered Charlie telling me it got too cold in his box for him to stay there all winter, and I wondered if he was confusing the chill in the tunnel with the chill in his soul. This was a place where you could have a lot of chill in your soul.

I was starting to get short of breath from the climb and was about to stop for a bit when I came to another side-tunnel, this time with a definite white arrow pointing into it. I turned into it, sorry to leave the reassuring touch of the steel rail. I was swimming in thick blackness now. I moved forward a bit more slowly, sweeping the flashlight around a lot, pushing one hand out in front of me to grope at nothing. Somewhere up ahead, I could hear the faint gurgle of rushing water. Storm sewer, probably. Not a good thing to walk into.

The passage ended in a great black hole, which I assumed dropped to a main storm sewer line somewhere far below. But before that, there was a slightly wider spot in the floor and a messy campsite. I was there.

As promised so long ago, there was a cardboard box big enough for a person to sleep in, "under the wye-duct." It had a tattered sleeping bag, some clothes, and a few rags in it. They smelled like mildew. In front of the box was a small Coleman camp stove, some assorted full and empty tin cans, a green glass wine jug, and other junk not so easy to identify. Several candles sat in various kinds of holders with wax dribbled all over them. And behind it all, in a niche in the wall, was a box, a heavy white cardboard box of the sort that offices use to archive their paper files. But this one, I positively knew, contained something else. I had found Charlie Victor's frag box.

I lifted the lid and found Addendum Number One to Charlie's last will and testament, sitting on top of a big pile of cash.

Then I heard the noise.

Fire in the Hole

It came from far behind me, echoing back up the unseen rock walls. It wasn't a boom, exactly, but it wasn't a machine noise, either. I went back to the place where my tunnel joined the bigger one, killed the flashlight and looked around the corner. The light at the end of the tunnel, the door opening, tiny as it had been, was gone. What I had heard was somebody slamming the door.

I could hear voices now, too, but not well enough to make out what they were saying. Fairly young voices, male, wise cracking but insistent. The goon squad from the scene at the motel, and this time I had no shotgun to point at them.

And why had they shut the door? *Because they have night vision goggles, and they know you don't, dummy.* Shit.

I ran back to Charlie's squat and put the lid back on his box. Then, as fast as I could, I dug a hole in the soft sand floor with my hands, shoved the box in it, and pulled Charlie's big sleeping-box over the top. Then I scuffled the area where I had dragged it and got the hell out of there. I didn't know what my plan was, but being found at the campsite seemed like a very bad idea.

I went back to the main tunnel, killed my flashlight again, and groped my way across to the steel conveyor frame. As quickly as I could in the dark, I worked my way down into the lower framework and against the back wall. Then I crawled uphill maybe another dozen yards or so, banging various parts of my anatomy on the steel, and finally stuffed myself into a hollow in the limestone wall. I pushed some loose sand into a heap in front of me and settled down to wait. It wasn't much of a hiding place, but it was as good as I could do. I had to count on people not looking too closely into the jumble of angle irons and chains. And if they all went into the campsite cavern, maybe I could slip past them and work my way back outside. Maybe. It would have to do.

The voices began to get louder. I pulled my jacket up over my head, to hide my face and eyes, and worked on quieting my breathing.

Bring back memories, does it?

What?

Detroit, boyo.

Who the hell…?

What, has it been so long that you've forgotten the sound of me lilting voice already?

Jerp?

Himself. How've you been, lad?

This is crazy; you're dead.

Picked right up on that, did you? Of course I'm dead. I couldn't very well be here if I wasn't, now could I?

You're not. You came out of a cup of the Prophet's doped coffee. You're nothing but a piece of abnormal brain chemistry.

I've been called worse, I suppose.

No kidding. Since you're here, though, I'll tell you that I'm sorry I abandoned you in Detroit. I mean, I didn't want to, but you said—

Hush it now, then. I bled to death behind the wheel of the Mercury, is the thing. That's what I did. I didn't burn up. But if we'd ha' gone straight to the hospital, I'd bled to death before we got there, too. The thing of it is, I forgave you before I even drew me last breath. Time you forgave yourself, you hear?

I hear.

It's time and a half, and that's the truth of it. Can you do it?

I have to say, I needed to hear that, Jerp. But yes, I can do it. Two days ago, I'd have said no, but I had a sort of awakening, in an alley up on the Iron Range.

An awakening?

Call it a sea change.

Ah, one of them.

Now it's not only possible, it's easy.

That's the stuff, then.

Thanks.

Don't give it a thought, lad. So how are you getting on here, then?

Here? Not so well.

Not about to join me, are you?

No. I'll die soon enough, like anybody else, but not today and not here. I don't know what I'm going to do, exactly, but I know that much.

Now you're talking, lad.

He sure is.

And just who the hell is this, then?

Jesus, I don't believe this. It's a regular party. That's Charlie. You two have a lot in common; he's dead, too.

I may be dead, Humboldt, but I ain't gone. You want I should take care of those goons for you?

I don't think you can scare them, away, Charlie.

Oh, I can do lots better than that. Sit tight; I think you'll like this.

Sit tight, he says.

You wouldn't happen to have a drop of the pure, in a hip flask or some such, now, would you?

You can't drink; you're dead.

I meant for yourself

Losing my mind is bad enough, Jerp. I don't think I'll add getting drunk.

Suit yourself, lad.

Far down the tunnel, voices that were altogether too real replaced the ones in my head.

"Hey, there's a string going down this one."

"So?"

"So, I bet it's a trail marker."

"Could be. Or it could be a string. Dipshit. Are there any tracks?"

"Hell, this whole place is nothing but tracks. And in the soft sand, you can't tell the old ones from our own."

"What's that smell? Sort of like—"

"Hey, I saw the string jerk!"

"Jesus, me, too! Run it down fast, before our man has a chance to pull it all in!"

"You want me to stay and keep watch in the main tunnel?"

"What for? We know where he is now. Let's move it!"

There were a lot of scuffling noises and some clatter of gear. It and the voices gradually got more muted, until I couldn't make out the words any more, even though they were shouting now. Then for a short while, everything was silent.

And then there was the loudest explosion I have ever heard, accompanied by a flashbulb illumination of the whole place. After half a second or so, there was another, and then a third. Charlie's string had led straight to a whole cluster of booby traps.

Soft dust rained down on me, and for a long time the whole tunnel seemed to ring like a piece of steel on an anvil.

After a while, when I heard nothing more, I went back to Charlie's campsite and made the appropriate adjustments to the box, then put it back where I had first found it. Then I walked back out. The door at the bottom of the tunnel had blown back open, and the draft that I had felt when I first walked in was blowing smoke and dust into the side passage where the explosion had been. I stopped and watched it swirl in the beam of my flashlight for a while, thinking it was beautiful. It looked like deliverance.

Then I was outside, squinting into the daylight. Looking at my watch, I saw that less than an hour had passed since I had first opened Charlie's padlock. Amazing stuff, time. I still had enough of it to brush the dust off myself and maybe get my hearing back to normal. If my hands stopped shaking, that would be nice, too.

I did not hear any more voices from the tunnel, either of soldiers or ghosts.

Shots in the Dark

Anne showed up an hour or so later, just as promised, with a staff photographer, a sort of angular young woman named Chris. She wore jeans and a lumberjack shirt and vest and had a brown ponytail poking out of the back of a baseball cap. She made me think of the skipper of a swordfish boat.

"Anne tells me good things about you," she said as she shook my hand.

"How nice of her. Maybe some time you'll share them with me."

"Maybe not," said Anne. Then she looked at the still-open door to the cavern and gave me an arched eyebrow and a very hard look.

"You said you were going to wait for us, Herman. If the scene isn't original, I can't——"

"I think somebody else got here ahead of us," I said. It wasn't *quite* a lie, but it wasn't really an answer, either.

"You think it's safe to go in?"

"If we're careful. There was an explosion about an hour ago, and nobody has come out since then. I think somebody walked into one of Charlie's booby traps."

"Maybe we should wait for some police or fire people. The Bomb Squad. Chris, do you want a vote?"

"You know me, Anne. If there's a picture in there, I'm going. And if the authorities go in ahead of us, they'll shut us out, for sure." She started fooling with some of the gear that she carried in her vest, which seemed to be all pockets.

"Then we're off," said Anne.

"Just a little," I said, "and it hardly shows."

"Video cam for openers, I think," said Chris. "Mr. Jackson, it would be best if you went first, so there's someone in the picture for scale. Here's an extra battle lantern for you."

She handed me the biggest flashlight I have ever seen, and we set off to find the Wizard.

I was just as glad the others were behind my back, since I couldn't tell how good a job I was doing of pretending I hadn't been there before. When we came to the branch cavern that had smoke and dust still drifting back into it, I explained to them about the string and the white powder.

"Let the Bomb Squad go down that passage," I said. "Later, though. Charlie wanted us to go the other way."

And when we finally came to Charlie's squat, I managed to be as surprised and delighted as everybody else. Chris switched to a digital SLR with a big flash and photographed me pointing at the frag box, then checking the lid for wires or other trip devices, and finally opening it and holding up the hand-written note that was on top of the money, then some of the money itself.

"Do we dare take it outside?" said Chris. "I mean, it could be like a crime scene or something."

"I'll worry about that, if you don't mind." Agent Krause, right on cue.

"Would you identify yourself, for the record?" said Chris, switching back to her video camera and swinging it around.

"I am Special Agent Krause, of the United States Secret Service."

"Nice to meet you. We are—"

"You are the person who is shutting off her camera. This site and that box are evidence in an ongoing official investigation, and they are strictly classified. Shut it off now, unless you want to lose it."

"Nice to see you again, too," I said. "Where's your partner?"

"He's chasing what he foolishly thinks is a hot lead, down in Swede Hollow. Seems he had an anonymous phone call." She went over to the box and peered inside it.

"But you came here instead?" said Anne.

"Apparently my anonymous phone calls are better than his."

Good old Agnes.

Kraus pulled out the note and read it in the light of her own flashlight. She smirked. Seeing her do so, I stifled the urge to follow suit.

"Good stuff, Agent?"

"None of your business, Jackson. Tell you what, though: you can carry it outside for me. We're leaving this place, people. Now. You over there, is your camera off?"

Chris pointed it at her and said, "The little red light is off. See?"

I thought the little red light looked as if it had a piece of black electrical tape over it, but I saw no reason to tell Krause that.

"Let's go," said Krause.

And we did. I led the parade back to the real world, carrying the frag box, with Agent Smug close behind and Chris and Anne bringing up the rear. About halfway back, there was another problem with the light at the end of the tunnel. It didn't get shut this time, but somebody stepped in front of it. I recognized the silhouette of the man I now knew to be Sergeant Major Robert Dunne. He had his phony cop uniform on again, and both it and he were looking burnt and bloodied.

You think you used enough explosive, Charlie?

There didn't seem to be anything wrong with the submachine gun Dunne was holding, though.

There was no way I could jump out of his field of fire, so I did what I hoped was the next best thing: I shone my light in his face and tried to close the distance between us. I didn't get very far.

"Point that light someplace else, or I'll blow you and it both to hell."

I pointed the light at the floor. Behind me, Krause did the same. But she, too, was moving up.

"I thought I told you to shut your operation down and get out of town," said Krause.

"As a matter of fact, Agent, you did not. In your typical arrogant manner, you ordered us to take our operation out of the public eye, quote-unquote. And I would say this is about as far out of it as we could get. I believe you're holding what I came here for, Jackson. Bring it here. Krause, you stay where you are."

"Where's the Colonel?" I said.

"Say again?"

"Colonel Rappolt, your boss."

"You know about him, do you? Impressive, for a dipshit civilian. But you obviously don't know much about the Army."

"How's that?"

"Colonels do not go on treasure hunting ops. And they do not do their own killing. He watched it, but he didn't get any licks in. He just spat on the guy afterward. And once the bum was dead, the colonel was done with it all. He didn't care about the box the guy told us about when we were beating on him. But I do. I just lost four good men looking for it. So give it up, now, and don't get cute."

"Me? I wouldn't think of it." I took a last step toward him and pretended to trip on a conveyor frame, dropping the box and falling on top of it. I was hoping to make a play for his gun, but Krause was too fast for me. The momentary distraction was all she needed to get her skinny automatic out of its secret hiding place and put about a dozen rounds into the sergeant major. Personally, I thought she was overreacting, but I can't honestly say I didn't approve.

I did wonder, though, if I would ever get my hearing back again.

Aftershock

When we got back out to the daylight, Anne called 911 before Krause could think to tell her not to. Soon we had a mob of police and fire people to contend with, including the Bomb Squad and a crime scene team. I even got to meet the elusive homicide cop, Detective Erickson, who turned out to be a fairly likeable guy. He and Krause were old buddies, it seemed, and he did nothing to stop her from leaving with Charlie's box. She also got to keep her weapon, and she confiscated the memory card from Chris' video cam.

"How can they do that?" said Chris.

"It's evidence in a conspiracy case," I said. "The Secret Service has had the power to seize that for as long as there has been a Secret Service."

"I bet we never see any of it again," she said.

"She promised I could have the money back, as soon as it's done being evidence," I said, "since I'm Charlie's legal heir."

"What will that be, a year or two?" said Anne.

"If ever," I said, thinking about the black hole that Krause had threatened to have me thrown into. Other things could be thrown into it, too. "And even if I get the money back, I'd bet the video and the note are permanently gone."

"Good thing nobody thought to take the memory card out of my SLR."

"Don't say that too loud," I said, "until we get clear of this place."

◇◇◇

Eventually we did get clear, finally running out of people who wanted to debrief and/or intimidate us. We all went down to Lefty's then, to do a bit of debriefing of our own. Anne stopped by her office on the way and got a laptop, and soon we were looking at an enlargement of the paper from Charlie's box. Chris had done a perfect job of shooting it. It was written on the back of a copy of Charlie's will, with some kind of fairly blunt felt-tip pen, printed all in caps.

DEAR HOBART

I ALWAYS KNEW YOU WOULD BE THE ONE WHO WOULD FIND THIS. THERE ISNT ENOUGH HERE TO BUY THE HIT ON THE PRESIDENT, BUT TAKE IT TO THIS GUY CALLS HIMSELF HOOK AND SEE WILL HE MAYBE DO IT ANYWAY CONSIDERING HOW THINGS WORKED OUT. YOULL FIND HIM AT THE ST. PAUL HOTEL UNDER THE NAME OF EDDIE BARDOT. HE MIGHT HAVE A COUPLA OTHER NAMES TOO. I COPPED SOME OF HIS CREDIT CARDS SO YOU CAN SEE THE OTHERS. THANKS FOR EVERYTHING

YOUR FRIEND CHARLIE VICTOR

"Who's Hobart?" said Chris.

"That's me," I said. "Charlie always called me something that started with H and had two syllables, but that's as close as he ever came to remembering my real name."

"How much money was there in the box?"

"I didn't have time to count it, but I thought it looked like about five thousand."

"And who's this Bardot person?"

"Who knows?" I shrugged. "Maybe a real assassin, maybe just a con artist. Krause won't care."

"So that's it, then," said Anne. "Agent Krause gets her big bust—"

"She could use one," said Chris.

"Oh, nasty," I said. "Correct, but nasty."

"She gets her big *collar*," said Anne, "and the guys who killed Charlie are all dead."

"Except for Rappolt," I said.

"Oh, yes. Him. Did you mention him to the police?"

"No. I figured there was no point. He's back in wherever he's officially supposed to be by now, with a ton of plausible deniability in front of him. And no way the Army investigates a full colonel on the say so of a mere civilian."

"You're probably right. I don't have enough hard data to use him in my write-up, so how much less is anybody in authority going to pursue it? Oh, well."

"I trust it's a usable story anyway?"

"Oh, it's a hell of a story, Herman."

Anne's story ran two days later. The Secret Service, of course, pressured her editor about the need for secrecy in the assassination case, and he partially agreed. She was not allowed to say anything about the hit man named in the note, nor about any hit man, period. She was allowed to tell about the tunnel and the box, but only as a secret stash of money from unknown sources.

But that was enough. She wrote a very solid piece about Charlie's and his father's murders and their connection to the Vietnam War. It had sensational crime reporting, human interest, history, and just a hint of conspiracy, and it ran on the front page. She also did a sidebar on the lives of homeless people, with a picture of Glenda. That ran in an interior section of the same issue. She wanted to do another one on the abuses of power by the Department of Homeland Security, if only to get back at Agent Krause for stealing her video, but her editor wouldn't buy it.

We celebrated the printing by going out to dinner at a sports bar that superficially resembled the dance hall in Eveleth. They didn't have a band, though. For dancing and other activity, we had to go back to my townhouse. Later, we sat on the big couch in front of the fireplace, watching the gas log pretend to burn itself up and working on a bottle of my best Scotch.

"Seems like it was a long way for you to go, just for a story in one issue of the newspaper," I said.

"Sometimes it happens that way."

"Was it worth it?"

"False modesty does not become you, Jackson. What you mean is were *you* worth it. I shouldn't have to tell you so, but yes. But the story? Of course it was. There's always a bit of a letdown after a big story, though. It feels as if you never really quite knew as much as you would have liked before you wrote it."

"Maybe you'd have written it the same way anyway."

"Maybe. I'll never know. The thing about Rappolt bothers me."

"You mean that you couldn't include him in the piece?"

"No, that he gets off scot-free and nobody can do a thing about it. Doesn't that bother you?"

"Actually, he didn't quite get off. I had my hacker friend send an email to him, with a cc to his superior, telling him that his operation is blown and all his people dead."

"So, what will happen?"

"I don't know. His hometown is Kansas City. I thought I'd watch the local newspaper for a while at the Central Library, see if there's anything about him."

"You can do that online, you know."

"You can do a lot of things online, Anne, but that doesn't necessarily make them any better. I like tactile events. I like touching something besides a mouse."

"I noticed." She gave me a sly smile.

"Is that a complaint?"

"Not on your life."

"Anyway, whatever happens with Rappolt, Charlie wouldn't have cared, one way or the other."

"How can you be so sure of that?"

I let out a huge sigh, took my arm back from where it had been wrapped around her shoulders, and stood up. I had just made a very risky decision, one that was most unlike me.

"I'm about to give you a gift, Anne. It's a hell of a gift, and I'm betting a lot on your not taking advantage of it."

"You're talking like a soap opera, Herman. What are you giving me that is so precious?"

"The truth."

I went to my desk in the corner of the dining room, unlocked the center drawer, and took out a stained and crumpled sheet of paper. As I handed it to her, I said, "This is what was really on top of the money in Charlie's box."

"What was *really* there? But how could you have changed it? I mean, I saw you pick the other one up."

"A lot of things are possible in a dark tunnel, Anne. Did you wonder at all why Charlie would have written the note on the back of a copy of his will?"

"I guess I didn't think about it. Maybe that was the only paper he had."

"Wrong. It was the only paper *I* had with *his* fingerprints on it. So that's what I had to use for the forgery. This, however, is the McCoy."

She put down her glass of Scotch and read:

Dear Hubert,

I figured you would find this if anybody could. That's why I wrote that will. Once, I would have told you to take the money and use it to kill some people. A whole list of them. But I finally lived long enough to learn some things. I learned that blood feuds are no damn good. And I learned that the way that you stop them is just to stop.

I'm sick of the killing and the planning to kill and the hate. I want it to end with me. So take the money and do something good with it, okay? Maybe you can buy a bond for some homeless person.

That's a joke.

Thanks for all your help over the years. I'm proud to have known you.

Your dead friend,

Charlie

◇◇◇

"You're right," she said. "He wouldn't have cared about Rappolt. In fact, it sounds as if he knew about him and still didn't care."

"And by not caring, he may have finally found his way out of the jungle."

"That's nice, Herman. I wish I could write it. What are you going to do with the money, assuming you ever get it back?"

"Actually, I didn't wait. I gave a free bond to a guy named Vitrol Wilson, who is a guaranteed skip. The question is what are you going to do with that piece of paper?"

She looked at it again. Then she got up, walked across the room, and threw it into the fire.

"Would you like to dance, Herman?"

"I'd love to."

◇◇◇

The next day we held a memorial service for Charlie, down in Connemara Gulch. As his only heir, I had donated his remains to the med school at the University of Minnesota, but we solemnly buried his fatigue jacket and dog tags in a place by some small trees and marked the spot with a cross of baking powder. It took a while for the word to spread, but we eventually drew about twenty raggedy people for the event.

I had brought six bottles of wine with screw tops and a huge bag of White Castle hamburgers, but nobody was allowed to have anything without first standing over the grave and saying a few words. Some of them were actually quite moving. Apparently Charlie was well liked, even though he himself never admitted to liking anybody. The guy named Mingus, whose neck I had stood on only a few nights earlier, produced a harmonica and played "Amazing Grace" while each of the homeless people threw a handful of dirt into the hole and said "ashes to ashes," or something like that. One of them actually knew the Twenty-third Psalm, which he recited with some passion. One said, "Home is the soldier, home from the sea," and then got a look of major confusion and consternation. Another said, "There's a lot more of us laying down than there is up a-walking around." I shot him a quick glance to see if it might have been the Prophet.

Anne, true to her word, had brought a dozen copies of the newspaper with Glenda's picture in it. She gave them to her and showed her where to find the article.

As she looked at it, her eyes started to tear up.

"That ain't me! Why you printing somebody else's picture with my name? Dear, sweet suffering Jesus, I don't look like that!"

She looked again, squinting. "I don't, do I?"

"I'm sorry, Glenda. I thought you'd be happy to see—"

"Oh my God. I was never really beautiful, but I was at least… My God amighty. Where the hell have I got to?"

The tears were streaming freely down her face now, and soon her body was racked with sobs. Mingus put his harmonica back in his pocket and opened a bottle for her.

"Here you go, babe. Have a drink and forget about it."

She looked at the extended bottle for a long time, her crying subsiding a bit. Finally she said, "I don't think so."

"Sure, you do. It'll make everything okay. Don't it always?"

"I gotta go," was all she said, shaking her head vehemently. She gathered up her newspapers, clutched them to her bosom, and walked away.

I guessed it was a day for atonement and rebirth. I hoped so, anyway.

Epilogue

With Eddie Bardot snatched off the street, Wilkie was able to persuade Frank Russo to come back for his trial, after all. So the twenty-five thou I had taken out of Charlie's box, the first time I was in the tunnel, was pure gravy. I was back to playing with the house money. I gave Agnes her back pay and a week in advance for good measure. I didn't have the five K that the feds took, of course, but that was okay. They left town with Eddie in cuffs, just as happy as if they had good sense. He, presumably, was not so happy, and that was worth something to me.

Not long after that, there was an obituary in the *Kansas City Star* for a Colonel John Rappolt. Apparently he had done what a lot of self-important career officers do when they see their entire world fall apart. He had shot himself. So even though Charlie said he didn't care, I figured that all the shadows from his personal jungle were finally gone.

I wasn't sure if mine were, though, and I needed a detached, third party perspective to straighten out the issue. One morning, I headed north out of the Twin Cities, then crossed the St. Croix River into Wisconsin and went east on Highway Eight, across the recently harvested farmlands and into the brown and black late autumn countryside. I was going to a place that I visit seldom but think about often, all the way across Wisconsin and into Upper Michigan. Redrock Prison is its name, and it was where my uncle Fred was doing his fourth term for bookmaking.

After the usual pleasantries, I told him all about Charlie and his box and how I wasn't sure I had done enough truly to lay him to rest.

"Lemmie tell you a story, nephew," he said.

"Okay."

"Back about forty years ago, there was this guy, name of Eddie Feigner, was the fast-pitch king of softball. He could throw a softball, underhand, a hundred and twenty miles an hour, so fast the ref couldn't even see it. He was just the pure stuff, couldn't be beat."

"He was too good to play with any regular team, so he used to play traveling exhibition games, like the Harlem Globetrotters did in basketball. He traveled with just three other guys, a catcher and two fielders. They didn't need any basemen, see, 'cause Eddie would strike everybody out, but they had to have four men on the team so they had enough people to bat with the bases full. They called themselves 'The King and his Court.'"

"I seem to vaguely remember something about them."

"Yeah, I think I might have taken you to a game once when you were little. Okay, so anyway, here's our boy, at the end of the ninth inning in some nowhere little town. He's up by one run and there's two men out and he's got two strikes on the last batter. But he don't throw the ball. Instead, he's pacing around on the mound, looking worried. So the catcher goes out to talk to him.

"'Hey, man,' he says, 'we're one pitch away from winning this thing. Throw it, already.'

"'I gotta tell you,' Feigner says, 'I ain't got nothing left. My arm is shot. I'm not sure I can even get the ball to the plate, much less throw a strike. I think we gotta concede the game.'

"So the catcher thinks for a while and comes up with a plan. 'Gimmie the ball now,' he says, 'and I'll hide it under my chest protector. Then I'll go back to home plate and you pretend to throw the ball, like always. I'll whack the ball into my glove like I just caught it, and we'll see what the ump says.'

"So that's what they do. Feigner fakes throwing the pitch, the catcher fakes catching it, and the ump yells, 'Stee-rike! Yer outta here!'

"And all of a sudden, all hell breaks loose at home plate. The batter is screaming at the ump and kicking dirt on his shoes and the ump is pushing him with his chest and they're both gesturing with their hands and getting red in the face. The catcher wants nothing to do with any of that, so he walks away and goes back out to the pitching mound.

"'What's going on?' says Feigner.

"'Ah, you know,' says the catcher. 'Same old, same old. The batter thinks it was low and outside.'"

I laughed. "Cute, Unc, but what's the point?"

"It's not done yet, okay?"

"Sorry."

"So a year or so later, they're playing the same team again, and the same batter comes up in the bottom of the ninth. This time Feigner's arm is fine, but he throws the guy four balls, walks him. So the catcher goes out to the mound.

"'What the hell are you doing?' he says.

"'Paying for my sins,' says Feigner.

"'Yeah? Gee, Eddie, that's really nice. That's a fine thing to do.'

"'Thank you,' says Eddie.

"'You're welcome. Don't do it anymore.'

"And he didn't."

And neither did I.

Author's Notes

Minnesotans will be quick to note that I have taken some liberties with both time and place settings. Most of the Saint Paul settings are real, including the abandoned tunnel under Kellogg Park, but anybody trying to locate Lefty's Pool Hall or Nickel Pete's pawnshop will find himself on a fool's errand. The Ramsey County Jail moved from its location on the Mississippi River bluff several years ago, but in Herman Jackson's world, it is still there and always will be. It lets him keep his office downtown. The Iron Range is largely the way it was fifteen years ago, when I used to spend a fair amount of time there. Today, there is almost no trace of the original town of Mountain Iron. The bus station in Eveleth is a real historic reference, though it, too, is now gone. I got off at that station once in May, and the piles of plowed snow were still higher than the parked cars. The VFW bar is pure fabrication.

With history, I have been more scrupulous. The events that triggered the 1967 race riots in Detroit are well documented, and I have not altered them. My scenes in Vietnam are largely composites of the many stories told to me over the years by coworkers or classmates who were there.

The characters, of course, are another matter. If they bear any resemblance to anyone living or dead, it is a matter of pure coincidence, and nobody would be more astonished to discover it than I.

TRUANCY
ORIGINS

TRUANCY
ORIGINS

ISAMU FUKUI

A Tom Doherty Associates Book
New York

TOR®

This is a work of fiction. All of the characters, organizations, and events portrayed
in this novel are either products of the author's imagination or are used fictitiously.

TRUANCY ORIGINS

A Tor Teen Book
Published by Tom Doherty Associates, LLC
175 Fifth Avenue
New York, NY 10010

www.tor-forge.com

Tor® is a registered trademark of Tom Doherty Associates, LLC.

Library of Congress Cataloging-in-Publication Data

Fukui, Isamu, 1990–
    Truancy origins / Isamu Fukui.—1st ed.
        p. cm.
    Prequel to: Truancy.
    Summary: Relates how Truancy, an underground movement determined to
bring down the Mayor's goal of control through education, began with the birth of
twin boys who grew up to take divergent paths after being adopted by the Mayor.
    ISBN-13: 978-0-7653-2262-3
    ISBN-10: 0-7653-2262-5
    [1. Brothers—Fiction. 2. Twins—Fiction. 3. Totalitarianism—Fiction. 4.
Education—Fiction. 5. Counterculture—Fiction. 6. Fantasy. 7. Youths' writings.]
I. Title.
    PZ7.F951538Tt 2009
    [Fic]—dc22

                                                                            2008035627

First Edition: March 2009

Printed in the United States of America

0 9 8 7 6 5 4 3 2 1

I dedicate this story
To Francis Yuan
For being my friend
Through all the times
When no one else would

CONTENTS

TRUANCY ORIGINS

PROLOGUE ··· SIBLING RIVALRY

The Mayor spared a glance out the window of his office. It was night now, but the lights of the City never died, defying the dark skies with their persistent glow. *Night.* City nights were usually chilly. The Mayor, who detested humidity and heat, always welcomed the nights. For good measure he also kept his office air-conditioned to the point where the air felt stale and metallic—but *cool,* at the very least.

So where is this damn sweat coming from?

Frustrated, the Mayor reached up to his forehead and wiped off the glittering drops that had accumulated there. He clenched his palms, only to realize that they were shaking. Mentally steadying himself, the Mayor prayed that the dim lighting would be enough to conceal his perspiration from the small, gray eyes that faced him. The eyes silently observed his every move, and as they did, the Mayor felt a strange, unfamiliar feeling in his gut. The Mayor grimaced. It was almost as if . . .

And then it hit him. The sweat, the shaking, the feeling—could it be *fear?*

The Mayor had not been accustomed to fear for many years, not since he had begun governing what he had always thought of as *his* City. But now those cold, unblinking eyes served as a reminder that it was not his City after all, that there were people out there to whom he was just a pawn.

Taking a deep breath, the Mayor laid his folded hands down upon his desk. Across the polished wooden surface, in spite of the dim light, the watchful eyes glittered, and the Mayor recognized both intelligence and menace in their sharp gaze. For several minutes, the room remained completely silent, save for the low, consistent hum of the air conditioner. No words were said, and yet the silence managed to convey a clear message. The Mayor knew that he was not in charge here, not now.

It was astounding, the Mayor thought bitterly, that an eight-year-old girl could exert such a presence.

"I hope you don't mind me saying that your visit, pleasant though it is, was . . . unanticipated," the Mayor said, choosing his words cautiously. "I had not heard that your father was sending his daughter on city inspections. In fact, I must confess that I didn't know the government had been conducting any city inspections at all lately."

The girl's gaze intensified at the breaking of the silence, but the Mayor was confident that he had chosen the right words. There was nothing malicious in that gray stare. Not yet at least.

"My father has no illusions about my capabilities, and he believes that it's best for me to expand them through firsthand experience," the girl replied, her voice as slick as oil. "But I'm afraid that you have misjudged my purpose here, Mr. Mayor. This is not an inspection—we are quite aware of how well your city has performed. I might go so far as to say that your work has been exemplary."

The Mayor did not acknowledge the proffered compliment, though his eyes narrowed. He hadn't really thought that it was an inspection, but if it wasn't a reprimand either, what could it possibly be? There was something odd going on here, the Mayor knew, and it filled him with that unpleasant sensation that he now associated with fear.

"As you know, we like to protect experimental cities like yours from exposure to potentially contaminating influences," the child continued. "That is why we have not formally conducted inspections for years now. As far as your citizens know, your small operation is the *only* government they are subject to, and we'd prefer it stay that way. But we do appreciate your success—it has been thoroughly documented by our agents in the populace."

The Mayor leaned back in his chair in an attempt to appear relaxed, even as a few more beads of sweat trickled down the back of his neck.

"Then why are you here?" the Mayor asked bluntly.

"My father has sent me as a courier, Mr. Mayor. I'm here to drop off a . . . sensitive package," the girl replied, and the Mayor reflexively drew back as he saw something unsettling stir across the child's features. "I know of your reputation for respecting secrecy, so I believe it safe to tell you that my father has recently sired two sons. Twins."

The Mayor forced a smile to conceal his dismay. If these new brats ended up anything like their older sibling, it could only mean more trouble for him and his City.

"You must convey my sincere congratulations to your father. I couldn't be happier for him," the Mayor lied.

The atmosphere of the room abruptly changed. The girl's head snapped forward, her face contorting as her small hands gripped the armrests of her chair so tightly that her knuckles turned white. The Mayor instinctively re-coiled, and a stir at the far end of the room reminded him that the girl's bodyguards were present, prepared to kill at the child's command.

"The twins are illegitimate," the girl snarled. "They have no father."

The Mayor was taken aback as the girl's composure suddenly slipped, malice echoing in her voice, fury clearly etched on her young face. In that one moment of shock, the Mayor briefly wondered how anyone could possibly be so serene one moment and so feral the next. But as swiftly as the outburst had come, it had gone, and the child was again calmly collected, staring at the Mayor with those stormy eyes, her voice as cold and as smooth as ice.

"Unfortunately, my father and I have had a disagreement about the infants. He has refused to . . . properly dispose of them." The girl's eyes glinted. "After some . . . debate . . . it was decided that it would be best to entrust the children to the care of another."

Upon hearing those words, the Mayor felt a sudden wave of panic threatening to overwhelm him. He was not a stupid man; he knew where this was going, and he *definitely* did not like it one bit. Grinding his teeth together, the Mayor waited as the girl continued.

"The children need to live comfortably. They also need to be kept from causing trouble. And who could possibly be better suited for both tasks"— the girl smiled faintly—"than the Mayor of the Education City, whose system has never failed to control a child?"

The Mayor blanched, his calm façade in ruins.

"If I may—" the Mayor began hoarsely.

"I'm afraid that you may *not*," the child interrupted as she drew two rectangular pieces of plastic out of her pocket and placed them on the Mayor's desk. "You needn't worry about finances. My father has set aside a generous amount of funds for their personal use. These cards will grant access to accounts containing one hundred million each in government currency. Two hundred million in total. It's enough to maintain a small army, and should be more than enough to assure that they will live comfortably."

"Money is not an issue . . ." the Mayor began to protest.

"Then there should be no problem," the child said. "The decision is final. You will find these . . . orphans . . . outside in the hallway. You will adopt them and raise them. You are expected only to keep them in good health, out of the way, and, most important, out of trouble." The girl smirked now as she rose from her chair. "Allow me to convey my sincere congratulations to *you*, Father."

Before the Mayor could renew his protests, the girl had already turned her back to him and begun walking away. As the girl reached the door to the Mayor's office, she was flanked and then followed by the two armed bodyguards that, up until that point, had been doing their most convincing impersonation of statues. The Mayor watched their shadows recede out of sight through the open door, dazedly wondering how he had been left speechless by a child barely taller than his own desk.

For one suspended moment, the Mayor remained motionless in his padded armchair, wishing that he could sink into the soft folds of leather to escape the troubles that had so suddenly been foisted upon him. But before he could convince himself that the girl's visit had been a bad dream, a shrill, wailing cry from the hallway cut through the chilled air of his office. Unmistakably the cry of a baby.

The Mayor forced himself out of his seat, and, in an almost dreamlike stupor, stumbled over to the doorway. Blinking as his eyes adjusted to the brighter light of the hallway, he found that the shrill wail doubled in volume. The Mayor forced himself to stand straight. Then he saw it—the source of the cries, a crib resting in the hallway, containing two infants that looked to be about six months old. The noise came solely from a baby lying on his back, bawling as loud as his little lungs could manage. The other child, in stark contrast, was completely silent, but not at all inactive. He was crawling around the edges of the crib, exploring the bars with his fingers, and occasionally reaching outside them with tiny arms as if by doing so he might escape.

The Mayor found himself inexplicably awestruck by the sight, so much so that he barely heard the cries of the first baby. Then he was snapped out of his reverie by the rough sound of the clearing of a throat. The Mayor looked up, and was surprised to see the girl and her bodyguards still standing at the far end of the hallway, watching him strangely.

"I trust that everything is in order?" the girl called over the cries, dislike visible on her face even at a distance.

The Mayor didn't answer, but instead looked up at the girl's purely light complexion, and then down at the babies, who clearly had a yellow tinge to their skin.

"What are their names?" the Mayor suddenly demanded. "Tell me their names!"

At this, the girl slowly approached the Mayor, still flanked by her bodyguards. No longer caring if he was in any bodily danger, the Mayor patiently waited until the eight-year-old stood right under him, exactly level with the Mayor's waist.

"Their mother named them," the girl explained, gesturing towards the crib. "The noisy boy is Umasi. The restless one is Zen."

With that, the girl spun around and walked away as though she had just completed a casual errand. The Mayor didn't know whether or not he would ever see the girl again, but in that instant he swore to himself that he would do everything within his power to make sure that the children called Zen and Umasi would never meet their half-sister. He looked down at the crib again, and for an instant was unpleasantly surprised to find the child named Zen staring up at him with dark eyes that already seemed to be assessing, analyzing, sizing him up. The infant's stare reminded the Mayor altogether too much of the vicious gaze of his older sibling. Rattled, the Mayor looked instead at Umasi, who was still crying loudly. Gingerly, the Mayor picked Umasi up and cradled him in his arms as best he could. Almost instantly, the wailing subsided, and the Mayor found another pair of dark eyes looking up at him curiously, and in them the Mayor saw intelligence, yes, but also innocence that sparkled so clearly that it was unmistakable.

The Mayor swayed his arms, rocking Umasi to sleep. As he did so, he couldn't help but notice Zen's eyes tracking his twin's every movement. Only when Umasi had finally fallen asleep and been placed back in the cradle did Zen stir, crawling back to his brother's side, where he also promptly fell asleep.

Maybe this wouldn't be so unpleasant after all, the Mayor thought as he watched the sleeping babies. But already guilt encroached upon his conscience. These children would have to be put through school. The City's schools. Schools meant to ensnare the children of others would now be used on his own. If he could, he would have saved them from that hell of his own design.

But that was impossible. Education in this City was absolute.

"Forgive me, you two, for what I'll do to you," the Mayor murmured quietly. "You will suffer, but it'll be for your own good."

On that day, the City's schools had all reported perfect attendance. It was a day when the City knew no truancy. But that night, the Mayor willingly accepted two unfamiliar children as his own, and welcomed them into his City, a City that he also valued as his child. He had no way of knowing that in that crib slept the inevitable undoing of his City.

When death lies ahead . . .

. . . it's natural to look back.

You looked . . .

. . . didn't you?

Yes. Yes I did.

So did I.

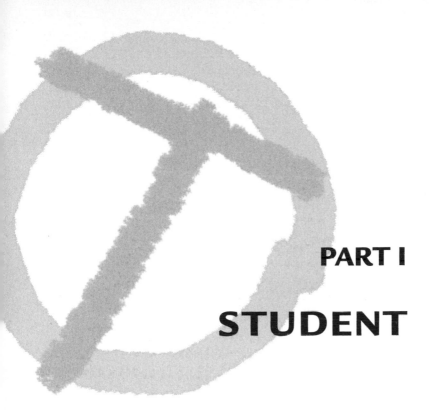

PART I

STUDENT

1
FILIAL PIETY

T he fifteen-year-old boy slowly turned a page of his textbook, relishing the crisp sound of the shifting paper. He had never really liked social studies, though this passage on the subject was not actually an uninteresting one. The topic was agriculture, something that one did not often observe within the City. The student couldn't help but find something whimsical about the idea of vast spaces with no buildings and few people. Small garden terraces were one thing, but large areas that existed solely only to grow plants? It was an alien notion, though obviously a necessary one; after all, the City had to get its food from somewhere.

The boy absentmindedly took a sip from his bottle of lemonade and sloshed it about in his mouth. Produce imports into the City had increased by five percent in one particular year . . . grain shortages had occurred on three separate occasions due to rural drought . . . the City had once issued migration permits allowing select citizens to move out onto outlying farmlands . . . that program had been canned the next year owing to an excess of volunteers, and the existing volunteers were forbidden to return. The boy inscribed notes on all of it into his binder mechanically, sipping his lemonade as he went.

He paused only once, taking the opportunity to zip up his jacket and adjust his glasses. Chilly winds had begun making their way through the concrete ravines of the City, and the student was seated outdoors, upon a backless bench in his school courtyard. Thumbing down the pages of his book to prevent the wind from ruffling them, he watched idly for a moment as leaves flew by in a flurry of ruby and gold. He had always been fond of the fall season, as it was rarely ever hot or cold enough to be truly uncomfortable.

Satisfied with his fleeting break, the student returned to his textbook, taking another swig of lemonade as he did so. The chapter he was reading hadn't been assigned by his teacher yet, but he found that working ahead of the class schedule often paid off. Besides, he never did have anything better to do during his free periods.

The boy was soon completely immersed in the text, lost among the figures, statistics, and historical minutiae. He became so focused on the reading, in fact, that he didn't notice the sound of running footsteps behind him . . . until one of the feet connected squarely with his back.

The boy was flung forward, landing face-first on the hard ground. His textbook and binder landed in shambles to his left; his bottle of lemonade flew to the right and came to rest in a large, sticky puddle of its own contents. The shock disoriented him. His glasses flew several feet away, leaving him with a blurred perception of the world. Even so, he knew what was coming next, and instinctively tried to lift himself off the ground. A hard kick to his ribs floored him again, leaving him to clutch his side in pain. Before he could attempt any other movements, a heavy boot came to rest atop his head. It wasn't applying much pressure yet, but the message was clear, and the boy remained still.

"Hey guys, looks like we've found ourselves one of the princes of the City!"

"Which one is it? They look the same to me."

"Don't be stupid, this one has short hair and glasses," a third voice snarled, this one belonging to the owner of the offending boot. "It's obviously Umasi."

"Not Zen," the first voice said, disappointed.

"No, not Zen," the owner of the boot agreed. "But I can't say that I like this one much either. He's a real teacher's pet. Always sucking up in class. Isn't that right, Umasi?"

Umasi realized that there was no right answer to the question and opted to remain silent. But even as he clamped his mouth shut, he could feel anger bubbling up inside him. It was not a rational, focused anger, but more of a general fury that he knew could prove more harmful to himself than to his assailants. Umasi forced himself to be calm, even as his silence prompted the owner of the boot to remove it from his head and instead seize a fistful of Umasi's hair.

"Your brother's got quite an attitude, you know that?" the boy said as he yanked Umasi upright. "Thinking he can run around like he owns the school and everyone in it, just 'cause his daddy's the Mayor. What about you? Does it run in the family?"

Umasi shook his head stiffly, his teeth grinding against each other behind sealed lips. Tears of shock and anger ran down his face, mingling with the dirt that had rubbed onto him from the ground. This reaction produced hearty laughter from the trio.

"Aww, you made the baby cry!"

"Anyone got some tissues?"

"I think he's had enough," the third bully said. "I'm done wasting time here. Let's let him off easy this time."

Without waiting for a response from his cohorts, the brute roughly shoved Umasi to the ground again, holding his head right above the newly formed puddle of lemonade.

"You like that stuff so much, why don't you have some more?" the boy suggested. "Lick it up. We just want you to drink a tiny bit, and we'll let you go."

Umasi remained silent, but didn't move. As hard as he tried, he couldn't act rationally. Just a drop of the lemonade, dirty though it might be, wouldn't do him much harm, and would save him a world of trouble. But what was left of his pride and dignity wouldn't allow him to do it, and with the idea of fighting back being so obviously suicidal, Umasi was paralyzed with indecision for several agonizing moments.

"Come on, do it!" the boy ordered again impatiently.

Slowly, hesitantly, Umasi lowered his head as the boys jeered behind him. He halted just above the puddle, breathing deeply to steady his nerves, fighting one last battle with himself. But he would never know what the results of that struggle might have been, for another voice chose that moment to make its presence known.

"Excuse me, gentlemen, but it appears as though you've confused me with my brother over there."

The three bullies spun around, instantly forgetting all about Umasi. Sitting up shakily, Umasi turned around as well, to see the three boys staring almost dumbstruck at a fourth. The new center of attention wore a black windbreaker jacket over his gray school uniform, with matching black boots and a backpack slung over one shoulder. His sleek, dark hair was tied back into a simple ponytail, and his cold, intimidating gaze radiated both strength and menace.

For a fleeting second Umasi saw fear on the faces of his tormentors, but it swiftly passed, replaced by dogged determination.

"Zen," the first boy spat.

"Correct," Zen agreed, leaning against the brick wall behind him.

"Still growing out that girl's hair?" the second boy jeered.

"That would seem to be the case, wouldn't it?" Zen replied, his glinting eyes surveying each one of them thoroughly.

"There's three of us this time," the third boy warned. "Think you can take all of us at once?"

"Probably," Zen said, his gaze coming to rest upon the first boy, who reflexively took a step back. "But the real question is 'Are you brave enough to find out?'"

There was a moment of silence, as all three of the bullies faced the same indecision that Umasi had experienced moments before. On one hand, Zen had made a challenge that couldn't be ignored. On the other, each of them had experienced humiliating defeat at his hands before. But with them outnumbering him three to one, there was no way for them to back down without losing face. Almost simultaneously, the three boys reached the same decision and lunged forward from all sides, charging Zen with arms outstretched.

Theirs would prove to be a very painful mistake.

Zen shed his backpack and smoothly ducked the first boy's assault from the left. He then stepped forward, bringing his fist arcing upwards into the boy's belly, the whole motion taking less time than it took his backpack to hit the ground. The impact of the punch was tremendous, and the hapless boy made a noise halfway between a whimper and a wheeze, followed by a gurgling sound as Zen jabbed at his throat, cleanly tipping him backwards like a domino.

Zen was still in motion and changing targets even as the first boy fell. Deftly seizing the second boy's oncoming arm to deflect the blow, Zen grasped the boy's shoulder and yanked, using the boy's own momentum to send him crashing right into the brick wall. The last boy was more cautious, pausing a few feet in front of Zen before attempting an ungainly kick. Zen grabbed the boy's leg and kicked the other out from under him. The boy, finding it suddenly impossible to stand, fell onto his back. Hard.

Seeing that the first boy was showing signs of stirring, Zen seized the opportunity to deliver a swift kick to his ribs, insuring that he wouldn't be reentering the fight anytime soon. By that time, however, the second boy had already risen from the ground, blood dripping from his nose. Letting out a roar of rage, the boy charged forwards, quickly but clumsily. Zen remained still until the last moment. Then he sidestepped, catching the boy's leg with his foot and delivering a blow to the boy's back with his elbow. The boy dropped to the ground face-first. This time he did not get up.

By now the third boy had also risen, and attempted to attack Zen with a running kick while his back was turned. Hearing the boy's footsteps, Zen gracefully spun aside, swinging his arm around in an arc as the boy's leg lashed out. The boy was already unbalanced, and as Zen's palm came into contact with the boy's head, Zen was able to comically swat him aside. The boy fell sideways, landing humiliatingly in the sticky puddle of lemonade.

"You might want to dry that off before your next class," Zen suggested as he passed by his soaked victim. "You know what the teachers say about bringing drinks into the classroom."

The dripping boy did not respond, but rather sputtered and swore loudly as he rolled over and out of the puddle before coming to a rest, his chest heaving. Meanwhile, Umasi found that he could do nothing but sit there as Zen approached him, the three groaning boys strewn over the ground behind him like fallen leaves. A sudden breeze kicked up, sending the actual leaves flying forward like confetti, the brilliant colors streaming all around Zen.

In that moment, Umasi thought that it was the most impressive thing he had ever seen in his life.

Zen wasn't even breathing hard. He scooped up Umasi's glasses, then calmly pulled Umasi up, dusting his brother's clothes off in the process.

"So, how're you doing?" Zen inquired as Umasi wiped his eyes and face with his sleeve.

"I'm—"

"Minor scratches to the face, dirt everywhere, maybe some slight bruising if you're unlucky, and, judging by how you keep clutching them like that, some sore ribs," Zen observed, handing Umasi his glasses. "All things considered, you're fine, and lucky. Those fools back there don't have the guts or the ability to do anyone serious damage."

"Did . . . did you do *them* any serious damage?" Umasi asked tentatively as he slid his glasses on to look over Zen's shoulder at the three motionless boys.

"Nothing that a trip to the school nurse can't cure," Zen replied. "One of them has a bloody nose, and that's probably the worst of it. I do imagine that their egos have taken a blow, however."

"Aren't you worried that they might tell on you?"

"They might," Zen said. "Not that I would particularly care. But frankly, I doubt that they would."

"Why's that?"

Zen cocked his head and grinned at Umasi. It wasn't a pleasant grin, but rather one that managed to be both vicious and cheerful at the same time.

"If you were in their position, would *you* want anyone else to know what happened here?"

"No, definitely not," Umasi admitted.

"Good. Now here, hurry up and wash off your face. I've got some water with me—it's much more useful than that lemonade you're always drinking." Zen drew a bottle out of his jacket and thrust it into Umasi's arms.

"Why the rush?" Umasi inquired as he rinsed off his face and wiped it again with his sleeve.

"Because it's almost time for biology class," Zen replied. "Why do you think I came looking for you?"

Umasi froze, then turned to stare at Zen.

"We're not late, are we?" Umasi asked.

"As of now, I doubt it," Zen answered. "But if the clock I saw on my way here was accurate, we probably don't have much more than three minutes left."

"We'll never make it," Umasi groaned. "Help me get my stuff together."

Umasi dived to retrieve his textbook as Zen picked up the binder and unceremoniously shoved its contents back into place. The two brothers briskly returned the items to Umasi's backpack, which was still lying on the bench where Umasi had been seated. As Umasi zipped up his backpack and clumsily fitted his arms through the straps, Zen walked over to his own backpack, seized it by one strap, tossed it into the air, and slid his arm through a strap as it came down.

"What about them?" Umasi asked, gesturing towards the fallen thugs, who were only now beginning to stir.

"I'm sure that they'll be able to come up with some interesting excuses when their teachers ask them why they're late," Zen said. "But I doubt that you're in a similarly inventive mood, so perhaps we should hurry up."

Umasi did not object to this reasoning, and followed Zen at a run towards the subdued brown school doors. The school building itself was made out of reddish bricks, and seemed to have been literally styled after a prison. The few windows of the school were tiny, rectangular panes cut infrequently into the sheer brick face. The building's sole concession to flashiness was right above the plain main doors of the school—the number one, wrought of some kind of shiny metal, with a sign beneath it declaring proudly that the building housed the school of District 1.

As they ran through the massive courtyard, Umasi noticed that area was already mostly empty, with only a few students still running for the doors as Zen and himself were. Umasi briefly wondered how he hadn't noticed the silence, even from his secluded corner over at the farthest end of the yard. Silently scolding himself, Umasi swore that he'd be more alert next time. As they reached the doors, another student heaved them open and rushed inside. Zen's foot snapped forward, stopping one of the doors, allowing Umasi to go in first.

Upon entering the building, the two quickly presented the backs of their arms to the waiting security guards. All students in the City had a unique identification tattooed onto their arms. The Educators, who ran the City and its schools, made sure that students were scanned whenever they entered or left school, so that they could be kept track of.

After the security guards had cleared them to pass, the two brothers ran through the dimly lit hallways and stairwells so fast that everything seemed a blur. Finally, just after the bell rang, they reached their classroom. Umasi was out of breath as he stumbled through the door, but Zen was coolly collected.

"You two are late," the teacher observed as they entered.

Umasi, knowing better than to respond, quietly headed towards his assigned desk. Zen, however, paused by the doorway to make an ironic bow towards the teacher.

"My most *sincere* apologies, Mr. Benjamin."

The teacher scowled, knowing that he was being mocked.

"For that, Zen," Mr. Benjamin snapped, "homework for the whole class is *doubled*, just so they can be mad at you. If you're expecting special treatment because of your father, you've got another thing coming, boy. Now follow your brother's example and take your seat."

"So be it," Zen murmured as he walked over to his desk, taking the angry glares of his classmates in stride.

Satisfied, the teacher turned to face the blackboard and wrote noisily upon it with a piece of chalk. Umasi had already unpacked his bag and was doing his best to look attentive, though he couldn't help but glance at Zen out of the corner of his eye. If Zen had a fault, it was his attitude towards academics; he was already scribbling idly on a piece of paper, his sharp eyes wandering everywhere but the blackboard.

"Okay, class." Mr. Benjamin finished writing and turned around. "While you copy down these notes from the board, I'll be going around to hand back your last tests."

Umasi wasted no time in flipping to a fresh sheet of paper and copying the notes down industriously. He unconsciously leaned forward as he worked; even with glasses it was sometimes difficult for him to see, and his handwriting was fairly small. With his attention buried in his binder, time passed quickly for Umasi. It wasn't long before the teacher came around to place a paper on his desk.

"Excellent work, Umasi," Mr. Benjamin commended.

Umasi inspected his test paper, noting his perfect score with satisfaction. There was always something about being rewarded with a good score after rigorous study that made him feel . . . content. Remembering that not everyone was so easily satisfied, Umasi glanced over at Zen, who was just now receiving his paper. Zen barely gave it a glance, shoving it into his binder indifferently—but Umasi knew from the dirty look that the teacher gave Zen that the grade couldn't be good.

Umasi had always wondered about his brother's academic indifference. Umasi knew that Zen was smart. In fact, outside the classroom Zen sometimes made him feel slow and stupid by comparison. And yet, Zen's test scores were mediocre at best, he often got in trouble with the teachers, and he never seemed able to pay attention in class. The only time that Umasi had ever asked Zen about it, Zen had told him "academics have little to do with intelligence," and then gave him such a severe look that Umasi had never asked again.

At least Zen was smart enough to behave before he got in serious trouble, Umasi reflected. Some of their classmates were still shooting Zen dark looks over their extra homework, but Umasi had heard of other classes having entire tests failed owing to one student's misbehavior. Umasi shook his head at the unfairness of it all and turned towards the teacher, who had begun speaking again. The rest of the class passed uneventfully, and once the ending bell rang Umasi joined Zen outside in the hallway. As he walked out the door, Umasi felt a dull pain throbbing in his ribs. It wasn't seriously discomforting, but it was enough to remind him of what had transpired out in the courtyard. As he leaned against the wall of the hallway for a moment, Umasi felt a firm hand on his shoulder.

"Are you sure you're all right?" Zen asked.

"I'm fine," Umasi assured. "It's just the bruising acting up."

"Well then, let's get going," Zen suggested. "School's out, and I've had enough of this place for today."

The dull throb in Umasi's side showed no signs of ceasing, and he found that he couldn't help but agree with Zen. The hallways were crowded and noisy now, and the two brothers had to shove their way through the masses to get to the entrance. As they did another boy called out, hurriedly pushing his way through the crowd.

"Zen! Just the guy I wanted to see," the boy said. "I heard you got jumped outside."

Zen nodded. "The usual suspects. Apparently they couldn't find me, so they decided to go after my brother instead."

"Idiots." The other boy snorted, ignoring Umasi completely. "I saw one of them in my history class just now. Kid had a hell of a bloody nose."

"Becoming personally acquainted with a brick wall will do that to you." Zen smiled.

"So you didn't have any problems with three of them?"

"They're pushovers, Gabriel," Zen said dismissively. "You've never had any problems dealing with them yourself."

Umasi felt left out during the conversation, something that he'd gotten used to over the years. The student that Zen was talking to, Gabriel, was a dark-skinned boy that Umasi had seen once or twice in the hallways, but he hadn't learned his name until now. At school Zen seemed to know everyone, and everyone knew him, for better or worse. If anyone knew Umasi, it was usually due to the novelty of him being the twin brother of a more infamous student.

"Good job, man," Gabriel congratulated, slapping Zen on the shoulder. "You know I'd have helped if I were there."

"Of course," Zen said as the crowd around him seemed to swell. "It's time to go. I'll see you around."

"Watch yourself, Zen!" Gabriel called as he vanished back into the packed crowd.

Zen and Umasi reached the doors and allowed the security guards to scan their arms. Moments later, they burst through the doors and outside into the open air. The current of moving students, almost like a river, swept them away from the school and down the street towards the subways that most students used to travel to and from school. The two brothers, however, fought against that current and emerged from the masses at the other end.

They proceeded down the street and around the corner, a route that no other students took. They had insisted to their father on being allowed to walk at least as far as they would have to to get to the nearest train station, and so they had several blocks to travel before reaching a tiny parklike enclosure at the intersection of two forked streets. The leaves on the trees there were also turning gold, and the potted plants were just beginning to wilt. There were tables and chairs that the boys usually sat at while they waited, but today their limousine was early, its chauffeur already waiting with a door open.

"Hello, boys, how was school today?" the chauffeur greeted. "Any better?"

"Marginally," Zen replied as he slipped into the limo, sliding his backpack off so that it rested next to him.

"It was good," Umasi lied as he followed suit, his ribs still throbbing.

"Great to hear!" the chauffeur said as he slid into the driver's seat, shutting the door behind him.

The limousine started up and began making its way through traffic towards the Mayoral Mansion. Zen rolled his window down, and soon the wind rushing into the car sent loose strands of hair billowing off his head like black smoke. As the buildings and other cars passed by, the two brothers remained silent, gazing out opposing windows, absorbed in their own thoughts. Had they shared those thoughts, they would have found that each of them was disgruntled with school, though for vastly conflicting reasons. But neither of them had any reason to discuss school with the other; after all, for as long as both of them could remember, this was how life had always been.

For Umasi especially, it was impossible to imagine living any other way.

2

BEHIND THE SCENES

H ow goes the implementation of the new program?"

"Initial reports would suggest very well, sir. We sent the instructions to the teachers in a random order over the course of the entire month to avoid any student suspicions. Some teachers have only recently received the directions, of course, so we should have more comprehensive data within a few weeks."

"I trust that there were no complaints from the teachers?"

"Nothing filed officially."

"But of course you cannot prevent gossip."

"Of course."

"How about the student reaction?"

"That's where things get interesting, Mr. Mayor. Firstly the negative effects—we've seen the expected loss of student morale, as well as an overall grade decrease across the board, both of which seem to be a direct result of the program. Also, observed physical altercations between students shot up by seven percent."

"And the positives?"

"The tactic produced immediate and dramatic results. Punishing entire classes for any one student's misbehavior effectively turned the rest of the class against that student. They punish their own even more effectively than we can directly. As a bonus, so far no students have yet been observed to blame the teachers or us."

"Give me a rundown on the statistics."

"Overall marked classroom behavior improved by thirteen percent. There was an especially significant improvement in overt outbursts, with only twenty-seven having been reported the entire month. It seems that even if a class is not subject to the tactic themselves, word spreads quickly."

"Excellent, sounds promising on every count. Tell the board to continue the regimen and observe its effects over an extended period of time."

"Yes, sir. Also, the concept committee has produced another proposal that you might find interesting."

"Give me a summary."

"In short, we'll restrict students to one room during their free periods. We'll enforce this using the security guard patrols rather than teachers. Consistent harassment during free periods should apply an interesting new level of pressure that we've not yet explored."

"It's getting late. Have the proposal on my desk by tomorrow morning, I'll review it then."

"Consider it done, sir. Are you heading home now?"

"Yes, my sons are waiting for me."

"If I may be so bold as to ask, sir . . . do you ever notice our policies having effects on your sons?"

"All the time. Do you have any children?"

"No, sir."

"You should hope that it stays that way. You don't ever want to have to go home and look your kids in the face after a day of this work."

"I love my job, sir."

"And so do I. But I also love my sons, and I find it . . . difficult . . . to reconcile the two."

It's really not that hard, you know," Umasi said, looking up from his desk.

"Speak for yourself," Zen snorted, lying back comfortably on his bed.

Umasi sighed as he looked back down at the two lists of math problems spread out on his desk. One was his, and the other was Zen's. It had become routine for Umasi to do the homework for both of them. Zen never seemed able to do his on his own, and Umasi had decided that it saved time if he did it all himself rather than coaching his uninterested brother.

As Umasi went to work on the problems, Zen began tossing darts at a board hung up on a wall. The room was large, and shared by the both of them. It had been divided down the center by an invisible line that they had both agreed to after a dispute when they were younger—one of the few times Umasi could ever recall quarreling with his brother. One half was host to Umasi's bed and desk, which held various stacks of books, paper, and writing utensils. Zen's half also had a desk, though it was mostly empty. The dartboard was hung up on Zen's side, and a large dresser, which held both their clothes, rested right upon the border, half of it on either side. Next to the door were a bunch of pegs where they hung their jackets, and Umasi knew that Zen kept a baseball bat and unused chess set under his bed. Everything was very orderly. Their interests might have been different, but they both had an inclination to keep their things organized.

As Umasi continued working, the darts that Zen was throwing made a low *thunk* each time one slammed into the board. Out of the corner of his eye, Umasi couldn't help but notice that Zen was managing to precisely hit the rim of the bull's-eye with almost every shot, forming a ring around it with his darts. As impressive as the display was, however, Umasi found it rather annoying.

"Could you stop that?" Umasi asked, looking up from his work. "It's distracting."

"If you say so," Zen replied, tossing his last dart at the board, where it struck the midst of the circle that he had formed with all the previous darts.

"Thanks," Umasi said as he turned back to his work.

"How're your ribs feeling?" Zen asked, changing the subject.

"Better," Umasi answered, not taking his eyes from his paper. He knew where Zen was going to steer this conversation, and he wasn't very fond of that particular subject.

"You know the only way you're going to get them to stop messing with you is to fight back for once," Zen advised, putting his hands behind his head as he stared up at the ceiling.

"Too bad I'm not as tough as you," Umasi murmured, scribbling down another answer.

"You took the same self-defense courses that I did," Zen pointed out. "You should've been able to escape, at the very least."

"Those were the only courses you were better at than me, remember?" Umasi countered.

"Yet you still passed," Zen replied. "I'll admit there *is* a difference between training and real fighting, but you're never going to find out how big that difference is for you if you don't try at all."

"I don't want to try," Umasi muttered, sharpening his pencil.

"And why's that?" Zen asked, sitting up straight and looking over at Umasi.

"Because I don't like fighting," Umasi answered, his eyes remaining focused on his papers.

"Well that's obvious," Zen snorted. "But you don't like getting pounded either."

"I guess that makes me a pacifist then, doesn't it?" Umasi suggested.

"Pacifism is a losing attitude," Zen said derisively. "Look where it got *you*—beaten up on the ground with your head in a puddle."

Umasi was now starting to get annoyed—probably what Zen was after in the first place. Whenever Zen was bored, which was often, his favorite pastime seemed to be aggravate the nearest person within earshot.

"Do you want me to finish this or not?" Umasi demanded, turning around and gesturing towards their collective homework.

"Of course!" Zen replied with mock surprise. "Don't tell me that our little chat managed to interfere with your work ethic."

"Don't play dumb," Umasi scolded. "Why don't you help for once? Go get some lemonade, I'm thirsty."

"I don't think that we have any left."

"Then go out and buy some, it's not like you have anything better to do," Umasi suggested, turning back to his work. "Dad's going to be home for dinner soon. At the very least I can drink it then."

"Point taken," Zen said, sliding out of his bed and walking over to the dresser, upon which rested two shiny plastic cards. "Of course you don't object to me using your money, right?"

"Go ahead, it's not like either of us are going to run out anytime soon," Umasi pointed out.

Zen laughed at that, and then picked up both of the cards. One of them had the letter *Z* scribbled on it, and the other a *U*. Ever since their father had entrusted the cards and their accounts to the twins, on their thirteenth birthday, they'd been sure to mark them so as not to confuse them. Two years later, they had hardly managed to dent the massive sums at all—not that they had tried much, of course, as they were both modest spenders. Still, for one brief moment, Zen enjoyed the feeling of the plastic in his hands, knowing that he held more money, and consequently more power, than most of the wealthy in the City ever saw in a lifetime.

And then he dropped the card marked *Z*, pocketed the one labeled *U*, and strode out of the room.

Y ou sick or something? You don't have to do this if you're too weak."

Red gritted his teeth and forced himself to his feet, ignoring the merciless aches in his gut. Untamed brown strands of hair dropped in front of his eyes, obscuring his vision as a sudden wave of pain forced him to double over slightly. Glaring at his companion, Red straightened up slowly.

"Who, me? I'm fine," Red lied. "It's not like we're robbing a bank. I'm ready to go any time, unless *you* wanna chicken out, Chris."

Chris raised an eyebrow.

"Whatever you say, man, but you look ready to collapse any moment now. You're damn lucky you fell in with my gang, else you'd probably be dead by now."

"I don't need you," Red snarled, his body tensing. "I did fine by myself for *years*."

Chris and Red stared each other down. Chris had the advantage in height and weight, and had the support of most of the other vagrants in their group, which was no small feat, all things considered. However, Red, at least, could tell that the boy was a coward at heart. Red wasn't scared of him, and would not allow himself to be bullied.

A few more tense moments passed, and then Chris backed down, a conciliatory grin spreading across his face.

"All I meant was that you're better off with us than without, Red," Chris said. "And since you ain't run off yet, you probably agree, yeah?"

Red nodded grudgingly, relaxing slightly himself.

"Good then, let's go," Chris said.

As soon as Chris turned, Red shuddered and grasped his knees, another wave of pain racking his body. Despite the setting sun casting a warm orange glaze over the streets around him, Red couldn't help feeling cold. The air was getting chillier every day now, and the leaves in the park had been dying. Winter was near, and judging from the increasingly savage pain in his gut, Red knew it would be the worst one he'd seen yet. It was the reason why, after years of hacking it alone, Red had decided to join up with Chris' gang.

Then, as suddenly as they had come, the sharp pains faded away. Forcing a grin as Chris glanced back at him, Red began walking, cursing his appendix as he did. For a long time he had ignored the pains, dismissing them as hunger pangs; after all, he rarely, if ever, enjoyed a full stomach. When they grew worse, Red convinced himself that something rotten he had eaten was to blame. A few weeks later the pain had still not subsided, and Red had begun to accept that something else must be wrong with him. He didn't actually know if his appendix was the problem, but he liked the word, one that he vaguely remembered learning about back when he still attended school. It had been three years since he had last sat in a classroom—three years since he had become a vagrant. He was sixteen now.

Taking a deep breath, Red followed Chris down the empty sidewalks of District 7, an abandoned district—one of the many miniature ghost towns within the massive City. The entire City itself rested upon a large island, surrounded by two rivers and, on its west side, the ocean to which they flowed. That landmass was divided up into districts, from 1 to 57, and these districts in turn formed the City. Districts with low populations in poor neighborhoods often fell into disrepair, and every so often the Mayor's Office would order these districts evacuated and sealed off with fences. These districts had been a blessing to the vagrants of the City, who used the emptied buildings to hide from the Enforcers—uniformed officers who maintained law and order in the City and often hunted down vagrant children.

For the past few days Red and his companions had camped out in District 7. The Enforcers had recently swept the area, meaning that they wouldn't be back for a while. There was only one rival gang around, which meant that, despite their sole competitors growing increasingly belligerent, they could spend most of their energy on basic necessities rather than fighting. But most important, District 7 bordered on the bustling District 5, from which the vagrants were able to steal a decent amount of food.

As Red slipped into a dark back alley, a rich scent reached his nostrils, and he paused to savor the smell. Driven by hunger, he and Chris swiftly proceeded down the alley until they came face-to-face with a crude wooden barricade—one of the fences that had been erected to separate District 5 from the abandoned District 7. Red crouched down next to Chris to wait. On the other side of that barricade, he knew, was an alley where a restaurant dumped its trash.

"I'll be waiting here on lookout," Chris said. "You go on in and bring us some food."

Red narrowed his eyes.

"Aren't you coming?"

"Nah, today's not my turn. You're kinda new, this your first time out with me, yeah? Well this is how we roll," Chris said. "'Sides, you wouldn't even know about this place if I hadn't told you about it."

He had a point there, but Red wasn't about to let it go. None of the other members of the gang had ever mentioned this, and Red knew that if he gave in and fetched Chris food without complaint, he'd be pegged as a pushover.

"Listen, Chris," Red said, standing up slowly. "I'm going to go along with this now because I like the crew. But if screwing me out of food gets to be a regular thing with you—"

"How am I screwing you out of food?" Chris said defensively.

"Well you're not gonna be sticking your neck out to get it, are you?"

"Stop it," Chris said, taking a step backwards. "You're getting first pick, yeah? And we'll take turns at this. Next time you go out with a partner, I'll make sure that you're the one looking out."

Red might have been hungry, but he wasn't stupid. He knew that "next time" Chris wouldn't be his partner. Chris would be off with one of the others, pulling the exact same stunt with them. The kid never intended to risk *his* neck at all, Red realized in disgust. Smart, but slimier than a maggot.

Still, though Red wasn't stupid, he *was* hungry.

The only way to settle things now was to fight Chris right then and there, and Red didn't see anything to be gained from that. Red quickly decided that so long as he got his turn at lookout, it didn't really matter who the partner was. Mentally cataloguing the incident for later, Red nodded at Chris, and then turned towards the restaurant entrance. Chris, looking thoroughly smug, turned and walked over to the relative safety of the other end of the alley, standing watch on the off chance that someone might come that way.

It wasn't long before Red heard someone open a door and drag stuffed trash bags outside. As soon as the person stepped back into the restaurant and shut the door, Red bent down and removed a large wooden board from the bottom of the barricade that hadn't been nailed down properly. Red wormed his way through the resulting hole, unbothered by the filth of the alley floor. Emerging on the other side, Red fell upon the black trash bag resting on the ground, tearing a hole in its side so that he could rummage through its contents.

Much of the trash was useless stuff like napkins and empty cans, but Red was persistent in his search, and soon he had amassed a pile of scraps—a chicken bone with some meat still attached, a tin dish with a decent chunk of pie left in it, and a corncob that was only half eaten. Red grinned at his findings and wasted no time in devouring what he had found. A sharp hiss from behind the fence reminded him of his other duties, and he rolled his eyes as he gathered up some more scraps for Chris.

When he was finished, he crawled back out the way he came, replaced the wooden board, and presented Chris with the scraps he had collected in the tin dish.

"Good job, kid, you're all right with me." Chris' eyes glinted strangely as he said this, and Red didn't believe his words for a second.

Still, Red wasn't bothered, not by having to feed an overgrown maggot like Chris, and not even by having to eat trash. His motivation was survival, not pride. After all, only the proud could be humiliated. What use did he have for pride? As a vagrant, pride could only get you killed.

And besides, it wasn't bad, as far as trash went.

P ass the gravy, please," Zen requested.

"Here you go," Umasi replied, handing Zen the gravy tureen.

"Thank you." Zen poured a generous amount of gravy over his roast beef and mashed potatoes before setting the tureen back down onto the table.

"Don't forget to eat your salad," the Mayor reminded, eyeing Zen's plate.

"Now, Father, have I *ever* forgotten to eat my salad?" Zen asked reproachfully after he swallowed a bite of roast beef. "Deliberately eschew, yes, but forget? Never."

"Don't confuse the issue. Meat and potatoes all the time isn't healthy."

"Confuse the issue?" Zen used his fork to mix the mashed potatoes with gravy. "You needn't treat this like a policy debate, Father."

"You're right, this isn't a debate," the Mayor agreed. "Eat your salad."

"If you insist." Zen shrugged, spearing a piece of lettuce with his fork.

Umasi smiled as he took a sip from his glass of lemonade filled from the carton Zen had gone out to buy earlier. Dinner was one of the few times when he could count on seeing his father and his brother together, which was usually an enjoyable event. Umasi and Zen had always known that they were adopted, but they neither remembered nor needed any other parents. Though the Mayor worked most of the day and was sometimes absent for long meetings, Umasi often forgot that he was adopted at all. To the twins, the Mayor was their father, absolutely.

"Umasi, how'd you get that scratch?" the Mayor asked, peering across the table at Umasi.

Umasi froze, halfway through the motion of bringing a piece of roast beef to his mouth.

"What scratch?"

"The one on your face," the Mayor said.

"Oh," Umasi began, thinking quickly, "I tripped in the courtyard today."

"Tripped? Was there a hole or something? A brick out of place?" the Mayor asked. "I could get it fixed if so."

"No, Dad, I was just careless," Umasi insisted, which had some truth to it.

"I see," the Mayor said, turning back to his meal. "Well, be more careful next time."

"Right, right," Umasi promised.

Out of the corner of his eye, Umasi saw Zen smirk at him. Both of them knew exactly why they would never tell their father about any fights they got into: They both had to deal with their reputation among their peers as the Mayor's sons. If word went around that they were going home and tattling to their father, they would never hear the end of it. Well, at least not until Zen personally silenced every critic.

"So, how was work today?" Zen asked, glancing at the Mayor as he cut another piece of roast beef.

"Good," the Mayor replied, stiffening. "And how was school?"

"It was . . . fine," Zen said, noisily crunching down on some lettuce.

Umasi looked back and forth between Zen and his dad. For some odd reason that Umasi had never understood, the Mayor never seemed comfortable talking about his work with his sons. On the other hand, for reasons that Umasi completely understood, Zen was never comfortable talking about school with his father, though Zen made a great effort not to let it show.

There were a lot of secrets there at that table, Umasi realized, only half of which he was privy to.

The rest of the meal passed with idle conversation about current events in the City. Umasi joined in a little, though not much. Dinner conversation tended to turn into a sort of intellectual sparring match between Zen and his father. Umasi always thought it entertaining to observe, but not so much to actually participate in.

"Oh, undeniably," Zen said, wiping his mouth with his napkin as he pushed his empty plate away. "But wouldn't it be more cost-effective to offer free property in the abandoned districts and allow any takers to handle the renovations?"

"That's been suggested before, but even if it does cost us more in the long run, it's more efficient to fix up the districts ourselves and then sell the property," the Mayor replied. "Renovations done by normal citizens tend to be shoddy, and require evacuation and repair again within a few years."

"That's a good point," Zen admitted. "But if you have these districts supervised by citizens, there will always be someone around to keep the vagrants out."

"The vagrants have never really been a significant problem," the Mayor said dismissively. "If they start to bother a neighborhood, we just send in the Enforcers and they scatter like rats."

"If you say so." Zen shrugged.

"Well now, have you both finished your homework?" the Mayor said, looking back and forth between Zen and Umasi.

Zen flashed Umasi a knowing look before responding.

"Yes, of course," he replied.

"Good, then you should probably think about heading to bed early," the Mayor suggested. "You're always too tired in the mornings. An extra hour or two will do you good."

Without much better to do, Zen and Umasi decided to heed this advice as an attendant came around to collect the dishes. They both knew that it wouldn't make them much less tired the next day, but then again, few things ever did. School just had a way of sapping the strength and spirit out of a person.

3

CROSSING THE LINE

U masi and Zen awoke the next morning, groaning as though they hadn't gotten any extra sleep at all. By the time the limousine delivered them to school, they were both quite testy. Their moods were somewhat improved when they entered their first-period classroom, where they found that their regular teacher was absent and that a substitute had filled his place.

Substitutes were always a bit of a wild card, though students were usually glad to see them. Few substitutes dared to actually try to teach anything, lest they interfere with the real teacher's syllabus. Some substitutes, however, *would* attempt to teach something, but lacking proper knowledge about the class and its subject, would succeed only in wasting everyone's time. Still others neither taught nor allowed a class to fool around, but were just strict for the sake of being strict.

And so all the students in Umasi's class waited in trepidation to see what type the substitute would be. Umasi's spirits fell as he determined that the woman, who had declared her name to be Ms. Hill, fell into the last and least desirable category. She looked like she was taking a bite out of a lemon with each name as she called the roll. Umasi sighed and removed his glasses so that he could rub his tired eyes. It became painfully clear that the substitute would rather be elsewhere as she came upon a name that appeared to give her difficulty. She frowned at the list so deeply that her face wrinkled like a prune, and paused for several long seconds before taking a stab at it.

"You-mashy?" Ms. Hill called out.

Umasi was used to his name being mispronounced, both intentionally and unintentionally, though he never found it any less irritating whenever it was botched. Still, he knew that teacher was referring to him, and that was all that really mattered in class. He was about to brush his annoyance aside and announce that he was present when an indignant voice cut him off.

"What'd you call him?" Zen said loudly.

Umasi's heart dropped as he heard his brother speak. There was no need for him to do this, to risk getting himself into serious trouble over something so petty. Turning to look at his brother, Umasi shook his head desperately in an attempt to dissuade him. Zen ignored him and instead crossed his arms over his chest as he glared at the teacher.

Ms. Hill instantly rounded on Zen. "Is there a problem?"

"Yeah, that's not his name," Zen replied bluntly.

Ms. Hill inhaled, inflating her chest like a blowfish as her eyes widened with outrage.

"You are *incredibly* rude, you know that?" Ms. Hill snapped, letting her breath out all at once.

"I could say the same for you," Zen countered.

Umasi cringed. Ms. Hill stared. Zen looked utterly unconcerned.

"You are really hideous," Ms. Hill said in a shocked tone. "I suppose you never make mistakes?"

"At least I have the decency to acknowledge when I do."

There was complete silence. Umasi, along with the rest of the class, stared at his brother in disbelief. Ms. Hill's jaw hung wide open as she gaped at Zen blankly. Her ears had received Zen's message, but her brain was refusing to process it. Everyone knew that Zen had crossed the line, and they all waited to see what would happen when Ms. Hill returned to her senses.

"You better make good with me now," Ms. Hill said at last, seething, "or I will call security on you!"

"Make good with you?" Zen asked amusedly.

"I've never met a student who was so hostile and rude!" Ms. Hill was shaking with anger now.

Zen raised an eyebrow, and Umasi knew that his brother was silently laughing at the teacher's hypocrisy. Umasi, on the other hand, wasn't laughing at all. His brother had a knack for aggravating teachers, but he'd never done anything like this before. Umasi knew that Zen wouldn't apologize. Once he started something, he always saw it through. This time, though, Umasi didn't even want to imagine how far that would be.

Surprisingly, however, Zen's next utterance was an attempt at reconciliation.

"We've both had rough mornings," Zen pointed out to Ms. Hill.

"That's probably true . . . but *I* am the adult," Ms. Hill said. "You are a student, and I am a teacher. When I was growing up, I was taught to respect adults!"

"Respect should never go one way," Zen said. "If you have to force someone's respect, then you've probably lost it forever."

Ms. Hill stared at Zen as though he were a stubborn stain that she would dearly love to wipe away, but couldn't, no matter how hard she scrubbed.

"But we are not equals!" Ms. Hill sputtered. "I'm your superior!"

Zen sighed and scratched his head with one hand, which meant that he was frustrated.

"If you had just corrected—" Zen began.

"I DON'T NEED A CORRECTION!" Ms. Hill suddenly screamed, losing all traces of self-control.

"Look at this from another point of view—"

"I DON'T NEED TO SEE YOUR POINT OF VIEW!" Ms. Hill shrieked as she stormed over to the classroom phone.

Zen watched Ms. Hill with apparent indifference as she gripped the phone with shaking hands and called for security and the Disciplinary Officer. She flashed Zen a triumphant grin as she hung up, but the grin soon faded as Zen yawned. Zen's indifference served only to infuriate Ms. Hill even further—but Umasi knew that that was Zen's intention.

Umasi, for his part, was terrified. Disciplinary Officers were high-ranking Educators who meted out punishment for all sorts of infractions. Their inspections were feared all throughout the City, for they were the only ones who had the authority to expel a student. The luckless District 1 School, being where it was at the heart of the City, was probably the only school that had a Disciplinary Officer on duty at all times.

Umasi couldn't help but feel guilty as he sat in his seat sweating. If it weren't for him, Zen wouldn't have gotten into trouble. By the time a uniformed security guard showed up in the classroom doorway, Umasi was cringing. Zen calmly went along with the guard as he was escorted down to the Disciplinary Officer. Zen did, however, spare Ms. Hill a defiant smirk as he left, which calculatedly put the substitute teacher in a bad mood for the rest of the period . . . if not the entire day.

As the bell rang, Umasi raised his head and groggily slipped his glasses back on. Rather than spend the rest of the period worrying about what horrible punishments Zen might be facing, he had decided to take a nap. The substitute, who was still fuming in her chair, didn't object, and there wasn't much else to do. The rest of the students had been far from talkative after watching Zen's awe-inspiring display.

Umasi wasted no time in seizing his backpack and joining the queue to leave the class. As soon as Umasi stepped into the hallway, a low voice addressed him.

"Hey."

Startled, Umasi froze in midstep. His abrupt halt triggered an instant pileup in the doorway, and a number of students began to open their mouths to complain. A second later, they all shut their mouths without saying a word as they realized who had just spoken.

"Perhaps we should talk a few feet to your left," Zen suggested, eyeing the congestion of students. "You seem to be blocking traffic."

Umasi didn't need to be told twice. He hurriedly backed aside, allowing the procession of students to slowly leave the classroom, all of them casting reverent looks at Zen as they passed. Umasi knew why—Zen's standing up to the teacher like that wasn't something any of the students were likely to forget before the day was out. Zen had awed the whole class, largely because all of them had dreamed at one point or another of doing what he had actually done.

Zen nodded at each of the students in turn as they passed, and then finally exchanged glares with Ms. Hill, who exited last and didn't stick around to maintain eye contact. As the substitute strode away without saying a word, the hallways filled with students on their way to their next classes. Now no one paid any attention to the twins as they huddled together by the wall.

"Did you get expelled?" Umasi asked, voicing his worst fear.

"Expelled? For that?" Zen snorted. "Don't be ridiculous. I just told the Disciplinary Officer that the substitute was making fun of my dear brother's name, and that I got called down for standing up for him."

"And he just let you go?" Umasi said incredulously.

"Oh, he asked a few more questions and I told him what he wanted to hear," Zen said. "They added a note to my record, of course, and I suppose that they'll notify Father. Speaking of which, I don't think Ms. Hill knew who our father *is,* but the Disciplinary Officer surely did."

"I guess you were lucky," Umasi said, relieved. "Why did you do that, anyway?"

"I wasn't in the best of moods," Zen said, scratching his chin. "And that substitute got on my nerves from the start. Besides, I've always wanted to do something like that, but I've never had a good excuse."

"But that *wasn't* a good excuse," Umasi protested. "It didn't bother me that much, really."

"Well, by the time I was through telling the story, I'd made it sound like she had thoroughly bullied you." Zen grinned. "And I did get away with it in the end, didn't I? Success is what makes a good excuse."

"I guess you're right," Umasi conceded, sighing deeply.

Umasi realized that the hallway was just about empty now, and he cast his gaze upwards at the clock hanging on the wall. He turned rigid upon seeing the time.

"We're going to be late!" Umasi blurted.

Zen looked at him without saying a word, and as Umasi glanced at his brother's eyes he realized that Zen had some crazy idea, and that he would inevitably be drawn into it.

"Speaking of things that I've always wanted to do . . ." Zen began slowly.

"No. You're not thinking of cutting class, are you?" Umasi demanded.

"How perceptive," Zen's eyes glinted. "But you're only partly right. I think the both of us deserve a good day off. Let's cut *all* of our classes for the day."

"Impossible. We can't," Umasi said.

"Why not?"

"You've just been down to see the Disciplinary Officer!" Umasi hissed. "If you get into trouble again, right after that . . ."

"The Disciplinary Officers don't handle attendance," Zen said dismissively. "That's an entirely different department. He'll never even find out."

"But what will Father say?" Umasi demanded.

"Father is busy with his work, and probably will be until dinnertime," Zen pointed out. "I doubt that he'll find out until the next attendance report, if I don't manage to tamper with it by then."

"But . . . but the limo will be waiting!"

"It wouldn't be the first time we decided to walk home. When we don't show up after a while the driver will go on his way."

"Rothenberg's been stepping up the Enforcer patrols. What we'll be doing . . . it's illegal!"

"So is killing, but hey, people still die." Zen shrugged.

Umasi opened his mouth to renew his protests, but even as he did the bell rang again shrilly, indicating that they were both late for class. Umasi slowly shut his mouth and looked over at Zen, who was now smirking triumphantly. Umasi suddenly realized that Zen had meant to keep him talking until they were both already late for their next class. It was too late now, and Umasi knew it.

"All right, fine," Umasi sighed, admitting defeat. "But how are we going to get out? If the security guards scan us, they'll know that we're cutting class."

"Oh, that's easy," Zen said confidently. "Follow me."

With no other choice, Umasi followed Zen as he led him to one of the dim staircases and down to the basement, where the cafeteria and gymnasium were located. Instead of heading to either of those places, however, Zen led Umasi down a side corridor he had never ventured down before. The fluorescent lighting gave the basement an eerie ambience as they walked through the hall, mercifully without running into anyone. At the end of the corridor, Umasi saw a forklift and what looked like loading trolleys grouped around a big set of double doors. Large signs on the doors warned that an alarm would sound if they were opened.

"These are the service doors. They bring in all the supplies and food for the cafeteria through here," Zen explained. "Ignore the signs, that alarm is actually broken."

"How do you know that?" Umasi asked.

Zen cocked his head and glanced over at Umasi, the fluorescent lighting flickering oddly overhead.

"You should really try to make more . . . friends," Zen suggested. "They can be useful on occasion."

"I'll keep that in mind," Umasi murmured.

With that, Zen shoved the doors open, and despite everything Umasi cringed, half-expecting the alarm to ring. After several seconds passed and nothing happened, Umasi opened his eyes to see Zen holding one of the doors open with an "I told you so" look. Embarrassed, Umasi straightened up and cleared his throat as he looked out at the inviting sunlight.

"Let's go," Umasi said.

"After you," Zen replied, spreading his arms gallantly.

After a moment's hesitation, Umasi broke into an excited run and burst outside, blinking to adjust his eyes to the sunlight. He discovered that he was standing in a small, overlooked corner of the courtyard. Hearing the door shut behind him, Umasi spun around to see Zen walking towards him, rubbing his hands as he took a deep breath of the crisp, cool open air.

"They ought to hold classes outdoors," Zen said wistfully. "I can't remember the last time I breathed fresh air in a classroom."

"Yeah . . . so, should we just go straight home?" Umasi asked.

"I don't see why not. It's not like there's much else to do right now," Zen observed.

"Well, we could . . . uh . . ." Umasi glanced around, looking for ideas. His gaze came to rest upon a large billboard advertising an upcoming movie. ". . . see a movie, like that one there! I've been wanting to see that!"

"Umasi"—Zen looked up at the billboard impatiently—"that movie comes out months from now."

"Oh, right," Umasi said, spotting the date on the ad. "Sorry."

"Everyone makes mistakes," Zen said. "Listen, Umasi, when the film comes out we'll see it together. Opening day, first showing. In the big District 1 Theater."

"Really?" Umasi blinked. Zen didn't make promises like that very often.

"Really." Zen nodded. "But seeing as it's not out now, I think that we'd best be on our way."

"Of course," Umasi agreed. "Lead the way!"

Umasi was soon struggling to keep up as his brother led the way out of the courtyard and onto the streets. As they walked beneath the shadows of the towering buildings that lined each street, Umasi had to admit that Zen's idea had been a good one. Umasi for once got a chance to look at every building and appreciate its uniqueness, from its colors to its bricks to its windows and its height. Umasi couldn't remember a time when he hadn't been too rushed to spare the buildings anything more than a passing glance.

"Look at that." Zen pointed as they crossed a street.

Umasi followed Zen's finger and looked up to see the greatest building of them all—Penance Tower, a massive skyscraper that dwarfed every other building in the City. Catching the morning sun, its distant windows glittered, a hundred times more radiant than flashbulbs. The tower lay at the center of District 1, a government building from which everything from the City's stop signs to its bridges was managed remotely. Umasi had seen it before, of course—it was so tall as to be impossible to miss. But he had never seen it in such an impressive light, and stood staring at its glittering form for several dumbstruck seconds before Zen yanked him forward and out of the way of oncoming traffic.

The rest of the trek passed quickly for Umasi, for he saw nothing that could equal the impressive sight of Penance Tower. As they walked, Umasi was uncomfortably aware that some adults turned their heads to look suspiciously at the twin students, but none of them were concerned enough to interrupt their own business to mind someone else's. Before long, Umasi and Zen arrived at the sizeable Mayoral Mansion. The guard at the gate raised an eyebrow when he saw them, but said nothing, as he wasn't being paid to ask the Mayor's sons any questions.

"Today is a Friday. I think Dad is probably working at home," Umasi realized as they walked across the fancy marble floor of the lobby.

"Even if he is, he'll just shut himself up in the conference room for hours as usual," Zen said. "He never comes out until after five at the earliest."

They pushed open the polished wooden doors into the foyer of the mansion, and then Umasi froze.

"What's wrong?" Zen asked, turning back to look at Umasi.

"Have you ever been . . . curious about what Father does at work?" Umasi said. Maybe it was the liberating thrill of cutting class, but he found himself feeling unusually brazen.

"He holds meetings and runs the government," Zen said, looking away.

"No, that *is* his work," Umasi said. "I'm talking about what he *does* at work. He never talks to us about it. He gets nervous and changes the subject whenever we ask. If I've noticed it, then you've definitely noticed it too."

Zen spun around to glare at Umasi through narrowed eyes.

"What exactly are you suggesting?" Zen demanded softly.

've reviewed the proposal."

"What are your thoughts, sir?"

"Interesting, though potentially expensive. We may have to hire additional security guards to make it effective enough to produce results."

"Well, we do have the budget for it, sir."

"Indeed, which is why I'm giving it the green light. I want the program up to speed within a week, with initial progress reports the week after."

"Consider it . . . done . . . sir, did you just hear that?"

"Hear what?"

"I could've sworn I just heard something outside the door just now. . . ."

"It's probably that blasted maid again or something. Now pay attention—you're too easily distracted."

"I'm sorry sir."

"Accepted. Now, I've been drafting a little proposal of my own in my spare time."

"I'm all ears, of course."

"It's very simple—immediate school banning of all items not pertaining to a student's education. It would of course include any nasty recreational devices that students have been using to distract themselves."

"That's . . . quite a radical proposal, sir."

"And I think that's exactly what we need right now. Small, subtle, incremental changes are fine, but our most effective experiments in controlling students have always been our boldest."

"What justification are we going to give for this?"

"The usual one. We'll label the items a threat to student safety and be done with it."

"A threat to safety? Do you think they'll buy that?"

"No one complained when we classified scissors and compasses as weapons."

"Well actually . . ."

"No one complained *officially*."

"So how are we to enforce this?"

"With metal detectors and mandatory searches."

"Won't that be . . . expensive?"

"Like you said, we do have the budget for it."

Umasi sat there in stunned silence, one ear pressed tightly against the door to the conference room. Next to him, Zen quietly stood up to leave, an unreadable expression on his face. Not wanting to hear any more, Umasi held his glasses in place so that they wouldn't fall off as he rose hastily and trotted after his brother. Zen paid him no attention, walking away wordlessly, his fists tightly clenched. His own head swimming, Umasi struggled to find something, anything to say that might make sense of what they'd just heard.

"What . . . what are you going to do?" Umasi asked.

"I'm going to get to the bottom of this," Zen replied in a cold, hard voice.

"Zen . . ."

At that, Zen spun around, and Umasi took a step back. Umasi had thought he knew his brother, but the face before him was a stranger's. It wasn't angry, it wasn't sad—in fact it displayed no emotion at all. It was unpredictable, unreadable, and that scared Umasi. But what absolutely terrified him was the look in Zen's dark eyes, a look that he had never seen before, one that screamed of danger, louder every second.

And then Zen broke eye contact and stormed off, leaving Umasi to stand all alone, too stunned to notice the tears running down his cheeks.

Everyone's here, yeah?"

"I think so."

"Zack, Raphael, James, Scar, Niles, Walker, Red?"

"They're here, Chris, and so are all the others."

"Wait a sec, what about Gil?"

"Gil? Anyone seen that kid?"

"Last I saw him was two days ago."

"Yeah, I ain't seen 'im in a while either."

Chris seemed to ponder that for a moment, then shrugged.

"He knew where we were supposed to meet. He ain't here, which means he's either run off or dead," Chris said. "Either way, he ain't none of our business anymore."

There was a murmur of assent, and Red made a mental note not to be late to any of these little gatherings. Tonight the gang had taken refuge in an abandoned underground parking garage in District 8. Such areas were favored gathering places for vagrants, as they provided shelter from the elements, open space to build small fires inside garbage cans for heat, as well as a good hiding place from the Enforcers. In here the only dangers were usually each other.

Chris and his gang might have working together to survive, but fights even within the group weren't uncommon. A misunderstanding over a scrap of food, an attempted theft gone wrong, even verbal arguments that got out of hand—all of these could result in fights, and these fights often turned fatal. Red had been lucky so far, as he usually got along well with the other vagrants; he wasn't obnoxious, had little that was worth stealing, and—being the newest in the group—was something of a novelty.

"All right, James and Walker watch the exits. That other group of pansies has been getting catty lately."

"Chris, do you think that Gil might've run into them?"

"Does it matter? Just watch that exit. If they got the guts to show up, we'll give 'em a piece of our minds. Who's leading them these days anyway?"

"Last I heard it was a kid named Glick."

"Bah, they go through a new leader every week, those guys."

Slowly but surely the vagrants began to make themselves comfortable in their temporary shelter. Bonfires were lit, scrounged food was—very carefully—traded, and guarded conversations broke out. Some vagrants had blankets, others even had soft drinks. Red, who had neither, rested near a particularly large fire, trying not to think about the pain in his abdomen as the other vagrants around him swapped tales about the legendary Vagrant Ghost.

"I swear it, I saw her!" the vagrant named Niles insisted as the others looked at him skeptically. "It was maybe two months ago, I was just minding my own business, and bam! She appears out of thin air! Completely pale, with glowing red eyes and this living chain that coiled around like a snake!"

"Did you eat anything funny that day?" Red asked.

"No! I swear, it was real as you are!" Niles insisted. "Her chain struck me between the eyes and knocked me out!"

"It knocked you out?" A brown-skinned vagrant snorted. "Are you sure she didn't float around in the air making wailing noises before vanishing through a wall?"

"You're not funny, Raphael!" Niles snapped. "A hundred other vagrants have seen her too. I tell you, the abandoned districts are haunted!"

"Fairy tales," Raphael said dismissively. "Some half-starved vagrant sees a stray cat and thinks it's a monster. Happens all the time."

Niles and Raphael continued arguing for a few minutes, though the debate never heated up to the point of violence. Meanwhile, feeling an uncomfortable pang in his stomach, Red slowly forced himself to his feet and reached for a brown paper bag containing half a slice of pizza that he had been saving. As he picked up the bag, however, he knew that something was wrong. He tore it asunder, and a strangled growl escaped his throat. The bag was empty. Someone had stolen his food.

Suddenly, the other vagrants around the fire quieted, staring at him as they realized what must have happened. Like a contagious disease, the silence slowly spread throughout the entire garage as the other vagrants turned to see what was going on. Red glared around at all of them, and quickly spotted a boy whose shirt had a visible drop of sauce on it. Looking closer, Red recognized a large vagrant who went by the name Zack. Zack hastened to wipe his mouth with his sleeve, but it was too late —Red had seen the grease shining on his face.

Aside from the crackle of flames, the parking garage was now completely silent. Red and Zack stared each other down, unblinking. Everyone knew what was coming; they just didn't know who would act first.

And then Red lunged, snarling like a mad dog. Zack leaped forward to meet him, but Red's greater momentum slammed Zack back onto the ground as Red pounded at his chest. Zack tried to shove Red off, but Red slammed his forehead down onto Zack's face. For a moment Red saw stars, but when they cleared he found that blood was pouring from Zack's nose. Letting out a howl of rage, Zack flailed out with thick arms, catching Red in the face and chest. In retaliation, Red seized one of Zack's arms and sank his teeth into it as hard as he could, eliciting a scream of pain from his victim.

This was not a clean, honorable fight. This was a battle to the death, and Red intended to use every weapon he had. Moments later Red rose, spitting blood. Zack leapt to his feet, clutching his injured arm, a wild look in his eyes. With arms now outstretched, Zack barreled towards Red, who ducked and slammed his knee into Zack's groin. Zack yelled in pain again, and managed to lash out once, catching Red in the abdomen before falling to the ground himself, clutching his privates.

Searing, unimaginable pain shot through Red's body. The agony he had been feeling in his gut for the past few weeks was nothing, *nothing* compared with what it felt like to be punched in that sore spot. Cursing his appendix loudly, Red struggled to his feet despite the pain, kicking Zack in the groin as he tried to rise as well. As Zack lay groaning on the ground, Red seized the nearest burning barrel, and with strength he didn't know he still had, overturned its fiery contents on top of Zack. Zack's struggles suddenly doubled as he thrashed about wildly, trying to put out the flames.

And so Zack never realized that Red had jumped, not until Red's feet came slamming down onto his neck with tremendous force. As if from far away, Red heard a strange gurgling sound beneath him . . . and then silence. Stepping away quickly lest he catch fire as well, Red clutched his aching abdomen, which was still sending sharp pain through his body. As he blinked tears from his eyes, Red looked around at the other vagrants. Most of them stared at him for a moment before hastily looking away . . . though Red couldn't help but notice that Chris continued to stare at him, eyes glittering in a way that sent chills down his spine.

U masi shifted restlessly in his bed, buried under layers of warm blankets. The mattress was comfortable and the pillows were soft, not to mention that it had been a long day. Yet try as he might, Umasi couldn't get himself to sleep. Agitated, he moved again, placing his pillow under his chin.

He could hear the faint sounds of Zen's steady breathing, and knew that his brother must already be asleep. Umasi, however, couldn't stop thinking . . . no, couldn't stop *worrying* about what had happened that day. Could their father, their own father, really be intentionally trying to make them suffer? Not just them, but every student in the entire City? It seemed absurd—what would be the point? And yet Umasi couldn't think of any other way to explain what he and Zen had overheard.

Umasi turned over on his side, wrapping his blanket around himself as he did so. He wasn't as worried about what they had heard as he was about Zen's reaction. In that brief, frightening moment, Umasi had seen something dangerous stirring in Zen's eyes. It had swiftly faded, but Zen hadn't been the same all day. Distant. Isolated. Cold. Umasi hadn't attempted to talk with him—he still remembered the fear. That unfamiliar, irrational fear he had felt in that moment of revelation.

He had been afraid that Zen might strike him.

Zen had sworn to get to the bottom of it. What could that mean? What was he planning? Umasi couldn't help but shiver, despite all the blankets. For some reason he dreaded the idea of facing the uncertainty of the next day. He didn't want to fall asleep, as it meant that he'd have to awaken the next morning. What would Zen do? What would he find? Umasi knew it might be serious, and yet he didn't know what to do about it. He could sense that disaster was coming, and yet couldn't do anything to prevent it, or even warn others about it. If only he hadn't come up with the stupid idea of eavesdropping in the first place.

Umasi shivered again. All of a sudden, he felt chilly all over. His arms couldn't get enough heat, no matter how tightly he pressed them against his chest. Everything, his thoughts included, now seemed distant and vague. He faintly heard himself groaning, as if it were a faraway echo. He felt almost separate from his body and all its sensations . . . except the cold. That persistent, clinging iciness.

And then Umasi felt a pang of terror so overwhelming that he bolted upright, his heart racing. The room was completely unlit at night, and his eyes couldn't see anything, even accustomed to the gloom. And yet Umasi was certain that something terrible was lurking about—or else why would he be so frightened? And then memories began to flash before Umasi's eyes. Failing grades. Bullies chasing him. His father, yelling. A cockroach, still moving after being crushed. His glasses, shattering as they fell to the floor. Falling from a balcony in the mansion, seeing the floor rushing up to meet him . . .

Eyes. Enormous, cold, hateful eyes set into a pale face, staring down at him as he wailed inside the crib. Then the glare faded away, and then that's when Umasi saw it.

For one fleeting moment, he caught a glimpse of a head concealed by a dark hood. Then suddenly, Umasi felt as though he had been set on fire. And then he knew no more.

4

Parental Control

H ow is he, Father?"

"He seems to be a bit delirious, but it's nothing too serious. Just a regular fever."

"The weather *has* been getting cold lately."

"Well, it's not even winter yet . . . though your brother has always been rather fragile compared to you. Don't tell him I said that, by the way."

"Wouldn't dream of it. So, what should we do for him?"

"He just needs to stay in bed, drink lots of juice, take his medicine, and rest. I'd watch over him myself . . . but unfortunately I've got some important work to do today that I can't put off. I'll have the staff look after him. You should too, but be careful not to catch what he's got."

"Well that goes without saying."

"Good boy. I'll try to be back early today—call me if there are any problems. You have my number."

"Of course."

Umasi heard a door shut, as if the sound had echoed over to him from a great distance away. The voices had ceased talking—what had they been saying again? He couldn't concentrate. Everything seemed disorganized and unclear, as if his normally neatly arranged thoughts had been dunked into a pool where they could float about erratically, bumping off one another. It took him a while to realize that he felt hot. Fever. The voices had said something about fever. That must be it.

He felt something cool and wet being applied to his forehead, soothing the fires in his head. Attempting to make some sense of what was going on, Umasi forced his eyes open to find that everything was a confusing blur. Cool trickles dripped down his face, and he realized that someone had put a wet towel on his forehead. Blinking to rid himself of a drop of water that had landed on his eyelid, he opened his eyes again to see a blurry shadow standing over him. The shadow reached down towards him and he felt something being slipped onto his face. The next thing he knew, Umasi saw Zen's face looking down at him emotionlessly. Glasses, Umasi realized. Zen had put his glasses on him so he could see.

"No . . . no school?" Umasi mumbled.

"You're still out of it, I see," Zen commented. "No, no school. Today's a Saturday, remember?"

"Oh," Umasi groaned, lucid enough to realize that he was both sick *and* not missing any school.

"Do you recognize who I am?"

"Yeah," Umasi croaked.

"Well, then, you're not completely delirious," Zen observed. "Nonetheless, you're to stay in bed for the rest of the day. Leave everything to me."

"Leave . . . what?"

"*The truth,*" Zen whispered, leaning forward as his voice took on a dangerous tone. "I'm going to investigate Father's 'work.' I'm going to find out what he's really been up to for all these years."

Umasi wasn't of a mind to fully grasp the import of Zen's words, but something about them triggered alarms in his head.

"No . . . no, you mustn't . . ." Umasi protested.

"You don't know what you're saying." Zen laughed. "The maids will be up soon with some drinks and medicine, and then you'll get some rest. It'll do you some good. You shouldn't even be conscious, really—take a nap. By the time you're sober, everything will be taken care of."

"No . . . don't . . ."

"You needn't worry your fevered head about this, Brother," Zen said. "I can do the thinking for the both of us."

Umasi struggled to renew his protests, but his throat was too dry to speak without discomfort. The next thing he knew was the familiar, ringing sound of a door slamming shut—a sound that he knew, even in his fevered state, meant disaster.

*Z*en shut the door behind him and strode off, his footsteps muffled by the thick carpeting. How convenient it was, he thought, that Umasi would end up falling ill today. He wouldn't have to worry about his brother second-guessing him, not to mention that the mansion's entire staff would be dedicating themselves to treating Umasi's fever. With that in mind, Zen quietly proceeded to the small janitor's room, where he knew a large number of keys hung upon one wall. Zen swiftly examined them all before carefully selecting one and slipping it into his pocket. He then climbed up a wooden spiral staircase to the top floor of the mansion, where he proceeded to a large mahogany door.

Zen first tried the brass doorknob, but found it locked. He hadn't expected it to be open, but even the Mayor was careless sometimes. Still, Zen had come prepared, and he smiled as he drew from his pocket the master key that he had retrieved from the janitor's room. It could unlock every door in the mansion, and it was the only key, besides the one the Mayor carried personally, that could unlock the door before him. Zen slid it into the lock, turned it, and without hesitation entered the Mayor's study for the first time in his entire life.

Zen shut the door behind him and flipped a switch on the wall to turn on the lights. His eyes were greeted with a warmly lit room with varnished wooden panels and classic decor. The wall opposite the door was lined end-to-end with bookshelves, all stuffed with teaching literature. To the left side stood a large desk stacked high with papers, a computer, a telephone, and neatly arranged writing utensils. Zen was about to proceed over to the desk when the right wall caught his eye. He walked over to inspect the large bulletin board that hung from it, and as he realized what was pinned up upon the board, his fingernails suddenly dug painfully into the palms of his hands.

The board was strewn with drawings, school papers, tests, report cards, all of them demonstrating absolutely outstanding work over the course of many years. Every one of them bore Umasi's name, every one of them bore comments praising Umasi's efforts. Zen searched the entire board long and hard for something, anything that he had done, but there was nothing. Nothing at all. But more sickening to Zen than that revelation was the realization that he *hadn't* produced anything worthy of being placed upon the board. Zen did not cry; he didn't even twitch. Yet something snapped inside him, and as he spun around to approach the desk, years of repressed bitterness filled his heart.

Tests? Homework? Grades? Useless, petty things! Zen knew that he, unlike his twin, had talents geared for greater things than that. Someday, someday soon, Zen knew, he would show his father—no, show the *entire City*—exactly what he was capable of. If he surpassed them all, who then would be left to grade him?

Zen seized the nearest document on the Mayor's desk and examined it. Then he seized another, and another, his features darkening with every sheet. Every page detailed plans, schemes set forth by the Educators. Everything was there, in painstaking detail—from a program that locked student bathrooms in order to establish their use as a "privilege" to a ploy for teachers to release students late for class so that they could get in trouble with the next teacher. Seemingly everything, big or small, that Zen had ever hated about school lay there on that desk, but the one question he couldn't answer was *why*? Why go through so much trouble to make children miserable? What was the *reason*?

Zen was so obsessed with the search for this answer that he barely noticed it when he came upon a sheet of paper different from all the others. Inspecting it, he realized with a jolt that it was his latest report card, stating that he'd passed everything by a thread. But that wasn't right, the report card Zen had received said he'd failed a few classes! Then realization hit, and Zen felt his bitterness redouble. All this time, his father had been changing his grades. Why? Did the man think that it would *motivate* him?

Zen crammed the report card into his pocket and carefully replaced the rest of the papers before clenching his fists. He had to be absolutely sure before he acted. He knew their crimes, but now he *needed* their motive, and he obviously wasn't going to find that here. For that, there was only one last place that he could look.

Red jerked awake at the sound of gunfire. He was instantly alert, crouching down behind a fallen chunk of concrete as he tried to get a bearing on what was happening. All around him the other vagrants were already fleeing, weaving around more concrete slabs and pillars as they dodged bullets. Even as Red watched, one of his companions caught a bullet in the back, cried out, and fell to the ground. Red immediately understood. No vagrant group in the entire City had guns. This had to be an Enforcer raid.

Red weighed his options. Considering the utter chaos unfolding in the garage, it was clearly every man for himself at this point. Red glanced around. Chris was nowhere to be found, and that suited him just fine. Red didn't think that the Enforcers had spotted him behind the concrete just yet, and the garage was very dark; none of the lights had been working for a long time, the vagrants' fires had been put out in the night, and only faint, distant daylight flickered in from the entrances to the garage at both ends. Of course, the Enforcers would have flashlights, but they couldn't be everywhere at once. Red smiled as he looked around. Another reason the vagrants had favored the parking garage was the numerous sturdy concrete pillars that provided cover.

Red decided not to go for one of the direct exits. As enticing as the daylight was, it probably meant more Enforcers were waiting there to pick off runners. Instead, as soon as he heard the closest Enforcers firing at another target, he leapt out from behind the fallen concrete slab and darted behind a pillar. As soon as he thought it was safe to move, he darted behind another one, and another, slowly making his way deeper into the garage towards the door he knew led to a stairwell. Once he escaped to the ground floor, he would have more options.

With his goal blazing in his mind, Red darted for another column, but this time a flashlight briefly passed over him.

"There's another one!" a voice shouted.

Red swore under his breath, and then abruptly broke into a run through the dark forest of pillars. Other flashlights began skirting the area around him as loud footsteps pursued him, but he knew they'd have a hard time getting a good shot at him.

As gunshots rang out and bits of concrete began flying off the surrounding pillars, Red suddenly came up with a risky plan. With the echo of the garage, the Enforcers wouldn't be able to tell whose footsteps were whose. As soon as Red passed behind another slab of concrete and temporarily out of the Enforcers' sight, he froze, his back tightly pressed against the pillar in the complete darkness. The Enforcers ran past, their flashlights darting everywhere but behind them.

As soon as he was sure that the last Enforcer had passed him, Red quietly slid around the column and doubled back the way he had come as fast as he could without making much noise. He had spotted a small Dumpster the previous night, and upon reaching it he was pleased to discover that it was still full of trash. The trash was old enough to smell rancid even to Red, which was really a good thing: if it smelled bad to him, then the Enforcers probably wouldn't bother digging too deep.

"Where is he?"

"We lost him," an authoritative voice said, echoing throughout the garage. "He may have backtracked. What's the kill count so far?"

"Seven at the last tally, sir."

"We were told to expect more than twice that. We definitely missed some. Spread out and search the area. Shoot anything that moves."

Holding his breath and shutting his nostrils, Red dived into the Dumpster. He would have shut the lid, but was worried about the noise it would make. Instead, Red allowed himself to sink beneath a thin layer of trash, so that he was still able to breathe through the pockets of air between the distasteful objects that made up the garbage. As he waited, completely still, Red thought about what he'd just heard.

These days Enforcer raids were far from uncommon, but it wasn't often that they knew exactly where and when a group of vagrants would be hiding out—and it was even rarer for them to know how many to expect. Enforcers generally discovered them either with routine sweeps . . . or when they were tipped off. Red thought about the missing vagrant that had been mentioned the night before. Could it be that the boy had betrayed them?

The Enforcers hadn't always pursued the vagrants so brutally, but ever since a man named Rothenberg had become their Chief Truancy Officer, they had begun cracking down, offering generous rewards to any vagrant that turned in others. They had killed hundreds and turned more against each other. Rothenberg's name had become more feared and hated than any other among the vagrants.

Red's thoughts were interrupted and he allowed himself a groan inside the Dumpster as the familiar ache in his gut returned. It was getting sharper, more painful by the day, and the only comfort Red could find in that was the possibility that he might actually be dying.

Someday, someday soon, Red knew, he would be free of all this. But until then, all he could do was his best to stay alive. His only ambition was to prove to be as stubborn a victim for the City as he could.

Zen strode up the steps of City Hall, a wrapped box clutched in his hands. All around him adults passing in and out of the building shot curious glances at the unusual sight, but Zen paid them no heed, keeping a bright expression upon his face. As he pushed open the glass doors of the entrance and stepped onto the checkered marble floor of the lobby, he was met by a security guard, who recognized him immediately.

"Zen!" the guard greeted. "What brings you here?"

"I'm here to see my dad." Zen smiled pleasantly. "He's here, isn't he?"

"Oh yes, he came in a few hours ago." The guard nodded. "He should've just started his meeting right now, but I'll call him to let him know you're here."

"No, no, please don't, sir," Zen said. "Today's a special day for him, and I wanted to surprise him." Zen held up the wrapped box.

"A special day?" The guard scratched his head. "It's not his birthday today, is it? Thought that was last month."

"Come now, mister, you're prying into family secrets." Zen frowned. "Father won't like that at all."

"Oh! No, it was my mistake to ask, sorry, I didn't mean to . . ." The guard trailed off, sounding flustered. "Tell you what, son, why don't you just go on up and see your dad? You can surprise him all you like; I won't let him know you're coming. His office is on the fifth floor, I'm sure you know the way."

Zen's face split into a decidedly uncharacteristic smile. "Thank you very much!"

Without waiting for a response, Zen darted through the lobby, through the busy crowds of people, past the stainless-steel doors of the elevator, and into the linoleum-tiled stairway. As soon as he was alone in the stairwell, his smile vanished, his carefree strides were replaced by a stiff gait, and his bright expression smoothed into a flat, emotionless face. Sometimes, Zen thought to himself, the stigma that came along with being a child could actually prove useful. Zen ran up the stairs two at a time until he reached the fifth floor.

Then, taking a deep breath, Zen pushed open the stair doors and made his way towards the Mayor's Office.

You may all have noticed that I've not called a cabinet meeting for quite a while until now," the Mayor said, folding his hands together upon the oval conference table at which they were all seated. "This is because, on the academic side at least, everything has been proceeding exemplarily. Indeed, though we're only barely into the school year, it is shaping up to be one of our best thus far."

"So then what has occasioned this, sir?" one cabinet member asked.

"If you'll refrain from speaking out of turn, I will tell you," the Mayor said. "If you'll remember, six months ago we promoted an Enforcer named Rothenberg to the position of Chief Truancy Officer. Since then he has used most of his increased budget for a citywide crackdown . . . but on vagrancy much more than truancy."

All heads around the table nodded; every Educator was familiar with Rothenberg and his exploits.

"Actually, vagrancy levels *have* in fact been dropping." The Mayor smiled wryly. "This is due in large part to the fact that Rothenberg's men have been killing them all. It appears that it has gotten to the point where even Enforcers have been filing official complaints about it. Some of them have guilty consciences, others worry about the legality of such wholesale slaughter."

"Well, one of those is easily addressed, sir," a cabinet member said quickly. "It is entirely legally sound. If you'll recall City Code 916 . . ."

" '*If deemed necessary, Enforcers may shoot miscreants in abandoned districts so as not to expose the inhabitants in the surrounding vicinities to danger.*' Yes, I'm quite familiar with my own laws," the Mayor said. "The issue here is not the killings—it's one man unilaterally taking action that might upset the entire system."

"I for one think that he has the wrong focus," one cabinet member said. "The vagrants are no threat to our society—they're already outcasts of our system; the dredges, the failures. What we should be worried about is curbing *truancy*. Shouldn't the Chief Truancy Officer be mainly focused on catching *truants*?"

"Not at all," another member interjected. "Job titles aside, you're losing sight of our larger purpose. The reason we exist and the only objective we're to pursue is *control*. To me, the vagrants represent the ultimate defiance of our cause—the only individuals in this City that we *cannot* directly control. Their extermination would go a long way towards making ours the truly ideal society."

"Please, you can't honestly believe that," a third, elderly member said, snorting. "A society that requires regular, bloody purges to maintain control is about the farthest thing from perfect that one can imagine. In fact, isn't that just the thing that we're trying to prevent? Conflict and bloodshed?"

"We're not talking about the vagrants forming an uprising here," the second member countered. "That's unthinkable, of course. But the fact is that the vagrants are a stain upon our otherwise spotless City, and they need to be wiped out. Rothenberg understands this better than you—he's seen it all with his own eyes. He personally goes out on patrols and raids."

"Likely because he enjoys the slaughter," the elderly member said disapprovingly.

"Look at this practically," the first member said impatiently. "The vagrants pose absolutely no threat to our control. They are disorganized, starved, and can't stop fighting each other over scraps. What's more, they are feared, hated, and held up as the ultimate bad example. We've made them the demons of this City—they are what every student fears becoming, what every parent fears their child could become. Exterminating them would be expensive, and deprive us of a powerful tool."

"I say that Rothenberg is the real threat," a fourth member said quietly. "A single officer making such momentous decisions on his own? It sets a bad precedent. He is within his legal boundary as of now, but he is pushing it. Others might start wondering how far they can push their own boundaries. If we don't rein him in, we might conceivably lose control of the Enforcers—and *then* we'd have serious problems."

"But if we do rebuke or demote Rothenberg," a fifth member protested, "it would look as though we're acceding to the complaints. This might inspire others to complain, to challenge our rule more often."

"Good points, all." The Mayor sighed, creasing his forehead with thought. "I confess that based on what little I've seen of the man, I've never had much liking for Rothenberg. But his record speaks to his ability to get things done."

"The *wrong* things," the third member murmured.

"That may or may not be the truth," the Mayor conceded. "To make a decision right now would be rash, I think. We need to take our time to devise a way to deal with this without jeopardizing our control."

"It is certainly the most dangerous threat we have faced in a long time," the fourth member warned.

"Perhaps," the Mayor allowed. "It's quite definitely the greatest danger to our control right *now*, at any rate."

At that very moment, outside the door of the office, Zen noiselessly withdrew himself from the door and stood up solemnly, his brows creased with silent menace as a twisted smile spread across his face.

"My dear, dear father," Zen whispered as he walked back towards the stairs. "You have no idea what kind of threat your *control* has just invited upon itself."

As he reached the stairwell, Zen paused by a garbage can to throw his fake present away. Then, without a second glance, he entered the stairwell as an insane idea began to take shape in his head.

5

The Origin of Truancy

U masi flipped the pages of the book, not really reading the words at all. As a matter of fact, he wasn't even wearing his glasses; they lay to his side, on a wooden stool that also supported a large pitcher and a cup. He didn't think that he could concentrate enough to read even if he did have them on. He wasn't exactly sure what time it was, but he knew it must be late evening already. He certainly felt as though he had taken a long nap.

The last thing he remembered was being fussed over, fed some soup and foul-tasting medicine, and then being told to rest—a request that he had readily obliged. He had awoken feeling much better, and his temperature had been taken before he'd been assured that his fever had gone down. All of that was fine, but what was bothering Umasi was what little he remembered of what had happened *before* that.

At first Umasi had been content to believe that Zen's plans had been part of his many nightmares, but Zen hadn't been in to see him at all that day, and none of the mansion staff had seemed to have seen Zen either—unusual, and more than a little worrying. As the minutes ticked by, Umasi became more certain that Zen really had gone and done something crazy in search of "the truth." And so Umasi was a nervous wreck as he waited there in his comfortable bed, flipping the pages of a book to keep himself distracted.

As Umasi reached the end of the book and slammed it shut, a loud noise assaulted his ears. His head snapped towards the door, where he saw Zen entering. Umasi reached for his glasses, and as soon as he put them on he quickly wished that he hadn't. Zen towered over him, staring down with a dangerous, excited gleam in his eyes.

"What happened?" Umasi asked.

"It's all true," Zen hissed. "They really are . . . they're the ones responsible for everything wrong with school!"

"You mean . . . it's all intentional?"

"Of course it's intentional!" Zen exploded. "They document this stuff, meticulously! They plan these things like experiments, as if we were lab rats!"

"But why would they?" Umasi asked. "It makes no sense!"

Zen turned to glower at a bare wall of their room, as if seeing something hanging from it that Umasi could not.

"I wondered that myself, and that's what I sought to discover today," Zen muttered, as though to no one in particular. "It's all about control, about maintaining their supposedly perfect society." He spun around to point at Umasi. "They're trying to make us dependent on their instruction! Through the schools they punish individuality, they make us faceless prisoners with only the faintest illusion of freedom!"

Zen's newfound fervor was frightening to behold, and Umasi was surprised to find that he had the nerve to reply to his brother's rant.

"But . . . isn't what they're doing just maintaining law and order?" Umasi argued. "They're just keeping the peace. I mean . . . without the schools all sorts of miscreants might run amok."

Zen looked at Umasi incredulously.

"Brother, in case you're missing something, we're talking about a government destroying self-learning in order to force its citizens, its children, to become dependent on their system!" Zen said heatedly. "Are you supporting psychological torture for the purpose of suppressing independent thought?"

Umasi had no answer to that, though some dark corner of his brain began to suspect that Zen was going crazy.

"Your schoolwork, your grades, all your precious achievements, all it represents is complicity!" Zen snarled, turning back to face the wall once more. "School is not meant to educate. It's meant to dominate! But they won't have it all their way. I'll make sure of that."

Zen was calm again, and glanced over at Umasi.

"I hope you feel better," Zen said quietly, changing the subject. "I think I will retire today—I'll leave you to your thoughts."

And Umasi certainly had plenty of those.

H ey, you!"

Red tensed, leaping back off the wall he'd leaned against when his pains had started acted up. Snapping his head around, he was dismayed to find a vicious-looking vagrant approaching him with obviously hostile intent. Though Red didn't recognize the girl, he knew that the odds were that this was a member of the rival gang that had been causing Chris trouble lately. The attacker was wielding a rusty knife in her hand, but Red was fairly sure that he could outrun her, unless . . .

Red glanced back over his shoulder.

Damn.

Two more vagrants were walking up the narrow street behind him, unarmed, but both larger than he was. Red took a deep breath, turned sideways so that his back was to the wall of a building, and kept an eye on both of the approaching parties. As he did, Red wondered how he could've been caught in such a simple and obvious trap; he must really be slipping. Red silently cursed his appendix as he prepared for the inevitable confrontation, wishing that he'd stolen something to eat since escaping from the underground garage.

"Hey guys, what's up?" Red grinned at the armed vagrant.

The vagrant tossed her knife from one hand to another as she closed in on Red, not returning the smile at all. Instead, she looked at her two approaching buddies and called out to them.

"Isn't this one of Chris' little rats?" she asked.

Red winced at that. He still didn't feel anything but wary as far as Chris was concerned, not to mention that he hadn't seen or heard from his gang since the escape from the parking garage. Red had grown increasingly convinced that someone had betrayed the group to the Enforcers, and was now entertaining the possibility that he might have been the only survivor, though he doubted it; Chris' bunch was notoriously good at staying alive.

"Beats me. Anyways, it don't matter if he is or if he isn't. He sure ain't one of us."

"What should we do with him?"

"Kill him," the girl said immediately. "The weather's been gettin' cold lately. All I got are rags, and I like the look of his shirt."

"Hey, we ain't too fancily dressed ourselves," one of the boys protested—and it was indeed the truth.

Red rolled his eyes. His clothes, picked up off the street and from garbage piles, weren't "fine" even by vagrant standards, but if he wanted to live through the winter, he'd need them. Also, they were just about the only things left that he actually owned. Red knew that if the thugs had any sense, they would've attacked him without wasting any time, but they obviously didn't think that Red had a chance at escape. Overconfidence—a cardinal sin among vagrants.

"See, I think I like his pants. Those are some warm-looking pants," a boy observed. "Lemme get the pants and you can have the shirt."

"Which one of his pants, nitwit? He's obviously wearing more than one!" the girl snapped.

"The kid is like an onion, with all those layers," the last vagrant chuckled. "And he smells like one too!"

At that, Red decided to make his move. As one of the boys doubled over with laughter, Red lashed out with one foot, catching the thug squarely between the legs. No reason to play fair, Red thought as the vagrant dropped to the ground squealing. Knowing that he had precious little time left to act, Red tackled the girl, seizing her wrist with both arms and twisting as hard as he could. His adversary let out a shriek as she dropped the knife.

Red dived, seizing the hilt of the weapon just before the third assailant could get his hands on it. As he pushed himself painfully to his feet, Red saw the disappointed vagrant charging him like a car with its breaks cut. Red didn't hesitate, thrusting the knife forward with a yell. There was a scream, and something warm and sticky poured over Red's hand. The vagrant dropped to the ground, writhing in agony as a scarlet stain spread across his filthy clothing.

By then the other two attackers had risen and were about to lunge, but upon seeing what had happened to their comrade they skidded to a halt, eyeing the blade apprehensively. Red forced a grin even as bile rose in his throat.

"By the way, yeah, I'm with Chris," Red said as cockily as he could. "Go back and tell whoever's leading you guys this week not to mess with us."

And with that, Red spun around and ran. He had never really been very devoted to Chris' crew—now less so than ever, as he didn't know if the gang even existed anymore. Still, Red knew that strength in numbers, or even the illusion of it, could be very intimidating among vagrants. And sure enough, the thugs let him go, glaring at his receding back.

Wiping the bloody knife on his pants, Red slipped it between his belt and his pants as he fled. Red was pretty good at running, even with the persistent aches in his gut. Night was just setting in, and it didn't take him long to vanish down a maze of back alleyways on the streets of District 7.

Zen crammed the last spoonful of cereal into his mouth, glancing across the table. Umasi looked weary this morning, and Zen couldn't help but notice that he'd barely touched his toast. The maids had insisted that Umasi's fever had passed, but to Zen it looked as though his brother hadn't gotten any sleep at all the previous night. Zen vaguely realized that he should be concerned, but his newfound obsession had seized him like a fever of its own. All he could think about was what he had seen and heard the day before, and so, done with his breakfast, Zen wasted no time in darting off alone. He wasn't in any mood to be bothered, and he had a feeling that there was a good chance that Umasi would want to do just that.

Arriving at his destination, Zen turned the knob and pulled the door open as he flicked the light switch on the wall. Rows upon rows of jackets, shirts, and other articles of clothing were illuminated before him, forming a forest of garments. Zen looked around the hallway first to make sure he wasn't being watched, and then plunged into the mess of outfits, shutting the door behind him. He needed a private place to work and to hide its products—somewhere he could be sure that he wouldn't be disturbed or discovered. This was a difficult need to fulfill in the Mayoral Mansion, watched over as it was by countless staff.

Moments later, Zen was crouched down upon the floor between a set of navy blue jackets and a row of overlarge leather coats. It really wasn't a room so much as it was a glorified clothes closet for garments that no one wore more than once or twice a year (if ever). It smelled odd, but it was quiet, comfortable, and absolutely private. No one, not even the cleaning staff, ever had a reason to open this particular closet. Zen smiled, remembering hiding from Umasi in this closet back when they used to play hide-and-seek. Umasi never did find him.

At that thought, Zen frowned and narrowed his eyes. Umasi, being the curious brother that he was, would come looking for him sooner or later—and it wouldn't be a game, and there wouldn't be any head start. If Umasi managed to find or follow him to the closet . . . well, Zen decided, he would just have to make sure that didn't happen. It wasn't that Zen didn't trust Umasi. When the time came, Zen knew that he could count on his brother's help. After all, no matter how reluctantly, Umasi had *always* gone along with Zen's crazy ideas. The problem in Zen's mind was that Umasi was not as cautious or vigilant as he was, and Zen was taking no chances about letting something slip before he was ready.

And then there was the billboard in their father's study.

Zen shook his head to clear that troublesome thought, then bent down and spread his papers upon the hard wood floor. He began poring over a large map of the City, divided by district. Checking the map against a printed list, Zen began highlighting all the abandoned districts with a red marker. He worked with furious speed, as if seized by a sudden madness. In no time at all, the entire map had been marked, and Zen turned his efforts towards a long roster that he had printed out from the computer in his father's study.

The names on the roster all belonged to students—the worst students, or so they had been flagged by the Educators. These were the underachievers, the troublemakers, the truants of the City. For a whole hour Zen sat there on the floor examining each student's profile, crossing off or circling each name he came upon. Some of the students he determined were genuinely dumb or violent, but on the opposite end of the spectrum there were innocents: students who meant no harm but simply ended up in the wrong situations at the wrong times. Others, however, Zen judged were probably like him—proud spirits at heart, lashing out at an oppressive system.

Now he would give them all an opportunity to lash out together.

Zen had started from the top of the list, which was in alphabetical order, and was eventually startled to discover his own name upon it. Startled, but not displeased. The roster had flagged him as uncooperative, a distractive influence, and, most recently, a truant. Zen smiled grimly. Everyone in the

City spoke the word "truant" with a certain amount of disapproval, if not revulsion, as if that one word summed up all that was scorned by education—and maybe it did. But they didn't know the truth, and he did. Why should he be ashamed to be a truant? If the Educators' system was wrong, then wasn't failing it *right*?

"Yes," Zen muttered to himself, " 'Truant' is a title that I'll be proud to bear."

At that, Zen froze, contemplating what he had just said. Seized by sudden inspiration, he interrupted his checking of the roster and grabbed a fresh sheet of lined paper. Steadying his hand, which had begun to tremble with excitement, Zen touched a pen to the paper and slowly scribbled a header at the top:

The
TRUANCY

Truancy. *The* Truancy. Zen stared down at the word. He knew that no one would yet see on that paper what he saw, but he also knew that it would only be a matter of time. That word, Zen realized, was the seed that he would grow into something powerful and terrible enough to consume the entire corrupt City. Joyous excitement exploded in his chest, prompting him to laugh—and he did so gladly, feeling more thrilled than ever before in his life. His mirth was limited to the closet, thoroughly muffled as it was by the heaps of clothing, but to Zen it felt as though it reverberated throughout the entire world.

An hour later, Zen exited the closet, flipped its lights off, and shut the door. Inside the closet, hidden within the pockets of a large fur coat, were all the documents that Zen had worked with and produced on that fateful day. It was enough to leave the pockets bulging, and Zen knew he would return to work some more that night.

Zen smiled inwardly. He had never been half as productive with his schoolwork.

That night Umasi found himself restless for the third night in a row, though this time it was worse than ever. He couldn't even shut his eyes, but rather remained upright in bed, transfixed upon the splotch of blackness where his brother should've been sleeping, but wasn't. Zen had vanished for most of the day, and Umasi had no idea where he'd gone. It wasn't like Zen to vanish like that without telling him anything, and Umasi couldn't remember the last time Zen had slipped out of bed for *any* reason. He was sacrificing precious hours of sleep . . . and to do *what*? These strange new behaviors seemed . . . alien, as if the brother Umasi had always known were now a complete stranger.

Umasi couldn't even begin to imagine what Zen was working on, but he knew that Zen couldn't have just idled the entire day. He had almost asked Zen straight up what he had been doing, but nothing about Zen had invited conversation that day. Umasi knew that it was the uncertainty that was killing him—knowing that something was happening, but not knowing *what*. And so he hung there in the darkness, torturously dangling between ignorance and enlightenment.

Unable to stand it anymore, Umasi got out of bed, shivering slightly as the cool air hit his skin through his thin pajamas. Slowly, he walked over towards Zen's bed. And walked. And walked. Strange, Umasi thought, he didn't remember Zen's bed being so far away. Suddenly, a gust of freezing wind assaulted him, forcing him to shut his eyes to protect them from the sting. When he opened his eyes again, he found himself sitting at a desk in a classroom.

Umasi blinked. The room was empty except for him, Mr. Benjamin, and a silhouetted student sitting in the front row. The teacher was writing something on the blackboard, and Umasi reflexively began to copy it down. But as soon as Umasi seized his pen, he found that he couldn't concentrate. No matter how hard he tried, whatever was on the board just wasn't interesting enough to keep his attention. Frustrated and bored, Umasi began scribbling idly until he felt a hand touch his shoulder. Umasi looked up, and a wave of panic surged through him as he saw Mr. Benjamin glaring down at him.

As Mr. Benjamin began to shout, Umasi found his gaze drawn to the other student in the classroom. The boy seemed not to notice his plight, completely intent on copying down what was on the board. Umasi blinked again, and found that Mr. Benjamin was no longer shouting, but handing back tests. Umasi stared at his score, a sixty, and then glanced over at the other boy, who was smiling ear-to-ear at a hundred. This wasn't fair, Umasi realized. He *knew* that he was smarter than the other boy. All the other boy was doing was repeating what the teacher wanted him to, like a trained parrot.

Angry tears began welling up in his eyes. Umasi blinked them away, and found that he was standing in his room. His father was yelling at him, and though Umasi could not hear the words, he knew that he was being told to be more like the other boy. As his father fell silent, Umasi turned to find the boy looking up at him from his desk, surrounded by piles of finished homework.

"It's really not that hard, you know," the boy said condescendingly.

"Speak for yourself," Umasi retorted.

The other boy smiled at that. "Come on, let me help you."

"Help me do what? Be more like you?"

"Why not?"

"Because I'm *not* you!" Umasi screamed. "I can't be someone I'm not! I can't be like you! I don't *want* to be like you!"

"But don't you see how happy I am? Don't you see how easy things are when you sacrifice your pride? Here, let me show you."

Umasi was back in school, Ms. Hill screaming that he was an inferior as the other boy sat back at his own desk, unscathed. Then his father appeared, presenting the other boy with a new bike for his outstanding report card. Umasi relived memory upon memory, but from a new perspective. Their first day of high school . . . the last test they had taken . . . their third-grade report cards . . . his own birthday. Always the other boy was there, a model student, an ideal son, a flawless example of mindless obedience. Everyone loved that other boy, everyone showered him with praise and affection—the way one might pet a well-behaved dog.

"Enough!" Umasi shouted. "You're right—it's easy to sacrifice pride, which is why I won't do it!"

"That's too bad for you," the other boy said sadly. "Because then you'll never be happy in this City."

The words were like a slap in the face. Umasi heard the truth in them, a truth that robbed him of his breath and flooded him with hopelessness. For a moment Umasi felt certain that he would just give up, that he would just lie down and die . . . but he was not so weak as that. Frustration, bitterness, and hate quickly filled the void in his heart, driving him towards a logical, yet mad, conclusion.

"If I cannot be happy in this City"—Umasi laughed—"then I'll just destroy it! I'll make a City that suits ME! I will rule the City, and there's not a single soul in it that can stop me!"

The other boy vanished before his rage, and Umasi felt exhilarated, liberated, free for the first time in his life! All the hatred that he had bottled up through his ordeals came pouring out—hatred for the adults, for school, but most of all for the other boy, who he could never be. . . .

And then Umasi woke up in a cold sweat. As he sat up in his own bed, gasping for air, warm tears ran freely down his cheeks—for he knew that other boy was himself.

6

LEARNING A LESSON

Umasi adjusted his glasses and looked over at Zen's desk. His sleep had hardly been peaceful, but Umasi had awoken on Monday morning with a remarkably clear head, along with some troublesome feelings. Though he couldn't remember precisely the details of his dreams, Umasi had retained enough of the emotions to feel pity for Zen. What's more, for some reason he felt terribly uncomfortable with himself.

Umasi shook his head. While he was somewhat disappointed to return to school, he was glad that he'd have the chance to keep an eye on his brother. Umasi never did see Zen return to bed, and couldn't know exactly how much sleep he'd had gotten—but Zen's general inertness, the dark rings under his eyes, and his sluggish movements all indicated that the answer was "not much." Umasi's sympathy now outweighed his curiosity, and so during their free period Umasi had dragged Zen to a hallway bench where he could rest—or so Umasi had thought. It hadn't taken long for a pair of security guards to accost them, rudely awaking Zen as they screeched at him for violating student boundaries.

Umasi had forgotten about the recently instituted "free period rooms" simply because it didn't make any sense to him considering that benches had been laid out in the hallways for student use. But in light of Zen's revelation, Umasi now understood the true purpose of the seemingly pointless rule. Some of the bitterness from his dream—Zen's bitterness, Umasi sensed—had followed him into consciousness, and for a moment Umasi considered defying the guards. Ultimately, Umasi decided that it wasn't the right time to make a stand, especially since he was worried that Zen might do something rash. However, Zen merely rose, flashed the guards a chilling "just you wait" smile, and then lumbered off to rest in the nearest bathroom.

It was probably the most unpleasant place in the entire building to take a nap.

Still, Zen didn't seem to mind, and Umasi was glad that he had avoided getting into trouble. The rest of the free period passed without incident, leading them into science class. By this point Zen still looked so tired that Umasi had begun to wonder whether his brother had gotten any sleep the previous night at all. Remembering his ominous dream, Umasi resolved to ask Zen about what he'd been up to when they got home. That decided, Umasi unpacked his binder as the teacher began talking.

"Can anyone tell me what these are?" the teacher asked, gesturing towards a cage placed upon her desk.

"Rats," came the monotonous, choral reply.

"Yes, but these are not normal rats," the teacher declared. "Can anyone tell me what's wrong with them?"

Silence.

"Zen, how about you?"

Out of the corner of his eye, Umasi saw Zen jerk up his head, which had been lolling upon his desk like a wayward beach ball. Umasi knew that the teacher was punishing him for being exhausted; putting one's head down in class was an invitation to be called upon, a simple tactic that was uniformly effective in getting students to act awake. Renewed pity surged through Umasi as Zen glared at the cage of rats.

"Their eyes are red," Zen murmured. Indeed, the rats' eyes *were* blood-red.

"Yes," the teacher conceded, sounding disappointed as Zen's head dipped a few inches. "Anything else?"

"They're white," Zen added, his head sinking a bit further.

"Correct," the teacher admitted. "These are albino rats. Can anyone tell me what that means?"

Seeing a chance to divert the teacher's attention from his brother, Umasi raised his hand—predictably the only one to go up in the entire sleepy classroom. The teacher didn't hesitate to take the bait.

"Yes, Umasi?" The teacher pointed an approving finger at him.

"It's a condition caused by recessive genes. It can be inherited from the parents, or sometimes occur through random mutation," Umasi explained as Zen's head flopped silently down onto the table once more.

"Very good." The teacher nodded. "And what does it do?"

"It prevents the body from producing pigment, which is what gives it its color," Umasi quoted the textbook, watching Zen lazily raise his own textbook to shield his sleeping head from view. "Aside from sensitivity to sunlight and some vision disabilities, albinos are just as physically fit as regular members of their species."

"Excellent," the teacher exulted, turning back to face the class as a whole. "Albinism can afflict mammals, reptiles, fish, birds, and amphibians. Individuals with albinism usually appear white, and in many species the eyes appear red due to the underlying blood vessels showing through."

The teacher's predatory gaze began to sweep around the room, coming dangerously close to spotting Zen's head buried in his textbook. Thinking fast, Umasi raised his hand again. The motion caused the boy next to Umasi to mutter "suck-up" under his breath, but Umasi ignored the snide remark, as the sudden movement had succeeded in catching the teacher's eye.

"Are there albino people?" Umasi asked. He knew the answer, but out of desperation had seized upon the first question to come to mind.

"As a matter of fact, there are, though you'll seldom see them, especially in this City." The teacher pursed her lips, as if discussing a distasteful subject. "In human albinos, the eyes are usually blue more often than red. Human eyes are typically deep enough to cover the blood vessels, though there are exceptions in certain types of lighting."

Umasi continued to jot down notes mechanically, keeping an eye on his brother's condition out of the corner of his eye. What the teacher said next, however, stopped Umasi dead in his tracks.

"However, all albinos regardless of eye color have significant vision problems that make them unfit for education, and thus unfit for normal life in this City," the teacher finished. "It's unfortunate, of course, but students must conform to education and not the other way around."

A moment of tense silence followed, indicating that some students in the class disagreed with the teacher—though no one cared enough to speak up. Then the silence was shattered by an outburst from the most unexpected of persons.

"Unfit for life?" Umasi demanded. "How can you say that?"

For a moment the teacher was taken aback at a model student arguing with her, but she quickly rallied and responded with a note of anger in her voice.

"Education is the most important aspect of any child's life. There is no place in this City for an educational liability," the teacher said. "Some of these people can't even do as much as look at an overhead projection. Their handicap guarantees substandard grades. It's unfortunate, like I said, but they are unfit for school, and if you're unfit for school, you're unfit for society!"

"That doesn't make sense!" Umasi retorted. "You can't judge a person's worth based on their grades alone!"

By now all the students in the class had shaken off their weariness, staring at this new phenomenon—a teacher arguing with her favored student. Out of the corner of his eye, Umasi spotted Zen looking at him with a mixture of surprise and approval.

"You can in this City!" the teacher snapped. "And *you* need to show more respect! I'm surprised at you, of all people, talking to a teacher like that!"

"I'm sorry," Umasi lied, "but if education isn't meant to conform to the needs of students, what should it conform to?"

"The rules. And the rules are that a student is worth no more than their grade," the teacher said flatly. "It's harsh, but it's the truth. And unless *you* want your personal value to decrease, I suggest you hold your tongue."

Umasi did was he was told, but fumed on the inside. He wasn't sure what had set him off like that. The teacher *had* upset him with her callous statements, but he had never been one to talk back to a teacher, no matter what. Still, somehow his anger felt *good,* as though a long-dormant part of him was finally asserting itself. Umasi smiled; maybe losing your temper once in a while wasn't so bad after all. Then he remembered the anger from his nightmare, and his smile vanished, replaced by a thoughtful look.

Zen was up to *something,* he knew, which was good; Umasi now agreed that something had to be done. And Umasi had the utmost faith in his brother. Zen's plans were always effective ones. Whatever it was that Zen was planning, Umasi resolved that he *would* make his brother tell him about it.

And maybe, just *maybe,* Umasi would help him.

I've looked at the latest proposition."

"And?"

"It's unacceptable."

"I had a feeling you'd say that, sir. Do you mind if I ask why?"

"Not at all. Reinstating physical punishment is completely counterproductive. It's a regression, an insult to decades and generations of progress."

"Our system did start with it, sir."

"And that was before my time, if you'll recall. Since then we've refined our methods so that we don't have to be so . . . *crude.*"

"Crude methods can be effective."

"And destructive. There *will* be official complaints from all sides with something as blatant and dramatic as this. Not to mention that our more subtle tactics have produced much better results."

"If this were phased in over the course of several years, even decades . . ."

"It wouldn't be worth the trouble, or the risk. We have much more promising venues to pursue."

"And I imagine that you're concerned about your own sons."

"I wouldn't be much of a father if I weren't. As a matter of fact, I'm not much of a father anyway—I hardly have time to see them these days, and when I do, it's clear that our work has been taking its toll on them."

"It taken its toll on all of us at one point."

"A common rationalization."

"I know, sir. And I don't actually support the proposition, I was just curious."

"Oh?"

"Yes. I . . . apologize for lying to you before, sir, but I actually *do* have children."

"I see. And why didn't you tell me?"

"If you'll forgive me sir, I just wanted to know if your heart was in the right place."

"I've fired others for less, but as one parent to another I can understand your concern. Besides, I knew you were lying."

"You . . . you did, sir?"

"I personally examine the backgrounds of all my staff, no matter how minor they are. But now that you've come clean, I can assure you that though some have accused me of lacking a heart, my intentions *are* noble."

"I believe it."

"Good. Now, let me see if I recall correctly . . . you have one daughter and one son, right?"

"Yes, sir, their names are Tack and Suzie."

Satisfied with his work, Zen collected his papers into neat piles, rolled them up, and then stuffed them into the various coat pockets hanging above him. He was making good progress; by now he had to use six different jackets just to hold it all. He had lists detailing every conceivable item he'd need, their exact costs, and how he might procure them. He had circled critical government buildings on his map. He had even determined which potential Truants would be most beneficial to his cause.

Zen didn't think that funds would be a problem. With his and Umasi's special accounts combined, they easily had enough to sustain a sizeable army for a decade, if not longer. And Zen knew that there would be ways to generate income and offset expenses once the Truancy was established. In a few days, he would finally be ready to pass the point of no return—to leave home, hit the streets, and see the abandoned districts for himself. After he'd secured reliable hideouts, the recruitment could begin.

Zen stood up and stretched amidst the various garments. Allowing himself a deep sigh of satisfaction, he made his way to the door, pushed it open . . .

And found himself face-to-face with Umasi.

"Greetings," Zen said, swiftly masking his surprise.

"What were you doing in there?" Umasi asked innocently enough, though Zen could see Umasi's eyes narrow slightly behind his glasses.

"Homework," Zen said.

"I see," Umasi said. "Well, that's odd, because I have your homework here. I just did it for you, as a matter of fact."

Umasi held out a roll of papers, which Zen slowly reached out to accept before changing his mind halfway through.

"Thanks for the thought," Zen said, withdrawing his hand and narrowing his eyes, "but I think we both know that I won't be needing them."

"Quite so," Umasi agreed. "What are you up to, Zen?"

Zen contemplated Umasi for a second before smirking.

"I suppose there's no reason not to tell you now. After all, in a few days it'll all begin."

"What will?"

"The Truancy."

"Truancy?"

"*The* Truancy," Zen corrected. "The organization that will stand against the Educators."

"How can I help?" Umasi asked without hesitation, prompting another smile from Zen.

"You won't need to do much, of course," Zen assured his brother. "I will need your account card, but frankly you're not much good in a fight and—"

"Wait," Umasi interrupted, frowning. "What do you mean by 'fight'?"

Zen looked at Umasi incredulously.

"Fight, battle, conflict, war, whatever you want to call it," Zen explained as though Umasi were dumb. "What, did you think that the Truancy would be all pickets and picnics?"

"Why not?"

"Why not?" Zen repeated. "Surely you're joking. You can't possibly hope to change anything in this City that way."

"You can't know that until you try," Umasi pointed out.

"And if you try and fail, enormous effort would've been wasted only to have the Educators crack down so hard that you won't be able to piss without having something breathing down your neck," Zen spat.

"Then why not wait until we're adults?" Umasi suggested. "Then we'll be treated like real people, we'll have the same rights—"

"No." Zen shook his head firmly. "I will not fall into that trap."

"What do you mean?"

"Don't you see? That's the greatest part of their system, it's their safety valve!" Zen hissed. "Oppressed peoples might overthrow their tyrants, but not if they can count on *one day joining the oppressors*! The City does just that, and it works! Those that harbor rebellious thoughts in school eventually grow up, forget what it was like not to be treated like a real person, and then dismiss the suffering of the next generation as a childish phase. The oppressed can't *wait* to become the oppressors, and some of them will even defend inequality so that they can someday enjoy it themselves."

Umasi stared at Zen, clearly disturbed by the passion with which Zen uttered every word. Either that, Zen thought, or perhaps he was more disturbed by the realization that every word Zen spoke was the truth.

"This is an eternal cycle of cruelty, and *I* will not be part of it," Zen continued darkly. "If I am to cause suffering, I will do it on my own terms, not theirs."

"But if you're as devoted as you say you are, you'll remember your goals, your ideals, and carry them even into adulthood."

Zen hesitated at that, just for a moment. It wasn't like Umasi to maintain an argument for this long.

"And what if I do?" Zen laughed. "What if I do succeed in toppling the Educators, securing freedom for the students? What then? I'll become their protector, their *rescuer,* a wizened parent that guides the dumb child, a devoted shepherd that protects the vulnerable flock! If I rescue them and they are unable to do so themselves, I, the adult, will be the superior and they the inferiors. The cycle will start all over again!

"You see, Umasi," Zen continued, "it must be done now, while we're still children. If we wait too long, we'll become them, and even if we defeat them they will have won. Students need to secure their own freedom, to prove their own worth and demonstrate their own strength. Only when children genuinely dominate the adults can you say that something has changed. We have to act before it's too late."

Umasi let out a sad sigh. "And this action would involve bloodshed."

"There is no other way."

Umasi breathed deeply, as if readying himself for an impossible task. Then his head rose and he looked Zen straight in the eye.

"Then I'm sorry, Zen, but I can't be part of your Truancy."

Zen stared, his eyes wide, and Umasi realized that for the first time in his life, he had made Zen speechless. Umasi felt his heart squeeze painfully at the look of infinite betrayal in Zen's eyes, but still managed an apologetic smile as he turned to walk away.

"You said it yourself, Brother," Umasi called sadly. "I'm a pacifist."

U masi finished buttoning his pajamas and lay down upon his bed, his hands folded behind his head. He took a deep, calming breath before shutting his eyes. He couldn't believe it. Umasi had been so sure that Zen couldn't possibly be planning murder, and yet that was exactly what he had been doing all this time. Umasi was tempted to believe that Zen couldn't possibly know what he was getting into, but he knew Zen too well to accept that. What's more, Umasi still remembered the anger of his dream, the unspeakable hatred and the clarity it had brought—or rather, the insanity.

None of his nights had been untroubled for the past few days, and now that it was bedtime again, Umasi was sure that the ominous nightmares would return. And yet, oddly enough, he found that he simply didn't care anymore. Maybe it was because he had enough to worry about while awake, or maybe he'd finally begun to embrace the nightmares, horrible though they might be. Whatever the reason, it was almost as though he had become numb to nocturnal emotions. For a moment, Umasi idly wondered if he was going crazy himself, just as he suspected Zen was. Then he nodded off to sleep.

It came as no surprise to Umasi when he opened his eyes to find himself floating in perfect darkness, save for a strange, faint glow that seemed to issue forth from his skin, revealing swirling smoke all around him. Umasi examined his luminous self interestedly, and barely reacted when a shadowy figure, revealed by Umasi's own glow, began approaching him.

"So, you've finally found some nerve," the silhouetted figure observed. "That's good. Now that you've got it, why don't we have a straight conversation for once?"

"Who are you?" Umasi asked calmly.

The figure laughed faintly, but did not answer.

"I think you know who I am. Really, I'm surprised that you've tolerated me for this long, Umasi," the boy said. "Your brother grew out of me a long time ago. You should've been rid of me years back. After all, you always were the more dangerous of the two."

"Me? More dangerous than Zen?" Umasi asked.

"Oh yes—with you, innocence and goodness are just shoddy coats of paint over a canvas of menace," the boy said. "At the core, you're no less perilous than your brother is. More so, in fact."

"No."

"Denial. That's childish. The same blood flows in your veins, and the same pride inflates your heads, whether you flaunt it or not." The boy chuckled, and Umasi thought he caught a glimpse of familiar features beneath the shadow. "Don't you feel the blistering of your pride every time you are humiliated? Don't you fight a losing war against your own outrage every time you are treated unjustly?"

Umasi gritted his teeth, but did not respond.

"Not to mention," the figure added, "that you're both horribly unpredictable—insanity runs strongly in your veins. It must be a family heritage."

"Insanity?"

"How else to explain all this?" The boy laughed. "Am I not proof that

you're completely out of your mind . . . though admittedly in a very different way from your twin?"

"What are you?"

"You sound frustrated. Well, that's progress, I suppose." The boy chuckled. "Am I making you angry, Umasi? Don't worry—when you try to re-
press emotions, anger is always the first to slip through. Your temper tells
me that I'm doing my job."

"What are you!" Umasi shouted again, louder.

"I am you, Umasi, and I am weak." The shadow spun around and began
walking away. "In the end, either you will conquer me . . . or I will conquer
you."

7

STANDING HIS GROUND

Several days had passed since Umasi confronted Zen. In that time winter had officially arrived, bringing with it the first snow of the year. Of course, snow in the City rarely amounted to much. It had to fall in extraordinary amounts to even accumulate on the streets, and the City's snowplows were so effective that Umasi had never seen a blizzard so terrible that the roads couldn't be cleared for school the next day.

And so while Umasi sat at his desk alone in the room he shared with Zen, the snow had already come and gone, leaving only chilly air behind. Absentmindedly, Umasi scribbled down another answer upon a sheet of lined paper. Homework had become an almost calming ritual for him, as the problems it presented now seemed so trivial when compared with his real problems.

Realizing that he'd made an error with one answer, Umasi hastily erased it with the back of his pencil. Umasi smiled as he swept the resulting shavings away. If only it were so easy to erase mistakes from his life. Umasi continued working, mentally preparing himself for what he knew was coming. Earlier that day, Zen had told him to meet him on the roof of the mansion. The deadline for the proposed meeting was drawing close, and Umasi had felt a need to gather his thoughts.

He knew what Zen was going to ask, and he had been anticipating it for days. As Zen undoubtedly had spent his time preparing his plans for the Truancy, Umasi had spent his time working up the resolve to tell Zen no once and for all. He had imagined every possible argument or plea that Zen might make, and was ready to counter them all. Umasi knew that this would be perhaps the most important decision that he would ever make in his life, and he had already made his choice. In the past, Zen had never failed to drag Umasi along into his plans, but this time Umasi was determined that things would be different.

With that thought, Umasi pressed his pencil down onto the paper so hard that the lead shattered. Sighing, he swept the pieces into the garbage can and glanced over at the clock on his desk. It was now or never, Umasi realized as he rose from his chair. He would have to face Zen sooner or later, and he'd decided that *sooner* would be preferable, before things got worse *later*.

Realizing that it would be freezing up on the roof, Umasi reached out automatically for the coat pegs as he opened the door. His hand latched on to an olive green jacket, which looked rather ugly but felt warm enough. As Umasi made his way towards the roof, he shut his eyes, feeling calmer than he thought he would. Maybe it was all the preparation and self-assurances, but whatever the reason, he simply didn't worry about what was coming next. He knew that he was strong enough for this.

This time, he would stand his ground.

"I just wanted you to know that everything is ready. All the preparations are complete," Zen said as he lurked in the shadow of a large vent. "The Truancy will be born tonight."

Umasi stared out at the City skyline. The setting sun cast vibrant red and gold hues over the varied buildings, and the windows caught the rays and reflected them like a thousand blinding gemstones. Umasi took a while to respond, feeling the warm glow of the sun wash over his face, countering the chilly winter winds.

"Then I wish it good luck, and hope that its creator doesn't get killed or imprisoned in the process," Umasi replied at last, his eyes fixated upon the sunset.

"Is that all?" Zen demanded.

"Should there be more?"

"Apparently not," Zen murmured. "So you're really not coming with me after all."

"No, I'm not," Umasi said as the cold winds ruffled his short hair. "I'm no killer."

"And you won't even come for my sake?" Zen asked almost pleadingly, a tone that Umasi had never heard from his brother before. "You won't even have to fight if you don't want to."

Umasi felt his gut churn. Zen was really going out of his way to accommodate him; he genuinely wanted them to stick together in spite of everything. But Umasi already knew that would never work. No matter how much it hurt the both of them, this was the way it had to be.

"I'm sorry, Zen. I sympathize with your motive, but I can't support your proposed methods," Umasi replied firmly. "There's no reason that you have to fight, either. It's not too late—you can turn around and walk away. Just forget about it all. Live a normal life."

"A normal life?" Zen scoffed. "Here, life is whatever they tell us it is. On a whim they can teach us a fabricated history, change the norms of society, whenever and however they want."

Umasi was silent. After all, there was truth behind those uncomfortable words.

"You can't talk me out of this, Umasi," Zen warned. "I know that you pride yourself on being meek and weak, but I'm no doormat. Imagine how I feel—finding out that everything I've ever believed has been a lie . . . finding out that I was used and betrayed, betrayed from the day that I was born . . . and betrayed right up until this moment, by my own brother, no less."

Zen swung his head around to glare at Umasi, who could feel his brother's gaze burning into the back of his head. Umasi shut his eyes and did not respond. He couldn't even begin to imagine how to explain to Zen that he knew *exactly* how he felt.

"We are all forced to endure unspeakable injustice, and now that the two of us know it for what it is, we have a chance to show everyone else!" Zen argued. "Open your eyes and look at the City! We hold its entire fate in our hands. Together, we can change this City for the better!"

"Having the power to change the City doesn't give us the right to," Umasi said, his eyes still shut behind their glasses.

"No, it gives us the obligation to," Zen countered.

"You don't know that you'll succeed."

"I won't find out until I try."

"Then try, Zen," Umasi said, opening his eyes in time to see a streak of dark purple tinge the skyline. "I won't stop you. But I won't help you."

Zen's nostrils flared, and the shadows concealing him lengthened as the sun slipped farther over the horizon.

"I trusted you, Umasi," Zen said. "Even after finding that the whole City had betrayed me, I trusted you. Only one person did I dare turn to . . . only to find that *again* I am betrayed." Zen laughed, and Umasi shivered as a particularly chilly gust of wind washed over him. "I guess I have to thank you, Brother. You've shown me that I can't count on anyone else. I will wait no longer. If I alone am to be the first Truant, then so be it."

"You're out of your mind," Umasi murmured.

"Am I?" Zen wondered. "Perhaps you're right. But if this is madness, then I prefer it to the delusions of sanity. And if you had any pride, you would agree."

"It's not a matter of pride."

"No, not for you it isn't, I suppose." Zen examined Umasi, as if suddenly seeing him in a new light. "You're *scared*."

"Not just for myself," Umasi said defensively. "I'm worried about *you*."

"Not a pacifist, just spineless after all," Zen muttered, now addressing himself. "It was a mistake to try to involve him. He hasn't got the guts for this."

"You don't have to do this, Zen," Umasi pleaded. "Think of the danger, the odds you're going up against."

"It's better to risk death, serving my own will," Zen said quietly, "than to live this life in invisible chains."

"You're willing to die over this?"

"And kill over it too."

"You're mad at me, aren't you?"

"Now, why would I be mad at you?" Zen asked sarcastically.

"It's not just because I'm not going with you." Umasi insisted. "You're . . . resentful about how I've always done better, been happier, in school. You've always been."

"I have no idea what you're talking about," Zen said coldly. "If you ask me, all that study has addled your wits. Stick to crunching numbers, Umasi. You're good at reading books, not people."

"You don't mean that."

"And you obviously don't know me," Zen snarled. "To be honest, I prefer it that way."

That ended the conversation, and Zen stormed off the roof. Umasi, however, lingered, watching the last rays of sunlight slip over the horizon as the whole City was wrapped up in the darkness of night.

U masi was worried about what Zen's manners would be like at the dinner table that night, but needn't have been. Zen was unusually upbeat, as though their tense exchange on the roof had never happened at all. Umasi wasn't naïve enough to believe that Zen was being genuinely friendly, but he was still glad for the opportunity to have a civil conversation with his brother. In fact, as the meal progressed Umasi found himself increasingly eager to go along with Zen's act.

"Greens?" Umasi asked Zen.

"Let's do an exchange."

The Mayor claimed to believe in a balanced diet, though in practice what he really meant seemed to be "the more green stuff, the more balance." As a result, there was a great variety of greens on the dining table, almost enough to conceal the platters of meat. But even with such a wide selection, Umasi instantly knew that Zen would want the bowl of string beans, while Zen in turn passed him a platter of spinach. As they made the exchange, the Mayor looked at them both with interest.

"Have you boys been practicing reading each other's minds?" the Mayor asked, smiling.

"Hardly," Zen said. "You don't have to dine with Umasi that often to memorize his tastes. They're just that predictable."

"So are yours, Zen." Umasi raised an eyebrow.

"I don't deny it." Zen smirked, devouring a string bean whole.

"Well," the Mayor said, "I'm glad that you two are getting along so well. I'm sorry that I haven't been able to spend much time with you boys lately, but things have been very busy at work."

Zen frowned. "Oh, I don't doubt that."

Umasi was not pleased by this particular change of subject, and quickly grasped for something else to talk about.

"Uh . . . so . . . um . . . hey, Zen, what are you going to do after dinner?" Umasi asked.

"I don't know." Zen glanced at Umasi. "Perhaps play a game?"

"Play a game?" the Mayor interrupted. "I know that it's a Friday, but do you really have the time for that? How's your homework coming?"

"Oh, my work is coming along just fine, Father." Zen grinned. "I think you'll find that I've been doing a lot of research lately. On a wide variety of subjects."

Umasi shifted uncomfortably in his seat, catching Zen's hidden meaning.

"That . . . that's nice, Zen . . ." Umasi said. "Which game were you thinking of playing?"

Zen raised his eyebrows at Umasi.

"I was thinking of a strategy game," Zen said. "Preferably a cooperative one. You know, so that we can play it together."

The Mayor interrupted again. "A strategy game? You shouldn't be playing games too much. Isn't there something more constructive for you to do?"

Zen smiled. "Trust me, Father, I'm going to get many constructive things done in the coming days."

"Ah, you know, Zen, maybe you shouldn't try that game," Umasi said. "It seems pretty difficult. You might lose."

Zen shrugged. "Oh, we might lose, I'm sure. But the point would be that we tried."

The Mayor looked sharply at both Zen and Umasi. "Speaking of trying, I happened to receive the latest attendance report today. There better have been a mistake, or I'd be very disappointed with the both of you—just because you are my sons doesn't mean you can break the rules as you wish! Do you know what a serious thing it is, to be a truant?"

Umasi felt an instinctive surge of panic, but Zen remained completely calm.

"Believe me, Father, I was disappointed that day as well," Zen said quietly. "It was all my fault, though. I coerced Umasi into going along with it.

But I assure you, it won't happen again . . . *ever*. After all, I do indeed know how serious it is, to be a Truant."

Umasi shook his head as Zen and their father exchanged words about the evils of truancy, leaving him totally forgotten. At least it now felt like old times, Umasi realized. He had probably spoken more during that dinner than he had at any five others combined.

Watching his brother, Umasi couldn't wait for the dinner to end as the look in Zen's eyes grew increasingly dangerous. And yet, at the same time, Umasi dreaded what might happen once dinner was over.

T his feels . . . strange, Zen noted idly as he zipped up his backpack. *Am I really going to do this to Umasi? Have things changed that much?*

Though he kept asking himself those questions, he already knew the answers. After all, they had been so obvious for quite a while, and Zen was not in denial. It had all started with the revelation and the betrayal, the boundless outrage slowly boiling inside of him. It festered, growing stronger over time. Zen was perfectly capable of thinking and planning rationally, but only in the service of his intoxicating obsession. It mastered him, consumed him. A relentless fixation, it lay in wait in the dark corners of his mind, omnipresent and omnipotent. It knotted his guts, it blackened his heart, and it poisoned his thoughts.

It was the greatest feeling he had ever experienced.

He couldn't escape it.

He didn't *want* to escape it.

Am I going insane? Zen wondered as he shifted the backpack aside. *Or returning to sanity?*

Zen reflected on what he was about to do, and then burst into laughter at a sudden realization. This was nothing new after all. He was simply going to fulfill a dream that he had always had. What student had never dreamed of rebelling against school? But he, among all the students of the City, had the ability to realize that dream. All he had been missing was justification, motivation, the drive to set it all in motion. . . .

And now, at last, he had it.

Zen smiled grimly and reached for the black windbreaker jacket hanging from a peg, buttoning it around his neck, leaving the sleeves loose so that it splayed behind him like a cape. Zen then slung his backpack onto his shoulder. Its original school contents had long since been emptied out upon the floor, replaced by more practical items. He was dressed warmly, with a black sweater and two other layers besides. He clenched his fists, savoring for a moment the new feeling of freedom and empowerment coursing through his body.

Then the door opened, and Umasi entered the room, staring at Zen.

"You're not here to play a game," Zen observed, folding his arms.

"No, I'm not," Umasi agreed, walking over to his desk. "Were you going somewhere?"

"I still am."

"I see," Umasi said, looking away. "You know, I've had an idea. What if we confronted Dad about this? Do you think we might be able to change something?"

"No." Zen snorted. "He views us as lab rats."

"You can't honestly believe that."

"It's the truth!"

"So you're really determined to do this then?" Umasi asked, his voice strained. "Without even trying anything else?"

"You and I both know the answer to that," Zen replied as he retrieved a baseball bat from under his bed and began examining it. "And what about you? Is your decision final?"

Umasi sighed, still unable to face Zen.

"When I see classmates and teachers, I see lives, Zen. I'm not like you. I can't see them as calculations or part of a greater scheme," Umasi said. "I'm not going to take part in anything that'll end those lives."

Zen quietly walked behind Umasi, still examining his baseball bat.

"So your final answer is no?"

"That's right." Umasi nodded as he sadly looked down at the pages of schoolwork strewn across his desk.

"I'm afraid it's your choice to make." Zen sighed. "But just one thing, Brother . . ."

"What?"

"I'm sincerely sorry about this."

Before Umasi could pick up on the danger in those words, Zen raised the baseball bat and brought it crashing down upon Umasi's head. Umasi crumpled to the ground, rendered unconscious by the blow. Zen bent down to examine Umasi, and after satisfying himself that his brother was merely asleep (and would remain so for a while) he proceeded over to the dresser.

Resting atop it, in their customary places, were the two account cards labeled *Z* and *U*. Zen ran his fingers over one, then the other, before seizing both and slipping them into his pockets.

It would really begin that night, Zen exulted as he exited the room and made his way down to the lobby. As he slipped out a service entrance of the mansion to avoid the watchman, he felt the cold, liberating winter air hit his face. He pulled the hood of the windbreaker over his head and then headed straight for District 7, the closest abandoned district on his map.

At last, there would be no more waiting.

He would finally teach the City the meaning of Truancy.

Dear Sirs,

I know that it has been some time since my last report. As always, no news tends to be good news, especially in this City. I must admit that when I was first assigned here, the idea of using academics to control a population seemed absurd to me. But after years of seeing these Educators at work, I cannot help but be impressed. All signs indicate that this City and the methods behind it have been successful. Civil unrest is unheard of, violent demonstrations nonexistent, and open rebellion a fairy tale. My personal recommendation is, and has long been, that we adopt this City's philosophy immediately. However I understand that my opinion is not the one that matters concerning that greatest of steps.

As for the two children entrusted into the Mayor's care, I have not had an opportunity to meet them myself. However, and you must forgive my editorializing, I believe that the Mayor is as fine a guardian as we could have hoped for. Of course, he is dedicated to his work, and his results are more impressive than any Mayor before him—but at the same time he seems to possess a genuine sympathy for his adopted sons. Indeed, this attachment is no secret among his staff. I will continue to monitor the situation, but thus far I have been given no reason not to believe that the boys are in excellent hands.

Your Servant,
207549627

PART II

VAGRANT

8

AWAKENING

A sudden spasm of pain jerked Red awake. He didn't get up immediately, but instead shut his eyes and groaned loudly in protest. As if in response, the pain prodded him again, harder, forcing him to sit up. Red winced and clutched his gut, which swiftly gave him a third agonizing jolt, insuring that he was really conscious.

"Okay, okay, I'm up," Red complained, stretching his back and limbs.

Red had seen better days. The winter was already proving to be a nasty one, and the first snowfall days ago had been murder on his stamina. The City's snowplows did not clear out the abandoned districts, and the last of that first snow had only melted the day before. Without the relative safety provided by the gang, Red had taken to sleeping in a different place every night. To do so, Red had to trudge through wet snow, sogginess penetrating all three layers of his clothing. Wet, freezing, alone, and hungry. Not the best of combinations.

On the other hand, Red had also seen worse days, but he didn't really like to think about those. Ever.

Cursing his appendix as he finished stretching, Red felt his stomach growl. Only in their absence had Red realized that he'd gotten used to Chris' gang sharing information about what food sources were safe at what times. Without those tips, it had been especially difficult to find edible things, and though the snow had faded, Red didn't foresee it getting any easier. The only bright side was that Red had recently overheard a couple of other vagrants talking about Chris. Apparently the boy was still alive, along with at least some of his crew. Still, Red had no idea where to find them, and any search for them could also lead him right to their rivals, who probably hadn't gotten over their last encounter with Red.

Red's stomach growled again, punctuated by an especially sharp stab of pain in his gut. Red slapped at the general area of his appendix and scowled at the resulting agony, his mind drawn back to practicality.

"All right then," Red muttered. "I'll just have to feed myself."

Before he awoke, Red had been sleeping in the stairwell of an abandoned office building in District 8. He found that even without heating or lights, it was relatively warm and dry, and no one had discovered him there. Ignoring the complaints of his body, Red raced down the stairs to the ground floor and quickly exited the building. Jogging steadily, it didn't take him long to run across District 8 and reach the border of the lively District

5. As he ran, he tried not to pay much attention to the dead and largely crumbling buildings. Maybe the hunger was playing tricks on his mind, but he didn't like the way they seemed to leer at him in the pale morning sun, their dirty, clouded windows staring like dead eyes.

As Red reached the border of District 7, he slipped down another back alley, running down it until he reached a chain-link fence. Using the links as footholds, Red swiftly climbed over it, his heart beating faster as he dropped down into an alley of District 5. Already he could hear and see glimpses of people walking on the sidewalk—simultaneously his predators and his prey.

Silently edging down the alley, Red tried to gauge the number of people treading the sidewalk. He quickly determined that it wasn't busy enough to be a weekday; he'd lost track of the days a long time ago. This was a mixed blessing. On one hand, he would have been harder to pick out in a large crowd. On the other, if he were discovered, he'd have a much better chance of escaping through a sparse crowd. In any case, he didn't have much of a choice. There was no way he could afford to wait around for a day or two.

With his angry gut prodding at him to hurry up, Red took a deep breath and sniffed the air as he inspected the street as best he could. There didn't seem to be any food stands around, so there was no way for him to directly steal something to eat. Still, Red smiled; there were always the pedestrians passing by the mouth of the alleyway. Spotting a well-dressed elderly man with a wallet sticking out of his pocket, Red sprung into action, slipping out of the alley and onto the streets. No one seemed to notice him, or at least didn't care enough to point him out. That was typical; Red found that citizens of the City usually tried to ignore him, which was really the best treatment that he could expect from them.

Red and the man in front of him waited at a street corner for the stop sign to change, along with a number of other people bunched up tightly in the queue. When the light did change, the elderly man, along with the rest of the group, rushed forward across the street trying to make up for lost time, leaving Red all alone on the curb. Red grinned as he slipped the man's wallet into one of his pockets. No one had seen a thing.

Red next targeted a woman who was busy talking on her cell phone. As she walked along, oblivious of her fellow pedestrians, Red sneaked up behind her and drew her wallet from out of her handbag. Unfortunately for him, however, this time he was spotted, and a man grabbed his arm before he could pocket his plunder.

"Got you!" the man shouted triumphantly, turning to look for the woman whose wallet Red had stolen. "Miss! Hey miss, this brat stole your wallet!"

Red didn't panic, but rather watched amusedly as the clueless woman walked on, still chattering into her phone. The man attempted to get her attention again, but as he did Red suddenly jerked his arm free and made a run for it. The man let out a shout of outrage and ran after him, but Red could tell that he would never catch up. He was old and fat, and Red still prided himself on being able to run pretty well.

Dashing down an alley that Red knew would lead back to District 8, he spared a glance behind him just in time to see his pursuer skid to a halt. Red grinned to himself. None of the citizens of the City were willing to pass into the abandoned districts; only the Enforcers ever pursued vagrants into those forbidden areas.

As soon as Red was safely standing back upon the empty, noiseless streets of District 8, he drew the wallets out from his pocket and inspected the contents. He was pleased to find a decent bundle of cash in both wallets, but less pleased to see a number of account cards. He knew that the cards probably had access to more money than he could ever dream of getting his hands on, but attempting to use them could easily tip off the Enforcers even if it worked.

Still, the cash suited Red just fine. Hopefully he could make it last him through winter, though he doubted that it would. At worst, he could always attempt the same thing again. He'd always gotten away with it so far, and besides, he found the art of stealing to be a refreshing escape from monotony.

But as the adrenaline and the excitement faded, Red abruptly realized that his stomach was still grumbling. He didn't feel safe spending the stolen money just yet, and that still left the problem of what he was supposed to eat.

Zen chewed the piece of beef jerky slowly, enjoying the juice as it ran down his throat. It wasn't anything he'd order in a restaurant, but it tasted all right, if a bit on the salty side. In any case, he wasn't really concerned about the flavor of his rations; the most important thing for him was that the stuff took forever to go bad and was fairly nutritious.

After taking a swig from his water bottle, Zen reached inside his backpack and seized a bag of dried apple slices. He popped a few into his mouth, then washed them down with more water before standing up straight to survey his surroundings. He had slept quite comfortably in the interior of a run-down car he'd found in District 7. There was evidence of someone having slept there before, but whoever it was had long since moved on, and Zen wasn't about to be picky about his bedding.

Zen slung his backpack back onto his shoulders and left the car behind, walking along the empty streets, carefully examining each building he passed. Finding a small shop with its windows and doors boarded up, Zen drew a hammer out of his bag and smashed the boards to pieces until he could get in. The interior was a crumbling mess, but it was roomy enough and would serve for Zen's purposes. Taking a can of red spray paint out of his pocket, Zen methodically sprayed a small symbol inside the doorway of the building, where no one would spot it unless they were looking for it.

The symbol was a red circle, with the letter *T* slanted clockwise contained within it. Zen marked the exact spot of the shop on his detailed map of the City, and then proceeded to search. Soon he would fill all the safe houses he had marked with supplies, so that the Truants would never have to remain still. They would be able to strike without warning and vanish into the abandoned districts, hiding in any of a hundred different locations.

As he worked, Zen felt an airy, liberating feeling within him, an excitement stemming solely from his newfound independence. It wasn't a sudden or fleeting sensation, but rather the lightening of a spirit that had finally freed itself from bondage and had begun forging its own fate.

Zen found himself so caught up in his blissful work that he never once gave a thought to the brother he had left behind. Zen stood completely alone and felt all the more powerful for it. Others would join him later, he knew, but for now it was just him against the City, and he couldn't wait for the first battle to be fought.

H ey, Rothenberg, sir!"

"What is it now?" Rothenberg grumbled, ambling over to the patrol car with a paper cup of coffee in hand.

"We've gotten some complaints in from District 5. Looks like there's a vagrant running loose there, pickpocketing people right off the street."

"In broad daylight?" Rothenberg raised an eyebrow.

"Looks like it, sir."

"Those animals get bolder every day." Rothenberg smiled, his grip tightening on the coffee cup. "Do we have a description?"

"Wild brown hair and ragged clothes, that's all that the guy got a good look at, sir," the Enforcer replied.

"It's a start." Rothenberg nodded as he got into the car. "District 5 isn't too far away. Let's go."

"Do you think that the vagrant will still be hanging around there?" the Enforcer asked skeptically as he started the engine.

"You don't know these kids like I do." Rothenberg chuckled, a deeply disturbing sound. "If this one successfully pulled off something like this, he won't be satisfied with just a few wallets. He'll strike again, maybe even today."

"And if he doesn't?" the Enforcer inquired, navigating his way through tight traffic.

"Then we'll do a sweep of Districts 7 and 8," Rothenberg said. "Flush him out and maybe nail a few of his dirty little friends too."

"Yes, sir."

Rothenberg leaned back in his seat and watched the buildings on either side pass by. He loved doing this, actually getting out onto the streets and participating in the hunt for vagrants. Desk work reminded him too much of his old stint as a teacher, an experience that he did not remember with much fondness. While he had enjoyed being able to lord over rooms full of uppity teenagers, he had taught drawing. *Drawing.* Few things bored Rothenberg more than watching kids scribble away without any semblance of talent. He had hated the subject with all his guts, but his limited talents hadn't allowed him to teach anything else.

Fortunately, his notoriously strict treatment of his students attracted the attention of the local Disciplinary Officer, who had facilitated a career change to the Enforcers. From there he had served with distinction and enthusiasm, quickly rising through the ranks until he had earned the prestigious position of Chief Truancy Officer.

Rothenberg took a sip of coffee. If only his private life had worked out as well as his professional one. His wife just hadn't understood that being a parent meant being a City official. The Mayor had said it himself: The role of a parent in the City was to enforce the will of the Educators upon each individual student. Rothenberg believed to the core of his being that this duty meant keeping them in line and making them constantly mindful of their place. His wife, on the other hand, had strongly objected to Rothenberg's ideas about discipline.

It was all that damn kid's fault, Rothenberg thought as the car stopped at a light. When Rothenberg became an Enforcer, he began spending much more time at work, leaving his wife at home to spoil their son. Then came the daughter, and when no agreement could be reached about her upbringing his wife actually took the girl and left. Even worse, she'd left their worthless son behind.

Rothenberg's grip tightened on his coffee. He didn't want to have anything to do with that kid. The boy had ruined everything—and Rothenberg had told him so, many times. But with his wife gone Rothenberg was free to experiment with his brand of discipline, and as far as he was concerned it had definitely made progress. The boy didn't talk much anymore, didn't get into trouble, and generally took care of himself, leaving Rothenberg free to do what he really loved—hunt the vagrants.

Rothenberg grinned wolfishly. There was something incredibly satisfying about identifying, tracking, and finally dealing with a vagrant. Mere truants simply weren't as fun; they were still students, so you couldn't shoot them, and what fun was hunting down rebellious teenagers if you couldn't administer the ultimate punishment when you caught them?

Rothenberg took another sip of coffee. He had always thought that students were treated too softly, almost like equals. He was determined to remind them that they had no rights, and he would put them in their place by force if necessary.

The patrol car screeched to a halt, and Rothenberg's partner unbuckled his seat belt and stepped out of the car and onto the sidewalk of District 5. Rothenberg quickly followed suit, feeling his heart start to beat faster at the very thought of a chase. Rothenberg grinned again, fingering the handle of his gun and the hilt of his knife. It was time to put a miscreant in his place, six feet beneath the ground.

Umasi slept fitfully. With no blankets to cover him, the winter's chill managed to reach him in his dreams, where he found himself standing in the midst of a strangely silent blizzard. His head throbbing, Umasi struggled against the snow, but found only an infinite expanse of white all around him. Freezing winds battered at him cruelly, ice melting at his touch and seeping into his garments. Never until now had Umasi, who had never lacked for warmth, realized just how much he hated the cold.

Without warning, a particularly powerful gust of wind slammed into him, knocking him off his feet. Within seconds, as though it had been waiting for him to fall, the blizzard had covered him with a snowdrift. Umasi fought, but could not stop the white from washing over him, and he cringed, expecting to suffocate at any moment. A second passed. And then two.

Umasi opened his eyes, finding himself warm and unharmed in an impossible landscape. Everything, absolutely everything was white, with not a shadow or a blemish to distinguish one patch of ground from another, nothing to indicate where a wall or ceiling might begin or end. This was no snow-covered landscape—just pure, infinite whiteness.

As the panic and fear slowly left Umasi, some rational corner of his mind told him that it was all a dream. As if on cue, a dark figure emerged from the whiteness, marring its perfect plainness. Umasi glared at the boy who seemed to bear his face. The boy, dressed in an overlarge dark green winter jacket, smiled in greeting.

"Well, I don't think that either of us saw that coming," he said conversationally.

"Saw what?" Umasi demanded.

"Oh, come on, haven't you figured it out? Why you're here?"

"Because I'm dreaming."

"Right, and why are you dreaming?"

"Because I'm asleep?"

"And, Umasi, *why* are you asleep?"

"What kind of stupid question is that?"

"One that you can't seem to answer," the boy observed. "Why don't you get up now and take a look? Or are you going to let your brother have everything his own way?"

With that cryptic statement, the boy smiled again and pulled the hood of his jacket tightly over his head so that it cast his face into shadow. Before Umasi could respond, the boy waved an arm in farewell—the jacket's sleeves were long enough to conceal his hands—and Umasi could feel himself gradually rising into consciousness.

Stirring and forcing his eyes open, Umasi found his vision blurred and his head hurting terribly. Rubbing his eyes furiously, Umasi forced himself to sit up, feeling dazed but knowing that he was awake at last. Instinctively he groped around for his glasses, and as he put them on he realized that he was lying on the floor. Wondering what he was doing there, Umasi confusedly looked over at Zen's bed to ask his brother about it.

The sight of the empty bed brought it all back to him, like another blow to the head. Fully alert now and feeling a fresh surge of panic, Umasi forced himself to his feet. Zen was gone. Gone for real. This was no nightmare, and there would be no waking up. Zen had run away from home and was going to kill people, maybe a lot of people.

Umasi expected to be paralyzed by indecision, but to his surprise he found that he knew exactly what he would do. He would not stay here, wasting away in school as disaster brewed outside. He would not stay here to be interrogated by his father. He would not stay here, helpless as he had always been.

He would go after Zen.

He would make his brother see reason if he could, and stop him if he must, but Umasi knew he couldn't allow Zen to carry out his plans. Looking around his room, Umasi moved with unusual swiftness. He seized his backpack and turned it upside down, dumping all of his school materials out of it. He then approached the dresser to get his account card . . .

Only to find it missing, along with Zen's.

Umasi stared at the dresser in disbelief. He knew that the cards had both been there the night before. Umasi knew it was impossible that they could've just disappeared, unless . . .

Umasi's face hardened. *Zen.* Umasi found it difficult to believe that his brother could have resorted to theft, but there was no other explanation.

Swearing under his breath, Umasi opened a drawer in the dresser and seized a small bundle of cash bills. He stuffed them into his backpack along with a blanket before proceeding down to the kitchen. He threw a bunch of food haphazardly into the backpack as well, and then, after a moment's hesitation, also included a long, sharp kitchen knife.

He then quickly returned to his room, threw on some warm clothes, and slung his backpack over his shoulders. He was about to leave, but at the last minute a small tinge of regret stayed his hand as he reached for the doorknob. Father. The Mayor would lose not one, but both sons at the same time. Despite all that the man had done, Umasi felt that he owed him at least a final farewell.

Frowning, Umasi spun around and approached his desk, taking out a fresh sheet of lined paper and a bold marker. Hastily, he scribbled a brief note and left it prominently placed on the desk, where it would quickly be found.

> *Dear Father,*
> *I know everything. Zen knows everything. He has run away. I'm going after him. I won't be back. Good-bye.*
>
> > *Love,*
> > *Umasi*

As Umasi opened the door, he spared one last look at his old life. And then he was gone.

9

APPLES AND ORANGES

R ed eyed the fruit stand as he walked amidst the crowd, his stomach grumbling in anticipation. His better judgment had argued against returning to strike District 5 so soon, but he was emboldened by his previous success, and his stomach had prevailed over that better judgment. There were many stands in the City that peddled fresh fruit, but as far as Red was concerned, the one in his sights was the greatest. The modest display of produce looked to Red like a feast from paradise, all of it within about twenty paces of his grasp.

Red continued walking along with the flow of pedestrians towards the fruit stand. It would be a risky maneuver, he knew, as there wasn't an immediate escape route available. Still, Red was fairly sure that he would be fast enough to make it to a border alley across the street, provided that enough pedestrians remained indifferent; after all, running away was still his area of expertise. Once he made it to the alleys, Red knew he would be safe. No one but an Enforcer would dare chase a vagrant into an abandoned district.

His mind made up, Red readied himself as every step brought him closer to the stand. Red saw a woman stop to buy some cherries from the proprietor—a perfect distraction. Drawing up to the stand at last, Red swiftly grabbed a plastic bag from the stand's supply and piled into it a heap of apples and oranges, the two closest fruits, before either the woman or the proprietor could notice that he was a vagrant.

And just like that, Red was off like a rat, the plastic bag full of fruit slung heavily over his shoulder as he ran. A moment later Red grinned as he heard the expected cry of outrage from the proprietor.

"Stop that kid! He's a thief!"

Red's grin quickly faded, however, as he was *not* expecting to hear what came next.

"Out of the way! Give us a clear shot!"

Red spared a backwards glance and felt his blood run colder than the winter air. There were two men in blue uniforms, holding pistols and running towards him at top speed. *Enforcers.* Red thought he had been running as fast as he could, but his legs instantly doubled their effort at the sight.

Then a gunshot went off, and he could hear screams.

"No, you idiot, not with civilians around! Chase him into District 8!" a deep voice shouted. "If you'd hit anyone the Educators would've served you up in the school cafeterias!"

"Sorry, Rothenberg, sir!"

Red found that he could yet run a little faster upon hearing the name Rothenberg. Up until that moment, he had never known exactly how much he and all vagrants had come to fear that name, but now that he was actually being pursued by the man himself, Red found a sick feeling of dread building up in his already-suffering gut.

"Watch where I'm going? How about you watch who you're talking to!"

"Get out of his way, urgent Enforcer business!"

In spite of everything, Red managed a grin. Apparently the Enforcers had bowled over some angry pedestrians in their haste to get at him.

And then he reached the open mouth of the alley, the walls spread to either side like welcoming arms. Red darted in without a moment's hesitation. From the sounds of angry cursing and argument behind him, Red knew that he'd probably have plenty of time to make good his escape. He smiled to himself as he proceeded down the alley, slowing down to an almost leisurely pace.

And then he froze, stunned by what he saw before him.

Standing there, motionless save for slight shivering, was a very pale, hauntingly thin girl with filthy black hair that messily fell down to her shoulders. She seemed so incredibly *small* that at first Red thought the girl must be about ten years old, but he quickly decided that she was more like thirteen, albeit extremely thin and hunched over, making her seem unnaturally tiny. All of these things were odd by themselves, but none of it was what had frozen Red in his tracks.

It was the eyes. Even in the dim lighting of the alley, the eyes were an icily light blue, as if they possessed a pale luminance in and of themselves. They were wide open, unblinking, as if permanently fixated upon some invisible horror that only they could see. With one brief glance into those icy orbs, Red could see unspeakable pain, shock, and fright in those eyes, enough to send shivers down his spine. Whatever this girl's story was, Red pitied her instantly.

Shaking himself out of his stupor, Red reached into the plastic bag and drew out an apple, which he thrust into the girl's hands as if to buy off that icy stare of hers. The girl didn't move, and gave no indication that she had noticed Red or his apple at all.

And then loud, angry voices and heavy footsteps approached the alley, and Red's survival instinct kicked in. He quickly glanced farther down the alley. The path seemed to branch off into two different directions, which would force the Enforcers to split up, unless . . . Red scanned the sides of the alley and spotted a fire escape that led up to the roofs of one of the buildings. Perfect.

"You should run," Red advised, turning to look back at the girl. "Enforcers are coming, you can't stay here."

She didn't seem to hear him, and much to Red's concern simply remained staring straight ahead with those haunting blue eyes.

"You might get killed if you stay here!" Red warned urgently, shaking the girl with one arm. "You have to run!"

The angry noises drew closer now, almost to the mouth of the alley, and Red groaned as he released the girl. Left with no other choice, he dashed over to the fire escape. Climbing as nimbly as he could—and he wasn't bad at climbing—he just managed to slip up onto the roof as the two Enforcers plunged into the alley below. His heart beating wildly, Red peered cautiously over the edge of the building, his curiosity refusing to let him leave until he found out what would happen to the strange girl.

Red held his breath as the Enforcers slowed to a halt down below.

W ell, what have we here?" Rothenberg said, rubbing his hands together at the sight of the helpless vagrant.

"Looks to me like an accomplice to that thief," his partner said, seizing the girl's arm and squeezing so tightly that she dropped the apple instantly. "Will you handle the questioning, sir?"

Rothenberg didn't answer at first. Instead, he slowly bent down to retrieve the apple, contemplating it for a moment. Then he suddenly snapped upright, shoving the apple into the girl's face. The girl flinched, but didn't make a sound as Rothenberg leaned over to look her in the eyes, their faces separated by no more than an inch.

"There was a boy here," Rothenberg said with deceptive calm. "He *stole* this apple. Where did he go? Which path did he take?"

Still watching from up above, Red tensed, ready to bolt at a moment's notice should the girl give him away. But mystifyingly, seconds passed without the girl saying anything. She merely continued to stand silent and motionless. Red wondered at this behavior. Was she trying to repay him for the apple by keeping quiet?

No, Red decided a moment later, after examining the girl's features. She was just *scared*. Too terrified to speak. He could tell by the way her icy eyes widened, how she stood stiff like a board, petrified.

"Answer me!" Rothenberg boomed, his furious words echoing throughout the alley.

Red could see the girl cringe, her eyes widening even further at the Enforcer's outburst. Another tense moment passed, and still the girl said nothing. This time Rothenberg smashed the apple into the side of the girl's head, causing flecks of apple to fly everywhere.

Red gritted his teeth in anger, and for one reckless moment entertained the idea of announcing his presence to the Enforcers below. But no, there was nothing to be gained from that. If half the stories about Rothenberg were true, he'd just kill the girl first and then come after him.

"If you do not answer me, I will hit you again, harder," Rothenberg said bluntly.

Red clenched his fists, furious at the injustice occurring below him. Rothenberg surely knew that his efforts were only terrifying the girl further, making her only less likely to talk. But Red knew enough about Rothenberg to understand that that was probably what the Chief Truancy Officer was really after.

As if to punctuate this thinking, Rothenberg at that moment chose to make good on his promise, and slammed the hard apple onto the girl's head again, harder, eliciting a whimper but no answers.

Red felt a sudden surge of guilt. If he hadn't given the girl that apple, perhaps none of this would be happening. A moment later, he scolded himself for thinking that. He knew what was going on. Having failed to capture him, Rothenberg was instead taking his frustration out upon the first helpless child he could lay his hands on.

The girl had begun to tremble visibly, dazed by the blows. Rothenberg slowly shook his hand to free it of mashed apple. For his part, he thought he was doing good. If there was one thing that Rothenberg couldn't stand, it was a disrespectful child, and wasn't fear the ultimate sign of respect?

Rothenberg now spoke again, this time his voice so deadly that Red hugged his arms to his chest as chills spread across his body.

"Hold her still," Rothenberg ordered his partner, who obediently seized the girl firmly by both shoulders. "We'll get some answers out of her, one way or another."

Rothenberg reached for his belt and drew something shiny out of a small sheath. As it caught the dim light of the alley, Red suddenly realized what it was.

"You *bastard*," Red breathed.

It was a knife. At the sight of it, the girl's blue eyes widened even farther, and for the first time a tear ran down her cheek. By now, however, she was so overcome by fright that she couldn't do so much as whimper, much less talk—not even to save her own life.

"See this?" Rothenberg said, bringing the knife up to the girl's face. "This represents your last chance to cooperate."

Red shook with silent rage. The sight below was horrifying even to eyes as experienced as his—and yet he couldn't look away. The worst part for him was that he could be nothing more than a spectator; there was nothing he could do now that wouldn't result in both him and the girl dying. And as a vagrant, one's own survival *had* to be the first priority. Had to be.

But none of that made it any easier for Red to watch what unfolded below.

In one quick motion, Rothenberg made a cut across the girl's left cheek. It was shallow, but the wound stretched across her entire lower face, ending at the bottom of her chin. Red knew from a glance that the ugly gash would disfigure her for life at the least. Her tears, now pouring freely, mingled with her blood. Red silently cursed himself, wishing that he were good at more than just running away, certain now that he'd be watching the innocent girl die right before his very eyes.

And then, without warning, the impossible happened.

It was strange, Umasi thought, how one could be walking along the crowded streets of a bustling City, surrounded by people on all sides, and still manage to feel completely alone. He had only very rarely explored the streets outside of District 1, and though he could navigate his way through the City well enough by its street signs, he felt as though he were in a completely alien world as soon as he had passed out of his familiar neighborhood.

Umasi had been in a hurry to leave District 1 in order to avoid being recognized by anyone he knew, but as he meandered aimlessly through District 2, the unfamiliarity of his surroundings quickly brought home to him the seriousness of his situation.

He was all alone now. There was no turning back, and there would be no one to help him anymore. Somehow, the full weight of that realization failed to impress itself upon Umasi. It was an awful lot to take in all at once. After all, in just one day, his entire world had been shattered at its very foundations. The previous day he had been a normal student buckling under the weight of his responsibilities. A normal student, burning with anxiety as his brother planned mass murder, while contemplating how his own father had been using him as an experimental guinea pig.

Well okay, so maybe some things were better now.

But on the other hand, he was a vagrant. Umasi shuddered at the term. Neither student nor Truant, he'd done the unthinkable—fled from his comfortable home without knowing where to go. What was he going to eat? Where was he going to sleep? How was he going to find his brother? What was he going to do if he did?

Umasi paused at an unfamiliar street corner, realizing that he hadn't thought things through before running out the door. Zen must've faced the same questions himself, Umasi knew, but his brother had had weeks to answer them all and more. Umasi adjusted his glasses absentmindedly as his brows furrowed with thought. Where would Zen have gone? Umasi knew that Zen didn't trust anyone enough to stay at someone's house, and he surely wouldn't have risked sleeping in a hotel. He couldn't even sleep on the streets without risking being seen, unless . . .

The abandoned districts.

Umasi frowned at his conclusion. Every child in the City was taught never to go near the abandoned districts, overrun as they were by thugs and vagrants who would kill you for the clothes off your back. But if Zen was prepared to go there, Umasi was prepared to follow.

But this presented a new problem for Umasi: *Which* abandoned district would Zen go to? It was a baffling question. Umasi knew that there were dozens of abandoned districts throughout the City, but he didn't even know which ones they were. He couldn't exactly go back home to research the subject, nor would he be safe visiting a public library to find out . . . and it definitely wasn't the type of question to just ask any random stranger off the street.

Umasi sighed. He *really* hadn't thought this through very well.

Racking his brain for any recollection of the number of *any* abandoned district, Umasi suddenly remembered a current events homework that he had done the previous school year. The assignment had been about the City's docks, and Umasi had written about District 13, a waterfront district replete with run-down piers. The district had recently been declared abandoned, and while District 13 wasn't exactly nearby, it wasn't impossibly far from District 1 either.

His mind made up and a destination finally decided, Umasi straightened up, adjusted his glasses, and began the long trek towards the abandoned District 13.

It was as good a place to start as any.

en examined the alley with interest as he walked along it. City alleys tended to be dark, dirty, and smelly, and yet Zen knew they would prove to be one of his most valuable resources. The countless, narrow passageways in the back alleys of the City connected many districts, and entire armies could easily travel through or hide in them. Such alleys had never completely been charted on any map. Zen imagined that the vagrants of the City would have a better understanding of them than anyone else.

The vagrants. Zen had given them a lot of thought lately. They were a sizeable population with little reason to love the Educators or the Enforcers. They knew the abandoned districts better than anyone else, and anyone tough enough to survive under their conditions would probably be formidable fighters. The only problem was their trustworthiness, or perhaps their lack of it. He knew that he could recruit large numbers of vagrants just with the promise of food, but how many of them would be left after eating their fill and running off with whatever they could carry?

And so Zen had decided that, while he would definitely need to incorporate groups of vagrants later, he would need to start with more reliable dissidents who could form the core of the Truancy. He had already contacted a number of students on his list of potential recruits, and had over a dozen that were ready to join him at a moment's notice, with many more giving his offer some serious consideration.

In the meantime, however, Zen would continue to devote his time to making sure that his army, when it arrived, would have suitable lodgings, equipment, and knowledge of their new environment.

Suddenly, as Zen continued walking down the narrow alley, he heard a voice talking in the distance. An adult voice. Zen tensed and began proceeding very cautiously, the words becoming clearer with every step.

"There was a boy here. He *stole* this apple. Where did he go? Which path did he take?"

So, there was a thief on the loose around here, probably a vagrant. Whoever it was that was doing the talking had taken the time to pursue that thief, to the edge of an abandoned district, no less. Zen frowned. It had to be an Enforcer, and he knew that those typically patrolled in pairs. There would be at least two up ahead.

"Answer me!"

Zen grimaced at the noisy utterance. It was so loud that even its echo was deafening.

A moment later, Zen heard a strange sound that seemed to be a combination of a *crunch* and a *squish*. Whatever had produced that noise could not have been pleasant.

"If you do not answer me, I will hit you again, harder."

Zen smiled grimly. So the noble Enforcer was using some persuasive questioning. Judging by the sound, the Enforcer had probably smacked whoever he was interrogating with the apple that had been mentioned.

Zen was getting pretty close now, and the sound of the second impact was sickeningly clear when it came.

"Hold her still. We'll get some answers out of her, one way or another."

His curiosity fully roused, Zen quietly slipped his backpack off and drew a knife from his jacket pocket. He wanted to see what was going on for himself.

"See this? This represents your last chance to cooperate."

The voice was now perfectly clear, unobstructed . . . and as Zen rounded a bend, he saw them. The alley he lurked in seemed to merge with a wider one that bent off at an angle, forming a fork in the path. Right in his line of sight stood two uniformed Enforcers and a small, pitiful vagrant girl. One of them was holding the girl in place by her shoulders while the other held a knife up to her face. Neither of the Enforcers had seen him, focused as they were on their helpless victim.

The Enforcer with the knife immediately caught Zen's attention. He was a large, middle-aged man who had clearly shaved his hair some time ago. Since that last haircut, the man's large, bulbous head had managed to sprout mostly red bristles, though some looked to be turning gray. The man's eyebrows and small but thick mustache were also a dark red, precisely the color of fresh blood. He seemed to have a bit of a paunch, but was otherwise fit, and his impressive frame made him look quite formidable— much more so than his partner, who seemed to define the word "average." What's more, the way the redheaded Enforcer spoke and carried himself indicated to Zen that he was the leader of the pair.

Zen's eyes glinted in the shadows at the prospect of what he was about to do. He might even enjoy bringing the Enforcer down.

Then, right as Zen prepared to act, the Enforcer flicked his hand. Zen raised his eyebrows. The Enforcer was so tall compared with the whimpering girl that he had to bend down to bring his knife to the level of her face.

Zen swiftly decided to change tactics and gripped his knife loosely, getting a feel for its weight in his hand. Both the Enforcers were armed, though neither had their hands anywhere near their guns. They were both so confident, so secure in knowing that they were at the top of the food chain on the City's streets, that they had allowed themselves to get completely careless.

I hope you've had your fun, Zen thought, fingering the handle of his own knife. *Because I'm about to have mine.*

Zen looked up again. The girl was both bleeding and silently crying now. For a moment Zen felt a tiny hint of sympathy flicker in his embittered heart, but it was swiftly replaced by anger.

Zen stood up from his hiding place in the shadows, bent his arm back, and hurled his knife through the air like a dart. Zen didn't even need to make sure that the knife hit the Enforcer holding the girl; he knew that it would. Instead, Zen lunged straight for the larger man as his partner let out a cry of shock, and then another of pain as the knife buried itself in his back, bringing him to the ground.

Rothenberg had only just begun to redirect his attention, an astonished look on his face as he glimpsed Zen darting towards him like a living shadow. Zen used his momentum to launch himself into a jump kick that caught Rothenberg right in his paunch. The forceful blow knocked the air from Rothenberg's lungs, and the brutal Enforcer was flung hard against the brick wall, his own knife falling from his large hands. Still in motion, Zen reached out with one arm and seized the knife by its handle before it hit the ground.

At that range, Zen didn't even need to look to send the second knife flying right into the smaller Enforcer's throat.

Dispassionately, Zen spared one moment to admire his handiwork. The smaller Enforcer was still writhing on the ground, one knife in his back and another in his throat, but that struggling soon ceased. Zen noticed that the recently deceased Enforcer had managed to draw his pistol before the second knife had reached him. Zen swiftly seized the gun and then brought it around to point at the forehead of a stunned Rothenberg, who froze clumsily with one hand halfway towards his own firearm.

His eyes cold and hard, Zen deftly reached down to relieve Rothenberg of his gun and then swung his leg in an arc, catching Rothenberg aside the face and bowling the Enforcer over.

"If you want to avoid a painful death, then get out of my sight," Zen said, brandishing both weapons to show that he was deadly serious.

Rothenberg fumed for a moment, feeling a familiar rage building up inside him as he prepared to spring into action. A moment later, his fury dissipated, replaced by an emotion that was definitely not familiar for him.

Fear.

If any other child had spoken to him like that, if any other child had said those words to him, if any other child had dared to strike him, Rothenberg would've retaliated regardless of the consequences—and he might have had a chance, for Rothenberg's speed and physical prowess had been notorious among the Enforcers he'd trained with.

But this boy, his dominant posture, his menacing appearance, and his pitiless eyes all served to strike a chord of fear in Rothenberg that he had never known before in his life. For one suspended second, Rothenberg was paralyzed with terror, all logical thought having failed him. By the next, he had already sprung to his feet and was running out of the alley as fast as he could, stumbling in his haste to get away.

Meanwhile, Zen crouched down by the body of the first Enforcer, contemplating what he'd done. It was the first time he'd killed a person. He'd thought he'd feel guilty about it. Or at least remorseful. Or *something*. But try as he might, he couldn't feel anything about it.

How odd.

Zen straightened up and slipped both guns into his pockets. Maybe there would be time for emotions later. Turning around again, Zen abruptly found himself facing the girl that he had saved. She was still bleeding profusely, and stood rooted to the spot, though her icy blue eyes were now fixed upon Zen. Zen walked up to her and examined her limbs and face.

"So, how're you doing?" Zen asked casually.

The girl's eyes widened at his voice, but she didn't answer.

"Some nasty bruises all over your body, though they don't look that fresh. Scraped ankle as well as some other minor scratches, all old injuries. Visible malnourishment and perhaps chronic insomnia. Bad gash across the face—not a deep wound but there's a lot of blood loss," Zen observed as he ripped a piece of cloth off his shirt to use as a bandage. "I'm no doctor, but that cut will have to be disinfected, and you'll probably be scarred for life—perhaps in more ways than one. But all things considered, you're lucky just to be alive."

The girl remained silent and still as Zen retrieved his backpack and drew out a water bottle, which he used to bathe her gash. Using the strip of cloth torn from his shirt, Zen bound the wound tightly, taking care to leave her mouth uncovered in case she'd care to speak.

"So what's your name?" Zen asked as he finished binding the wound.

The girl looked at him, and something in her icy eyes flickered and thawed.

"I'm Noni."

Before Zen could respond, Noni visibly relaxed for a brief second, and then fainted, falling to the ground like a limp rag.

Zen raised an eyebrow.

"Well, I was about to ask you if you can walk," Zen said to the unconscious girl. "But I don't think that's necessary now."

Red continued staring downwards as the mysterious boy slung his backpack over his shoulders, scooped the girl up into his arms, and began walking back down the way he had come as though what had just transpired were completely ordinary.

He killed an Enforcer!

Red still couldn't believe what had happened. The only thing convincing him that it all hadn't been a hunger-induced hallucination was the fact that the Enforcer's body was still lying there in a pool of blood. Red was tempted to climb back down there and touch it to make sure that it actually existed, but he still had just enough judgment left to hold him back.

Red shook his head to clear it. He would need to think long and hard about what he thought he had seen. It was unheard-of! Someone, a kid no less, had taken down not just one, but two Enforcers—killing one of them at that! Thanks to its ruthless educational system, crime was more or less unheard of in the City, and the worst that Enforcers typically had to deal with were mere truants and vagrants. Vagrants especially had a short life expectancy; they rarely reached adulthood, and anyone who resisted the Enforcers usually had a life expectancy of about thirty seconds at best. And yet . . .

He killed an Enforcer!

Red began questioning his own sanity. A murderous child emerging from the shadows to attack adults? If it were real, if Red hadn't gone completely nuts as he knew some vagrants did, then it could only mean trouble. Winter had only just begun, and the Enforcers would be out for blood if one of their own had really been killed. Things could only get uglier from here, Red knew.

Still, Red wouldn't be shedding any tears over the dead Enforcer. The two men had richly deserved what they'd gotten, as far as Red was concerned. It was just a pity that the mysterious boy hadn't killed Rothenberg as well. Digging into his bag of fruit, Red pulled out an apple and began munching it. He was pleased that the girl had gotten away. She hadn't done anything to deserve what was done to her.

Sobering, Red realized that Rothenberg would probably radio for help. Maybe he already had. For all he knew, every Enforcer in the entire City could be descending upon his location at that very moment. Still munching on his apple, Red forced himself to his feet and began to run, the rest of his fruit slung over his shoulder. He needed to get away from here— somewhere far, far away. If things were about to get as bad as Red thought they would, Chris' gang would hardly be able to offer him any protection. He'd flee to one of the upper districts, maybe even as far as the twenties or thirties. Red didn't really care where he went, so long as he wasn't in the way when the Enforcers came to exact their revenge.

And so Red found himself running yet again. He really was good at running. But try as he might, Red couldn't forget that the other boy hadn't run. The kid, whoever he was, had stood his ground.

He *killed* an *Enforcer*!

Rothenberg ran through the crowd, ignoring the angry complaints of the civilians that he bumped into as he pressed his radio to his ear. Now that he was a safe distance away from that damned demon child, his fear had faded, replaced by outrage and anger. What the hell had happened back there in that alley? His partner . . . dead? An Enforcer? Killed by a boy? A kid? An inferior?

Impossible! Unthinkable!

But it had happened.

Except no one seemed to believe it.

"Can you please reconfirm the suspect's description, sir?" the voice on the radio asked patiently.

"What in education's name is wrong with you?" Rothenberg bellowed. "I told you twice already! It's a teenage boy, black clothes, long black hair, and dark eyes! Is there something wrong with your hearing? Did you lose your ear in the line of duty?"

"No sir," the voice said. "An ambulance is on its way. Can you tell us how badly is your partner injured?"

"How bad is he injured? How bad is he *injured*? He's dead! That's how bad he's injured, you idiot! Dead! How many times do I have to say it?"

"So this young boy just sprang up from the shadows?" The Enforcer on the other end could not conceal his skepticism. "And he killed your partner, right in front of your eyes? With just a knife?"

"Now you're getting it!" Rothenberg shouted. "It took you long enough! Where is that damned backup?"

"We've sent a call out for all District 5 officers to head to your location, sir," the voice said. "We've also posted a lookout for the suspect you described—"

"Just the District 5 officers?" Rothenberg roared. "I can count those on one hand! Listen to me, idiot: Get every last Enforcer in the entire lower half of the City down here! We're going to sweep every inch of Districts 7 and 8! We're going to find that kid even if we have to burn those districts to the ground! That's an order, do you hear me? Get *everyone* down here *now*!"

There was a pause.

"Chief Truancy Officer Rothenberg, sir, please stand by. We're transferring your communication."

"Transferring? What?"

Rothenberg growled angrily as a click on the other end indicated that he was now talking to someone new.

"Listen up, you uneducated fool!" Rothenberg snarled. "If this doesn't concern getting every Enforcer in the City down here at my disposal, then I don't want to hear it!"

There was another pause, and then Rothenberg felt both his anger and ego deflate rapidly.

"CTO Rothenberg," the new voice said darkly. "This is the Mayor."

Rothenberg gulped, a motion that made him look like a goldfish gasping for air.

"My apologies, Mr. Mayor," Rothenberg said, bringing his voice back under control.

"Save your apologies for later, Rothenberg," the Mayor snapped. "I need to see you in my office, immediately."

"But I didn't know that it was you, sir!" Rothenberg protested. "The man I was talking to didn't tell me who he was transferring me to!"

"Stop that blubbering, I'm not going to fire you," the Mayor said.

"Then . . . why do you want to see me?"

"It's about the . . . *suspect* that you claim attacked you."

*Z*en swiftly bore Noni through the dark alleys of District 8, heading towards the closest hideout that he had been able to find that day. As he walked, he contemplated how unnaturally light she felt. He wasn't sure exactly how much she weighed, but it couldn't have been much; it was like carrying a feather. That was fine with him, though, as it made carrying her all the easier.

Zen began to consider his earlier actions, debating whether or not it had been a good idea to tip off the Enforcers and Educators so early on. He had done so mainly for two reasons. First, he was sure that his father would get Umasi to spill everything that he knew anyway. And secondly, it had been hard to resist the opportunity to give those men what they deserved. Still, the Enforcers would be on high alert now, looking for him specifically. He would have to tread carefully.

Zen spared a glance down at his live burden—barely live, at that moment. She wasn't quite skin and bones just yet, but she wasn't far from it either. Not only that, but her clothing also seemed painfully thin for the weather; if she didn't starve to death, she quite possibly would've frozen to it. And then there were the fading bruises all over her body. *Someone* had mistreated this girl before the Enforcers, Zen noted. It was surprising, really, that she was still alive.

She was tougher than she looked, Zen concluded. In time she might become physically formidable—but Zen had a hunch that her mental and emotional wounds ran deeper than her physical ones.

Zen now began to wonder why exactly he had been compelled to bring her along with him. She wasn't an enormous burden, and could become a useful asset in the future. But on the other hand, no matter how light, she *was* a burden, and a significant responsibility, and he wasn't even sure that he'd feel guilty if he left her behind. He was finding it hard to feel guilty about anything of late.

Zen looked back down at Noni once more. Her dark hair was filthy and matted and hadn't been cut in a while. Her abject thinness left her looking disturbingly gaunt. She was dressed in rags and hauntingly pale. But despite all that, Zen was certain that under better circumstances she had the potential to look pretty . . . and yet he knew decisively that he possessed no physical attraction for this bedraggled girl. So then what was it?

Perhaps it was just curiosity, Zen postulated. Or perhaps some part of him was still capable of sympathy, and wouldn't allow him to leave her to die. Perhaps he needed an assistant—someone he could trust, and who would in turn trust him absolutely. That would fit. Zen could no longer count on his brother, but something about Noni made him feel confident he could count on her.

Whatever the reason, Zen decided then that he would accept her well-being as his responsibility. This was no casual decision; whenever Zen resolved to do something, he always saw it through to the end. He would take this traumatized victim, lying helpless in his arms, and he would see her become someone truly powerful—someone who could outlive him.

11

A re you absolutely sure that's what the child looked like?"

Rothenberg suppressed a growl, frustrated at having had to repeat his story for maybe the tenth time over the past few hours. If he had been anywhere but here, in the Mayor's Office, he probably would've thrown a tantrum. Merely being in the presence of the Mayor had sent a chill down Rothenberg's spine. Then again, that might've just been the air-conditioning, which had bafflingly been kept running even at the onset of winter.

"Yes, sir." Rothenberg nodded. "I'm positive."

"And you're telling me that he *killed* an Enforcer?"

"Yes, sir, my partner," Rothenberg said, leaving out the embarrassing detail about how the boy had used Rothenberg's own knife to finish the job.

The Mayor sighed, rubbing his eyes tiredly as he leaned back in his chair. Rothenberg said nothing, but watched the Mayor confusedly. He had met the Mayor only in passing before, but the City's leader had a reputation for being tough and unyielding, not weary and feeble. What's more, Rothenberg couldn't even begin to imagine what the Mayor's personal interest in the murderous boy was.

"Do you have any children, Rothenberg?" the Mayor asked suddenly.

Rothenberg frowned, wondering what *that* had to do with anything. The question made him uncomfortable, largely because he never ceased wishing that the answer were no.

"I keep one son, sir," Rothenberg said. "His name is Cross."

"Cross," the Mayor repeated idly. "That's a fine name. Well, Rothenberg, you know what it's like to be a father, and you've already met *him* in person. Whatever else can be said of you, no one disputes that you have a knack for getting things done. I'm going to entrust you with a very secret, very important task."

"You can count on me, sir," Rothenberg promised immediately, sensing an opportunity for a promotion.

"What you learn now cannot be repeated to any other individual," the Mayor said, looking sternly at Rothenberg. "There are absolutely *no* exceptions. Do you understand?"

"Perfectly, sir."

The Mayor regarded Rothenberg for another moment, as if second-guessing his own decision. Then the Mayor shook his head and picked up a sheet of lined paper from his desk and held it outstretched. Rothenberg accepted it, and quickly realized that there was a note scribbled on the paper. The Mayor watched calmly as Rothenberg's eyes widened as he read.

"Are you beginning to understand why I've called you here?" the Mayor asked dryly.

"The boy that attacked me . . . you think it was one of your *sons?*" Rothenberg exclaimed, still examining the paper with disbelief.

"The description you provided matches that of Zen, who is mentioned in that note that his brother left behind," the Mayor explained as he folded his hands together to stop them from shaking. "It seems that he discovered an Educator secret, and has reacted . . . rashly."

"So we proceed in hunting him down and killing him?" Rothenberg asked eagerly, if a bit foolishly.

"Out of the question," the Mayor snapped, glaring at Rothenberg. "I've already instructed the Enforcers to ignore your report and your prior orders. Officially, this 'attack' never happened. If anyone asks, the story is that you had a few too many drinks when you made the call—your temperament at the time would certainly support that notion."

Rothenberg's nostrils flared like a bull's, but he kept his silence as the Mayor continued glaring steadily at him.

Before the meeting, the Mayor had pulled up Rothenberg's records and discovered that the man had a history of aggression problems dating all the way back to school . . . where corporal punishment had been used to curb his violent tendencies. The Mayor envisioned the Enforcer as a sort of hound dog—useful for fetching things, but it had to be kept on a short leash, lest it kill rather than track.

"Let's get to the point," the Mayor said. "I want you to locate and arrest the boy who attacked you, but he must be brought back to me *unharmed*. I cannot emphasize enough that this whole thing must remain secret. No one can know that he's missing, and no one can know what he's done."

"You want me to handle this all by myself?"

"Of course not." The Mayor snorted. "You'll have *all* the Enforcers' resources at your disposal. Just ask for anything, and you'll get it. But remember, no one, and I really mean *no one,* can know what your agenda is."

"What about the boy who wrote this letter, this"—Rothenberg looked down at the paper once more—"Umasi. What about him?"

"I expect that *he'll* be back in a day or two," the Mayor said confidently. "It's Zen that I'm worried about. But if you can bring in both, that'll be even better."

"And what happens when I succeed?"

"*If* you succeed," the Mayor emphasized, looking Rothenberg straight in the eye, "I'll see to it that you get promoted all the way up to Chief Enforcer. Just remember that if anything happens to either of my sons, I will hold you personally responsible."

"Don't worry, Mr. Mayor," Rothenberg assured. "I'll bring them both back unscratched."

"You better, Rothenberg," the Mayor said, turning his chair around so that his back faced the Enforcer. "Or you'll wish you never graduated from school."

S o, how is it?"

Noni looked up at her rescuer, who was now placidly sitting across from her. She imagined that he was talking about the canned soup that she had, very tentatively, been sipping. For some reason, she felt secure in the boy's company, intimidating and dangerous though he was. But even so, she couldn't stop her spoon from shaking as she tried to answer.

"It's . . . good . . ." Noni managed to reply as she brought another quivering spoonful to her mouth, thinking that it was the best thing she had ever tasted.

Noni had awoken in an unfamiliar room, someplace warm, resting upon something soft. It was dark, and she wasn't sure if it was night or day. She was confused at first, not knowing where she was or how she'd gotten there. But soon it all came back to her—the boy with the apple, the angry men, the knife. Noni shuddered. But then there was the other boy, the one who had hurt the men, the one who had stopped them from hurting her! But he wasn't there when she awoke.

She had felt scared then, all alone in the dark on a makeshift bed of rags, wondering if she'd been abandoned again. She clutched her blanket to herself, staring into the darkness with wide, unblinking eyes, twitching at every shadow, every creak of a floorboard, imagining a massive man with a knife coming for her again. But then her rescuer had returned, bearing proper bandages and stinging ointments and other things he used to treat her wound. Now it was bound up and didn't feel so painful anymore. He had mended her other cuts too, but more than that, his presence alone made her feel better somehow. Here was a monster more frightening than all the others . . . but this one was on *her* side. Scary people had never been on her side before, but now that one was, she felt safer than she could ever remember being in her whole life.

Now she was eating canned soup that he had warmed over the stove. She was so used to being cold that the warmth had felt strange to her at first, though it was immediately welcome. She thought that it was chicken soup of some sort, but it seemed so long since she'd tasted real food that she'd forgotten what it was like. But already she was feeling more *alive* than she had ever since . . .

Noni blinked back sudden tears. She couldn't even remember what came after "ever since," and yet even thinking about it made her cry.

"Why are you crying?" the boy asked dispassionately.

Noni liked it, how the boy didn't seem to show any emotion. She wished she could be more like that.

"I don't know," Noni said timidly.

"Can't remember?"

Noni nodded.

"You've probably got some unpleasant repressed memories. Sometimes they're better kept that way," the boy speculated, sounding as though he were speaking out of boredom. "Of course, that can't be all that's bothering you, but I've no way of knowing the rest."

Noni liked that too, how he came out and said everything to her face. He made no effort to hide his thoughts, obviously because he didn't care about anyone hearing them. If he hated her, she knew he would tell her without hesitation, and the fact that he hadn't was enough to convince her that he *didn't* hate her . . . not like everyone else had.

"Anyway, you've been physically patched up as well as circumstances allow, and I think we've handled the malnutrition problem for now," the boy mused. "The only issue remaining appears to be the insomnia, and the only way to deal with that is for you to get some rest."

Now that he mentioned it, Noni began to realize how very tired she really was. Her eyes remained wide, but stung from the effort. She had been so frightened for so long that she didn't know when she had last gotten any real sleep. The boy began to lead her back over to the heap of cloth upon which she had been laid to rest, and she freely followed along. She eagerly lay down and managed to pull a blanket over herself as the boy stood up and slinked over into a dark corner where a bunch of documents had been spread out.

As he went, Noni suddenly remembered to ask something that she'd forgotten.

"Um . . . sir?" she said tentatively.

"Yes?" The boy turned his head around halfway to look at her over his shoulder.

"What . . . what should I call you?" Noni asked, her voice pitifully small.

The boy seemed to hesitate for a moment as he crouched there in the shadows. Noni cringed, immediately worried that she had somehow upset him with her question. But the boy merely shook his head with indecision as he turned fully around.

"I suppose that 'sir' will do for the time being," he said. "Now go to sleep. We'll have friends joining us soon."

"Yes, sir," Noni said obediently.

U masi groaned in spite of himself and attempted to rise. He was swiftly rewarded with a brutal kick to the gut. As he crumpled back to the ground, a worn boot stomped on his back, and then another assaulted his ribs. The pain from the impacts was persistent, throbbing, and Umasi knew that if he survived he'd be black and blue all over.

As he lay on the ground, Umasi bit back a moan as he realized that the beatings he had received on the school courtyard might as well have been slaps on the wrists. The brutal force behind these blows had been unimaginable to him just days prior. He had never understood what it meant to be attacked by people who didn't hold back, people with no mercy or restraint.

But he did now.

"Think we should kill him, Raphael?"

"No way man, take a look at those clothes and the backpack. Kid ain't no vagrant—he's a student. The Enforcers would torch the whole district if we killed him!"

"Psh, let 'em come, they'll never find us."

"You crazy, James? You forgotten the parking garage already? Chris would throw a fit if he knew you were thinking about bringing the Enforcers down here."

"Fine, whatever, let 'im live. If he *is* a student, he sure picked one hell of a place to go on a field trip."

"Come on, he's had enough and we're already late. The others might've ditched us by now."

Umasi again repressed the urge to moan and rolled over at the sound of receding footsteps. His injuries punished him for every movement, but he refused to make any sound that would betray his weakness. Opening his one eye that wasn't swollen shut, Umasi vaguely saw two boys running off with his backpack containing all of his supplies. The vagrants rounded a street corner, and then they vanished. Umasi felt a nasty sensation welling up in his stomach, but he clenched his fists and forced the vomit down. The only food he had left was inside his stomach, and he couldn't afford to lose that now.

Life on his own wasn't what he thought it would be.

Umasi wasn't sure exactly what he had been expecting, but what he felt now was much worse than anything he'd experienced in his troubled dreams. It was despair, shame, guilt, disappointment, and a hundred other negative emotions all rolled into one. He had never felt worse in his life.

His only consolation was that he had taken the beating without moaning, without betraying his weakness. There had been a time when degrading himself wouldn't have mattered to Umasi, but in that moment when he had first faced possible death, with his life at the mercy of two who had none, he realized that he had nothing else left to defend but his pride. And so he had.

Umasi ruefully wondered if it was just his luck that sucked or if District 13 was to blame. Whatever it was, he had barely stepped within the boundaries of the abandoned district before the two thugs had appeared, both large, ragged, with a feral look in their eyes.

"Hey kid, that's a nice backpack you got there," the first vagrant had complimented.

"Uh . . . thanks?" Umasi had replied warily.

"Welcome. Now hand it over."

"Wh-what?"

"I don't think he heard ya right, Raphael," the second thug had observed. "He ain't givin us the pack."

"Maybe this'll teach him to listen!"

And with that, the vagrant named Raphael had punched Umasi hard in the chest, flinging him against the wall of a building. His glasses had been cast from his face by the impact, and the other vagrant quickly trampled them underfoot. Seeing that, and having been tossed around like a rag doll, Umasi had snapped. Before he knew what he was doing, Umasi had struck back for the first time in his life, kicking viciously at his assailant. Caught up in his sudden madness, Umasi had forgotten everything he learned in his self-defense classes, attacking fiercely, but crudely.

Maybe that was why they had beaten him so hard.

The first vagrant had taken the blow well, staggering back a few paces as his partner lunged for Umasi. Umasi had slid his backpack off in order to move better, and then threw a punch at the second thug, who backed up just in time to avoid it. Then the first ruffian reentered the fray, seizing Umasi by both shoulders and slamming him against the brick wall. His partner then joined in, using Umasi as a punching bag, and the rest was history.

There had been two of them, sure, but it didn't stop Umasi from feeling pathetic about how easily he'd been beaten.

In an attempt to suppress tears of rage, Umasi focused on his injuries. Damn, did it hurt everywhere. He'd been bruised all over, and he thought that he was bleeding but wasn't exactly sure where. He didn't think that anything had been broken, but he felt so incredibly tired, a weariness that ran deeper than just his muscles. He would rest for a while, here. Not die,

Umasi reminded himself, just rest. And maybe later he'd get up, leave the accursed district, and then . . . what? Return home, lesson learned?

Home, where he'd exchange his freedom for comforts and safety? Home, where everything would be so easy, and yet so hard, all over again?

Both of Umasi's eyes snapped open.

No.

He had no home.

He had run away once already, and he wouldn't run back again.

Umasi allowed himself a painful smile with cracked lips. Even as he lay there, curled up and shivering on the dirty ground, he now felt an insane sort of pride. He wasn't going to give up. If he survived, then there would be no more running for him. He would face his problems, and find his brother or die trying.

lad that you could join us, Gabriel! Everyone else has already arrived, and some of them were beginning to voice concern."

"Sorry, Zen, I had to dodge a few Enforcer patrols on the way here."

"Yes, I've received a lot of complaints about those. Did any of them spot you?"

"I don't think so, but this whole district's been crawling with them from what I've seen. Think they're on to us already?"

"Doubtful. They're probably just searching for me—I did kill one of them yesterday, after all."

"What? Already?"

"Indeed. Come on in, the others have already been briefed in your absence."

"Lot of people in there I've not met yet?"

"Some of them I've only met today for the first time myself, actually."

"And you trust all of them?"

"None of them got caught by those loud and obnoxious Enforcer patrols, so they pass the test of minimum capability. Only time will tell how reliable they'll be. From their academic profiles, and the occasional interview I conducted over the phone, I've decided that these would make the most promising inaugural Truants. Certainly, few of them have much to lose."

"Well, Zen, I trust your judgment."

"I do appreciate that. By the way, I must ask you not to refer me as 'Zen' anymore. I think it prudent that my real name not be associated with the Truancy in any way."

"All right, I just hope you know what you're doing."

"So do I, Gabriel. After all, if it turns out that I don't, then we're all dead. Every last one of us."

"Now, there's a cheerful thought."

Zen laughed mirthlessly as he led Gabriel farther into the building where he'd been hiding since the previous day. It was a nondescript brownstone on a street of nearly identical-looking houses, and save for the Truancy symbol concealed inside the doorway, nothing made it stand out among the others. By all appearances, it defined "inconspicuous," and was therefore a perfect place to hide from the Enforcer patrols.

As they entered a small, dimly lit chamber, Gabriel found himself facing a room full of unfamiliar faces. Zen wasted no time in introducing Gabriel to the other newcomers. The first that had arrived was a brown-skinned boy named Amal, who looked friendly and intelligent. The second was a dark-haired and brooding boy named Aaron, who barely spoke a word during the introductions. In third place was a skinny kid named Max, who was looking around a little dazedly, as if unable to believe what he was doing. In dead last was Ken, a fatigued boy who had had some difficulty arriving undetected.

"Would you like some hot chocolate, Gabriel?" Zen offered as Gabriel shook hands with the others. "We've made some to ward off the cold—this building has running water, but no heating or electricity, I'm afraid."

"No, thanks," Gabriel said. "I had a narrow escape with one of the patrols and my stomach is still unknotting."

"Well, you're certainly not alone." Zen gestured at the other Truants. "Aaron and Max declined refreshment as well."

The two Truants he named both nodded briefly at Gabriel, but said nothing. There was a lot of palpable tension in that room, and a lot of nervousness.

"Well, my friends, you must be wondering how exactly things will work around here," Zen observed. "I won't keep you in suspense. As all of you know by now, we are going to fight the Educators. I believe that we have always known in our hearts that they were our enemies, that this conflict was inevitable—but in their ignorance they have never regarded *us* as anything more than scum, let alone a threat."

Gabriel nodded at that, as did all the other Truants. They all knew personally how deep the Educators' contempt for them ran. None of them had any love left for the Educators, especially in light of what Zen had revealed to them.

"I won't make any illusion about what this struggle will entail," Zen said. "You will have to kill. You may very well die. All of you understood this before you came, and yet you came anyway. The only promise that I can make you now is that no sacrifice that I ask of you will ever be without purpose."

Gabriel believed that. No matter what people might have said about Zen, no one ever accused him of being wasteful.

"You may think that you will be able to handle it now," Zen continued, "but it is possible that you may later want to change your mind. This will not be allowed. Once you are a Truant, you can never return to being a student again. Attempting to do so would endanger yourself and all of us. If you run, the Enforcers will undoubtedly try to capture and interrogate you . . . provided that we don't get to you first."

Gabriel smiled grimly at that. Even within the confines of school, dark rumors about the Enforcers and what they did to the vagrants managed to spread. Even if they were exaggerated, Gabriel had no doubts about the Enforcers' brutality.

"We may be old by the time this struggle is over," Zen warned, "so it is important that we never lose sight of what we're fighting for—a City where we would have been equals. I myself left school only a few days ago, and yet already the memories of it are fading. But we cannot forget the true nature of school, for when that happens the Educators will have truly succeeded in their goal—turning us into them.

"We've not known each other for a long time, but we all share a common enemy, and a common goal," Zen said. "That's enough to make us comrades. No matter the outcome, from this day forward we will pursue that goal and fight that enemy together. From this day forward, we are that which the Educators fear most.

"From this day forward, we are the Truancy."

It wasn't the type of speech designed to produce applause, but Gabriel and the other Truants clapped anyway. Zen's words had been solemn and yet thrilling at the same time.

"So, mister, if you're to be our commanding officer, what should we call you?" the boy named Amal asked. "You never did tell us your name."

"My real name will be kept secret for obvious reasons," Zen explained. "Until I devise a permanent alias, you may refer to me simply as 'Z.'"

"When are we going to see some action, Z?" the one named Aaron asked.

"It would be wise to avoid direct confrontations with the Enforcers for now," Zen said. "But we will be exploring District 13 tomorrow to find some alternative hideouts—these Enforcer patrols are quite inconvenient, and I think that the docks can offer promising shelter."

The Truants all nodded mechanically at this. Zen wasn't surprised that there weren't any more questions just yet. The previous day they had been at home with their families, and now here they were, plotting armed rebellion against the institution of school. It must have seemed somewhat absurd, if not surreal. The boy named Max had his eyes glued to the floor now.

But most of the other Truants had begun to mill about, talking among themselves, getting to know each other better. Gabriel was the only one of them that Zen had known from school, but they were smart enough not to act chummy with each other; it would give the impression to the others that Gabriel was a one-man member of an elite. And that sort of separatism was dangerous.

Zen was confident that the five newcomers, Gabriel included, were likely to shape up well. He had selected this first group very carefully, as the beginning could make or break the entire future of the Truancy. The students he'd chosen not only had a history of "disrespecting authority," but many of them had useful talents as well. With that in mind, Zen approached a dark-haired Truant sitting alone in a corner.

"You, Aaron, is it?"

"That's right."

"You're good with electronics, correct?"

"Good enough to get me into the City-Wide Science Talent Search," Aaron said gloomily. "But not good enough to save me when I got nailed for plagiarizing. In humanities, not science," he added quickly, catching Zen's eye.

"What would it take for you to make . . . say . . . an explosive trigger?"

"Not much. A TV remote. Maybe a radio. Hell, if you got me, like, a washing machine timer, I could rig up a time bomb. I can't help as much with the explosive part, though."

"This apartment building is safe and relatively large—there's plenty of junk lying around. I want you to salvage whatever you can. In the meantime, we'll be combing the abandoned districts very soon. We'll get everything you list and more," Zen promised. "As soon as you have enough to start working, I want you to prepare as many triggers as possible. Do you think you can rig up proximity explosives?"

"That'll be harder, but—"

"Work on it. I'll get you any raw materials that you need. Are there any particular tools you'll require?"

"Well, it'd be nice to have—"

"Draw up a list, get it back to me as soon as possible," Zen said briskly. "We don't have time to waste, my friend. The Educators have no idea what we're up to, but sooner or later they're going to figure us out. When that happens, I want it to be too late for them to stop us."

"I'll do my best," Aaron said, looking Zen in the eye. "Who knows? Maybe now they'll appreciate my talent."

In response Zen gave a curt nod and a grim smile. Zen had picked his comrades well after all. While Aaron's ability would prove to be the most useful in the immediate future, the majority of his handpicked rebels could contribute some sort of specialized work. Any who couldn't would be assigned to patrol duty, scavenging parties, and scouting work. Eventually, however, Zen knew that the latter would have to outnumber the former. He had his specialists, but he would soon need soldiers.

Zen had lately been giving increasing thought to the vagrants of the

City. Obviously, few of them would be suited for specialized work, but they were tough, subtle, and had an intimate knowledge of the City streets. If he could just insure their loyalty, they would make perfect soldiers. Zen resolved that he would work on that.

"Hey Z, who's that over there?" Gabriel asked, snapping Zen out of his revereie.

Zen followed Gabriel's finger until his eyes came to rest upon the small figure, half-covered by blankets, in a corner that no one had noticed until then.

"Her name is Noni," Zen explained as few other Truants glanced at the corner with interest. "She was attacked without provocation by the Enforcer that I killed. She's still recovering from her injuries, but when she's healthy she will join us."

Noni rested quietly in the corner, though she eyed the newcomers with trepidation. Now with all eyes on her, she began shivering violently, a reaction only partially due to the cold.

"Are you sure she'll be up to it?" Ken asked skeptically. "Fighting, that is. I mean, she doesn't look too good to me. How bad is it under those bandages?"

At that pronouncement, Noni's shivering doubled, and she shut her eyes as she pressed her arms and legs to herself even tighter. A few of the Truants began to look alarmed, but Zen acted swiftly before the girl could become any more distressed.

"Gentlemen, for your very first, and admittedly very inglorious mission as Truants, I would like you to help move some boxes downstairs," Zen said. "You'll find the supplies in the main hallway—everything that I was able to sneak in past the patrols. Kindly take them down to the basement."

The other Truants didn't argue, and quickly filed out the door, which Zen took to be a good sign. A few of them cast curious glances at Noni on the way out. The frail girl was now a pitiful, shivering lump under the blankets. As soon as the last of the newcomers filed out the door, Zen shut it and walked over to Noni, drawing something out of his coat.

"Their intentions were good, but obviously you don't like that injury being spoken of or seen. You also don't seem to like the cold much," Zen observed, to which Noni nodded. "I have a solution to both those problems."

Noni's shivering abated slightly as she looked up hopefully at Zen, who then showed her the item he had taken from his coat—a large, black scarf. Zen swiftly wrapped the scarf around Noni's head so that it completely obscured the lower half of her face from the nose down. The injury was concealed, and what's more, Noni now felt much warmer.

"Thank you," Noni mumbled from behind the scarf.

"Thank me the day you're ready to take that off," Zen said, gesturing towards the scarf.

And with that, he left the room, leaving Noni alone to ponder his words.

U masi staggered along the streets of District 13, leaning against the buildings to his left for support. His ears and fingers had become painfully cold, alternating between stinging and numbness every few seconds. His cheeks burned from the chill, and his limbs had all gone sluggish, their injuries from the day before numbed by the cold. He was still decently clothed, as his two attackers had neglected to take his jacket, but even with it on the cold seemed to seep right through to his core. Umasi shuddered, both from the weather and from the knowledge that winter had only just begun.

But even worse than the cold was the hunger. It had long since ceased to ache in his stomach, becoming a dull, numb sensation instead. It enfeebled his motions, clouded his head, and blurred his vision worse than it already was. Umasi would've liked nothing better than to just lie down and rest right where he stood, but he had a feeling that if he did, he would never get up again. So Umasi forced himself to continue moving, wandering through District 13 in a daze.

Right now Umasi was struggling to reach the border of District 12, a living district where he might be able to find some food. District 13 was a long way off, and he had no real hope of making it, though he had no choice other than to try.

Suddenly, as Umasi stumbled around a corner and the border came into sight, he froze. Umasi's glasses had been shattered beyond repair, and his vision clouded by hunger, but his eyesight was still good enough for him to make out what was unfolding in front of him. Two blurred figures were viciously attacking each other, a box containing what appeared to be an entire pizza pie lying forgotten beside them.

Umasi's other senses swiftly kicked in, and over the intoxicating scent of food, he realized that the two vagrants, a girl and a boy, were talking as they fought.

"You and the rest of Chris' pukes can all go to hell!" the girl snarled, punching the boy square in the belly.

"If we do," the boy wheezed, clutching his stomach as he slammed his shoulder into her, "it ain't gonna be you that sends us there!"

"I got this fair and square!" the girl shrieked, gesturing at the pizza box as she was knocked backwards by the blow. "You touch this, and the rest of us will kill all of you!"

"We ain't scared of you!" the boy jeered, advancing upon his foe. "What's this I heard 'bout one of your guys getting whacked the other day?"

"I was there; your kid had a knife!" the girl spat, swiftly slamming her elbow into the boy's face. "None of you can fight for shit unarmed!"

"Tha's funny, 'cause we ain't got no knives, and it wasn't us that killed any of you jackasses," the boy said, grabbing his injured face with one hand while blocking a punch with the other. "But I'm about to, right now!"

"Well then you're off to a pretty pathetic start, aren't ya?" the girl taunted, lunging forward as she threw another punch.

At that moment, Umasi almost shouted out a warning, for he could tell what was about to happen from the boy's pose. As the girl lunged, the boy suddenly lurched forward to meet her. Her fist connected with his chest, but the boy just grimaced and took the blow, both of his own arms lashing out in an instant. A moment later the boy had the girl by the throat. Umasi stood transfixed in horror as the girl thrashed about wildly, kicking, flailing, trying to pry her assailant's hands from her neck. The boy's arms shook with strenuous effort, his face contorted in ruthless determination. The girl began making the most horrible sounds Umasi had ever heard, an increasingly faint gagging and hissing as her last breaths escaped her lungs.

Only when the girl fell silent and her movements ceased did Umasi shake himself from his trance. In that moment, something snapped inside of him, just when he had fought back against his two assailants. But this time, he became the attacker. Roaring to announce his presence, Umasi lunged at the other vagrant, who immediately spun around in confusion. Umasi might have been starving, but the other boy had just finished a fight to the death and was barely standing himself.

With strength that he never knew he had, Umasi tackled the boy, slamming him down onto the hard asphalt. Momentarily stunned by the impact, the boy could not react as Umasi slammed his elbow into the boy's face the way the girl had done. Reeling from the blow, the boy flailed out with his fists and feet, but Umasi barely noticed as he rained punch after punch upon his victim's head. Snarling with fury, the vagrant forcefully rolled them both over so that he came out on top.

Umasi, however, never allowed the boy to exploit that advantage. He swiftly slammed his forehead up into the other vagrant's face, and something cracked sickeningly as the boy let out a scream of pain and rolled off of Umasi. Umasi showed no mercy, standing up and kicking the other boy while he was still down. The vagrant ceased shouting and clumsily shot to his feet, glaring at Umasi, his face a crimson mess.

The vagrant charged at Umasi in a frenzy, but instead of lashing out with his fists as Umasi expected, he instead clamped his jaws down upon Umasi's shoulder. Umasi roared in outrage and lunged forward, driving both of them to the ground, though Umasi's fall was cushioned by his opponent. Not letting up for an instant, Umasi then drove his fist into the other vagrant's already bruised belly.

That did it. The other vagrant let out a moan and writhed pitifully on the ground. Suddenly realizing what he was on the verge of doing, Umasi shot to his feet, staring at the other boy in horror. Abruptly noticing Umasi's absence, the other boy scrambled to his feet and staggered away as fast as he could, his hands covering his bloodied nose. Umasi was left alone, gasping for breath on the lonely street.

Clutching his shoulder, Umasi slowly approached the fallen girl who had been left behind. He searched for a pulse, though he knew that he would not find any. It was the first time that he had looked upon death, and yet it already seemed as though they'd always known each other. Umasi hugged his arms to his chest, and his shivering intensified. There was something about witnessing the awful finality of it all that chilled him worse than any blizzard could. Who had the girl been? What had driven her to this end? What else might she have become had the circumstances just been a little different? Umasi didn't know, and never would, and that thought filled him with unspeakable sadness.

Then, in that darkest and coldest moment, Umasi remembered Zen's casual words, spoken in passing.

So is killing, but hey, people still die.

Bizarrely, Zen's voice dried his tears and lifted his spirits. The girl's story had ended, and there was nothing he could do about that now. But Umasi still had yet to see his own story, his mission, through to the end. Glancing over at the pizza box, now lying abandoned on the sidewalk, Umasi felt a rumble in his stomach. He crawled over to it and began stuffing himself. He ate and ate and ate, until he was sure he'd be sick if he ate another bite.

Umasi grimly closed the box, saving the remaining slices for later as he walked back towards the riverside. He felt drawn towards the docks and their view of the open water, freezing wind notwithstanding. The sun was setting now, and the skies were a dark blue streaked with fading rays of yellow. Umasi imagined that it would look very scenic, reflected in the water.

But as he walked, all Umasi could think about was the body that he'd left behind. He now wondered if he would ever find his brother, or if he would end up like the girl, his story lost forever—just another whimper in the chorus of screams that was the City.

Rothenberg turned up the heat dial on his car dashboard as he drove through a gate leading into District 7. Taking a quick sip of coffee before placing the cup back inside its holder, he leaned back in his seat and proceeded through the empty streets of the abandoned district. In spite of himself, a smile spread across Rothenberg's face. He felt completely at home here, inside his comfortable car, doing what he loved most—hunting vagrants. Granted, he wouldn't be able to kill the two particular kids he had been sent to find, but at least he would be rewarded handsomely for finding them—rewarded with the realization of all his wildest dreams.

Not to mention that *all* the Enforcers were already at his beck and call. He could certainly get used to that.

The Mayor had been true to his word: No sooner had Rothenberg arrived at Enforcer Headquarters than he had discovered that the instructions to obey him had already gone out. That had been yesterday, and since then Rothenberg had had a dozen separate patrols thoroughly comb the streets of District 8. Meanwhile, Rothenberg had decided to take District 7 all for himself. He didn't actually expect to find the Mayor's sons here by himself, but he felt like doing some private hunting. He was still fuming over being humiliated the day before, first by that brown-haired brat and then by the Mayor's son, and now he had an opportunity to take it out on the vagrants.

Just then, Rothenberg turned a street corner and spotted two shadowed figures running from his patrol car. Though dusk had already settled and the children were hard to see in the dim lighting, it was obvious that neither had a ponytail. The first kid was running very fast, so much so that Rothenberg wasn't sure he'd be able to hit him. The other, however, was weighed down by what appeared to be a hefty backpack he'd slung over one shoulder.

Rothenberg smiled. The Mayor's runaways might be off-limits, but all the others were fair game.

Rothenberg lowered his car window and stuck his head and gun outside, aiming at the slower, clumsier silhouette. He fired once, the gunshot roaring throughout the empty street as the fleeing figure crumpled to the ground with a yelp. Rothenberg let out a cold chuckle, then opened his car door and stepped out to examine his catch as its companion vanished around the corner.

It was a fairly large vagrant boy, and Rothenberg noted with some satisfaction that his shot had caught the kid right in the head. The ragged, filthy child looked like typical street trash to Rothenberg, but there was one thing that seemed out of place: The backpack that the boy had been carrying looked relatively new. It was probably stolen goods, Rothenberg decided as he spun around and began walking back towards his car.

Without checking to see what was inside the backpack, or bothering to do anything about the boy's body lying there, Rothenberg reentered his car, rolled up the window, and sipped more coffee before resuming his hunt. The vagrant he'd shot hadn't been one of the Mayor's sons, and that was all that the Enforcer really cared about—especially since he wasn't keen on lingering outside of his heated car for too long. After all, the weather had been getting rather chilly lately.

13
FAILURE

The day was cloudy and overcast, and yet strangely bright, casting a gray sheen over District 13. The river reflected the gray hue, and thanks to especially strong winds the surface of the water resembled a thrashing sea of living silver. Zen found that he rather enjoyed the sound that the waves made as they crashed against the various docks and piers of the district, but he had little time to appreciate the scenery.

Today was, as planned, the Truancy's first excursion, and though he didn't expect any trouble, it wouldn't do to be careless. They hadn't had any difficulty moving through the districts that stood between District 8 and District 13; they had split up into pairs and looked utterly unremarkable as they walked along the streets. Amal had paired with Gabriel, Max had paired with Ken, Aaron had stayed behind to build triggers, and Zen had taken Noni along with him.

Noni hadn't been very talkative so far, though Zen hadn't expected her to be. She had, however, opened up enough to ask a few questions about their surroundings as they went along. Having food and rest for a change seemed to agree with her, and her wounds were already showing signs of healing. Zen believed that suffering spawned strength, and he was certain that Noni would someday become very powerful indeed. He was, however, beginning to worry that she might become too dependent upon him.

And so Zen kept a formal distance as the two traversed the empty streets of District 13, gray light illuminating their path. Zen discovered a large apartment complex that would someday be perfect for housing hundreds of Truants, and Noni carried a sack filled with materials to return to Aaron. Slowly but surely Zen, with Noni close behind, made his way towards the river—towards the docks, piers, and riverside warehouses that he was sure could offer up useful tools and materials. Everything went exactly according to plan . . . now they rounded a corner and the river itself came into sight. It was there that Zen saw something crouching down by a pier that made him freeze in his tracks.

Satisfying himself that it wasn't an illusion, Zen ordered Noni to remain where she was, and then he strode forward to speak with the person he had never expected to meet again in his life.

Umasi had gotten up late, and only then with the greatest reluctance. His body ached, his mind felt sluggish, and his memories of the previous day had not yet dulled. His dreams, however, had been untroubled for a change. Perhaps that was because his old nightmares were tame compared with the one that had become his life, Umasi thought grimly as he spat in the river to rid his mouth of its bitter taste.

Feeling his stomach grumble in complaint, Umasi wearily reached for the nearby pizza box. He quickly pulled out one of his remaining slices and began sucking on it hungrily like a Popsicle. The slice had very nearly frozen solid from the cold, but Umasi didn't complain; he knew that he was lucky to have it. By the time he was halfway through the slice he was feeling a little better, well enough to pay attention to his surroundings. It was then that he noticed what looked like an indistinct shadow gliding towards him.

Hastily swallowing his latest bite of frozen pizza, Umasi cautiously raised himself into a crouch. The blurred figure drew closer, taking on an unmistakable humanoid shape. Umasi tensed, ready to fight if he had to. But moments later the figure came into focus, and Umasi's jaw dropped in disbelief.

"Zen?" Umasi gaped as the black-clad figure drew up to him, jacket billowing in the strong wind.

For a brief moment, Umasi wondered if he had already gone completely mad, or if his vision was perhaps worse than he had thought. But as soon as the figure opened its mouth, Umasi realized that he was neither hallucinating nor blind.

"Umasi. You look different without your glasses." Zen's eyes narrowed as he examined Umasi's ragged form. "What are you doing here?"

"I've been looking for you!" Umasi exclaimed delightedly, unable to believe his luck.

"Is that so?" Zen said. "Have you changed your mind then?"

"No," Umasi said, his smile fading. "I thought I might be able to convince you to stop."

"Stop?" Zen suddenly laughed at the absurdity of it all. "You came out here at random, completely unprepared, just to try to *stop* me?"

Umasi hesitated for the briefest of moments.

"Yes, I did."

"You're serious," Zen observed incredulously. "And how exactly did you propose to stop me?"

"By . . . talking some sense into you."

"How can you talk sense into me if you're the one that's deluded?" Zen demanded. "Surely even *you* aren't so naïve as to believe that I'd stop now."

"Wishful thinking, maybe," Umasi conceded. "But I can't just watch you go through with this. It's not too late, you can just forget about everything and come back!"

"Not too late?" Zen repeated. "There's already blood on my hands, Brother."

Umasi was stunned. It couldn't be. It had only been a few days, hadn't it? It had felt like years to Umasi, but he was sure that he'd only awoken on the street four times so far. Surely Zen hadn't managed to *kill* anyone in that time?

"You can't mean . . ." Umasi choked.

"Yes, yes, I killed an Enforcer," Zen said impatiently. "That one truly deserved it, though, I'm sure you'd agree if you'd seen him."

His worst fears confirmed, Umasi felt an indescribable horror welling up inside him as he remembered the death he'd witnessed the previous day. Suddenly feeling sick, Umasi stumbled back a few paces as he stared at his brother as if truly seeing him for the first time.

"So as you can see, Umasi," Zen continued, "if you want to get in my way . . . you're going to have to fight me. Are you prepared to try it?"

Memories of dark dreams that he had thought he'd long forgotten flitted through Umasi's mind. Zen was really going to destroy the City. Countless lives might be ended if this *one* were allowed to continue.

When is a threat so great that life should be taken to stop it?

Who had the right to even answer that question?

Umasi abruptly shook his head. "Not me."

"Still trying to occupy the moral high ground, are you?" Zen raised an eyebrow as he looked Umasi up and down. "By the looks of it, you've become quite the hypocrite in the short time I haven't known you. Or do you mean to say that all of that blood is your own?"

Following Zen's gaze, Umasi stared down at himself, something he hadn't done since he'd run from home. His clothes were already filthy and torn, bruises in various stages of healing covered his body, and scattered bloodstains were clearly visible on his clothes and skin. Some of that blood was his, yes . . . but Umasi realized, with jolt of self-loathing, that Zen was right: He *had* shed the blood of another.

"You see, Umasi, you're not *really* a pacifist. Even you have to fight for something on occasion." Zen smirked. "You just use that term to hide yourself from reality, to avoid conflict. You're just a coward."

Zen's words stung Umasi more than either of them thought they would. Umasi felt his fists clench unconsciously as he realized that there was some truth in them. Zen was right. He had been a coward. He was scared of getting hurt, and even more scared of hurting anyone else. All this time he had been running away from his problems, not trying to solve them. He had talked of peace, but had done nothing to achieve it.

Umasi grimaced. His cowardice would end here.

"All right," Umasi said grimly, "we'll settle this your way."

Zen looked slightly surprised, but not displeased.

"Didn't think you had it in you," Zen said as he walked forward. "Let's make this interesting, shall we?"

Umasi tensed as Zen approached, but then watched in confusion as Zen walked past him and towards the docks. Looking around, Zen spotted and picked up two thin metal pipes that had been left lying around. They were slightly rusted, but Zen knocked them against each other and found that they were perfectly sturdy. Tossing one to Umasi and keeping the other for himself, Zen nodded to his brother and walked farther along the waterline. Puzzled, Umasi followed until Zen reached one particular pier that stood out from the others.

This pier had been mostly demolished, with all of the boards that had once made up its surface long since torn away. However, the thick wooden columns that had held up the boards remained, their exposed heads stoically remaining above the water. Years of neglect had not been kind to the columns; the tips of many were broken off, some had sunk to the point of vanishing underwater, and others were bent sideways like a diagonal splinter marring the silver face of the water. The columns were each about two feet thick and spaced about three feet apart.

As a whole, the massive wrecked pier formed a uniquely challenging terrain, and with a growing sense of trepidation, Umasi realized what Zen was up to. As if to confirm his suspicions, Zen elegantly leapt onto the closest pillar, then continued making short hops until he was a good ten pillars deep. Only then did he turn around, both feet planted firmly upon the tiny surface beneath him as he raised his pole towards Umasi.

"Well? Do you still intend to stop me?" Zen leered.

"Yeah," Umasi answered, suddenly bereft of confidence.

"Then come and get me."

Umasi took a deep, calming breath, and then stepped forward. As his foot touched down upon the first column, he felt a strange thrill travel up his body. Hopping over to where Zen now stood watching him, Umasi realized that while Zen had made it look easy, maintaining his balance and calculating jumps from pillar to pillar was incredibly challenging. More than once Umasi felt sure he would slip and plunge into the river below, which sloshed about with increasing violence, as though eager to claim the intruders over its surface.

A powerful gust kicked up, and suddenly a fierce wind battered Umasi's body and screamed in his ears. None of this was helping him stay upright, and as he felt the river's cold foamy spray on his face, he realized that he might fall without Zen having to lift a finger. The short poles they wielded weren't very dangerous on their own, but they were more than enough for either of them to tip the other into the icy water.

Trying not to think about the consequences of losing, Umasi made one final leap, and found himself standing upon the column right in front of Zen. Zen grinned and performed a dignified bow as a particularly large wave splashed behind him, framing his figure with a silvery spray that glittered in the pale light.

"Are you ready?" Zen asked.

"Yes."

"Actually, I don't think that you are." Zen smiled. "But we'll soon find out, won't we?"

And with that Zen brought his pole swinging towards Umasi without any warning. Instinctively, Umasi raised his own pole and blinked surprisedly as it blocked the blow with a loud *clang*. Unfazed, Zen lashed out again, this time at Umasi's legs. Umasi quickly brought his pole downwards to parry the attack, feeling pleased with himself as Zen's pole noisily bounced back.

Zen, however, seized the opportunity to leap diagonally over to another column with almost catlike agility, now facing Umasi's exposed flank. Seeing the danger, Umasi quickly hopped sideways and landed safely on another column as Zen's pole cleaved the air where he had just been standing. Looking as though he was enjoying himself, Zen leapt diagonally again onto a short column, and then forward onto a taller one, bringing him adjacent to his brother. As he made his last leap, he also brought his weapon swinging upwards towards Umasi, who easily batted it away with his own pole.

Umasi and Zen eyed each other for a few tense seconds, and then Umasi decided to try to imitate Zen's tactic. He made his first diagonal hop successfully, dodging Zen's wild swing in midair. But as he made the second jump, a powerful gust of wind battered him, nearly tipping him over as he landed haphazardly on a pillar diagonal to Zen's.

Seizing the momentary advantage, Zen jumped to a column next to Umasi and lashed out with his pole, catching Umasi in the ribs and further unbalancing the hapless brother. Teetering dangerously, Umasi managed to hop to another column to regain his balance. Just then, a large wave rose up, threatening to engulf Zen's pillar. Recognizing the threat, Zen leapt into a magnificent cartwheel over open water, his hand touching down on the column that Umasi had just abandoned, propelling Zen feet-first towards the column upon which a stunned Umasi currently stood.

With reflexes he didn't know that he had, Umasi hopped backwards clumsily as Zen slammed down upon the pillar. Umasi was almost surprised to find himself safe as Zen took a moment to recover from the complicated maneuver. However, with a quick glance behind him, Umasi realized that he was now at the very edge of the shattered pier, and nothing now stood between him and the angry waters of the river. He had no ground behind him to retreat to.

With a shout of defiance, Umasi suddenly lunged towards Zen with his pole outstretched, determined that one or both of them would end up taking the plunge. Zen, however, was already in motion even before Umasi jumped, and swiftly landed upon another column with a smirk of satisfaction. It was only then that Umasi realized that Zen hadn't been dodging Umasi's attack.

A powerful wave washed over the pillar as Umasi landed, soaking his pants and sneakers. Umasi let out an involuntary gasp; it was as though his legs had suddenly been encased in ice. Roaring in frustration, Umasi stamped his numb feet upon his pillar, bothered more by his careless blunder than by the freezing sensation.

"I bet you wish you applied yourself more in gymnastics class now, don't you, Brother?" Zen asked, still spotless despite all that had happened. "You never did get the hang of cartwheels."

"You're just messing around," Umasi realized bitterly, grip tightening on his pole as he turned to face Zen.

It was at that moment that Umasi realized that they had an audience. Standing far behind Zen, all the way back on dry land, was a thin, pale girl with a black scarf thoroughly wrapped around the lower half of her face. Umasi didn't recognize her, but knew that she could only be one of Zen's new Truants.

"Her name is Noni. You might call her my assistant," Zen said, not needing to turn around to understand what Umasi was looking at. "I believe that I told her to remain behind. Apparently, she has found that order difficult to follow."

"I never thought you the type to show off for a girl," Umasi said scathingly. "Will I be invited to the wedding?"

Zen raised an eyebrow.

"Oh, now you're trying to make fun of me," Zen said. "That just won't do."

Umasi and Zen faced off once more, glaring at each other as the river frothed around them in approval. Umasi made the first move, lashing out at Zen's head with his pole. Zen deftly blocked the blow with his own weapon, then thrust it forward at Umasi's belly. Umasi quickly parried the attack, then swung again, this time towards Zen's legs. Zen noisily blocked again. They continued to exchange blows as they stood, unmoving, upon their respective columns, their metal weapons glinting in the pale gray sunlight. With an especially loud *clang,* both of them suddenly found themselves in a deadlock, each of them attempting to push the other into the water with brute strength.

Zen knew that he could win easily now, if he brought all of his considerable strength and energy to bear against his half-starved brother. But he didn't just want to win this fight—he wanted to break Umasi's spirit so completely that the boy would give up and return home, never to challenge him again. And so, to Umasi's surprise, Zen abruptly ended the deadlock by actually retreating back a column.

Breathing heavily, Umasi eyed Zen. He took his brother's withdrawal to be a sign of weariness, something that he didn't feel thanks to all the adrenaline coursing through his veins. And so, foolishly, Umasi jumped forward in his eagerness without bothering to consider the circumstances under which his brother had chosen to retreat.

As he sailed through the air, a particularly strong gust of wind swept over Umasi's body, upsetting his balance. The wind also kicked up another sizeable wave, which crashed against the column that Umasi was jumping to, making it slick with water as Umasi came tumbling down. Knocked off-balance by the wind, Umasi teetered there on the brink for one suspended moment, a look of horror on his face. Then Zen lightly tossed his pole, striking Umasi in the chest, who plunged into the water with a great silvery splash.

For a moment there was silence, save for the whistling of the wind and sloshing of the river. Then Umasi's head surfaced, and after a great gasp for air, let out an earsplitting shriek. Zen's lips curled into a smile. The water must've been even colder than he had thought. Still, maybe now his brother would learn his lesson at last.

Then, at that inopportune moment, what remained of Zen's conscience chose to wonder if what he had done was necessary, if he had to have picked such an unfair environment. Refusing to address his own doubts, Zen watched impassively as Umasi desperately grasped hold of a nearby column and hung on for dear life. As Umasi's teeth began chattering, Zen suddenly wondered if his brother's life might actually be in danger. Then he shook his head. Umasi would surely return home now, where he would be safe. Zen couldn't afford to second-guess himself. He had no time for guilt or doubt.

His mind made up, Zen spun around and made broad steps from column to column, all the way back to solid asphalt, where Noni stood staring admiringly at him. Zen turned around and addressed Umasi, who was still clinging desperately to the pillar.

"Pathetic! I wasn't even trying!" Zen called as Umasi gasped and shivered.

"I thought that you might at least be entertaining! You're just a waste of time after all!"

Umasi shuddered as another wave washed over him, refreezing the parts of his body that had just been warming up again. But he didn't so much as look at his brother as he spoke.

"You're so pathetic that you can have your money back," Zen continued as he drew a plastic account card from his pocket. "I think you'll find that I've not spent too much of it. Run back home, or try to buy yourself a house if you feel like it. I really don't care."

Zen tossed the card lightly onto the ground where Umasi could easily retrieve it, and then spun around and began walking away.

"Are we leaving, sir?" Noni asked, tugging on Zen's sleeve.

"Indeed. It's a shame that we have to cut our operation short, but at least this has not been a completely fruitless venture," Zen answered, casting a glance back at Umasi's struggling form.

"Will . . . we come back?"

"I might send someone along later to examine the docks more thoroughly," Zen said speculatively. "But for now, I've grown rather tired of them."

And with that, Zen began walking faster. Noni stopped to watch him go for a moment, and then quickly ran after him, trailing closely behind with a worshipful light shining in her eyes.

Sputtering and shivering, Umasi climbed up upon a slanted pillar, using it as a ramp to a fully upright column. From there he carefully crawled across the other pillars, all the way back to solid ground, the wind laughing in his ears every inch of the way. His soggy clothes now clung tightly to his body, which was now thoroughly numb from the cold. After experiencing that freezing water, Umasi almost felt warm now. Almost.

Determinedly focusing on his chilled limbs, Umasi tried and failed to avoid thinking about what had just happened. He had been so sure that he could beat Zen, so confident that he could make Zen see the error of his ways. Now that he had resolved to fight, he had thought himself formidable, as though some hidden power had been unleashed. What a joke.

Zen had just been toying with him from the start.

And all Umasi had accomplished was getting humiliated at his hands.

What had he been thinking? Umasi berated himself over and over as he realized how stupid he had been. He was half-starved and slowly freezing to death while Zen was well fed and rested. What's more, Zen was a born fighter with much more experience. It had always been up to him to protect Umasi. How could Umasi ever have imagined beating him in a fight?

Umasi shook his hair free of water, knowing that it was getting cold enough to freeze him solid if he remained still. As he stretched, he suddenly spotted something on the ground—his account card, still resting where Zen had left it. Umasi picked it up, and upon touching it a sudden surge of anger coursed through him. He was so pathetic that Zen had shown him *charity*. Nothing could've infuriated him more at that moment, and nothing could've been better calculated to demolish his pride.

As the last vestiges of his dignity eroded, an unearthly scream ripped forth from Umasi's lungs, the demented howl of a tortured soul. Umasi screamed again and again, until he had shed all of the many emotions that had built up inside him. Only then, at last, did he collapse, exhausted in every way.

Umasi remained there for a long time, contemplating the unfathomable depths of his failure, even as gentle snowflakes began to float down from the sky to the ground upon which he lay.

A little way removed in District 15, Red frowned, idly brushing a few white flakes from his hair. It was snowing again, which to Red meant more soggy clothes and difficult travel. Letting out a sigh that immediately crystallized into mist, Red began trudging along an alleyway that would bring him to the live District 16. The one benefit of heavy snow was that it made moving through living districts safer; people tended to stay indoors if they could help it, and it was hard to tell a vagrant apart from a normal citizen in a blizzard.

In the few days since he fled District 8, Red had traveled at night, and only then with the utmost caution, expecting to be caught with every movement he made. Enforcer patrols had seemingly doubled of late, and he knew that the district he'd left behind must be swarming with them by now. District 15, being as large as it was, had offered him a small peace of mind. Here, on the silent streets, with the river nearby, the memory of an Enforcer being murdered by a child seemed distant and dreamlike.

But it had been real, Red reminded himself, and even now he was still running as far away from District 8 as possible. He had managed to scrounge up a few scraps that he'd saved in a brown paper bag that he clutched at his side; it would be enough to last him through a night or two of travel. Lost in mental calculations of how far he'd be able to get in a day, Red was not looking as he rounded a corner, and he abruptly collided with another individual.

Cursing himself for his inattentiveness, Red instantly went for the rusted knife concealed in his belt. The other person, whoever it was, had let out a yelp of surprise, meaning that at least Red wasn't the only one caught unawares. Snarling at his adversary, Red prepared to fight, to kill, to do whatever he had to do to survive. Then his enemy spoke, and Red froze with his hand on the hilt of his knife.

"Red? That you?"

Recognizing the voice, Red backed up and blinked, getting a good look at his foe for the first time.

"Chris?"

"Good to see ya again, man," Chris said, his pose relaxed, though his eyes remained wary. "We thought you was a goner for sure."

"What're you doing out here alone?" Red said suspiciously. "Were you coming from District 16? Why aren't you with a partner?"

For a moment Chris looked annoyed by the questions, but he quickly recovered and answered smoothly.

"Well, we just ain't got enough people to go out in pairs anymore," Chris explained. "Lost a bunch since we got scattered. But most of us who're left are back together now, and we've been recruiting. Speaking of which, how'd you like to stick with us again?"

Red narrowed his eyes. It was a tempting offer, but something about it didn't seem right. It wasn't like Chris to just welcome him back without expecting something in return.

"Why are you so eager to have me back all of a sudden?" Red demanded. "It was hard as hell to get in the first time. Things changed that much?"

"Well . . . you and Zack had that little disagreement . . . then 'bout half of us got cut down in the parking garage . . . James got shot by an Enforcer a little while back, or so Raphael said when he caught up with us today . . ." Chris recounted, scratching his neck. ". . . and Niles just got the crap beaten out of him. The kid crawled back yesterday all busted up, expecting us to baby 'im. He's out of the gang, of course. Also those wimps, the ones that got a grudge against us, they've been causing a bit of trouble lately. So we got a few spots we need to fill, yeah."

Red considered Chris' explanation. It made sense. They could obviously use Red and Red could use them. But still, something kept nagging at the back of Red's mind that made him wary about the whole thing. It took him a few moments to realize what it was.

"All right, I guess I'm in," Red said. "But something was bothering me, back in the parking garage."

"What, being shot at? Yeah, bothered me a bit too." Chris chuckled, an oily, unpleasant sound.

"No," Red said. "The Enforcers there knew exactly where we were, when we'd be there, and how many of us to expect. There's only one way they could've known all that. Someone must've sold us out."

At that, Chris froze. For a moment, Red thought he saw a look of panic flit across his face, but then it smoothed out as usual.

"I hadn't thought of that," Chris admitted. "But if you're right, it must've been Gil. The kid went missing right before the raid, didn't he?"

"Yeah, he did," Red said slowly, having already considered that possibility. "But still—"

"What's that you got in the bag there?" Chris interrupted, gesturing at the paper bag that Red clutched at his side.

"What, this?" Red said, the previous topic completely forgotten.

"Yeah, that!"

"Food," Red admitted, turning around as he hastily tied the bag to his belt.

"Well, why don't you . . . you know . . . share?" Chris suggested. " 'Cause you're going to be one of us again and all, we ought to celebrate a bit. Split the wealth and all that. That's how we roll, ain't it?"

For a few seconds Red said nothing, seemingly contemplating Chris' words. Then he spun around, his rusted knife suddenly drawn, his face a mask of rage. Chris, who hadn't noticed the weapon until that moment, reflexively stumbled backwards.

"Remember what I said about screwing me out of food, Chris?" Red snarled, inching forward with the outstretched blade.

"Stop, man, you're overreacting," Chris protested, backing up. "Wasn't like I was ordering you or nothing, it's just . . . well, since we're crew, I thought you might share! Course if you don't want to, that's cool too," Chris added hastily, as Red showed no signs of stopping.

"I was fine with sticking with the gang again, Chris," Red growled, "but I don't see any point if you're gonna try to starve me to death!"

"Come on, I didn't mean it like that!" Chris cried. "Give us a chance, man, we'll make it up to ya, I swear! Stop, okay? Stop."

Red stopped advancing, a look of disgust on his face. Red didn't buy Chris' repentance for one moment, and he was certain that the moment he let his guard down Chris would happily stab him in the back. Still, Red didn't want to murder someone who was begging for his life. Chris visibly relaxed once Red stopped moving, though he kept a wary eye on the knife, which was still threateningly raised.

"Look, we're moving on all the way up to District 25 as soon as we can," Chris said. "Word is there's a grocery store there with security issues—we can get in the loading dock, we'll have a feast. You ain't gonna get a second chance at something like that. You in?"

Red lowered his knife, but did not say anything. He brushed at his hair again distractedly, only to realize that he was covered in a thin sheet of white. The snow had really begun to fall in earnest.

"Or maybe you'd rather take your chances with this storm on your own?" Chris added shrewdly.

Red thought about that for a moment. Then he slowly slid the knife back into his belt.

"All right. Lead the way."

14

Personal Demons

For a whole day and night, the entire City had been blanketed by white, its buildings obscured by a snowy veil. The flakes had fallen ceaselessly, becoming one of the worst blizzards in the living memory of the City. But as far as the students were concerned, it might as well have been a single snowflake—for, as the Mayor had duly promised on television, crews had worked day and night to clear the roads. School had not been canceled.

But Umasi neither knew nor cared about all that.

Umasi fingered the card in his pocket, and then hastily withdrew his hand as though burned. He had taken it with him, and yet, tainted as it was by Zen's charity, he could not bring himself to use it, not even to save his own life. Umasi's clothes had lost some of their dampness over the night, and Umasi was getting used to how uncomfortable they felt. The chill had nearly frozen the fabric as well as the flesh beneath it, and stray snowflakes constantly threatened to dampen the clothes anew.

Umasi had spent the night under a large tree in the Grand Park of District 20, the largest park in the entire City, a place where no one would go during a snowstorm, and where he was unlikely to be found even if they did. Umasi considered it a small miracle that he'd been able to walk in a daze all the way from District 13 to District 20, but he had collapsed shortly after reaching the tree. Some part of him genuinely had not expected to awake again.

But he had, and so now he sat upon a lonely park bench, the storm having abated, though the snow still remained. Umasi's hands gripped his arms tightly, fingers digging roughly into his shirt as they scrabbled almost desperately for warmth. Before sitting down, he had painstakingly wiped the snow off the rough wooden bench, though he'd since discovered that the job had been incomplete; some stubborn flakes remained only to melt spitefully and seep into the seat of his pants. His red eyes watered and stung from the freezing air, which, like a calculating enemy, bit furiously at every inch of his exposed skin. And as Umasi sat there shivering, a deeper, more complete cold penetrated him so deeply that Umasi had forgotten that there was such a thing as warmth, let alone that he had once felt it.

But more paralyzing than the cold was his own weakness. Part of him was still too proud to accept his brother's spiteful aid, even if it meant dying. Another part was terrified by what he might have to do to survive, content to perish in denial if only to avoid facing reality. Then there was his despair, the sinking feeling that there was no point to trying to survive, no purpose to be served by living. A thousand weaknesses had frozen him solid before the cold ever reached him, and so Umasi just sat there, helpless to do anything to save himself.

Soon, worse than any pain, Umasi's body had now become numb, and the hunger that had pierced him so sharply before subsided into an ominous, distant prodding. His throat was bone dry, and each ragged gasp of freezing air ravaged his lungs. Somewhere, tucked into a dark crevice of his mind, Umasi's instinct screamed at him to search for warmth, something to eat, even to lick the snow for its moisture . . . but his body had passed beyond the point of obeying his mind's feeble pleas.

Umasi leaned forward, and his agonized eyes swelled. He ceased moving, and his jaw grew slack. He sat there on the brink for seconds that seemed like days . . . until finally his tortured eyes slid shut, and what will he had left finally succumbed to the cold.

That's quite enough of that, Umasi."

Umasi's eyes snapped open, and then blinked.

White. All he could see was white.

Raising a hand to rub his eyes, Umasi was convinced that he was hallucinating. Opening them again, he creased his brow in frustration.

There was no change. The ceiling, his surroundings, the floor upon which he sat, all of it was one continuous landscape of white so pure that he couldn't tell where the walls stood, or where the ceiling ended . . . or indeed if there were walls or a ceiling at all. Disoriented, Umasi climbed to his feet, noticing immediately that he felt odd . . . *warm*, he realized, a sensation that had become alien to him. But that only made sense, after all; there was no snow here in this infinite blankness, nor wind, nor cold. His clothes were dry, his blood was warm, and his joints no longer cried out in pain as he moved his limbs.

"But on the other hand, of course, none of this makes any sense at all," said a voice that was not his own.

Umasi looked around. There was no sign of the person who had addressed him, the figure that he had nearly forgotten, the boy he had hoped never to meet again. But that boy had spoken, and he was right again; the last thing Umasi remembered was treading the border of death on a bench in a park. Waking up to find himself impossibly healthy in an impossible place could mean only one thing.

"This is another dream, isn't it?" Umasi called out, hearing his voice echo strangely through the boundless space.

"Well, of course," the voice replied from behind him.

Umasi spun around and found himself facing what seemed to be . . . himself. The boy before him had clean clothes, glasses, and a backpack. He looked well fed, sheltered, naïve. On top of it all he had a warm-looking, hooded olive green jacket that concealed most of his face and stretched all the way down to his winter boots. In spite of himself, Umasi couldn't help but feel resentful in the boy's presence.

"So is this a good dream, or a nightmare?" Umasi asked, surprised only at how casual his own voice sounded.

"Well, how would you tell one from the other?" the boy wondered.

"Nightmares are frightening," Umasi answered simply.

The boy's smiled approvingly.

"I suppose that's true," he agreed. "Dreams, like lives, are defined solely by our reactions to them."

"So then what's this?" Umasi asked again. "A dream or a nightmare?"

The boy cocked his head, contemplating Umasi with bespectacled eyes.

"Obviously, it's whatever you make of it! I just hope that you don't make as big a mess of it as you did with your life."

"What's that supposed to mean?" Umasi demanded.

"Well, you're dying, aren't you?" the boy said bluntly. "You're too proud to save your own life, too afraid, too depressed, too ashamed, too *weak*."

"So what's your point?" Umasi asked, gritting his teeth. He didn't care much for this boy, and cared even less for how right he was.

"You're pathetic," the boy said sadly, "and it's killing you. I can't let that happen."

"Because you'll die with me?" Umasi guessed shrewdly, folding his arms.

"I *am* you, Umasi," the child reminded, "and I am weak. But I want to help you."

"If you're so weak, how can you possibly help me?"

"Isn't it obvious?" the figure said, betraying a note of impatience. "I am everything that cripples you, everything that holds you back . . . and that makes me the worst enemy that you will ever face."

"You—"

"Now you know who I am, and why you must best me. Isn't that enough?" the boy interrupted. "You were supposed to be a good student, but you never learned that if you can't master yourself, then you will master *nothing*."

The figure raised his hood above his head, casting his face into shadow. Then he waved his arm upwards in an arc, and from thin air a long procession of polished swords emerged, their blades all pointing downwards. In the space of an instant, the line swiftly expanded as far as Umasi could see, and then the boy waved his arm sideways. The single row of swords multiplied into many, the sky suddenly filled with countless suspended blades stretching as far as the eye could see. As a finale, the child raised his arm straight up, and the swords multiplied again, this time spreading upwards to create several layers of glittering blades.

"But I don't want to master anything," Umasi protested, gazing upwards at the impossible display.

"Oh, but you do," the figure insisted as he stretched his arm out sideways, a single sword floating down so that its hilt slid neatly into his outstretched palm. "You once wished to master school. You now want to master your brother's ambitions. If you awake, you will wish to master the cold, or else you will welcome death . . . out of a desire to master your own life at last."

"I don't welcome death," Umasi said as a second sword fell haphazardly from the sky, unceremoniously burying itself in the white ground at his feet.

"Then prove it," the boy said, pointing his sword at Umasi. "You can only truly appreciate anything, even your own life, after you've had to fight to keep it. And now you *will* fight, something you've only just begun trying in life."

"Wait a minute—"

But Umasi had no time to finish his sentence. The figure, suddenly silhouetted, lunged at him impossibly fast, covering the sizeable distance between them in a split second as though he had shot through the air without touching the ground at all. Without fully knowing what he was doing, Umasi seized the hilt of the sword at his feet and instantly brought it around to block the shadow's attack. The sheer force of the collision caused Umasi to stumble backwards, but the attack was parried.

"Your movements are clumsy and your blows lack conviction," the phantom observed as he slashed at Umasi again, "but your reflexes, at least, are sharp."

"Thanks, I think," Umasi grunted as he parried the blow, backing up warily.

"Does my sword scare you, Umasi?" the boy taunted, lunging at Umasi again as he brought his sword down in a vertical slash.

"I'd be stupid if it didn't!" Umasi shouted as he lifted his sword to block the new attack, backing up even farther.

"True. Only the insane or foolish are truly fearless. But what is it about my blade that frightens you?" the shadow pressed, doggedly continuing its assault. "Do you fear being cut? Feeling pain? Bleeding, perhaps? Or do you just see a sharp edge and know to be afraid?"

"How am I supposed to know?" Umasi demanded angrily as he backed up clumsily to avoid a series of fierce slashes aimed at his waist.

"The first step towards conquering your fear, Umasi, is *understanding* it," the boy said patiently, knocking aside a feeble attack by Umasi. "They say that you fear the unknown, and there is truth in that. More significant, however, is that fear *is* the unknown."

Umasi said nothing but gripped the hilt of his sword, raising it challengingly as he glared intensely at his spectral opponent. The boy regarded Umasi for a moment, his blade lowered at his side. A split second later, he lunged, his body suspended horizontally in midair as it swung its sword around in a powerful arc at Umasi's neck.

"Understand the nature of weapons, and you will be undefeatable."

Umasi had been anticipating an attack and easily blocked the blow, but the attack possessed such impossible force that the next thing Umasi knew, he was hurtling backwards through the air like a rag doll.

"Understand the nature of death, and you will be immortal."

Umasi hurtled through the air disoriented, and the wind rushed in his ears as he plummeted—but despite all that, the boy's echoing words couldn't have sounded clearer; they whispered at him from all directions as if their source was inside his own head.

"Understand the nature of failure, and you will be *unstoppable*."

Umasi finally hit the ground, his right shoulder slamming down first and taking the brunt of the blow. After that initial impact, Umasi bounced once and then rolled a few more painful yards before coming to rest, chest heaving as his newly battered limbs ached.

"So, tell me Umasi," the figure called mockingly from a distance. "What is this? A dream, or a nightmare?"

Umasi forced himself to his feet as his muscles groaned in protest, raising the sword that he had somehow managed to grip even as he was thrown through the air.

"I'm . . . not . . . scared!" Umasi breathed defiantly.

Umasi lunged, rushing recklessly at the smirking figure. His bones rattled painfully with each heavy step that he took, and even as he increased his pace, he knew that his efforts were hopeless. Still, Umasi ignored himself and only continued to charge at his motionless foe, his sword stubbornly raised.

"There's brave, and then there's careless," the boy chided. "It's time that you learned the difference, Umasi. Bravery can be a strength. Recklessness is never anything but a weakness."

In spite of this warning, the shadow remained perfectly still as Umasi hurtled towards him. Possessing none of the boy's impossible speed, Umasi had only covered half the ground between then when suddenly what felt like a wall of freezing wind slammed into Umasi, bowling him over.

"Having problems?" the boy asked sympathetically, looking completely unaffected by the gale. "You haven't been able to lift a finger against the cold while awake, I'm not surprised that it's the same here."

Umasi's eyes widened, and memories of ice and chilling cold came rushing back. Umasi suddenly found himself shivering, his eyes shut and head aching furiously as the relentless wind pounded at him. Still he stood his ground, but moved no farther even as the wind subsided, paralyzed by indecision. He felt a heavy feeling in his heart, and as his limbs grew numb he realized that he had failed.

"Beaten so easily?" the boy said, disappointed. "Come on, we can't have that."

The figure swiftly swung his sword three times through thin air, and there was the whistling of something sharp rushing through the air. Umasi opened his eyes and saw nothing . . . and that's when he felt something like wind slice right through his shirt and skin. A instant later, the pain erupted and Umasi stared downwards to see three long gashes across his chest. The wounds were shallow, but they bled profusely, were white and numb with sudden cold.

"Well now, I see that you're moving again," the boy said cheerfully. "At least the vagrants have already taught you to struggle when someone threatens your life directly."

Umasi's head snapped up as he glared furiously at his enemy, pain and cold forgotten as he readied his sword. The boy smiled back, and then took a single step forward. There was a sound of billowing wind, and then a powerful gust propelled the boy through the air with even more speed and force than ever before. Bracing himself, Umasi stood his ground and arced his blade around at his oncoming foe. Their swords collided with the impossible force that Umasi had come to expect, but this time he gritted his teeth and dug his feet into the ground, even as the freezing wind that had propelled his opponent forward slammed into him. Umasi was pushed back, but not thrown.

"Better!" the boy exclaimed, again swinging his sword diagonally at Umasi.

Umasi blocked the blow, but there was more force behind the deceptively casual attack than any before it. Taken completely by surprise, Umasi was flung into the air again, his ascent aided by another gust of wind that followed in the sword's wake. However, this time Umasi swiftly recovered from his shock and, feeling completely calm as he soared through the air, performed a midair somersault before landing elegantly on his feet. The boy looked delighted as Umasi turned to gaze at him serenely.

There was a moment of perfect stillness, and then the boy's arm snapped forward, launching his sword like a bullet. Umasi neatly sidestepped the projectile as his enemy outstretched his arm again to catch another sword that descended from the sky as if by unspoken command.

Umasi lunged again, but this time his steps were steady, his breathing was even, and his mind was focused. The boy, however, grinned confidently as Umasi charged, and raised his new sword lazily in defense. Umasi's eyes narrowed, and he struck as soon as he came within range. The two blades clashed, and for a moment nothing happened.

Then Umasi's blade began to crack, and then shattered into a thousand glittering pieces as though it were made of glass. The boy laughed, and swung his sword at Umasi's neck. Umasi blocked the blow with his bare hilt alone, and his opponent's laughter was suddenly cut short as he outstretched his arm to grasp a new sword that obediently descended from the sky. A determined gleam shone in Umasi's eyes as he tossed the old hilt aside, and the boy frowned beneath his hood as he launched himself into the air, flying up to seize one of the many swords still hovering above.

"That wasn't bad, Umasi," the boy admitted, "but now is when your real test begins."

"No," Umasi disagreed quietly.

"No?" the boy asked, suddenly sounding uncertain.

"No," Umasi repeated firmly. "I don't know if this is a dream or a hallucination or even an afterlife . . . but I do know that this is no nightmare."

"And why is that?"

"Because I'm not afraid of you at all," Umasi answered simply.

"That's admirable, but Umasi," the shadow warned, "don't forget that even the fearless can die."

The boy suddenly shot downwards at Umasi, and as he did there was a burst of black smoke from which emerged three identical figures, each wielding a sword. Umasi managed to block the first blade, dodge the second, only to have the third hit its mark, cutting deep into the side of his waist. Two of the shadows faded away into black smoke, but the third pointed his sword at Umasi—a sword now dripping with blood.

Umasi clutched his side, feeling the unpleasant fluid stain his clothes and hand. The pain was surprisingly bearable, but the bleeding was bad. Combined with the cuts he had suffered earlier, Umasi knew that this wound could mean trouble. What had happened to those old cuts, though? They were hardly hurting at all. Umasi looked down at his shirt, and his eyes widened. No torn fabric, no blood, no wounds . . . but why?

Because I forgot about them! Umasi realized, looking up at the boy, who he now imagined was grimacing under his hood. *This is my dream, aren't I the one in control here? Wasn't I always the one in control of this, and my life?*

"That's not a bad conclusion," the boy conceded, addressing Umasi's unspoken thoughts. "However, you overlooked something."

"And what would that be?"

"While nightmares are entirely out of control," the boy explained, "no one can fully control their lives or their dreams either."

Umasi lunged forward at the same time as his enemy, and their blades slammed together with tremendous force, though neither was fazed. As they sprang apart, both swords began to crack, shattering like glass, leaving behind only useless hilts. The boy called down another sword from the sky, but Umasi skipped backwards a step and then lightly leapt high up to where the swords lay suspended in the air. Seizing the hilt of one of the swords, Umasi used its stationary hilt to swing himself around so that he plummeted down towards his foe, pulling the sword down with him as he fell.

The boy smiled ominously, and a distant howling announced the impending danger. As Umasi plunged downwards, a powerful, freezing gale slammed into him. But to Umasi's elation, the wind had seemingly no effect; it did not slow him, it did not chill him, it didn't do so much as tug at his hair. It was as if the wind never touched him at all. Reacting quickly, the boy slashed his sword through the air twice, invisible blades of wind slicing again through the air. But this time Umasi simply swung his sword sideways, and a powerful gust swept aside the unseen attacks.

By now Umasi had almost reached the ground, and the boy had but a split second left to dodge. Shooting backwards like a bullet just as Umasi swung his sword downwards, the foe managed to evade the blow, though Umasi cut a long gash through his jacket. Umasi himself landed softly on the ground, straightening up to eye his opponent calmly. For a moment the boy idly examined his cut jacket, and then laughed, a sound that boomed strangely throughout the white emptiness.

"What's so funny?" Umasi asked curiously.

"Well, you've certainly overcome some weaknesses," the boy admitted. "But you just have so many that I hardly know how to proceed. Let's try your confusion, shall we? That's a common fatal flaw."

"What do you me—" Umasi began, and then stopped as he looked down.

The ground had not changed in appearance—it was still a plain, pure white. But as Umasi began to fall, he realized that somehow the ground hadn't been ground at all—or at least it wasn't ground anymore. It was interesting, Umasi thought placidly as he fell, how this space really had no walls, no sky, no floor at all.

But enough of that.

Umasi didn't know how or why he could, nor how or why he knew he could—he only knew that he did. His descent first slowed, and then stopped altogether as Umasi hovered calmly in midair. Looking up, he could see the dark figure floating, waiting for him. Umasi allowed himself a small smile, and then shot upwards towards his enemy, enjoying the feeling of incredible speed as he flew through the air. As Umasi drew closer, the boy erupted into a familiar burst of black smoke, from which emerged another three, all swiftly plunging down to meet Umasi.

Umasi easily spiraled to the side to evade the first figure's sword, slicing neatly through its middle as he did. The attacker erupted into black smoke as Umasi blocked the second shadow's sword and then swiftly plunged his own through its hood. As the second figure also dissipated, the remaining boy swung his own sword at Umasi with tremendous force, but Umasi lazily blocked the blow, holding his sword with only one hand.

There was a cracking sound, and a moment later the boy's sword shattered into glittering, useless shards. The shadow stared at the remaining hilt as though it had betrayed him, and then glared at Umasi's own sword as if expecting it too to shatter at any moment. When it didn't, the boy scowled and shot back up into the air, flying towards the massive cloud of swords with Umasi in close pursuit.

The shadow grabbed a sword as he flew through the cloud, and then seized a second and slammed them together. The two swords fused as easily as if they were made of clay. But he wasn't done yet; as he flew past more layers of swords he seized two more and added them to his increasingly huge weapon until he held in his hands a massive claymore nearly as tall as he was. Glancing down at the pursuing Umasi, the boy suddenly began spiraling around like a corkscrew with his sword outstretched, cutting through dozens of swords all around him. These broken blades fell downwards in a glittering, deadly rain.

But Umasi didn't waver, and as he passed through the steel hail, the blades clattered against each other and bounced off him harmlessly, none of them giving him so much as a scratch. And so he calmly emerged from the cloud of swords unscathed, and the boy spun around to see him still in pursuit. In that moment, Umasi could've sworn that he saw a triumphant grin flit across the boy's hooded face. Then the shadow ceased its ascent, and instead plummeted towards Umasi, massive sword outstretched.

The huge blade cast an ominous shadow over Umasi, but Umasi felt a strange, peaceful calm in the place of all the fear, doubt, confusion, and general internal chaos that he had become used to. As Umasi drew closer to the source of the darkness, its shadow shrank, and Umasi raised his small sword to meet the enormous one that fell towards him.

The two blades met, but there was no clash. Both Umasi and the boy watched in delight as Umasi's sword cut neatly through the claymore like paper. An instant after he had severed the massive blade, Umasi angled his sword sideways to cut his foe as they passed each other by. For a moment, Umasi and his opponent were both suspended motionless in midair.

And then Umasi found himself on hard, white ground once more, standing back to back with his enemy. There was no trace of swords, either in their hands or in the sky—just pure, white emptiness. Out of the corner of his eye, Umasi saw a hooded head turn towards him, and he saw lips move, speaking to him, asking him a question. Umasi could not hear what was being said, but nonetheless he nodded.

The boy then burst into black smoke for the last time, swirling around Umasi in farewell before dissipating for good.

And then Umasi shut his eyes, and all that was white turned to black.

Dear Sirs,

I did not expect to be contacting you again so soon. However, anything out of the ordinary in this City tends to stand out, and lately I've seen some troubling signs in the Mayor's office. I have nothing but suspicions as of yet, but activity in the office has suddenly and inexplicably increased of late. In particular, we had an Enforcer named Rothenberg in here a few days ago. The man has a brutal reputation, and it appears as though the Mayor has given him a special assignment of utmost importance and secrecy.

Again, all I have is pure conjecture, but I felt it odd enough that you should be informed. I'm almost certain that the Mayor is hiding something, though admittedly I have no idea what it is or how serious it might be. Perhaps some of your other observers in this City will be better placed to investigate? I will await further orders concerning this matter.

Your Servant,
207549627

PART III

MAVERICK

15

A Second Chance

*W*ith weather like this, I wonder if there's any point to refrigerating these trucks.

Suppressing a shiver, Red shook his shoulders to dislodge some stray snow that had fallen on him as he climbed into the back of the truck. All around him other vagrants worked in silence, taking care not to intrude upon each other's claim. For once, Red admitted grudgingly, Chris had been true to his word. Since rejoining the gang they had safely made their way up to District 25, where they had indeed been able to break into the loading dock of a supermarket. As a bonus, the blizzard had even snowed in the business, and without any employees around, the whole store was ripe for the picking.

Apparently they weren't the only ones who thought so. By the time they had arrived, a number of other vagrants were already swarming over the trucks and crates. Amazingly, however, no fights had broken out; none of the other vagrants seemed to belong to a rival gang, and everyone was more interested, at least in the short term, in feeding themselves rather than fighting with others when there was plenty to go around.

"Grab as much as ya can, take as long as ya want," Chris had said. "If any of them wanna cause trouble, we'll sort 'em out."

As he worked, Red glanced over at the boy working next to him. He didn't think he'd ever met the kid before, which wasn't surprising considering that Chris' group rarely ever ventured into this part of the City. Still, there was something strangely familiar about the boy—the shape of his face, his vaguely yellow skin, his dark hair . . .

Red dismissed it as his imagination and turned back to the matter at hand. He seized upon a package of uncooked bacon and stuffed it into his bag with the rest of his pilfered goods. As he did, a potato slipped out of Red's hand. Red was about to retrieve it when the boy's arm shot out, seized the potato, and held it out to Red in one fluid motion.

Red stared at the proffered tuber while the boy continued gathering his own fruits without sparing him so much as a glance. Red hesitantly accepted it and didn't ask any questions, though a dozen new ones were now brewing in his mind. The boy's simple act of generosity was unheard of among vagrants. What's more, the boy's speed was unusual for a starved vagrant—not impossible, to be sure, but unusual, especially considering how scrawny the boy looked.

Now doubly curious, Red continued filling up his sack while watching the boy out of the corner of his eye. The boy was completely silent as he worked. In fact, he was so unnaturally relaxed that it was almost as though he were in a daze. But upon closer inspection, Red saw a sharp awareness glittering in those dark eyes . . . along with something else hiding deeper beneath the surface—something decidedly dangerous.

Red shook his head and refocused on his food. The kid didn't seem to pose any immediate threat, and Red was content to ignore him. The boy, for his part, seemed perfectly unconcerned with everyone else inside the garage. For a while the tenuous peace held, and Red had nearly filled his bags to burst when the sound of footsteps announced new arrivals.

"You!" an infuriated voice cried out.

All heads turned to see what was going on. There, glaring at Chris, stood a vagrant that Red recognized as one of the three who had cornered him with the knife he now carried in his belt. Moments later, a half-dozen other vagrants slipped through the space under the garage door. Among them was a boy Red knew as Glick, their leader. Realizing what was happening, a number of Chris' cohorts began rallying together, though Red chose instead to watch from inside the truck like the neutral vagrants.

"Glick," Chris greeted. "You still leading this bunch then? That must be some sort of record for ya guys. Grats on going a week without snuffing it."

"Thanks, but I think you were the ones really setting records this week, Chris," Glick retorted. "How many of your buddies did you manage to get killed? 'Bout half? We'd be happy to add a few more if ya like."

"You like to talk about numbers, Glick, but there's more of us than you," Chris said—and he was right; the small group assembled around him narrowly edged out the handful that stood with Glick. "Did you come all the way up here to die? Can't say I blame you—I wouldn't wanna live with a face that ugly either."

"You idiots got the Enforcers swarming all over the lower districts," Glick accused. "We decided to check this one out, only it looks like you're stinking things up here too."

Chris and Glick stared each other down, the vagrants on either side fidgeting restlessly. The tension in the room seemed ready to explode at any moment. Reaching slowly for the knife at his belt, Red waited. If a fight broke out, he had decided to join in. It wouldn't do to have Chris' gang lose; after all, some among Glick's crew might recognize him.

Then, to everyone's utter shock, a gunshot rang out, and Glick fell to the floor, dead. Red blinked in confusion; he was sure that none of Chris' crew had a gun. For a moment the rest of the vagrants seemed equally baffled, until the garage door abruptly slid upwards to reveal a number of larger, uniformed figures.

"Enforcers!" Chris shouted almost gleefully as more shots were fired into the tightly massed gangs.

The children all reacted instantly. Some, like Red, spun around to assess the situation. Several Enforcer patrols, their car sirens now flashing outside, were storming the garage. Other vagrants, like the strange boy who had sat next to Red, didn't bother to look around at all, but instead dived out of the truck and towards whatever cover they could find.

The latter had the right idea.

"Rodents! Pests! Scum!" Red could hear an Enforcer shout as bullets slammed indiscriminately into the truck. "You'll pay in blood for those goods!"

A vagrant crumpled to the floor next to Red, pierced by a bullet. The sight prompted Red into action. Lunging for cover behind some wooden crates not far from the truck, Red experienced an unpleasant sense of déjà vu at the chaos unfolding around him. Dozens of vagrants were already moaning on the ground or, worse, lying completely motionless. Chris was nowhere to be found. Feeling the weight of his bags, Red realized that he was carrying too much to make a clean escape. Now wasn't a time to be greedy. Without hesitation Red dropped all but one bag and reached for his knife.

As the nearest Enforcer approached his hiding place, Red prepared to leap out and stab the man in the back. There was once a time when he wouldn't have dared try it, but he had since seen for himself that Enforcers could be killed. But just when he was about to lunge, his wrist was caught in a firm grasp. Spinning around, Red found himself face-to-face with the strange boy he'd seen earlier. Red opened his mouth to ask what the hell the kid thought he was doing, but the boy cut him off by shaking his head solemnly.

Red shut his mouth and lowered his weapon. There was something about the boy's gaze that forbade argument. The Enforcer, in the meantime, had already passed by and was now reloading his weapon. Red glanced over at the distant garage entrance, unsure of what to do. Red's companion, however, showed no such indecision. Standing up abruptly, the boy seized a potato from the floor and hurled it. The tuber slammed into the Enforcer's pistol just as he finished reloading it.

The gun went off, and the man screamed in pain, having shot himself in the foot.

Even before the projectile found its mark, the mysterious boy had already leapt into action, lunging towards the Enforcer and body-slamming him against the wall before he could recover. Red's jaw dropped as the boy seized the writhing man by the shoulders and slammed him against the wall again, dropping him to the ground.

"Let's go," the boy called at Red over the persistent sound of gunfire. "The others are going to notice pretty soon. Two stand a better chance than one."

Red nodded, not in any mood to argue with the formidable stranger.

The boy seized the fallen Enforcer's gun and made a dash for the entrance, his bag of food slung over his shoulder. Red quickly followed suit, jumping over stacks of crates as he ran. Just as they reached the exit, they heard an Enforcer shout behind them, and bullets began flying in their direction. Red and the stranger managed to duck out of the garage and onto the snowy streets as bullets slammed into the pavement around them.

Red dived behind an Enforcer's patrol car, the other boy joining him as they watched other vagrants scramble away. Some unlucky ones were quickly cut down, staining the snow crimson. Red winced as a particularly nasty spasm of pain jerked through his gut. He knew there was no chance of evading pursuit, as the snow was more than thick enough to leave clear footprints.

"Do you know your way around here?" the boy asked suddenly, causing Red to jerk in surprise. He'd almost forgotten about his enigmatic companion.

"Uh, kind of," Red answered. He was new to District 25, but he'd gotten a good look at the nearby alleys on his way in.

"When those guards try to leave the garage, I'll make them keep their heads down," the boy said, holding up his stolen weapon. "I'm not sure how many shots it has left, and I won't be trying to hurt them, but I will be able to buy you some time."

"Time for what?" Red asked confusedly. Surely not even this kid was noble enough to sacrifice his own neck so that a stranger could escape.

"This street is on a slant. Go up to the corner and kick a garbage can down," the boy ordered. "After that, run somewhere we can lose them, and I'll follow."

The plan sounded sensible to Red, and it would allow him to make a run for it no matter what happened. Red sprang to his feet and ran for the street corner. At first he could hear the snow crunching beneath his feet, but those sounds were soon drowned out by gunshots. Looking behind him as he ran, he saw a couple of wary Enforcers peer out from behind the safety of the garage walls, firing at the car behind which the armed vagrant now crouched.

The boy sprang up and fired back twice, forcing the adults to duck for

cover again. Red noticed that, true to his word, the kid's shots weren't landing anywhere near the Enforcers, though the men weren't in any position
to realize it. Red found such behavior remarkable, if more than a little
strange. As far as Red was concerned, alive and blameworthy was preferable to dead and admirable.

With that in mind, Red came upon the street corner and scrambled over
to the lump of snow under which a garbage can had been buried. Excavat-
ing the cylinder as fast as he could with his bare hands, Red winced as he
heard more gunshots ring out. Finally breaking the can out from its icy
prison, Red quickly turned it on its side and gave it a kick in the right direction to get it started.

Red spared just a moment to watch as the garbage can rolled on down
the sidewalk, gathering snow into its surface as it went. A second later he
was sprinting towards an alley across the street, bag still slung over his
shoulder. The other boy, realizing that Red had succeeded, sprang out from
behind the car and followed. The guards, seeing their prey make a break for
it, leapt out from behind their cover as well.

Just in time for a massive cylinder of snow to flatten them like a giant
white rolling pin.

Red heard confused yells and angry shouts coming from behind him,
and he could only assume that the ploy had worked. Soon he was back
within the familiar maze of alleyways, and paused to take a breath, certain
now that the other guards would pursue some closer, clumsier, and slower
target. He was beginning to relax when he felt a hand on his shoulder,
nearly giving him a heart attack.

"It's me," a familiar, calm voice said.

Red spun around and found himself facing his impromptu ally. For a
moment he wondered why he had been so surprised; the kid had said that
he would be following. Then Red realized that he hadn't heard the boy approaching at all, a discomforting realization for the seasoned vagrant.

"That was some quick thinking," Red said.

"Thank you," the boy replied. "You were impressively fast yourself."

"Uh . . . thanks," Red said, that strange feeling of familiarity returning
as he examined the boy again. "By the way, have we met before?"

The boy's eyes narrowed, and Red suddenly felt uncomfortable under
the scrutiny of those dark orbs.

"No, I don't believe we have."

"Well . . . my name is Red," Red said, unable to think of anything else.
"It was . . . nice working together?"

"That it was," the boy agreed. "My name is Umasi."

"Well, Umasi, no offense, but I have to meet up with the rest of my gang," Red said. "Or whatever's left of it by now . . . again. Anyway, we'll be better off with two separate tracks in case the Enforcers come around."

"I was about to suggest that myself." Umasi nodded as he turned to leave. "Good luck reuniting with your friends. Maybe I'll see you again sometime, Red."

"Maybe," Red said, racking his brain for any hint of where he'd seen the retreating boy before.

As the boy vanished from sight, Red shrugged and plunged deeper into the darkened alleyway. At least this time Chris had identified a place for the gang to meet, Red thought. If they'd been scattered again he was sure it'd have meant the end of the crew. Satisfied by knowing that they would re-group, Red didn't bother to wonder how the Enforcers had found the gang in the first place.

It was only long after they had parted ways that Red finally remembered where he had seen someone similar to Umasi before. The boy had dressed better, been cleaner, talked differently, and had longer hair . . . but there was an unmistakable, striking resemblance between Umasi and the boy that Red had seen murder an Enforcer. Were they the same person?

No, they hadn't acted anything alike. Was it just two of them? Or were there perhaps many of them running around? What could it all possibly mean?

Red had no way of answering those questions, but as he arrived at his gang's rendezvous point in the lobby of an abandoned hotel, he felt a chill run down his spine to go along with the bitter pain that had resurfaced in his gut.

Umasi munched on a carrot thoughtfully as he walked along the alley. He wasn't sure what nutrients were in the root, and he had never really been a fan of vegetables. Still, he was going to be picky. He really wanted to try some of the meats he had recovered, but most of it was raw and he wasn't sure it'd be a good idea to eat them that way. Wondering how he might get a fire going at all, let alone in the aftermath of a snowstorm, Umasi instead opted to finish his carrot and bite into a hard potato next.

Umasi knew that he could live as comfortably as he wanted with his ac-count card, yet something kept him from returning to society. He had got-ten over being humiliated at the docks, and his vagrant appearance didn't bother him either. It was more like he felt at home in the abandoned dis-tricts, where only his strength stood between him and death.

After he had awoken from his deathlike trance in the park, Umasi forced himself to his feet, staggered out of the park, and walked through the snowy streets of District 20. He had felt strangely detached, somehow, from the rest of the world—yet he had never felt more alert and aware in his life. Wandering up towards District 25, he had overheard two vagrants talking about looting a grocery store. Knowing that he probably had to eat soon or never again, Umasi had followed them to the site.

Wiping vegetable juice from his chin, Umasi began gnawing on a wedge of cheese. Not all vagrants were that bad, he'd realized. The brown-haired boy he had teamed up with to escape the Enforcers had been as honorable as could have been expected. The boy could've ignored Umasi's instructions and left him to the Enforcers, but he hadn't—though Umasi had not believed he would. Umasi sensed that under different circumstances, the guy might've been a dependable, upstanding citizen.

Umasi suddenly frowned as he recalled something the boy had told him. He had mentioned that he recognized Umasi from somewhere, but Umasi was certain that they had never met before. Then Umasi froze, halfway through his cheese. There *was* one other person in the City who looked like him, wasn't there? Umasi furrowed his brow, recalling memories of a conversation on a rooftop, of a fight at the piers, events that seemed to have happened a lifetime ago.

Zen had already been spotted by vagrants, Umasi realized. It made sense that his brother would seek their aid. After all, who knew the underbelly of the City better than they? Who had greater reason to hate the Educators?

It was just as well, then, that he would no longer be a vagrant, Umasi decided. The time had come for his wandering to end. He would seek out a place secluded from the rest of the City, somewhere where he could contemplate what to do next, and perhaps he would feel comfortable enough to spend his money at last. With that resolved, Umasi felt as though he truly had died there on that bench in the park. Now he'd gotten a second chance at life, and he didn't intend to waste it.

Rothenberg stretched his neck as he walked up the flight of steps. The hunt for the Mayor's children hadn't been going very well at all. The searches had all yielded nothing, and to make matters worse, the boy the Mayor had expected to return home hadn't. The Mayor had been getting anxious, and after their latest exchange Rothenberg felt he needed to relieve some stress. And so he headed home, to his apartment, for the first time in a week. He rarely ever did go home, preferring to sleep at Enforcer Headquarters or even in his patrol car. But every now and then, it was . . . therapeutic, to return to his apartment and remind himself that his methods did work.

Rothenberg slid his key into the lock and turned, slamming it open loudly as he entered.

"Cross, where the hell are you?" Rothenberg bellowed. "Get out here, right now!"

Rothenberg almost smiled at the frantic sound of scuffling as a twelve-year-old boy with short, neatly trimmed red hair rushed out to meet him. The boy's pale complexion was marred by freckles, and he was slightly out of breath as he stood there before Rothenberg. This was Rothenberg's son, though Rothenberg didn't like thinking of the boy that way. To him, every child was either a student or a vagrant, and this student just happened to be his responsibility to discipline.

"Sorry Dad, I—" Cross began, panting.

"WHAT DID YOU JUST CALL ME?" Rothenberg roared, smacking the boy across the face.

The blow was powerful enough to fling Cross to the floor, where he clutched his stinging cheek and avoided looking at his father, who suppressed a satisfied smile. Cross hastily stood up, wincing as he did so.

"I'm sorry . . . sir," Cross said.

Rothenberg seized Cross by the scruff of his neck and raised him up like a rag doll. Cross didn't resist, and Rothenberg glowered at him for a moment before sniffing the air exaggeratedly, as a dog might.

"Do you smell anything, boy?" Rothenberg demanded.

"No, sir, I don't," Cross said confusedly.

"THAT'S THE DAMN PROBLEM!" Rothenberg shouted. "Where is dinner? Why haven't you prepared it yet?"

"I'm sorry, sir," Cross said, "I didn't know that you were coming home tonigh—"

"Talking back to me, are you?"

Rothenberg punched him in the stomach. Cross groaned and crumpled to the ground, looking extremely small as he forced his jaw shut. He knew exactly what would happen to him if he vomited on the floor.

"Get up, or I'll give you something to really moan about," Rothenberg said.

Cross scrambled to his feet obediently, his face now inscrutable.

"Go get that dinner ready. It better be fast and it better taste good, boy," Rothenberg snarled. "I've had all that I can stand of disrespectful children. I'll make sure you students learn your place whether you like it or not."

"Yes, sir," Cross said emotionlessly as he spun around and walked to the kitchen.

Rothenberg sighed. He was feeling better already.

Walking over to the dining room, Rothenberg sat down at the table, propping his feet up as he did so. In the kitchen he could already hear cooking noises, and soon he could smell it too. He was pleased that there weren't any noisy sobs to go along with the sounds of pots clanging and water boiling. His disciplinary methods really were making progress.

Just then Rothenberg's cell phone rang from his belt. Sighing, Rothenberg unhooked the device and flipped it open.

"Chief Truancy Officer Rothenberg speaking. What's the problem?"

"Sir, we may have a lead on that special case you've been working," the voice on the other end said.

"Oh? Do tell," Rothenberg said, sitting up straight.

"There was a robbery up in District 25 today. We ambushed a bunch of vagrants looting a grocery store—one of our informants told us about it beforehand. It took a while to get in position due to the weather, though, so we only caught them at it after they'd damn near stripped the place."

"What's that got to do with my investigation?" Rothenberg demanded.

"One of the Enforcers at the scene swears that he spotted a child who matches the description of one of the suspects you're looking for," the Enforcer on the phone explained. "We only just found out about it. I thought you'd like to know as soon as possible."

"Hm . . . could be a coincidence, or it could be the break we've been looking for." Rothenberg smiled. "Did we capture any other live witnesses?"

"None of the apprehended vagrants survived their wounds, sir," the Enforcer replied, "aside from our informant, who we turned loose before we knew he might've seen something important. We won't be able to question him until he contacts us again."

"Well then we're just going to have to go out and hunt down new witnesses," Rothenberg said. "If we catch one, I'll want to handle the interrogation personally. Rothenberg out."

And with that, Rothenberg shut his phone off and returned it to his belt. They had a lead. Maybe not a very good one, but at least it was something that he could work with. All hunger forgotten, Rothenberg sprang up from his chair and made for the door, feeling the thrill of the hunt course through his veins. As he exited the apartment, he quietly shut the door behind him without a second thought.

At that moment Cross entered the dining room wearing an apron and holding two dishes full of steaming pasta, sauce, and meatballs. For a few seconds the boy just stared at the empty room, his face still unreadable.

But as he turned around and returned to the kitchen, a single tear slowly slid down his stubbornly blank face.

oni whimpered quietly, her wide eyes frantically searching all around
the darkness of the room. She wasn't looking for anything in particular,
but she knew that there must be all sorts of nasty things lurking in the
all-encompassing shadow, things that wanted to hurt her. Several feet away
she could hear the steady breathing of the great and frightening creature
that had become her guardian and savior, the terror that trumped any
monster out to get her. She was sure that there was no enemy, no challenge,
nothing that he couldn't overcome.

But he was asleep now, and who was left to protect her?

Tossing around in her sleeping bag, Noni wondered how long she had
been lying there, awake and terrified as everyone else slept peacefully. She
was just being stupid, she told herself. There was nothing to worry about.
Really.

Then she froze in panic as her eyes skimmed over a particular patch of
darkness. It looked like all the others. Except that she was sure that she had
seen something *move* there. But no, that was silly, wasn't it? How could she
see anything move when she could barely see her own hand waving in
front of her face? But then again, if something *was* moving, creeping towards her, she would never know until it was too late. . . .

And then something creaked, and a million horrible thoughts about what
might've caused it flashed through Noni's mind. Trying to calm herself, Noni
rationalized that it was a run-down, abandoned apartment, of course something would creak. But then again, *something* had to have caused the
noise . . . and she couldn't know what it was, thanks to this infinite blackness.

Maybe it was just a rat.

Or maybe it was a huge man with a knife.

Noni stifled a squeal and ducked fully inside her sleeping bag, using it
like a cocoon to shield her from the night. For many minutes she trembled,
her terror overwhelming her. There was no escaping the darkness, the
blank canvas upon which her imagination painted horrible images. Not
even when she closed her eyes could she get away from it.

Finally, unable to take it any longer, Noni came to a decision. No matter
how mad her protector might be if she woke him, it would be better than
facing the endless darkness and the infinite horrors it held all alone. Nervously, she crawled out from the shelter of her sleeping bag and over to the
slumbering monster near her.

"Sir?" Noni whispered, tapping Zen on the shoulder.

Zen was instantly upright and awake, his eyes darting around the room reflexively. Sensing no immediate danger, he slowly turned his attention towards Noni with such alertness that she wondered if he had actually been asleep at all.

"What is it?" Zen asked.

"I . . . I can't sleep," Noni said.

Even in the dark Noni could feel Zen's eyes upon her, examining her, scrutinizing her through the shadows. It was a vaguely chilling feeling that raised her neck hairs, but it was oddly comforting at the same time.

"Why can't you sleep?" Zen asked, not stirring an inch.

"The dark . . . it scares me."

At this, Zen stood up with shocking speed, towering over Noni. In the darkness of the room, Noni was struck by how Zen seemed like a massive shadow masquerading in the shape of a man. The shadow reached down to grasp Noni's hand, pulling her upright with ease, as she offered no resistance.

"So you say that this darkness scares you?" Zen said quietly.

"Yes." Noni bowed her head in shame.

The shadow swiftly gripped her shoulders and turned her towards what some rational corner of her mind knew was just a wall, but to her seemed like terrible, endless blackness. Noni didn't feel afraid this time, not with those strong hands gripping her shoulders, powerful and reassuring. But the dread still hung in the air, ready to descend upon her the moment the hands abandoned her to the dark.

"You see darkness, and you fear it simply because you do not understand it, because you do not know what it hides," the shadow explained.

Noni could do nothing but nod rapidly in agreement.

"But you should know, Noni, that when you look upon something that frightens you, it will look back at you," the shadow said. "What do you want it to see? A shivering, whimpering girl? Or an unmovable, strong silhouette, every bit as mysterious and frightening as the darkness itself?"

The strong hands released their grip, leaving Noni alone to face the dark. Noni braced herself for a wave of fear and panic, but after several moments she realized that it wasn't coming. Slowly, but steadily, Noni stood up to her full height for the first time in years. She stood straight, silent and unmoving. She no longer felt scared.

"Remember, no matter how frightening your foe is, you can always make it afraid of you," Zen said. "Go to sleep, Noni. Light will return soon, and there will be a lot to do when it does. We will be visiting the vagrants tomorrow."

But Noni was no longer listening. She remained standing, for how long she did not know. She simply looked at the darkness, and the darkness looked at her, and as it did she felt as though they had come to an understanding. And when Noni finally lay down again, she had no trouble getting to sleep.

The winter dawn was pale and streaked with gray as Umasi climbed over the crude wooden wall. Grunting as he landed on his feet, he paused to rest for a moment, his breath misting in the frigid air. Looking around at all the abandoned buildings, Umasi decided that it was very unlikely that any other vagrants had decided to take shelter in this particular district.

District 19 was a relatively small, long-abandoned district surrounded on all sides by flourishing live districts. Any vagrant who took root in District 19 would have to get food from one of those busy districts, and ran a huge risk of being discovered. If they were caught, or if the Enforcers did a sweep, there was nowhere to run except the live districts, making it one of the most dangerous in the entire City. Just getting to District 19 unscathed was a challenge in and of itself, one that Umasi had overcome by moving before dawn and in the aftermath of a blizzard.

But it had been worth it. Umasi knew that he could enjoy true privacy here, a place forsaken even by the vagrants. He strolled down a lonely street, under the pale gray sky as the rising sun cast rays of pink and orange onto the snow. Cool wind stirred around him, whispering to him—the only sound to break the perfect tranquillity. Umasi paused in a blissful moment of appreciation. He had never paid much attention to the wind before. For as long as he could remember, its wail had been been drowned out by the cacophony of men and machines.

Here, in this lonely part of the City, the world itself seemed changed. As Umasi stared down the vacant sidewalk, he realized just how used to the company of other people he had been. For the first time in his life, Umasi understood that silence could be more impressive than the loudest noise.

Umasi took an uncertain step down the street, feeling as though he were sleepwalking through a dream. On either side of him, the pale light made the worn buildings seem ghostly and dead, and years of filth had long since discolored their façades. But though bricks had fallen and glass had shattered, the buildings still stood strong, confident that they would endure longer than those who had abandoned them.

It was in the shadow of one such building, staring up at the ghostly sky, that Umasi found himself enjoying the feeling of the cold air on his skin. The winter no longer stung him, the long shadows no longer scared him, and an unfamiliar sensation now flowed through him, speaking to him of contentment and possibility. Was this what it was like to be truly free? Was this what Zen was seeking? If so, Umasi felt that he finally understood his brother's struggle, misguided though it was.

Umasi shut his eyes, and the pastel sunlight crept over him. As it did, he felt his heart lighten. Slowly drawing a small plastic card out from his pocket, Umasi did not wince but smiled. District 19 could not have been a home for long to any vagrant, but unlike the vagrants Umasi had all the resources he could possibly need, and all the time in the world to use them.

Umasi now understood that he was home. There was no school here, no teachers, no father. He had fallen through the cracks of society to escape the grasp of education. Here, the world was serene and beautiful, as though it had never known the chaos of civilization. Here, there was no life to interrupt his own.

With that thought, Umasi heard the echoes of old words that he had once been told seemingly ages ago.

On a whim, they can teach us a fabricated history, or even a new reality.
A district devoid of life . . .
Here, life is whatever they tell us it is.
And yet more alive than any other in the City.

kay, I'll ask *again*. Is this one of the vagrants that you saw loot that truck?"

"I don't know, sir. He might be. Like I said, I didn't get a good look at all of them."

"Listen, this vagrant was found in possession of food stolen from that supermarket. The stickers were still on the damn things. Now, I didn't bring you all the way down here to give me some pathetic excuses about not having gotten a 'good look.' "

"What exactly do you want from me, sir?"

"It's about time you asked. I want you to tell me that you recognize this kid, and then get the hell out of my sight!"

"Well . . . now that you mention it, the boy does look kind of familiar. . . ."

"That's good enough for me. Now get going, I have a prisoner to interrogate."

The Enforcer obligingly left the room, looking slightly scandalized. Rothenberg paid him no attention. Instead, he glared through the one-way mirror into the dimly lit room where the captive vagrant sat handcuffed to a chair. An Enforcer patrol had apprehended the boy in District 22, apparently fleeing from the abandoned District 25.

Rothenberg snorted. He'd thought that all the vagrants knew better than to travel straight through inhabited districts. But then again, these children *were* the ones that had trouble learning lessons.

With that in mind, Rothenberg opened the door to the secluded room. If the child was difficult enough, he might even enjoy this. After all, the hardest lessons were always the ones most worth teaching.

"Our witness just identified you, boy," Rothenberg growled. "He saw you loot that produce truck with all those other vagrants."

The boy paled. Rothenberg frowned. So, this one was a coward after all.

"Th-that's impossible!" the boy sputtered. "That can't be right, man, I bought these in a store!"

"Oh really?" Rothenberg said skeptically. "Where?"

"Some market somewhere, I don't remember exactly!"

Rothenberg slowly rubbed his temples. As entertaining as it sometimes was, he really wasn't in the mood for this brand of stupidity right now.

A second later, Rothenberg's bricklike fist slammed into the boy's face, knocking him and the chair to which he was still handcuffed to the floor. Rothenberg crouched down to examine his handiwork. The boy's nose was bleeding, and his eyes were wide with shock. Rothenberg smiled. So, he was still so fast they never saw it coming.

"I'll ask just once more," Rothenberg said, bending down so that his head hung mere inches above from the boy's face. "I'm getting tired of repeating myself today, and if I have to ask again, I promise that it'll hurt a lot worse than what you just got. Now, if you want to come out of this with all your limbs intact, you'll tell me where you got those vegetables."

"Okay, okay, I'll talk," the boy said. "Look, I just traded with this kid for 'em. I gave him some old socks, he gave me the food, I didn't do nuthin' wrong!"

"What was his name?" Rothenberg demanded.

"I dunno, we vagrants ain't exactly big on names," the boy said. "But I know that he was part of Chris' gang!"

"Oh?" Rothenberg said. "And who's Chris?"

"Just some slimeball, I don't want nuthin' to do with 'em, but food's food and one of his guys had some!"

"How big is this gang?"

"Dunno, you Enforcers keep killing bunches of those guys, don't ya?"

At that, Rothenberg's eyes narrowed. The only gangs that the Enforcers were able to cull on a regular basis were the ones with informants in them. As the implications of that began to dawn on Rothenberg, he noticed the vagrant looking at him shrewdly.

"Is that helpful or sumthin'?"

"It might be," Rothenberg conceded as he stood up. "Very well. If your information pays off, you'll be keeping your limbs after all. Until then, you will continue to enjoy the . . . hospitality . . . of the Enforcers."

And with that, Rothenberg left the room, ignoring the child's declarations of thanks. His subordinates *had* mentioned that they raided the grocery store because of an informant, hadn't they? But Rothenberg hadn't known that it was a gang behind that robbery. He still wasn't sure if the Mayor's brats had joined up with the gang, or if they just happened to be robbing the same place at the same time, but Rothenberg now had a feeling that if he found that gang he'd find the boys.

All Rothenberg had to do now was wait for the right informant to make contact . . . or hunt down this "Chris" and his gang by himself.

It was a depressed group of vagrants that gathered around a bonfire that evening. The sky had just begun to darken, allowing the massive flames to cast long, flickering shadows over the filthy ground. A few of them were lucky to be alive, having narrowly escaped the grocery store to rejoin the rest of the gang in District 15. Many had not been so lucky, and now, because they were leaderless again, morale had hit rock bottom. One of the vagrants had wrapped himself in a dirty blanket and sat next to the fire, glumly feeding it planks torn from a nearby building. For a while the crackle of the fire was the only sound. Then a vagrant sitting under a broken streetlamp addressed the boy with the planks.

"We shouldn't let the fire burn that high, someone might notice the smoke."

"Shut up, Frank, I'm cold."

"He's right," another vagrant said. "Glick would never have let you make it that big in the first place."

"Yeah, well Glick's dead now, isn't he?"

"Just stop feeding the damn fire!"

"You gonna try to make me?"

"Guys, cut it out!" Frank shouted. "You gonna let us fall apart just 'cause Glick stopped a bullet? You gonna let Chris' gang win?"

"You wanna be the leader, Frank? Chris' gang was right; the way things are going you'd be dead in a week."

"If you think they're so right, why don't you go run off and join 'em?" Frank said, firing up at once.

"Maybe I will!"

"Yeah? Well I don't think they take dead members!"

Frank and the other vagrant were now on the verge of blows. Before violence could break out, however, an unfamiliar voice spoke up.

"Excuse me, gentlemen," said the voice, slick as oil. "As fascinating as your little drama is, I have an urgent matter that requires your attention."

The vagrants all spun around. A strange figure walked towards them, clothed all in black with a windbreaker jacket billowing behind him like a cape. At his side walked a thin girl wearing a winter coat, a black scarf wrapped firmly around the lower half of her face. The vagrants immediately avoided eye contact with her; something about that icy stare was highly disconcerting.

"Who the hell are you?" the vagrant with the blanket demanded.

"You may call me Z, and this is my assistant, Noni," Zen said, gesturing at the rigid girl beside him. "Where is your leader?"

For a few moments the vagrants boggled at the pair, unable to believe their suicidal foolishness. Then the silence was broken by the same boy as before.

"I dunno where you get off, askin' questions like that," the vagrant snarled, casting his blanket aside. "But you look kinda rich, and that means coming here was the worst mistake of your life!"

With that, the vagrant lunged at Zen with outstretched hands, grinning with yellow teeth. Zen seized the boy's arm, turned, and hurled the vagrant over his shoulder. The vagrant hit the ground hard, swearing loudly. The other vagrants all sprang up, preparing to rush the intruders. But at that moment, dark shapes emerged from all sides, and the vagrants realized that they weren't alone.

As the figures approached the bonfire, the firelight threw their features into sharp relief. They all appeared clean and organized, but of more immediate interest to the vagrants were the weapons that they all held in their hands. Most of the newcomers wielded sharp knives that reflected the dancing flames, and a few even bore pistols. The vagrants quickly chose to sit back down, realizing that they were at the mercy of these strangers.

"Where is your leader?" Zen repeated.

There was silence.

"Surely someone can shed some light on the subject," Zen said, a note of impatience entering his voice.

"He got killed," the vagrant named Frank explained at last.

"How fortuitous." Zen smiled grimly. "Well then, since the position of leader appears to be vacant, I nominate myself. Any questions?"

There was another brief silence. Then a bold vagrant crouched in a corner stood up.

"Who the hell are you?"

"*That's* a fair question," Zen admitted. "I have already given you my name, but what I am called matters much less than who I am. I am the leader of the Truancy."

"The Truancy?" the boy repeated. "What's that?"

"Us," Zen said, spreading his arms to encompass everyone present. "We are the Truancy, and we have precisely three things in common. We are all children, we all fight the Educators, and we are all determined to set things right in this City."

"What's wrong with the City?" one of the vagrants by the fire demanded.

"Take a look at your situation and you'll have your answer," Zen said. "No matter what your reason for being here is, I highly doubt that it was by your own choice."

A few of the vagrants nodded at that, and all of them now seemed to be paying close attention.

"You are here because the Educators want you to be here; you are here by their design," Zen continued. "You were not compatible with their system. Therefore, you are a liability to them, and must be hidden from view or else made example of. Your fate has been tragic, and students throughout the City are warned that they must obey or else end up like you."

"So why're you here?" the first boy demanded.

"To offer you a choice," Zen said. "You can accept the fate the Educators have condemned you to, or you can defy it, as we have. I can give you the means to fight back, food to stave off hunger, and warm shelter to return to. Make no mistake, you will be fighting a war, but I do not believe that it will be any less dangerous than your lives are now—and you will no longer be outcasts, but proud Truants. And should we prove victorious, we will cast down the Educators and you will be revered and admired throughout the City."

Firelight glinted in many vagrants' eyes. Zen almost smiled, but knew that any celebration would still be premature. Sure enough, one of the vagrants then spoke up.

"Fighting the Educators? That's crazy talk, man. There's *thousands* of Enforcers, we'd be up against the entire City! There ain't no way you can take on the entire City!"

"To the contrary, my friend," Zen responded, "there may be thousands of Enforcers, but there are a *million* students and vagrants in this City. The Educators are only the masters of the City because those children consent to be ruled. I do not intend to take on the entire City—I believe that the entire City will take on the Educators. It doesn't take much to start an avalanche. If you join us, others will follow, and together we will *bury* our enemies."

"Having a ton of people won't do you no good if all you got is a few pistols and knives," another vagrant said, snapping his fingers. "Them Enforcers won't even notice you if that's all you got."

In response, Zen calmly drew what looked like a TV remote from a pocket of his windbreaker. Pointing the remote outwards, he pressed the power button with his thumb. For a moment, no one knew what to expect. Then chaos erupted all around them.

An abandoned car was flipped over by the force of one explosion, and the first-floor windows of a nearby building were shattered by another, sending glass flying like hail. Water spouted into the air as a fire hydrant was blown from the sidewalk, and a number of trash cans clanged noisily as they were bent out of shape and slammed against the walls of an ally. Vagrants screamed, and a few tried to run, but were shoved to the ground by perfectly calm Truants. Soon the dust settled, and everyone present realized that the explosions, while close enough to be very noticeable, had not been close enough to do them any harm.

"I counted four blasts, Aaron," Zen said calmly to one of the nearby Truants. "If I am not mistaken, that would mean that two of the bombs failed to go off."

"Sorry, Z, could be that the other two are out of range," Aaron said, scratching the back of his neck. "Should I try it at a shorter distance?"

"That would be appreciated," Zen said, handing the remote over.

As Aaron vanished down an alley, Zen turned back to the vagrants, who were all gaping at him, dumbfounded.

"The noise will likely have attracted attention," Zen said. "So I hope that you are satisfied concerning our arsenal."

By now some of the vagrants had recovered their wits, and the one named Frank actually got up and approached Zen with a shrewd look on his face.

"Things that go boom are good and all, and we got a glimpse of that fancy fighting of yours," Frank said. "But how do you students do in a real battle? We're as tough a group as you'll find in this City, but even we've been having trouble with another gang. It's 'cause of them that we're in this mess. The bastards are led by a kid named Chris. If you can take care of them, I'll follow you to hell and back."

A number of the vagrants murmured in approval of this idea, and some of the Truants shifted uncomfortably. Zen however, remained impassive.

"Essentially, you're trying to bargain with me," Zen observed. "I, however, do not make compromises. That said, with or without you, I will be offering your current rivals the same opportunity that I have offered you. Should you both accept, I will expect you to get over your little feud."

"And if they refuse?" Frank demanded. "They'd sooner kill than cooperate with anyone."

"Should that be the case, I will destroy them," Zen said in tones of steel.

As if to punctuate the statement, some distance away two more explosions shook the ground. Noni folded her arms and glared at Frank, who looked somewhat perturbed by the latest blasts and the girl's frigid gaze.

"The Truancy is only just getting started, gentlemen," Zen said. "Food, shelter, a cause to live for, these are the things it has to offer. You can pledge your loyalty to the Truancy and fight the Educators for control of the City . . . or you can remain vagrants and fight each other for scraps. I have nothing more to add. Follow me as you wish."

With that, Zen spun around and began walking away. The other Truants fell in line behind him. For a moment the vagrants stared at their receding backs. Then, as one, they leapt up to follow, forming another line beside the veteran Truants. As they walked, Zen was pleased to hear snippets of conversation floating up from between the two columns.

"The guy's kind of strange, but he's dead serious, you'll see."

"When do we get to eat? I ain't had anything in days."

"He actually killed an Enforcer with just a knife! That's how we got our first guns, see?"

"The other vagrants call me a liar, but I'm telling you, I saw the ghost with my own eyes just a few days ago! She's as real as they say!"

"I never got expelled myself, but I was getting there. Another year, maybe, and I might've been one of you."

"So ya joined this bunch 'cause you got caught copying? Funny, I got kicked outta school for the same thing!"

"My old teacher used to say you guys killed people and ate them, but he was just full of it, right?"

"You," Zen said suddenly, pointing back at a vagrant in the column, "come here for a moment."

Realizing that he had been summoned, Frank rushed forward to march at Zen's right. Noni glanced at him with icy eyes from the left.

"What's your name?" Zen asked.

"Frank."

"Well then, Frank," Zen said, turning to his new recruit, "where do you think we might be able to find that rival gang you mentioned?"

17

W e got the worst luck in the City, guys, the worst."

"Don't be stupid, Walker. We're lucky this many of us got outta that mess."

"Yeah, yeah, I know, don't lecture me."

"Hey, anyone seen Raphael today?"

"Yeah, Chris, he went out scrounging early this morn."

"Good, thought he might've run off or something."

"Who, Raphael? Nah."

Red sighed and huddled closer around the fireplace, uninterested in participating in the conversation. One benefit of the hotel lobby they'd been hiding in for a while now was that it actually had a real fireplace, so they had something with which to cook their stolen food. In total, ten of them had survived to regroup. Red considered it a small miracle that even that many had gotten away from that slaughterhouse. Red glanced over at a corner, where Chris was still talking animatedly with some of the other survivors.

Given the time to think about it, Red had become increasingly wary of Chris since the second Enforcer ambush. Aside from Chris being a generally slimy character, Red had realized that whenever there was trouble, Chris was suspiciously absent. He longed to voice his suspicions, to seize Chris by the collar and tell him exactly what he thought of him—but he couldn't. Unwilling to change leaders at this dark hour, the gang stuck by Chris, and Red knew it would take further upheaval to change that.

"Whose turn is it to bring some snow in today?" Chris asked.

"Walker's," came the collective reply.

"Go get something we can melt into water, Walker," Chris said.

Walker grumbled and grabbed a bucket sitting on the floor. The hotel's electricity and water no longer worked, and so it was up to some unlucky soul to go out each day and dig around for some clean snow—something that was increasingly hard to find. In the City, it didn't take long for a fine layer of grit to accumulate on top of snow, a filth that only grew more pronounced over time as the snow began to melt.

"It could be worse," Chris said, turning back to address the other vagrants. "We lost a lot more people than this in the parking garage, dunno how many of you were around for that one."

"Raphael was there, wasn't he?"

"Yeah, and Red too, I'm pretty sure," Chris said, and Red could feel the boy's slippery gaze on his back. "Say, Red, us survivors are pretty lucky, aren't we?"

Red was spared having to reply because at that moment, Walker's alarmed shout reached their ears, followed by loud swearing. Red leapt to his feet along with the others and dashed outside. As they tumbled out the door, they froze staring in disbelief.

Raphael's body lay sprawled in a splotch of crimson snow. The blood seemed to have came from a bullet wound in his chest. Judging from the tracks and the trail of crimson, the body had been dragged and left here, on their doorstep, on purpose. Red looked up at his comrades. Some looked depressed, others shocked, though most were angry. This was an obvious challenge, and they all wanted to know who had issued it.

Gingerly seizing Raphael's body by the legs, Red began dragging the body indoors. It was morbid work, but it had to be done, and soon the other vagrants joined him. As they worked, they began to whisper to one another, speculating about who could have done it. As far as they knew, no gang had gotten their hands on a gun.

"Maybe the vagrant ghost did it!" Walker suggested unhelpfully.

"This isn't a time for jokes!" Red snapped.

Indoors, Red turned the body over. There, attached to Raphael's back, he discovered a note, just as he suspected he would. He snatched it up, and as the other vagrants realized what he had, they all gathered around.

"The Truancy requests your immediate presence four blocks down," Red read aloud.

"The Truancy?" Walker repeated. "Who the hell are they?"

"Never heard of them," Red muttered. "Think that's what Glick's gang is calling themselves now that their boss is dead again?"

"They ain't got the guts to pull something like this!"

"Maybe they got a leader with balls this time."

"Ne'er mind who dey are, what're we gonna do 'bout 'em?"

"That's obvious," Red said, standing up. "We go out and show them who's boss. If we let them think they can kill us whenever they want—"

"That's stupid, man, you saw that wound, they got a gun!"

"What're they gonna do with just one gun? We'll take it from 'em!"

"I say we give 'em what they gave Raphael! Red's right, show 'em who's boss!"

"Speaking of who's boss, where are you going, Chris?" Red said suddenly.

Chris, who had been slowly sneaking towards the door, froze like an icicle, a guilty expression on his face as all heads turned to him.

"Nowhere," Chris said hastily.

"You slimy little worm," Red snarled, suddenly furious. "Were you trying to run? Or just going to call your Enforcer friends for help?"

At that, pandemonium broke out. Some vagrants began shouting all sorts of accusations at Chris, their long-suppressed complaints now unleashed. Others shouted in his defense, screaming threats at Red instead. In no time the two sides seemed ready to fight to the death, and any sense of camaraderie quickly devolved as insults grew personal and the entire gang threatened to break out into one big free-for-all. Seeing the hopeful look on Chris' face as their leader watched the madness unfold, Red found himself shouting louder than he thought himself capable of.

"SHUT UP!"

The other vagrants did just that and turned to stare at Red.

"Think about it, guys, this sneaking little rat is never around when there's trouble!" Red said, pointing at Chris. "You saw him just now, trying to slip out like he always does. He's a coward!"

"Just stop, okay?" Chris said as the other vagrants began murmuring to each other.

"He's always trying to take advantage of us, have us bring him food like he's some sort of king," Red spat viciously. "When was the last time any of us were on lookout while he risked his neck? When was the last time he risked his neck at all?"

"Stop!" Chris said again, his voice suddenly high-pitched.

"The Enforcers always know how many of us there are, where and when to find us," Red continued, "and Chris is nowhere to be found when they do! I'd bet anything that this rat's been selling us out! It probably makes him feel special!"

"STOP!"

Chris lunged at Red, who felt a thrill of satisfaction as they both hit the ground, wrestling for each other's throats. Red had been expecting Chris to attack him, and he intended to take full advantage of the opportunity it offered. All around them, the rest of the gang formed a silent circle, realizing that their collective fate was about to be decided.

As they thrashed about on the ground, neither combatant was able to gain the upper hand. Chris had size on his side and was driven by desperate rage, but Red was clearheaded and fierce in his own right. The two rolled under a large wooden table, and Red, who had been pinned under Chris, lashed upwards with all his might. Chris slammed against the bottom of the table, stunned long enough for Red to shove him off to the side. Scrambling out from under the table, Red swiftly overturned it, bringing it crashing down upon Chris as the vagrant leader attempted to rise.

Parts of the table, which had become rickety after years of neglect, broke off from the impact, and Chris struggled to extract himself from the mess. Red seized a broken table leg and swung it at Chris, who hastily raised a chunk of the tabletop to block the blow. Both leg and tabletop shattered as they struck each other, and Chris flung his pieces into Red's face to send him reeling back a few paces.

Trying to press his advantage, Chris charged at Red, who seized a tall lamp and swung it around to meet his oncoming foe. The lamp head slammed into Chris' face, the bulb shattering as Chris yelped in surprise and tipped over. Not letting up for an instant, Red swung the lamp around and brought its base crashing down onto Chris' prone body. Chris squealed like a stuck pig, raising his arms uselessly to fend off any more blows.

"Stop! You can't do this! Stop!" Chris whined. "Please, I didn't mean it!"

Red struck Chris with the lamp again, and the would-be leader curled up into a fetal position, his cries of "Stop" growing fainter and more pitiful with each utterance. Red stared down at the lump in disgust, then shook his head and lowered his weapon. All around him, the vagrants stared as though seeing Chris for the first time. Some looked shocked; others were revolted.

As soon as Red turned his back, Chris stopped whining and glared up at his enemy with a look of pathetic loathing. But he did not rise, and Red didn't spare him another glance. Instead, breathing heavily, Red straightened up and looked around at the other vagrants.

"All right," he panted, "now let's go show this Truancy what we're made of."

Zen tapped his foot lightly as he stared up the empty street.

"Are you sure that they'll come?" Zen asked.

"They're not gonna turn down a challenge like that," Frank said. "I mean, Chris isn't known for being brave, but if he doesn't come the rest of his gang will."

"Good, because the alternative is approaching them in their own lair," Zen said. "That is something I would prefer to avoid if given a choice."

"It's too bad the kid—what was his name, Raphael? Too bad he didn't want to play nice."

"If he had not attacked you on sight, there would have been no need to kill him," Zen agreed. "However, that is not how it panned out. Thus, here we are."

"Here" happened to be the end of a street that, unlike most in the City, did not connect with any others. It merely stopped, forming a jutting rectangle surrounded on all sides by buildings. The district had long been abandoned, and its oddly configured streets had never been renovated. A veritable maze of alleyways cut through the neat blocks so randomly that even vagrants had difficulty keeping track of it all. Zen had picked the perfect place for an ambush, though he did not think the vagrants would see it as such. He expected them to rush into the trap believing that they were cornering their victims.

Zen glanced around one last time to make sure that all the preparations had been made. Frank, Noni, and he were the only ones out in the open, but out of the corner of his eyes he could see Gabriel giving him a thumbs-up from the shadow of an alley. Within the alleyways, Zen knew, would be a number of other Truants keeping an eye on every possible path to and from the site. Aaron, though no longer present, had already tested and set up a number of explosives just in case, though Zen did not intend to detonate any of them today. The former vagrants, now new Truants, lay in wait in the surrounding buildings. They had adjusted well to life as Truants; given food, a chance to wash, new clothing, and a good night's rest, they seemed like new people altogether, and got along surprisingly well with the veterans. Zen had decided that Frank should remain visible, and so he stood by Zen's side along with Noni, who occasionally shot icy glares at him. Everything was in place, Zen decided—except Chris' vagrants.

As if on cue, a motley collection of ten vagrants rounded the street corner and began advancing up the road. Zen was amused to see all sorts of junk being wielded as weapons; pipes, bricks, planks—one boy had what looked like a tall, broken lamp. Zen smiled. If all went well they would soon have much better weapons to use. And if it didn't . . . well, then no amount of lamps would save these vagrants.

"Is this all there is?" the boy with the lamp called as the group drew closer. "This is the Truancy?"

"Indeed." Zen bowed graciously. "We are the Truancy, and we're pleased to make your acquaintance. I must apologize for our disagreement with one of your members—we were unable to convince him to stop attacking Frank here, so I had to persuade him with my gun."

Zen casually began retying his ponytail, his shoulders raising his windbreaker so that the gun on his hip was clearly visible. Some of the vagrants hesitated at the sight; indeed, the boy with the lamp froze completely when he got a good look at Zen. Still, they seemed to have the advantage in numbers, so all of them stood their ground. But when next they spoke, it wasn't to Zen.

"Frank?" one of the vagrants said incredulously. "Frank from Glick's bunch? Is that you? What the hell happened to you? You look like a student now!"

"Glick is dead, so is the gang," Frank said bluntly. "But we're definitely not students, we're Truants now."

"Who are?" another vagrant jeered. "You three? We're terrified. When we came out here we was expecting a real gang or something, not three idiots with a gun!"

"There are actually twenty of us present, and more who are not," Zen said. "Perhaps if you took a look around you might begin to understand the situation a little better."

As if against their will, the vagrants' heads turned, and now many of them really did look scared. Zen didn't blame them. Emerging from the alleys and buildings were seventeen more Truants, all equipped with some sort of formidable weaponry, all healthy and well clothed. The vagrants gaped, for they recognized the faces of some of their old rivals among the Truants who now surrounded them. Zen glanced over at Frank and saw a look of pure delight on his face. He could tell that the boy was struggling hard not to gloat aloud.

Just as the vagrants seemed to be steeling themselves for one last, desperate charge for freedom, Zen cleared his throat and spoke, stopping them in their tracks.

"Before anyone attempts anything foolish, I should make it clear that I do not intend to kill any of you unless you force my hand. The Truancy is not some vagrant gang out to kill over the contents of garbage cans."

"Then what is the Truancy, eh?" one of the vagrants demanded.

"If you would sit down and listen for a few minutes," Zen said, "I will tell you."

Red sat rooted to the spot, still staring in shock at the boy who was now declaring himself to be the leader of a rebellion against the Educators. It wasn't the boy's weapon, his wild ambitions, or even the ambush that had stunned him; it was the boy himself. Red had instantly recognized the mysterious child who had appeared from the shadows to casually murder an Enforcer. Red had always known that the boy—who had just introduced himself as Z—was trouble, but he had never expected that trouble to involve him.

Shaking himself from his stupor, Red cautiously began looking around. The other vagrants were all sitting in rapt attention, all previous enmity forgotten. With a surge of fury, Red spotted Chris skulking about at the back of the crowd. Red hadn't known that the boy had tagged along, and thought that he had a lot of nerve to do so. Gritting his teeth, Red looked back up to examine Z's companions. Red had never seen Frank before, but with a jolt, Red realized that the girl standing next to the Truancy leader was the one he had given an apple to in that alley on that fateful day. There was no mistaking those icy eyes. At the same time, Red found it difficult to recognize her because she looked . . . different. Her hair was no longer matted, but straight and glossy. She was wearing new, clean clothes, and a black scarf was tightly wrapped around her face. But more than that, her pose, rigid and strong, made her seem like a completely different person from the shivering, terrified little girl that Red remembered.

Red sank closer to the ground and looked away, worried now that the girl might recognize him. As the boy who called himself Z began talking about resources and mentioned something about unlimited funds, Red saw a greedy expression flit across Chris' face. Red smiled wryly; Chris might be foolish enough to try to exploit this bunch, but Red certainly wasn't. He had a sharp instinct for detecting danger, and this Truancy set off every alarm that he had.

Just by looking around at the faces of his fellow vagrants, Red could tell that he was alone in his distress. His compatriots were obviously captivated by what the Truancy was offering. Seeing their former rivals turned overnight into a clean, well-fed, well-organized fighting force had made a deep first impression, and they now coveted that kind of change for themselves as well. Red grimaced. Z was now discussing how he planned to make a base of operations in District 15. If Red waited around until the end of the speech, there was no doubt that he'd be overruled, and then possibly killed.

The only thing he could do, Red decided, was what he did best: run.

And you called Chris a coward, a nagging corner of his mind jeered. *Look at you, sneaking off at the first sign of trouble!*

It's not like they'll be needing me, Red told himself. *I wouldn't be doing anyone any good if I stuck around to be killed; it's not the same thing.*

With that thought, Red dispelled his doubts and slowly, carefully, began inching towards the cover of the nearest alley. Largely hidden by the bodies of his fellows, Red managed to reach the mouth of the alley undetected. Red glanced around. The Truants themselves no longer seemed to be watching the crowd, but rather paying attention to their leader's speech.

Steeling himself, Red took a deep breath and slipped into the alley, pausing for the briefest of moments to see if anyone had noticed. No one had. Hope welling up in his chest, Red got up and began walking away as quietly as he could. Soon he turned a corner and was out of sight from the street. Breaking into a run, Red began to feel pretty good about his chances. Then a startled voice yelled at him from a side alley.

"Hey! You! Hold it right there!"

Red glanced down the passage and saw a thin Truant running at him, pistol held aloft. Red swore under his breath and began running as fast as he could. He hadn't expected the Truancy to have anyone watching the alleys; clearly this group meant business. The boy chasing him continued to shout warnings, and Red knew that at any moment he might start firing. Ducking behind a corner, Red thrust his leg out as his pursuer came into sight, tripping the boy. As the Truant fell, his gun went off. Knowing that the others would have been alerted by the noise, Red hastened to take advantage of the precious seconds he had bought. With another burst of speed, he darted around the next corner . . .

. . . and slammed right into a brick wall.

Rebounding from the collision, Red clutched his injured face. The corner hadn't been a corner at all, but rather an indentation in the alley wall. Red swore loudly, trying to regain his footing, but it was too late. The pursuing Truant had gotten to his feet and was now raising his gun. Red's legs suddenly failed him, and he fell back onto the ground. His hands trembling, Red shut his eyes, knowing that at last, after all the running he had done in his life, death had finally caught up to him.

Then there was a swish and the tinkling of metal. The Truant let out a yelp of surprise, followed by a dull thud. Red's eyes snapped open just in time to see the glint of a chain as it was drawn back into a white sleeve. Almost involuntarily, Red's eyes slowly followed the sleeve until he found himself staring awestruck at its owner. Red blinked, but the vision did not vanish.

Standing over the now-unconscious Truant was a beautiful girl. Everything from her snowy hair to her almost pearly skin was astoundingly pale. Even her clothes were whitish, though rips and soot were visible on the fabric. A white headband held back her hair, which fell just long enough to skirt her jawbone. A thin white sweater, its sleeves tied together, was draped around her neck like a mantle. As this vision of grace looked down at him, Red knew that he was looking upon the mythical vagrant ghost.

In the dim light of the alley, the spirit's eyes had appeared the faintest blue. But as she turned around, they caught the bright setting sun and turned a deep red, the color of blood. Rendered speechless by this entrancing phenomenon, Red numbly realized that all of the wild stories he had laughed at were true. The phantom looked down at Red with ruby pupils, and then uttered one word in a soft, sympathetic voice.

"Go."

Red didn't need to be told twice. Scrambling to his feet, Red spun around and ran, his heart thumping wildly in his chest. Behind him he could hear the clinking of chains, and when he looked back over his shoulder he found that the alley was empty, save for the unconscious Truant.

His mind now racing as fast as his heart, Red could not help but wonder if madness was his punishment for cowardice. But if it was real, at least the ghost had appeared to be on his side. No one else in the City was anymore.

"And now that you know what the Truancy is, I can tell that many of you are interested in becoming a part of it," Zen said.

No one contradicted him. Some vagrants nodded; a few even grinned.

"So then, who is your current leader?" Zen asked.

At this the vagrants began looking around. After a few moments, they blinked and glanced at each other as they reached the same conclusion: Red had disappeared. Zen cleared his throat impatiently. On the verge of panic, one of the vagrants pointed at Chris. Slowly, all the others copied him, and a slow grin spread across Chris' face.

"Are you Chris?" Zen asked.

"Yep, that's me."

"Do you pledge your loyalty to the Truancy?"

"Well, I suppose—"

At that moment the sound of a gunshot rang out from the nearby alleys. Some of the vagrants looked around in alarm, and even the Truants were suddenly wary. Zen narrowed his eyes, and then pointed to the side, singling out two Truants.

"Gabriel, Ken," Zen said, "go check it out. I believe it came from near Max's position."

"Gotcha," Gabriel said, darting off into an alley with Ken close behind him.

"As we were discussing before being rudely interrupted," Zen said, turning back to Chris, "do you intend to join, or not?"

"Well, it's a tempting offer," Chris said, scratching the back of his neck. "And your cause is noble and all that, but what . . . you know . . . *incentives* are there?"

"He's giving you food, clothes, and a safe place to sleep, fool," Frank said, unable to contain himself any longer. "That's a lot more than you were ever able to provide for your gang."

For a moment Chris looked ready to make an angry retort, but Zen cut him off before he could open his mouth.

"Frank may have spoken out of turn, and he may have been blunt. That does not, however, stop him from being right," Zen said, folding his arms. "If you have a specific request to make, Chris, make it a clear one."

Chris' face seemed to puff up as fear, anger, and greed all fought each other for dominance. In the end the latter prevailed, and Chris was unable to restrain the eagerness in his voice as he spoke the question that had clearly been on his mind for a while.

"Will we get paid?" Chris asked.

"Should you handle your responsibilities satisfactorily, you will be rewarded, yes," Zen said slowly. "I would caution against spending too often, though, as the living districts are going to become a very dangerous pla—"

"Please, can I get an advance?" Chris interrupted, his voice suddenly sweet. "It would motivate me more. After all, I'm bringing all these people too, ain't I?"

Zen's eyes narrowed, and a few of the vagrants shuffled uncomfortably at the behavior of their reinstated leader. Before Zen could respond, Ken and Gabriel reappeared from the alley, supporting the limp figure of Max. They dragged the unconscious Truant to Zen's feet and laid him out upon the ground before standing at attention.

"We found him knocked out back there," Gabriel explained. "Looks to me like he took a blow to the head."

"A very clean hit to the forehead, in fact," Zen muttered, crouching down to inspect the fallen Truant. "Whoever did this does not seem to have intended to cause him permanent harm. Is his weapon missing?"

"No, sir, got it right here," Ken said, holding up the pistol.

"Good," Zen said, straightening up. "I'm sure that he'll be able to enlighten us about what befell him when he wakes up. On the off chance that it was an Enforcer spy, however"—Zen now turned to face the vagrants—"we will be leaving now. You all know what I offer, and you can follow me or not. The choice is yours."

With that, Zen turned and made for a nearby alleyway. He was quickly joined by the other Truants, some of whom materialized out of other dark corridors and abandoned buildings. Ken and Gabriel picked Max up again and began to follow, and a few vagrants sprang up to help. The rest fell in line behind Zen. Leading the way for them was Chris, the treacherous glint in his eyes growing brighter with every step.

18

A FATEFUL ENCOUNTER

Red stared up at the sheer wooden barrier, reeling from the enormity of what he was about to do. For days now he had been running, fleeing from human sight. Ever since his miserable attempt at leadership, he no longer felt safe in the company of any vagrant; there was no telling how far the Truancy's influence might already have spread. It had not been as easy as one might think, to hide from everyone and everything, when every abandoned district had its own vagrant population.

As the rising sun peered over the horizon, Red clenched his fists, fingernails digging into the palms of his hands. Had it really come to this? Was he going to seek refuge in District 19, supposedly the most perilous location in the entire City? No vagrant could stay in that forsaken district for long, surrounded as it was by dangerously live ones, and few were daring enough to approach it at all. If the Enforcers got a whiff of a vagrant in there, it really would be the end. And yet, Red felt that he would be safer there than in any other abandoned district, where so many varied threats were lying in wait.

It was better to stay isolated for as long as he could, Red thought, than to risk the company of others when everyone had become a potential enemy. District 19 would be either his salvation or his undoing, and Red knew that he had no choice but to find out which it would be; dawn had come, and if a pedestrian saw him he was as good as dead. At least he had been lucky enough to get this far without being spotted, something that Red took to be a good sign. He had never been very superstitious, but ever since his brief encounter with the vagrant ghost, he had felt that fortune was prepared to intervene on his behalf every once in a while.

A ray of sunlight washed across Red's face, and he turned to find the sun almost completely risen. The citizens of the City would be awakening soon. Seized by a sudden feeling of desperation, Red gripped a plank jutting out from the crude wooden wall and swiftly scrambled over onto the other side. He unceremoniously fell to the ground with a mixed feeling of pain and triumph, the former coming from the elbow that had taken the blunt of the fall, and the latter coming from the fact that he was finally safe . . . for now.

Zen stood before a flower shop in the abandoned District 15, admiring the wooden floor of its interior through the large show window. The window took up most of the shop's façade, which would, when he moved in, allow him to see what was going on out in the street at all times. The shop had obviously been uninhabited for some time, but it remained secure and comfortable enough for his purposes. Already Truants were carrying various crates and boxes inside it, and Zen held a can of red spray paint ready at his side.

Things had been going well for him and the Truancy in the few days since they'd added former vagrants to their numbers. Their small army was growing larger every day as both vagrants and students continued to join the fold. Admittedly Max had not been the same since having been discovered unconscious (he kept insisting that he'd been attacked by a ghost), but Zen had reassigned him as a mechanic, and the boy was proving to be very handy with tools. With help from the former vagrants, the Truancy had established a number of hideouts all over the City, and had moved on to acquiring enough weapons to wage war. Zen had even found himself living quarters that were to his liking in the form of the flower shop, and yet, despite all of his successes, he felt oddly hollow.

Brushing off the feeling, Zen shook his can of paint violently, held it up to the window, and sprayed a large red circle onto it. Then Zen sprayed on a T, turned slightly clockwise, within it. This was the mark of the Truancy. Examining his work, Zen began shaking his can again. It would need another coat of paint to stand out properly.

"You've definitely got artistic talent, Z."

Zen spoke without turning as he carefully applied the second coat. "It's not like you to flatter anyone, Gabriel. Is there something that you wanted to ask?"

Gabriel came forward to stand next to Zen, unabashed as he gazed at a number of Truants carrying what looked unmistakably like guns wrapped in sheets into the flower shop.

"Well, now that you mention it, I *was* wondering where you got all these weapons from," Gabriel confessed.

"Well, I won't go into specifics, Gabriel," Zen said. "But let's just say that with enough money, gaps can be made even in Enforcer inventories."

"Speaking of money, it looks like the new leech is back for more," Gabriel said, gesturing to the side. "Didn't you already give him the damn advance he was begging for?"

Zen glanced at what Gabriel was pointing out to him, and frowned. Walking towards them with a huge smile on his face was the former vagrant leader named Chris. Zen had always been wary about the boy's avaricious attitude, and things he'd heard about him had not allayed his suspicions.

"Indeed I did," Zen muttered. "Twice. I wonder what he wants now. If you'll excuse us, Gabriel?"

"Of course," Gabriel replied, casting a dark look at Chris' approaching figure.

"Hey, Z, thanks for the money!" Chris said as he slid up next to Zen. "I really appreciate—"

"And yet I note that it hasn't increased your productivity at all," Zen observed. "I seem to recall that you promised that you would actually follow your own self-imposed recruiting schedule if I paid you once."

"Well, yeah, but—"

"And when your own deadline came around, you had nothing but excuses for me," Zen continued. "Yes, you told me you were adjusting, but even your subordinates were more efficient than you."

"Look, just stop, okay? Stop."

"And now I hear that your efforts are actually *diminishing*," Zen said. "In fact, I think that you may actually be scaring vagrants away. So let me make one thing very clear: Whatever you're about to ask me, it better not involve satisfying your greed."

"Well, it isn't," Chris said, sounding angry now. "I was tryin' to be polite, but if you're gonna be rude so will I. I'm going to take a break from this stupid crap."

Zen turned around to look at Chris incredulously.

"You must be joking."

"I'm not, and it's not funny," Chris said, glaring. "You have me shut up here, working like a dog, not even allowed to go wherever I want, I had more freedom as a vagra—"

"Listen to me very carefully," Zen hissed. "I've been more than lenient with you up until now—"

"Actually no, you haven't," Chris interrupted. "You've been a real asshole, actually."

"What do you think this is, a field trip?" Zen said. "Do you see the rest of us lounging around and whining? I ask no more of anyone than I ask of myself. You *will* go out recruiting tonight. Otherwise, if you're going to continue to put us all at risk because of your inadequacy, then perhaps the Truancy isn't for you."

So strong was the venom in Zen's quiet words that Chris was silent for several moments. When he did speak up, it was in a shaky tone, yet still accompanied by an angry glare.

"Yeah, maybe it isn't," Chris spat. "Just remember that either way, I got your money."

And with that, Chris spun around and stormed off, looking as though he'd like nothing better than to attack anything that got in his way. Gabriel silently returned to Zen's side, looking disapprovingly at the raging boy. Zen seemed thoughtful for a moment, and then he turned to Gabriel.

"Gabriel, I want you to keep an eye on our new friend Chris," Zen said.

"I've heard a few interesting stories from his former subordinates, and I'm beginning to fear that he may be more dangerous than I had anticipated. Follow him when he goes out tonight. I'd prefer that he not know what you're up to, but keep track of him no matter what. Can you do it?"

"Gladly," Gabriel muttered. "Shall I start now?"

"Please."

The next moment, Gabriel was gone, darting up the street as if he were Chris' shadow itself. Zen watched him go, then he pulled open the door of the flower shop. Inside he found equipment ranging from pistols to body armor all resting upon the wooden floor, swathed in white sheets. He admired the impressive cache, made a few mental changes to his long-term plans, then cast his attention elsewhere.

Zen glanced over at a stack of crates upon which Noni was sitting, swinging her legs and looking thoughtful as she watched Truants working outside through the glass display window. Her health had improved. She was no longer haggard, her shoulder-length hair was now smooth instead of frazzled, and most promisingly, she no longer stared at the world with wide-eyed fright.

Coming to an impromptu decision, Zen reached over and picked up a box he had had brought in with the weapons.

"Noni, come here," Zen ordered.

Noni slid down from the crates and walked over to Zen, looking up at him curiously.

"Sir?"

"How well do you think you can aim with these?" Zen asked as he opened the box to reveal a target and dart set exactly like the one that had hung in his room in the Mayoral Mansion.

"Not very, sir," Noni answered.

"Well, now's as good a time to practice as any."

Realizing that the soapy water was losing its heat, Umasi reluctantly rose from the tub and reached over to a nearby stool for a towel. As he exited the bath, wisps of steam rose with him and coiled their way to the ceiling. Ignoring the sudden chill as he left the water, Umasi hastily dried himself off, pausing only for a moment to savor the refreshing sensation of being *clean*.

It was more than just a hygienic matter. Umasi now felt more energized and alert than he had in a long time. Casting a glance at the bathwater, Umasi noted that it was nearly black with soot. Well, that was hardly surprising. Soon after deciding to settle down in District 19, Umasi had realized that it had been a long time since he'd had a bath.

While there was still running water in District 19, Umasi hadn't been able to find a building with a working boiler. Consequently, he had been forced to boil his own over a stove in large pots. It had been tedious work, but well worth it in the end. It was just too bad that the water didn't keep its heat for very long in this weather.

Humming idly to himself, Umasi drained the tub and donned some new clothing—not just some new rags from a Dumpster, but actually *new* clothing. He had gone shopping out of necessity the previous day, discreetly withdrawing cash at one location before spending it elsewhere. Aside from a heap of groceries and a fresh wardrobe, he had also bought things like soap and blankets. It had taken several trips to carry it all, but Umasi had enjoyed feeling like he was creating a new life for himself.

Now dressed in a simple white sweater and warm khaki pants, Umasi left the bathroom and entered the living room of the apartment he'd claimed for his own. It was rather dirty with disuse, but he expected that he'd have ample time to clean it up later. On one table rested all the groceries that he'd bought the previous day that wouldn't fit into the still-working refrigerator, and on another rested packs of alcoholic lemonade—a beverage he'd never tried before, but had bought on a whim.

Right now Umasi wasn't interested in either pile, and instead walked over to a kitchen counter to seize a sports bottle and attach it to his waist. He then proceeded to the door, where he donned a new pair of boots before stepping out of the apartment and onto the streets of District 19. Umasi was pleased to see the pale morning sun set the remaining snow aglitter. No one plowed the streets of District 19, and he rather liked the crunch that his boots produced as they trampled the snow underfoot.

Enjoying the crisp winter air, Umasi began to jog around the district, retreading along the footsteps he had left the evening before. He might not have been a vagrant anymore, but having had to struggle for his life had instilled in him a strange need to stay active—and so he jogged, feeling more refreshed with each passing block.

After he had run far enough through the snow to leave his muscles burning and his chest heaving, Umasi paused to take a break, sitting down upon a doorstep as he took a swig from his bottle. He was about to return to his jog when he thought he heard something. Freezing in place, Umasi listened closely. Yes, there it was, a crunching sound, clearly made by footsteps, drawing closer. But that was impossible. No vagrant in their right mind would seek refuge in District 19.

Umasi frowned. What if it was an Enforcer, come to try to bring him back? The footsteps didn't sound quite that heavy, though, and he was sure that no Enforcer would be exploring an abandoned district alone, on foot no less. It *had* to be a child. But would it be a vagrant or one of Zen's Truants?

A moment later, the source of the noise rounded the block and stopped short as it spotted Umasi. Umasi, for his part, wasn't able to see the boy as anything but a blur at a distance; his eyeglasses were one relic of his past that he had yet to replace. But as the boy approached slowly, as if unable to believe what he was seeing, Umasi realized to his surprise that he had met this vagrant before. It was the kid from the supermarket raid—Red, he had said his name was.

Red stopped short a few feet away from Umasi, and Umasi took the opportunity to examine him up close. The boy was covered in dirt, streaks of black concealing what would have, under better circumstances, probably have been a handsome face. His head was covered with wild, untamed brown hair, which matched his amber eyes. He was unnaturally scrawny, but something about him testified to a hidden strength. The look on his face and in his eyes spoke of great maturity and intense hardship.

Umasi was amused to see that Red had a look of complete shock on his face. Apparently the vagrant was more surprised by this reunion than he was.

"Hello there," Umasi said as he stood. "I didn't expect to be getting any visitors around here. I understand that vagrants consider this a risky place to be."

"Yeah," Red managed, seemingly uncertain that the person before him wasn't a stress-induced hallucination.

"Are you lost?" Umasi inquired.

"Uh . . . I don't think I am," Red replied, flustered.

"Well then, you must be here on purpose," Umasi reasoned as he held out his bottle. "Care for a drink?"

Chris fumed as he strode along the darkened streets of District 13. Nearly all the vagrants of District 15 had already joined the Truancy, and so it had fallen to him to recruit in the lower districts that he was so familiar with. He hadn't taken well to this task; after being in charge for so long, running around like some errand boy seemed more ignominious to him than eating trash. And that kid Z had the nerve to complain about Chris' performance. Didn't he understand that he was lucky that Chris had helped him at all? Didn't he understand what Chris could do?

Apparently not, and so Chris had decided to show him. Approaching a run-down phone booth, Chris furtively glanced around to make sure he was alone. Seeing no one in the growing darkness, he quickly began dialing a very special number. He had powerful friends, and the Truancy would soon pay the price for insulting him. His only regret was that that bastard Red had seemingly vanished, and would not be there to die with them.

"This is Enforcer Headquarters, how can I help you?"

"Yeah, this is Chris, I'm an informant," Chris said, smiling into the receiver. "I'd like to—"

"Let me forward you to our tips division."

Chris felt a flash of annoyance, but kept his cool as his call was transferred.

"Yes?"

"This is Chris. I'm a regular, my name should be down on the list."

"Ah yes, yes it is. We were very pleased with your last two tip-offs. Over two dozen vagrants killed, very impressive. Do you have more vagrants to turn in?"

"Better," Chris said, unable to contain his excitement. "I need to come into a station again. I got some *very* interesting information you should hear."

"Hold on a second, Chris," the operator said. "It seems that Chief Truancy Officer Rothenberg has left a note concerning you. It says to let you know the next time you make contact that he needs to meet you in person as soon as possible."

"R-Rothenberg?" Chris said, feeling a jolt of fear at the name. Then he laughed at himself. Why was he afraid? Rothenberg was on his side! What's more, the man actually needed him! "Tell Rothenberg I'll see him first thing tomorrow, then. They'll notice me missing if I go tonight, I think."

"He will be expecting you," the operator promised before cutting the line.

Chris hung up and grinned in triumph. If the Enforcers had been pleased before, they would be ecstatic now that he could deliver an armed rebellion to them on a silver platter. It was only a matter of time now until Chris could retire to the living districts under Enforcer protection.

With that pleasant thought in his head, Chris proceeded to his original destination. Until he could get the Enforcers to come along and mop up the Truancy, he would have to play along with their little game. This meant continuing to go through the motions of recruiting vagrants. Deep into District 15, Chris soon found what he was looking for; the smoke and firelight stood out in the otherwise abandoned district. Before making himself visible, Chris approached silently and peeked out at the camp from behind a corner.

Small fires had been ignited in garbage cans and metal barrels, and around them milled about an assorted bunch of vagrants. He could tell from their behavior that they were not a gang; they were too guarded for that, and yet they seemed somewhat familiar with each other. The camp was typical of vagrants: someone built a fire, and its warmth drew others like moths. Even as he watched, a vagrant wearing a winter jacket with a hood pulled over his head appeared from a nearby alley and moved in to warm his hands around a fire. Deciding that it was safe enough, Chris made his move.

"Hey there, guys!" he said cheerfully, moving out into the open. "Nice, cozy place you got here."

The vagrants all spun around to stare at him.

"Who are you and what do you want?" someone demanded, voicing the question that was obviously on all of their minds.

"Relax, guys, I'm on your side," Chris said. "I'm Chris, but right now I'm talking for the Truancy."

"The Truancy?" a vagrant repeated. "What's that?"

"A rebellion," Chris replied. "A bunch of kids out to beat the Educators. Hard to believe, yeah, but these people are serious. They like to talk about freedom and good stuff like that—but between you and I, there are much better reasons to join up."

"And what're those?" another vagrant demanded.

"Guns. Food and drink. Warm beds," Chris said. "But of course, if things later go south, I, probably like most of you, would ditch, and take what I can with me."

"So you'd just screw your buddies, after all they do for you?" the hooded vagrant demanded from his place by the fire.

"Hey, just pointing out that there's nothing to lose here," Chris said defensively, raising his hands in a placating gesture.

"And what would the Truancy ask of us in return?" a vagrant demanded.

"Just that you fight the Educators and their Enforcers," Chris said, a statement that sparked murmurs among the group. "And also that you take orders from the boss, a guy that likes to be called Z. He's tightfisted with money and thinks he's cleverer than he is, but I guess he's a match for the Educators." Chris yawned. "So, if you're interested, all you have to do is come to District 15. The more that come along together, the better the chances are that Z will reward m—I mean, us."

And with that, Chris made an ironic salute and spun around to leave the camp. As soon as Chris was out of sight, excited conversation broke out among the vagrants. Most of them did indeed know each other, and many seemed wary of the Truancy and especially the one claiming to be its messenger. One of the vagrants, seeking a fresh opinion, turned to address his neighbor, the quiet boy by the fire whose face had been obscured by his hood.

"Hey, you, I ain't seen you around before," the vagrant said. "Whaddya think 'bout that guy? Is he nuts or what?"

"I don't think he's nuts," Gabriel answered, lifting his hood for the first time that night. "But I do think he's a traitor."

Yeah, yeah, so then I told him I wasn't going to help him kill anyone!" Umasi said, his voice slightly slurred as he took another swig of lemonade liquor. "And what do you think he did then?"

"Wait, wait, don't help me, I know this." Red furrowed his brow in thought as he took a sip from his own bottle. "Did he . . . uh . . . I dunno, do a dance?"

"No!" Umasi shook his head violently. "Zen, he doesn't dance. No, no, he hit me over the head with a bat, that's what he did!"

"He didn't!" Red gasped in disbelief.

"He did," Umasi insisted mournfully. "And then he ran off, and I chased after him, and a few . . . a few snows later, and I end up here."

Red paused to digest the boy's story. It was a strange and wild tale, almost as fantastical as Red's encounter with the vagrant ghost, and yet he didn't doubt its truth for a moment. The alcohol they had been sharing might have had something to do with that, but even when he was completely sober Red had felt, somehow, that Umasi was completely trustworthy.

At first Red had been too stunned at meeting Umasi again to question his hospitality, and so far Umasi had been nothing but generous and had asked nothing in return. Normally Red would've been suspicious of such selfless behavior, but as strange as Umasi was, he wasn't tripping any of Red's internal alarms. He seemed almost as good as Zen (the boy Red now knew was his twin) had been bad. In fact, Red actually found his company to be enjoyable. He couldn't remember the last time he had been able to sit around another human being and not worry about being killed or robbed.

It was night now, and the two of them sat by a large bonfire they had built in the middle of the street outside of Umasi's apartment. Umasi's speech had been rather guarded when Red first encountered him, but a couple of bottles later they found themselves much more talkative. Umasi had wasted no time in telling Red his story, and Red had been relieved to find out that the boy named Zen was human after all, if especially dangerous. Now that he knew who led the Truancy, Red felt assured that he had had a narrow escape by evading it.

After explaining his brother's saga, Umasi's story began twisting and turning, taking a few detours along the way, and they soon found themselves a bit distracted.

"Bubble gum is cool," Red said, "but not as good as . . . what did you say this stuff was?"

"Hard lemonade," Umasi replied, reading the label.

"Yeah. Alcohol. My dad, see . . . he didn't drink much . . . at least not that I ever saw," Red said, putting his bottle down for a moment. "Always working, you see."

"My dad . . . well, being Mayor and all . . . didn't exactly get to see much of him you know?" Umasi said as he took another sip from his bottle. "But I never thought he'd . . . he'd betray us like *that*. I always thought he loved us."

"Man, you got it bad, you did," Red acknowledged. "I had a good mom, I think. She was always saying that going out and getting exercise and fresh air and all that was important. Then when I did she'd tell me to get back in here you miserable boy and finish your homework."

"I never had a mom, not that I can remember," Umasi said. "Adopted and all that . . . I think my real mom named me and my bro, though. Zen got the better name, I think. I'm not too fond of my name, did you know that?"

"Yeah, well I'm named after a . . . what do you call those things . . . a color," Red complained. "It's like . . . my parents got real lazy . . . or drunk. Might as well have named me . . . purple or something."

"Red's not a bad name," Umasi insisted. "It's like . . . Ted, but with an R."

"Funny, I never thought of it like that," Red said as he took another swig. "So . . . uh . . . how long have you been out here, like as a vagrant?"

"Now that you mention it, I think . . . I think it was like . . . what, a few weeks?" Umasi said. "I could've sworn it was longer, but I guess it only felt that way."

"Yeah I lost track myself, you know," Red murmured. "I'm pretty sure it's been at least two winters besides this one, though. You always remember the . . . that cold stuff . . . *snow*."

"Two years, man, that's rough," Umasi said. "I barely been one for a week, and it was . . . it was . . . was awful, I think."

Red and Umasi continued drinking in silence as the bonfire flickered and cast dancing shadows through the snow. The silence stretched on and on, until both of them had nearly gotten through an entire other bottle. Suddenly a bolt of pain shot through Red's gut, and he doubled over in agony. Umasi looked over at him.

"You all right?" Umasi asked, suddenly sounding much more sober than he had mere minutes ago.

"I'm . . . I'm fine," Red replied as the pain faded. "It's just that damn ape . . . no, appendix. It's acting up again."

"Appendix?"

"Yeah, at least, that's what I think it is. Who knows?" Red spread his arms as if asking the City in general.

"It's been bothering you for a while now?"

"Yeah, getting worse all the time." Red nodded gravely.

"Maybe you should see a doctor."

"Impossible." Red snorted. "Million problems with that . . . you're a silly guy . . . besides, I'm fine, I got plenty of life left in me."

"I dunno, you look pretty sickly to me." Umasi's speech slurred anew with a fresh gulp.

"Sickly?" Red waved his bottle angrily. "I'm the fastest vagrant in this entire City! No one can outrun me!"

"That so?" Umasi smirked. "I bet I can beat you in a race!"

"You're on!" Red shouted, leaping to his feet. "I'll . . . I'll beat you so bad . . . you'll be like the tortoise in that racing story!"

"The tortoise won," Umasi pointed out.

"The weasel then!" Red hiccupped as he stumbled around the bonfire. "Let's go! We'll see what animal is faster!"

"Yeah . . . real fast," Umasi agreed, swaying slightly. "But maybe, you know, we might could do that . . . later . . . kind of not in the mood now."

Red pondered that suggestion for a moment.

"Yeah . . . yeah . . . later sounds good." Red decided, as he sat back down. "I'm feeling kind of . . . tired . . . now that you mention it."

And with that, Red tipped over and collapsed, alcohol coursing through his veins and throbbing painfully in his head. In the brief moments of consciousness that followed, Red heard only one distinct sentence, spoken close by his head, and he thought that he recognized Umasi's muttering voice.

"Man, he's a lightweight for sure."

And then he passed out.

19

SETTING TRAPS

Huffing, Umasi ran up the steep incline of the street, trailing just slightly behind Red. It had been several days since the vagrant had shown up in District 19, and Umasi never ceased to be surprised by how fast he could run. As far as sprinting was concerned, they had very quickly established that Red was superior. Since then they had taken to running long, elaborate marathons through the streets of District 19, and Umasi found that he stood much more of a chance with these long-distance races.

As they reached the top of the paved hill, Umasi saw that they were coming up on one of the many obstacles that had naturally formed over the years: a run-down building had collapsed, creating a miniature mountain of debris right in the middle of the road. Far from going around it, however, the two boys tackled the problem head-on, scrambling over it as fast as they could. Umasi was able to find better footholds in the mess than Red, and slid down the other side with a small lead.

"Passed you!" Umasi taunted over his shoulder.

"Not for long!" Red shouted back as his feet touched down on smooth pavement again.

The weather had warmed slightly since Red had shown up, and though the air remained chilly, the sun was bright and the skies were blue. All the snow from the great blizzard had melted. This, in addition to good food, had seemed to do wonders for Red's constitution. True to his promise, Red sped up and was soon running evenly with Umasi. By this point they were both breathing heavily, a fact that wasn't lost on either of them.

"Want . . . to slow . . . down?" Umasi suggested between breaths.

"Are you . . . getting . . . tired?"

"You're the one . . . that fainted . . . the other day," Umasi pointed out, causing Red's face to live up to his name.

"I just . . . had a few . . . too many drinks," Red insisted.

"Lightweight."

"Tortoise."

"Remember . . . the hare . . . took a break," Umasi pointed out.

"Good point," Red admitted, slowing down to a jog.

Umasi followed suit, and the two continued their trek through the empty streets at a slower pace. As they ran, Umasi cast a furtive glance over at his newfound friend. The amber-eyed vagrant looked quite civilized after just a day or two of baths and new clothes. His health and stamina had also improved noticeably during their runs, though he still complained about his painful appendix.

Umasi hadn't realized how much he missed human company until Red showed up. There was just something about being able to have open conversations that refreshed his spirit. Umasi could relate to this troubled vagrant. No matter how much dirt covered him, Umasi recognized that Red was a good person at heart. Of course, that raised an awkward question in Umasi's mind, one that he hadn't yet felt comfortable asking.

Umasi glanced over at Red, who seemed to be admiring the abandoned urban scenery. It was probably better to satisfy his curiosity now and get it out of the way.

"So, Red," Umasi said, "how did you end up becoming a vagrant? Why did you run away?"

Red blanched.

"I didn't run away," he said after a moment's pause. "I was forced out."

"By your parents?"

"No." Red shook his head. "By the Educators. I was expelled."

"Why?"

"For cheating," Red said darkly. "It was my fault. I deserved it. I was stupid."

"Did you just peek at someone else's test or something?"

"Nah. I let a friend peek at *my* tests for the entire term. My homework too. He would've been thrown out with a failure if I hadn't helped him. But the teacher eventually caught on, and the rest is history."

Red's voice was bitter as he relayed the story. Umasi glanced over at him. Cheating was one of the most vilified acts in the City. Any student found guilty of it, or even suspected of it, was lucky to avoid expulsion, and if they did the Educators made sure that word of their misdeeds would follow them like a curse.

But as Umasi dwelled upon Red's fate, he realized something. It was as if a ray of light had cut through the darkness the Educators had cast in order to illuminate the truth.

"Red," Umasi said, "you didn't do anything wrong."

Red turned to look at Umasi in surprise. "What?"

"Helping someone else at great risk to yourself, with no guarantee of a reward?" Umasi said. "That sounds more like generosity to me."

Red blinked at that.

"Generous or not, it's still a crime."

"It's a crime because the Educators say it is," Umasi said, "but who is the victim?"

"Well," Red said uncomfortably, "say someone who earned his grades alone applies for something and gets outdone by someone I helped. You have a victim there."

"Imagine that you help a needy friend get a job over the head of someone who tried alone," Umasi said. "Would you have done a wicked thing?"

"But that's not the same thing, tests are supposed to—"

"In both cases you have a victim of competition," Umasi said. "Should you really be condemned for helping a friend over an obstacle at great risk to yourself?"

Red had no answer to that, but jogged on in silence, apparently deep in thought.

"Risking your own neck to help someone when you *know* you could be punished and vilified for it," Umasi continued, "*that* shows spirit, the very thing that the Educators seek to break. They can only completely succeed when there is no selflessness like yours left to challenge them." Umasi turned to face Red. "Red, my father did you a great wrong, and I'm sorry that it landed you here."

"You know," Red began, "all these years the Educators had me convinced that I got what I deserved. But now I'm not so sure."

"Few people deserve what you've gone through," Umasi said, shaking his head. "It's all wrong. This entire City is wrong."

The two continued to jog in silence for several moments after that, the only noise their footfalls upon the bare asphalt.

"Yeah, well, enough about my debatable past," Red said. "What about you? You're just out here because of what your brother did, right? No matter how you look at it, you've been squeaky clean compared to me."

"My brother is guilty of enough crimes for the both of us." Umasi frowned. "The Educators may be wrong, but he's the farthest thing from right that there is. I could've stopped him before. I *should've* stopped him before. I didn't, and now every time he kills it's just as much my fault as it is his."

"Now, that's just stupid," Red said. "He's your *brother,* and from what you said you weren't nearly as strong back then as you are now. What were you supposed to do?"

"Tell someone. Fight him. Sabotage his efforts. Anything, really," Umasi said. "I was a coward. I was too afraid to even try."

"But that's all in the past now, huh?" Red said.

"That's right." Umasi nodded. "I'm not so weak anymore."

"Well, strength and fighting isn't everything," Red said. "Let's see how much faster you've gotten, shall we?"

Without warning Red launched into a sudden sprint, darting forward like a rocket. After a moment's pause, Umasi gave pursuit, his legs a blur as he struggled to catch up.

"That was a dirty trick, you cheater!" Umasi said with mock anger.

Red just laughed, and Umasi joined in. As they ran, neither of the two children could remember a time when their hearts had felt quite so light.

So, you must be Chris."

Chris licked his lips as he looked across the sterile table at his interrogator, a massive man with nearly shaven, graying red hair that he knew must be Rothenberg. A single bulb hung from the ceiling, illuminating them both, and Chris couldn't help but sweat under the vicious gaze of the towering Enforcer.

"I asked you a question, vagrant!" the man shouted, slamming a fist against the table.

"Yes, yes, I'm Chris!" Chris squeaked. "You . . . you're Rothenberg, right?"

"No," Rothenberg said in a dangerous voice. "To you, I am 'sir,' 'Chief Truancy Officer,' or 'Mr. Rothenberg,' got it?"

"Yes, sir, Mr. Rothenberg!"

This meeting was not off to the start that Chris had hoped for. They were currently in the District 14 Enforcer Station, a locale that Chris had frequented as a vagrant, and one that was conveniently close to the Truancy's hideout in District 15. He had managed to slip away while supposedly gathering materials from abandoned houses, and he knew that he wouldn't be missed for at least another hour. When he marched into the station, he had expected to be treated as a hero. Instead, he'd been hustled into a dark interrogation room by a group of special Enforcers who identified themselves as Rothenberg's team. Chris had quickly been joined by their redoubtable boss.

"So, Chris, when you called you mentioned that you had some interesting information for me," Rothenberg said. "Did you mean that you wanted to lead your little rat pack to the slaughter again?"

"No, sir," Chris said, excitement overtaking his fear. "Better."

"Let's hear it then," Rothenberg said, a note of eagerness in his voice.

"There're these kids, these crazy student dropouts," Chris said. "They . . . they're forming a rebellion against the Educators! And they've let me join them!"

Rothenberg stared. Then he laughed for a moment, before stopping abruptly and raising his fist again.

"Listen carefully boy," Rothenberg said, "I have no patience for lies."

"It's no lie, I swear it!" Chris insisted. "This clean kid came outta nowhere with guns and knives talking about a rebellion. He called it the 'Truancy.' He said his name was Z, I think it must be his initial or something."

"The leader's initial . . . is Z?" Rothenberg repeated.

"Yeah . . . does it mean something to you?" Chris asked.

"It might. What does this boy look like?"

"Uh, long dark hair, dark eyes, kinda yellowish skin," Chris said. "Talks like an adult or something, wears all black from what I've seen."

Rothenberg's fist moved, and Chris cringed before realizing that Rothenberg was pumping it in the air as if in triumph. Chris stared at the uncharacteristic display. Then, as if suddenly realizing how silly he must look, Rothenberg froze and brought himself back under control.

"So, Zen is playing rebel now, is he?" Rothenberg chortled. "That's cute."

"He—Zen, that is—calls it the Truancy," Chris said, mentally cataloguing what he knew must be Z's full name.

"I don't care what he calls anything," Rothenberg said impatiently. "Where is he now? This supposed leader?"

"He's set up a base in District 15," Chris said, "but, well, he's got a lot of guys around . . . and guns, and I think I heard them talking about bombs."

"They can talk about whatever they like." Rothenberg snorted. "I'll just send in a bunch of patrols to scare them off and grab the head brat."

"Sir, I think you should be a bit more careful," Chris said. "Both of the times I turned in my gang the Enforcers showed up with too few people and a bunch escaped. So maybe . . . maybe . . ." Chris faltered, seeing Rothenberg's eyes narrow.

"Watch who you criticize, boy," Rothenberg growled.

"Ye-yes, sir," Chris said, wilting under that gaze.

"But if you think that they're so dangerous, I don't see any reason not to go in full force," Rothenberg said, his tone brisk now. "I'll send in more than enough patrols to exterminate every vagrant in the City, but I'll need you to provide an opportunity for us to snatch that leader. I want him alive. Can you help with that?"

A genuine smile spread across Chris' face.

"I'd love to, sir."

"Excellent." Rothenberg handed Chris a cell phone. "My personal number is in there. When the time is right, let me know, and they'll never know what hit them. Now, you better get back to the other brats before they notice you're missing."

"Sir, there's . . . well . . . my payment?"

"Bring Zen to me alive and I'll set you up for life."

"In a living district?"

"In a living district," Rothenberg said distastefully. "Now get out of my sight."

Chris hastened to comply as the door to the room slid open on cue. Rothenberg remained in his seat for another minute, excitement coursing through his body. The vagrant's story about a rebellion had sounded insane at first, but Rothenberg realized that there *was* one boy who had managed to kill an Enforcer, right in front of him no less. Now the kid was actually trying to gather others to do the same. Rothenberg laughed. What foolishness. He knew where they were. Now he would simply wait for the ideal moment to move in, slaughter this ridiculous "Truancy," and return its lunatic leader to his father.

R ed raised his plank to block Umasi's, the two pieces of wood colliding with a dull *thunk*. Breaking the deadlock with brute force, Umasi gave a shove that sent Red staggering back. When they began this sparring match, Umasi had warned that he wouldn't be holding anything back. Even so, Red hadn't expected ferocity like this. Umasi was relentless, pressing the fight so aggressively that Red was almost convinced that Umasi was out to kill him.

Red's reflexes were good enough to parry the next attack, but before he could riposte, Umasi swung his board back again to slam painfully into Red's shin.

"Ouch!" Red yelped, hopping backwards on one foot.

Without pausing for a moment, Umasi lunged again, thrusting forward to catch Red right in the chest, shoving him backwards so that he fell flat on his butt. Sitting prone on the ground, Red gingerly rubbed his knee as Umasi brought his weapon to rest lightly on top of Red's head.

"Okay, okay, I give up," Red conceded as he dropped his own plank. "Man, if that's how you *practice* fighting, remind me never to make you mad."

"Sorry," Umasi said, suddenly looking embarrassed. "I may have overdone it a bit. Are you all right?"

"Yeah, I've been worse," Red said, standing up to highlight the point.

Satisfied, Umasi walked over to where two bottles of lemonade were cooling in a stubborn patch of snow that hadn't yet melted. He sat down and opened one for himself, then tossed the other to Red.

"So Umasi," Red said after taking a gulp, "what made you want to fight in the first place?"

Umasi looked troubled by the question, but answered anyway.

"I don't want to feel inactive," Umasi explained, "not after all I had to do as a vagrant."

"So your brother doesn't have anything to do with it?"

"I didn't say that."

"So you want to get strong and beat your brother," Red observed. "Is that for the good of the whole City, or is it about you?"

"Probably some of both," Umasi answered after a moment of thought.

"Well there's nothing wrong with self-satisfaction, but people don't forget nobility," Red said. "Just take a look at the vagrant ghost, for example."

"The *what*?" Umasi raised an eyebrow.

"The vagrant ghost," Red repeated. "She's a legend among the vagrants—or at least, I thought she was. Lots of people told me they've seen her, but I never believed any of it until I saw her myself."

"You did?" Umasi said skeptically.

"Yeah, the day I got away from your brother," Red said. "She saved me from a Truant who had a gun."

"What did she look like, then?" Umasi asked, examining Red's face as though expecting a joke.

"Pure white, all over," Red said. "Except the eyes; they were blue, but then they flashed red. And she had a chain, that's what she used to knock out the Truant, I think."

"How can a ghost knock anyone out?"

"Well I suppose the chain was solid enough," Red said thoughtfully. "She didn't touch him at all, of course, from what I saw. Then she disappeared."

"Even if you weren't hallucinating," Umasi said amusedly, "what's it got to do with nobility?"

"Oh, well, you know," Red said, "since she saved me I kind of assumed that she wanders the City trying to help people . . . or something like that. Why else would she stick around, on the streets of all places?"

"Maybe because she's not real?"

"Have it your way." Red shrugged. "If you stick around in the abandoned districts long enough, maybe you'll see her too. Back on topic; when are you actually going to stand up to your brother?"

"I don't know," Umasi said. "When I'm ready."

"If you ask me, I think you're ready now," Red said. "You're just too busy trying to convince yourself of it."

"What're you suggesting, then, that I go looking for him this very minute?" Umasi asked.

"Well I dunno about *that*," Red said, glancing up at the setting sun. "It's getting late, and I'm getting hungry. How about tomorrow?"

"Tomorrow?"

"Sure, why not?" Red replied. "From what you just showed me back there, you're damn ready to take on anyone one-on-one if it comes down to that."

Umasi hesitated for a moment, then looked over at where Red's weapon lay discarded and creased his brow.

"You might have a point," Umasi said. "But there's still the problem of finding him."

Red smiled. Finally, an opportunity for him to feel helpful.

"Well you see, about that . . ." Red began. "When your brother was giving his little speech, he did mention a little place where he was setting up headquarters."

"You mean . . ." Umasi suddenly sat up very straight.

"Yeah, I know where your brother and all of his buddies are." Red nodded. "Or at least the district where you can find them."

"Can you tell me how to get there?"

"Of course," Red replied with a grin. "And I'm coming too, whether you want me there or not."

Umasi stared at Red for a moment, and then a slow smile spread across his face.

"I haven't known you for all that long, Red, but it's been long enough for me to know that you're a good friend," Umasi said. "Thanks."

Red felt color rushing to his cheeks. It was kind of embarrassing, but so meaningful, being called a friend after having lived for so long without any.

"I'm honored" was all he could say.

You're certain of this?" Zen asked as he gazed out the flower-shop show window.

"Completely," Gabriel nodded. "He's working with the Enforcers, all right, and from what I overheard when he was on the phone last night, he's been doing it for a while."

"I don't doubt it, but I'd like to be sure before I act," Zen said. "You say he actually entered an Enforcer station?"

"No mistake there. I even got a look at the guys he'd been meeting when they came out after him. Hell, I recognized one of them. The huge bastard with red hair, Rothenberg. I've seen him on the news before."

"Rothenberg? Interesting," Zen mused. "I can only conclude that my dear father was desperate enough to send that mutt out to retrieve me."

"So what are you gonna do about all this?" Gabriel demanded. "The Enforcers might be here any minute now."

"I doubt it." Zen shook his head.

"But how can you be sure?" Gabriel pressed.

"I would in fact be worried about Rothenberg barging in here today," Zen allowed, "*if* I didn't believe that he would wait on Chris' word."

"So what do we do?" Gabriel asked. "Take Chris into custody now?"

"No, Gabriel, our friend Chris has offered us a unique and valuable opportunity," Zen said with a faint smile. "We can turn this to our advantage. This is the chance I've been waiting for to make our debut to the Enforcers."

Gabriel looked at Zen strangely. "I'm not following."

"It's rather simple, really," Zen explained. "I will now be able to dictate when and where we fight, and be certain that the Enforcers will show up to fall into the trap."

"How?"

In response, Zen pointed outside the window. Gabriel looked out and spotted Chris talking with another former vagrant.

"You're going to feed him false info," Gabriel realized.

"That's right. I'll provide the Enforcers with an opportunity that they can't resist." Zen nodded. "Would you be so good as to bring Chris to me?"

Gabriel hastened to comply, and moments later Chris stood before Zen, a look of anticipation on his face.

"You wanted to see me?" Chris said.

"That I did," Zen agreed, his voice pleasant. "I've come to believe that the reason you've not been fitting in so well is that I've been giving you unsuitable tasks. However, I think I've finally found a job that fits you—something simple, but very important. You see, tomorrow I will personally be moving to a location on the edge of this district, where I hope to establish our permanent Truancy headquarters."

"So what do I do?" Chris asked.

"You'll be leading my personal bodyguards," Zen said. "It won't be too much work, I assure you—there'll be no more than four for you to manage."

"Only four guards?" Chris repeated, unable to keep the eagerness from his voice.

"I want to travel inconspicuously," Zen explained. "Any more than that and we might attract attention. We're still no match for the Enforcers, you see. It'd be a disaster if even just one patrol spotted us."

"And we wouldn't want that, of course," Chris said, licking his lips. "Will I get paid for this?"

"Oh yes, I'll give you double what you've already received as soon as we arrive safely at our destination," Zen said. "Does that sound good to you?"

"Yeah," Chris nodded, "sounds great. I'll do a *very* good job tomorrow, promise. Where exactly are we going again?"

Zen provided the location, and shortly afterwards Chris left the flower shop, an enormous grin plastered on his face. Through the window Zen could see Gabriel shoot Chris a nasty glare before returning into the shop.

"How did it go?" Gabriel asked.

"Perfectly," Zen replied, all traces of his smile gone. "We've got work to do now. I want you to *discreetly* pass along some very special orders to every combat-ready Truant we have. Here's what needs to be done . . ."

Fifteen minutes later, Gabriel exited the flower shop, intent on his mission. Zen watched for a moment, then turned to Noni, who had made a habit of sitting atop the crates in a corner of the shop, motionless and soundless like a shadow.

"This is how you let enemies set the very traps they fall into, Noni," Zen explained as he gestured vaguely out the window. "Do you understand?"

Noni nodded, and Zen smiled.

"So, how've you been doing with those darts?"

In response, Noni seized one from her side and hurled it across the room towards the target, where it cleanly struck the bull's-eye.

20

THE WAR BEGINS

A n excellent job, Chris," Zen said as he held out a thick wad of bills. "I'm glad that our journey was uneventful."

"It was nothing. The Enforcers don't patrol this district much anyway," Chris said as he took the money.

Chris could barely contain his elation. Contrary to what he had said, he knew that no less than ten Enforcer patrol squads were on their way to surround them right now—much more than enough to subdue the four Truants and their leader. Everything was going perfectly according to plan. Chris made sure to tell the Enforcers to wait until they reached this point to attack, so he had even been able to collect his reward from Zen.

Chris wondered why Rothenberg was so determined to capture the boy alive. He was certainly nothing special; the dimwitted fool had no idea what was about to happen to him, and here he was, *paying* Chris to sell him out. The very idea alone sent shivers of joy running down Chris' spine.

"Well now, since I'm in charge of the guards, I think that they should all have a good look around for danger, just in case," Chris suggested, glancing over at Zen for approval. "I'll stay here, though, of course."

"It's your call," Zen said lazily. "You *are* in charge, after all."

"Go on, scram," Chris said, shooing the other Truants away. "Check out the buildings or other streets or something."

As soon as the other Truants disappeared from sight, Chris glanced over at Zen, who seemed to be admiring a building over to the side. Chris grinned. This would be easier than he thought. Drawing a pistol out from the pocket in which he had stowed it after Zen gave it to him at the start of their trek, Chris quietly approached Zen from behind.

Chuckling slightly at the irony of using a weapon Zen had provided against Zen himself, Chris lunged, seizing Zen in a headlock with one arm while he brought his pistol to the side of the boy's head with the other.

"What're you doing, Chris?" Zen asked, sounding much calmer than Chris had expected him to.

"Don't ask, I don't owe you any explanations," Chris spat. "The Enforcers are on their way. Just sit tight and don't make any trouble, and I won't have to kill you here."

"So, you sold us out," Zen observed.

"Sold you out?" Chris laughed. "Sorry to break it to you kid, but you're a joke. Rebelling against the adults? It's ridiculous, you can't possibly think that anyone believes in that nonsense. *Anyone* would sell you out, if they had the chance and the right price."

"That's really what you think, is it?" Zen asked mildly.

"Yeah, it is," Chris said. "Where do you think everyone else is? They'll cut and run the moment they hear the sirens. It's over. This silly game is *over.*"

"Well, I don't know about that," Zen said, sounding almost amused. "There seem to still be a few players left."

It was then that Chris saw them. Truants, emerging from their hiding places in dark alleys, empty buildings, even a manhole. The four body-guards had also returned, and altogether there couldn't have been less than two dozen armed Truants standing there, surrounding him, glaring at him with grim expressions. Chris felt a shiver travel down his spine as he spotted Noni among them, her icy blue eyes seeming to pierce right through him. Chris quickly forced a laugh and tightened his grip on the trigger.

"You're all fools!" Chris shouted at the silent Truants. "The Enforcers are going to slaughter you if you don't drop those weapons! Stop, got it? Stop!"

His words didn't seem to impress the Truants at all. Instead they began to close in on him.

"Stop! I'll shoot your leader!" Chris threatened. "I mean it, stop!"

Zen laughed, and Chris' blood ran cold.

"By the way, Chris, I believe I forgot to mention that the gun I gave you isn't loaded."

Chris froze, then pulled the trigger in desperation. Nothing happened. Frantic now, Chris pulled it again and again, to no avail. Zen smiled, then drove his elbow backwards into Chris's gut, knocking the traitorous Truant backwards and to the ground.

"How did you know?" Chris raged. "Who told you?"

"You're entirely too predictable, my friend, and far too greedy for your own good," Zen said as the Truants closed in on Chris. "Take this filth somewhere where he won't be able to embarrass us any further, and then dispose of him."

Gabriel and Frank stepped forward to drag the traitor off, looks of intense satisfaction on both their faces. As he was taken away, Chris shouted "Stop! Just stop!" at the top of his lungs until Frank punched him in the face, silencing him. Moments after the three were out of sight, a single gunshot rang out, marking a truly ignominious death. The ugly display concluded, Zen turned around to face the rest of the gathered Truants.

"The Enforcers will be here any minute now," Zen warned. "How are the upper preparations?"

"Everyone is in place as you specified," the Truant named Amal said. "We're on the rooftops along every possible street they can come at us from."

"Ground support?" Zen asked.

"Aaron's explosive traps are set and we're all in place."

"Very well then," Zen said, rubbing his hands together as sirens suddenly began to sound from nearby. "Let us prepare to greet our guests."

The Truants tensed, gripping their weapons tightly. Zen smiled confidently. Now was the moment of truth.

"At last, our war is about to begin."

Heh, that definitely looks like trouble," Red said, leaning around the corner of the alley as a volley of gunshots rang out. "Maybe following the sirens wasn't such a good idea after all."

"I can't believe things have gotten this bad," Umasi muttered as another explosion boomed in the distance. "It's like a war zone down here."

"That's exactly what it is," Red agreed. "But I gotta hand it to your brother—he sure caught those Enforcers with their pants around their ankles."

His curiosity piqued, Umasi peered out from behind the cover of the alley, and caught a glimpse of a flaming Enforcer patrol car belching black smoke as uniformed bodies lay scattered across the ground. One struggled to rise, but more loud gunshots sounded, and he dropped back down, completely motionless. The sight made Umasi sick, and he withdrew his head with disgust on his face.

"This . . . this is just *senseless*," Umasi breathed in disbelief. "How can he do this?"

"Best ask him yourself, eh?" Red said, trying not to pay too much attention to what was going on not too far from where they sat. He had seen plenty of death and murder in his time, and yet this *still* disturbed him.

"Yeah, but where is he?" Umasi muttered. "He could be anywhere in this mess. He might not even be here at all—these could just be some of his cronies."

"This is his district," Red said. "I'm sure he'd defend it himself, right?"

"I suppose he's that kind of guy," Umasi allowed as another explosion and some distant screams reached his ears. "But that doesn't help us find him."

"Maybe we should split up," Red suggested. "We'll find him faster if we both look in different places."

"It's too dangerous." Umasi shook his head. "There might be some trigger-happy Truants out there, and the Enforcers will *definitely* shoot you on sight."

"You can take care of yourself, and I've been giving Enforcers the slip for years," Red said. "I've spent too much time running away from things. Now maybe I can do some good. I mean, your brother would hear me out before shooting me, right?"

"I . . . don't think he'd kill an unarmed kid without asking questions," Umasi admitted.

"Then what's the problem?" Red asked.

Umasi thought about it for a moment, and then nodded.

"All right, let's go," Umasi said. "At this rate we're going have to stop him as soon as possible."

"Good luck!" Umasi heard Red calling as he plunged down another alley.

Steeling himself for what was to come, Umasi proceeded down a different alleyway, hoping to circumvent the entire battlefield. The passage he chose was dark and cramped, and with each explosion bits of debris would shake loose from the long-abandoned buildings. Occasionally he was able to catch glimpses of what was going on through passages that led to the street, and none of what he saw was pretty. From what he could gather, the Enforcers had attempted to surround the Truancy on all slides, dividing up their forces in the process. Apparently the Truants had placed explosives on the roads to blow up the cars as the Truants picked off any survivors. Umasi was beginning to wonder where all the Truants were when he turned a corner and abruptly found himself facing one who was busy shooting down a side alley.

"Hey, who're—" the Truant began, noticing Umasi.

He never finished the question. Umasi lunged, tackling the boy to the ground before he could bring his weapon to bear. He punched the Truant between the eyes, stunning him. Just in case, Umasi grabbed the pistol and tossed it into a nearby garbage can. Footsteps echoed behind him as more Truants came to investigate the disturbance. Umasi set off at a run, diving around an alley corner as soon as he got the chance. When the footsteps drew close, Umasi sprang out from his hiding place, tripping one Truant and slamming his elbow into the oncoming face of another.

"You ain't one of us!" the Truant cried as he stumbled backwards, clutching his face.

"Correct," Umasi agreed, punching him in the stomach.

"You with the Enforcers?" the other Truant demanded from the ground.

"Nah," Umasi said, turning to face the questioner. "I'm just a maverick."

In the narrow and gloomy alley, neither of the Truants were willing to use their guns for fear of hitting each other. Instead, the one who'd tripped scrambled back to his feet, seizing a loose brick as he rose. Umasi ducked as the Truant attempted to swing the brick at him, and then punched the Truant in the belly, causing him to double over. Umasi seized the boy's shoulder with one hand, and then shoved his back with the other, sending him flying forward into his comrade. At that moment, the first Truant Umasi had encountered came into view, apparently having regained consciousness. The boy jumped over his fallen allies, and Umasi braced himself for the attack.

Just then another massive explosion shook the ground, and this time there was a great crumbling sound from above. In spite of themselves, Umasi and the Truants looked up just in time to see a number of bricks shake loose.

"Oh shi—" one of the Truants began, just before a brick struck him on the head.

Umasi leapt backwards, avoiding the rest of the masonry as it came tumbling down onto the screaming Truants. For a moment Umasi feared that they might be dead, but one by one they began to stir and groan under the bricks. Satisfied, Umasi turned to proceed down the passage.

But as Umasi rounded another corner, he found himself staring at a dead end. Gritting his teeth, he realized that he didn't have any other choice; he'd have to brave the battle in the streets if he wanted to have any hope of finding Zen. Backtracking, Umasi leapt forwards just as a particularly deafening explosion went off. A moment later, Umasi's eyes widened as an Enforcer car was sent flying through the air towards him, crash-landing against the opening he'd been approaching. It burst into flames that leapt out towards Umasi, who quickly retreated as he felt the heat on his face, his path thoroughly blocked.

Running back to the next closest side alley, Umasi found this one blessedly free of flaming vehicles. He plunged out into the open, blinking for a moment as he adjusted to the sudden light, and then found himself standing in the midst of utter chaos. Wreckages of other cars already littered the streets, huge plumes of smoke billowing out from their metal carcasses. Enforcers had taken cover behind these smoking wrecks, firing at Truants who were ducking in and out of alleys and building windows. Without hesitation Umasi darted towards a nearby wreck, coughing as he was enveloped by its fumes. As he slipped behind the car, hoping to use it as cover as he advanced, he found himself crouching beside a terrified and coughing Enforcer.

"Wh-who are you kids?" the Enforcer sputtered at Umasi, groping around on the ground for his fallen pistol.

"Oh, I'm not with them," Umasi said, gesturing in the Truants' direction.

"Y-you're not?"

"No." Umasi shook his head, and for a moment the Enforcer looked hopeful. "But I'm not with you people either," Umasi added apologetically.

With that, Umasi shoved the man to the ground and kicked him in the temple. Seizing the pistol that lay a few feet away, Umasi disposed of the weapon inside the smoking car. Then a shot rang out, and Umasi could feel the wind as a bullet passed right by his ear. Turning to see a large silhouette advancing upon him through the smoke, Umasi seized the fallen Enforcer's truncheon and launched himself over the car and to the safety of its other side in one fluid motion.

More shots rang out, but only slammed into the car as Umasi crouched behind it. As the silhouette came into view around the corner of the wreck, Umasi lunged, swinging the truncheon at the figure's head before it got a chance to see him in the smoke. The man staggered back, and Umasi swung again, this time hitting a kneecap, causing his victim, who Umasi could now see was a uniformed Enforcer, to fall to the ground. Then Umasi was off like a bullet, dashing out of the smoke cloud and over to the next car.

Behind him he heard an explosion go off, but not like any of the ones the Truancy had set off. Umasi looked over his shoulder and saw that the car he had just fled had combusted, the Enforcer apparently having fired a stray shot into its gas tank. Hoping that the man was okay in spite of everything, Umasi dived behind the next patrol car, this one remarkably intact despite having crashed into a fire hydrant. The hydrant was spraying water high into the air, causing a faint rainbow effect to cut through the smoke and air. Umasi peered through the car window, and grimly realized that its occupants had been either knocked out or killed by the crash.

By now Umasi had reached the corner of an intersection, and a moment later another Enforcer patrol car came into sight from a perpendicular street. Tires screeching, it swerved dangerously before coming to a halt right before the intersection. Two Enforcers tumbled out of it and begin firing upwards, their shots quickly returned as Umasi realized the Truants must have soldiers on the rooftops. For a moment it looked like a stalemate as neither Truant nor Enforcer was able to hit the other. Then Umasi saw an explosion rock a building right above the Enforcers, and large chunks of masonry fell down like a brick avalanche, burying the Enforcers and their car. Umasi knew there would be no survivors under that mess, and despite his horror he felt a sort of morbid admiration for the Truancy's effective tactics.

Just then, an out-of-control patrol car began charging down the street, swerving haphazardly. Umasi leapt out of the way just in time as it slammed into the other Enforcer car he'd been crouching behind. More shots rang out. Umasi dashed around the street corner and into another smoke cloud. He knew that if Zen was here, he had to be close; the gunshots had become increasingly rapid as he got deeper in. In the middle of the smoke cloud, Umasi suddenly saw two dark figures struggling hand-to-hand. Moving in closer, he saw that it was an Enforcer swinging his truncheon at a Truant, who was dodging nimbly.

Umasi darted in and swung his own truncheon, slamming it into the back of the Enforcer's head. The Enforcer stumbled forward, and the Truant kicked the man in the face, sending him sprawling on the ground. Before the Truant could utter his thanks, Umasi swung at him too, knocking the boy upside the head. The boy staggered back, dazed, and Umasi seized the opportunity to sweep the Truant's legs from under him. Umasi then tossed the truncheon aside as he continued running, leaving both Enforcer and Truant groaning on the ground behind him.

Umasi found himself close to another alley as he emerged from the smoke. Shaking his head in an attempt to clear the ringing from his ears, Umasi ran forward to the cover of the alley. As he slipped in, he suddenly stopped short, feeling a jolt of stunned elation. There, standing in the alley with a smoking gun, was Zen.

Umasi's elation was swiftly replaced by horror, and his heart nearly stopped as he realized what exactly it was that Zen was standing over.

Rothenberg stared in disbelief at the receiver as another frantic voice on the radio turned to static. His coffee lay spilled on the ground some distance away as he grasped his radio in one hand and a Truant's neck in the other. The boy had tried to shoot at him from an alley, but Rothenberg's aim had not deteriorated since his promotion. He'd shot the kid in the arm and then captured him easily. Yet Rothenberg now felt paralyzed, unable to think about anything else except how mad the world had suddenly become.

Rothenberg had lagged behind as the rest of his small task force had moved in to surround the Mayor's son and his handful of supposed "bodyguards." The boy Chris had promised an easy pickup; the four guards would be scattered, and their leader held at gunpoint until they arrived. Rothenberg had almost gone ahead in person, but had decided not to when the arrest would be so routine, so easy.

Too easy, apparently.

Rothenberg cursed aloud and squeezed his captive's neck tighter, causing the unfortunate boy to sputter pathetically.

"What is this?" Rothenberg snarled at the child. "What do you brats think you're playing at?"

"We're . . . Truants . . . and you're . . . going to die," the boy choked out, and then spat in Rothenberg's face.

Rothenberg roared in outrage, dropping his radio and wringing the rebel's neck like a stuffed animal. Several moments later, Rothenberg dropped the limp body to the ground as a subordinate Enforcer ran up to him, looking pale and horrified.

"What's going on?" Rothenberg demanded. "What the *hell* is going on?"

"It's the task force, sir," the Enforcer explained. "The patrols that went ahead apparently all set off some sort of explosives while driving to the pickup point."

"Well, what do the survivors have to say for themselves?" Rothenberg asked menacingly.

"There don't seem to be any survivors, sir," the Enforcer said. "Lots of gunshots and more explosions, but we can't raise anyone on the radio anymore."

"Dammit!" Rothenberg kicked the dead boy's body in frustration.

"If I may suggest something, sir," the Enforcer said, "I think we should scour the rest of District 15. We might catch some of them as they return to their base, and the informant did say they'd holed up somewhere in District 15 for now."

"No, you idiot!" Rothenberg raged, kicking the body again. "Don't you see? It was a trick, that brat Chris was playing us all along. Holed up in District 15—hah! Who knows what other nasty surprises they've planted there for us? They just lured us out here so that they could ambush us! The boy's info was phony from the start!"

"If you say so, sir," the Enforcer said. "What should we tell the Mayor?"

"Nothing," Rothenberg snapped. "Keep this quiet for as long as you can, I'll talk to him myself when I have to. Now get out of my sight."

With that, Rothenberg stormed back to his patrol car and slammed the door shut, breathing heavily in his fury. He had been made a fool of today, by kids, no less. Nothing could have enraged him more than that. A dark expression gathered on his face as he ran a large hand over his bristly head. He might have lost this one, but he'd even the score, no matter how many dead children it took.

Zen sighed and fired another shot into an Enforcer's motionless body, just to be sure. Things had gotten a little hairier than he'd anticipated. He had not expected the Enforcers to be able to penetrate this far through their explosive traps, but from what he'd seen, things had gone well for the Truancy nonetheless. He had not seen any Truants fall, though Zen knew that there would have to be a casualty or two when the smoke cleared.

Having sent Noni up to scout out the battle from a rooftop above, Zen had battled the two Enforcers that had reached him all alone. All the other Truants had stuck to their assigned positions, where Zen believed they would be more effective. He was on high alert, having just concluded a fierce battle, and so when he heard footsteps approaching him from behind he didn't hesitate. Acting on instinct, Zen spun around and fired. The gunshot rang throughout the alley, and a figure crumpled to the ground.

But as Zen bent over to inspect his victim, he was dismayed to see that it wasn't an Enforcer, but an unarmed boy he didn't recognize. He was sure it wasn't a Truant, whose faces he all knew by now. Perhaps it was just a vagrant that had been in the wrong place at the wrong time. Twinges of guilt wormed their way through Zen's conscience, but he quickly suppressed them. He couldn't afford to get emotional now, not at such a crucial juncture. It had been an accident. Unfortunate, but not intentional. Reassuring himself with those thoughts, Zen straightened back up.

And saw Umasi staring at him with wide-eyed shock.

Slowly, disbelievingly, Umasi crouched, staring at his fallen friend. Red still stubbornly clung to life, his chest heaving up and down, but there was a lot of blood, and Umasi knew he was doomed. With one hand, Umasi turned Red's head to face him, and found that Red's eyes were still open as he breathed in pained gasps.

"It's all right . . ." Red breathed, bringing a hand to his appendix. "Hit me here . . . it hurts . . . less . . . now . . ."

Red's voice trailed off feebly, and Umasi numbly looked at Red's wound, which was too high to have actually struck the appendix. Still, Umasi couldn't find the words to correct him. He couldn't find any words at all. He could only watch as, one increasingly ragged gasp at a time, Red's life faded out there in the alley, right before Umasi's eyes.

Silently, Umasi rose, eyes fixed on the boy he'd known for only a few days, and yet one he counted as his only friend. He might've stayed there in shock forever, if Zen had not spoken up at that moment.

"He was collateral damage," Zen said coldly. "Nothing mo—"

Umasi's fist slammed into Zen's chest. Zen's eyes widened in shock, the wind completely knocked out of him. The next thing he knew, Umasi's foot connected with his gut, shoving him backwards, leaving him sprawling on the ground. Zen looked up at Umasi and froze, suddenly feeling true terror for the first time in years.

Zen had never seen his brother like this before. Umasi's face was contorted with rage, his dark eyes shining with fury as he advanced upon Zen's helpless form. Zen quickly scrambled to his feet, throwing a quick punch at his oncoming assailant, only to have his wrist seized effortlessly. Before Zen could move, Umasi lunged forward headfirst, slamming his forehead into Zen's face.

Zen crashed against the brick wall behind him, his nose bleeding as Umasi brought his knee forcefully up to collide with Zen's ribs. Zen gasped in disbelief and pain as Umasi proceeded to punch him repeatedly in the belly. As he wheezed, Umasi seized Zen by the neck and threw him to the side. Winded, Zen landed on the ground clutching his gut.

Looking around the alley, Umasi spotted a rusted crowbar lying on the ground. He seized the weapon and spun around with grim determination, prepared to finish his brother once and for all . . .

And suddenly found himself staring into a pair of wide, icy, pleading eyes.

"Get out of the way," Umasi said in a low, dangerous tone.

Though the girl who stood before him had a black scarf wrapped around her lower face, Umasi recognized her as the one Zen had called Noni when they met at the pier. She refused to budge, staring at Umasi with those disturbing blue eyes. He growled menacingly, raising the crowbar above his head. The girl flinched slightly, though she didn't move an inch.

"GET OUT OF THE WAY!" Umasi roared.

In response, Noni stretched her arms out to either side, shielding Zen. Zen looked completely thunderstruck as he stared up at the girl that had interposed herself between him and his brother. Umasi snarled with frustration and stepped to the side, trying to get around Noni. She matched his movement, always placing herself between him and Zen no matter where he moved.

Finally, Umasi raised the crowbar again in aggravation and brought it swinging down at the stubborn girl.

"Noni, move!" Zen shouted.

She didn't listen, shutting her eyes as she waited for the blow.

It didn't come. Opening her eyes, she saw the scary boy breathing heavily as he glared at her, the crowbar quivering an inch from her head. Then tears began running down the boy's face, and he dropped his weapon to the ground where it clattered loudly. Crying quietly now, he walked over to where the dead child now lay in a pool of his own blood, and gently lifted the body and slung it over his shoulder.

Ignoring the blood spilling all over his clothes, Umasi spun around and walked out of the alley, his shoulders still heaving with silent sobs as he went. Noni did not lower her arms until he was safely out of sight.

21

Umasi opened the box of matches with shaking hands. Everything was ready, at last, yet he couldn't bring himself to finish it. Red had been a friend when he had none, the only one to stand by him as he confronted his own brother. But Umasi had failed in the end, and his friend had died for nothing at all. Gazing over the edge of the pit that he had dug in the soil of an abandoned construction site, Umasi looked down at the body that lay within, resting atop a neat pile of planks that he had arranged.

There should have been a funeral procession, Umasi thought, or an acknowledgment of some sort. But there had been nothing for Red. No one knew, and no one cared that this particular life had been lost that day. No one except Umasi, who had carried the body back alone, through empty streets, under lonely bridges, until he had finally returned to District 19, his home.

Few vagrants ever died with someone to mourn them. Red, at least, would have one person see to his funeral. Umasi knew that parting words were appropriate, but he struggled to find some that fit. In the end, he decided upon the simplest.

"I'm sorry," Umasi murmured as he looked down at the friend he had failed. "I know that you wouldn't have blamed me, but I'm sorry."

With that, Umasi solemnly lit a match and tossed it down into the pit, where it quickly ignited the gasoline that he'd poured over the wood. Soon all of it was ablaze, tongues of flame dancing upwards, slicing through the darkness, sending sparks flying upwards to join the stars. Umasi, however, continued only to gaze down into the heart of the fire and the body that burned within it.

Soon black plumes of smoke began to rise, and a horrible smell—acrid yet sweet—reached Umasi's nostrils. He didn't flinch—not from the stench, or from the heat that seared his skin, or the smoke that stung his eyes. He remained perfectly motionless until the last of the flames had died down, leaving only glowing embers and a pile of ash.

Umasi sighed, and the cool wind seemed to sigh with him. He had thought that cremating the body was the best thing to do. He wasn't sure if Red would've minded rats gnawing at his corpse, but Umasi hadn't been able to bear that thought. Now that it was over Umasi had decided to bury the pyre anyway.

Umasi picked up a shovel and cast the first dirt down into the bottom of the pit. The embers still flickered at him as he worked, but he paid them no mind, as his was elsewhere. He should have felt sadness. All he could find was anger. He wanted nothing more than to swear on that grave that he would put an end to Zen, that he would make sure that no one in the City would ever have to feel such anger again. His brother had truly become a monster, a murderer, and there was no longer any question of reasoning with him.

And yet Umasi *hadn't* killed Zen. Not even when he had the chance, not even in the moment of his greatest fury. It had been the girl with the icy eyes who had cooled his madness that day, when she had been prepared to give her life for Zen's. But Umasi had had time to think about the battle he had witnessed, the madness that he had traveled through. Beliefs he had claimed to hold for years had been tempered in the heat of battle, and Umasi knew now that he was sick of death. That if he faced Zen again, alone, nothing was likely to change.

Killing was a step he wasn't prepared to take, perhaps a step that he would never be prepared to take. Perhaps Zen would truly be unstoppable. Zen was the war bringer, and Umasi, being the pacifist, was in no position to stand in his way.

"Too bad, Red," Umasi said as the light of the remaining embers cast his face into shadow. "I won't be avenging you after all."

With that, Umasi spun around and returned to his apartment, the last of his anger dissipating as he lit the stove and began brewing lemonade.

Rothenberg sipped halfheartedly at his mug of coffee, not enjoying it in the least. He really was in a foul mood.

This was not an uncommon occurrence. Rothenberg's fickle temper was as legendary as any of his other traits, and ordinarily people would just avoid him, knowing that he'd cool off soon enough. But today hadn't been an ordinary day, and his disposition was uncommonly foul. It wouldn't have been so bad if his hopes for the day hadn't been so high, but having come so close to his goal only to be humiliated instead had plunged him into a truly dangerous mood.

And Rothenberg's mood was usually a good indicator of how long some poor kid had left to live.

"I'm going out," Rothenberg announced to the rest of Enforcer Headquarters as he slammed his coffee down onto a desk.

"Where exactly are you going, sir?" one man asked.

"Hunting vagrants," Rothenberg said as he stood up and went for his coat, "and then I'm going home."

Nearly everyone in the room shivered at that pronouncement. Ever since Rothenberg had been given unlimited power among the Enforcers, rumors had gone around about Rothenberg's thoughts on parenthood.

"But, sir, what about the investigation?" an Enforcer asked.

"We've already doubled the patrols and planned thorough sweeps of all abandoned districts," Rothenberg muttered as he slid his coat on. "That's enough for today, it's not like there's anything else we can do."

"Shouldn't we at least be running down some leads or som—"

"WHAT LEADS?" Rothenberg roared. "WE'VE GOT NOTHING! NOTHING AT ALL!"

The whole room was silent. This kind of behavior had hardly ever been seen at Enforcer Headquarters, and it had certainly never been displayed by a commanding officer before.

"Our best lead led to a trap, and all we've got to show for weeks of effort are a bunch of wrecked cars and dead men," Rothenberg continued. "The sweeps begin tomorrow, and if it's war they want it's war they'll get, but until then I've got vagrants to deal with."

More silence. The Enforcers all knew that when Rothenberg worked himself up into a frenzy he could go out on patrol all night long without sleep. One bold Enforcer took a deep breath and opened his mouth to speak, but Rothenberg quickly cut him off.

"Save your breath," Rothenberg snarled. "Not even the Mayor could get me to stay here now."

Just then, another Enforcer burst into the room, interrupting the exchange as he panted, clutching a cordless phone.

"Sir!" The Enforcer saluted, holding out the phone. "It's the Mayor. He wants to talk to you. He says it's urgent."

Rothenberg shut his eyes and willed himself not to start smashing things in frustration. He could *feel* his subordinates silently laughing at him. Suppressing a snarl, Rothenberg snatched the phone out of the other Enforcer's hand and brought it up to his ear.

"Hello?" Rothenberg said.

"Mr. Rothenberg," the Mayor greeted coldly. "It's been a while since you've bothered to update me on your search."

"There hasn't been all that much to report, sir," Rothenberg lied, shooting glances around the room as if daring someone to contradict him. "We've been running down a few leads, but we don't have a location yet."

"Is that so?" the Mayor mused. "Then I suppose you can explain the disturbance today in District 15?"

Rothenberg swore under his breath. How had the Mayor found out so quickly?

"An exaggerated case of friendly fire," Rothenberg said through gritted teeth. "The boy armed a few starving vagrants, and the Enforcers got trigger-happy."

"And that would explain all the Enforcer patrol cars that were destroyed?"

Rothenberg grimaced.

"I don't know what to tell you, sir," he said at last.

"How about the truth?" the Mayor suggested coldly.

There followed an uncomfortable silence as Rothenberg was rendered speechless, sweat beginning to run down his neck. When the Mayor spoke up again, his voice had a dangerous edge that hadn't been there before.

"I am not pleased with you, Rothenberg," the Mayor said. "Let me make it clear now that I don't buy any of your excuses. Luckily for you, I'm not so interested in the truth. In fact, I don't even *want* to know what exactly happened today."

"Thank you, sir."

"I'm not finished," the Mayor snapped. "What I *am* interested in, and what you've failed to do, is see my sons safely returned home. I will be sending one of my aides to keep an eye on your progress. You have three more weeks, Rothenberg, and be glad that I'm being that generous."

With that, the Mayor hung up, leaving Rothenberg clutching his receiver so tightly that his knuckles turned white. Rothenberg glanced around at the other Enforcers, all of whom were looking at him expectantly. Rothenberg let out a deep rumbling sigh and clenched his fists.

"All right," Rothenberg said, "our workday's been extended a few hours. Let's get back to it."

*Z*en stood in the center of the flower shop, under the single lightbulb that was all that cut through the darkness of the night. Though he was not the tallest Truant present, he seemed to tower over all the others as he rapidly issued orders. Despite their victory, there had been little time for celebration. Now that the conflict had started in earnest, Zen had no doubt that the Enforcers would be stepping up their operations, and that the Truancy would have to match them to survive. As he finished discussing their stock of explosives with Aaron, Zen turned to give Gabriel a new assignment, stubbornly ignoring the injuries he had sustained at the hands of his brother. Zen had resolved not to think about *those* until he'd done what needed to be done.

"Who is he, exactly?" Gabriel asked as he looked down at the photograph that Zen had presented.

"He's called Ralph, but his name isn't important. What's more significant is that he's *technically* the Chief of the Enforcers," Zen said.

"Technically?"

"I've done a little investigation, and it seems that our notorious friend Rothenberg has been temporarily given complete control over the Enforcers to aid him in his . . . search," Zen explained. "That would create a conflict at the highest level of command, and *that* simply won't do for a functioning organization. I can only presume that the Mayor has ordered Ralph to step aside to allow Rothenberg to pursue his search. That would explain his recently acquired habits, at any rate."

"What habits?"

"He tends to frequent one particular bar in District 9 these days," Zen said. "It seems that he's taken to drowning his woes in drink. Having his power stripped has not agreed with him."

"So that's why you want us to take him out in District 9," Gabriel observed.

"Exactly." Zen nodded. "When he stumbles out in his usual stupor, he'll hardly be in any condition to make a fuss. Make sure that there are no witnesses, and then take him out."

"This guy hasn't done anything to us," Gabriel said uncomfortably. "I haven't heard of him ever killing anyone."

"Don't go soft on me, Gabriel," Zen said sharply. "It was by this man's hand that Rothenberg was promoted into a position to slaughter the vagrants. Ralph knew the type of man Rothenberg was. He just hired him to do the bloody work he didn't want to take responsibility for himself."

Gabriel frowned. It seemed that no one was truly innocent in this City.

"All right," Gabriel conceded. "But why not go after Rothenberg himself?"

"Several reasons," Zen said. "Firstly, while he is not quite stupid, he does have the fatal flaws of overconfidence and underestimation. He keeps expecting frightened runaways, not an armed rebellion. Consequently, he can only bungle to our advantage until, perhaps, he is forced to face reality.

"Secondly, he's much more dangerous than the real Chief at present. Aside from his considerable Enforcer protection, he is renowned for his own physical prowess and marksmanship. I caught him by surprise once, but were he to be cornered alone again, it would take someone of extraordinary cunning and brutality to match Rothenberg," Zen said. "Finally, he's notoriously unpredictable. He follows no exploitable patterns. He rarely even goes home, except to beat his son."

Gabriel grimaced at that final pronouncement.

"I've already provided the details and the names of individuals you'll be working with," Zen said. "This will be an easy operation, but also an important one. The Enforcers will learn that they are not safe even when off-duty. If you have no more questions, you may go."

Gabriel nodded again and threw a quick salute—not because he was required to, but out of genuine respect—and then spun around and left the flower shop. Barely taking time to catch his breath, Zen turned to address a waiting Frank.

"Frank, you and the other former vagrants know the abandoned districts better than any of the other Truants," Zen said, to which Frank nodded. "Therefore, this most important assignment will fall to you. The Truancy's future success depends on turning the City's abandoned districts into safe zones where we can be relatively safe from Enforcer scouts."

"I don't understand," Frank said, frowning.

"It means that you will form a number of tiny crews to establish a presence in every abandoned district in the City," Zen said patiently. "Not for long-term occupation, not to establish bases, but to heavily mine these districts with explosives—and whenever possible, attack Enforcer scouts and patrols."

"If we're not gonna use 'em, what's the point of mining these districts?"

"To make the Enforcers fear them," Zen said. "I want them to think twice about entering an abandoned district. I want them to know that they cannot do so lightly. Otherwise they would simply systematically search the City, and find and destroy our hideouts within weeks."

"What if the Enforcers come in a big group?"

"If you've had time to prepare the traps, then you will be able to inflict far more damage on them than they will to you," Zen said. "The goal here is to cause maximum damage with minimum cost. Take whatever Truants you need, and speak to Aaron about the explosives. I want you to move out tomorrow—I have no doubt that the Enforcers will have begun sweeping the abandoned districts by then. This is a race for control, and if we lose then we will have nowhere to hide. Do you understand?"

"Yes, sir."

"Excellent. If you have no more questions, you may go."

As Frank left, Zen let out a tired sigh and looked around. The shop was nearly empty, all the other Truants with orders having already left. Slumping slightly, Zen walked over to a small folding chair in a dark corner of the shop and sat down. Over in another corner, Noni was quietly stealing glances at him as she threw knives at a wooden target. She had very quickly graduated from darts.

Zen shook his head and leaned back to think. Zen's guts still churned like butter every time his mind strayed to his latest encounter with Umasi.

Up until that battle Zen had not spared his brother a second thought, certain that he'd given up and gone home long ago. His sudden reappearance mystified Zen. Umasi no longer looked like a vagrant, and yet he clearly had not returned to being a student. So what had he been up to? What had he become? It frustrated Zen, having known Umasi all his life and yet not being able to understand or recognize him anymore.

Zen thought about the brown-haired boy that he had killed, the one that had set everything in motion that day. Had the boy been a friend of Umasi's? Zen did not recognize him, but it was the only thing he could think of that would explain Umasi's unprecedented reaction. Did Umasi even know that it had been an accident, that Zen hadn't meant to do it? Had he seen what had happened? Didn't Umasi realize that Zen was—and here Zen's gut churned most violently, for he could barely admit this to himself—sorry about what he had done?

No, Zen decided, definitely not. No wonder he had been so upset then. But what really bothered Zen was how easily Umasi had managed to beat him. Yes, Umasi had taken him completely by surprise, in more ways than one. But Zen had barely been able to put up a fight. That was unlike him. It had been as though his limbs had frozen, his mind blanked. It was as though he'd been paralyzed by . . . by *guilt*.

Zen shook his head like a dog drying himself of water. Little though he liked to dwell on it, he knew that he deserved what he'd gotten. Perhaps that had been why he could not fight properly. But still some credit had to go to Umasi, who, aside from his uncharacteristic ferocity, had demonstrated a fighting prowess Zen had never expected of him. Gone was the naïve and weak boy he'd humiliated on the piers, and in his place had risen something undeniably powerful.

Zen clenched his fists. The next time he met Umasi, if there was indeed a next time, he swore he would hold nothing back, for he knew that their next fight would be to the death. After all, this one had very nearly ended with his. The crowbar that had almost done it now lay in a dark corner of the shop as a grim souvenir. Zen glanced over at Noni, who had retrieved her collection of spent knives and resumed throwing them at the target anew. Her determination to protect him had shocked him. As far as he knew, no one else had ever literally been willing to die for him. It was a strange feeling, and not an unpleasant one, though when Zen had told Noni to get out of the way it had only partly been out of concern for her.

Zen hadn't wanted anyone to interfere, not on his behalf, not even to save his life. He didn't like being saved, or protected. It was an irrational pride of his, but one that he cherished deeply. To him, there was a sort of sanctity about a battle between two people, one that absolutely had to be preserved. If it came down to another confrontation between him and Umasi, he would make sure that it would truly be just between the two of them.

"Ten lemons, one and a half cups of honey, and half a gallon of water." Umasi read aloud from his list, checking each item on it against a pile of ingredients assembled on the counter. "Looks like I didn't miss anything."

As he began making his favorite beverage himself for the first time in his life, Umasi contemplated what he would do now. If he could not kill Zen, then any attempt to stop him was doomed to failure before it began. Zen had already proven his resolve. He would not stop until killed.

"Cut lemons into halves . . ." Umasi muttered as he sliced the yellow fruit, blinking as juice spurted into his eye.

"You're willing to die over this?" Umasi had asked.

". . . then thoroughly squeeze the juice out . . ."

"And kill over it too" had been Zen's reply.

Umasi still didn't understand why Zen had shot Red. He knew that Red couldn't possibly have done anything to provoke him, but perhaps Zen had mistaken him for an enemy? No, Zen's enemies were the Enforcers. Umasi shook his head, stubbornly refusing to believe that his brother was so far gone that he had simply murdered a defenseless boy without reason.

"And you obviously don't know me."

With a particularly violent squeeze, Umasi wrung the last lemon, noting that he now had about three-quarters of a cup of juice, and then set aside the empty peels. Glancing over at the recipe again, Umasi began to read the next step aloud.

"Combine the water and the honey in a saucepan . . ."

"You can't talk me out of this, Umasi."

". . . and heat until completely dissolved," Umasi finished, setting the saucepan atop the stove as he poured the two appropriate ingredients into it.

For a moment Umasi glanced at the dancing flame of the stove. Reminded of Red's funeral pyre and the killer who had necessitated it, Umasi reflected on how disturbing it was, to see the brother he knew so well vanish for a while, only to reappear as a complete stranger.

"To be honest, I prefer it that way."

Before long the honey had dissolved nicely in the water, until only a consistent syrup remained. Umasi shut off the stove, and then looked to the next step.

"Pour the resulting mixture into a pitcher . . ."

"Were you going somewhere?"

". . . and then add the lemon juice."

"I still am."

"Refrigerate and serve cold."

Umasi smiled wryly as he poured the separate ingredients into the pitcher. Cooling the drink certainly wouldn't be a problem—he could stick the drink into the refrigerator—but it would be just as effective to bring it outside, which was what he intended to do. Picking up the hot pitcher with cooking mittens, Umasi gingerly carried the lemonade outside, where he already had a stand waiting in the glow of a streetlamp.

"You've shown me that I cannot count on anyone else."

Making the stand had been the work of a few minutes. He'd simply unfolded a table and two chairs in front of his makeshift apartment, and then placed a plain sheet and stacks of plastic cups on top of the table. To complete the effect he added a cardboard sign to the front upon which he had scribbled "Lemonade—1 Bill."

"You won't even have to fight if you don't want to."

Umasi placed the pitcher down on the stand with some pride and stood back to admire it all. It was majestic in its simplicity, a place where he wouldn't mind spending the rest of his days . . . and perhaps he would do just that. He spontaneously resolved that everything he was, everything that he had become, would be tied to this spot.

"It's not a matter of pride."

Having waited long enough, Umasi poured himself a cup of the still-warm lemonade and drank deeply. It had turned out well, and would only get better as it chilled. As Umasi finished, he wiped his mouth and let out a placid sigh.

"Open your eyes and look at the City! We hold its entire fate in our hands."

He would spend as long as it'd take, here in the peace of District 19, merely pondering the fate of the City, even as his brother sought to master it. There was no hiding from it anymore. Umasi knew who he was, and he was a pacifist at heart.

"Still determined to conquer the City, eh, Brother?" Umasi muttered to himself.

"Then try, Zen. I won't stop you. But I won't help you."

Rothenberg stormed along the streets of District 18, not even wanting to know what time of night it must be. He had spent tedious, fruitless extra hours slaving away at Enforcer Headquarters, planning his aggressive new campaign. He was exhausted, but he knew that there would be no sleep for him just yet. Rothenberg sorely felt a need to unload some of his stress onto Cross.

Rothenberg breathed into his hands to warm them as he walked. Off duty as he was, he'd left his favored patrol car behind. The cold didn't bother him too much, however, as he had dressed warmly and traveled more stealthily on foot anyway—all the better for sneaking up on any vagrant foolish enough to cross his path. Indeed, Rothenberg was so tense that he found himself desperately wishing that one of them *would* show themselves, but he was consistently disappointed.

Rothenberg scowled at the City in general, lit only by the faint orange glow of streetlamps. It wouldn't be long now; his apartment was only a few blocks away. As he walked, Rothenberg idly reflected upon how the neighborhood was almost as silent as an abandoned district at night. With that in mind, Rothenberg carelessly turned a corner and looked up, expecting only more empty sidewalk and pavement.

And that's when he saw it.

Rothenberg stared, and then rubbed his eyes, wondering if he was more tired than he'd thought. But it was still there, an unearthly, pure-white figure, crouching down as it examined a garbage can. As Rothenberg continued to gawk, the figure jerked its head up to stare back at him, and Rothenberg felt goose bumps prickle all over his body. The apparition had the appearance of a young girl, except it was unnervingly pale, *impossibly* pale. As she crouched directly under a bright streetlamp, Rothenberg could have sworn that her eyes flashed red.

Then that moment, which had seemed to be frozen in time, thawed abruptly, and the white figure darted around a corner and out of sight with shocking speed and grace, never making a sound. Acting on instinct, Rothenberg pursued the fleeing figure, drawing his gun. As he rounded the corner, he heard a strange metallic tinkling. The next thing he knew, something slammed into his forehead with calculated force, causing him to stagger backwards, momentarily stunned. Before he could even react, his pistol was knocked from his hand by a similarly precise blow.

Rothenberg looked up in confusion, wondering what it was that had hit him. Then he saw the pale figure, standing luminously under another streetlamp, a metal chain wrapped around her left arm, its end dangling from her right hand. The chain swayed slightly in the wind, tinkling as it did. The spectral figure didn't say a word, but glared piercingly at Rothenberg before spinning around and vanishing in the direction of District 19.

Rothenberg was left to stand there, wide-eyed, for several long minutes, unable to believe what had just happened. Wondering if it might all have been some mad delusion, Rothenberg glanced behind him where, sure enough, his pistol lay uselessly on the ground. His effortless defeat was real. That meant that the chain that had struck him was real . . . and that the impossible girl that had wielded it . . . was *real*.

All of a sudden Rothenberg realized just how cold it was out there on the streets, far from the comfort of a car heater. He actually shivered, and knew that no amount of heat would help him. What he just experienced had chilled more than just his flesh.

And as he stood there shivering on the sidewalk, Rothenberg couldn't help but be convinced that he had literally seen a ghost.

Dear Sirs,

There has been a fortunate turn of events since my last correspondence. The Mayor has assigned me to observe the Enforcer Rothenberg. While I suspect that the Mayor may be trying to remove me from his presence, I am not distraught, for this may be a perfect opportunity for me to shed some light on Rothenberg's activities. Unfortunately I am not yet privy to the secret behind his mission, though I have discovered that whatever it is, it's been consuming an incredible amount of resources—enough to personally concern the Mayor. I hope to question the man in person soon—perhaps I can leverage my new position to get some answers.

As a personal addendum, I would like to inquire about the possibility of having my own family relocated out of this City. My children have been born and raised here, and for this reason I do not expect my request to be granted. However, I cannot help but notice that this City's education has been taking its toll on them. I understand that that is the point of this City, but as a parent, I find it difficult to accept that point in good conscience.

Your Servant,
207549627

PART IV

PACIFIST

22
Fog of War

og.

It rolled across the waters surrounding the City in the early morning, the citizens awakening to find their whole world shrouded in gray. An unusual quiet now hung about the City, any sound strangely muted. In most parts of the City, people still walked the streets, children still attended school, but all of them felt, somehow, that they were but shadows in the endless gray.

For Umasi, fog, like sunlight, had always been a natural phenomenon to take for granted. Now with little else to occupy his attention, Umasi realized that he had never noticed fog descending like a carpet upon the streets, nor had he ever known it to be thick enough to reduce his world to a gray blur. He walked alone through the streets of District 19 as if through a dream, and whatever he could make out in the mist thoroughly awed him.

Umasi felt very small and isolated, as though he were the only person left in a world of infinite gray. It was a humbling feeling, and Umasi sighed as he breathed deep of the mist, feeling at complete peace with the City. It was in this state of mind that he walked back to his stand in silence, tendrils of fog swirling all around him. But as he rounded the corner he came to an abrupt halt.

A gray figure, shrouded in mist, was rummaging through the contents of his stand. Umasi called out through the fog.

"Excuse me, that's mine!"

As if on cue, the fog parted slightly, and Umasi's blood froze as he got a proper look at who was raiding his stand.

It was a slender girl that Umasi guessed to be around his age. Her features were elegant and soft, but her expression was cold as she glared at him over her shoulder. What had shocked Umasi was that from her headband to her legs, the girl was almost completely white. As she rose, a thin sweater whose sleeves she'd tied around her neck fluttered gently behind her. Her eyes appeared as a faint blue in the pale light of the fog, and Umasi thought that he saw in them both compassion and strength.

The girl spun to face him fully, and the snowy hair that fell to her jaw swirled like a blizzard. Something tinkled lightly. Umasi noticed that a large metal ring attached to the end of a chain dangled down from within her left sleeve. Flickering in and out of visibility in the swirling fog, the pale girl seemed almost ethereal. It was then that Umasi believed the girl must indeed be a spirit—that Red had been right all along—that what stood before him was the legendary Vagrant Ghost, exactly as Red described her.

"Pure white, all over. Except the eyes; they were blue, but then they flashed red. And she had a chain . . . If you stick around in the abandoned districts long enough, maybe you'll see her too."

Frozen in shock, Umasi could think of nothing but what Red had said. Then he recalled something he had once heard in a classroom, the words flitting out at him from hazy memory, as if from someone else's life.

"In human albinos, the eyes are usually blue more often than red—human eyes are typically deep enough to cover the blood vessels, though there are exceptions in certain types of lighting."

The truth came crashing down upon Umasi, and he laughed out loud as his wits returned to him. He knew now the secret behind the "ghost." At that moment, the pale girl abruptly lashed out with her chain, swinging it in an arc towards his head. Now fully alert, Umasi ducked easily, knowing that the worst such an attack could do was knock him out. The girl drew the chain back skillfully, catching the ring at its end with her right hand.

"I know you're not a ghost!" Umasi called out, irked that his opponent remained silent.

The albino stiffened, but did not reply. Instead, with a lightning-fast motion she sent the chain shooting straight towards him. Umasi dodged to the side. The large ring at the end of the chain struck the ground with a metallic clink. The girl drew the chain back again and began twirling its end around rapidly, stirring the fog around her. As she closed the gap between them, she sent the chain flying out repeatedly with impressive force, her motions fluid and graceful. Each of her attacks was followed swiftly by another, resembling something like a dance, though Umasi had little time to admire it. He was being forced to dodge so rapidly now that he himself resembled a very clumsy tap dancer.

In spite of himself, Umasi was getting irritated. He had come to think of District 19 as his fortress, his private lair. Being attacked and made fool of within it did not sit well with him, and all the calmness he'd been trying to cultivate was quickly collapsing around him. Thinking to end the battle quickly, Umasi's hand lashed out and seized the metal ring the next time it whizzed by his head. Ignoring how his hand stung from the impact, for one brief moment Umasi believed that he'd won.

Then the albino did something completely unexpected. As he caught the ring, she allowed the chain to slacken and snapped her arm up and down, sending a complicated loop over Umasi's arm. Before Umasi could realize what was going on, his arm was entangled and she had yanked the chain.

Umasi hit the ground face-first. As he lay, humiliated, on the asphalt, he realized that his adversary had relaxed a bit, as though she thought it was over, and that a part of the now-loosened chain had coiled around the girl's foot. Knowing that he probably only had seconds before she realized her mistake, Umasi abruptly pulled on the chain with all his might. He was rewarded with a yelp as the girl also fell to the ground.

Umasi took the opportunity to shake himself free of the chains and leap upright, but his foe was already starting to rise as well. Darting forward, Umasi tackled her—and found himself in a position that was both warm and embarrassing.

The girl struggled beneath him for a moment. Finding that she could not loosen herself, she glared up at Umasi. Her pale blue eyes were slitted as she spoke for the first time.

"Get off me."

An involuntary shiver traveled down Umasi's spine. He sprang up immediately. Her voice was cold, like freezing wind and stormy water. To him it was as elegant as, and even more powerful than, her chain had been.

"Well, sorry," Umasi said. "If you wanted food so badly, you could've asked."

"And you'd share?" she demanded, sitting upright.

"Of course," Umasi replied. "Do I look like I'm starving?"

She regarded him carefully.

"No, you don't. Why is that?"

"I thought you were hungry?" Umasi said. "Over here. I'll explain after you eat."

With that, Umasi began walking towards his apartment without sparing the girl a second glance. She sat there on the ground for several moments, contemplating his receding form with an inscrutable face. Then the slightest of smiles tugged at the corner of her lips, and she cautiously began to follow.

What interesting weather we're having," Zen observed, attempting to gaze out the store window, only to find it completely misted over.

"Do you think Gabriel succeeded, sir?" Noni asked from her dark corner.

"Barring any unpleasant surprises, I expect that he has," Zen replied. "He's due back any minute now. I suppose that we'll soon find out for certain."

Noni merely nodded at that, but didn't stop staring at him with those piercing blue eyes. That stare had become unnerving in its intensity, even to Zen, and he tried not to think too hard about what might be behind it. Zen knew very well that he could afford no love but for the Truancy. That was the price that his role exacted, and it was one that he'd already paid. He had to be in utter control of his emotions at all times, or else all was lost.

"Noni," Zen said suddenly, "it's rude to stare."

Noni's normally pale complexion flushed very pink, and she began to stutter out an apology, which Zen ignored.

He could tell that she was hurt, and he felt a certain amount of regret at that. Noni had come a long way from the shivering skeleton he'd rescued in that alley, and had even repaid Zen by saving *his* life. Zen guessed that she was now able to walk among confidently among the other Truants because she had built an emotional wall to protect herself. The problem was that she seemed to have built it with Zen on the wrong side, for he would now have to extricate himself from that position.

Just then, Zen spotted a dark shape approaching through the window, and stood up, glad for the distraction.

"Well, that can't be Gabriel's team. I wonder who it is," Zen said. Noni gave no response, save to slip further into the shadows.

The door soon swung open to admit the truant named Amal, who looked slightly out of breath.

"Just got word from Frank," he explained. "He says they've set up crews in all the abandoned districts from 5 to 15, and will have covered twice that many by tomorrow. But he says that manpower and explosives are limited, so he wants to leave out the districts that are least likely to be searched or most easily surrounded."

"I'll leave that up to his discretion," Zen said. "Tell him to keep up the good work. Also, inform Aaron's team that we should have acquired a new shipment of raw materials by tomorrow, so they should start using up whatever they have."

"Yes, sir. Oh, speaking of Aaron, one of the chemists he's found cooked up something you ought to see," Amal said. "It's a smoke bomb. Saltpeter and sugar or something, could be nifty."

"Possibly, though it would be quite redundant in this weather," Zen observed, glancing out the misted window again. "Ah, it looks like Gabriel's team is returning at last. I'll inspect the new bomb later, you are dismissed."

Amal gave a short bow, and then turned and walked out the door. Before it could close, a tired but triumphant-looking Gabriel slipped in, quickly saluting Zen before flashing a satisfied smile.

"I take it that you were successful?" Zen said.

"Very," Gabriel exulted. "It went better than expected, and some of the new guys really proved themselves. See, after we took the guy out, some more people from the bar started coming our way and almost raised the alarm."

"How did you resolve that problem?"

"Two of the vagrant recruits ran out and picked their pockets," Gabriel said, chuckling. "Then they dashed off in the opposite direction, and the stupid adults followed. The suckers were yelling and cursing enough to wake the whole district, but they all went the wrong way."

"Did everyone escape successfully?"

"Yeah, even the decoys." Gabriel nodded. "Hell, we even got the people's wallets in the end."

"Very good," Zen said. "The ones responsible for the distractions can divide up the wallets' contents evenly. They certainly earned it, at any rate."

"They'll be glad to hear that." Gabriel grinned, then turned serious. "Do you think the Enforcers know already?"

"If they don't now, then they will soon," Zen replied, turning towards the window once more. "Our friend Rothenberg won't be happy. I can only hope that his search parties try poking around in one of Frank's districts next."

ir, we had a very specific search schedule planned out," the Enforcer said. "Why reschedule *all* the teams to check District 19?"

"I don't need to explain myself to you," Rothenberg said irritably. "Just look under every brick in that district. I want every inch of it gone over with a microscope."

Rothenberg glared up at the other Enforcer with bleary eyes as he drained the last drops of coffee from his cup—his fourth one that morning. Rothenberg hadn't gotten much sleep the previous night. Upon arriving at home, he had uncharacteristically gone straight to bed. Images of the ghost he'd encountered haunted him all night long. Even when he had managed to fall asleep, the spectral figure had appeared in his dreams, winding its cold chain around his neck, telling him that this was his punishment for all the vagrants that he'd killed.

Rothenberg shuddered and slammed his cup back down upon the desk. The other Enforcer now looked slightly concerned, but decided to speak anyway.

"Sir, some of the search parties have already gone out," the Enforcer said. "We don't have any resources to spare, and even vagrants rarely ever go to District 19, so I don't see why—"

"I have my reasons!" Rothenberg snapped, mumbling something under his breath about murderous spirits. "Don't ask questions, just do it."

The Enforcer now looked more concerned than ever, and Rothenberg got the impression that the man thought him to be insane. Rothenberg growled. He wasn't crazy. Yes, ghosts weren't supposed to be real, but he had *not* been hallucinating the previous night. Whatever it was that he had seen vanish towards District 19, he wouldn't rest until he'd hunted it down again and killed it somehow—even if it was already dead.

"Very well, sir," the Enforcer said reluctantly. "I'll arrange for a couple of patrols to examine the area tonight."

"No!" Rothenberg snarled. "I want a full task force devoted to this, and I want them on it *now*. Get it done, quickly!"

A sudden commotion erupted outside the office. Both Rothenberg and his subordinate stared at the door, and a moment later it burst open to admit a harried-looking man. He was pale-faced and out of breath as he shoved a sheet of paper into the other Enforcer's hands. Rothenberg stared at the both of them, his impatience rising as he saw his subordinate's eyes widen at whatever was on the paper.

"What is it?" Rothenberg demanded.

"I'm sorry, sir." The Enforcer sighed. "It looks like your search of District 19 is going to have to be delayed."

"Why, what's going on?"

There was no response, only uncomfortable silence. The news was apparently so bad that neither Enforcer wanted to deliver it.

"Tell me, dammit!" Rothenberg snarled dangerously.

The other Enforcers looked at each other nervously, and then one spoke up.

"Chief Enforcer Ralph was murdered today," he explained. "The evidence suggests that the kids we're looking for had something to do with it. And . . . the Mayor's aide is coming tomorrow. He's going to want answers."

Rothenberg stared blankly, wondering if the man was joking. Seconds passed, and no one laughed. Rothenberg grimaced, then slammed his fists down on the desk. The others jumped. The Chief Enforcer, *murdered*? With the Mayor's aide breathing down his neck there was no way that he would get away with a ghost hunt now.

"All right then," Rothenberg breathed. "Call off the District 19 search. Let's get on this before the Mayor's lapdog gets here."

Umasi watched as the strange girl devoured her second sandwich with astounding speed. The two of them were sitting on opposite sides of the lemonade stand. So far, she had downed four glasses of lemonade and an entire sandwich as though they were nothing. Somehow, she still managed to look dignified, almost graceful as she did so.

At first she had seemed so tense that Umasi feared she might vanish into the fog if he so much as twitched. But as she ate, she seemed to relax a bit. For his part, now that she was no longer attacking him, Umasi felt a sort of grudging admiration for the girl. You could tell a lot about a person when you fought them, which was perhaps why so many friendships followed conflict. The girl's style and weapon of choice had spoken of determination, grace, and power, tempered by a strong desire not to cause more harm than necessary. In some ways, though Umasi was reluctant to admit it, she was what he wanted to be.

"So, what's your name?" Umasi asked.

"I don't have one."

This was such an odd answer that Umasi blinked, wondering if she was snubbing him. Though her voice had been cold and guarded as usual, the clarity of her unblinking gaze convinced Umasi to give her the benefit of the doubt.

"Why not just give yourself a name?"

"I've never needed one."

"Then what am I supposed to call you?"

"What makes you think that I'll be staying long enough for that to matter?"

Umasi could actually feel his face turn pink.

"With the way you eat I'd expect you to be here all day."

"You have enough food to last all day?" She raised her eyebrows as she wiped her mouth with the back of her hand.

"I thought you were leaving?"

"Did I say I was?" she replied frostily.

"You certainly implied it."

"Do you want me to leave?"

Umasi hesitated at that, and for a moment he thought that he saw a trace of a smile flit across the girl's face.

"Let's try this again," he said finally. "I find that having a name is convenient, but if you don't want one, that's your business. Mine is Umasi."

"That's a nice name."

"You're the only one who seems to think so," Umasi said wryly.

"Well, I don't know that many names," the girl conceded. "I can't say that I've made many friends in my life."

"Then . . . then why do you trust me?" Umasi asked, tentative for the first time. "We did fight, after all."

The girl hesitated for a moment, as though marshaling her thoughts.

"You can tell a person's true character after they've had you at their mercy," she said. "You had me at yours. Actions are louder than words."

Umasi thought about that first bit of wisdom, and resolved to remember it. He felt that it applied to the relationship between students and teachers in the City, among other things.

"You had me for a moment there too," Umasi said. "That trick you used to trip me up was well executed."

"Thank you."

The girl hesitated for a moment.

"The first instinct is always to grab the chain," she explained. "If you do, it just becomes a contest of strength, so I had to find ways around it."

"And that one worked. I merely got lucky," Umasi said.

"No, I was careless." She shook her head. "Had you been a different type of person, I might be dead or worse by now."

"So you really believed that you were fighting for your life?" Umasi said. "I somehow got the impression that you were . . . well, it was like you didn't want to seriously hurt me."

Now she really did smile, however faintly. Then it was gone.

"I didn't," she admitted, "but I wasn't holding back. If I can beat someone without harming them, I'd prefer to. Usually people are . . . they're afraid of me. The whole ghost thing. So I never *had* to kill, only disable."

Umasi contemplated her philosophy, and found that it intrigued him. Was it possible to fight without restraint, and yet do so without any intention of inflicting harm? Apparently so; the girl had pulled it off admirably, with a nonlethal weapon and noble intentions. Umasi marveled at how she had developed such an approach after all that she must've suffered. Umasi contemplated his guest. Her sleeves had slid up far enough for Umasi to see that she had no number or bar code tattooed upon her pale arms, as was standard for all students in the City.

"You don't have a student number," Umasi pointed out as he filled another cup of lemonade and pushed it towards her. "Why is that?"

The girl cocked her head as she accepted the drink, as though momentarily confused. Then she glanced at Umasi's arms, and upon spotting his number her face fell.

"Oh, *those*," she murmured, taking a sip from her cup. "I never got one. I was never allowed into school at all."

The undisguised regret he heard in her voice struck a chord in Umasi. He knew that the student numbers weren't anything to be proud of, nor were they a pleasant thing to bear—but on the other hand some students in the City were content with their miserable existence. With slight shock, Umasi remembered that he had once been one of them. But the girl before him would never get to decide for herself, never know what it was that she had been missing.

Unless he told her.

"You shouldn't let school bother you so much," Umasi said. "In this City, the price of knowledge can be steep."

The girl looked up from her drink curiously, her steely shell completely forgotten for the moment.

"What're you talking about?"

Umasi sighed and poured himself a cup of lemonade. The last person he'd confided in had ended up in a fiery grave. Was he ready to share those secrets with someone else? No, Umasi decided as a lump rose in his throat, not yet.

"I . . . know I promised to explain, but I don't think I'm ready to talk about it now," Umasi said. "Sorry to disappoint you."

The albino looked at him strangely for a minute, and then shrugged and downed the rest of her lemonade in one smooth gulp.

"Well, as you said, you did promise to explain," she said, setting her cup back down onto the stand. "I suppose I'll just have to wait until you're ready to do so."

Umasi blinked in surprise, and then found that he was smiling, of all things.

"Well then, welcome to District 19, milady." Umasi bowed slightly in his seat. "I hope that you enjoy your stay."

23
WITHOUT A NAME

T he night sky had just been broken by a tinge of orange when two Enforcer patrol cars turned a corner and proceeded cautiously down an empty street. The Enforcers carefully scanned each crumbling house as they passed by, though they saw nothing moving in the predawn darkness. In other parts of the abandoned District 7, they knew that other patrols would be combing the streets just as they did. Though none of them expected to find anything, they kept up the tedious job until the eastern skies glowed in the dawn.

Just as the two patrols passed by what looked like an empty soda bottle on the side of the road, an explosion ripped through the darkness, instantly reducing one of the cars to nothing but fiery wreckage. The two Enforcers in the other car scrambled out, frantically looking around for their assailants. Gunshots rang out, and before the Enforcers could even tell where they were coming from, one had already fallen. The other, panicked at the loss of his partner, ran for a nearby alley, desperate to escape. A moment later he was consumed by another fiery explosion.

The radio left behind in the untouched Enforcer car blared with frantic queries, and then panicked shouts. All throughout the rest of District 7 more explosions and gunshots went off, and by the time the sun rose over its streets, not a single Enforcer was left alive in the whole district.

A ll dead?" Rothenberg said incredulously. This was not the news that he wanted to wake up to.

"Yes, sir," the Enforcer replied, shifting uncomfortably. "We sent five patrol teams in to sweep District 7 as planned, two reported that they were under attack, and all of them are now missing."

"Then that might be where they're hiding!" Rothenberg said. "Send in a bigger force, everything you can throw at it!"

"Well, we immediately sent every patrol we had available, and even deployed a helicopter for aerial surveillance," the Enforcer said. "They recovered all the wreckage and most of the bodies, but set off a few more explosives. Two more men were killed, one more injured, and no sign of any of these self-proclaimed Truants."

"Nothing? No sign at all?"

"No, sir, they seem to have covered their tracks well. We simply didn't have the manpower for a door-to-door search of an abandoned district, and if the group that did it is still there, it would be so small that it'd be like a needle in a haystack. Besides, I doubt that District 7 was intended to be their main hideout anyway."

"What makes you say that?"

"A single routine patrol in District 5 failed to report in on time. We sent the helicopter over the area. It wasn't hard to find; great smoking wreckage in the middle of the street. It looks like it fell into the same kind of trap as the District 7 sweep. We didn't dare approach that one on the ground in case we set anything else off."

"Great," Rothenberg snarled, "call off the other sweeps for now. If they've mined 5 and 7 to hell, I'd bet anything that they've done all the others as well. We're going to have to rethink our entire strategy. We'll need to go one district at a time with more men, more cars, we're going to have to be thorough and—"

"Having problems, Rothenberg?" a new voice asked.

Rothenberg spun around and glared. He had been standing in his office with the door open as he received the bad news of the day and had not heard the newcomer entering the room. He was surprised to see that it was not another Enforcer bearing grim tidings, but rather a man in a brown leather jacket with short brown hair and a neatly trimmed mustache and beard.

"Who are you?" Rothenberg demanded.

"My name is Jack," the man said. "I'm one of the Mayor's aides. I was told that you would be expecting me."

Rothenberg's heart skipped a beat. He was tired, and in the flurry of bad news and plans that had to be rethought, he had completely forgotten about the Mayor's aide. The other Enforcer seized the opportunity to excuse himself, leaving the two men alone in the office.

"You look tired, Rothenberg," the aide said. "Have you been getting enough sleep lately?"

"Of course!" Rothenberg replied. "And I don't see how that's any of your business."

As a matter of fact, Rothenberg hadn't slept more than a few hours a night since he had encountered that ghostly apparition in District 18. The pale figure had continued to haunt his dreams, each time worse than the last.

"Well, the Mayor would certainly like to be assured that you've been well rested. After all, he seems to think that your assignment is highly important," Jack said, narrowing his eyes. "On that note, what exactly are you doing, Rothenberg?"

"Has the Mayor briefed you on my assignment?"

"On the basics, yes, but not on what exactly you are looking for."

"Well, then, I can't help you," Rothenberg snapped. "It's not a big deal anyway, just normal Enforcer business. We've got it all under control, don't worry about it."

"Normal Enforcer business?" The aide raised his eyebrows.

"That's right."

"Then might I ask why you've been neglecting all of your other normal assignments?" Jack asked, gesturing towards Rothenberg's desk, upon which a mountain of untouched paperwork rested.

Rothenberg scowled. "The Mayor's assignment takes priority."

"I was under the impression that you had the Mayor's assignment 'under control,'" the aide said.

"We do!"

"Then why not see to your other responsibilities now?"

"How do you know that I was not about to?"

"Is that the case? Well then I apologize for interrupting, please go ahead." Jack sat down in Rothenberg's chair and leaned back as though daring him to do it.

Rothenberg knew he had been challenged, but he would not back down, especially not from this skinny, pompous assistant. With a look of pure malice, Rothenberg seized the first folder on the top of his towering work pile and stormed from his office. A routine foster child issue, Rothenberg realized as he opened the folder. He'd been assigned the case because it was in District 18, his home district. It would make for an easy break until he could get back and properly lead his men without any damn aides breathing down his neck.

There was a soft tinkling, then something whooshed through the air. Reacting instantly, Umasi dived out of the way just in time as the chain struck the ground he had occupied a moment before. Forcing himself into a roll as he hit the hard asphalt, Umasi smoothly returned to his feet a second later. His pale opponent twirled her chain around for a moment as she drew it back, and then abruptly lashed out again.

Umasi ducked this time, feeling the wind on his hair as the chain passed an inch overhead. In the few hours that they had been sparring, he had accumulated both a great respect for the chain as a weapon, and a large collection of bruises. The girl's eyes glinted scarlet in the bright sunlight, and her chain wrapped partially around her before swinging back and unwrapping in a powerful horizontal sweep. Umasi was forced to drop to the ground to avoid it, and before he could rise the chain had doubled back in an arc, slamming down hard on Umasi's back. Umasi crumpled for a second, feeling the cold asphalt beneath him. He smiled wryly as he rose, rubbing his back.

"Nice one," Umasi conceded. "I managed to dodge seven strokes that time, I believe?"

The nameless girl nodded. "You're getting better at reading my movements."

"Not by much," Umasi said. "I can never tell what you're going to do until the last minute."

"It's a difficult weapon to predict," she said, "but it's better for countering. You're just dodging right now; if you were attacking me it'd be harder."

"So how am I supposed to beat it?" Umasi asked.

"Look for an opening after a failed attack," the albino said, bringing her gaze back down to Umasi. "Do you want to take a break?"

"That sounds good." Umasi bowed, feeling worn out.

The girl curtsied and walked off into the middle of the empty street by herself. Umasi watched her go. All they had done so far was duel, and occasionally discuss tactics. The topic of Umasi's secrets had not come up yet, and Umasi could tell that the albino was patiently waiting for him to bring it up. Umasi had no doubts about her trustworthiness. He was not as naïve as he had once been, and knew that his physical attraction to her was only natural—but his admiration for her went deeper than that. Her philosophy, her strength, and her self-control had all struck chords in Umasi. Here was an individual who was truly at peace, ready to accept life or death as it came, content to go unacknowledged by the world.

Deep in thought, Umasi moved to sit down on the doorstep of an abandoned building. Meanwhile, the pale vagrant launched into a flurry of graceful motions. A rapid clinking sound reached Umasi's ears, and he looked up to see her chain flitting through the air so rapidly that it seemed to be everywhere at once. It really was like a dance, Umasi thought, the chain constantly in motion, striking down invisible enemies with its rhythmic movements. The chain glittered in the sun, and it almost appeared as though she were wielding a string of light. Umasi could only stare, mesmerized, realizing that the girl had her eyes closed.

"How do you do that?" Umasi asked in awe.

"Hm?" The pale drifter abruptly ceased her movements, opening her crimson eyes as she allowed the chain to fall like a puppet whose strings had been cut.

"Move so perfectly without looking," Umasi clarified.

"Oh." The girl looked slightly abashed, though not displeased. "My eyesight's not very good. Sometimes it's easier to rely on my other senses."

"My vision hasn't been so great since I lost my glasses," Umasi said. "Which senses do you use instead?"

"Touch, mostly," she explained, "though hearing helps too. If you practice listening for long enough, you can hear each individual clink in the chain. Then it becomes a bit like playing music, I suppose."

"You must've been practicing with that for a long time."

"I've probably had it for longer than I haven't." She nodded. "It's a part of me now."

Umasi hesitated in asking his next question, but only for a second.

"How long have you been alone out here? Out on the streets of the City, I mean."

The pale girl seemed to freeze for a moment, her red eyes narrowing as they stared at Umasi. Umasi tried to meet that crimson gaze but could not, looking down at the pavement as he awaited his sentence. But when she finally began to speak, her voice was not admonishing, but gentle.

"I don't know for sure anymore," she said. "But I think it was since I was about eight. It's been maybe six or seven years since then."

"How did you survive all that time?" Umasi asked. "A matter of days nearly killed me. I can't imagine trying to last for so long. . . ."

"For a while it was pretty bad," the girl admitted. "Eventually, though, I found that most people were scared of how I looked. That kept me safe, so from then on I tried acting as scary as I could, and they'd all run away in the end."

"So that's how the legend of the Vagrant Ghost got around," Umasi murmured. "But didn't anyone know who you really were?"

"No." She shook her head. "Eventually there wasn't anyone I couldn't scare away. For the longest time I was . . . lost . . . in the role."

Umasi contemplated a life like that, forced into pretending that you were a monster in order to survive, unable to let anyone know that you were human. Umasi shuddered, realizing that he'd gotten off quite easy in life.

"You mentioned that you've only been out here for a short while," the girl said, her ruby gaze searching Umasi's face. "How did you hear about me?"

"My friend," Umasi said. "His name was Red. He'd been a vagrant for a long time. When I first settled down here in District 19 he was my only companion. He said that you saved his life."

"I don't often do that," she said. "When was this?"

"It'd be just a few days ago, really," Umasi said. "He had brown hair, and was being chased by a boy with a gun."

"Ah." The girl inclined her head. "I remember. I'm glad that he got away."

There was a heavy silence. Umasi couldn't bring himself to tell her that her efforts had been in vain, that he had gotten Red killed after she had risked her life to save him. Then comprehension dawned in her eyes, and she spoke again.

"What happened to him? Why isn't he still here?"

"He was killed by my brother," Umasi said bitterly.

"Your brother?"

Again Umasi found that he could not speak. The girl continued to look at him, a gentle wind stirring her snowy hair. There was silence as Umasi lost himself in dark thoughts, and then suddenly the spell was broken.

"You've heard the story of my life, more or less," the albino said. "Can you tell me the rest of yours now?"

Umasi nodded, having expected the question and already decided to answer. It was only fair, after all.

"It might take a long time," Umasi said. "But I suppose that we've got plenty of that."

And so, taking a deep breath, Umasi related his story, from beginning to end, right up until the moment that he came across the girl without a name at his stand. For her part, the girl listened in respectful silence, though at times her eyebrows would rise in surprise, or she would bite her lip in concern, or her eyes would betray visible sympathy. The sun was setting and her eyes were blue once more by the time Umasi finished, but by then he was certain that he couldn't have asked for a better audience.

After checking his folder again to make sure that he had the right address, Rothenberg strode up the steps to the doorway of the brownstone apartment and knocked. Resolving issues between foster parents and their children was a mundane Enforcer duty, but that suited Rothenberg just fine after weeks of increasing chaos. From what he'd gathered from the case file, the subject was a fourteen-year-old boy living with a couple that had already made several complaints, though the child's orphanage had vouched for him each time.

The door swung open, and Rothenberg suddenly found himself staring down into a pair of venomously green eyes.

"You must be Edward," Rothenberg said.

The boy blinked. His emerald eyes made a striking contrast to his short blond hair and long, thin eyebrows. His features were soft and his skin pale. He was clothed in an unremarkable gray student's uniform, which struck Rothenberg as odd since it was dark now, far past school hours.

"Yes, sir," Edward replied. "May I please ask who you are, sir?"

Even Rothenberg could find no fault in a question phrased so politely.

"I am Enforcer Rothenberg," said Rothenberg imperiously. "I am here responding to a complaint made by your foster parents. Where are they?"

"If you would please wait a moment, Mr. Rothenberg, I will go get them," Edward said.

Moments later, two haggard-looking adults stood on the doorstep. Rothenberg introduced himself, and the woman turned to her husband.

"Dear, could you please go keep an eye on the boy? Who knows what he might be putting under your pillow this time."

The man gave a grim nod and left purposefully. The woman introduced herself as Elli and hastily invited Rothenberg into the sitting room. He accepted the offer of coffee and sat down in a chair opposite her as she began to relate her tale.

"Well, we've had him for a year now," Elli explained. "But honestly we've been trying to get rid of him for months. The orphanage just won't take him back, they say we've agreed to care for him for the duration and that's that. They also stick up for him every time . . . *every* time." Elli's face grew furious. "He must've done a good job on those orphanage nuts."

"So his parents died, did they?" Rothenberg asked.

"Yes, and he was sent to the District 18 orphanage. We thought . . . we thought we'd be doing good, you know? Taking care of a parentless kid. And we've never had children ourselves. Probably never will now, after all this." Elli laughed bitterly.

"The record says that you've filed over a dozen complaints about the boy," Rothenberg noted, looking down at his folder. "And that the Enforcer in each case—"

"I know, I know, they always side with him!" Elli said, suddenly looking panicked. "You've got to understand, you have to believe me! He sneaks out at night, breaks curfew to do who knows what, and you wouldn't believe how many complaints I get from other parents about him! He . . . he's even threatened my husband and me!" Elli added, sounding truly frightened. "He's threatened to *kill* us, and we have to leave him alone because . . . well, I think he'd do it!"

"The child seemed respectful enough to me," Rothenberg said, and from him this was the highest praise.

"You don't understand!" Elli wailed. "He does this every time a visitor comes around! Always a polite act, and sometimes he tells them that we'd been abusing him, and they believe him! We got dragged down to the Enforcer station for an inquiry!"

"*Have* you been abusing him?" Rothenberg asked. "Personally you'd have my utmost sympathy if so, I firmly believe that—"

"No, no, no we haven't!" Elli insisted. "No one ever believes us! Not the

Enforcers, not our neighbors, not even our friends! He's a monster, and a damn clever one too! We keep asking the Enforcers to arrest him, to take him in, bring him back to that damnable orphanage, but he ... one time ..." Elli's voice lowered to a frantic whisper. "He actually planted a gun under my husband's pillow! Damned if I know how or where he got it, but he put it there, I'm sure of it, and he reported us to the Enforcers! My husband spent two months in detention for that, and we're lucky it wasn't longer! Do you know what that did for our reputation? Have you asked what people think of us now? I swear I haven't laid a hand on that boy, but sometimes ..."

At this point Elli seem so overcome by anger and fear that she could not speak, her face puffing up like a red balloon. Rothenberg watched amusedly, unsure of what to think. On the one hand Elli seemed so desperately frantic that Rothenberg found it hard to believe that she was lying. On the other, what she was saying seemed so outlandish, so unlike the boy Rothenberg had met, that Rothenberg had indeed convinced himself that she was lying to get the boy out of the house. Rothenberg shrugged. If they wanted the brat gone that much, he'd oblige them.

"You believe me, right?" Elli said suddenly. "Please say you believe me, Mr. Rothenberg!"

"To be honest, I don't." Rothenberg frowned as Elli groaned. "However, I don't need to either. I am going to return Edward to the orphanage anyway without interviewing the boy."

"You ... you are?" Elli said, a faint note of hope in her voice.

"I am," said Rothenberg, "because you seem to want him out very badly, and the idea of ruling in favor of a child is repugnant to me."

"Thank you, thank you so much!"

But Rothenberg was no longer listening. He was staring behind the woman at the flight of stairs, down which Edward was now dragging a packed suitcase, his foster father trailing a cautious distance behind.

"Hello again, Mr. Rothenberg!" Edward said brightly from the stairs. "Will we be leaving now, sir?"

"How did you know—" Rothenberg began.

"Oh, don't be surprised at that, he probably figured you out and what you would decide the moment he saw you," Elli said bitterly. "Always two steps ahead. He's a bright boy, if only he didn't ... wasn't ..."

"Well, I don't think there's any more to be said," Rothenberg declared as he stood up. "We'll be going now. Good luck to the two of you."

The couple thanked him all the way to the door, where Rothenberg waited for Edward to catch up and begin following with the suitcase. Rothenberg didn't spare the boy a second thought, and they walked under orange streetlamps in silence. Then Rothenberg stopped short, recognizing the street that they were on. He wasn't sure why he was so surprised—it was District 18, after all—but he began glancing around frantically at every shadow, for it was here that he had seen the ghost with his own eyes.

When no phantasm presented itself, Rothenberg remembered something that the couple had mentioned. He slowly crouched down so that his face was level with Edward's. Edward had been watching the man cautiously. At such a distance Edward could not help but notice the dark rings under his eyes, as well as a general appearance of dishevelment.

"You out here a lot at night, boy?" Rothenberg whispered.

"Fairly often, sir," Edward said. "Even when I'm not running errands, I sometimes go for walks myself . . . before curfew, of course."

"Good, good," Rothenberg said distractedly, running a hand over his scalp. "Tell me this, then: Have you ever seen a pale girl with red eyes on the streets around here, coming or going to District 19, carrying around a chain?"

Edward wondered if the Enforcer was drunk, or if he was playing some sort of game. Unsure of what answer the man was looking for, Edward decided to go with the truth.

"No, sir." Edward shook his head. "Haven't seen anything like that."

At that, the look on Rothenberg's face turned ugly. The next thing Edward knew, the Enforcer slapped him hard enough to send him staggering.

"You lying brat!" Rothenberg snarled. "I've never heard so many lies from a kid before in my life. I'm going to tell the orphanage that you're a lying, thieving, vandalizing miscreant. Maybe that'll teach you."

Edward winced and rubbed his stinging cheek as he struggled to keep his fury under control. Patience, Edward told himself. Patience. Give him what he expects to hear.

"But sir, that's not true," Edward protested.

"You shouldn't be complaining," Rothenberg said. "Be glad that I'm not going to go through the trouble of arresting you for lying to an Enforcer. There's a war going on, boy—hell, you should be happy that I don't shoot you right now."

With that, Rothenberg seized Edward by the arm, dragging him along. As they walked, snowflakes began to fall from the sky, visible only as they fluttered under the streetlamps. Rothenberg looked more disturbed than ever, casting furtive looks at every patch of darkness that he passed, muttering under his breath about ghosts and war and rebellious children. So self-absorbed was Rothenberg that he never saw the grin on Edward's face, a twisted smile as the boy imagined a thousand horrific things that he would someday like to do to this brutish Enforcer.

Edward did not hate this man, though he did envy him. Edward envied his power and the freedom to abuse it. His various petty misdeeds gave him only fleeting satisfaction; the best he could do was manipulate someone in a position of power. He coveted that position for himself, the constant liberty to treat those under him however he wished. After all, if there was one thing that his unfortunate life had taught him, it was that justice had no meaning unless you had the power to define it yourself.

24

THE BIRTH OF ZYID

Snow had fallen during the night, and early the next morning Umasi decided to go to the trouble of making a warm bath. After he was done, his nameless guest had asked to use what was left, and he had of course consented. One of the things that had struck Umasi when he first met her was how *clean* she was for a vagrant. He wasn't sure what her secret was, but he hadn't thought it polite to ask, and instead exited the apartment to give her some privacy.

Only after she emerged did he understand that she had in fact been dirty before. She looked like a person transformed, like glass turned into diamond. Her skin and hair, which he had thought white before, had really been dull gray compared with how they were now. When the pale sunlight struck her hair, she seemed like an ethereal goddess rising up from the snow.

Umasi complimented her on her appearance, but noted that it was a shame that she couldn't wash her clothes as well. She then mentioned that she'd never been able to buy any for herself, making do with whatever gray or white rags she could find. That gave Umasi the idea of going clothes shopping, something that he'd never considered doing before in his life. Up until that moment, buying clothes had been something to do out of sheer necessity and nothing else. He wasted no time in approaching his companion with the idea.

"Shopping?" she frowned. "I told you, I can't afford—"

"I'll pay for you."

"No you won't."

"It's not charity, you know. It's just doing a friend a favor."

"It . . . what?" she sputtered, momentarily disarmed.

"Come on!"

For the first time since he'd met her, the pale girl looked taken aback, but she didn't protest as Umasi led her along by one arm. Though she talked to no one, and pointedly ignored all the stares she attracted, she otherwise seemed strangely comfortable among other people. When they got to the store, Umasi remembered that he didn't have the faintest idea about picking outfits, and so he urged his companion to do it for the both of them. The albino was reluctant at first, but after she got a chance to examine the nearly endless aisles of clothing, she soon seemed almost to be enjoying herself.

The pale girl quickly chose plain white garments for herself, replacing everything but her headband. She then set about picking Umasi's attire. Her new white sweater, tied around her neck like her old one, billowed behind her as she moved from aisle to aisle. Umasi ended up with several simple sets of clothes of different light colors, a theme that suited him. He now wore plain khaki jeans, and a long-sleeve white shirt with a buttoned-up collar, over which a beige vest had been added. His worn, dirty green jacket had been discarded, and a long white scarf was tied loosely around his neck so that its ends could flow behind him.

Umasi quickly paid for everything, not wanting to be seen in the living districts for longer than necessary. Just as they were about to leave the store, the nameless girl spotted a case of sunglasses. She chose two pairs of a simple black design that didn't seem very popular.

"What're these for?" Umasi wondered.

"Remember what I said about not relying on sight?" she asked as she slipped hers on. "These will probably work better than blindfolds. They dim your vision instead of removing it altogether, so you can keep them on all the time."

"Constant practice." Umasi nodded. "It's a good idea, but black's not really my color."

"Oh?" She raised her eyebrows.

"Yeah, my brother's the one who likes and looks good with black, so—"

"Aren't you twins?"

"Not identical, and—"

At this point she put a hand on her hip and looked at him sternly.

"Umasi, the rest of your clothes are practically white. Are you going to let your brother decide everything you wear? Or are you going to let me do it?"

"Are those my only choices?" Umasi asked meekly.

"Yes." She smiled.

"All right then, milady." Umasi slipped the sunglasses on.

And so Umasi left the store looking quite striking, though his companion still attracted far more attention for a variety of reasons. Neither of them looked remotely like a vagrant anymore, and it was already after school hours, so though many heads turned, no one bothered the pair as they made their way back to District 19.

As they walked through the snow, Umasi began to get a strange, unreasonable feeling that his new outfit wasn't as warm as the old one—a notion that he quickly dismissed because the clothes he was wearing now were decidedly thicker than those that he'd abandoned. But by the time they reached the District 19 fence, he was visibly shivering.

"Are you all right?" the nameless girl asked, removing her sunglasses.

"Yeah," Umasi insisted, "just a bit cold and tired right now."

"Cold and tired?" she repeated. "You didn't throw out that old green jacket yet, right? Maybe you should wear it again for now."

"Yeah, that's a good idea," Umasi agreed, sliding into the jacket only to realize that it wasn't doing him much good. "I just think I need to lie down under some blankets and get some rest."

"You haven't been up all that long," the albino pointed out. "You shouldn't be worn out already."

"Maybe it's all this snow, I don't know," Umasi murmured. "Will you help me over the fence, milady?"

She obliged him and gave him a boost over the wooden barrier. He dropped down unusually clumsily onto the other side. As he rubbed his sore back, Umasi numbly realized that he wasn't thinking very clearly. Chalking it up to his inexplicable weariness, Umasi staggered to his feet and began making his way back towards the lemonade stand. His nameless companion gracefully slipped over the fence herself a moment later and swiftly caught up to him.

"You're not like yourself," she said, eyes narrowing. "I think you might be catching a cold."

"Milady, I've been dunked into the river and come out into a blizzard without getting sick," Umasi said wearily. "I don't think a few flurries are going to get to me so easily."

"It was a miracle that you survived before," she conceded. "But that doesn't make you invincible."

Umasi had nothing to say to that. He simply walked back to the apartment and immediately slipped under a pile of blankets that he had made his bed. But even with the warmth of the thick cloth, he only grew colder with each passing moment. Despite the chills, it didn't take his weariness long to lull him to sleep, and so he never noticed the pair of blue eyes that watched him in growing concern.

Gesturing forward with two fingers, Rothenberg glared at the other Enforcers, some of whom were looking decidedly nervous. Outside, the sound of explosions continued to rend the air, some off in the distance, others uncomfortably close by. At Rothenberg's command, the other Enforcers rushed forward into the abandoned apartment and began shouting as they knocked on doors. They were rewarded with yells of surprise, and Rothenberg felt a surge of triumph. The brats were here!

Rothenberg had returned to Enforcer Headquarters late the previous night, and had been simultaneously pleased and outraged to find the

Mayor's aide asleep in his chair. While Rothenberg had lamented the loss of his seat, he was happy that he wouldn't have to deal with the man, and even happier that his last orders had been followed in his absence. A massive task force moved out to take District 7 by storm.

Forgoing sleep and driving all thoughts of specters and phantoms from his mind, Rothenberg hastened to join the task force. When he arrived, his eyes were met with a scene of total destruction: Every few blocks patrol cars and bodies littered the otherwise empty streets, smoke rose in great gray and white plumes, shouts both from nearby and over the radio echoed in his ears. But though their casualties were mounting, it had not been in vain; one of the children was seen fleeing to this building, and so Rothenberg personally led a team in to flush him out.

"Truants! This is the Enforcers! Surrender now or we'll kill the lot of you!" Rothenberg roared as one of his men kicked a nearby door in.

In response, a gunshot rang out and the Enforcer who had kicked the door down crumpled in the doorway. Leaping into action, Rothenberg peered into the room and fired at the center of the dark figure within. His victim let out a yelp and crumpled to the ground, but another sprang from behind a closet, forcing Rothenberg to duck back as bullets soared his way. Rothenberg fired back blindly into the room, and then chanced a look. The Truant had taken cover behind an overturned desk, just as he expected. Seizing his chance, Rothenberg charged into the room and leapt over the desk, tackling the boy before he realized what was happening. Rothenberg roughly slammed the Truant's head against the ground, rendering him motionless.

Rothenberg rose and looked around the room, breathing hard. It was now unoccupied, though a small pile of what Rothenberg suspected were crude explosives rested in a corner. From the sounds throughout the building, Rothenberg knew that his fellow Enforcers were fighting similar battles. Running back out into the corridor to join them, Rothenberg drew his radio from his belt.

"Remember, if you see our primary suspect, apprehend him alive at all costs!" Rothenberg shouted for the umpteenth time that morning. "We need him alive!"

It was a purely precautionary reminder. Rothenberg did not expect to encounter the Mayor's son in this small hidey-hole where only a handful of Truants seemed to have settled in. Indeed Rothenberg did not expect to find the boy in District 7 at all. Still, Rothenberg was taking no chances about accidentally shooting him. He didn't even want to imagine what the Mayor would do if one of his sons turned up dead.

As Rothenberg lunged for the stairs, a deafening noise split the air, and the entire building began to quake. Over the ringing in his ears, Rothenberg heard panicked shouts on his radio.

"They're setting off their entire supply of bombs!"

"They must be crazy!"

"Everyone out, the building's gonna collapse!"

Rothenberg took those last words to heart, turning tail and dashing out of the building as fast as he could. As he ran out into the street, he turned and looked up to see flashes of more explosions inside the building. He raised his arm to shield himself from falling glass, and then, with a great tremor and crumbling sound, part of the building collapsed in on itself, sending dust and debris cascading to the ground. Other Enforcers emerged from the entrance, coughing and sputtering as they reached the open air.

Rothenberg smiled for the first time in days. It had come at a high price, but this was a victory for the Enforcers; the Truancy had now been completely eradicated from District 7, and he was one step closer to cornering their lunatic leader. Rothenberg rubbed his hands delightedly and then reached for his radio. His duty to the Mayor had been done for the day. Now it was time to hunt down the ghost of District 19 and earn some peace for himself.

And sometimes, they would . . . they would threaten me with a gun. . . . I was so scared, but then the Enforcers took it away, and after that Mrs. Elli got angry, very angry, and . . . and . . ."

At this point Edward buried his face in his hands, his shoulders heaving with fake sobs. One of the orphanage matrons patted him gently on the back, exchanging grim looks with all the others who had gathered around Edward's bunk as he related his tragic tale of abuse at the hands of his foster parents.

"Awful, isn't it? I read about the gun arrest in the papers, but I didn't recognize the name. Poor Edward. Why do all the awful things have to happen to the best children?"

"Taken down to the Enforcer station for an inquiry, were they? It must've been bad, that's not something the Enforcers do every day."

"If I'd known what those two devils were up to, I'd have marched right up there and taken Edward back myself. Those irresponsible Enforcers—I knew that they kept asking us about Edward, but they never properly told us what was going on! Outrageous, we had a right to know!"

"If you ask me, those foster parents ought to be locked up for good. Discipline is one thing, but threatening a child with a gun, I ask you . . ."

"At least you're safe with us now, Edward. After all that's happened to you, I think we'd better keep you here and out of foster care. Why don't you get some rest?"

Edward stammered out his thanks, and with a final reassuring pat on the head, the matrons filed out of the room and flicked the lights off, leaving him alone in the dark, windowless dormitory. The moment the door shut, Edward's miserable face rearranged itself into a satisfied smile, and he slid out of bed and crept over to a floorboard that he knew was loose. Lifting it up, he examined his hidden trove and was delighted to find it exactly as he had left it. There was an assortment of cash that had been acquired illicitly here and there, a scrapbook filled with newspaper clippings about his various misdeeds (none of them correctly attributed to him), a set of keys that would access every room in the orphanage, a sharp, polished knife in a sheath, and at the very bottom, a loaded handgun daringly stolen from a drunk Enforcer.

Edward smiled and dug out the scrapbook before replacing the floorboard and returning to his bed. From his suitcase, he almost lovingly drew out a fresh bundle of newspaper clippings, all collected during his time with his latest foster parents. He carefully added them to the scrapbook, pausing briefly to chuckle over the article about his foster father's arrest. Once he finished, he plopped down on the bed and began reading through the scrapbook from beginning to end. It was a favorite pastime of his, reliving the acts of notoriety that served as a distraction from his otherwise mundane life.

The next day, Edward knew, he would have to go to school, for not even the kindly matrons who loved him so dearly would permit him to miss classes. Still, unlike most students of the City, Edward had no fear of school; its teachers were easy to please and its assignments were trivial exercises in memorization. Indeed, Edward's teachers had often told him that he was a model student, and Edward saw no reason to correct them, for that misunderstanding made his life so much easier.

Having reached the end, Edward shut his scrapbook and carefully replaced it beneath the floorboard. Few people with power over Edward could ever guess at the contents of that book he hid so carefully, for it spoke of a nature far more dangerous than anything else under that floorboard could ever be.

U masi awoke, and an involuntary moan forced itself out of his parched throat. His mouth was dry, his thoughts were a jumbled mess, and his body was racked with cold even as his face burned with heat. Through the muddy haze of confusion, two memories rose up into his consciousness.

One was of him boasting how he'd survived the river and a blizzard without falling ill, and the other was of the last time that he had been sick, back in the comfortable Mayoral Mansion, where he'd fallen ill from nothing at all.

Zen had taken care of him then, Umasi remembered dimly. He had helped him, and then turned towards madness in the same day. But who was here to help him now? Would he be able to get better on his own?

Suddenly, he felt something cool and wet being applied to his forehead, soothing the fires in his head. Attempting to make some sense of what was going on, Umasi forced his eyes open to find that everything was a blur. Cool trickles dripped down his face, and he realized that someone had put a wet towel on his forehead. Blinking briefly to rid himself of a drop of water that had landed on his eyelid, he opened his eyes again to see a blurry shadow standing over him.

And then it hit him.

"Milady?" Umasi murmured uncertainly.

"I told you that you were catching a cold," she chided. "Here, take this. You'll have to drink some to swallow it, so try to sit up a bit."

Umasi felt something being placed in his mouth, and a second later two arms propped his body up enough so that he could swallow a mouthful of water. Then the arms fluffed his pillow and laid him down again. A soft hand began petting the top of his head soothingly, and Umasi soon found himself slipping off into unconsciousness again.

From then on Umasi awoke every few hours, only to fall asleep again shortly thereafter. He only felt worse each time he opened his eyes, but his misery was allayed by the pale girl who never seemed to leave his side. Sometimes she would place a fresh wet towel on his forehead, other times she would coax more medicine or some juice down his throat. Once she added another layer of blankets on top of him. Sometimes he felt that her treatments helped, other times they didn't seem to have any effect. But always her gestures and care alone made him feel better.

By the time the sun went down, and what little sunlight that seeped through the window had faded, Umasi's fever was nearly unbearable. No matter how many blankets were piled on, he couldn't stop shivering as he writhed in discomfort. His hands scrabbled all around his body, desperately trying to warm it all at once. He hadn't eaten anything since the morning, and yet he felt no hunger. His fevered mind wondered if he could possibly die to a cold of all things.

And then, still in the throes of delirium, Umasi imagined something impossible. His blankets stirred, lifted, and a gush of cold air racked his body, causing him to shiver violently. Something heavy, soft, and warm slipped on top of him as the covers sank again to the floor. For a moment Umasi was sure that he was suffering a hallucination. Only when gentle arms wrapped around him was Umasi convinced that what was happening might be real. Forcing his eyes open, Umasi saw a pair of pale blue eyes, barely an inch away, looking back at him with unmasked concern.

"Wha . . . what are you doing?" Umasi murmured weakly.

"Shh," the girl replied, resting her head under his chin. "I owe it to you."

"You . . . don't . . . owe me this," Umasi protested feebly.

"You gave me food when I was hungry, shelter when I was weary, and friendship when I was lonely," she whispered. "If I want to give you warmth when you're cold, that's my business."

Some stubborn part of Umasi's consciousness wanted to protest again, but the miraculous warmth melted away his chills and calmed his troubled mind. Her presence and her heat brought him such comfort that the rest of his consciousness surrendered without a fight. His heart racing, Umasi slid an arm around her back and blindly buried his face in her silver hair. He could feel her heartbeat reverberating clearly through her body, beating much more steadily than his own.

And so for one fevered night, Umasi forgot himself.

So, the Enforcers are getting serious at last," Zen mused.

"That's right, Z," Gabriel agreed. "There're only a few survivors from District 7 that got out in time, and they're reporting that the rest are probably dead. Enforcers are swarming over the entire area like ants, checking every building."

"I trust that the Enforcers are being made to pay for every inch of District 7 that they search?"

"Yeah, the survivors figure that the Enforcers set off *all* the mines." Gabriel nodded. "And the crew themselves made one hell of a last stand at their hideout—they blew their entire remaining stock of explosives rather than come quietly. Frank sent a message saying he can see the smoke all the way from District 13."

"A noble sacrifice," Zen murmured. "And Frank is attentive as always, I'll have to visit his outpost soon. I must admit I hadn't expected Rothenberg to be so wasteful. Something must have prompted this. The Mayor has probably put pressure on him, maybe set a deadline. If he's willing to continue spending resources like this, he must be desperate."

"Should we be worrying about this?" Gabriel asked.

"Perhaps. Our casualties are relatively few and their examples are valiant, but any losses at all are bad for morale. The Enforcers have a lot more men to waste than we do," Zen reasoned, glancing out the store window and into the night. "Indeed, this type of brute force is least favorable to us."

"So what're we going to do about it?"

"We need to spread out faster, and remain unfixed," Zen said. "The crews will need to start falling back at the first sign of Enforcer approach. We clear out when they come, and when they're finished setting off our traps we move right back in and plant them all again. We undo any progress they make. We'll need to track their movements as best we can— every second of forewarning counts."

"But if we're going to scatter and hide for now, it'd be best to scrub out those Truancy symbols," Gabriel suggested, nodding towards the one Zen had painted on the window. "Or perhaps move the real hideouts to places that don't have one."

"No." Zen shook his head. "The symbols can be surprisingly hard to remove, short of painting then over. As for moving, I've gotten rather . . . comfortable . . . in this place. If the Enforcers approach this shop, we will give them more to worry about than a few mines."

"So what are your orders, Z?"

"Get people out into the living districts to track Enforcer activity," Zen said without hesitation. "Tell the crews to assume that the Enforcers might come calling at any time, and to fall back if they do. They better have escape plans prepared, and every crew should always have a lookout posted at all times. Also, tell Amal that I need to see him here in one hour. I have an important job for him."

"All right, Z, I'll take care of it," Gabriel promised with a salute.

Zen frowned. Something had been bothering him and he'd just remembered what it was.

"Don't call me 'Z' anymore, Gabriel," Zen said. "The abbreviation is beginning to tire me."

Gabriel raised an eyebrow.

"Have you picked a new name for yourself already?"

"I'll get back to you on that," Zen promised. "*Tonight,*" he added, seeing the look of skepticism on Gabriel's face.

"If you say so," Gabriel said, spinning around to leave the shop.

Zen looked thoughtful as the Truant shut the door behind him. He had been putting off many things, and this was one of the last of them. For a while now he had felt irked by being addressed as "Z"; it was merely an abbreviation of his old name, and he hated the way it sounded. Right now the Z still stood for Zen, and he knew that people would never have died for the student Zen—and yet that day people *had* died for him, for the first time. It was a milestone now that he thought about it, and yet Zen still felt oddly detached from their deaths. He quickly brushed that thought aside;

he *did* appreciate their sacrifices, sacrifices made for a person who was certainly no longer the student Zen—so what would the letter stand for now?

He began tossing ideas around in his head. Nothing came immediately to mind, and so he idly began stringing *Z* together with other letters of the alphabet. After several moments of this, he hit the combination *ZD*. Something about it felt right to him. He ran it over and over again in his head, faster and faster. ZD . . . Zeede . . . Zeed . . . *Zid.* Yes, that sounded sharp, unique . . . but it looked too short, like his old name. After a second of thought, he mentally slid a *Y* into place, and suddenly found himself with Zyid. At last, Zen thought, he could wholly abandon that last trace of his old life—his name. He would bury the boy he once was, and transform himself into more than an individual. "Zyid" would be an icon of power, a title to be feared and respected.

"Noni," Zen said suddenly. "I've decided on a name you can address me by."

"What is it, sir?" Noni asked.

Zen nodded at her steady response. He had noticed that a thin veneer of ice now seemed to form over the girl whenever she spoke. Zen found that he wasn't unhappy about it, as he could tell that within that frosty cocoon she was changing, growing stronger. He vaguely anticipated the day when she would emerge from it.

"The name is Zyid." Zen spoke the name aloud for the first time, eager for another opinion.

For several long seconds, Noni had none.

"If it's all the same to you," Noni replied at last, "I'd like to keep calling you 'sir.'"

Zen looked at her for a moment, and then shrugged.

"As you wish."

25

Y ou don't seem very pleased to hear from me, Mayor."

That's because I'm not, the Mayor thought.

The cold eyes that regarded him still had that powerful presence that the Mayor remembered from years ago. It made little difference that the eyes were projected from a computer screen, and belonged to a woman thousands of miles away. The girl had grown up into a young woman who looked just as formidable, and perhaps even more dangerous, than she had at the age of eight. The Mayor suppressed a shudder, talking solace in knowing that his sons, related to this woman by blood though they might be, were not yet as perilous as she.

The Mayor knew that the fate of the City rested on this conversation, and that it would take every ounce of acting prowess he had to fool this woman. The Mayor's sole comfort was that the Government couldn't possibly know everything yet, or else armed troops would be marching through the streets of the City even as they spoke.

"I was merely a little surprised," the Mayor said. "You must understand that this is highly irregular."

"Well, I confess that it's not every day that my father asks me to check up on your little experiment."

"And for sound reasons," the Mayor said stiffly. "I have nothing more to add to the reports that I send."

"I am aware of that."

"Then what's this all about?" the Mayor demanded.

The gray eyes glinted, and the Mayor felt his stomach contract in dread. He knew what was coming next.

"My estranged brothers."

The Mayor forced his face to remain impassive even as fear and doubt flooded his mind. They couldn't have found out already, it was impossible. Hardly anyone in the City itself knew about it, the Mayor had made sure of that.

"What about them?" The Mayor asked mildly.

The eyes narrowed, their gaze boring into him through the screen, and the Mayor suddenly felt like a lab specimen being dissected upon a table.

"Let's just say that my father is concerned," she said. "Do you remember the money accounts that my father set up for the boys?"

"Yes," the Mayor answered. As a matter of fact, he had been worrying about those ever since he discovered the cards missing along with his sons. Money was power, and who could tell what two children might do with so much of it? The accounts were outside of the City, beyond his jurisdiction, and he was powerless to do anything to shut them down or even see how much had been spent.

"Well, it just so turns out that the monthly financial reports were being reviewed the other day when an . . . anomaly was discovered," the woman said. "My father was contacted by the treasury, of course, and was assured that it was no mistake."

"And what was the nature of this anomaly?" the Mayor asked warily, though he suspected that he already knew the answer.

"It seems that someone has withdrawn an astounding amount of money from one of the accounts," she replied. "The other has also withdrawn more than usual, though not nearly as much as the first. My father presumes that you have a satisfactory explanation."

The Mayor flashed a mechanical smile. This, at least, was a question that he was prepared to answer, having spent weeks of sleepless nights thinking about it.

"Oh, *that*," the Mayor said. "You almost had me afraid that there was a serious problem."

The woman raised an eyebrow, prompting the Mayor to hurry along with his explanation.

"The boys are now of an age where they should start becoming responsible with their own money," the Mayor said. "I have allowed them to make investments of their choice in the City. Of course, they have more money to experiment with than the typical child, but at least one of the two thinks big."

"I see," the young woman said, a thin smile creeping across her face. "Well, I think that my father will be satisfied with that . . . but one thing, Mayor, off the record, and just between the two of us."

"What?"

"You don't fool *me*."

Then the screen went blank, plunging the room into darkness. The Mayor was left to sit there alone at his desk for the rest of the night, breathing heavily as his heart raced. He would return to normal only long after the sun had risen.

en gazed out the shopwindow as the sound of wooden clacking reached his ears. The bright early-morning sun had melted away the last of the snow that had fallen a few days ago, and the day was shaping up to be the warmest of the winter thus far. Outside in the street, a number of Truants were engaging in friendly duels with each other, wielding crude wooden swords that Zen had allowed them to make for well-deserved recreation. These Truants had accomplished a lot in a short time, and there was no doubt left in Zen's mind that they had the potential to succeed in a way the Educators had never dreamed possible.

Zen was proud, but not *of* them or what they had done. To be proud of their accomplishments would be to lay some claim to them, no matter how small. Zen had decided to leave that particular brand of arrogance to the parents of the City. Instead, Zen was proud of the things that he had done himself, chief among them assembling and leading the formidable Truants before him. As if to punctuate this feeling, Zen suddenly spotted Amal approaching the shop, a look of triumph on the boy's face.

"We got what you asked for, Zyid," Amal said as he entered the shop and held out a large rolled-up paper.

Zen smiled. The new name that he had picked for himself didn't sound normal to him yet, but he didn't mind the novelty of it. Besides, he was certain that in time his invented name would feel more natural than his given one.

"Excellent," Zen said, taking the paper and unfurling it. "How did you manage to obtain it?"

"We marched right into City Hall and said we were doing research for a school project," Amal said. "It's not like they had any reason not to believe us."

"You've done very well," Zen said, placing the paper down onto a table. "Take the rest of the day off. I'll need to see you here tomorrow at eight for another assignment."

Amal bowed out of the shop, and as he left Gabriel slipped in through the door to give his first regular report on Enforcer movements. As he approached Zen, his eyes caught the paper that the Truancy leader was inspecting. Gabriel forgot what he was there to do as recognition struck.

"Say, aren't those—"

"The blueprints for our good old District 1 School?" Zen finished without turning around. "Yes, yes they are."

"What are they for?"

"All in good time," Zen said, rolling the blueprints up again. "These will not be put to use until our friend Rothenberg is removed from the picture."

"You're planning to go after him soon?" Gabriel raised his eyebrows.

"Oh no." Zen shook his head. "If my guess is correct and the Mayor has set Rothenberg a deadline, we will not have to. As soon as that deadline expires, or the Mayor loses his patience, Rothenberg will be removed from power, and then the Mayor will finally discover the extent of what he's been covering up. That's when our struggle begins in earnest."

"What's Rothenberg been covering up?"

Zen turned around and cocked his head at Gabriel.

"The existence of the Truancy, of course. If you were in Rothenberg's position, would *you* want the Mayor to know what we've been up to?"

Gabriel knew that the question was rhetorical, and saw no need to answer it. Instead he asked a different one.

"What do we do until Rothenberg is gone?"

"We continue to fight him," Zen replied. "I expect that as he grows increasingly desperate, Rothenberg's attacks will become more dangerous and reckless. We will make as big a dent in the Enforcers as possible so that they will already have a healthy respect for us when the Mayor inevitably takes over." Gabriel nodded at that. "Now, I believe you were here to update me about the Enforcers' daily movements?"

"Thought you'd never ask. It looks like they're going to move in numerical order. A massive task force swept District 8 about an hour ago, but our guys got out in time and we didn't lose anyone," Gabriel said. "However, some of our patrols in the inhabited districts are reporting that a smaller task force is heading elsewhere, and Frank can't understand it because it's not even a district that he expected them to search. We haven't laid any mines there."

"I need to stop putting off that visit to Frank," Zen muttered. "Which district was he referring to?"

"District 19."

There was a brief moment of silence, and then Zen's eyes glinted as he barely held back a smile.

"District 19?" Zen repeated. "I wonder what mad whim sent Rothenberg there. He can search that district all he wants, he won't find anything. Not even a vagrant would live in that forsaken place."

Well, that certainly looks like trouble," Umasi observed.

"I wonder why they're here," the nameless girl mused. "Do you think they're after you?"

Umasi wondered the same thing himself. The two children were crouching atop a District 19 rooftop, looking down at the streets below. Several blocks away they could see a large procession of patrol cars traveling from block to block, with dozens of uniformed Enforcers scrambling around like blue ants. Umasi silently thanked the bright sun for melting the snow that would've otherwise left tracks.

Umasi had only recently been allowed out of bed. For a few days his companion had gently but firmly insisted that he rest, feeding him herself at every meal. Umasi had been somewhat baffled by her kind treatment, but he was grateful and hadn't thought to protest. He still wondered exactly how much of what he remembered from those delirious days had been real and what hadn't. Some of it certainly seemed too unlikely to be true.

"I doubt they know I'm here for sure, but they probably are looking for me or my brother," Umasi said. "And even if they aren't, they would love to arrest me anyway . . . unless my father's given them permission to shoot me on sight."

"He might permit it, but I won't," his companion said, her crimson gaze fixed on the Enforcers. "We should leave while we can. It looks like they are trying to surround the district."

"I'd like to be able to come back when this is all over," Umasi said uncertainly. "They're still pretty far from the lemonade stand. We have a good chance of hiding it before they get there."

As soon as he suggested it, Umasi felt bad about fussing over such a minor thing when both their lives could be at stake. Still, the stand was precious to him, it was home, and he was sure they could save it in time. Umasi glanced at his companion, who was frowning slightly, but not objecting. Her next word surprised him.

"Okay," she said reluctantly.

Knowing that there was precious little time to waste, the two of them scrambled over to the edge of the building, jumping down onto a series of rusty fire escapes. They ran down the steps and climbed down the metal ladder at the bottom to reach the ground. They then made their way back to the lemonade stand as swiftly as they could.

Umasi was relieved that he hadn't made any lemonade for the day, for it took only a quick trip in and out of the apartment to stuff all the paper cups and the pitcher itself into a garbage bag, which he then tossed into a nearby alley where it wouldn't look out of place. He thought he might've heard something crack as he placed the bag down, but now wasn't the time to make a fuss. The lemonade taken care of, Umasi scrambled to deal with the stand itself.

Meanwhile, his companion had vanished into the apartment, and by the time he entered to check up on her, he found that any evidence that someone had lived there recently had already been dragged off into the basement or tossed into more garbage bags, which joined the others in the alley. Umasi was glad that he had not bought any furniture for the rickety apartment. All in all, it had taken them less than five frantic minutes to finish the job.

"They're almost here," the albino said, glancing at the end of the street. "Maybe two, three blocks away."

"How do you know?" Umasi asked.

"You just have to listen."

Umasi blinked at that, then he paused and allowed his frenzied pulse to steady, shutting his eyes as he strained his ears. To his surprise he found that she was right: there were clearly voices, footsteps, and the low hum of a car engine headed their way.

"Guess we can't go back that way," Umasi muttered. "It's probably too risky to try to going around them as well. We'll just have to go the opposite way."

"That will take us to District 20."

"Yeah," Umasi nodded. "But I don't care what district we end up in as long as we get out of here safely."

"Well said," his companion murmured.

Their minds made up, the two children darted down the street, around the block, and made straight for the nearest barrier separating Districts 19 and 20. Umasi glanced at his companion, who was proving to be a very fast runner, barely breathing hard as her sweater fluttered behind her. It didn't take them long to reach the wooden barrier, still with no sign of Enforcers in sight. They skidded to a halt just before it, slightly out of breath. They could now hear honking and rumbling and all the other typical sounds of the City, but none close enough to have come from directly behind the fence. Nonetheless, the nameless girl still eyed the wooden barrier warily.

"Someone might spot us going over," she said. "It's early morning. Students are heading to school now."

"That street is never very busy, there probably won't be anyone around," Umasi said. "In any case, we have no other—"

"Shh!" The girl pressed a finger to his lips.

Umasi was confused for a moment, but then he heard it as well: two voices on the other side of the fence, rapidly approaching. Umasi felt another surge of appreciation for his companion; if he had climbed over, he might've dropped right on top of their heads. Umasi was now so intent on listening that as the unseen pedestrians passed by them he caught a snippet of their conversation.

". . . I still don't get why you're walking me to school, Dad."

"You may be used to going by yourself, but you're still only thirteen years old. It's perfectly normal for parents to walk their children at your age."

"But why aren't you at work?"

There was an uncomfortable pause.

"The Mayor himself has recently given me a special assignment. I don't follow a strict schedule anymore."

"You mean you got suspended?"

"No, I did not get suspended," the voice snapped. "Stop changing the subject. Even if I were not an Educator I would still be your father, and I can walk you to school whether you like it or not."

"So are you going to walk Suzie to school too?"

"She's still young enough to take the bus, and I think that's quite enough questions from you for one morning. But since we're answering questions now, I have a few to ask about your last report card. . . ."

By this point the voices had already grown so faint that Umasi had to strain to hear them, and their footsteps had also seemed to have faded. His companion, however, remained wary for a few more seconds before finally giving him a nod of approval. Umasi scrambled over to the wooden barrier, using the boards jutting out from it as footholds as he climbed over. He was relieved to land on his feet, and even more relieved to find that the street was indeed empty of people. A moment later, the nameless girl gracefully slid over as well, joining him at his side.

"We made it," Umasi said, relieved. "Where do we go now?"

"I know a place where we can stay," the pale girl said.

"You do?" Umasi blinked.

"Yes," she said, looking away as though fighting a battle with herself. "This is an odd request, but could you wear both pairs of sunglasses while I lead you?"

"Both sunglasses?" Umasi repeated.

"It'll work like a blindfold, but won't look so odd." The albino turned to look at him again. "The place that I'll be taking you . . . I've never shown anyone before."

Umasi hesitated, but only for a moment. The request was odd, but he could see that this place, wherever it was, was very important to her. He trusted this girl implicitly, and she hadn't asked any questions when he wanted to hide his stand. The least he could do was grant her wish for secrecy.

"All right," Umasi said, fishing his sunglasses out of his pocket. "Let's go."

His companion's ruby eyes sparkled as she handed him her pair of sunglasses, which he awkwardly doubled up with his own and slipped onto his face. He soon found that the effect left him nearly blind, though he could vaguely make out the faintest outline of the world around him. He was sure that there was no way he could find his way back even if he tried. The pale girl slid her hand in his and tugged, leading him along.

The trip through the noisy, live district wasn't as uncomfortable as it might've been, as the albino proved to be a careful and considerate guide. Still, Umasi did manage to bump into things a few times and nearly tripped on the edge of the sidewalk once. He also had the nagging feeling that people around him were staring, even though he couldn't see them. Eventually, the noises of the City seemed to die away, and Umasi had the feeling that they were now in another abandoned district, though he couldn't be sure.

Finally, the girl released his hand, prompting Umasi to reach up and slide both sunglasses off of his face and into his pocket. He found himself looking up at a dirty, run-down brownstone with another rusted fire escape. He glanced at his companion, who merely smiled back and began climbing the metal ladder. Umasi followed suit, thinking that they were headed for the roof. But at the third floor, the girl stepped in through a shattered window. Umasi followed and found himself in a dark room with only faint light from the broken windows to illuminate the rubble strewn about the floor. Umasi felt as though he was traveling through a cave as he followed his guide, who led him over to another window, this one with a rope ladder leading down.

His guide gracefully descended the ladder, and Umasi followed, not fully paying attention to where he was climbing. But as he hit the ground, he froze, awestruck. They now stood atop the roof of a small building wedged between two taller ones, giving the peculiar impression that he was at the bottom of a valley, with small mountains to each side. All around there were flowerpots filled with soil, and dead vines scaled the walls to either side. Umasi could see the wilted remains of plants that would bloom again in the spring. A few skeletal trees had caught some unmelted snow, which glittered in the pale sunlight.

While no flowers remained, dozens and dozens of icicles glistened instead, hanging from windowsills above, from tree branches, from every ledge imaginable. These glittering prisms were still in the process of melting, their droplets catching the light like a sparkling rain. Over to one side, a pipe had been broken, the frozen water that had once spewed from it still unmelted, leaving a frothy cascade suspended in the air.

It was a small slice of paradise in the midst of a City where too much was ugly. But Umasi couldn't stop himself, despite strenuous effort, from thinking that the most beautiful thing in the garden was the pale girl that stood beside him, outshining all the radiant white around her. With difficulty, Umasi shook himself from his stupor and gave his surroundings a closer inspection, the cold turning his cheeks red.

He realized that this garden had obviously been used as a dwelling for some time. Rusty pots and pans were stacked among some flowerpots in one corner, and near the broken pipe Umasi could see a washcloth and a bar of soap. Before it had frozen, it had been a shower. Umasi noted that that must be why the pale vagrant had seemed so clean. A bundle of blankets in a corner indicated a bed to him, and though he wasn't sure where she slept when it rained he guessed that it would be somewhere in the cavernous building that they had passed through.

"Is this where you've lived all these years?" Umasi asked at last.

"It's as close a thing to home as I'll ever have." The girl nodded. "You're the first person I've ever shown it to."

"I'm honored, milady."

The albino turned her head to look at Umasi again. She spent several long moments just looking at him, to the point that Umasi began to feel embarrassed. Then a soft breeze flitted through the brick canyon, blowing a few strands of dark hair into Umasi's eyes.

"Your hair is getting longer," she observed.

"Yeah," Umasi agreed, flicking the rebellious strands away with one finger. "I haven't gotten it cut in a while. It's getting a bit annoying, actually. My brother is the one who likes it long."

"If you want, I can cut it for you."

"You can?" Umasi asked, looking over at his companion in surprise.

"I've had to cut my own for most of my life," she reminded him. "A simple bowl cut would work for you, I think, and that wouldn't be hard to do at all."

"How's that work?"

"Just as it sounds. May I try it?"

"Anything you want, milady," Umasi said, and meant it from the bottom of his heart.

She smiled at him, and Umasi thought that there was a knowing look in her eyes, as though she understood just how deeply he meant what he'd said. Then she was off, rummaging through the neatly arranged pile of old pots and pans until she found one that met her approval. It was a fairly deep pot, and slightly rusty, though it fit Umasi's head perfectly. Before placing it there, however, the girl first produced a comb and a pair of scissors, and then gently parted Umasi's hair down the middle so that it framed his face. Then the pot went on, and Umasi soon felt a snipping sensation.

The girl gently cut off all the hair that protruded from beneath the pot. The dark, severed hairs fell onto Umasi's shoulders and lap, some even sticking uncomfortably to his neck. By the time the pot was lifted and a small, cracked mirror placed before his eyes, Umasi noted that he had a neat and precise appearance about him that he'd never had before.

"How do you like it?" she asked, helping him brush off some excess hair from his neck—a simple gesture that sent goose bumps down his body.

"Much better, thank you," Umasi said. He stood up to shake the remaining hair from his shoulders.

"Good." The girl stretched as she lay down on the bare ground. "Running from the Enforcers made me a bit tired. Take a nap."

Umasi hesitated for a moment, then joined her on the ground as bidden. It occurred to him that his spotless clothing might get dirty, but he hadn't forgotten his days as a vagrant and knew that a little soot wouldn't do him any harm. Staring up from within the brick canyon, he realized that the sun's light had already begun to fade; it was neither light nor dark now, but a lukewarm blue. A soft hand sought his, and together the two of them lay there in perfect peace until the light finally vanished, giving way to darkness.

Only then did Umasi return to his senses, and his hand released its grip as he sat up abruptly.

"The Enforcers are probably gone by now," Umasi said. "I wonder if we should go back."

Then Umasi felt a tug on his sleeve, and he turned to see his companion smiling impishly at him.

"What's the rush?" she asked, pulling him back to the ground.

Backpack slung over one shoulder, Edward listlessly walked back towards the orphanage, dirty snow lining the street on either side. As he walked, he noted that the day was already dying, its bloody red light spilling all over the City. The winter days were short, but it was still unusual for most students to get out of school at sunset. Edward, however, had been encouraged to take extra elective classes by his teachers. He had obliged them, of course, though he resented the time wasted upholding his image.

None of the other orphanage students got out as late as Edward did, and so he mostly had the street to himself. Occasionally a car or another pedestrian would pass him, but by City standards this route, running right next to an abandoned district, was a lonely one. That was one of the few things that Edward liked about it. Pausing for a moment at a curb, Edward turned and looked down the street, noting the crude wooden barrier that had been erected to block it off. That way led to District 19, and Edward spared the barrier a hard glance before moving again.

District 19 was a direct neighbor to District 18, and had long been abandoned. As far back as Edward could remember, the houses visible above the fence had been empty. Edward had never seen anyone walking the streets of that district, though he had peered over it on occasion. More than once he had been tempted to scale the fence completely and see what he might find in that forbidden place, but each time he concluded that the risks outweighed any potential gain.

As Edward idly kicked an empty soda can out of his way, he became aware of the sound of sirens. Enforcer sirens. Edward looked around cautiously, involuntarily touching his hand to the spot on his cheek where that Enforcer named Rothenberg had struck him. He would never forget that blow, he knew. In time he would dish out many more like it himself.

It took Edward more than a moment to realize that the sounds were not coming from District 18, but rather from his left, from *behind* the wooden barrier. Edward froze in confusion and excitement. Nothing ever went on in District 19, certainly nothing important enough to warrant the presence of Enforcers. Seized by a thrill of curiosity, Edward grabbed a newspaper dispenser and dragged it over to the wooden barrier. A passerby stared at him as he worked, but said nothing even as Edward pushed the dispenser against the fence. Standing on top of it, Edward was just barely able to peer over the edge, and what he saw only increased his interest.

Several blocks into the abandoned district, dozens of uniformed men and women were scrambling in and out of buildings, going from door to door and hastily searching every apartment. Enforcers, beyond a shadow of a doubt, and Edward couldn't imagine that the Enforcers would waste valuable resources on a blind sweep through the entire City. They were obviously looking for something important, something they thought might be in District 19 . . . but what? What secret could District 19 possibly hold that would justify such a search?

With a jolt, Edward noticed that on one of the buildings the Enforcers had set up a small surveillance camera to watch the fence. Edward quickly withdrew his head, wondering if it had alerted anyone. Deciding that it would be best to leave before that question was answered, Edward leapt down from the newspaper dispenser and ran off. At school he was known for being an athletic boy, and he was soon out of sight of the fence.

Minutes later, he reached the orphanage unhindered, though the images of what he had seen still filled his mind as he greeted the matrons politely and entered his private dormitory. He felt excited as he had not been for a long time. He had stumbled upon something secret, something important. What had merely been a whim before now had a newfound urgency. There was more to District 19 than had previously met his eyes, and as Edward sat down on his bed, deep in thought, he resolved to cross over that fence as soon as it was safe to do so. If there was indeed something important hiding within District 19, Edward vowed that he would be the one to find it.

N ight had fallen, and with it the stars had come out, clearly visible from the hidden garden. Lying on his back, Umasi enjoyed the gentle rustling of the wind, the twinkling of the stars up above, and most of all, the conversation he was now having with his companion. It was not casual, for they discussed deep secrets that had never been shared before, but the words flowed so naturally that they hardly thought about what they said. It was as if they were spinning bonds with threads of words, and those bonds, not the words, were what Umasi cherished.

". . . so back when I was in school I used to get bullied all the time," he said. "They would make fun of my name. . . . I never liked my name, my brother's is much better. Anyway, he was the one who would always protect me, Zen was. He was my only friend, or as close to one as I had. I was always an outcast in school."

"I was an outcast from birth," the albino said. "My parents, I think, knew what my fate would be, but they raised me anyway until the time came. Maybe they hoped I would get in, I don't remember anymore. The Educators evaluated my 'condition' and decided that I couldn't possibly learn like a normal student. I was expelled by default . . . never had a chance."

"That was wrong of them."

She said nothing, but merely kept looking up at the sky, the glittering stars reflected in her blue eyes.

"I've been wondering, though," Umasi continued, "your parents . . . they gave you a name, right?"

"Yes."

"Why don't you use it?"

"They gave me a name in the hope that I would be able to live a normal life," she explained. "That hope was futile. I have no number. I have no name. To this City I may as well have not existed, and I am content that way."

"It matters to me that you exist," Umasi said. "Did you really never talk to anyone else?"

"Occasionally," she replied. "Obviously, I tried to avoid people. The only ones I ever approached were starved or crazy, and usually thought I was a monster or an angel. It's hard to say which frightened them more. A few attacked me. That's how I began experimenting with the chain."

"I remember how isolated I felt sometimes, and that was back when I had a brother, a father, countless people that I was in contact with every day," Umasi said. "The only reason I wasn't violent was because I was a coward. But you're completely at peace, even when shunned by the entire City. Why is that?"

She was silent for several long moments, and Umasi turned his head to look at her. She was even more striking in the starlight than she had been in daylight. Her skin and hair seemed to possess a pale magical luminance of their own.

"I think it was because I always clung to words," she said at last. "I rarely had anyone to talk to, but I had the papers and books that I salvaged. They were anchors to humanity when I couldn't be seen. I also had a dog once . . . before the Enforcers cracked down on strays. Without them I might've ended up like the worst vagrants of this City."

She gestured up at the empty and abandoned apartment that they had to travel through to reach the garden, and Umasi understood that that must be where she kept her treasures. It made sense to him, and it explained why she spoke with such literacy compared with other vagrants he had encountered.

"Someday we should visit a bookstore," Umasi suggested. "I never read much besides what my teachers told me to."

The albino hesitated in answering, and for the first time Umasi saw a troubled look on her face. That more than anything worried him, and suddenly he felt afraid of what her next words might be.

"I won't be staying with you forever, you know."

He'd been expecting that, but Umasi's heart still sank. A few clouds, black against the night sky, slowly floated in to obscure the stars. Umasi wondered why he was so surprised; he had known from the start that the nameless girl was an independent spirit at heart, that it was extraordinary she had stayed as long as she had. But even so, he had become used to her calming presence, her musical voice, her fragrant smell, her gentle touch . . . Umasi cringed. The thought of separation was suddenly unbearable.

"When are you going to leave?"

"Sooner rather than later," she replied. "You and I are too free to be happily bound to each other. We could never remain together. Go and chase your own dreams, whatever they may be."

"I only ever have nightmares," Umasi said bitterly. "Zen is the one with all the dreams."

"You're always talking about your brother," the girl said suddenly, looking at him intently. "What about you?"

"M-me?" Umasi sputtered. "What's there to say about me?"

"Can't you think of anything?"

"I . . . don't trust myself to judge myself," Umasi said. "Why don't you tell me?"

"The good and the bad?"

"Yes, please."

"I might break your heart."

At that Umasi hesitated for several long seconds, but then he plunged on without even realizing it.

"My heart is yours to break, if that's what you want to do with it."

His nameless companion looked at him with soft but searching blue eyes. Then, evidently convinced of his sincerity, she took a deep breath.

"You're naïve, almost to the point where you might be mistaken for ignorant," she began. "You're a coward at heart, afraid of doing things that need to be done. You're arrogant—don't give me that look, it's true! You've got it in your head that you're going to be the one to save the whole City, when you barely managed to save yourself!"

Umasi winced. The words hurt, but he had asked for them, hadn't he?

"You've been pampered all your life and it's made you lazy. You're also immature in many ways, but I think they all tie back into your naïveté." The girl began ticking points off her fingers. "You're not dumb, but you don't apply your intelligence to anything practical. All you've ever used your head for was to add numbers and satisfy teachers. Really, in some ways you're just like all those other sorry students you mentioned." Umasi shut his eyes at that comparison, but did not cover his ears. "You're also a hopeless optimist, and it makes you gullible. Ah, and you expect the world to be all compassionate when you yourself try to act tough. Telling others to do something while refusing to do it yourself . . . is there a word for that?"

She looked questioningly at Umasi, whose throat now felt dry.

"Hypocrite," Umasi croaked.

"Yes, you're a hypocrite." She nodded sagely. "So that's what that word means; I could never figure that out before. Oh, and there is your unhealthy obsession with your brother, but I think you already know about that. That's about it. Was that what you were looking for?"

Umasi somehow managed a nod. He had never felt so worthless in his life.

"Good." She smiled faintly and patted his head. "Your list of good traits is shorter, but at least you have one. You're sweet, in your own way, and generous. And deep down there you've got true strength. Even you haven't realized that yet, but I think you will, someday. I certainly do, at any rate."

"So you love me?" Umasi asked in a half-serious tone, though he yearned for a serious answer.

The pale vagrant gravely turned her soft blue eyes onto him, and he suddenly felt very squeamish.

"You weren't like anyone else I've met," she said, avoiding the question. "I couldn't scare you, for one thing. And you were accepting, for another. I'd nearly lost faith in people, having been away from them for so long." She smiled and looked heavenwards. "You showed me that there's still good in this City. I'm glad that I met you."

"But not glad enough to stay?"

She glanced back at him again and her eyes, though dry, were sad. The dark skies above were now fully masked by storm clouds.

"No, Umasi," she said quietly, "not glad enough to stay."

26
FADE TO WHITE

The day was murky and overcast as Edward strode down the street, casting furtive glances at the other passersby. It was Sunday, and not many people were out in this part of the district, but he was taking no chances. Today he intended to find a way around that surveillance camera, and it wouldn't do to have anyone seeing him hanging around District 19. As he drew closer to the fence that separated Districts 18 and 19, the crowds steadily began to thin, until Edward was completely alone on the block as he approached the final stretch.

As Edward was about to round the last corner to reach the fence, he heard the unmistakable sounds of a scuffle. Slowing down as a precaution, he peered around the corner and saw two bullies attacking a third student, a smaller boy who looked a little younger than Edward. Judging by the groceries that lay scattered on the ground, Edward figured that the boy had been returning from the supermarket when the bullies struck.

Typically, the streets of the inhabited districts of the City were safe. The Educators' system tended to produce well-behaved, tolerant children who grew up into similarly well-mannered adults. But there was always a small minority belligerent enough to cause trouble, but smart enough to avoid expulsion—at least for a while. District 18 had a largely innocent population just like any other inhabited district, but unfortunately for the luckless boy around the corner, it also included its own menacing minority.

As Edward watched them fight, he thought that the victim was doing rather well, all things considered. He threw punches and kicks at his larger tormentors as wildly as he could, but eventually one of them managed to lock his arms behind his back, and that was the end of that. Edward briefly considered waiting for them to finish and just get out of his way so that he could get on with his business. However, when a whole minute passed without the bullies showing any signs of relenting, Edward lost his patience. Sighing, Edward picked his backpack up again and strode around the corner.

"Are we going to have a problem, or are you all going to get the hell out of my way?" Edward called out.

The two bullies glanced up at Edward with undisguised contempt on their faces.

"Mind your own business, blondie. Get outta here before you end up like this kid."

"That sounds like a raw deal." Edward yawned. "Here's a better one. You get out of my sight now, or I will remove you from it."

"Isn't this kid from one of the lower grades, Jim? He's got quite a mouth on him."

"Guess his parents never taught him when to keep it shut."

"My parents, being the extraordinary fools that they were, are dead," Edward said impatiently. "Get out of my way unless you want to join them."

"Hah! I remember now, he's one of those orphan kids!"

"Yeah, I bet he—hey, whaddya think you're doing, blond boy?"

In answer to the question Edward plunged his fist into the speaker's face. With a roar of outrage, the other miscreant, named Jim, aimed a punch of his own at Edward. A moment later, Jim stumbled forward clumsily, having hit nothing but air. Edward let out a snort of derision at his foe's bumbling. Growling now, Jim lunged and swung at Edward's face.

This time, Edward ducked and slammed his elbow into Jim's stomach. Jim howled in agony and fell to the ground, his own momentum having carried him right into Edward's blow. As Jim lay cursing and writhing on the sidewalk, his companion rose to his feet and stared at Edward in stunned disbelief.

"You stupid little blond!" the boy snarled.

He lunged, intending to tackle the smaller Edward to the ground. Edward reacted faster than expected, leaping backwards out of the way before his foe could realize what had happened. There was a suspended moment of shock as the bully realized the enormity of his blunder, and then he crashed painfully to the ground face-first.

"My name's not Blond, fool," Edward said as he kicked the fallen bully in the ribs. "It's Edward. Remember it."

The bully snarled incoherently for a second, and looked like he was about to spew a vicious retort. Then Edward kicked him in the ribs again, and he resumed moaning unintelligibly. Edward moved back to the boy named Jim, who sprang painfully to his feet at Edward's approach and ran as fast as he could. Edward did not give pursuit, and a moment later the other miscreant was up and running as well.

"Thanks . . ." a weak voice called out from behind Edward.

Edward spun around to see the miscreants' victim lying on the ground, his red hair ruffled and dirty. Edward noted that the boy's eyes were nearly swollen shut, and that even if they were not, this pitiful kid was hardly likely to betray him to the Enforcers.

"I didn't do it for *you*," Edward said as he proceeded over to the wooden fence. "You were just as much a part of the nuisance as they were."

"You . . . aren't thinking of going into District 19, are you?"

Edward ignored the boy and proceeded to climb the fence using its irregularities as footholds. This was a different stretch of fence than before, but as Edward reached the top and looked around, he spotted another camera pointed right at his position. Swearing under his breath, Edward dropped to the ground again.

"It looks like there's going to be another blizzard," the boy said tentatively. "You should get indoors."

With that suggestion the boy gathered up his groceries and staggered away. Ignoring him, Edward walked one block down and, as he expected, found no camera there. He figured that the Enforcers had set up surveillance every other block, and only around this area, which was close to the gate they'd have used to enter the district.

Edward was considering going over the fence right then and there, but then a snowflake drifted before his eyes. Looking up, Edward frowned as he realized the boy had been right; the snow was now starting to fall in thick sheets. If he were to proceed into District 19 now, there would be little chance of him finding anything in a total whiteout. Edward smiled in spite of himself. That was his typical luck, wasn't it?

Edward began making his way back to the orphanage, the snow stinging at his face, the wind howling in his ears. The trip hadn't been a waste; he now knew how to enter District 19 undetected. He intended to do just that as soon as the blizzard was over.

A re you sure you want to do this?"

"Yes. I want to know if I've learned anything."

"And perhaps a few bruises to remember me by?"

"If you really are leaving today—"

"I am."

"—then why not? We'll part the same way we met."

"Fighting?"

"Fighting."

"Very well, if it means that much to you. Don't hold back."

"Yes, milady."

Their gazes locked, and Umasi and his opponent slowly began circling each other, crushing the fresh snow beneath their feet. All around them the blizzard raged, endless curtains of white falling to cover their tracks even as they were made. The howl of the wind was so loud that their voices had been raised in order to speak, and the snow so thick that Umasi could barely see his adversary as she blended in perfectly with the white. Her chain clinked slightly as it slid down from within her sleeve, and Umasi's knuckles were as white as hers as he gripped his improvised wooden sword.

Then simultaneously they came to a stop, and Umasi lunged forward, bringing his sword down in an arc at his opponent. To his surprise she did not dodge, but held a length of chain taught between her hands, bringing it up to block the blow. As the two weapons clashed, she pushed the wooden sword back over Umasi's head and behind his back, trapping it there, reminding him of something she had once told him.

"It's a difficult weapon to predict, but it's better for countering. You're just dodging right now; if you were attacking me it'd be harder."

Before Umasi could even think about a way out of his uncomfortable plight, she had shoved forward with her knee, roughly bringing him to the ground. For a moment Umasi struggled there in the snow, and then the chain was gone, his sword suddenly free. Umasi leapt back to his feet, but as he looked around frantically he saw nothing but endless white. His foe had vanished into the blizzard like a wraith. He froze, bracing himself for the attack he knew was sure to come.

He didn't have to wait long; a moment later a tinkling chain cut through the white, swooping straight for his head. Umasi ducked and lunged towards the spot it had come from, but when he reached it he found nothing. Nonplussed, Umasi turned around just in time to see the chain strike him on the forehead. Umasi saw stars for a moment, and then, swearing loudly, fell back on his behind as the chain vanished again.

He got to his feet cautiously, and over the howling wind Umasi thought he heard laughter. This time he was able to spot the oncoming chain just in time, and knowing better than to try grabbing it he dodged instead. Frustrated, Umasi wondered how he was supposed to fight back against an enemy that he could not see or predict.

"You just have to listen."

Remembering those words, Umasi froze in place and hastily drew one of the pairs of sunglasses from his pockets, willing his pounding heart to be still. He placed the glasses before his eyes, and as his sight was plunged into darkness, listened intently. There was nothing but the moaning of wind, the patter of snow, his own heavy breaths, the blood pumping through his veins, the tinkling of an oncoming chain . . .

Umasi jumped reflexively, and heard the chain swoosh by mere inches from his head. Umasi smiled, and snow blew into his open mouth. He could not see, but he was no longer blind.

Crunch, crunch, crunch.

The sound of his footsteps in the snow was now almost deafening to his ears as he moved towards the origin of the attack, ears straining desperately for any sound of other movement.

Crunchunch, crunchunch, crunchunch.

Realizing that his footsteps seemed to have an impossible echo, Umasi stopped, his own feet falling silent, though the sound of others clearly persisted. His foe seemed to realize that she had been discovered, for the steps abruptly grew rapider.

Crunchcrunchcrunch—swoosh!

He knew the chain was coming, but this time Umasi did not dodge, but struck with his wooden sword, knocking the ring aside and to the ground. As the chain was noisily dragged back, Umasi lunged forward at the source, swinging his sword sideways just as the end of the chain returned to its mistress' hand. In a split second the albino drew a length of chain taut, barely managing to block the blow. Umasi felt elated at finally having been able to strike at his foe, but then she spun and kicked him in the chest, sending him staggering back a few paces.

Recovering quickly, Umasi swiftly brought his sword to bear again, but this time she hurled the chain so that it caught on his weapon, wrapping around it several times before coming to a rest, the metal ring dangling, weighing it down. Umasi feebly tried to swing his trapped sword, but in one graceful motion his foe stepped forward and elbowed him in the stomach. The pain was crippling, and Umasi knew that he didn't stand a chance with one of his hands busy clutching a useless weapon.

Without hesitation Umasi cast aside his sword and blocked the girl's next punch with his arm. The move had clearly been unexpected, for he was able to lash out and land a glancing blow, granting him an opportunity to slip something into her pocket unnoticed. Grunting in surprise, the girl leapt backwards and spun around, swirling like the snow, and then she was gone, vanished again into the blizzard. For a moment Umasi thought that he would be annoyed, but to his surprise he realized that being thwarted had not bothered him at all the entire fight. Understanding came crashing down upon him harder than the blizzard. He had achieved the same peace as she without even realizing it.

Her pacifism was not naïveté, as his had been before when he was a student, but rather the opposite. They had now seen enough of the City to know how cruel it could be, yet had come to terms with it. He did not seek defeat, but rather knew how to accept it and its consequences, if it came. He could not be moved, he could not be fazed; he had learned the nature of her strength, and it did not come from aggression.

He heard her long before she struck, stepping out from the blizzard as though she'd been part of the snow herself. Umasi ducked her chain, and then threw a fierce pair of punches. This time, however, in a blurrily fast motion she let the chain slip over his first wrist, looped it around the second, and then pulled the chain taut to trap them together. His hands now hopelessly entangled, she threw him easily over her shoulder. Umasi attempted to struggle as he hit the ground, but then he felt the sole of a shoe pressing lightly on his throat, and he knew he had lost.

But he smiled anyway, because for the first time he was wholly untroubled by defeat. He raised his hands in submission, the pressure on his throat was removed, and he stood up to give the victor a deep bow. She curtsied back, drew her chain around her arm, and then leaned forward to kiss him on the lips. It was just a peck, nothing more, but suddenly the howling wind and icy cold seemed very, very distant to Umasi.

"Does that mean you love me after all?"

He instantly wished that he could inhale those words right back into his throat, for he knew what her answer would be—but at the same time, he was deeply relieved that he had said them. The girl, for her part, cocked her head and smiled.

"Is there a correct answer to this question?"

"I may have been a good student, but I never studied that subject," Umasi confessed. "I don't know."

She laughed—a gentle sound like the tinkling of glass that drowned out the fierce roaring of the wind. Closing the gap between herself and Umasi, she traced a slow circle around his heart with her finger.

"Let's not make this complicated," she whispered into his ear. "I imagine that to love someone you have to care about them more than you do yourself."

"That makes sense," Umasi murmured, suddenly feeling as though he were in a trance.

"If it's true"—her voice was now serious—"then no, I don't love you, Umasi. I've never loved anyone in my life, and I don't think I can learn how to now."

"That's not true." Umasi shook himself out of his stupor. "You helped me, even when you had nothing to gain. And I can see it in the way you fight. You haven't been selfish—you're the most selfless person I know."

"I suppose that you could be right," the girl said before turning to look straight at Umasi. "But what about you, Umasi? Do you love me?"

Umasi froze for a long, hard second under her gaze, and then, struggling to rationalize what was utterly irrational, he forced himself to think. No, as infatuated with her as he was, he didn't believe that he cared for her more than he did himself. And so he spoke the first thing to come from his mind, and not from his heart.

"No, I don't love you either."

"Mmm . . ." the girl mused, only the slightest trace of disappointment in her voice. "It's probably best that way."

"At least you know that you're not the only selfish one," Umasi teased.

It felt as though an intense pressure had been lifted from his head. The burning, obsessive longing whose existence he had never acknowledged dissipated, leaving both clarity and loneliness in its wake. He felt clear-headed and lucid once more, but cold and empty at the same time.

Then the albino laughed pleasantly, and for the briefest instant Umasi felt emotion grip him again, though it faded swiftly with her laughter.

"I will miss you, you know," she said as she drew away.

"And I you."

The girl curtsied one last time, and then spun around and briskly walked away into the snow. She paused only once, having remembered to utter the simplest, yet perhaps the most important, thing that she had to say.

"Good-bye, Umasi!" she called.

"Farewell, milady," Umasi whispered, his words lost to the wind as he bowed with deepest respect.

At that, the girl vanished into the blizzard for good. Instead of turning away, Umasi remained firmly rooted to that spot until the snow buried him up to his ankles. Darkness fell swiftly in the middle of winter, and as the shadowy snow swirled all around, Umasi realized that it was as if she had never even been there at all. The girl had left behind no evidence of her presence, not even a name to be remembered by . . . and yet Umasi knew that he would never forget her.

Cursing the weather, Rothenberg drew the hood of his warm jacket lower as the blizzard howled all around him. Each step through the increasingly deep snow of District 18 felt like hard labor, and after a long day of work Rothenberg felt exhausted. Still, he was in good spirits. His new campaign of attrition was producing results, his Enforcers steadily securing more districts each day, though casualties were mounting. What's more, the task force he had dispatched to District 19 had turned up empty-handed after a thorough search. Even surveillance cameras had caught nothing but some dumb kid, and Rothenberg had now convinced himself that he might have imagined the ghostly encounter. For the first time in a long time, Rothenberg was looking forward to a good night's sleep. Yawning, Rothenberg looked up to check what street he was on, and then his blood turned cold.

He was again staring at a pure white girl, the very same apparition he had encountered before, the one whose existence he had just begun to allow himself to deny. Her clothes were different now, new, clean. She no longer looked like a vagrant, but seemed whiter than the snow that swirled around her. Terrified, Rothenberg reached for his gun with a shaking hand, but by the time he'd drawn it the ghost had vanished, swallowed up by the endless white.

Rothenberg shook his head and plunged forward. He had to know, he had to, and this was his one chance. Reaching the spot where the ghost had stood, Rothenberg stared down at the snow-covered ground, marred by fresh footprints. What kind of ghost left footprints? Rothenberg began following the tracks as fast as his legs could carry him through the deep snow. Ghost or monster, it didn't matter; what he had seen had not been natural, and he was determined to discover its secret.

The footprints led on through the night, until they finally turned and vanished into a narrow alley. Rothenberg swore as he looked into it; the snow had not accumulated in this tight space, and the footprints had simply disappeared. Adrenaline now thundering in his veins, Rothenberg began backtracking, breathing hard through his nose like a bull. He could not know where the girl had gone, but he intended to do his damnedest to find out where she had come from.

The snow was now falling so heavily that the trail was growing harder to track, but Rothenberg was able to follow the increasingly faint footsteps to the fence that divided Districts 18 and 19. With a jolt of horror, Rothenberg saw a clear depression by the fence where the girl had fallen after crossing over. Rothenberg's shiver had nothing to do with the cold. His task force had searched District 19, searched it thoroughly. There was supposed to be nothing, nothing, how could they have missed . . . ?

Rothenberg shook his head again. There was no use contemplating the ineptitude of his subordinates. If they refused to find anything, then he would do it himself. Seizing footholds in the wooden fence, Rothenberg scrambled over it, muttering an oath as he fell on the other side. His displeasure vanished, however, as soon as he realized that the tracks were still visible for some distance. Scrambling to his feet, Rothenberg continued following the footsteps until they faded into complete obscurity. Surrounded by the silhouettes of massive, dark buildings, and with endless curtains of snow falling all around him, Rothenberg suddenly felt very small (a rare occurrence indeed) as he stumbled farther into the district. And then he saw it, rubbing his eyes for fear that he was hallucinating or that he had stumbled into some sort of dream. Directly under a single orange streetlamp, covered by the newly fallen snow, was a stand with a cardboard sign still visible above the snowline. It read "Lemonade: 1 Bill."

Rothenberg staggered forward and reached out to touch the stand, brushing snow aside to reveal paper cups and a jug of frozen lemonade. It was all real, weird, and more than a little eerie. Rothenberg looked around again. There were depressions in the snow that might have been more footprints, but so much had fallen since that it was impossible to be sure. His task force had definitely not found this stand when they searched the district, so where had it come from? Had someone come and set it up for no reason after the Enforcers had left? Who could have done it? A vagrant could never afford it, a student would never have dared it . . . could it then possibly have been one of the Mayor's sons? No, that was absurd; one of them was playing soldier, and Rothenberg was sure that the other was dead by now, though he was smart enough to keep that opinion to himself.

That ghost or whatever it was had something to do with the stand, Rothenberg decided. Something sinister and unnatural was at work in this district, he was convinced of it. Suddenly the wind began an eerie wail, and Rothenberg glanced around frantically. The swirling, shadowed snow seemed to Rothenberg like dozens of white monsters dancing in the darkness, beckoning him to join them. Seized by an irrational panic, Rothenberg spun around and ran for the fence as fast as he could, the haunting wind pursuing him every step of the way.

27
EDWARD

dward awoke just after dawn and retrieved his knife from under the floorboard, hiding it in his belt; his gun would have been too big to conceal. After stealing some breakfast from the kitchen, he slipped out of the orphanage. He knew that his presence would not be missed; the staff was well aware of all the extra courses he took, and they never begrudged him an unannounced trip to the library. Or at least that was where he always told them he was going. To be fair, it was occasionally true. Occasionally. Most of his real destinations would have landed him in deep trouble with the staff and even the Enforcers, and today's second attempt to search District 19 counted as one of them.

Edward was pleased to see that most of the roads in District 18 had already been cleared; the City's snowplows were as efficient as ever. With hardly anyone walking the streets so early, Edward had little trouble reaching a safe part of the fence that divided the two districts. This time he climbed right over the wooden fence, dropping easily onto the soft and unplowed snow on the other side.

Edward stood up, brushed flakes from his uniform, and looked around. Snow blanketed everything in sight, sparkling faintly in the pale morning sun. There were no visible footprints, indicating that Edward was the first to walk this part of the district since the blizzard ended. That suited him fine. He wasn't sure how much truth there was to the rumors about murderous vagrant packs, but he wasn't eager to confirm them.

Edward began making his way through the district, but was slowed down by the deep snow. Still unsure of what exactly to look for, Edward glanced around as he went, though he was fairly certain that anything worth finding would stand out the moment he saw it. It had occurred to him that the odds of finding anything were slim, because if the Enforcers hadn't already found it, Edward stood little chance of doing so alone. Still, he was prepared to return as many times as need be to confirm that District 19 had nothing of interest to offer.

Despite his frequent wanderings, this was Edward's first time in an abandoned district, and it seemed almost eerie to him, an urban landscape devoid of life. Eyeing the ramshackle buildings all around, Edward hoped that he wouldn't have to enter them, as some of them seemed unstable. Just then, Edward's foot crunched into the snow again and he froze. This step had felt different. Stooping down, Edward inspected the ground. There was a sort of depression in the snow. Looking up, Edward saw a number of similar depressions riddling the street ahead. It was difficult to tell, but they seemed to be grouped together in pairs, almost as if some massive man had come running through during the night, and the blizzard had since covered the tracks.

Edward stood up and looked around, wary. If his hunch was right, and someone had recently passed by, then District 19 might be more dangerous than he suspected. At that moment, a voice spoke from behind him, and Edward nearly jumped out of his skin.

"You've been searching for a long time. May I ask what you're looking for?"

Edward spun around, prepared for a fight. Then he froze, for what stood before him now as not a vagrant, but a strange boy wearing black sunglasses and a smirk.

Y ou look awful."

"Mind your own business."

"I thought we'd settled this, Rothenberg. Your physical and mental state *is* my business."

Rothenberg grimaced, his cup of coffee cold in his hands. Despite having had no sleep at all following the previous night's haunting excursion into District 19, he hadn't been that troubled until the Mayor's aide had showed up. Upon returning to Enforcer Headquarters, he had been greeted with the news that some of the scouts he had deployed on foot had managed to enter District 13 without setting off the explosives that were designed to take out vehicles. One of them had spotted signs of recent Truancy activity, and so Rothenberg had found himself facing a once-in-a-lifetime opportunity to corner a large group of the kids in their own lair. Rothenberg had just begun to plan the attack when Jack had shown up with his usual determination to get in Rothenberg's way.

"What more do you want from me?" Rothenberg demanded. "I'm here, I'm doing my job, I'm making progress—"

"I've seen no evidence of this supposed progress."

"Look at the search plans!" Rothenberg said. "Look at the patrol activity! Look at the abandoned districts we've already secured!"

"I've seen the search plans, and frankly the disappearing patrols are more worrying than anything else," the Mayor's aide said. "It's hard to know how much progress you're making, Rothenberg, if you don't tell me what you're searching for or how close you might be to finding it."

"We're getting close," Rothenberg insisted. "If the reports I got today are true, we might even find it today. We've been securing the abandoned districts, and I think we might finally be up to the one we're looking for."

"Securing the abandoned districts from *what*?" Jack demanded.

"You know damn well I can't tell you that," Rothenberg snarled. "Go back and tell the Mayor that my strategy is working fine, it's just a matter of time."

"All I ever see are the same task forces going into the abandoned districts and coming out with fewer patrols than went in. I think the Mayor is going to want a more detailed explanation."

"Listen," Rothenberg said, "I've got some important information that we're going to act on, and I'm going to be extremely busy. Now you can go back and tell the Mayor whatever you want, but if he wants me to succeed then he'll get you out of my goddamn hair. I can't plan a major raid with some pompous assistant breathing down my neck!"

"A major raid?" Jack repeated, eyes narrowing.

Rothenberg scowled and said nothing, realizing that he had already given away too much. It wouldn't do for the Mayor or anyone else to suspect that a bunch of kids were planning rebellion. As pathetic as it might be, the very whisper of open resistance would mean serious trouble.

"I'm going to leave you to plan this 'raid' of yours, Rothenberg," the Mayor's aide said, "and I will hold off on my report to the Mayor until the end of the week. But the deadline is approaching and the Mayor is growing impatient. Pray that you have some results to show him soon."

With that, Jack turned around and left Rothenberg's office, his brown leather jacket slung over one shoulder. Rothenberg fumed for a moment, and then pressed a button on his desk to summon a subordinate who ran in with a salute.

"How go the preparations?" Rothenberg demanded.

"We've completely surrounded District 13 from all sides that are in contact with a living district," the man said. "We moved in one patrol at a time using different routes, just like you ordered. We've stayed out of the neighboring abandoned districts because we don't want to set anything off that might let them know we're coming, so there's a small chance that we might see some escapees when we move in. But if we do it fast enough I think that possibility is slim."

"Agreed," Rothenberg muttered. "Do we have that helicopter support I requested to track any runners?"

"Yes, sir, and the advance scouts have already identified likely escape routes."

"Excellent." Rothenberg stood up. "I would go myself, but every second counts. As soon as the last patrols are in position, move in and attack from all sides. Unless we find our primary suspect, I don't want a single survivor to leave District 13."

When Umasi awoke the sun was already beating down through a window of the apartment. Umasi blinked, then reached to the side for his sunglasses. As his hand found two separate pairs, Umasi remembered that he had forgotten to return one to his nameless companion. That remembrance triggered another memory, and he smiled. She had never noticed that during their last fight, he had slipped his account card into her pocket.

Dragging himself out of bed, Umasi dressed and prepared a light breakfast. As he worked he glanced over at the counter, where piles of bills now lay stacked, all recently withdrawn from his account. When things calmed down he would open a new account. But for now card or no, money was unlikely to be a problem for him.

His appetite diminished following his time as a vagrant, Umasi left his apartment after a light breakfast. The bright sun set the snow aglitter, but he knew it would take a while to melt it all. Nonetheless, Umasi decided to take a walk through the snow. He could not fully appreciate the transformed landscape through his sunglasses, but the trek would be good exercise and he had little else left to do.

As he walked through the district Umasi found that he had become familiar enough with District 19 to recognize some landmarks. Soon he came to a stop in the shadow of a building that he recognized as the one from which he and his nameless companion had observed approaching Enforcers. Remembering the view, Umasi felt a sudden impulse to climb back up the building and observe the district from above.

Swiftly scaling the icy ladder of the fire escape, Umasi breathed the open air on the rooftop and shut his eyes to listen to the world beneath him. He heard cars in the distance, and shouts, and crows, the urban birds of the City. Then his eyes snapped open, for he heard the unmistakable crunch of footsteps several blocks away. Umasi lowered his sunglasses, squinting across the snowy landscape. A lone figure was making its way determinedly through the snow. It didn't look like an adult, and Umasi thought that he caught a hint of gray—the color of a student uniform.

His curiosity aroused, Umasi returned to the fire escape and back to the ground as fast as he could. Slipping into the ground floor of an abandoned clothing store, he was able to look out of the show windows while remaining completely hidden himself.

As the boy passed by, Umasi was able to get a good look at him even through his shades. The student had soft features, with thin eyebrows that gave a shrewd and intelligent appearance. He seemed curious as he glanced around the district with green eyes, clearly looking for something. The boy stopped to inspect a depression in the snow, and Umasi felt a sudden urge to reveal himself. He knew that he should be careful about who he was seen by, but the other children he had confided in had proven themselves to be trustworthy. What's more, Umasi hadn't spoken to a student since before he had left home, and he now felt a keen longing to contact this gray-uniformed boy.

What was the worst that could happen? Umasi decided to throw caution to the winds as he silently stepped out of the store and into the open.

"You've been searching for a long time," he said. "May I ask what you're looking for?"

The boy spun around and for a moment Umasi was taken aback. The child's expression was positively dangerous, like that of a wild animal about to pounce, and his hand seemed to twitch towards his belt. Then the next moment it was gone, and he looked merely surprised, his thin eyebrows raised high.

"I'm not sure," the boy said. "It might be you."

"Could you elaborate?"

"I saw the Enforcers snooping around here yesterday. I figured that there must be something important hidden in here and I couldn't resist checking."

"You are aware, of course, that students are forbidden from entering the abandoned districts?"

"So then you're not a student?"

Umasi smiled in spite of himself. The boy was certainly no idiot.

"No. My name is Umasi."

"I'm Edward," Edward said, offering his hand. "I'm a student from the District 18 School, and a resident of the local orphanage."

"Pleased to make your acquaintance." Umasi shook the hand, already intrigued. If Edward himself had any curiosity about Umasi, he hid it well; Umasi instantly felt comfortable around the boy. "My lemonade stand isn't far from here. Would you mind joining me for a drink?"

You've been planning coming down here for a while, Zyid. Mind if I ask why it's so important?"

"It's not a long distance, and I was curious, I must confess," Zen said, tapping his crowbar on his shoulder. He had begun carrying it around as a reminder of how close he had come to death. "Having never had the chance to inspect this district thoroughly myself, I wanted to see what arrangements you've made here. After all, you've done an excellent job in setting up our mining crews all over the City."

"That's quite a compliment, coming from you."

"I never give idle praise," Zen said, his crowbar freezing in midair. "Our work is only going to grow more difficult from here, and we're going to have to adapt accordingly. For example, I believe that this hideout may now be too large."

Indeed, that was one thing that had struck Zen as he followed Frank up the stairwell of the hideout, sticking his head into the hallways on each floor. It was an elaborate operation; every other floor seemed to be occupied by Truants, some working on coordinating various crews around the City, though others were merely lounging around. The building was one of many cookie-cutter apartments of District 13 that used to be occupied by poorer citizens, though it was still in decent condition.

When he had first entered with Noni in tow, Zen had walked under a pristine green awning and through a pair of polished glass doors into the lobby. He had been offered the option of using the building's elevators—which were still functional—but had declined, instead choosing to take the tour on foot. Noni had split off on the second floor, drawn by a door that had been labeled SUPPLIES with a black permanent marker, leaving Zen alone to converse with Frank up on the seventh floor.

"What makes you say it's too large?" Frank asked as they stepped into the seventh-floor hallway.

"We want to be as discreet and as scattered as possible at the moment," Zen explained as he looked into one room where a number of Truants were operating a variety of communication devices. "We are aiming to outlast Rothenberg with a minimum of casualties. We cannot consolidate until the time comes when we have an army ready to take the Enforcers head-on."

"Well, I guess that makes sense," Frank said. "So how soon should we—"

Frank never got to finish his question, because at that moment a Truant burst out of one of the rooms of the hall, looking frantic. Spotting Zen, he let out something between a whimper and a cry of relief, and dashed over to the Truancy leader.

"Zyid!" the boy gasped. "Trouble, big trouble!"

"What is it?" Zen demanded.

"Some of our scouts in this district have spotted a . . . a huge number of Enforcer patrols . . . approaching our location."

There was a moment of stunned disbelief as Frank gaped at the boy. Other Truants that had heard him, or who had somehow sensed the change in atmosphere, also turned to stare. The building fell silent. Zen, however, remained as cool as dry ice.

"Any idea how they managed to get in undetected?"

"N-no, sir, some of our guys in the living districts reported one or two patrols moving by them at a time, but never more than that, and never following the same route—"

"How much time do we have until they reach us?"

As if in response, somewhere far below there came the sound of shattering glass and stamping feet. The Enforcers had broken in through the front doors. Loud footsteps issued from the stairwell, and the floor indicators on the two elevators started descending. The Truants were frozen, teetering on the verge of panic. Then Zen spoke up, his calm but urgent voice breaking the spell.

"Barricade the stairwell," he ordered. A number of Truants immediately scrambled to move furniture in front of the door. As they worked, Zen turned to Frank. "Are the elevators rigged to explode?"

"Well, yes, we planted explosives throughout the building, but—"

"Blow the elevators, and the elevators only," Zen said as he glanced at the floor indicators, whose numbers were now steadily climbing. "Now!"

Frank did not hesitate, pulling a cell phone from his pocket and selecting a speed dial. A second later two loud bangs issued forth from the elevator shafts, followed shortly by yells and distant crashes. The other Truants stared at the elevators for a moment; then something hard slammed against the stairwell door, instantly capturing their attention.

"Get a message to the other Truants inside the building," Zen said to Frank. "Tell them to barricade the stairs on every floor."

The banging on the door grew louder, and Truants scrambled to face the door, guns drawn. Some took cover within apartment doorways, others dragged out sofas and desks and other furniture to crouch behind. They looked scared, some of them were shaking, faced as they were with the utter hopelessness of their situation. Then with a swish of black Zen was among them, brandishing his crowbar and a pistol, and their fear was swept away.

"Behind that door may wait all the Enforcers in the City," Zen announced, "but the stairway is narrow and they can only come one at a time."

The banging on the door increased in volume, and the Truants tightened their grips on their weapons as they hung on to their leader's every word, his calm rationale lending them confidence.

"Five Enforcers or five hundred, it will make no difference; push onto the stairs, and retreat to the roof."

A series of deafening gunshots rang out, and deep dents appeared in the door. The Enforcers were trying to shoot their way in, but the Truants were ready for them now.

"Some of us will die here today, but if it's your time to go, then there's nothing to do but make it theirs as well!"

There was a final thud against the door, and it budged slightly, pushing

back the furniture that had been pressed against it. The head of an Enforcer peered in through the tiny crack, and then fell away, pierced by a
bullet as the Truants let loose a vicious volley. The Enforcers redoubled
their efforts to push open the door, and with a loud creak the furniture finally gave way and the Enforcers burst into the corridor. They were met
with a withering storm of gunfire, but more Enforcers stepped over their
dead comrades and into the hall. A few Truants crumpled as the Enforcers
returned fire, but after another volley they fled back into the stairwell and
began radioing for backup. Over the thundering of footsteps in the stairs
and gunshots from the lower floors, Zen stood up, holstered his pistol, and
swung his crowbar.

"NOW!" he yelled.

Zen charged into the stairwell, slamming his crowbar into the nearest
Enforcer's face. The Enforcer let out a yell of pain, and Zen kicked the man
in the chest, sending him crashing down the stairs into his comrades. Other
Truants immediately ran out into the stairs and began firing down on the
prostrate Enforcers.

"Tell the Truants on the other floors to fight their way into the stairwell
and onto the roof!" Zen bellowed at Frank over the chaos.

Frank retreated back into the hall to relay the orders. Zen reached inside
a hidden pocket of his windbreaker and pulled out a brick sized loaf of
some solid white substance. It was crudely shaped, as though it were made
in a bread mold, and had a match sticking out of it. Zen pulled out a lighter
and lit the match, then dropped the brick down the stairwell. A moment
later there was a small explosion, and the entire stairwell began filling with
thick white smoke. There were shouts of surprise, and through the smoke
Zen bellowed his orders in case Frank had not yet managed to spread the
word.

"THE ROOF! GET TO THE ROOF!"

The call was soon echoed by a dozen voices, and not all of them were
Truants. The Enforcers now knew what they were up to, and a mad upwards rush began, no one able to see through the smoke. Shots fired wildly
everywhere, Truants and Enforcers alike toppled and fell, providing obstacles for the others that were ascending. At the very top of the stairs, Zen
found his way blocked by a pair of Enforcers who had gotten there before
him. Before they had identified him as an enemy the crowbar had struck
one upside the head, bringing him to the ground. But the other had already
raised a gun before Zen could react, and for a moment he felt sure that he
had made a deadly blunder.

Then something darted through the air and buried itself between the
Enforcer's eyes. It was a knife. As the Enforcer crumpled backwards, Zen

spun around to see Noni charging up the stairs, wielding knives she'd taken from the supply room, a number of Truants from the lower floors following in her wake. Zen felt a brief surge of pride, and then kicked open the door leading to the roof. A few Truants charged in ahead of him, and instantly fell to the ground; as Zen had suspected, more Enforcers had beaten them to the top. Not to be discouraged, the surviving Truants burst out of the thick smoke and into the open air of the roof en masse. Only a half dozen Enforcers were lying in wait, and after a few moments of vicious gunfire, they all lay dead. As Zen wiped his crowbar, he shouted instructions to all the other Truants.

"Drag the dead out of the way and secure the entrance to the stairs! We'll wait as long as we can for the other Truants, but if an Enforcer comes through, shoot it!"

The Truants moved the bodies of both friend and foe, and then took positions all around the open door. A few tardy Truants emerged, sputtering from the smoke, but right behind them came a number of Enforcers, who were cut down before they could return fire. For a moment it looked like they were safe; there was no other way onto the roof, and with the narrow chokepoint of the door they could hold off an army with their handful of survivors.

Then, over the din of the firefight, Zen heard a loud beating noise, and was seized by dread. Spinning around, he saw the helicopter just as it came into view above the rooftop. The helicopter itself had no weapons, and Zen could see right through the cockpit window. The pilot was unarmed, the chopper not meant for combat. Still, as other Truants turned to see what was going on, the mere presence of the flying machine seemed to inspire terror in all of them. Even Zen was worried, but he wasn't yet sure why. Then the helicopter seemed to tilt forward, its rotor head nearly skimming the rooftop. Zen abruptly realized what it was about to do, and in that moment made his own decision.

The other Truants scrambled for cover as the helicopter advanced, haphazardly attempting to slice them with its rotor head. Zen felt rather than saw Noni standing by his side even as imminent death roared towards them. In a clean, fluid motion, he drew a bottle with a rag stuffed in its neck from his windbreaker, lit the rag with his lighter, and then hurled the bottle at the oncoming helicopter. A second later the bottle burst into what looked like liquid flames, and suddenly the entire helicopter was alight. The helicopter banked upwards, flew shakily over the entire block, then plummeted out of sight some distance away, leaving behind a trail of smoke.

Noni let out a muffled gasp of delight, but Zen felt no elation, no sense of satisfaction as he turned around to face the ongoing battle. The helicopter was down and out, but the damage was already done. The Enforcers on the stairs had managed to establish a hold on the roof after the Truants had scattered, and now the firefight had resumed. Zen knew that more Enforcers would be charging up the stairs at that very moment, and that it was only a matter of time until they were hopelessly outnumbered. Making a hasty decision, he joined the other Truants who were crouched behind large metal vents. Noni followed, and Zen was satisfied to see Frank among the other survivors.

"This building is close enough to others to safely jump across to another rooftop," Zen said. "When I say go, we will all scatter. Everyone head for a different building, hide if you can find a safe place, reach the living districts if possible, and return to District 15 eventually—it's been fortified. Stay off of the snow; it'll betray your trail. Good luck, and GO!"

Zen timed his command to coincide with a brief lull in the fighting. The Truants scattered in all directions, Zen and Noni fleeing down onto a rusty old fire escape and into an abandoned brownstone. Though there was no sign of pursuit, Zen felt a dark feeling growing in his gut as they fled. This had once been a hideout of over thirty Truants, and the survivors had numbered less than a dozen. Zen felt no sadness, just frustration and anger. He had underestimated Rothenberg and his Enforcers, and the Truancy had paid the price. This was their first defeat, and Zen swore that it would be the last that Rothenberg would ever score against them.

"Tie."

"Pardon me?"

"Three move repetition. That means a tie."

Umasi blinked and looked down at the board, their previous moves flitting through his head. Edward was right. They had been playing chess with a set that Edward had brought the previous day, and this was the first time that Umasi had failed to win. He'd had the upper hand, but allowed himself to get careless, not even paying attention as he followed Edward's king with his bishop back and forth. Umasi offered his hand, not at all displeased at having snatched a draw from the jaws of victory. On the contrary, he was happy for Edward, who had confessed to being a novice at the game.

"Well played, Edward," Umasi said. "I've had a couple visitors before you, but I must say you're shaping up to be the most dangerous student of them all."

"You did well yourself, Mr. Umasi." Edward shook the proffered hand, satisfaction on his face.

"Would you like to go again, or shall we call it quits?"

"I think that a tie is a good note to end on."

"I can't argue with that. You've improved markedly since we started playing."

"Well, I've gotten to know your style."

"True. An unknown adversary is more intimidating than a familiar one."

Edward raised his eyebrows at the mention of intimidation, but said nothing as Umasi poured them both another cup of lemonade. It had been several days since Umasi had first hit it off with Edward, who had since proven himself at every turn to be a fast learner and an academic, if not his intellectual equal. During their first conversation at the stand, Umasi had listened in fascination as Edward had recounted his numerous scholarly achievements, enough to put Umasi's own to shame. Umasi pitied Edward in a way, ignorant as he was of the truth behind the City's schools, and yet he seemed so content that Umasi could not bring himself to shatter the illusion. Besides, Umasi could hardly be critical, as he had once taken pride in academics himself. Instead, Umasi had expressed their mutual affinity for learning, and Edward had returned the next day with a pile of various books that now rested beneath the lemonade stand.

Umasi would never have called Red or especially the nameless vagrant unintelligent, but necessity had forced them to focus their wits on survival while Edward seemed content to focus on expanding his knowledge. Edward's unusual sharpness was also compounded by a certain competitiveness that vaguely bothered Umasi. Upon finding out that Umasi knew how to play chess, Edward had brought the set the next day and now seemed almost obsessed with winning. To be sure, Edward seemed to bear his losses well, but Umasi could tell that they irked him by the angry look in his eyes and the way his jaw set at the end of each match. Umasi dismissed this as Edward's drive to improve. After all, Edward was nothing if not respectful, even taking to calling Umasi "mister."

In between games or intellectual discussions, Umasi and Edward would share information that was much more precious to the two of them. Edward was always keen on hearing more of Umasi's history, though Umasi recounted his life story selectively and cautiously. He was still wary about revealing the whole thing to anyone. For his part, Umasi was always eager to hear more news of the City, which Edward supplied both with verbal summaries and gifts of newspapers. Nothing in the papers indicated anything out of the ordinary, which had set Umasi somewhat at ease.

"So, what was it like, living with the Mayor?" Edward asked.

"Less exciting than you'd think," Umasi replied. "He was busy with work more often than not, and whenever I spoke with him he was just my father, not the Mayor."

"Yeah, but getting to live in the Mayoral Mansion, with so much important stuff going on around you," Edward said, "I'd have traded my entire life at the orphanage for five minutes with the Mayor!"

It almost seemed as though Edward knew more than he was letting on, but before Umasi could question it, Edward's words reminded him of something.

"Edward, why not tell me about your own life?" Umasi suggested. "You mentioned that you live at the orphanage. I admit that that sparked my curiosity."

In the time they'd known each other, Edward had struck Umasi as a singularly emotionless individual. Aside from the rare glints of frustration behind those green eyes, Edward seemed perfectly at ease in everything he did or spoke about. It was disconcerting, and Umasi was curious about what might be hiding beneath the shell. Umasi was almost certain that Edward would be hesitant about revealing his own past, but to his surprise, Edward replied almost immediately, as though he'd rehearsed it a hundred times before.

"My parents died when I was seven years old," Edward said. "I don't really remember them that well, but I'll never forget the night they died."

"If you're not comfortable—" Umasi began, but Edward waved his words away.

"It was their anniversary. My parents left me at home to go out for dinner. I wanted to come too, but it was their night and . . . and they left me with a babysitter," Edward said, his voice shaking now. "And they never came back. At first I thought they were late. The babysitter tried to put me to bed, but I refused to sleep until I'd seen them. The night dragged on and the babysitter left, I was all alone. And then the Enforcers came to my house, and told me there'd been a freak car accident . . . that three people were killed, and two of them were . . ."

"I'm sorry," Umasi said quietly as Edward's voice trailed off.

"And then I was sent to the orphanage, and the matrons were nice enough for a while. They never paid me much attention until the school got excited, of course, but at least they let me alone. Later I got placed in foster care and . . ." Edward swallowed. "It was terrible. My foster parents would get drunk and beat me for the smallest things, and my foster f-father would threaten m-me with a g-gun, and I missed m-my r-real parents so ba-badly . . ."

Edward stopped, apparently unable to go on. Umasi felt pity for the boy, and at the same time felt honored that such terrible secrets were being shared with him. Edward took a few deep breaths to compose himself, and then continued.

"Eventually, the Enforcers locked my foster father up, but that only made it worse when he got out," Edward said bitterly. "Finally . . . just last week . . . some Enforcer named Rothenberg came along and brought me back to the orphanage."

"Rothenberg?" Umasi repeated. "Chief Truancy Officer Rothenberg himself took you back to the orphanage?"

"Yeah, I guess." Edward nodded. "He seemed a bit crazy to me, actually. Kept babbling about ghosts, and he mentioned something about a war."

"War?"

Umasi felt as though he'd been doused with cold water. How could he have forgotten? He had really, truly forgotten, as though his last confrontation with Zen had been the end of it, as though it was all a thing of the past. He had allowed himself to become so insulated from the world that he hadn't even pondered what his brother might be doing now. Seeing the stricken look on his face, Edward stared at him with large green eyes that were no longer teary but sharp and suspicious.

"Do you know what Rothenberg was talking about?" Edward asked.

Umasi hesitated, then was seized by a sudden need to confess all that he had allowed to slip from his mind before. The dams broke and he spilled his entire story from beginning to end, leaving nothing out. Edward sat respectfully silent throughout the entire tale, and though Umasi thought he saw a glimmer of delight in those emerald eyes, he brushed it off as honor at being let in on the City's secret. By the end of the long story the sun was already setting and Edward had to leave. He thanked Umasi, promised to return the next day, and left with a spring in his step, leaving Umasi all alone to think at his stand.

Umasi remained there long after nightfall, under the spotlight of the streetlamp above, still unable to believe how careless he had allowed himself to become. He hadn't even given a thought to the idea that people were actually dying at the hands of his brother. Umasi felt a sudden surge of self-loathing; he had been so selfish, so lovesick, so eager to philosophize that he had ignored the real and tangible chaos ensuing all around him. He had meant to adopt his nameless companion's ideas, and yet he had forgotten the most important one of them—that pacifism must be tempered by realism.

Though Edward could not know it, his arrival had been like a breath of fresh air. Umasi was awake now as he had never been before. He would feel safe now in taking action, confident that he fought not with passion but with clarity. He would bring to bear all of the strength he had found since he'd abandoned education, strength that made him unrecognizable to anyone who had known him then. He was now ready to make his mark on the City, if only to erase his brother's.

If the Enforcers could not do it, Umasi decided, then he would have to be the one to stop the Truancy.

So what do you think, Zyid?"

"Difficult, but not impossible."

"I don't agree. We can't exactly march in through the front doors, can we?"

"On the contrary, that's exactly what I intend to do, Gabriel."

The two children stood side by side on a busy sidewalk, apparently gazing in through the show window of a toy store. Directly behind them, and clearly visible in the reflection of the glass, was the front entrance of the District 18 Enforcer Station. The boys were both appropriately dressed for the frigid weather, with neck warmers and woolen hats. Zen had actually worn his windbreaker for once, its hood pulled over his head to further obscure his appearance. None of the passing pedestrians spared them so much as a glance, intent as they were on reaching their destinations and getting out of the cold.

"I just don't see it, Zyid. It's an Enforcer station with who knows how many people inside it. We can't attack it head-on like that," Gabriel muttered.

"It's just another building, Gabriel," Zen said, folding his arms. "The doors are made of wood, and the guards are made of flesh and blood. They will yield to explosives and bullets quite easily."

"So will we, though. Aren't you worried about casualties?"

"Few things worth accomplishing are ever without risk, Gabriel."

Before Gabriel could reply to that, two more kids emerged from the passing crowd and joined them in front of the toy store. One of them was a boy wearing earmuffs and the other a girl with a scarf wrapped tightly around the lower half of her face. Both Gabriel and Zen turned their heads slightly to acknowledge the newcomers.

"What did the parking garage look like?" Zen asked.

"We saw at least two dozen vehicles with Enforcer license plates, and that's not counting the squad cars," Frank replied. "I say we're looking at maybe fifty to a hundred people in that building at any one time."

"And the construction work that we saw on our way here?"

"It's blocking an entire intersection," Noni answered quietly. "Anyone driving in would have to take a detour."

"That should slow down any reinforcements, but even so we can only expect a very small window of opportunity," Zen mused. "Probably a matter of minutes."

"How much damage could we possibly do in a few minutes?" Frank asked.

"Enough," Zen said.

"Why did you pick this place anyway?" Gabriel asked. "What's so special about it? What are you planning?"

"I have made the mistake of underestimating our friend Rothenberg," Zen said. "His raid on District 13 cannot go unanswered. We can no longer afford to wait until the Mayor replaces him—we must eliminate him ourselves as soon as possible."

"Then shouldn't we be looking at Enforcer Headquarters?" Gabriel pressed. "That's where he'd be, right?"

"Enforcer Headquarters has much tighter security, solid defenses, and hundreds of personnel. I believe that we have little hope of breaching that building right now," Zen answered. "The District 18 Enforcer Station is a much more viable target, and it's located in Rothenberg's home district."

"But how are we going to get him into the station?" Frank demanded.

"I do not believe that that will be difficult," Zen said. "We will merely pretend to give him what he wants."

"What he wants . . ." Frank repeated.

For several moments none of the children spoke as they thought, the sound of the pedestrians and cars in the street swiftly filling the void. Then, almost simultaneously, Frank, Gabriel, and Noni stiffened, having figured out exactly what Rothenberg wanted. It was Noni who spoke first, and for all of them.

"No!"

"You want to turn yourself in?" Gabriel added, flabbergasted.

"*Pretend* to turn myself in, Gabriel," Zen corrected, inspecting a box of building blocks in the show window.

"You're crazy. What makes you think they won't shoot you on sight?" Frank demanded, his years as a vagrant having taught him to expect nothing but bullets from an Enforcer.

"Aspersions on my sanity aside, I have not come to this decision on a whim," Zen said, his voice sharp. "I do not for a moment believe that the Mayor would allow Rothenberg to shoot me on sight. If I came quietly, he would want to find out how I know what I do, who else I have told, and what they are doing about it."

No one could find an objection to this logic, and Gabriel, who alone knew of Zen's parentage, wisely refrained from mentioning the other reasons which Zen had omitted.

"But how are we going to get away?" Frank asked, changing tack. "We're marching right into an Enforcer station smack in the middle of a living district."

"There's a subway one block away." Noni spoke to general surprise. "And District 19 is only five blocks away."

"Noni is correct," Zen said. "Additionally, I took note of the open manhole in the street. It seems to lead directly to the sewer mains. When we escape, we shall scatter. Most will take the subway, some will take the sewers, and some will flee to District 19."

"How many do you intend to take with you for this?" Gabriel asked.

"Two dozen," Zen said. "I do not underestimate our enemies, and we will need to cause enough damage and mayhem so that, even if Rothenberg survives, he will be finished when the Mayor hears what happened. Are we clear?"

The other Truants heard the finality in his voice and reluctantly began to nod. At that moment, the toy store's proprietor, who had been watching them through the window, came out of the shop to address them.

"You kids have been out here for a long time. Looking for anything in particular?"

"No, sir," Gabriel replied, "just trying to decide on a birthday gift for our friend."

"Well, why don't you come on in and look around?"

"That's very kind of you, but I'm afraid we must decline," Zen said quietly. "We were just about to go on our way. We're late for an appointment, you see."

"All right then, but don't hesitate to come back!"

"Don't worry." Zen smiled coldly. "We'll be back tomorrow."

With that, Zen turned and joined the crowd moving towards the subway station, the other Truants hastily following suit. As they walked together down the crowded street, Zen muttered something to his comrades that only they could hear over the bustling of the street.

"Tomorrow we strike Rothenberg down inside his own Enforcer station."

As Edward lifted up the loose floorboard that night, every nerve in his body tingled in triumph. After days of playing along with Umasi, he had finally gotten the whole story out of the boy, and what a story it was. In retrospect Edward realized that he had gone about it the wrong way. He had thought a display of intelligence would be enough to gain Umasi's trust. But after all, the key to cracking the boy's shell had been to put on an emotional display. As he replaced his knife beneath the floorboard, Edward nearly cackled aloud at how readily Umasi had bought his sob story.

While it was true that Edward remembered the night that his parents died, he had never had anything but contempt for them. The story about his foster parents had of course been nothing but his usual lies. And yet this compassionate fool had ate it all up, and in return had provided him with invaluable information. Having to act so pathetic had irked Edward a bit, but that was only the usual price of knowledge in the City, and Edward decided that it was more than a fair trade as he settled down on top of his bunk.

Student, Umasi had called him. Not just any student, but his most dangerous student. To his surprise, Edward found that he relished that title. Knowledge was power, which was why the Educators were so keen on having a monopoly on it. Edward knew that the so-called knowledge that the Educators fed their hapless pupils was useless drudge, but the information that Umasi had so carelessly given him was priceless. Edward had never really considered himself to be a pupil of the Educators, seeing as how they never taught him anything worth knowing. But Umasi had already given him knowledge that could make him more powerful than the Mayor himself, and so Edward was not uncomfortable thinking of himself as Umasi's student.

Seizing a blank notebook and a pen, Edward began scribbling down notes on everything he'd learned. Two of the Mayor's sons had gone missing, one of them currently wasting time in District 19 while the other led a secret rebellion against his father. The rebellion was called the Truancy, almost exclusively consisted of children, was competently led, and had already engaged the Enforcers and won on at least one occasion. Judging by the contents of recent newspapers, the Mayor was keeping everything under wraps—a big mistake in Edward's opinion—and Chief Truancy Officer Rothenberg was obviously in on the secret, possibly in a leadership capacity. Not bad, not bad at all for a day's work.

Edward neatly folded his notes and hid them beneath the floorboard as well. Now the question was how should he use the information, and how soon. Edward decided to wait. Patience often paid off, and there was more that he could yet learn from Umasi about the Truancy and its leader, about the Mayor and his Educators, and about how to destroy them both. But which one to side with? This was the key question remaining for Edward as he slid under the covers for the night.

There were so many ways that he could profit from this war. Would he join the Truancy and lend his talents in order to overthrow the Mayor? Wait for the Educators' darkest hour and then help them crush the uprising? Manipulate both factions against each other for his own ends? Edward decided not to rush into a hasty decision. The perfect circumstances for him to act would likely make themselves obvious in time. Meanwhile, Edward intended to continue playing along with the pacifistic fool, until he had gleaned all that he could possibly need to know.

Then, armed with that knowledge, he could at last make the City his oyster. But he would have to cover his tracks. The source of the information would be destroyed so that no one else could happen across it. Edward smiled as his head sank lower into the comfortable pillows. He would kill Umasi, and then go on to realize his dream of becoming the most powerful person in the entire City.

Dear Sirs,

While I do not like jumping to conclusions, and like the conclusions that I have reached even less, it is my duty to report that we may be seeing the first signs of serious civil unrest in this City—unrest that Rothenberg has been discreetly assigned to suppress. So far there is nothing to suggest a Class A Disturbance, and the public appears to remain both content and oblivious. However the signs are all troubling nonetheless; Rothenberg's Enforcer resources continue to vanish without official explanation, there are reports of strange noises and occurrences in the City's abandoned districts, and the Chief Enforcer was even murdered last week in what has been labeled as a bar fight—but if my suspicions are true this may have actually been an assassination.

Lately even the Mayor has become visibly distraught, his uncharacteristic behavior more pronounced. On the rare occasions that I have seen him he was pale and haggard, almost sickly, and reportedly his activity in the office has suffered accordingly. He has passed these symptoms off as a head cold, but I believe that it may be an indication of something much direr. I urge the Government to give this matter their highest priority, as even its critics agree that this City represents one of our greatest hopes.

Your Servant,
207549627

PART V

LEGEND

29

ULTIMATUMS

Rothenberg's breath came in short, excited bursts as he made his way up the stairs leading to the front doors of the District 18 Enforcer Station. It had been nearly a week since his raids had last produced results, and while the ambush in District 13 had left a number of Truants dead, his Enforcers had suffered expensive casualties in the process. The loss of the helicopter in particular had been difficult to sweep under the rug, and having to deal with the Mayor's aide peering over his shoulder at every turn, Rothenberg had despaired of meeting the Mayor's deadline.

So when the call came in that morning informing him that a boy identifying himself as the Mayor's son had walked into an Enforcer station and turned himself in, Rothenberg could hardly believe his luck. After all of his searches and efforts, could it possibly be this easy? Rothenberg's heart pounded as he shoved the doors open and ignored the greetings of various Enforcers. His logical side expected it to be a ruse, a mistake, but in spite of his reservations, a burning hope now filled his chest.

"Good morning, sir." A lieutenant saluted. "You're early, we didn't expect—"

"Where is he?"

"Uh, the prisoner?"

"Yes!"

"He's being held in the interrogation room. You were quite adamant about being the first to see him, so—"

Rothenberg never heard the rest of the sentence, as he was practically running for the interrogation room now. The District 18 station was one he knew well, as it was within his home district; in his haste, Rothenberg never paused to consider whether or not that might be more than mere coincidence. As he drew up to the sturdy door of the interrogation room, Rothenberg stopped to take a deep breath, then, with a shaking hand, turned the knob.

As he stepped inside, Rothenberg froze, gaping at the figure sitting at the polished metal table beneath the room's single lightbulb. Somehow, he managed to shut the door behind him as he entered, relief and delight coursing through him. There could be no mistaking those contemptuous eyes; this was the same boy he had once fled from in an alley. Handcuffed and in custody, the child still managed to exude a formidable presence, but this time Rothenberg did not feel the slightest trace of fear. They were on his turf now, and playing by his rules.

"Good morning, Rothenberg," Zen said, nodding politely. "I believe that this is the first time that we've had the pleasure of conversation."

Rothenberg ignored him. He knew that allowing a child to take control over a conversation only invited humiliation. Instead, Rothenberg began pacing around the room.

"Why are you here, boy?" Rothenberg asked.

"I need to speak with my father."

"Running back to Daddy after all?" Rothenberg snorted. "And here I was starting to think that you actually had a spine."

"The message I have for him is not for my benefit," Zen replied. "Indeed, it concerns the welfare of the entire City."

"What is your message, then?"

"For his ears alone, Enforcer."

"You test my patience, boy."

"And I expect you to score highly."

Rothenberg blinked at that, then set his jaw.

"Fine then, if you won't tell me why you're here, then I'll guess. You can't handle what you've started. It's grinding at you on the inside, because you know what your problem is, kid? You don't want to kill people."

"I'd have thought that our encounter in the alley would've indicated otherwise," Zen countered.

"Oh you're willing to do it, I'll give you that." Rothenberg smiled coldly. "But when it comes down to it, you don't want to kill—you just want something else and are willing to kill to get it. You don't enjoy it."

"Am I take it that you do?"

"You're damn right I do, boy," Rothenberg snarled. "Why do you think I have a reputation? Why do you think you're sitting in that chair while I stand here? Why do you think I've got this position?"

"Truthfully, I would chalk the latter up more to my father's senility than to your sadism."

At that, Rothenberg's face turned redder than his hair had ever been; his fists clenched as he tried to restrain himself. The Mayor had insisted that his sons remain untouched, Rothenberg reminded himself.

"You're just a stupid little kid after all," Rothenberg spat. "A rebellion? Hah! I bet that you were so caught up in your crazy little fantasy that you never stopped to think about what that meant. You're ending lives, boy. You're *killing*, and if you don't love your work, how can you ever succeed at your job?"

For the first time, Zen's composure slipped, and the boy seemed genuinely troubled as he sat there beneath the light, his face cast into shadow. Rothenberg smiled, but before he could comment, a deafening noise burst from outside the room. Rothenberg spun around, staring at the door as if by doing so he might see through it. Gunshots now rang out, followed by screams and other sounds of chaos.

"It seems that there is a problem that requires your immediate attention, Rothenberg," Zen said blandly. "Why don't you demonstrate how successful you are at *your* job?"

Rothenberg froze, then his mouth opened in a wordless scream of rage. As Rothenberg realized that he'd been outsmarted by this filthy child *again*, his restraint snapped. No longer caring about his ambitions, the Mayor, or the consequences, Rothenberg reached for his gun, intending to shoot the boy where he sat, to fulfill the fantasy he had had ever since their first meeting in the alley.

Before Rothenberg could bring his weapon to bear, the heavy interrogation table flew up at him, knocking him back a few paces.

"I spared your life once before, Rothenberg." Zen leaped to his feet, having overturned the table with his cuffed hands. "Don't expect such charity from me this time."

Before Rothenberg could utter a coherent response, Zen lunged, ramming into Rothenberg with his shoulder. Rothenberg was pushed against the wall, but this time quickly rebounded, kicking out at Zen, catching the Truant in the chest. Zen staggered backwards. Rothenberg swung his pistol around, but Zen swiftly seized the metal chair and swung it with all his might. The chair struck Rothenberg's outstretched hand as it pulled the trigger, and the shot went wild as the gun was knocked from his grip.

"You little bastard!" Rothenberg roared, enraged by the loss of his weapon. "You haven't got the nerve to kill me!"

With that, Rothenberg barreled forward like a freight train. His hands still cuffed together, Zen ducked and attempted to slam his elbow into Rothenberg's oncoming chest. Though the hit landed, Rothenberg gave no indication that he had been hurt, instead bowling Zen over so that they were both sent sprawling on the floor. Zen again seized the fallen chair and swung it at Rothenberg, who swatted it aside like a fly, sending it clattering off in a corner. Rising to his feet, Rothenberg seized the entire table, raising it high over his head. Zen dove for the fallen pistol, bringing the weapon up just as Rothenberg brought the table down in front of him. His body now shielded, Rothenberg charged forward, table-first. Faced with this oncoming wall of metal, Zen fired, and shot after shot clanged off the sturdy table as he vainly sought an exposed limb. At the last moment, his gun emptied, Zen fluidly leaped up and pressed his hands against the wall as his feet kicked out and connected with the table.

For a moment it seemed as though Rothenberg's momentum would crush Zen between the wall and the table, but Zen managed to absorb the impact, gritting his teeth as he pushed against the wall with arms and legs. Realizing what was happening, Rothenberg redoubled his efforts, his feet scrabbling to get a firm hold on the ground. But Rothenberg's strength could not overcome Zen's superior leverage, and after a few moments of intense struggle, Rothenberg was sent flying backwards as Zen dropped to the ground, fatigued and sore.

As Rothenberg hit the wall on the opposite side of the room, his head bizarrely seemed to clear, and he became aware of the distant shouts and gunshots that still issued from outside. Exhausted, Rothenberg took a moment to catch his breath and consider the situation. This whole thing had been a plot to kill him. It was the only thing that made sense. All conscious thought abruptly flew from Rothenberg's mind as he understood at last that his life was in danger. Survival instinct kicked in, and for the first time since the alley, Rothenberg felt afraid of something other than the supernatural.

At that moment as the door to the interrogation room slammed open, and Rothenberg nearly panicked. Turning to face the door, he was relieved to find himself facing not Truants, but two aghast Enforcers, neither of whom were armed. What fools, Rothenberg thought scornfully as he shakily rose to his feet. Still, they could give him the chance he needed to escape with his life intact.

"Ch-Chief Rothenberg, sir!" one of them sputtered. "We're under attack!"

"I can see that, you dolt!" Rothenberg snarled, gesturing at Zen's stirring form. "You two, take care of this suspect. Kill him!"

"Kill . . . him, s-sir?"

"You heard me!" Rothenberg yelled. "Kill him and get out of my way!"

"But where are you going, s-sir?"

"To take care of the problem," Rothenberg said, his voice low and dangerous. "Now, get out of my way. I won't say it again."

The two Enforcers stumbled into the room as Rothenberg staggered out into the hallway, shutting the door behind him. As he began to flee down the corridor, he thought he heard the two Enforcers he'd left behind screaming behind the closed door. Rothenberg shrugged it off; by the time the Mayor's son was finished with the two idiots, Rothenberg would be far away. Even as he ran, he was starting to feel back in control again, injured and spent though he was. With the Mayor's son occupied, there was no child left who could possibly get in his way. Rothenberg's fear gave way to a familiar thrill as he made for the back entrance, the pain from his wounds completely forgotten. He might have been retreating, but he was still the hunter here, not the Truants.

As the din of combat grew louder with every step, Rothenberg realized that some Truants must have slipped in through the back entrance as well. He smiled at the realization. He was aching to pay them back on his way out. In between spurts of gunfire, the shrill scream of the fire alarm could be heard, and sprinklers were soaking offices that Rothenberg passed by; there was a fire somewhere in the building. As the last corridor to the exit came into view, Rothenberg saw three Enforcers crouched behind the corner, exchanging shots with unseen enemies around the bend. Panting heavily, one of the Enforcers pulled back just in time to avoid a burst of return fire, then jumped as he spotted Rothenberg.

"Chief Rothenberg!" he shouted over the din, drawing the attention of the other Enforcers. "You're alive!"

"Keep your voice down!" Rothenberg said, just loud enough to be heard in the lull between shots. "How many are at the back entrance?"

"Far as we can see, only two, sir!"

"Only two?" Rothenberg grinned. "Well, then, what are you three dolts doing? You outnumber them! Storm their positions, take them out!"

"But, sir, they're well concealed!"

"It doesn't matter, there's two of them and three of you, and I'll be watching your back," Rothenberg insisted. "Go, that's a direct order!"

"Sir, you're unarmed—"

"I said that's a direct order!" Rothenberg snarled. "Get going or I'll kill you with my bare hands!"

The Enforcer paled, but quickly swallowed and turned to look at his comrades, who had been too busy firing back to hear the conversation. Regaining their attention, the Enforcer Rothenberg had spoken with indicated their new orders with a few hand gestures. The other Enforcers raised their eyebrows and looked up at Rothenberg, who nodded curtly. The Enforcers looked back at each other, and then, taking deep breaths, plunged out into the open together. Rothenberg wasted no time in taking their place behind the corner, and was unsurprised to hear gunfire followed by screams as the Enforcers he'd sent out to die fulfilled their purpose. Rothenberg licked his lips in anticipation as he saw a pair of shadows grow closer on the ground. Just as he'd expected, the two Truants clearly thought that their enemies had all been slain, and now rushed forward to search the building.

As the first Truant came into view, Rothenberg abruptly thrust his foot out. The boy's gun flew from his hands as he was sent sprawling to the floor. The second Truant halted in time to avoid tripping, but Rothenberg was up in an instant, body-slamming him before he could raise his gun. The boy was shoved to the floor, and Rothenberg stomped on his arm. Something cracked, and the boy screamed, letting go of his weapon. Rothenberg quickly confiscated the gun, and then turned to give the other Truant a kick to the head that knocked him senseless.

The hall was now littered with the bodies of the Enforcers he had sacrificed and the Truants he had incapacitated, but the exit was within sight. Satisfied, Rothenberg was about to take his leave when a gunshot rang out from the direction he had just come. Rothenberg dived, bringing himself up into a crouch behind the safety of the corner, his pistol bared and his nerves tense.

"Here!" a boy was shouting. "Back entrance, he's here! *Rothenberg is here!*"

With that, a single Truant boldly dived around the corner, pistol in one hand and a radio in the other. The boy frantically let loose three shots, none of which were well aimed, missing Rothenberg completely. In response, Rothenberg calmly raised his pistol and let loose a single bullet. The Truant crumpled in mid-run, letting out a yelp as he fell to the floor. Rothenberg fired a second, unnecessary shot, and then leaped up and made for the exit without so much as a glance backwards.

He was both relieved and disappointed to find that the back alley to the building was empty. Jamming his pistol into his belt, Rothenberg made for the nearest fire escape and began climbing. Years of chasing vagrants had taught him all about how to evade pursuit in the City, though this would be the first time that he would employ such knowledge himself. His bloodlust had been sated for now; his only remaining motivation was survival. As Rothenberg made it onto the roof of a building, the fear of imminent death slowly began to fade, only to be replaced by a different kind of fear as he contemplated the enormity of the disaster that had just transpired.

In spite of himself, Rothenberg groaned as he dashed along the rooftops. The Mayor was not going to be happy.

"Zyid, are you all right?"

Zen's head snapped up as he leaned against the wall of the hallway, tiredly rubbing his freed wrists. The door to the interrogation room rested open behind him, the motionless bodies of two Enforcers beneath him— one of them missing a set of keys that Zen had used to unlock his handcuffs. Breathing heavily, Gabriel and two other Truants ran up to him, concerned looks on their faces.

"I'm fine," Zen said, wincing as he forced himself upright. "There was a slight miscalculation on my part."

"Rothenberg?" Gabriel asked.

"He was formidable." Zen nodded, touching a hand to his sore ribs. "Even I underestimated him, after all. But it doesn't matter. He may not be dead, but he's finished all the same. What's our status?"

"We caught them completely by surprise," Gabriel reported. "It was easier than I ever hoped. Believe it or not, not many of the Enforcers were armed—I don't think they ever dreamed that they could be attacked here."

"Did we lose anyone?"

Gabriel hesitated, but only for a moment. "Amal is dead. We think he tried to stop Rothenberg from escaping. Two others ran into him as well—they're both injured, but not shot or anything."

"Have the injured already been removed from the building?" Zen demanded.

Gabriel nodded.

"Good," Zen said. "Make sure that they're with Frank and the subway group. Get them out of here as soon as possible." One of the Truants saluted and ran off to convey the order.

"And Amal?" Gabriel asked.

"Leave him."

"But—"

"He died fighting Rothenberg personally, as admirable an end as any of us could wish for," Zen interrupted. "Honor his memory, not his corpse. I take responsibility for his death. Now let's go."

Gabriel frowned, but nodded again as the Truant next to him shifted uncomfortably.

"Conceal your weapons," Zen said, businesslike once more. "As planned, I will be leading the sewer escapees. Gabriel, you will flee to District 19—split up as soon as possible. Frank will make for the subways, if he hasn't done so already. Go!"

Like the snap of a rubber band, the Truants sprung into motion, dashing through empty halls and past moaning Enforcers until they reached their comrades outside. Gabriel took charge of his group of five and made a run for District 19 just as the sound of approaching sirens reached their ears. Guns were stuffed into backpacks, safely out of sight. Within seconds the Truants had scattered and vanished, leaving the newly arrived Enforcers to gawk at the scene of destruction that had once been their impregnable station.

heckmate."

Umasi nodded as Edward stood triumphantly over the board. In truth, Umasi had seen Edward's victory coming several moves earlier, and had made no effort to stop it. Edward had greatly improved of late, and Umasi felt that his efforts deserved to be rewarded. As Edward grinned down at the pieces, however, Umasi began to question his decision to let Edward win. There was something strange, almost perverse, on the boy's victorious face.

"Is winning so important, Edward?" Umasi asked.

Edward blinked, and the unsettling expression on his face vanished, though for the first time Umasi suspected that it had merely gone into hiding rather than dying completely.

"Of course it is," Edward said. "If you're willing to settle for a loss, how can you ever be expected to be a winner?"

"Sometimes circumstance deals you a loss, and there's nothing you can do but accept it," Umasi advised.

"Recognize it perhaps," Edward conceded, "but accept it? That's for people with no pride."

"Pride is both a flaw and a weakness, Edward," Umasi warned. "If there's one thing I've learned from experience it's that no matter how strong and rigid you are, you can always be broken. Only if you are flexible can you be truly invincible."

Edward fell silent at that, and examined Umasi with an inscrutable expression. Umasi returned the gaze from behind his dark sunglasses. Before either of them could break the silence, a loud bang sounded in the distance, the sound carrying all the way over into the abandoned District 19. Both Umasi's and Edward's heads turned as softer but still distinct cracking noises followed.

"That's District 18," Edward observed.

"It's him."

"Your brother's work, Mr. Umasi?" Edward asked, an almost hungry gleam in his eye.

"I can imagine no other explanation." Umasi stood. "Come, let's see what's going on."

Edward made no objections as Umasi led him over to the nearest fire escape. Scrambling up onto the rooftop, they saw faint trails of smoke rising not too far off. Unable to see anything else, the two boys stood there and listened to several more minutes of distant gunfire. Then the shots fell silent, and Umasi's expression was grim as they were replaced by sirens.

"Unforgivable," he muttered.

"And he's practically doing it right in front of you too," Edward said with convincing sympathy. "Must be harsh."

"Wait. Over there. Do you see anything?"

Edward peered in the direction that Umasi was pointing, and could not help but break out into a grin. There, visible only as specs in the distance, were a handful of figures hastily climbing over the fence that separated Districts 18 and 19.

"Well, well. It looks like your brother is paying you a visit," Edward announced, then blinked in surprise. "But how did you know they were there? I thought your eyesight wasn't very good?"

"You just have to listen," Umasi said darkly, adjusting his sunglasses. "This will not stand. I will not have Truants in my district."

"We . . . could just ignore them," Edward said, as though he knew that Umasi wouldn't do anything of the sort. "I don't think they've seen us."

"This isn't your fight, Edward, and I won't ask you to join me," Umasi said. "Just tell me how many you saw."

"Six, and there's no need to shoo me away," Edward said. "If there's going to be any excitement, I want a piece of it."

"They will likely be armed, and . . . I've never seen you fight, Edward," Umasi said, looking over at his friend. "Are you sure that you—"

"Two-time City martial-arts finalist, remember?" Edward said. "I can take care of myself. *Trust me*," he added as Umasi looked like he might protest.

"Well then, perhaps that's just as well," Umasi mused after a moment's consideration. "I believe that they're splitting up."

Edward looked down again and saw that, sure enough, the figures had divided up into two groups of three and were quickly vanishing down opposite avenues.

"Shall we each take a group?" Edward suggested.

"You read my mind," Umasi said. "I'll take the bunch on the left. You take the ones going right. Be careful, Edward. Don't attack if you aren't sure you can take them."

"You needn't worry about that, sir," Edward insisted, his green eyes glittering.

Umasi gave a curt nod, then vanished down one side of the building, the ends of his white scarf trailing behind him. Edward watched him go, smirked, and then moved to intercept his own group. His heart thumped in excitement. At long last, he was going to see the fabled Truancy in action.

Gabriel and his two companions moved quietly, though their light footfalls seemed unnaturally loud in the relative silence of the abandoned district. It was probably an unnecessary precaution, seeing as how they were sure that they weren't being followed. Still, it wouldn't do to get careless; they had all been briefed on the dangerous position of District 19, though with the District 18 station in chaos it seemed unlikely that the Enforcers could surround District 19 in time. No, Gabriel was quite certain that they were safe. Their guns were safely stowed in their backpacks, and once they reached District 20 they could easily pass as students.

Gabriel sighed and spared a glance up at the beautifully clear skies. His eyes registered movement, a glimpse of white, then something huge had dropped amongst them. Before Gabriel could do more than shout in surprise, he was hit hard in the chest, the air flying from his lungs. Another blow sent him crashing to the ground, where he dizzily heard one of his comrades stammer out a single word.

"Z-Zyid?"

The air was abruptly filled with a shrill sound, and it took Gabriel a moment to figure out that the other Truants were screaming. One of them quickly fell silent. Then the other followed suit.

"How *dare* you commit murder on my doorstep?" a furious, unfamiliar voice demanded.

Someone was gagging now, and Gabriel forced his eyes open. There, holding one of the Truants up against a wall by the throat, stood an impressive figure clothed in light colors, the ends of a long scarf flowing behind him. His eyes were concealed by black sunglasses, giving him an enigmatic and dangerous appearance. Though the boy was like none he had ever seen before, Gabriel somehow thought he looked strangely familiar.

"When you first saw me, you believed that I was someone else," the enigmatic boy was saying. "What did you call me, Truant?"

"Zyid . . . he's . . . our leader . . ." the Truant gasped.

"So, that's what he's calling himself these days?" the boy said. "Where is he? Is he with the other group? Is he here?"

"No . . . not . . . here . . ."

The captor loosened his grip. "Then where is he?"

The Truant turned a little paler at that, but clamped his jaw firmly shut. Gabriel, recovering from the sudden assault, prepared to rise and fight to the death should the stranger tighten his grip again.

"I see," the boy said softly. "Well then, if you won't betray him, I have a message for you to convey to my brother."

The captive, clearly thinking that he was in the grasp of a madman, looked more terrified than ever. Something in Gabriel's head, however, clicked upon hearing the word *brother*. Gabriel shakily rose to his feet, his eyes widening in shock.

"I know you!" Gabriel gasped. "You're Umasi! You're Ze . . . Zyid's brother!"

"Correct," Umasi said without turning around. "You were with us at the District 1 School, weren't you? Yes . . . Gabriel, wasn't it? I remember now. Tell my brother that he is to disband the Truancy within two days, Gabriel, or I will set out to destroy it myself."

"You're siding with the Educators?" Gabriel said angrily.

"No," Umasi replied coolly, "I am siding with no one, and the Mayor will learn the difference soon enough." Umasi released his grip, and the captive Truant slid to the ground, sputtering. "Take your Truants and leave this place, Gabriel. Give up on my brother's mad ambitions. Go home, and you'll never see me again. Otherwise, the next time we meet, I will do whatever I must to protect the people of this City from the likes of you."

W h-who are y-you?"

"Why does it matter? You're about to die anyway," Edward replied lazily, advancing upon the prone figure on the ground.

The boy shook in terror as Edward bent down and smoothly scooped up a dropped firearm. To either side lay the already-unconscious forms of the two other Truants that Edward had accosted. Really, it had been almost disappointingly easy. In an effort to draw out the encounter, Edward had given up the element of surprise and allowed the poor fools to fumble with their backpacks for a few moments before his patience ran out. Even with that advantage, it had been over all too quickly. If this was the true strength of the Truancy, Edward thought disdainfully, then it would be all too easy to rub them out if he decided to side with the Educators.

"P-please, no, d-don't!" the boy stammered as Edward cocked the hammer of the pistol. "Please!"

The Truant's eyes were wide in terror, his arms shaking, cringing at Edward's slightest movement. Then, as Edward brought the gun up to the boy's forehead, he abruptly went limp, having fainted completely. It was a truly pathetic display. Edward paused for a moment to reflect on how he certainly wouldn't make any fuss if he were facing imminent death, and was about to pull the trigger when a shocked voice called out.

"What do you think you're doing, Edward?"

Edward looked up and blinked in surprise as he saw Umasi approaching with a look of horror on his face.

"I'm about to take care of this Truant," Edward replied, turning back to look down at his victim, finger tightening on the trigger.

"No!"

Edward sighed and looked up again. Umasi was in his face now, staring as though they had never met before.

"What now, Mr. Umasi?" Edward said impatiently.

"What did he do?" Umasi demanded. "Why were you about to kill him?" Edward blinked again. "He entered the district. I thought you didn't want any live Truants in here."

"I don't want any dead ones either!" Umasi said. "What were you thinking, Edward? I thought that you were smarter than this!"

For one fleeting moment, Edward was seized by a sudden urge to simply bring his gun around and shoot Umasi down where he stood. Edward fought down the urge. Umasi was still useful, though Edward now realized that that wouldn't last much longer.

"I'm sorry, sir," Edward lied, throwing the gun aside. "Apparently I misunderstood your wishes."

"How could you even think of killing someone on an assumption?" Umasi demanded, and then shook his head. "Edward, I'm impressed by your skill, but we're going to have to have a talk about killing later. Go home, Edward, and think about what you were about to do."

"As you wish." Edward nodded politely, and then spun around and left as Umasi began dragging the unconscious Truants towards the edge of the district.

As Edward walked, his brain rapidly went to work. Apparently Umasi took his pacifism more seriously than Edward had believed possible. What a fool. How could someone so knowledgeable be so stupid? Perhaps he had overestimated the boy, Edward thought. He was just another weak idealist after all.

Edward made a mental inventory of everything he had written in his notebook so far. It was more than enough for him to realize his dreams. The strategy games, the words, the exercises, none of the things Umasi had tried to impart meant anything to Edward. Edward had been after one thing—information, which he now had in spades. He had even seen the Truancy with his own eyes, and knew now that they were quite vulnerable. There was little if anything more to be gained by sticking by Umasi, who was showing the first signs of mistrust.

Edward climbed over the fence and dropped back into District 18, his thoughts turning to the gun he had cast aside, and the one that he still kept concealed beneath the floorboards. From now on, he resolved, he would carry it every time he met with Umasi. Sooner rather than later, Edward knew, he would have to put an end to their meetings for good.

Explain yourself!"

Rothenberg cringed. Never had he seen the Mayor like this before.

This was not the dignified and composed leader that the City saw on television. The man sitting at the desk across from him was apoplectic with rage, his face red, teeth bared, eyes furious. Very nearly intimidated into silence, Rothenberg found himself stammering as he spoke.

"I . . . I had him, Mayor! I had the boy! He w-was sitting right in front of me, close as you are now!"

"Do you take me for a *fool*, Rothenberg?" the Mayor demanded. "You may have been face-to-face, but if you really had him he would be here now! No, Rothenberg, *he* had *you*, and you were too blind to see it!"

"Mr. Mayor, I was *so close*, I've been producing results, I swear that—"

"Results? *Results?*" the Mayor shouted. "I've told you time and time again, the only result I care for is seeing my sons returned! Do you have any idea how much your so-called results have cost me? Do you think I have not heard of each and every casualty your search has suffered?"

"Casualties? I don't know what y-you're—"

"So you think me a fool after all!" the Mayor roared. "I've read Jack's reports. You spent days trying to cover up the loss of a helicopter, days that could've been devoted to searching! How did you manage to lose a *helicopter*, anyway? Was the pilot drunk? Were *you* in the cockpit? That would explain it!"

"No, I—"

"Never mind, that's not the point! As disturbing as your wasteful incompetence is, it's not the point!" The Mayor shook his head distractedly. "I don't know how he's doing it, but it's clear to me now that my son is making a fool of you. I should never have put you in charge of this search. You're fired. Get out of my office and await my punishment later."

"No!" Rothenberg said desperately, his dreams crashing in ruins around him. "Mr. Mayor, I . . . I . . ." Rothenberg cast around wildly for something, anything he could say, and his mind suddenly fell upon the mysterious lemonade stand that he had come across. "I located one of them, Mayor, I know where one of your sons is!"

"Oh? And where is that?" the Mayor asked coldly.

"District 19!"

"Is that so?"

"Yes! I saw . . . signs of one of them there, and my men report that that's where some of the attackers fled to. I'm sure of it! Your son is there!"

"Then why have you not sent any patrols to pick him up?"

Rothenberg opened his mouth to speak, but no words would come, and he shut it again, looking like a great fish gasping for air. The Mayor watched this display with cold fury, and then leaned forward in his chair.

"Very well, Rothenberg," the Mayor said in a soft but dangerous voice, "if you think one of my sons is in District 19, you will enter that district— *alone*—and bring him back to me. You have one day."

"What?"

"You heard me," the Mayor said. "If you're not lying, go get my son yourself. But I swear to you, if you do not have him here tomorrow, then you will never see the light of day again. Dismissed."

30
KINDRED SPIRITS

Would you turn off that damn siren? If there's anyone in that district they'll hear us coming a mile off."

"My apologies, Mr. Rothenberg."

"The flashing lights aren't helping either. Turn those off too."

"Regulations won't allow it, I'm afraid."

Rothenberg glared at the man in the driver's seat. The Mayor was insulting him, he knew, by sending this insufferable aide along with Rothenberg. What's worse, Rothenberg wasn't even being allowed to drive the single patrol car on its way to District 19. For his part, Jack looked quite smug at the wheel.

"Forget the regulations and turn the damn lights off," Rothenberg ordered. "And you're supposed to call me 'sir.'"

"Actually, the Mayor made it quite clear to me that you're no longer even an Enforcer," Jack said. "It hardly seems appropriate to call you 'sir' when a lowly aide like myself outranks you."

"You better watch yourself," Rothenberg warned. "If I come back today with what the Mayor is looking for, you can bet that I'll be Chief Enforcer again."

"The Mayor thought you'd say that," Jack said unconcernedly. "He also said he'd be surprised if you decided to come back at all."

Rothenberg fumed. So the Mayor was that determined to humiliate him, was he? But what burned worse than the insult was the knowledge that it was true. Rothenberg wasn't sure exactly what he was going to do, or even what he could do, but he knew that returning to the Mayor empty-handed was not an option.

"Tell me something, Rothenberg," Jack said suddenly, and Rothenberg looked at him in surprise. "What's out there that's so dangerous? What are you looking for?"

"The Mayor still hasn't told you, then? No, he wouldn't have, not an insignificant clerk like you," Rothenberg said scornfully. "It's between me and the Mayor alone, and you'll keep your nose out of it if you know what's good for you."

"You're an angry man, Rothenberg," Jack observed as he braked at an intersection. "Why do you hate children so much? Were you beaten when you were one?"

At that, Rothenberg's furious retort died on his lips, and the car interior was suddenly very silent. Sensing that he had unintentionally touched a nerve, Jack did not press Rothenberg further, and the rest of the ride passed in tedious silence. After what seemed like hours, the impressive wooden barrier surrounding District 19 finally came into view.

"We're here," Jack said as the car came to a halt. "I'm supposed to wait for you until sundown. I'm afraid that the Mayor told me to inform you that if you're not back by then he'll issue a warrant for your arrest. Good luck, Rothenberg."

"Worry about yourself," Rothenberg snapped, looking at the wooden fence through the windshield. "I'll be seeing you again. Count on it."

With that cryptic statement, Rothenberg flung the passenger door open and stormed out. Jack blinked as the man slipped over the fence and into District 19, then removed a cup of coffee from the car's cup holder and took a thoughtful sip. Whatever his task had been, Rothenberg had obviously failed and was now being punished for it. That was interesting. Interesting . . . and worrying.

Looking around to make sure that he was not being watched, Jack furtively removed a notepad from his pocket and began writing.

I cannot understand it. Didn't it bother you? The idea that you would be ending a life?" Umasi demanded. "How could you even consider killing someone defenseless like that?"

Edward bit back his snarled retort, and tried to force his voice into the normal polite one that he always used with Umasi. Edward had dutifully returned to Umasi as had become routine, but he had not expected to deal with this irritating and naïve interrogation. He had made certain to wear a jacket today, within which he concealed the gun taken from beneath the floorboards. Umasi was sorely tempting him to use it now, but Edward knew that that was a step he had to be very careful about taking. Who knew what other secrets Umasi might yet be hiding? Reminding himself that he was in control, that he could end Umasi's life at any time, Edward calmed himself and spoke. Still, despite his best efforts, a hint of impatience slipped into his voice.

"I've already apologized, Mr. Umasi. I'm not sure what else you want from me."

"I want to know how it happened!" Umasi said. "Until yesterday I had been convinced that you were a good person with a few quirks, but after what I saw yesterday I have begun to suspect that I am mistaken."

"How can you say that?" Edward said, feigning hurt. "Sir, everything I did yesterday was for you! I was just trying to do what you wanted! I misunderstood your intentions, yes, and I said I'm sorry! I don't know what else I can do!"

"Edward," Umasi said, "I'm honored that you were willing to kill for me . . . but at the same time, nothing could shame me more. I obviously have been remiss when speaking with you, for I must not have made my beliefs clear. When relating my tale I must've left out the most important parts."

"The most important parts?" Edward repeated, all thoughts of going for his gun suddenly forgotten.

"Yes." Umasi nodded. "I told you all the facts, or nearly all of them as best as I could remember. But I failed to relate the lessons that I had learned. You don't yet understand the true value of life, Edward, not like the two before you did. Sometimes it can be the only possession you have left. To steal it is the ultimate crime."

Edward nearly snorted aloud. This dribble was supposed to be important? Umasi intended to lecture him in some misguided attempt to appeal to morals that he didn't have? There was no profit in empathy, a lesson obviously lost upon Umasi, despite all of the boy's supposed wisdom. Some of Edward's annoyance must have shown on his face, for Umasi let out a deep sigh and hunched over the lemonade stand, hands folded pensively under his chin.

"You don't understand," Umasi repeated sadly. "Return to the orphanage, Edward. I find that I don't feel much like playing right now."

Edward gave a curt nod in reply, then stormed off, leaving Umasi to brood alone at his stand. As he turned the street corner, Edward quickly came to a decision. His patience had run out; he would give Umasi another day to get over the incident, but if Edward could not coax anything useful from the boy the next day, then their "friendship" would have to come to an end.

That decided, the rest of his trek towards District 18 passed in relative peace. He allowed his mind to wander and dwell upon what he would do when he eventually, inevitably, assumed control of the City. What had once been idle fantasy was now viable goal, and it felt *great*. So lost was he in his own dreams that it took Edward a moment to notice the sound of distant sirens approaching. When he did, he snapped back to full alertness.

He was only a block away from the barrier dividing Districts 18 and 19, and judging from the direction of the sound, the Enforcers were probably right on the other side of that barrier. But why were they here? They couldn't be looking for him; the orphanage had no reason to suspect that anything was wrong, and Edward was sure that he had covered his tracks.

That meant it was either a completely random search . . . or they were after Umasi. After a moment's consideration, Edward decided to ascend to a nearby rooftop in order to better judge the situation—a strategy that he admittedly would not have thought of if it hadn't been for Umasi.

The moment he reached the top, Edward scrambled over to the edge of the roof and looked down. He was surprised by what he saw. A single Enforcer patrol car had drawn right up to the wooden barrier and two Enforcers seemed to be talking inside. Then one of them, a massive creature, opened the passenger door and slipped out. He seemed to give the fence a long, hard look, and then began to climb over it with surprising dexterity. All of this was unfolding less than two blocks away from Edward's position, and he quickly ducked out of sight in case the Enforcer thought to look upwards.

Edward quickly weighed his options. This was a perfect opportunity for him to declare his allegiance to the Educators; he could lead this man right to Umasi, earning the gratitude of the Mayor himself, to whom he would offer his services in destroying the Truancy. Not a bad start to a career, but upon further consideration, Edward decided that it was too risky. Umasi would not be killed, but left free to warn the Mayor of his treachery. What's more, there was no telling that the Enforcer would not simply try to kill Edward and take the credit all for himself.

No, Edward decided, it was not the right moment to jump the gun. Instead, a different plan began to take shape in Edward's head. It wouldn't do to have the Enforcer stumble across Umasi's stand and risk having the boy returned to the safety of the Mayor's custody. What's more, after all the acting Edward longed to set his true nature loose, to prove, if only to himself, just what he was capable of. A single Enforcer in an abandoned district on his own—Edward couldn't ask for a finer victim than that.

His mind made up, Edward peered over the edge of the building again. The Enforcer was moving slowly, but following a set path. Running a few calculations through his head, he shimmied down the fire escape, then vanished down an alley as fast as he could. He had seen enough of District 19 to know something about its shortcuts, and managed to reach a distant block long before Rothenberg. Knowing that he had precious minutes to act, Edward looked around and swiftly spotted an old set of trapdoors in the sidewalk that provided access to the building's basement. The lock had long since rusted away, and Edward had no problem in flinging the doors open.

Seizing a heavy trash can from a nearby alley, Edward dragged it across the street and into the basement, making sure that it left a trail in the soot and dust that the Enforcer would be sure to see. He had to descend an irksome flight of stairs to reach the bottom, but once there he found it completely pitch black. He felt his way to an open door that led to another room and stowed the garbage can in there. Then he shut the door behind him, slipped beneath the stairwell, and drew his gun.

The trap was set. There was nothing more that Edward could do but to wait for the Enforcer to fall into it.

Though it would not be immediately apparent to anyone who walked into the flower shop, Noni could hear every word of spoken conversation uttered therein. Zyid was holding an urgent conference at the moment, with Gabriel, Frank, and a few other officers in attendance. Noni merely continued throwing knives at a wooden target, an exercise that had become trivial for her. She gave no indication that she was listening to what was being said, and Zyid never did either. But they both knew that she was. Every time a report was given and its messenger dismissed, Zyid would ask Noni for a recap and her opinions. She never failed in this regard, and though Zyid showed neither approval nor displeasure, she could tell that he was pleased.

Noni had natural talent for eavesdropping. She was used to observing without being noticed, though she was increasingly observing that others were in fact noticing her. She had been seen in battle more than once now, and Zyid kept her close. The Truants had taken note, and among the rumors that were whispered was the assumption that she had abilities that she did not. To avoid them, she maintained a cold and distant approach, and for some reason it seemed to work. She had earned some respect, but neither wanted nor needed any friends.

She had not participated in the celebrations of the previous night, when nearly all of the survivors of the assault on the Enforcer station had returned, giddy with success. There was a general feeling of accomplishment, of hope, now that they had proven that the Enforcers were not invulnerable. There had been an undercurrent of mourning for Amal, but the Truants who had once been vagrants were used to death, and the others were quickly growing accustomed to it. As for Noni, it didn't bother her. Her whole world was built on one person, and so long as he lived, she was secure.

Noni glanced furtively over at Zyid. He was now deep in conversation with Frank, Gabriel, and the other officers, serious looks on all of their faces. Zyid had let the Truants have their party the previous night, though he, like Noni, had taken no part in it. Noni wasn't even sure where he had gone. Then, midway through the celebrations, Gabriel's group showed up, the last to arrive. Noni had noticed immediately that something was wrong. Gabriel seemed grim, worried, and though all of his comrades were with him, many of them looked inexplicably pale. As if from nowhere, Zyid had appeared, hustling them off into a room for debriefing. Whatever had befallen them, Noni realized an hour later, could not have been good; Zyid emerged looking troubled, a rare expression for him.

The incident went unnoticed by the rest of the Truancy, and neither Zyid nor Gabriel or any of his subordinates had made mention of it as far as she could tell. Noni yearned to know what was so terrible that it could trouble Zyid, but she had not yet mustered up the nerve to ask. And so she watched in silence, out of the corner of her eye, as Zyid finished talking with his subordinates and sent them out of the shop. He seemed lost in thought for a moment, and then, as she knew he would, turned to her.

"So, Noni," he said, "I trust that you were listening."

"Yes, sir. You've contacted a student named Alex in the District 1 School."

"Correct. Have you figured out why?"

"You . . . before he died, you sent Amal to get blueprints for the District 1 School . . ." Noni recalled, to which Zyid gave an encouraging nod. ". . . so . . . so are you planning to attack that school?"

"More than just attack it," Zyid said, an intense glint in his eyes. "I intend to demolish it."

"You mean . . . blow it up?"

"Precisely," Zyid said, turning to examine the papers on his table. "With Rothenberg out of the way, we need to make our grand City debut on our own terms. I'm not sure how much the Mayor knows about us, but I will make sure that he does not doubt how serious we are."

"Yes, sir," Noni said, hesitating for a moment before plunging on with the question that had been bothering her for a day. "Sir, may I ask what Gabriel told you last night?"

Zyid looked up at her sharply, the very action itself a silent rebuke. "Nothing that need concern you, Noni."

"Is it . . . dangerous?"

"Very."

"Then I want to help."

"Appreciated, but unwanted. It is a personal matter. I will not tolerate interference."

Zyid's tone indicated that he would not accept any discussion on the matter, and Noni did not press him. But though she kept her silence, Noni came to a decision as she began throwing knives at the target again. No matter what he said, if Zyid ever found himself in danger, then Noni would be there to help in any way she could. After all, she knew that she could face any terror while at his side, but absolutely none without him.

Rothenberg slowly descended the stairs, not really paying attention to the strange trail that he was following. It looked like something heavy had recently been dragged along the ground, all the way down to the basement. Rothenberg didn't really expect it to actually be anything of interest, but there was little else to investigate without stumbling blindly around the district. As he had feared, District 19 looked different without the blizzard, and he had no idea where the lemonade stand had been before—if indeed it was still there at all.

No, Rothenberg no longer had any hope of satisfying the Mayor. Reality was unpleasant, but there was no denying it. Rothenberg was now weighing his options, wondering how best to get out of the mess he had found himself in. There wasn't much. If he tried to lie low within the living districts, the Enforcers would track him down; despite their failures in fighting Truants on their own turf, Rothenberg knew better than anyone what they were capable of. Returning empty-handed was not a happy prospect either, so what else was there? Rothenberg refused to even consider fleeing to the abandoned districts like a filthy child vagrant.

Scowling at the world and the foul hand it had dealt him, Rothenberg reached the bottom of the stairs. It was nearly pitch black down here, and Rothenberg knew that he was in some sort of basement. But no matter, the trail had led here and he was interested in what lay at its end. Stepping forward into the darkness, Rothenberg found a doorknob, which he turned to reveal an utterly dark room. Stepping into the inky blackness, Rothenberg felt along the wall for a light switch, found one, flicked it on . . .

. . . and heard a gun being cocked behind him as fluorescent lights hummed to life, illuminating the drab basement. Instantly alert, Rothenberg froze, cursing himself for his carelessness. Several moments passed and nothing happened. Rothenberg began to relax. Whoever had ambushed him clearly didn't mean to kill him just yet; that meant he had options. Rothenberg decided to wait and see what the person wanted.

"Well, what have we here, an Enforcer with the guts to work alone? What an uncommon phenomenon."

Rothenberg was startled by the voice—it belonged to a child! And yet it was different, very different, from any he had heard before. There was an undercurrent of cruelty, an unspoken promise of brutality in every syllable. It was chilling, not only in and of itself but because, after years of viewing them all as the same, Rothenberg was only just beginning to understand how different children could be. Instinctively Rothenberg's hand crept towards his gun.

"Not another inch, Enforcer, unless you'd care to get shot."

Rothenberg scowled and stopped his hand. Behind him the boy's footsteps began pacing back and forth. Rothenberg was being sized up. He found that that notion was alien to him. Being sized up by a child? What had become of the City?

"Hm, come to think of it, I believe I know who you are." The voice suddenly sounded delighted. "Yes . . . we've met before, haven't we? But you've never seen the *real* me, have you, Rothenberg?"

"What're you babbling about, brat?"

"Oh, so you don't recognize me after all?" the boy said with mock hurt. "Well, that's not surprising. You hardly seemed sober at the time. But I don't mind—I've heard quite a bit about you. The great Enforcer Rothenberg, the terror of the vagrants, the brutal man that the Mayor sent to war against his own sons!"

Rothenberg was surprised that the boy knew about his exploits, but he was shocked to find that the kid's voice was not filled with fear, anger, or even malice. Instead the voice now dripped with scorn and mockery, as if it were discussing a bad joke. Rothenberg clenched his fists angrily. He would make sure that this child, no matter who he was, paid for not showing more respect.

"Aside from your size, you certainly don't look like much," the voice continued, "so I suppose that I should commend you for getting this far."

"This is an abandoned district, boy," Rothenberg growled. "Who said you could come here?"

"Who said I could come here?" the voice repeated. "Why, I did."

"And do you think you can just do whatever you want?"

"Of course. You're not the brightest coin in the Mayor's purse, are you?" the voice mused. "If I feel like visiting an abandoned district, who's going to stop me? You? By all means, Enforcer, try it."

Rothenberg snarled incoherently, but did not move, silently acknowledging the boy's point.

"Do you really think you can get away with pointing a gun at an adult?" Rothenberg demanded, changing the subject.

"Oh yes—as a matter of fact, I believe I can get away with much more than that," the voice said. "I suppose that I should reintroduce myself. My name is Edward. Don't forget it again, Enforcer. Within a few years you and the rest of your colleagues will serve me . . . provided that you survive that long, that is."

"So you're not the Mayor's son?" Rothenberg said.

"That pacifistic fool?" Edward laughed. "Please. I have greater ambition than to rot in an abandoned district. I think you can identify with that. After all, the two of us are obviously kindred spirits."

"Oh yeah?" Rothenberg snorted derisively. "I don't think so."

"Oh, but it's true," Edward insisted. "We have much in common, you and I. We both care nothing for others, we are determined to realize our own ambitions, and we are both clearly prepared to resort to brutality to do so. Really"—Edward chuckled—"the only significant differences between us are our ages . . . and your relative lack of intelligence."

Rothenberg stiffened in shock at the insult, and in that instant his patience snapped, and his hand darted for his gun with astounding speed. Despite his encounters with the Truancy, Rothenberg was sure that Edward would not pull the trigger in time. The possibility that a *child* would shoot him in the back without hesitation, in cold blood, still did not yet occur to Rothenberg.

With most other children, he might have been right. With Edward, he couldn't have been more mistaken.

Edward didn't hesitate, carefully aiming his gun lower as Rothenberg reached for his pistol. Before Rothenberg could even draw his pistol from its holster, a deafening bang burst throughout the room, followed a moment later by an earsplitting shriek. Edward's lip slowly curled up into a satisfied smile as he circled around Rothenberg's writhing body.

"How careless of me—I think that I've shattered your kneecap," Edward said with mock concern. "I can't imagine how painful that must be. Not to mention that you might never walk on that leg again."

"You . . ." Rothenberg gritted in disbelief through his teeth, flopping about like an oversized fish. "You . . . you're just a . . ."

"Student? Child? Legal inferior?" Edward finished mildly. "True enough, I suppose—at least for now. But look at you, Enforcer, squirming about on the floor. To me, you're nothing but a worm."

Rothenberg snarled, and in a fit of irrationality, seized his fallen pistol, shakily raising it again. The motion was too clumsy, too slow to have any chance of success, yet Rothenberg performed it anyway in the defense of his ego.

Edward, of course, had no intention of allowing Rothenberg to pull the trigger.

"How rude of me," Edward said, "I forgot about your other leg."

Another deafening shot rang out, and once more Rothenberg screamed and thrashed about wildly on the floor. Both his knees now bled, staining his bullet-torn uniform dark red. Admiring his work, Edward chuckled to himself and kicked the gun backwards, out of Rothenberg's reach.

"That's right, wriggle about on the ground like scum!" Edward laughed. "You are a proud man, Rothenberg. We are both proud men. But how do you feel now, reduced to crawling at my feet!"

Rothenberg's eyes bulged, his nostrils flared, his breaths came rapidly as if no amount of air could satisfy his lungs. His arms reached feebly for Edward's legs, determined to do some kind of harm to the boy who had dared to so completely defy every expectation Rothenberg had of children . . . then he went limp, passing out from the pain and exertion.

Edward frowned at the Enforcer's loss of consciousness. He had expected the man to be able to put up with a little more than that. It was disappointing, really, that he wouldn't be able to feel anything else that Edward did. After just a moment's consideration Edward aimed his gun again anyway. He now wondered if Rothenberg might be awakened when shot, and there was no reason not to try.

Before Edward could decide on which body part to shoot next, his train of thought was suddenly interrupted by a new voice—calm, yet furious.

"What are you doing, Ed?"

Edward spun around to see Umasi standing in the doorway, Rothenberg's gun in his hand, pointed steadily at Edward. Edward was momentarily disconcerted by how completely Umasi had managed to sneak up on him, but the uneasy feeling soon passed. For all his strengths, Edward knew, this pacifist was no warrior.

"Mr. Umasi," Edward greeted, raising his own gun as he performed an ironic bow. "How kind of you to join us."

"How could you?"

"Come on, are you really that blind? Did you truly have no idea about who I really am? Obviously not," Edward observed, for Umasi was staring at him with a look of utmost horror. "Don't tell me that I scare you. Is the real me that fearsome?"

"Fear is the unknown, Edward," Umasi said in a voice from the grave. "No, you aren't frightening to me. On the contrary, I believe I truly know you now."

"You only think you do, Umasi."

"Do not think that you will get away with this."

"And who's going to punish me? You? Haven't I already proven that you're weak and foolish?" Edward crowed. "Look how easily taken in you were! After all you claim you've been through you're still naïve, eager to trust, *emotional*! Did you really think that my tears meant anything? I am not such a fool, Umasi! Not like you!"

"No, you're not like me at all," Umasi agreed. "I have never been pathetic enough to disguise myself as a friend and then flee after profiting from goodwill."

"Flee? I have no intention of fleeing, Umasi. You are a liability that needs to be dealt with." Edward smiled, finger tightening on his trigger. "You would weigh me down forever if you had the chance. But I won't let you hang on to my ankles—if something harmful is attached to you, sever it I say!"

"So you intend to decide this with bullets?" Umasi said, grip tightening on his own gun. "Afraid of meeting me in personal combat, are you? I don't blame you. You have never seen me fight. It is only natural to be scared."

"Scared? *Me*? You really think *you'd* stand a chance against *me*?" Edward gaped for a moment, and then burst into laughter as he tossed his gun aside. "Bring it then, Umasi. We both know you're not going to shoot me down in cold blood."

Umasi said nothing, but raised his gun to point at the ceiling. He fired, and with a shattering of glass and shower of sparks, one of the room's lights went dark. With a few more well-aimed shots, the room was plunged into total darkness, and Edward felt a moment's unease as he stood there squinting into the shadows. Brushing the feeling aside, Edward confidently braced himself for an attack, certain of his victory.

"Do you think that this is going to help you, Umasi?" Edward challenged. "Or are you going to run?"

"I have nothing more to say to you, Edward."

Edward heard Umasi's gun clatter to the ground, then there was a swoosh as something darted at him. Edward lashed out with his fist and felt a surge of triumph as it made contact. Then his wrist was seized and he was sent crashing to the ground. Scrambling back to his feet, Edward felt a bit of his confidence erode. A moment later, a foot connected firmly with his back, sending him stumbling forward in the blackness. Spinning around to face his unseen attacker, Edward seethed in frustration. The dark was more annoying than he had thought it would be. How could Umasi move so well when he was practically blind? What had he said before? Something about listening?

His heart pounding in his ears, Edward shut his eyes and struggled to hear something, anything. For a moment there was nothing, and then . . . There, to the left, noise! Edward pounced, outstretched arms swiping at thin air just as he realized that what he had heard was a clanking noise, and not the sound of a human. At that moment someone again zipped through the dark, and before Edward could react he was slammed to the side. Rebounding off a wall, Edward swung his fists randomly, breathing heavily, not knowing if he was even striking in the right direction. Then he stepped on something round, slipped, and crashed to the ground again.

Swearing, Edward scrabbled on the floor, searching for whatever it was that he had slipped on. Seizing upon what felt like some metal tubes, Edward realized that these were not only what he had tripped on, but also the same things that he had heard clanking earlier. Edward rose again, this time brandishing one of the tubes, and Umasi either let him get up or was too apprehensive to stop him. As he stood there, alone in the dark, Edward suddenly thought he heard a soft breathing behind him. Spinning around, Edward frantically swung his makeshift club, only to realize that he was lashing out at nothing, that his mind had been playing tricks on him.

Edward struck the ground with his pipe in frustration. Dammit! If only he could see! He would be winning, he should be winning! Cursing Umasi for his underhanded tactics, Edward strained his ears again, still hearing nothing but his own heaving breaths. Edward gave up and attacked the floor again in disgust. Useless! He was better than this pathetic creeping around in the shadows, ears twitching like some timid mouse. He was cunning, powerful, more formidable than anyone ever suspected, he was—

A fist slammed into Edward's chest, derailing his train of thought. Edward instinctively made a swipe with his free hand, and felt it snatch Umasi's sunglasses from his face. In retaliation a blow to the face sent Edward stumbling backwards. He feebly tried lashing out with his pipe. An unseen hand caught the weapon in midair, and Edward felt it deftly twisted from his grasp and sent clattering off. Edward hastily backed away, desperate to put some distance between him and his assailant. Reaching a corner, he hastily stuffed the stolen sunglasses into his back pocket and paused. All was silent again.

For the first time in his life Edward felt small and helpless as he stared blindly into the dark. Minutes ago he had been almost delirious with joy, an Enforcer at his feet, and seemingly the entire City his for the taking. Now his ambitions, confidence, and abilities had all abandoned him. He was frightened. Something creaked. Edward's heart pounded so hard that he could hear nothing else.

"Coward!" Edward shouted. "You were scared to fight me fair!"

In response strong arms seized Edward by the shoulders, and Edward cringed as he was hurled from his corner and onto the ground. Before he could rise, a foot stomped down on his back, pressing him against the floor, and Edward knew it was over.

"I would never have lost to you if there was light!" Edward raged at the unfeeling shadows.

"No, Ed." Umasi's voice was unfamiliar; cold and emotionless. "You were blinded by pride, not darkness. Someday you may learn humility, but until then . . ."

Something struck Edward on the back of the head, and his breathing eased as he was knocked unconscious.

". . . you will always be easily broken."

31

M an, this building's got a fireplace and everything, why don't we heat up a proper meal for once?"

"Something's got Zyid worried. That alert he sent out wasn't for nothing."

"Zyid can worry about whatever he wants; there haven't been any Enforcers in the abandoned districts since Rothenberg got the boot."

"Maybe there's something worse than Enforcers out there."

"What, you saying we should believe those stories about Zyid's evil twin? Please."

"I'm saying that we shouldn't be careless. Cold soup won't kill you, now sit down and eat it or Davis can have it when he gets back."

The discontented Truant reluctantly sat down and sniffed at the bowl of cold canned soup. His companion was already breaking off pieces of stale bread and dipping them into his own bowl, showing every sign of enjoyment as he ate. Listening to them both from the safety of a hallway, Umasi smiled faintly as he drew his ear away from the door. So, they were calling him the evil twin, were they? That was interesting, Umasi mused as he adjusted his sunglasses. The pair that he now wore had originally belonged to the albino. Edward had managed to swipe the other pair, and Umasi had not thought to recover it until it was too late.

The Truants inside the room began bickering with each other again, drawing Umasi's attention again. Umasi had judged that the one who wasn't being picky about his food was probably a former vagrant, and a sharp one at that. The other was no weakling, but he was careless, and Umasi wasn't particularly worried about him. Unbeknownst to either of them, the third Truant, the one they had called Davis, had snuck outside on the pretense of standing watch and had instead built a private bonfire to heat up his own meal. Davis was now unconscious, bound, and gagged in an alley outside, his weapons confiscated.

It had been several days since his fight with Edward, and the deadline that Umasi had given his brother had come and gone. After dragging the injured and unconscious Enforcer to the edge of the district, then carrying the equally unconscious Edward back to District 18, Umasi had set about preparing for his inevitable crusade against the Truancy. He did not for a moment expect Zen to yield to his demands, and so the night the deadline expired he had begun visiting the City's abandoned districts. Since then he had located and scattered three Truancy hideouts, and apparently he had Zen worried enough to put the rest of the Truants on high alert.

Not that it was doing them much good, Umasi thought to himself as the wary Truant finished his meal and announced that he was going to go check on Davis. Umasi brought himself into a crouch as the doorknob turned. The door opened, and Umasi pounced, relishing the startled scream as he slammed the Truant to the ground. He punched the boy between the eyes, knocking him out, and then smoothly leapt back to his feet. The other Truant was staring wide-eyed as his hands scrabbled across the floor for his gun. Umasi was on him in a flash, delivering a powerful kick to the temple that rendered him limp. Umasi paused briefly to make sure that his victims were indeed unconscious and had strong pulses, and then he went to work.

The guns were stripped of ammunition and thrown into a backpack along with knives and anything else that could serve as a weapon. The Truants' radios and cell phones were smashed beyond repair. The hideout's store of supplies and explosives was carried outside, into the middle of the abandoned street, where Umasi blew all of it up at once, sending an enormous tongue of flame lancing upwards. Only then, when the Truancy's work had been wholly undone, was Umasi's work finished. Satisfied, Umasi turned around and returned home to District 19, backpack slung over his shoulder. Umasi smiled as he went. Finally following the example he had long admired, he was fighting without restraint . . . but at the same time, at least for now, not fighting to kill.

As Umasi walked back through the living districts, allowing himself to become lost within the crowd of people, he looked up and found himself staring at a billboard advertising a movie that was coming out the next day. It took Umasi a moment to understand why the billboard felt so familiar, but then an old memory flashed out at him from a past he hardly remembered.

"Umasi, that movie comes out months from now."

"Oh, right. Sorry."

"Everyone makes mistakes. Listen, Umasi, when the film comes out we'll see it together . . ."

Umasi felt an emotional shock that sent him reeling, and for a moment he felt like the boy he had once been. Pedestrians stared as Umasi shook his head frantically. No, he couldn't let this happen now. When the time had come to deal with Edward, Umasi had known exactly what to do. He had fought his former friend without restraint, without mercy, without attachment or emotion. Now Edward was a thing of the past, a mistake that deserved no consideration. The time had come to deal with Zen, and Umasi would have to correct another mistake. He could not afford to allow his emotions to get in the way of what he had to do.

Umasi straightened up and slipped back into the crowd, his head clear once more. He would be there at the movie premier, but even if Zen was there as well, there would be no pleasantries to exchange. Fate had cast them as enemies, and they would play their parts out to the end.

So, another outpost has fallen?"

"District 36 this time. It was a small three-man outpost, they didn't stand a chance. They're sure it was just one attacker, there's been no sign of the other guy that jumped us in District 19. Same deal as usual—crew unconscious, equipment stolen, explosives detonated."

"My brother always was a stickler for consistency."

"Aren't you worried about this?"

"Not unduly. Our quarrel is a personal one. If I do not present myself to him, Umasi will seek me out in time. Until then there are much more pressing matters to deal with, such as our imminent attack on the District 1 School."

"Zyid, you might not be worried, but the other Truants *are*. The worse the gossip gets the more frightened they become. And let me tell you, it's getting pretty bad."

"You said you were sure that the Truants that were with you would keep their silence," Zen said.

"I did," Gabriel said, somewhat defensively. "It's the other Truants that are talking. You wouldn't believe some of the rumors they're spreading around. They think something supernatural is going on, that there's an exact opposite of *you* floating around the City attacking Truants. Someone even suggested that it's your evil twin—jokingly, of course," Gabriel added, for Zen had raised an eyebrow. "But seriously, who could blame them? I've *seen* him, Zyid. Back when we were at school I never thought you two looked that much alike, but he's different now. He's got the same kind of . . . presence, if you know what I mean."

"I think I do," Zen said. "How bad is it?"

"Well, the direct damage isn't irreparable—we've had to withdraw from a couple Districts and we've lost a lot of equipment, but he hasn't killed anyone yet," Gabriel said. "Still, it's doing a number on our morale. Like I said, the ghost stories they're telling have people spooked."

"And the solution?"

"Well," Gabriel said, "the common superstition seems to be that you're gonna have to take him out yourself. And realistically I'm not sure that anyone else can do it. I never even saw him coming, Zyid. There was a glimpse of white and then we were all down."

"For what it's worth, I've arrived at the same conclusion myself. There seems to be no other option," Zen said. "I will have to face him, and the sooner the better."

"You'll win, right?"

"As to that, I cannot say," Zen said. "Do whatever you can to quash the rumors, Gabriel. Our plans proceed as scheduled. Now, has Alex made final contact yet?"

"In the best way possible." Gabriel nodded. "I just met with him myself during his lunch break."

"If I recall correctly, the two of you knew each other when we were all back at school."

"He was in the same class, yeah, but I didn't know him well enough to call him a friend."

"No matter. Back when I first went recruiting I was certain that he would make a good Truant, which is why I had him stay behind for this one most important mission. Speaking of which, have there been any unforeseen complications?"

"No, he said the last of the charges are planted, but he seemed a bit nervous. He said it was kind of sudden for him, that it'd been a while since you first recruited him and he'd been starting to wonder if the whole Truancy thing was for real." Gabriel snorted, and then sobered up quickly. "Long story short, he's going to see it through, but he's got some last-minute reservations."

"I can't say that I'm surprised," Zen said. "Did you explain that no students would be put at risk?"

"No." Gabriel shook his head. "But I told him that you wanted to meet up with him personally before go forward, and he agreed. He sounded dead set on getting out of there, Zyid. I don't think things haven't gotten much better since we left."

"I don't think so either," Zen mused. "Did he agree to the time and place I suggested?"

"Yeah, the first opening-day showing of that new film, in the big District 1 Theater tomorrow, right?"

"Indeed."

"Any particular reason why you chose that time and place? That's just a matter of hours before we're set to attack, and District 1 might still be dangerous for you."

"At that time of night, I doubt that there will be much risk, or many people to overhear us during the movie," Zen said. "There are also other reasons that I made that choice, but I don't care to discuss those. As always your help is appreciated, Gabriel. Keep up the good work."

Understanding that he had been dismissed, Gabriel saluted and left. As the door shut behind him, the flower shop was abruptly plunged into silence. Zen brooded in silence for a few moments. Though he had not yet revealed it to anyone, he planned more than just a simple demolition with the District 1 School. With Rothenberg out of the way, he envisioned a massive, decisive battle—one that would teach their enemies fear, and introduce the Truancy to the Mayor in an unforgettable way. So far everything was going according to plan . . . even Umasi.

Zen had not expected his brother to meddle as overtly as he had, and Umasi had made himself an unacceptable variable, a big question mark in the Truancy's future. Zen aimed to correct that, provided that Umasi showed up for the movie. Zen believed that he would. After all, they had made a promise, and neither of them was known for reneging on those. They would be there the next day, and then the day after that the District 1 School would fall. The war between the Truancy and the Educators would begin in earnest, and Zen could be faced with the prospect of fighting both his father and his brother at the same time.

But Zen was determined not to let things go that far, to the point where the odds would be stacked against him. There *was* a way to kill two birds with one stone, to prune all but one branch off the family tree. The only question now was if Zen could defeat Umasi. Zen no longer underestimated his brother, and yet the thought of their meeting did not worry him; it was, after all, inevitable. With that in mind, Zen turned to address the shadow in the corner that had not moved a muscle since Gabriel's report.

"By now, Noni," Zen said, "I'm sure that a person as smart as you has figured out who exactly my 'evil twin' is."

"The boy you beat on the docks."

"And the boy who would have killed me, were it not for your intervention," Zen added. "Funnily enough, he actually *is* my twin, though I hesitate to label him as evil. No, he's merely grown up now, just like me. It's a pity that he's become an enemy when at last there is a resemblance between us."

"You beat him before, you'll do it again."

"I beat him once, and he returned the favor," Zen said, walking over to where the crowbar rested in the corner. He picked it up, and seemed to address it as he ran his hands over its surface. "So, we were opposite sides of the same coin after all. Best two out of three, Brother . . . the next flip will decide everything."

• • •

uch a thing to happen to the poor boy, after all he's been through . . ."

"Attacked by vagrants, here, in District 18 no less! Can you believe the nerve?"

"Have you filed a report with the Enforcers?"

"Of course, but you know them. They're too busy doing who knows what to bother cleaning up the vagrant mess."

"I'm telling you; whoever's in charge over there should be fired. I have half a mind to march up to City Hall myself and tell it to the Mayor."

"As a matter of fact, I heard that the Chief Truancy Officer lost his job just a few days ago."

"Really? Well maybe that's why the Enforcers are milling around like headless chickens."

Edward shut out the adults' conversation as they chattered noisily outside his door. After coming to on a sidewalk of District 18, Edward had dragged himself back to the orphanage, where the staff immediately noticed that he was sporting several prominent bruises. Edward wearily fed them a story about being attacked by vagrants, but most uncharacteristically felt no satisfaction even after they bought his lie and began fussing over him.

Regardless, the staff had insisted on keeping him bedridden, and as a result, Edward had actually missed a few days of school—a first for him, though at the moment he couldn't care less. He kept replaying his fight with Umasi over and over in his head. There was no denying it anymore: somehow, impossibly, he had miscalculated, misjudged, almost fatally. To continue to make excuses would be foolish; Edward had simply underestimated his mentor. The gap between them had been beyond his comprehension, so vast that he, for all his ego, had not even seen it.

Beneath the sheets, Edward's hand tightened around Umasi's sunglasses. They were a memento from the fight, the only physical reminder he had of what had transpired in that basement. As much as he wanted to destroy them, to cast them aside for good, he knew that he couldn't. The sunglasses carried humiliating, embarrassing memories, but they were important nonetheless, for they reminded Edward of his own failings.

Loosening his grip on the glasses, Edward forced himself to consider his options instead. Thanks to Umasi, the idea of entering the conflict now was untenable, and he no longer harbored any delusions about being able to attack Umasi himself; his pistol was lost, leaving him only with the knife beneath the floorboards. The only viable choice left was to wait it out and watch the conflict unfold; watch and wait for the right moment to act. The prospect of enduring perhaps years more of drudgery, living constantly in the shadow of his failure, was appalling to Edward . . . but what else could he do?

Then Edward blinked. If he was to wait, then what need was there to carry around the lessons he'd learned like a burden? Edward came to a decision. He knew a place, a secluded part of District 20's massive Grand Park, where he could bury the sunglasses until the time came when he would need reminders of the past in order to achieve the future of his dreams. He would continue to live as a student for as long as need be, for he was patient, and knew exactly what prizes lay at the end of the tunnel.

Edward smiled in the darkness, slipping the sunglasses onto his face. He had been beaten, but not thwarted. He had not, would not, give up on his ambitions for as long as he lived.

"And I *am* still alive, Umasi," Edward whispered to no one. "I wasn't the only one who made a mistake in that basement. You'll see. Just wait . . .

"Just wait . . ."

32
FINAL PREPARATIONS

The midnight premier had gotten a decent turnout, though by no means was it sold out. Zen and Alex sat together in the very front row, far enough from the rest of the audience so that their conversation would not be overheard over the noise of the movie. The film itself turned out to be a mindless action flick, though that made it loud and distracting enough to suit the Truants' purposes. His pale visage lit by the flickering screen, Alex looked troubled as he sipped through a straw from a cup of soda. Zen, for his part, kept his eyes fixed on the screen and picked at a bag of popcorn as they conversed.

"I don't want any other students getting hurt, Zyid."

Zen smiled around a mouthful of popcorn. Pale-skinned and dark-haired, Alex had always been considered socially awkward at school, though Zen had judged that the boy had a good character on the inside. It was satisfying to see that his judgment had been right again.

"Alex, the greatest tragedy that I can imagine would be the murder of one student by another. It is the Educators that seek to turn us against each other, not me."

"How do you know that there won't be any kids left inside?"

"It's *Sunday*, Alex. And even if there is a student there for some unfathomable reason, if everything goes according to plan the entire area will be evacuated before we detonate."

"How are you going to arrange that?"

"That is my business. You're going to have to trust me."

Alex shifted in his seat, but did not contradict Zen. The actors onscreen were now shouting, and both Truants patiently waited for the noise to die down. When Alex next opened his mouth, it was to ask a question.

"Are you sure that the explosives will work?"

"Provided that you placed them correctly—"

"I did."

"—then yes. Aaron assured me that they are perfect."

"And the trigger?"

"The remote should be effective within a thousand yards if the cell phone can't get a signal. Use the former only as a last resort, Alex; it's going to be very dangerous to get anywhere near that building."

"Is there anything else I should know?"

Zen casually flicked another piece of popcorn into his mouth.

"There may be a considerable Enforcer presence around the building right before our attack."

"What?"

The action onscreen had reached a climax, and a series of explosions illuminated Alex's dumbfounded face as the soundtrack thundered in their ears. Zen would have laughed if his sense of humor had been more accommodating.

"Don't worry about it, Alex. The Enforcers will be our problem, not yours. We will force them to retreat into the school. Then it will be your duty to detonate the explosives, unless you prefer that I do the honors. That's all."

"And what happens after that?"

"After that you return with us, should you choose to," Zen said. "I understand that your months of uncertainty and isolation in school must have been difficult. I regret that it was impossible to contact you earlier, but if you are successful now I can assure you that your sacrifices won't be ignored."

Alex looked away, both from the screen and from Zen's gaze. Looking back up at the film, Zen kept silent as he finished the last of his popcorn. He knew that Alex would accept. After all, it hadn't been so long ago that Zen himself had tasted the desperation of being a student—the constricting knowledge that no matter what he did, he would never be an equal in school, in the City, or in life, unless he became the person the Educators wanted him to be.

The only way out was utter obedience or outright rebellion. In Zen's mind, the choice was obvious for anyone with spirit.

"I'll do it. I'm coming back with the rest of you."

Zen nodded to himself. Evidently, Alex did have spirit.

"Then I believe that we've covered everything of importance, Alex. Sit back and enjoy the rest of the film."

A great tension seemed to drain out of the air between the two Truants, and Alex slumped in his seat as he stared blankly up at the screen. Zen, for his part, casually glanced over his shoulder, eyes scanning the rest of the audience. Everyone seemed fixated upon the movie, and no one seemed to have come in after the movie had started. There was certainly no one within earshot, at any rate.

Far from setting his mind at ease, this observation only troubled Zen. The rest of the film passed by quickly, and as the credits began to roll Alex quickly stood up, politely waiting for his leader so that they could leave together. However, Zen waved him off as he stood up himself.

"We have different destinations, Alex," Zen muttered. "Go on without me. There's something I have to make sure of."

Occupied with his own thoughts, Alex nodded and complied without question, leaving Zen to stand alone near the theater's exit.

When he had arrived early at the cinema, Zen had waited in a corner of the theater, positioned so that he could see every person who entered. Umasi would come, Zen was sure of that. Only long after the movie had started, with still no sign of his brother, did Zen finally sit down and join Alex in the front row. Now, as the entire audience filed out of the theater, Zen felt his unease increasing. Umasi was not among the crowd leaving the theater, nor was he among the few people that had stayed behind in their seats to watch the credits.

There was no way that Umasi could have seen him, Zen decided. And yet he was sure, somehow, that Umasi *had* been watching. The thought that he had been outmaneuvered already was deeply unsettling to him, but Zen never mistrusted his instincts. After a moment's hesitation, Zen drew a piece of paper from his pocket and taped it to the wall, where he was confident that Umasi would be able to find it.

His job completed, Zen buttoned his jacket around his neck and swept out of the theater as the windbreaker billowed behind him.

The projector flickered once and then died as the lights came on in the theater below. A teenaged theater employee got up and stretched briefly before changing the reels, just like he did every Sunday at midnight. As he worked, the boy glanced over at the unusual guest in the projection room, who had spent the entire movie staring down at the audience rather than at the screen. The guest was an odd kid —everything from his clothes to his mannerisms seemed off somehow—but he paid well, unlike the theater.

"If you don't mind me saying, you didn't seem very interested in the movie," the employee observed.

"I wasn't."

"Then why all this?"

"I was hoping to see someone here."

"Well, did he show up?"

"Oh yes, and I think he knows that I did too." Umasi stood up and reached into his pocket, his tone suddenly businesslike. "Our deal was half to let me into the projector room, and half when the movie was over. You kept your end of the bargain; here's the rest of mine."

The employee gratefully accepted the other half of the bribe and quickly counted it to make sure it was all there. Satisfied, he looked back up at Umasi, who was waiting with his arms crossed.

"Is everything in order?"

"Yeah, thanks."

"Good. Then remember, if anyone asks, I was never here."

"No problem, man."

With a nod, Umasi slipped out of the projector room and into the hallway outside. He'd been generous with the bribe; the boy now had enough to make his next summer vacation a memorable one, and neither knew nor cared what Umasi's motivations were. That was just the way Umasi wanted it.

As Umasi made his way down to the actual theater, the last of the audience filed out and made for either the exit or the bathrooms. Zen, Umasi knew, would be long gone by now. Neither of them intended to have their final showdown here, not in the middle of a crowded cinema. Yet Zen had left something for him, and Umasi knew what it would be before he even spotted it, taped to the wall of the theater. Without his glasses the small script appeared blurred, and Umasi tore it down from the wall in order to read it properly.

The message was concise, yet said all that needed to be said.

> *Brother,*
> *The District 1 School. Tomorrow at 4:00 pm.*
> *See you there,*
> *Zen*

Umasi contemplated the note for a moment, then shoved it into his pocket and exited the theater with the rest of the crowd.

It took Zen a couple of hours to return to the flower shop unnoticed. By the time he arrived, the dark streets were already filled with Truants, gathered together for one mission from every abandoned district in the City. Their complete numbers could not be discerned in the darkness, though Zen knew that there were precisely two hundred of them, divided up into divisions of twenty and then into groups of five. Each group had a captain, and every Truant was equipped with weapons and radios. They knew the plan, and now only awaited their orders.

It was the first time that the Truancy had ever undertaken an operation like this, and seeing the magnitude of it took Zen's breath away.

Noni was waiting for him as he entered the flower shop. She, like him, had garbed herself all in black, her hair drawn back into a simple ponytail. The scarf remained firmly wrapped around her lower face, though her icy eyes blazed with determination. Zen could see knives tucked away in her belt, and a gun holstered at her side.

"Are you ready, Noni?" Zen asked.

"Yes, sir."

"Then join the others outside. You're with group one. You'll be coming with me."

Zen could see a spark of delight flash in her eyes, and a moment later she was gone out the door. Zen strode over to the corner where the old crowbar rested, and he flipped it up into the air with his foot and caught it as it came down. Just then the door opened again, and Zen spoke without turning around.

"Is there a problem, Gabriel?"

"None on this end, Zyid. Is everything all right with Alex?"

"There were no complications. We move as planned. Are the preparations complete?"

"Just about," Gabriel replied. "The Truants await only your word."

"Then they shall have it."

Gabriel respectfully held the door open as Zen strode back outside into the darkness, where a soft but vast murmur had begun. The Truants were getting restless, and like a thousand leaves rustling together their whispers were each insignificant alone, but unable to be ignored when put together.

Zen smiled. Then he spoke, and hundreds fell silent. No school principal had ever commanded such genuine attention in the City. Even the Mayor himself could not claim to ever have had such a willing audience. Zen did not need to yell or bluster to be heard. His voice rang out through the silence, soft but strong, slick but genuine, powerful in its conviction, unwavering, uncompromising. It was the voice of one who would never allow himself to be an inferior again, and as the Truancy listened, it made that voice its own.

"Truants, think back to a few months ago, when every one of us here was *nothing*," Zen said. "We were capable only of what the Educators told us we were. 'Freedom is dangerous,' they said. 'This is for your own good.' Well, they were right about freedom—it is a dangerous thing indeed, for would-be oppressors above all. Their rule over us was not for our own good, but for their benefit. Not for our security, but for their convenience.

"In school nothing was ever expected of us but immaturity and grudging obedience. For the longest time I myself believed that students as a whole were capable of little else. But since I started the Truancy and fought by your sides, I came to realize that though some of us may have been expelled, none of us ever failed school. No, school failed *us*. It failed to treat us with respect, and so encouraged us to act as though we deserved none.

"We are capable of so much more than anyone ever suspected, and today we will prove it," Zen continued. "We will strike at the heart of the

Mayor's City, and all of its Enforcers may be waiting for us. This does not frighten me. I anticipate it. I want all of our enemies to see what I have; I want everyone to know the power of the Truancy. I want there to be no doubt left in their minds about who we are and what we can do. Rothenberg, with all his brutality, could not stop us, and the Mayor must know that he will fare no better."

With that, Zen raised his crowbar and spun around, leading the way into the fading night. Behind him the Truancy, two hundred strong, surged forward as one united shadow in the dark. There was no cheering. There was no celebration. Here was an army at march, single-minded in its purpose, like a black wave come to sweep the Educators out of power.

"Mark the calendar, Mayor," Zen said as he walked, "today is the beginning of the end of school."

U masi hung up the receiver, marveling that the pay phone still worked in District 19. Stepping out of the booth, he saw that the sun was beginning to rise as a yellow fleck upon the horizon. He watched his breath rise in swirls—there was just enough light for him to see it crystallize in the air—and crumpled up the paper that Zen had left for him, tossing it to the chilly winds. The message had been passed on, as Umasi knew Zen had intended all along. Umasi idly wondered if the Mayor would act on the warning, but knew that was no longer his concern. Either the Educators would save their school or they wouldn't.

Umasi began walking back to his lemonade stand. He wasn't entirely sure why he felt like playing into Zen's hands, but somehow it felt proper. Their family would have one last reunion before the end. Umasi turned a corner, and the lemonade stand came into view. In the middle of the street was a large heap, a mound of weaponry and explosives seized from the Truancy. Umasi paused to take in the sight. The pile was a testament to his campaign against the Truancy, but he knew it represented only a fraction of what the Truancy had become, and not even a speck of what it *could* become. Umasi knew what his responsibility was. He would do the duty no one else could. Umasi would destroy Zen, and without his leadership the Truancy, still in its infancy, could only wither like a plant pulled up by its roots.

Umasi knew that he could take his pick from the weapons in the pile, that there was enough firepower there to contend with anything that his brother's army might throw at him. Instead he pulled a simple switch out of his pocket, one that would detonate all the explosives in the pile, and the weapons along with it. Umasi had come a long way from being the weak and foolish boy that the Educators expected. He needed to rely on no strength but his own.

Umasi paused with his thumb over the switch, sparing a moment to acknowledge the three companions he had come to know during his adventures in the City. Each of them had helped shaped him in their own ways. Red's sacrifice had ignited the fight in his spirit. The nameless girl's discipline had helped him discover his own. Even Edward had taught him a valuable lesson; Umasi now knew to present the world with a cold and efficient face. Umasi did not know what lessons Zen had learned during their time apart, but for the first time in his life he felt that he was a match for his brother.

"Thanks, all three of you," Umasi said, tilting his head up to the lightening sky. "You've given me the strength to face him."

With that, Umasi thumbed the switch, and casually spun around as the pile was consumed by a fiery explosion. Silhouetted against the flames, Umasi strode forward into the sunrise, now blazing a bright orange. It was still early, but he wanted to get a head start on the day. It wouldn't do to fall behind.

After all, he had an appointment to keep.

How could it have come to this?
The Mayor lifted the lighter with a trembling hand as he lit the cigarette in this mouth. It was a new habit for the Mayor, but lately nothing else seemed able to distract him. Blowing the flame out, the Mayor clicked the lighter shut and relished the sharp click, audible even over the air conditioner. That damn machine got louder every day. It was falling apart, just like the rest of the City.

The Mayor took a ragged breath and let the smoke fill his lungs. Rothenberg had failed, but the Mayor now knew that he himself was to blame for trusting the man in the first place. The Enforcer had been found unconscious on the border of District 19, shot in both legs. When he had come to in the hospital, all he would babble about was some blond kid. The doctors said that Rothenberg would be able to walk again with surgery, but the Mayor had ordered them not to perform it. Rothenberg would remain a cripple, and the Mayor had half a mind to throw him in jail to boot.

There'd been no sign of his sons. Nothing at all. In the past few days the doubt had nearly killed him, but now at least he knew that they still lived. Several hours ago his answering machine had recorded a call telling him so.

The Mayor blew smoke from his lungs, then turned to eye the phone on his desk. For a moment he wondered if the message that it had received might not have been some sort of desperate hallucination of his; already he had forgotten most of its contents. The Mayor flicked the lighter open in agitation. There was only one way to find out.

For the second time that morning, the Mayor leaned forward and pressed a button on the machine. A painfully familiar voice immediately began to issue forth from it.

"I know that you've been looking for me," Umasi said. "I saw one of your people in District 19. Zen and I are both alive. He has assembled an army, the Truancy. He intends to overthrow you, and will destroy the entire City if he has to. I don't think that you can stop him. I'm not sure that anyone can . . . but I will try."

The Mayor clicked the lighter shut, and to him it was the sound of a magazine being loaded into a gun. An image sprung to his mind, so vivid that his drab office vanished from sight. Instead he saw grim-faced children gathered around lanterns and flashlights in the darkest corners of the City. They polished guns by lamplight, assembled and disassembled them. They were ready to kill, ready to die. The worst nightmare of every Educator brought to life.

"He is strong, Father—stronger than you ever suspected. But so am I, and tomorrow the two of us will decide who is better. There is so much that you don't understand about us, so much that you adults have forgotten. You are entirely too confident in wisdom that you do not have."

The Mayor recalled the report of the attack on the District 18 Enforcer Station, and for the first time pictured the scene in flames as his son fought Rothenberg. The Mayor cursed himself as he watched the struggle unfold; blinded by anxiety, *he* had unleashed this menace upon his City and sons. He was a fool. War had escalated before his very eyes, and yet he'd done nothing, pretended to notice nothing.

"Your search has failed. Tomorrow Zen will make his first move against you. You must protect the District 1 School. I will be the one to stop him. I am not on your side, nor am I on his. I fight for what both of you have abandoned. Someone must stand for the people of this City, and I will do it alone if I must."

The voice was so clearly Umasi's, and yet it was not the one the Mayor had known. There was strength and conviction in every syllable, and yet no warmth. The Mayor imagined what Umasi must look like now, a mature and noble figure shrouded in bright mist. The Mayor felt a surge of pride, along with an undercurrent of shame. Umasi had grown up not because of him, but in spite of him.

"Whenever I was troubled, you used to ask me if there was something wrong. I always insisted that there wasn't. I lied. There *is* something wrong with this City, Mayor, and all three of us know it now. If I die, Zen will recreate your nightmare in his own image. But if he is the one to fall, then I will see to it that you answer for your sins."

I'm your father. Call me Father, the Mayor thought in vain. The Mayor now saw the boys as they were the last time he had seen them, seated at the dinner table. It was a scene that had replayed in his mind many times before, but this time when the boys bade him farewell it carried an entirely new meaning, one that brought tears to his eyes. His lighter flicked open, and for one dark moment he was entirely lost in grief.

"Protect your school, Mayor. I will protect the City."

Those words jerked the Mayor up in his chair and out of his reverie. Being addressed by his title reminded him of his duty and cut through his grief like a bolt of lightning. His head unnaturally clear, the Mayor sprang into action. Seizing the phone from his desk, he quickly pressed the emergency button that would put him in touch with Enforcer Headquarters.

"Yes, Mr. Mayor, what can we do for you?"

The Mayor took a deep, steadying breath. The lighter clicked shut.

"Get every available patrol out to the District 1 School within the hour. Evacuate the immediate area. Prepare for war."

33

BROTHER AGAINST BROTHER

Even on the weekend, it was rare for any part of District 1 to be silent in the afternoon. But on this day, one part of it was as eerily quiet as an abandoned district. No one walked the streets of the nine blocks that had been sealed off, though countless Enforcers stood silent behind concrete barricades and parked patrol cars. They had been working all morning, first to evacuate the area, and then to seal it off with portable wooden fencing. All businesses and traffic had been shut down, the monolithic school at the very center of the area towering over the proceedings like a condemnatory giant.

Then came the defense preparations. The Enforcers didn't know anything about what they were supposed to be defending against, other than that the Mayor thought it was especially dangerous. Still they continued to dutifully erect the waist-high concrete barriers. Once the defenses were finished, the Enforcers stood quietly behind them, waiting for the war they had been promised.

When it began, not even an hour later, the Enforcers discovered that for all their efforts they were still unprepared. A patrol car at the western barricade was the first to explode, instantly throwing all the defenders into confusion. Though the attack was expected, the Enforcers found it difficult to grasp the idea of full-scale war in the City that they had dominated for so long. As the battle began in earnest, the Enforcers were shocked to find that their enemies were children. Their hesitation would prove fatal.

The initial attack came from the windows and roofs of the evacuated buildings, the Truancy somehow having managed to stealthily occupy them. Truants fired down at the Enforcer positions and tossed explosive cocktails between the rows of concrete. Trapped by their own defenses, the Enforcers tumbled over each other in their haste to abandon their position. As they fled, more Truants began emerging from other buildings, side alleys, even manholes.

The Enforcers had set up a strict perimeter around the area, but among the Truants were students from the District 1 School, unmatched in their knowledge of the neighborhood and its shortcuts. By the time the fleeing Enforcers had reached a second line of defense surrounding the school, a good ten percent of them had fallen, many having been outflanked by the Truancy. By now the Enforcers knew that they were fighting for their lives, and newly fortified with superior numbers, they were ready for a long fight.

As the Truants advanced and the battle wore on, it became clear that while the Enforcers had many advantages over the Truancy, what they lacked was the Truancy's leader. Black like the shadows, he swept through the battlefield like fear incarnate, firing with impeccable aim and brutally striking down stragglers with his crowbar. He knew that the Enforcers had been strictly ordered not to kill him, and he used it against them. As Zen leapt down from the roof of a truck and struck an Enforcer on the head, he noticed that some of the other squad leaders were finally arriving on the scene.

Gabriel was dual-wielding stolen pistols, and had taken cover behind a white van as he fired at the Enforcer barricades. The school took up the entire block, and the Enforcers had set up more concrete walling all around it. Like Gabriel, however, many Truants were now taking cover behind whatever they could and besieging the Enforcers from all sides. Zen wondered how well Gabriel could aim with his left hand, but even as he watched one, two, and then three Enforcers crumpled from Gabriel's shots.

Frank and his team of former vagrants had gotten a stroke of inspiration after seeing that one of the streets was on a downwards slant. They hotwired a car and set it to neutral, then drenched it with gas, set it on fire, and sent it rolling down the hill towards the Enforcer barricades. Enforcers dived out of the way as the car crashed and exploded spectacularly, and other Truants hastened to imitate Frank's idea. As the Enforcer lines were broken by the explosions, it became increasingly clear that the Truancy was winning the fight.

Satisfied, Zen turned away from the battle and made for one of the adjacent blocks, firing three quick shots across the street at an Enforcer that had turned his way. The Enforcer fell backwards, but Zen's gun clicked empty, prompting him to toss it away. Meanwhile, Noni had quietly sidled up beside him while he was surveying the scene, and she now fired fiercely at any Enforcer that so much as glanced at Zen. Her knives hadn't gotten much use, but Zen noticed that her marksmanship had markedly improved.

As Zen reached the block he was aiming for, he passed by the newspaper stand that Gabriel was now crouched behind. Gabriel saw him coming, and Zen waved back with uncharacteristic cheer.

"Never thought we'd be back here again, did you?" Zen greeted, gesturing back at their old school with his crowbar. "It's almost nostalgic!"

Gabriel, however, was all business.

"If Alex blows the building now, most of them will be buried anyway!" he shouted over the din of battle, pointing at the Enforcer positions around the school.

"I'm not taking any chances," Zen replied, his face and tone abruptly serious. "I want them to trap themselves first. If we're patient, not one will escape."

Gabriel nodded, then fired suddenly. Far behind Zen, an Enforcer was sent toppling backwards by the shot. Leaving Gabriel to continue the fight, Zen and Noni quickly rounded the block, out of the line of fire. There, as had been arranged, Zen saw Alex and Aaron examining some equipment as several other Truants stood guard. They all saluted Zen as he approached, and the Truancy leader couldn't quite place the emotion he felt as Alex presented him with a simple button trigger.

"I think you ought to do it, Zyid," Alex said. "Me . . . I don't think I—"

"I understand," Zen cut him off. "Does it work? Are you sure?"

"Positive." It was Aaron who answered this time. "I tested the signal myself."

"You've done well." Zen held out his hand. "I'll take it from here, Alex."

The boy looked even paler than usual as he handed Zen the trigger, but his voice was steady as he replied.

"Is everything going okay?"

"Yes. We've suffered some losses, but we have all the progress to show for it. The Enforcers can't hold their position for long. They'll make a break for the school at any moment now."

"And then it collapses on top of them."

"Indeed."

Alex turned, if possible, even paler, but again gave no other sign of his discomfort.

"Alex," Zen said sharply.

"Yes?"

"The City is no longer safe for you. You're past the point of no return. I think you know this."

"Yeah, I do."

"If there were another option I'd offer it to you, but you're one of us now." Zen offered his hand. "It's that, or wait for the Enforcers to figure out which student planted the explosives."

After only a moment's hesitation, Alex shook the proffered hand.

"I choose life, a life of my own," he said. "I chose it a long time ago."

"If that is your decision, then I'm going to have to ask you to leave all your reservations here," Zen warned. "After what you've done here today the Truancy may have a position of leadership for you, but you cannot have any doubts about who you are and what you need to do."

"I don't," Alex said, firmly this time. "I am a Truant."

"Glad to hear it."

Just then a messenger ran up to Zen, excitement etched on his face. "Zyid, the Enforcers are pulling back into the school. Should we cease fire?"

"No, they'd suspect a trap. Allow most of them to reach the school, but don't make it easy for them."

"Gotcha." The messenger turned and ran off to spread the orders.

"Looks like the battle's almost over then," Aaron observed, watching the messenger's receding back. "Finally."

"I hope we're all done before they get any reinforcements over here," Alex muttered.

"It looks like they brought in all the Enforcers from a half-dozen districts. Any reinforcements would have to come from quite a ways away."

"But it's still only a half-hour distance, tops. What do you think, Zyid?"

Suddenly the Truancy leader no longer seemed to be listening. Zen was looking around intently, as though searching for something that no one else could see. Realizing that he'd been addressed, Zen raised his hand for silence.

"You all know your orders and may proceed as planned," Zen said. "Leave me now."

"Huh?" Alex said. "But Zyid, what about—"

"*Now,*" Zen snapped.

The Truants hesitated for only a moment, but they knew from his tone that arguing wouldn't do any good at all. Reluctantly, the Truants turned and left, sneaking furtive glances back at Zen's motionless figure. Soon, all of them had disappeared around the block to rejoin the fray.

All except one. Zen glanced over at Noni, still standing faithfully by his side. She either didn't know or didn't care that Zen had meant to include her in his orders. But this time Zen would not allow her, or anyone else, to intervene on his behalf.

"Noni, I want you to go with the others."

Noni's head snapped around at him, and Zen felt an uncomfortable twinge as she stared at him in confusion.

"Why? What's coming?" Noni asked, her voice soft, but clearer than ever despite the scarf.

"If I am killed, the Truancy will look to you for guidance," Zen said, ignoring her question. "You belong with them. Not me."

"Sir . . . you're scaring me."

Zen looked down in surprise at the girl he had rescued from the alley, one who possessed strength and potential to match his own. And yet she couldn't see it, blinded as she was by her adoration of him. She had become dependent on Zen, and it was then that Zen realized that Noni could never be his successor, the future leader of the Truancy. Should he ever die, the chains that restrained her might be broken . . . or perhaps she herself would break.

It would have to be someone else, someone who was not only independent but someone that others could depend on. Zen vowed that if he survived, he would search for a suitable successor. But for now, there was nothing more he could do for Noni or for the Truancy. This was his struggle.

"Noni, go with the others," Zen said harshly. "That's an order."

"What's going to happen?"

"Nothing that you're a part of. Now *go*."

"But you don't even have a gun, how—"

"LEAVE!" Zen bellowed. "NOW!"

Zen saw the hurt in her eyes, but had already steeled himself against it. She turned, brushing against him, then began walking away. Zen watched her go without remorse. To stand above everyone else is to stand alone. And that was what the leader of the Truancy had to do, in the end.

Stand alone.

"You needn't have sent her away, Zyid. I wouldn't have hurt her."

Zen smiled at the familiar voice, and turned around to see a lone figure steadily approaching, its long white scarf fluttering in the chill wind. Zen made no motion to greet the newcomer, but gripped his crowbar tighter as his own windbreaker caught the breeze as well.

"You underestimate her," Zen said. "Who's to say that she mightn't have hurt you?"

"Someday, perhaps," Umasi conceded. "But she is not ready now—and certainly not ready for the burdens of leadership. The Truancy will end with you tonight, Zen."

"My name is Zyid now."

"So I've heard."

Zen waited for Umasi to speak again, but he didn't. The bright figure before him simply kept walking, maintaining a steady step as he drew closer. Zen searched for some trace of emotion on his brother's face, but found nothing but his own reflection in dark sunglasses. Whoever it was that now stood before him, Zen knew it was not the Umasi that he had known.

"No attempt at small talk, Umasi?"

"Is it common for enemies to exchange pleasantries?"

"Finally made up your mind then?" Zen narrowed his eyes. "That is most unlike you."

Umasi did not answer, but shifted his head up to gaze at the building that towered behind Zen. Gunshots, sirens, and other sounds of battle could still be clearly heard from around the corner.

"What do you hope to gain by attacking the school?"

"That *building*," Zen said, "that *institution* is already broken. I will merely make the structure reflect what's inside. Do you really mean to tell me that you'll fight to protect it?"

"My only purpose in coming here, Zen," Umasi said, "is to kill you."

The response was surprising in its bluntness.

"You're not going to tell me how wrong I am?" Zen said. "Lecture me on how misguided my ambitions are?"

"No."

Zen narrowed his eyes as an explosion behind him shattered one of the school's windows. The Enforcers had finished barricading themselves inside the besieged building, and the Truants would be starting their planned withdrawal at any moment.

"So, then you have learned something," Zen said, fingering the trigger concealed in his windbreaker.

"Many things," Umasi corrected. "I always was a good student."

"A good student?" Zen laughed humorlessly. "What has being a good student brought us, brought anyone, but mixed blessings at best and utter misery at worst? No pillar of justice can stand upon a foundation of disparity. School has nothing good to offer us. They only teach us the bad, by their example."

"I know."

"I don't think you do, Umasi," Zen said. "The system *worked* for you. You've never known what it's like to live without hope."

"Then why did you stay?" Umasi demanded. "Why would you sit back and allow yourself to suffer? I would have expected you to drop out."

Zen hesitated, knowing that the truth would hurt.

"If I had left," Zen said at last, "who would have protected you?"

Umasi looked as though Zen had slapped him.

"You stayed for me?"

"Who else?" Zen asked quietly. "Only for you, Brother. I was always ready to sacrifice for you."

For a moment both brothers said nothing, and the last distant gunshot rang out and gave way to silence. The Truancy had retreated, though the Enforcers remained inside the school for fear of an ambush.

"I'm sorry," Umasi said at last. "I appreciate everything you did for me more than you'll ever know. But it doesn't change my mind."

"I didn't expect it to," Zen said. "But now do you understand? Do you understand my side of this story?"

"I finally think I do," Umasi replied. "For you, this whole fight was always about school. But the thing is, Zen, for me . . . it was always about you."

"You would damn the City over our petty differences?"

"I will *save* the City, which is what you wanted to and should have done," Umasi said. "I admired you *so* much, Zen. For the brother I lost, and the person he was, I will save this City when you are gone."

"Such arrogance, Umasi," Zen whispered, his posture subtly shifting. "I have never presumed myself a savior. This City hardly needs one. No, what this City of education truly needs . . ."

Zen paused, then pressed the switch concealed in his coat. Behind him, several explosions rocked the school just as its front doors had begun to open. Glass shattered and bricks flew through the air, but for a moment the building still stood, casting its shadow over the brothers, imposing and indomitable as ever. Then it fell, as if in slow motion, collapsing in on itself like a house of cards, burying generations of misery along with the Enforcers. Dust and rubble was cast into the air like confetti, and to Umasi it seemed that one small shadow had lifted from a City shrouded in darkness.

". . . is *Truancy!*"

Momentarily awestruck, Umasi had forgotten about Zen. The crowbar cleaved the air like black lightning, yet Umasi dodged the surprise attack as though it had been rehearsed, countering with a swift jab. A wave of dust cascaded over the brothers as Zen twisted to absorb the blow with his shoulder. Suddenly they were engulfed by a storm of stinging wind and debris as what was left of the school reached out for them one last time. Hardly flinching, Zen swung his crowbar around, forcing Umasi to leap backwards out of the way, the ground rumbling beneath their feet.

"I never laid a hand on you, Umasi." Zen coughed as the rubble, but not the dust, began to settle. "It's something brothers are supposed to do, now and then. But you were just too pathetic, and I never did." Zen swung again, and smiled as Umasi effortlessly evaded the attack. "Perhaps I've been waiting for this all my life . . . waiting for you to be strong."

"Then I've kept you waiting long enough," Umasi admitted, ducking another attack and retaliating with a solid punch to the gut. "I apologize for the delay."

Zen grunted and staggered backwards, though his face showed no outward signs of pain. Indeed, Umasi had never seen his eyes sparkle with such excitement. Zen surged forward, the crowbar whipping through the dusty air in a whirlwind of impossibly swift attacks. Umasi, for all his agility, barely managed to keep up, and as one of the blows nicked his shoulder he realized that he might have underestimated his brother after all.

In truth, Zen had never fought so hard in his life, nor would he ever do so again. Unburdened by guilt or restraint, and unleashing years of repressed anguish, Zen felt liberated by their battle in a way that comes only once in a lifetime. For just one day, for just one fight, the full extent of his wrath was unleashed upon the City, and his brother.

Unable to find an opening in the blur of attacks, Umasi was forced to back up as Zen swung relentlessly. Diving aside to evade a particularly wide swipe, Umasi rolled on the ground and came up into a crouch. Without pause Zen came charging on, crowbar raised to strike. Feeling something digging into his knee, Umasi suddenly realized that the ground around him was littered with rubble from the school. Acting on impulse, Umasi seized a chunk of shattered brick and hurled it at Zen. The crowbar rent the air once and the brick shattered to pieces. Undeterred, Umasi began backing up again, bent over so that he could rapidly toss pieces of the demolished school at his attacker.

The tactic slowed Zen, but did not seem to tire him. Again and again the crowbar struck projectiles from the air so forcefully that sparks flew, and still Zen pressed forward, the madness in his eyes never dimming. The two brothers had nearly reached the end of the street now, and Umasi realized that he was being pushed towards an Enforcer barricade. Scooping up an armful of smaller rubble, Umasi hurled it all in one blurred motion.

Surprised by the sudden hail of attacks, Zen reacted as fast as could be expected, his crowbar knocking away every one of the projectiles. But just as Zen swatted the last brick with a feeling of triumph, Umasi's fist connected with his chest. Zen let out a roar of pain and shock. Seizing the opening, Umasi attempted to land a second blow, but Zen recovered in time to duck.

"Fast," Zen grunted as he struck with the crowbar, forcing Umasi to swing himself backwards over the low barricade. "Consider me surprised that you can fight so hard for no cause at all."

"And just what cause are you fighting for?" Umasi demanded, kicking the barricade at Zen. "Equality? Justice? Your own gratification?"

"I fight for all that have suffered," Zen replied, blocking the barricade with an outstretched foot, "in the name of education, because they were unable to fight for themselves."

"And I fight for all who will suffer because of what you intend to do. Look at this City, Zen!" Umasi spread his arms to encompass it all. "You presume to fight for everyone, but by doing so you put them all at risk. If the Educators will not yield it, are you prepared to watch the whole City burn?"

"You know me better than that," Zen accused, hurling the barricade aside.

"No, I don't," Umasi said coldly. "Not anymore. The brother I knew was never ruled by his fantasies. But you, Zyid, you're so caught up in your dream of a perfect world that you've forgotten the real one."

"If you don't know me," Zen snarled, lunging forward again, his jacket billowing behind him, "don't presume to understand me!"

The attack was so sudden and so fierce that Umasi had no time to dodge it. But a crowbar is not a sword, and has no bladed edge. As the weapon flashed towards him, Umasi raised his forearm, wincing as the two collided. Though in considerable pain, Umasi seized the opening and punched Zen hard in the face with his free fist.

"When was the last time you were out in the living districts?" Umasi demanded, clutching his forearm as Zen staggered backwards with a bloodied nose.

"We're in one right now, aren't we?" Zen said, wiping his face with his sleeve.

"This?" Umasi shook his head. "Thanks to your Truancy and the Mayor's Enforcers, this has become a place of death. But life is not yet so far from here, Zen. Perhaps if you see it, you might appreciate it before you die."

With that, Umasi turned and ran, his white scarf flowing behind him. Without hesitation Zen gave pursuit, every bit Umasi's equal in speed. The streets and buildings seemed more blurred than usual to Umasi as the wind rushed in his ears and the sidewalk flew beneath his feet. Minutes later, he came to a halt, and the world was normal again.

Umasi now stood on the edge of a crowd of people moving to and fro on the sidewalk. The barricaded area and the demolished school had been left behind. Here, neon store signs blended with traffic lights, their luminance cutting through the dimming blue of the winter sky. Beyond the sidewalk a massive four lanes of traffic formed one of the City's busiest streets, divided down the center by the tiniest concrete platform. Vehicles of all sizes zoomed along like a roaring metal river, and for the briefest of moments, Umasi stood there taking in the sight. Then instinct kicked in, and Umasi spun around.

He was just in time to spot Zen in mid-leap, crowbar poised to strike. Without thinking, Umasi jumped backwards, arms outstretched, shoving the pedestrians around him out of the way. Angry cries filled the air, but then Zen landed, his crowbar striking nothing but ground. Without pausing, Zen lunged forward again, sweeping his weapon around in a wide arc. Onlookers now scrambled to get out of the way of the two crazed children as they fought. Zen's ferocious strikes drove Umasi backwards into the street just as the traffic lights turned red and the traffic screeched to a halt.

Umasi placed his hand on the hood of a car and swung himself over it. Zen leaped on top of the hood and jumped down at Umasi, adding the full force of gravity to his attack. Umasi, however, leaped backwards atop another car's trunk, and as Zen came down, Umasi's foot snapped up, connecting squarely with Zen's chin. Staggering backwards from the blow, Zen hit the side of the car, arms splayed as the driver rolled the window down to yell. Pressing his advantage, Umasi leaped down and punched Zen in the stomach. With almost superhuman tenacity, Zen shrugged off the blow and shoved forward, slamming Umasi against the side of the second car.

"Damn kids!"

"If there's so much as a scratch on this car I'll have you arrested, you hear me?"

"This is why there should be school every day!"

"Where *are* the Enforcers? Didn't they block off the streets for something just a few blocks away?"

"Those two are *bound* to get run over, playing around in traffic like that."

Neither Zen nor Umasi heard or cared about the shouts and threats from the adult spectators. With enough space to swing, Zen struck with the crowbar again, forcing Umasi to slip back between a car and a van and onto the low concrete platform that bisected the four lanes of traffic. Zen gave pursuit, sliding himself over the hood of another car to land neatly on the platform. The concrete was barely two feet wide, not meant or safe for pedestrians, but the two combatants didn't care as they fought over what little footing there was.

Suddenly, as Umasi ducked one of Zen's fiercer attacks, the traffic lights flickered to green. All around them cars whooshed again, some honking indignantly at the children playing in the middle of the street. The brothers continued to struggle, as if safe in the eye of a swirling metal hurricane. As Umasi dodged Zen's umpteenth strike, Zen let out a roar of frustration that was lost to the noise of the cars, then slammed into Umasi, hoping to shove him into the path of the oncoming traffic. Umasi fell, but managed to twist aside to avoid certain death by mere inches. As he hit the ground, Umasi lashed out with his legs, catching Zen in the chest. Now it was Zen's turn to narrowly escape death as he stumbled backwards and was nearly crushed by a truck. As Zen regained his balance, Umasi leapt to his feet and dusted himself off, ready to continue the fight.

The light flashed red, and chaos gave way to calm. Zen swung his crowbar, and again Umasi dodged, this time leaping backwards onto the hood of a halted taxi cab. Zen brought his weapon crashing down, and Umasi jumped off the hood just before the crowbar smashed it, causing a sizeable dent. The cab door swung open, its red-faced driver beginning to yell. Zen calmly swung his crowbar back to hit the man upside the head, and then leapt over the cab to pursue Umasi, who ran not to the sidewalk, but to the pedestrian crossing at the edge of the intersection. As Umasi halted, Zen lunged, but Umasi merely caught him by the arms, fell onto his back, and then shoved Zen's body off with his legs. Umasi could hear Zen curse as he was thrown straight into the intersection.

What happened next occurred too fast for even Umasi to see how it happened. There was a series of loud noises, and by the time Umasi had returned to his feet, the intersection was consumed by a twisted, flaming wreck of metal, glass, and bodies. An eighteen-wheeler truck was overturned on its side, and cars were piled up like recycled cans, the lucky drivers struggling to extricate themselves from the mess.

For a moment Umasi held his breath, certain that his brother had perished in the wreckage. Then he saw a dark figure fleeing the carnage towards the sidewalk, and he knew. Umasi plunged after Zen, weaving his way around and through the devastation, ignoring the shouts all around him. Then he was on the sidewalk, the fire behind him casting him into shadow as one of the car's gas tanks exploded.

"Is this your answer?" Umasi shouted at the shadow on the sidewalk. "Tell me again how much of this City you're willing to watch burn!"

"As much as I have to, Umasi!" Zen roared, his face eerily illuminated by the flames. "Nothing in this City is indispensable! Not me, not you, not anyone!"

There was something unsettlingly familiar in Zen's tortured voice. It took Umasi several moments to recognize it, and he was shocked when he did.

"You're hurting," Umasi realized, his words startling Zen. "You hide it well—perhaps you haven't even noticed it yourself. But I can hear it, the silent screaming." Umasi closed his eyes. "You may yet discover your conscience before the end. I hope to spare you that pain. Just hold on, Brother, I will bring you the rest you need."

With that Umasi darted forward, ducking Zen's swing and striking his chest with a flattened palm. Now it was Zen's turn to be driven backwards as Umasi landed blow after blow, striking from such close quarters that the crowbar was nearly useless. Zen fought back fiercely, swinging calculatedly as he hopped backwards, blocking as many of Umasi's hits as he could with his free arm. Still, he could not halt Umasi's advance, and soon their fight took them down the entire block and under an overpass for pedestrians. Some adults scolded the two as they passed, but most were focused on the traffic pileup that the brothers had left behind.

As Umasi and Zen drew out from under the overpass, both had finally begun to show signs of wear and tear. Aside from the scratches and bruises that each one sported, sweat glistened on their brows, and their breaths had noticeably quickened. But they moved as fast as ever, and fought even harder. The two brothers were locked in mortal combat, focused on nothing now but their own struggle.

. . . And so neither of them noticed the young girl crouched on top of the overpass, pistol in hand. She brushed a lock of black hair out of her piercing blue eyes, and raised her gun. Noni carefully aimed the weapon at the unsuspecting Umasi, prepared to kill to protect her savior.

A second later, her gun went off.

34
ORIGINAL SIN

*W*hat's going to happen?"

"Nothing that you're a part of."

Noni ran, the wind whipping at her face, tugging at the edges of her scarf, threatening to reveal her weakness to a world that was blurred to her eyes. The rejection had sent tears streaming across her face, hot at first, but swiftly chilled by winter. She no longer remembered why she ran, or if she ever had a purpose to begin with.

What purpose could you possibly have? Noni demanded of herself. *You're useless. You always have been. Isn't that what your mother used to say?*

Mother?

The word stirred something in the murky depths of Noni's memory, something she knew should have remained undisturbed. A woman was shrieking obscenities as she beat her daughter. Empty beer cans littered the room. Something was missing from the filthy room. A person, a presence that Noni felt should have been there but wasn't. Was it a father? Did the girl even have one?

The woman hurled something across the room, and suddenly she was not a woman in Noni's mind, but a monster. The beast was accusing the girl of something now. Noni wasn't sure what it was but she knew the girl was innocent. The girl tried to protest. She was beaten for it. Suddenly Noni saw red, and she lunged at the monster in blind fury. Something struck her hard, and then all she saw was black.

She had fled at some point, Noni was sure of that. The girl had escaped from that life, if life it could be called, and had then vanished to the streets. Everything from there was like a long-passed nightmare, lost even to her own recollection. Her first clear memory was of the day she had been saved in an alley by an entirely different monster.

Her monster. Her savior.

Zyid.

In a flash, all became clear to Noni. Her eyes were dry, the world slid into focus, and she remembered why she ran. She stopped and stared. Across the street Zyid was fighting with the boy that he had called brother. Fighting, and losing. That realization shook her to her core, and in an instant she was running again, this time towards an overpass that would bring her right above the fight.

She wasn't supposed to interfere.

She didn't care.

Within moments she had taken her place on the walkway. All that mattered to her now was that Zyid would not die. Noni brushed a lock of black hair out of her eyes, and raised her gun. The time to strike was now. Zyid was on the ground, and some distance away Umasi stood catching his breath, clutching his wounded arm. It would be a clean shot, even from thirty feet at an angle. Noni carefully aimed the weapon at the unsuspecting Umasi, and prepared to kill to protect her savior.

A metallic tinkling filled the air . . .

Noni moved to pull the trigger, and something struck her hands with such force that the pistol flew from her grip. The gun went off from the impact, and then clattered off the edge of the overpass and down to the street below. Whipping around, Noni was just in time to see the weighted end of a chain fly back to its owner's hand.

Its owner was a girl of purest white, with eyes an even lighter blue than Noni's own. For a moment Noni was dumbstruck by the impossible sight, but her hands still stung from the chain and she immediately knew that this, at least, was no monster.

"Who are you?" Noni demanded as loudly as she could through the scarf.

"I'm his lady," the girl gestured down at Umasi, "and I don't have a name. What about you?"

"I'm Noni. Are you trying to help him kill Zyid?"

"I'm not here to help anyone." The girl placed a hand on her hip. "I'm just here to make sure that those two get to finish things themselves."

"I'm not sitting back and letting Zyid die!" Noni said fiercely. "Not even if it means dying myself!"

"Have faith in your boy. He didn't choose to fight alone because he expects to lose."

"But he said . . . he said that I'd have to take his place . . ." Noni said, her voice cracking. In that moment, she wasn't sure if she feared his death or her responsibility more. "He said that he might die!"

"Their fight is not about you, or me, or anyone else." The albino shook her head. "Don't you see that this is personal to them? Don't you see that this fight is *sacred* to them?"

"*He's* sacred to me!" Noni shouted, drawing her knife out from her belt. She normally wielded two, but had disposed of the other earlier. "I'm going to go help him, and don't try to stop me!"

The nameless girl blinked, and then took hold of the weighted end of her chain.

"If your heart is truly set on fighting for him," she said, "then your fight is with me. If I fall, no one will be left to stop you. Come at me, Noni!"

Noni didn't hesitate; the other girl was pretty, but she didn't look very tough. With a snarl Noni lunged forward, knife bared. The chain swung through the air in a wide arc, but Noni neatly deflected the end of it with her blade. As the end of the chain flew uselessly to the side, Noni struck, knife flashing from the reflection of a neon sign. With stunning reflexes the girl blocked the strike with the arm wrapped by her chain, and then pivoted to perform a graceful but powerful kick.

Noni was shocked to find herself sent flying backwards, but acted quickly to regain her footing, expecting another lash of the chain that never came. Instead the albino stood there in perfect calm, waiting for Noni to recover. Noni squeezed the hilt of her knife so hard that her knuckles turned white. It seemed impossible to her—even unfair, somehow—that someone so beautiful and delicate in appearance could be so strong.

"You're going to have to try harder than that, Noni." The albino smiled, toughness suddenly evident in her voice. "I didn't survive in the abandoned districts by losing fights."

"I'm a survivor too!"

Noni's words sounded childish and pathetic, even to her own ears.

"Survivors don't give up until it's all over," the other girl said. "Come at me again!"

Heeding the advice, Noni surged forward. This time as the chain came swinging towards her, she managed to snatch its end right out of the air. Feeling a surge of triumph, Noni kept running, the captured end of the chain held in one hand and her knife held in the other. Suddenly the other girl's arm whipped up and around, and before Noni knew what was happening she was falling face-first to the ground. Noni raised her hands just in time to protect her face, but the impact still hurt.

Scrambling to her feet, Noni saw the albino standing there as calm and collected as ever. Brushing the grit off her scraped hands, Noni realized that the other girl had looped the chain over her back, and then used it to trip her up in midstep.

"That was a dirty trick," Noni accused.

"When is fighting ever clean?" the other girl asked. "It can't be fair, one of us must always be stronger than the other."

"You're not stronger than me!"

"Prove it."

Again Noni charged. The chain swung once, but Noni deflected it with her knife. Next the chain shot straight at her like a projectile, and Noni dodged aside. Then before the other girl could reel the chain back in for a third strike, Noni lunged forward over the last few feet that separated them, knife outstretched. The albino moved her wrapped arm to block, but this time Noni was a step ahead. Noni smoothly tossed the knife from one hand to the other, and before the albino noticed the swap she had already blocked an empty hand.

Noni smiled in triumph. Then she slashed at her enemy's unprotected face. The attack drew blood, and the combatants leapt apart.

A moment later Noni felt a twinge of disappointment as she realized that her strike hadn't had precisely the intended effect. The albino had raised her unprotected arm to shield her face, and a crimson stain now appeared on the girl's white sleeve but nowhere else. Noni's disappointment was fleeting. The shallow injury might have been the only sign of her success, but for Noni it was vindication, evidence that her opponent was not so far beyond her that she was untouchable.

But though the albino was now panting softly, she didn't seem very concerned. She calmly lowered her arm, tore a piece of cloth from its cut sleeve, then bandaged her wound with it as Noni watched.

"I was wondering if you had red blood," Noni admitted.

"Have I satisfied your curiosity?"

"Not enough!"

Noni lunged without warning, and as she did the streetlights over the walkway flickered on, for the winter sun had now almost completely faded. All over the City, streaks of pale, bright light now undermined the dim aura of the cobalt skies. Tiny festive lights also flickered on, strung over trees and storefronts, but the two girls standing atop the lonely overpass had no time to appreciate the City's abrupt transformation.

The albino blocked Noni's arm with a length of chain held taut between her hands, then kicked to send Noni staggering backwards. She followed by smoothly swinging the chain upwards to shatter a streetlamp high above. Noni raised her arms to shield her face from falling glass, and as she did so the chain swung around again, this time slamming into Noni's unprotected flank. The whole maneuver had been executed in one fluid motion, like a dance.

Noni flinched as she took the hit, ignoring the sharp pain in her ribs and elsewhere. Seizing her chance to counterattack, she charged forward, nimbly ducking and weaving around two more strikes of the chain. Noni came within striking distance just as the other girl missed a third time. Seeing the opening, Noni felt a thrill of victory as she leapt and twisted in midair, aiming to plunge her knife into her enemy's belly.

In that instant, Noni saw something strange flash in her opponent's pale eyes. The next things Noni saw were stars, and she was sent reeling backwards from an incredibly fast strike to the face. For the first time the albino seemed angry, passing under a bright streetlamp as she stepped forward.

For a moment she appeared frighteningly ethereal, her hair radiant as her eyes flashed red. Then she was normal once more, and her chain shot forward like a snake.

The attack was too swift for Noni to dodge. The weighted end of the chain struck her on the forehead, but amazingly she did not lose consciousness as she fell backwards to the ground. Fighting the pain in her head, Noni sat up to see her enemy slowly advancing upon her. Acting on instinct, Noni groped for her knife, and upon finding it she hurled it at the other girl.

The albino casually swatted the knife out of the air with her wrapped arm, and the blade glinted as it tumbled off the edge of the bridge. Disarmed and defeated, Noni could do naught but sit helplessly in the other girl's shadow as she came to a halt in front of Noni. A chill wind kicked up, and Noni shuddered as it finally tugged her loosened scarf from her face, punctuating the completeness of her failure.

There was nothing to do now but wait for mercy.

To wait for death.

"I'm not going to kill you."

At that, Noni hung her head, for she had dreaded those words, dreaded being sentenced to live in disgrace.

"You were just stalling me all along, weren't you?" Noni whispered.

"Yes."

"You knew you wouldn't have to kill me."

"I hoped."

"I hate you!" Noni suddenly screamed. "Why can't I beat you? Why can't I be like you?"

"Why try to be something you're not?" the other girl asked, crouching down to Noni's level. "If you can find pride in who you are, success comes naturally."

At that, Noni swallowed and looked away. Several blocks down a fire crew was finishing putting out the flames from a crash, and a large group of spectators had gathered to watch. The scene barely registered in Noni's eyes. Noni had only one question left in her mind, now that it no longer mattered, not in the aftermath of her failure.

"Was I . . . wrong?"

"You made the same choice as many parents of this City," the albino said. "You fought only for the safety of your boy. I fought for the happiness of mine. It's not for me to tell you whether you were right or wrong; think about what *he* would have preferred. Have you been loyal to him . . . or just yourself?"

The question hurt, for the answer was obvious. Noni had betrayed the one she had claimed to love. Her heart sank, a terrible feeling compounded by the nagging reminder that her parents, she was sure, had never fought for her safety or her happiness. Seeming to sense her distress, the nameless girl crouched down and brushed the hair out of Noni's wet eyes. She opened her mouth to speak, and for a moment Noni winced, thinking that the girl was going to offer unwanted reassurances. Instead she said:

"You have nice hair. Do you mind if I braid it for you?"

Noni nodded numbly, and sat in silence as the girl slid behind her and gently began working with her hair. Now far off in the distance, Noni could see two specks, one white and one black, still fighting, unaware of what had transpired on the overpass. Somehow the distance brought home to Noni the fact that she really wasn't a part of that intimate battle, that she wasn't a part of Zyid's life . . . and that she never would be.

And so, as the strange girl finished braiding her hair into a ponytail, Noni truly broke out into tears, crying her heart out as she hadn't done in years. The other girl said nothing, but gathered Noni up in her arms and gave her a gentle squeeze.

It was the first motherly embrace that Noni had ever known.

The simple gesture was so shocking that Noni actually gasped. It was warm, more than warm. It spoke to her of acceptance, support, safety, and things that couldn't be put into words, things she had never known in all her life, that couldn't be imagined until experienced. She felt as though she could forever sleep peacefully in that embrace, and for the first time she knew what it was to be a baby in a crib.

For what seemed like eternity the two girls sat there in perfect silence, spectators of a greater battle that neither had any part in. Suddenly the sound of approaching sirens drew their attention, and Noni finally snapped out of her daze.

"So, more Enforcers are finally arriving," the albino murmured, standing up. "I'll have to keep them away from those two. Stay calm, Noni. No matter the outcome, your boy will be happier if you don't interfere."

Then in a blur of white she was off.

Like admonishment from the heavens, stinging hail began to fall as Noni sat there on the overpass, alone with her thoughts. The other girl had been kind, beautiful, strong, and graceful. Everything Noni wasn't, everything Noni wanted to be. The other girl hadn't failed her boy. Noni had failed hers, in more ways then one. Was it any surprise that Noni hated her? No, hated herself?

So as Noni helplessly watched the two specks slip from her sight and onto a distant ice-skating rink, she replaced the scarf around her face, so that she might again hide her shame from the world.

Though neither Umasi nor Zen would admit it, the two were exhausted by the time their feet hit the ice of the skating rink. Their heavy breaths froze into clouds, and hail had begun to fall in sheets, veiling the world and stinging any exposed skin. But all of this was a mere annoyance compared with the blows the two had already taken. Somewhere out there sirens were blaring, but like the ring of the school bell the sound no longer had the power to scare them. They had graduated from fear.

Nobody stood in their way as their fight reached the ice. This particular rink was a famous attraction of District 1, but was meant only for professional exhibitions, of which there were none that day. Zen had thrown Umasi over the barrier and onto the rink, then followed without hesitation. Umasi rose to his feet, and slowly, carefully, the two approached each other while trying not to slip on the ice. It was not unlike learning to walk for the first time, which, though they no longer remembered it, the brothers had also once done together.

Coming within striking distance, Zen lashed out with the crowbar, but Umasi ducked and threw a punch in response. Like lightning, Zen caught the oncoming fist with his free hand, and for a few moments the two combatants struggled to break the deadlock. They braced their feet against the ice, but pressed so hard that when the slippery surface finally caused their footing to give way, they were sent sliding in opposite directions.

As they came to a halt, the two realized that on ice their sure footing and refined movements were useless. The realization appealed to their more savage instincts, and suddenly their fight was no longer an elegant dance, but a primal struggle for dominance and survival.

Having regained some confidence in his movements, Zen surged forward across the ice as though he were skating and swung wide with his crowbar. Umasi dived feet-first, avoiding the attack and shooting straight at his oncoming foe. In Zen's haste to get out of the way, he slipped and fell. He hastened to rise, but as soon as he did he was met by Umasi's fist.

The punch was so powerful, the crowbar slipped from Zen's hands as he fell backwards and slid across the rink. For a moment he feared that he might lose consciousness, but the punishing hail on his face kept him awake even as it kept his eyes shut. Then Zen felt it—something pressing against his waist. Reaching for his belt even as he slid, Zen's numbly realized that it was a knife. Where had that come from, he wondered? He was sure that he hadn't brought a knife with him.

Then he remembered something, and suddenly everything became clear.

Noni had brushed against him before she left.

Zen didn't know how to feel about Noni slipping him a weapon without his knowledge, but he did know that to use it would be dishonorable. Yet he found that that didn't matter to him anymore. A moment later he lurched painfully to a stop, having bumped into the edge of the rink. Zen had been pushed beyond honor, pushed into a corner. All that mattered now was that there was a weapon in his hand, and he intended to use it.

Zen kept the blade concealed in the folds of his windbreaker as Umasi shot towards him, sliding swiftly across the ice. Zen took a deep breath, then launched himself off the wall towards his oncoming enemy. The two clashed at tremendous speeds. The knife flashed in a single, deft stroke, and blood splattered over the icy surface of the rink.

Zen and Umasi slid to a halt a few moments later, their backs to each other, and Zen casually wiped the knife off on his pants. The patter of hail striking the ground seemed deafening as a heavy silence grew between the two brothers. Umasi was the one to break it.

"What next, Zen?" he said coldly, removing his scarf to bandage his waist. "Will you pull out a gun and shoot me if that knife doesn't give you a sufficient advantage?"

"Spare me the lecture, Umasi. Brute strength means nothing without the will to win. This fight will be decided by ruthlessness."

"Rationalizations betray insecurity," Umasi said, turning around. "Let your actions speak for themselves, Zyid. In fact, they already have."

"This newfound pomposity of yours will do no good, Umasi . . ." Zen spun around and dived into a slide. ". . . not when you are dead!"

Prepared for the attack, Umasi jumped aside and hit the ice as Zen shot past with his knife bared. Sliding across the rink on his back, Umasi reached out with one arm and snatched Zen's fallen crowbar as he passed by, then used it to dig into the ice and skid to a halt. As Zen came charging towards him again, this time upright on both feet, Umasi leapt up and swung the crowbar so fast the air hummed. Zen blocked the attack with his knife, but was unable to control his momentum and slid right into Umasi, who promptly drove his elbow into Zen's face.

Zen dropped to the ground hard, but managed to make a swipe at Umasi's legs with his knife. Umasi leapt backwards but slipped, and both brothers raced to get back on their feet.

Zen was the first to rise, lunging at the unprepared Umasi. Acting on instinct, Umasi struck with the crowbar, hitting the hand that held Zen's knife. The blade went flying off to the side, but Zen hadn't been stopped. He tackled Umasi, sending them both sliding across the rink once more, locked in a savage embrace. They traded several blows, until Zen struck a stunning blow between Umasi's eyes. Then they were separated, just in time to crash into the base of the stairs that led up and out of the rink.

By the time Umasi had risen, steadying himself against the handrail, Zen was already running up the stairs. Not sorry to leave the ice behind, Umasi gave pursuit, feeling his limbs and lungs burn as a sea of lights swam into his hazy vision. He could make out Zen's dark silhouette crossing the street towards an enclosure dividing two lanes of traffic. There were trees there, bare of leaves now but wrapped in wires of festive lights, making them visible even through the darkness of Umasi's sunglasses. For some reason the world didn't seem so hazy anymore, and as Umasi looked heavenwards he realized that the hail had ceased.

The light changed, and traffic began moving, but Umasi didn't wait for it to stop. He plunged into the street, dodging honking cars again, nearly getting run over by a truck before finally reaching the other side. Though he was breathing harder than ever, Umasi straightened up and walked calmly into the small parklike enclosure where, he saw, Zen was already waiting for him amidst the glittering trees, plant pots, and small tables.

Zen had his back turned to Umasi, but Umasi could tell that he was holding something. To his tired eyes it seemed as though Zen was now clutching a rope of light, but Umasi knew that it had to be a length of festive wire torn down from one of the trees. The scene seemed oddly peaceful, now that the hail had stopped.

"Do you remember this place, Umasi?" Zen asked.

"No," Umasi replied, looking around again.

"This is where we used to wait for the chauffeur to drive us back to the mansion." Zen spread his arms. "I don't blame you for forgetting. It's been a long time."

Now Umasi remembered, and the memories came pouring back as if a dam had burst. He recognized everything; the tiles they used to draw on with chalk, the table they used to sit at, the tree they had once been scolded for climbing.

From here, we could always go home.

"Why did you bring us here?" Umasi demanded.

"Why not?" Zen replied. "Both of us are tired, Umasi. We can't afford to play much longer. There's no limousine coming to pick us up, and there's no home to go back to. For one of us, let this place be the start of a new beginning. And for the other, let it be the end."

Umasi swallowed a troublesome lump in his throat. Stanching the flow of memories, he concentrated instead on the bruises on his body, the gash on his waist and the aching of his muscles. His head felt like it was in a cloud. Zen was right; one way or another, their fight was coming to an end.

"So be it."

Zen smiled, then spun around, cracking the wire like a whip. Their final moves would be made at last.

Electricity crackled as some of the lights broke against the ground, but the wire was still live as Zen sent it shooting towards Umasi. Umasi dodged to the side and attempted to counterattack, but the moment he took a step forwards, the wire snapped at his heels. As Umasi drew back, Zen twirled the lights overhead, causing a dazzling effect, then lashed out again. Umasi ducked and leapt forward this time, but the wire swiftly doubled back, and he reflexively raised a hand to block it.

The wire cracked against his bare palm, and Umasi could feel tiny glass bulbs shatter painfully from the impact. Then came the jolt of electricity, worse than the sting of static, sending him reeling backwards in pain. Zen drew the wire back and then swung again, this time striking across Umasi's chest. That blow wasn't as painful as it could have been, cushioned by a sweater as it was, allowing Umasi the presence of mind to dodge the next crack of the wire.

Laughing now, Zen struck again and again, forcing Umasi to duck and weave but never allowing him to come too close. Sparks flew everywhere from the flurry of attacks, and Umasi, exhausted in both mind and body, couldn't imagine a way to defeat a weapon with such reach. Zen was saying something now, but Umasi couldn't hear the words. He was close, he knew, to the brink of death. A familiar place. Somehow, it made him calmer than ever, and for a moment he paused to listen.

Instead of Zen's words, he heard something strange filtering through the haze in his head and the noise of traffic and sirens. It was the distant tinkling of a chain.

"I can never tell what you're going to do until the last minute."

"It's a difficult weapon to predict, but it's better for countering. You're just dodging right now; if you were attacking me it'd be harder."

"So how am I supposed to beat it?"

"Look for an opening after a failed attack."

Umasi slowly began to roll up his sleeves. Zen was still talking; he hadn't yet noticed that something had changed with Umasi. Suddenly Umasi rushed forwards, and the wire swished through the air. With speed that surprised even him, Umasi dodged the attack and kept going. Zen lashed out again, and this time Umasi neatly deflected the blow with the rolled-up portion of his sleeves. As Umasi drew closer with his sudden, impossible speed, Zen panicked and swung wildly. This time Umasi jumped over the wire and onto a table, and Zen, with no time to recover from his failed attack, was left wide open.

He could only stare in disbelief as Umasi leapt off the table and down at him. There was a tremendous impact, and the next thing Zen knew, he was gazing upwards, his vision swimming out of focus. He felt a pressure on his unresponsive body, especially around his neck. There was a hand there, he realized. Cold and unyielding.

Then Zen's vision slid back into focus, and he found himself staring up into a pair of dark, triumphant eyes. Umasi's sunglasses had fallen off from the impact, and for the first time that night, the two brothers looked each other in the eye.

Zen had lost.

Umasi had won.

At last, it was over.

35

The Beginning

Late at night, in a dark and empty office at City Hall, a man sat at his computer terminal, illuminated only by the glow of the screen as he typed out an urgent message.

> *Dear Sirs,*
>
> *The situation here is far worse than I had ever suspected. I now have good reason to believe that this City is under siege by an unknown rebel organization, and that the Mayor has been deliberately concealing this fact. The District 1 School was allegedly demolished last month, but after having checked the records I found that no such demolition had ever been scheduled. What's more, dozens of Enforcer personnel have been unaccounted for since that incident. Rothenberg himself has been confined to a hospital ward with broken knees. Supposedly the Mayor has prevented him from receiving surgery that would allow him to walk again.*
>
> *Perhaps most alarmingly, I have discovered that the Mayor's surrogate sons are nowhere to be found. I am not sure how or if these mysteries are connected, but I do know that the boys have not been attending school for months.*
>
> *There is no time; I fear that my investigations may have already attracted the Mayor's attention. I request immediate Government intervention to secure this City, and recommend that the experiment be officially suspended. A separate investigation into th_*

"What's all this, Jack?"

The man froze with his fingers still on the keys. Hastily switching the monitor off, he spun around in his chair and straightened his tie.

"Just writing a report, Mr. Mayor."

"Oh I don't doubt that. It's a been a while since you last contacted our masters, hasn't it?"

Jack was careful not to let his sudden panic show on his face.

"What are you talking about, sir?"

"I know that you're a Government spy, Jack. Even if I hadn't known before, I would have after seeing the letter that you were writing."

Jack sat up in his chair, abandoning all pretense of innocence.

"How long have you known?"

"I always suspected," the Mayor replied. "But I was never able to prove it until recently. Your mistake was trying to use your position to conduct your investigation; while you were watching Rothenberg, I was watching you. You should have suspected that the appointment was a trap."

"So I should have." Jack nodded. "I guess that this letter won't be reaching the Government now."

"You know I can't allow it to."

"They'll find out anyway. If they haven't already."

"Perhaps, but I used to have the same job as you, Jack. I know how these things work. I doubt that there's a spy left in the City that I'm not keeping tabs on. In my opinion, the only way the Government could find out that there's a problem is if it goes public."

"Then since it no longer matters anymore," Jack said, "why not tell me what exactly the problem is? Where *are* your sons?"

For a moment the Mayor was silent, his entire body a grim silhouette against the faint light of the hallway.

"One of them is dead," the Mayor said at last. "I just found out yesterday."

"I'm sorry."

"Don't be, Jack. If anyone that works for me is at fault, it's Rothenberg." The Mayor's face contorted in anger. "The doctors say that they can fix him, but as far as I'm concerned the man will never walk again. Nor will he ever see anything but the sterile walls of his ward."

Jack shifted uncomfortably.

"So what happens to me?"

"You know what Government thinks of spies that get caught." The Mayor shrugged. "Procedure states that I'm supposed to fire you, and that you're supposed to sever contact with the outside."

"How convenient for you."

"I didn't make those rules, Jack, but I think that they work best for the both of us. I won't have to worry about you sending that report, and you won't have to worry about upsetting me."

Jack nodded slowly. He knew that the Mayor never made idle threats, and he also knew a good deal when he saw one. Turning around, he flicked the monitor on and deleted his partially written message. The Mayor gave a nod of approval when he was done.

"I'll see to it that you get a generous severance package," the Mayor said, turning to leave. "Go home to your family, Jack, and give young Tack my regards. I hope that your children lead happier lives than mine."

With that, the Mayor strode out of the clerk's office and over to the elevator that would return him to his own. Once there he sat down at his desk with a heavy sigh, and after a moment's indecision opened a drawer where a single sheet of paper was stowed. The letter had arrived in a plain envelope by normal post, and though he had already memorized every word, the Mayor unfolded it to read again.

> *Mr. Mayor,*
>
> *Zen is dead. I killed him. The Truancy he created lives on, but I will not fight it, or you, any longer. My part in this has already been played, and I intend to retire in peace to District 19. I do not want to see you, but you have nothing to fear from me so long as you refrain from invading my new home. Don't think too badly of me—I did what had to be done, so that you would not have to.*
>
> *Sincerely,*
> *Umasi*

As the Mayor slid the note back into the drawer, he reflected on how strange he felt. He had spent months in slow agony, waiting for bad news, but now that it had come it hurt less than he'd expected. The Mayor thought that he should be wallowing in grief and despair, but instead the emptiness within him had very quickly been filled with rage.

Zen had died because of the Truancy. The Mayor let that thought float at the front of his mind like a buoy, keeping him from sinking into despair. Had his heart not been broken, it would have told him that the thought was a lie, but for now he relished having a scapegoat. Rather than grieve, the Mayor needed to blame someone for his loss. He needed a focus for his anger.

And in the City, it was so much easier to blame children than to blame yourself.

"I will wipe them out," the Mayor swore, "even if I have to kill every last student in this City!"

The Mayor laughed as he flicked his lighter open. Things had become very simple now. There was no need for restraint or mercy anymore. A problem had arisen in his City, and he would solve it, any way he had to.

Zyid shut his eyes, gripped the solid piece of wood, and yelled as he lunged. The fake sword struck the mannequin, but he heard neither the crack of the impact nor the crash after the mannequin's head flew across the room and against a wall. All he felt was the recoil in his hands, the jolt that traveled up his arm and shook him to his very core.

Damn.

Zyid knew that he was still fast and that his blows were still powerful. He could muster up what looked like, to all others, genuine ferocity. Only he knew that it wasn't. His fire had burnt out. His defeat had been more than frustrating—it was devastating. Every time Zyid tried to summon up his will to fight, all he saw were Umasi's cold eyes staring into his, in that moment when he had felt true fear, that moment when he had faced death.

You're killing, and if you don't love your work, how can you ever succeed at your job?

That was it, he realized. The joy had gone out of battle. Never again would Zyid be able to fight like he once had. He felt diminished, weakened, a shadow of his former self. Umasi had not killed him, but Zyid knew he had been crippled for life. Would anyone notice? Perhaps not. Zyid was still so far ahead of most of them that they might not be able to tell the difference. But all it would take, Zyid knew, was one extraordinary person determined to kill him, and he would fall.

Ever since his defeat, Zyid had become acutely aware that someone would eventually finish what his brother would not. Umasi, Zyid realized, had not done him a favor by sparing his life. It wasn't just his fighting spirit that had been affected; he had begun doubting his actions, his motives, even himself and the Truancy he had started.

Lately, this doubt had begun to turn into regret, and regret into guilt, which he already had plenty of. After going for so long without it, Zyid was finally learning that no emotion was more self-destructive than remorse.

Zyid balefully picked up the mannequin's head and placed it back onto its body. It was far too late to go back, but he now knew that he couldn't continue all the way forward. His conviction had been shattered. He was no longer even sure that what he was doing was right . . . and how could he see it through when he was no longer certain?

Zyid looked out the window of the flower shop. Gabriel and Alex were having a mock fight in the street as other Truants gathered around as spectators. They laughed and cheered, oblivious of their leader's inner conflict. *They* were certain of their cause. They placed absolute faith in the Truancy, and in him.

Zyid's eyes locked on to a dark figure leaning against a wall in the shadows. Noni was there, watching the fight like the rest of them, probably sizing up the combatants. Zyid had noticed that she had changed, subtly, since the destruction of the District 1 School. She wore her ponytail in a braid now, and no longer questioned him about anything, nor did she try to protect him. Zyid wasn't sure what had brought about the change, but he wasn't fooled; he could tell that beneath the scarf and the icy barrier, Noni depended on him more than any of the others.

Zyid turned away from the window with a sigh. He knew that he could never abandon them, and so with a heavy heart he stood up to join them, resolved to play his part.

At least until one of them could take his place.

C ross stood and stared blankly around him, dazed. Just hours ago he had been at home cleaning the bathroom, alone as usual. Then came the knock on the door, and the next thing he knew he was standing in the entrance hall of the local orphanage with nothing but a small suitcase of his belongings. His father, he'd been told on the way, had been permanently crippled in the line of duty and wouldn't be able to take care of him anymore.

Cross had almost smiled at that last part.

At any rate, after a couple months, someone at Enforcer Headquarters had apparently remembered that Cross existed. They were nice enough to send an Enforcer to bring him to the orphanage, but not quite nice enough to warn him that they were coming. It was a lot to take in all at once, and Cross didn't yet know quite what to think or how to feel about any of it. The woman in charge of the orphanage had been nice enough when he arrived, though she seemed flustered at the prospect of finding somewhere to put him.

"We're completely full in all the other dorms, Mary," a janitor informed her. "Barely enough room to bring the vacuum cleaner through as it is."

Mary sighed theatrically.

"Thank you, Maxwell," she said, and then turned to Cross. "Well, nothing else we can do then, dear. We'll just have to put you in Edward's room."

Before Cross could ask who or what Edward was, Mary had seized his hand and began to lead him down a dimly lit side hallway. He was half-expecting to be put into a kennel with a dog, but when they came to a stop and opened a door he was instead greeted with a nearly empty dormitory that could have accommodated six. The lights were off, but the figure sitting alone on one of the bunks was clearly not a dog, but a perfectly normal-looking boy.

"Usually we let him have the whole space to himself," Mary whispered in Cross' ear. "I daresay after all he's been through the poor boy deserves some privacy. But you seem nice enough, I do hope that you two get along."

"Yes, ma'am," Cross mumbled.

"Is this the boy you were talking about earlier, madam?" Edward said, turning sideways to plant his feet on the floor.

"Yes, dear, I told you that we might have to put him in your room," she said anxiously. "Is that all right?"

"Of course. I know how much trouble it is for you, with all the other rooms stuffed full," Edward said. "I wouldn't want to inconvenience you any more than I already do."

"Oh not at all dear, not at all!" Mary said. "Cross here seems like a quiet child, I'm sure you'll get along well. Cross, this is Edward, you're going to be rooming with him from now on."

"Hello," Cross said quietly.

Edward got up and walked over to Cross, his hand outstretched. As Cross hesitantly shook it, he got a good look at Edward's face for the first time. In an instant he realized that they had met before, when he had been lying facedown on the street after being attacked by miscreants.

"Hi," Edward said warmly, reaching down to take Cross' luggage. "Nice to meet you. Please come in."

"Thanks," Cross muttered. He'd seen enough to know that Edward was the one calling the shots around here, and life under Rothenberg had taught him that it was smart to please the one calling the shots.

Mary, who had been watching carefully, beamed at them both.

"Well," she said, "I'll let you two get to know each other a little better. I've got some things to take care of now, but if there's anything you need just let me know."

"Thank you very much, madam," Edward called.

Mary smiled even wider, and then the door shut, leaving them both in relative darkness. Edward paused for a moment, and then turned to face Cross, his expression shrewd.

"Well, now that she's gone, we can speak frankly," Edward said. "You're that kid that got roughed up a while back, aren't you? That makes you one of the few around here who know the real me. It would be best to stay out of my way—but you already knew *that*, didn't you?"

"Yes."

"You're not stupid, I can see that much." Edward narrowed his emerald eyes. "And you're not afraid of me either."

"No," Cross agreed.

"You think you've seen worse. I like that," Edward announced, walking over to deposit Cross' luggage onto an unused bunk. "Just don't let it get to your head."

"I won't," Cross promised.

"And I believe it," Edward said, plunking down onto his bunk again. "Sit down, won't you?"

Cross obediently moved to sit on the bunk that Edward had chosen for him.

"I heard from the staff earlier that your father got hurt," Edward said. "What did he do anyway?"

"He is . . . was an Enforcer," Cross answered. "His name is Rothenberg. That's all I know, really. They didn't tell me anything."

At the name Rothenberg, Edward suddenly sat up, keen interest glinting in his venomous eyes.

"Rothenberg?" he repeated. "I don't believe in destiny . . . but this is quite the coincidence."

Cross blinked. "You knew my father?"

"We met. Twice." Edward smiled in a way that made most people shiver, though Cross seemed unaffected. "You interest me, Cross. Something tells me that we *are* going to get along a lot better than I did with your father."

"You know what happened to him."

"His time ran out," Edward said, leaning forward. "But that's not what's important, is it? Let me tell you what's going on in this City right now, Cross. And after that, I'll explain how *our* time is fast approaching."

The first warm rays of spring sunlight cascaded down onto District 19. Snow and ice that had until long clung stubbornly to rooftops and scaffolding finally bowed out to the light, melting gradually to form small waterfalls and brilliant sprays that glittered in the sun as they crashed down onto the streets below. The winter had passed, spring was here, and light had earned its place alongside the shadow.

Finally at peace, Umasi paused, allowing himself to admire the warmth of the sun and the sound of the water. For this day, at least, there would be no shadows over his stand—perhaps none even over the entire district. Having finally disposed of the last of his responsibilities, he felt truly free now, a wonderful sensation that seemed to bubble from the inside out.

Umasi wasn't exactly sure why he had delayed so long in writing the letter to the Mayor, but now that he had made his neutrality known, the last of his worries had faded. He could safely isolate himself from the rest of the world now, until the day he died, or until the coming war reached his doorstep. The Mayor would know better than to test him, and as for the boy who now called himself Zyid . . .

Leaning back in his chair, Umasi closed his eyes and thought back to the night it had all ended, and the words that had been exchanged after he had struck the last blow.

The world seemed a swirl of lights to the two brothers as they stared at each other on the icy ground. Zen's eyes were wide with shock, and seemed almost accusatory as they bored into Umasi's own. Umasi could see that Zen felt cheated, and why wouldn't he? Not once in Zen's life had his abilities ever failed him. Never had he been so completely defeated, or come up against an enemy that was stronger than he. But now, even though he had fought dirty and with every ounce of his might, Zen had still lost.

"How does it feel to be the victim, Zyid?" Umasi whispered. "I've always known what it feels like. But you, you never have. Is that why you lack a conscience?"

Umasi tightened his grip on Zen's throat, and watched as Zen's eyes went glassy as he choked and sputtered, clawing feebly at Umasi's hand. Then Umasi released him, and Zen was dragging deep breaths into his lungs, his chest heaving pitifully.

"I'm going to let you live, Zyid," Umasi said as he stood. "But I want you to remember this moment. I want you to remember it every time you take a life. I want you to remember what it is to be helpless, humiliated, and dying. Maybe then you'll understand why I chose not to go to war."

Umasi stooped to swipe his sunglasses from the ground and put them back on. The scarf tied around his waist had come loose, and he retrieved that as well before looping it around his neck. Then he faced Zen again, and Zen looked up in awe.

Umasi stood triumphant, indomitable, the ends of his scarf fluttering in the chill wind. His body was framed by the glittering lights all around him, which were reflected in his dark, enigmatic sunglasses. Though his clothes were torn in some places and stained red in others, Umasi only seemed stronger for all that he had endured.

In that moment, Zen thought that it was the most impressive thing that he had ever seen in his life.

"I will return to District 19. Stay out of my business, and I'll stay out of yours," Umasi said, snapping Zen out of his reverie. "I will tell the Mayor that my brother is dead. It's not so far from the truth anyway."

With that Umasi turned his back on Zen and began walking away. As Zen watched him go, his conscience finally kicked in, and the sudden pain nearly overwhelmed him with its intensity. As he began to relive every sin he had ever committed, something cut through the haze of guilt. It was anger, and Zen latched on to it in desperation.

"You're no brother of mine!" Zen screamed. "You never were!"

Umasi didn't so much as pause, but instead raised his hand to wave backwards in farewell. Infuriated, guilty, and eager for death, Zen painfully propped himself up with one elbow, shouting at the receding figure with all the menace he could muster.

"If *you* won't kill me, then no one can!"

At that, Umasi glanced back at Zen from over his shoulder.

"No," Umasi called. "Someday, another who can will rise."

Umasi kept walking, out of sight and into the glittering night. Meanwhile Zen lay alone, defeated on the cold ground, knowing that he had truly been left behind. Then the memories returned, and for the first time in his life, he cried.

You were right in the end, Brother.

Only now I wish that I were wrong.

Read on for a preview of Isamu Fukui's next book
Truancy City
to be published by Tor Books in 2010

PROLOGUE ··· NEWFOUND FREEDOM

The tent was sweltering as the young woman opened the flap and ducked inside. It had been particularly humid in this region, and her gray combat uniform was woven out of nylon cotton, a fabric that didn't perfectly insulate against the summer heat. Her troops liked to joke about the clothing getting hot enough to bake potatoes, but the woman herself gave no sign of discomfort as she sat down at her desk and thumbed on one of a series of monitors around her.

As the monitor flickered to life, a gaunt and disheveled man appeared onscreen. Recognizing the woman, the man scowled and squeezed a chrome lighter with one hand.

"*You.* I should have known."

"It's been awhile since we last spoke like this, Mr. Mayor," the woman said. "That was nearly four years ago, correct?"

"Not long enough. I would have preferred never to see you again."

The young woman smiled faintly at the monitor, her stormy gray eyes glinting.

"Don't tell me you haven't been expecting a visit from us, Mr. Mayor."

"Actually I'm wondering what took you so long," the Mayor said, flicking his lighter open. "Nearly a year since the rebellion went public? You're much slower than I'd heard . . . *Iris.*"

If the young woman was rankled by the mocking use of her name, she hid it well. Unperturbed, she leaned back in her chair and ran her fingers all the way through her dark, wavy hair, ending at the nape of her neck.

"If the decision were mine alone I would have come four years ago, at the first sign of trouble," Iris said. "Things are a bit different now. I had to make sure I was bringing the military with me."

"I heard you're a Lieutenant General now," the Mayor said. "Shouldn't you have that military in your back pocket?"

"If only." Iris sighed. "Sometimes I feel like it's the other way around."
The Mayor frowned and clicked his lighter shut.
"Why are you calling?" he demanded. "Why now?"
Matching the Mayor's shift in demeanor, Iris sat up straight. Her voice, once politely neutral, now turned cold and hard.
"I didn't wish for this conversation any more than you, Mayor," she said. "Procedure requires me to warn you that you have forty-eight hours to surrender yourself to Government custody and yield control of your City." She smiled wryly. "If you refuse—and I expect you will—then you will be detained and the military will achieve control by itself."
"Good luck with that. You'll need it." The Mayor laughed bitterly. "I take it that you're camped just across the river, then?"
"I'm afraid that's none of your business."
"Well then," the Mayor growled, leaning forward, "all I have to say to you and your wretch of a father is this—*come and get me!*"
Iris brushed her forehead with her knuckles in a mild show of annoyance. The Mayor sat stoically, clearly expecting an additional outburst of some kind. But when Iris spoke again, her voice was oddly hushed.
"Where are the boys? Are they still alive?"
At that, the Mayor's face flushed red with anger.
"I'll die myself rather than tell *you* anything about that."
The screen went dead. Iris slammed her fist against the desk.
"Yes," she muttered. "You will."

Who was that?"
The Mayor sighed and turned to face his guest, a boy sitting on the other side of his mahogany desk.
"A representative of the true Government of this City," the Mayor replied, "and someone I had hoped you would never meet. It's a long story."
"I've got time."
"But the City doesn't," the Mayor said sharply. "It's too late to explain the entire history of the Government, and frankly I don't know it all myself. What I can tell you is that they cannot be crossed. They are powerful beyond your imagination; their rule encompasses thousands of cities, and their military makes our Enforcers look like a joke."
"And this City is one of the many under their control?"
"Yes and no," the Mayor said. "This City is special—one of a few that the Government isolated decades ago."
"Why?"
"Because of a storm of civil unrest that nearly destroyed them." The Mayor flicked his lighter open. "It was before my time, so I don't even

know what the riots were about. But I do know that in the bloody after-math, the Government decided to take extreme measures to make sure that nothing like that would ever happen again." The Mayor smiled now. "The only problem was, no one could agree on which extreme measures to take."

The boy inclined his head.

"So they created the Cities as experiments."

"That's a bit misleading," the Mayor said. "The Cities were already there—the Government merely isolated them from outside influence and implemented a different philosophy in each. Until four years ago, this City was considered the most promising of all."

"And what was the philosophy behind this City?"

"It was simple." The Mayor clicked his lighter shut. "The founders be-lieved that *education* was the key to controlling a population."

Strapped across Iris's back was a black pole about three feet in length, which she now removed as she emerged from her tent. Pressing one of two buttons on it, she smiled as two metal ends instantly extended from ei-ther side of the pole, effectively forming a staff. Tapping one end against the ground, she glanced over at the shade where a colonel, a member of her staff, had been waiting.

The Mayor's guess had been correct—her tent was one of hundreds that formed a temporary encampment at the riverside. A mercifully cool breeze rolled across the water and over the camp as Iris approached the saluting colonel.

"All units are ready for immediate deployment, ma'am," the man said. "Will we observe the forty-eight hour grace period, or has the Mayor re-jected it?"

"The Mayor rejected it, but I don't intend to let him set our schedule," Iris replied, watching a beetle crawl across the ground. "Order a stand down from full alert."

The man looked surprised, but nodded anyway. "Yes ma'am."

Iris glanced at him. "Something on your mind, soldier?"

"I was wondering why we don't just overwhelm them, ma'am."

Iris nodded as the beetle stumbled over a rock. Some commanding of-ficers did not appreciate having their orders questioned. She, however, made a distinction between disrespect and curiosity, and felt that satisfy-ing the latter—though never the former—could make for a more effective army.

"Combined, the Educators and the rebels in that City have an estimated fighting force of twelve to fifteen thousand," Iris said. "It's enough to be a problem if we rush in blindly. We have only ten thousand ground troops to subdue any resistance and secure all fifty-seven districts against insurgent attack."

"But what do we gain by waiting?"

In response to the colonel's question, Iris gestured toward the river, and the man turned to look in that direction. Across the glittering water, the ominous shapes of skyscrapers loomed like giant tombstones. Many of them showed obvious signs of damage, and rising smoke plumes indicated that fighting was ongoing in the City.

"What you are looking at is nothing less than the complete breakdown of society," Iris explained as the beetle examined her shoelace. "That City was built upon education. Now that the very foundation of their lives has been challenged, those people don't know what to do with themselves or their newfound freedom."

"Freedom?"

"Anarchy, to put it plainly," Iris said. "It was inevitable the moment the rebellion gained traction. That City is in the middle of tearing itself apart. Once both sides are exhausted, we will move in and pick up the pieces at our leisure."

"So what are your orders, ma'am?" the colonel asked.

"Keep all forces on standby. No airstrikes, nothing that risks giving away our presence," Iris said. "However, cut all shipments into the City by another fifty percent."

The colonel looked surprised. "Why not cut them completely?"

"With no supplies, there can be no war," Iris said. "But if we reduce their supplies rather than cut them completely, they'll become desperate and go for each other's throats. By the time we move in, they'll be both exhausted and out of resources."

The man nodded. "And what about our assets within the City?"

For the first time, Iris hesitated. The beetle began skittering away. "Still no sign of our primary objectives?"

"None."

"Then tell the assets to keep looking."

"What happens if they're found?"

With precise restraint, Iris swung her staff, pinning the beetle to the ground without crushing it. She pressed the second button on the grip, and the staff discharged an electrical shock that instantly fried the insect.

"If either one of them is spotted," she said blandly, "inform me immediately."

1

Set(2)

rc 3.17.17 (0)

Truancy 2